A WANTED MAN

"I'm afraid I must insist on Mr. Jackson's company. You see, my employer doesn't want him anywhere near your charming influence."

Both the contessa and the envoy tensed, their fangs descending with an audible *flick*. "We are taking Mr. Jackson with us, with or without your employer's consent, sir," she said firmly.

Winn had had enough.

"There ain't a need to be so damn polite about all this," he growled. "Look here, Morpheus. I ain't goin' with you." Winn shifted his gaze to the vampires. "We done now? I thought we had a ship to catch."

"Not so fast, Mr. Jackson," Dr. Morpheus said, his voice dropping a notch with expectation. "Rathe has plans for you." The man began to swell, his belly growing. The buttons on his acid green vest popped off and flew in all directions.

The sound of ripping fabric filled the air. Beneath Winn the horse whinnied and shied backward, the white of its eyes visible. Winn tightened his hold on the reins. "What the hell—" he breathed.

Morpheus continued to swell, his grotesquely distended stomach shiny in the moonlight. He let out a blood-curdling yell as his abdomen split open from waist to breastbone and thousands of small, shining objects poured out of him onto the desert sand.

Winn wasn't about to stick around long enough to find out what they were. "Run!" he yelled.

Also by Theresa Meyers

THE HUNTER:
Book One of the Legend Chronicles

Coming soon

THE CHOSEN:
Book Three of the Legend Chronicles

Published by Kensington Publishing Corporation

The Slayer

BOOK TWO OF THE LEGEND CHRONICLES

THERESA MEYERS

ZEBRA BOOKS
KENSINGTON PUBLISHING CORP.
http://www.kensingtonbooks.com

ZEBRA BOOKS are published by

Kensington Publishing Corp.
119 West 40th Street
New York, NY 10018

All Kensington titles, imprints, and distributed lines are available at special quantity discounts for bulk purchases for sales promotion, premiums, fund-raising, educational, or institutional use.

Special book excerpts or customized printings can also be created to fit specific needs. For details, write or phone the office of the Kensington Special Sales Manager: Attn. Special Sales Department. Kensington Publishing Corp., 119 West 40th Street, New York, NY 10018. Phone: 1-800-221-2647.

Zebra and the Z logo Reg. U.S. Pat. & TM Off.

ISBN-13: 978-1-4201-2125-4
ISBN-10: 1-4201-2125-1

First Printing: April 2012
10 9 8 7 6 5 4 3 2 1

Printed in the United States of America

This book is dedicated to my Washington family.

To my dad, Ron.
Thanks for being the mad scientist in the family.
Your lab is going to change the world someday.
I'm very proud to be your daughter.

To my stepmom, Bonita Jay.
You are one seriously amazing woman.
Thank you so much for being part of our family
and loving my dad the way you do.

To Karla, Matt, David and Katie.
Some family you are born into, others you create.
You mean the world to me.

To Jenny, Terrel, Nate, Brennan and Tyler.
Thanks for being such a wonderful part of my life.

To my "little" brother, Tom, who towers over me.
I always knew you'd be a success.
That's just the kind of person you are.
I'm proud of you.

And, as always, for Jerry.
Because through good times and bad,
you've always been my hero.

Chapter 1

"Put down the gun, Hoss, 'fore I blow that oversized melon of yours to kingdom come." Winchester Jackson's cold, steady voice cracked through the canyon sure as a shot. Although Hoss Dalton, seated on his horse, had his rifle stuck under the leather flap of the stagecoach window, Winn knew the outlaw never robbed alone. Somewhere, hidden by the rock walls, sagebrush, and dead grasses of the canyon, Hoss's ragged band of fellow thieves lay in wait.

The stage perched precariously on the shaley edge of the dirt road leading from Carson City to Winn's town of Bodie. Inside, a woman whimpered and a small dog yipped.

This was getting old. It really was. And it was unlikely this would end well. Hoss was two bricks shy of a load and perpetually half-drunk. But then anyone who'd seen and done the things an old Hunter like Hoss had would want to drown himself in whiskey most of the time. "Hoss? You hear me?"

The female whimper was cut off instantly. Even the hot

desert air scented with creosote and sagebrush in the rocky chute of the canyon stood still.

Hoss turned slowly. His rifle, which was pointed at the occupants hidden within the dark interior of the steam stage, wavered at the I-won't-tell-you-again tone of the sheriff's voice.

Attached to the front of the stage, the mechanical horses, big copper beasts the size of Clydesdales, pinged, hissing steam through their venting nostrils as the metal and gears cooled.

Winn kept Hoss in his sights. The old man's eyes, rheumy from too much rotgut whiskey, flicked to the star-shaped silver badge on Winn's chest, his rifle slipping an inch. Sonofabitch, was the old fool going to shoot a stage full of people right here, ten minutes from town, for a measly payroll?

The brilliant sun hung white-hot overhead in a cloudless field of brilliant blue.

"Countdown is at three, Hoss. Drop that, or swear to God, I'll shoot you where you stand! Tommy Sutton? You stay right where you are!" he yelled. He didn't know if Sutton was there or not. Didn't have eyes in the back of his head either, but the rustle in the grasses off to his right stopped.

"Damn, Winn. You ain't nothin' like your old man." Hoss's tone conveyed his deep disappointment born of familiarity.

Winn peered down the length of his rifle barrel aimed at his quarry's heart. "Thank you for the compliment." Fact was, anything that distinguished him from his notorious outlaw father and supernatural Hunter, Cyrus "Black Jack" Jackson, pleased him enormously. He didn't want any part of that life. Not now. Not ever again.

"Cain't you jest let me go, for old time's sake?" Hoss and his group of bandits had once been Hunters alongside his father. But tough times had turned them from protecting humanity to protecting their own self-serving interests. They'd robbed this stage four times in the last month, hoping for a payroll run for the Black Gulch Mine.

Winn was damned if he was going to let it be five. He had a murder a day, sometimes more than one, to contend with in the rowdy mining town. Having the miners' pay stolen and travelers threatened on a regular basis was a pain in his ass. He'd stuck Hoss and his cronies in jail three times for doing exactly this. And every time, Hoss's nefarious connections had gotten them out. But enough was enough.

"If I let you go, then I wouldn't be doing my job, now would I? Get your hands where I can see them." Winn pulled down the lever on his repeating rifle, preparing it to fire.

Click. Click. Click. Click. Four other guns cocked and pointed at Winchester's head as the rest of Hoss's group emerged from the jagged, tan rocks of the canyon. A perfect place to stage a holdup.

Damn.

"Not this time, Winn." His wide smile a mess of gaps and yellowed teeth, Hoss stepped forward and pulled the rifle from Winchester's hands. "No one would have figured you for the rotten apple in the barrel. A lawman!" His lip curled with contempt. "That would jest make your pa spit nails."

Winchester resisted the urge to tug on the hardened tips of his heavily waxed black mustache, a habit he'd developed when agitated during his last five years as sheriff of Bodie. "My pa would have spit anything he could chew."

A metallic clink and rattle of gears alerted Winn that the steps of the coach were being lowered. "Stay inside," he shouted to the fool preparing to alight on a mountain pass with five armed men waiting mere feet away.

A rustle of taffeta accompanied a length of silky calf

and dainty half boot onto the first step. From the dim recesses of the stage stepped an elegant woman.

Winn felt a rush of unwanted heat as she emerged into the dusty sunlight. Dark, glossy curls were capped with a jaunty little top hat sporting a cloud of black feathers. Her expensive-looking bustled gown, the blue-black iridescent color of raven wings, hugged her slim waist and suggested a silhouette that was amply curved by nature rather than artifice. But more stunning than her figure was her face.

Seeing her beautiful, exotic features made Winn's heart knock uncomfortably and caused his palms to sweat. Sure he'd seen women. Plenty of them. But nothing like this roamed the likes of Bodie. Lips, a shade too full to be fashionable, and high cheekbones accented a pair of piercing whiskey-colored eyes that stole his breath away.

The woman's dusky beauty was both dark and alluring, but an undercurrent of danger surrounded her like a storm cloud charged with lightning. Upon the black kidskin leather of her gloved hand was a large ruby ring, which matched the blood-like droplets of rubies at her ears. Her every mannerism screamed wealth and privilege.

"Is there a problem, gentlemen?" Her voice was soothing and rich like warm honey, and her heavy Eastern European accent made "gentlemen" sound more like "zhentlemen."

Hoss gave an impatient jerk of his head toward the stage, even though his gaze lingered on the woman. "Wait your turn, missus. Get back in that coach. We'll have us a fine time when I'm done with my business." His suggestive tone made Winchester want to punch him—hard, and preferably more than once.

"I think not," she replied smoothly.

The hair pricked up porcupine fashion on the back of Winchester's neck as the scent of sulfur tainted the air. Something about this situation wasn't right.

He turned away from the woman, focusing instead on

taking down Hoss. Sure, he'd probably get shot by one of the Dalton gang, but if he did it right, it wouldn't be more than a flesh wound, and Hoss would take the brunt of his gang's shots. He bent his knees slightly, preparing to lunge at Hoss's middle, but before he could even move, all hell broke loose.

The woman's face warped, her brows protruded, her eyes turned crimson, and her full lips bracketed a pair of perfect, pearly fangs. She hissed, and every head turned.

"Vampire!" Hoss yelled to the others.

Taken off guard, they fumbled with their weapons, trying to exchange regular bullets for silver, but they weren't fast enough. In a blink she had stripped the Dalton gang from their horses and savagely ripped out their throats with her delicate gloved hands and razor-sharp fangs. In a cloud of dust, the horses ran down the canyon, back toward town, their frightened whinnies echoing off the rocks.

Only he and Hoss remained. Winchester grabbed his rifle out of Hoss's loose grip and trained the weapon on the monster in taffeta. She turned back, facing them, her lips slicked with bright red blood. The tip of her soft pink tongue stroked one fang, making Winchester's gut contract involuntarily.

"A bit rustic, and a little too well marinated in whiskey, but substantial," she said, as if discussing the vintage of wine. She pulled a black silk handkerchief from the sleeve of her gown and dabbed at the blood remaining around her lips and chin, removing the last traces of her unladylike activity.

"Well, don't just stand there, goddammit, shoot her!" Hoss yelled, shuffling behind Winchester. Winn stood his ground, the rifle pointed straight at the vampiress's heart. Not that it would do much good. What he really needed was a machete or a broadsword to lop that lovely dark-haired head from her slim shoulders.

"Don't come any closer," he warned.

She tilted her head slightly, like an inquisitive bird of prey, her eyes returning to their original amber color and her face returning to its regal profile. Only the fangs still remained.

"You have nothing to fear from me. Look around you, Hunter. Have I harmed the innocents in the coach? Have I harmed you? No. I took only the lives of those who were contributing nothing to your society in the first place. Hardly a crime." She peeled the soiled black gloves from her fingers one at a time, then tossed them into the air where they disappeared in a swirl of dark smoke.

Winn's finger rested heavy on the trigger, just needing a finite amount of pressure to fire the rifle at the vampiress. Only one thing held him back.

Everything she'd said was true.

He glanced at the wooden, steam-powered stagecoach. The occupants huddled inside, whispering and peering with wide, frightened eyes from behind the dusty leather window coverings, afraid to come out; but they were unharmed. Hoss's men lay in crumpled bloody heaps, and Hoss himself was still cowering behind him, but she hadn't attacked him.

"What d'you want, vampire?"

"I am the Lady Alexandra Porter, Contessa Drossenburg, emissary of His Vampiric Imperial Majesty, Emperor Vladimir the Fifth. I've come to seek out the eldest of the Chosen, Winchester Jackson. I was told he resides in Bodie." Her gaze flicked to the cluster of sun-bleached wooden and brick buildings down in the valley below, then drifted to the star on his chest. "Do you know him?"

"Lady, I *am* him."

Her eyes widened slightly. "Then we have business to discuss."

Winn slowly lowered his gun, but not his guard. Appar-

ently Hoss was stupider than he looked; he tried to wrestle the repeating rifle away from him. But Winn had lost his patience. He clocked Hoss on the side of the head with the butt of his rifle, and the other man slid unconscious facedown into the powder-fine dirt.

Winn glanced up at the vampire. "I don't do business with supernaturals."

She gave a shrug of her petite shoulder, her fangs retracting completely, leaving behind a row of even, white teeth. "I expected as much, but the emperor does not share my view. He thinks it is time for vampires to join with the Chosen if we are to defeat a mutual enemy."

"The enemy of my enemy is my friend?"

"*Da.* But perhaps it is best if we discuss this elsewhere." She threw a meaningful glance over her shoulder at the stunned occupants of the steam stage. "May I have your leave to glamour them? It is not safe for them to know so much. Don't you agree, Mr. Jackson?"

Much as he didn't like it, she did have a point. The last thing he needed was a stage full of frightened travelers to come rolling into Bodie spouting off about a vampire killing the Dalton gang. People, as a general rule, were panicky, stupid, and rash. And chances were ten out of ten, if the travelers talked, the town would come beating down his door demanding that he fix it. No, it was far better if she glamoured the lot of them and made them forget this unpleasantness had ever happened. He nodded his approval.

The vampire dipped her head as she bent in a curtsey, then gingerly picked up her skirts and turned back to the stage. The low, husky quality of her voice rustled like the taffeta she wore, sultry and smooth, completely absorbing the total attention of the travelers.

"You have had a most pleasant trip, with only the slightest delay for a mechanical horse that needed an application of oil," she said slowly. Winn tried to block out her voice,

but glanced over her shoulder to see the wide, glassy stares of the occupants of the stage. She certainly did know how to throw a glamour. Good thing he was practically immune.

That was the second thing Pa had taught Winn about hunting. The first had been never to trust a supernatural being. The Darkin were the scourge of the universe—children of the night—dedicated to eliminating humans so they could claim the earth for themselves.

No matter how elegant, sophisticated, or well-mannered the contessa seemed, she was still just a damn vampire, and sooner or later he was going to have to slay her.

The knowledge bit down deep and hard into his bones, refusing to let go. Winn silently cursed in four different languages. As the oldest Jackson brother, he'd been exposed to the life of a Hunter the longest. Pa had started drilling the rules into him from the time Winn could toddle.

Which made all of this so much worse. Because ten years ago he'd given it up, walked away, and vowed to stay good and gone from Hunters and anything to do with the Darkin. He'd tried to lead a normal life—be an upstanding citizen with a clean reputation—something neither of his brothers would know about. For while the Jackson brothers looked similar on the outside, with their pa's jet hair and broad shoulders and their ma's blue eyes and winning smile, they were as different as could be on the inside.

Winn turned away from her as she bid the travelers a kind good-bye. She shook their hands, and waved to them while the horses gained steam and began to huff and chuff, ready to resume their journey into Bodie.

It didn't help that his little brother Colt, the hothead of the three and a self-styled outlaw, had come waltzing in that afternoon, determined to locate their pa's long-lost piece of the Book of Legend. Winchester had told his little brother the truth. Only a Darkin could access the Book where Pa

had hid it. And, nothin', but nothin', was going to change his mind about taking up arms as a Hunter again.

White puffs of steam and darker smoke from the carriage's boilers mixed with the dust kicked up by the mechanical horses, creating a dark smudge in the otherwise cloudless clear blue sky as the stage clanked and rolled on down the hill into Bodie.

The vampire eyed him with a mixture of curiosity and respect mingling in the depths of her eyes. "You are not exactly what I expected, Mr. Jackson." She clasped her bare hands together, the dark ruby ring winking on the ring finger of her right hand.

"What'd you expect?"

The corner of her mouth tipped up in a way that made his skin seem to shrink a size, and he had to keep himself from leaning forward to sample those tempting lips.

"From the legends we've been told"—her gaze raked him over, assessing him— "someone bigger."

Winn's lips twitched beneath the edge of his mustache. "Is that so?"

Her long, tapered fingers lightly brushed the velvet rim of her expensive little hat, which was sheltering her face from the sun. "*Da.* But then looks can be deceiving." Even though she looked no more than twenty-five, she had to be an old and powerful vampire to be withstanding the intensity of the daylight.

"You got that right," he muttered. Strip a bustle, petticoats, and corset off a woman and you were often shocked at what remained. But not with her. He could tell.

"His Majesty would like you to accompany us to his main palace in Europe and join in recovering the second third of the Book of Legend."

"You know where another piece is?"

"We did. For six hundred years it had been stored within the royal castle. But recently it was stolen. If you are willing,

His Vampiric Imperial Majesty's envoy and I would like to return this evening to discuss retaining your services."

Winn pressed his lips together. He wasn't about to hire out to a vampire—imperial, majestic or otherwise. He didn't work *with* supernaturals, and he sure as hell wasn't about to work *for* them.

"Let's get one thing straight, Lady Drossenburg. If I decide to help you, and I'm not saying I will, it will be on my terms, and not because I give a rat's ass what your high and mightiness back home thinks. We clear on that?"

A fine little tic worked at the corner of her eye, but otherwise her face remained perfectly smooth. Clearly she was as uncomfortable with this little arrangement as he was. Good.

She bowed her head and dropped into an elegant curtsey, the pale dust marring the edges of her dark skirt. "Of course, Mr. Jackson."

"We'll meet at the jail in Bodie. Ten o'clock tonight suit you?" There was no point in making it too early. He'd need time to prepare, for one thing, and for another he wasn't exactly anxious to go it alone with two vampires, possibly more. It might be a diplomatic mission, but he wasn't some stupid, average hick. He'd been trained by the best Hunters around, and a man didn't forget hard lessons like those.

She rose from the curtsey and lifted her chin with a defiant tilt. The blood-drop earrings at her earlobes danced with the movement of her head, calling attention to the smooth, supple skin just below her ear. "As you wish. We shall see you this evening."

Winn nodded. He wasn't happy about the appointment, but saying so wasn't going to make the situation any better. With the coach gone, he had no idea how she planned to get back to—wherever she'd come from, or if she intended to walk the three miles into town. She strode, her bustle swaying, in a slow, graceful pace toward the open desert,

away from Bodie. One second she was there, a dark mark against the too-tan landscape, and the next she turned into a spiral of dark smoke that dissipated on the breeze.

"Damn vampires," Winn muttered to himself, looking at the mess she'd left behind. High overhead three buzzards, their naked pink heads barely visible, circled in the sky. He'd have to get a deputy to come out here with Mortimer Brewster, the mortician in Bodie, to collect the bodies of the Dalton gang before only their picked-over bones remained. Carefully Winn dragged the bodies closer to the rocks, making a tableau that looked more like the attack of a mountain lion.

Hoss groaned and stirred up a cloud of powder-fine dirt from the trail. Winchester grabbed him up by the collar of his shirt, hauling him to his feet. "Up and at 'em, Hoss."

The bandit shook his head and wobbled. "What happened?"

"You were damn lucky, Hoss. Damn lucky. This time."

"Where am I?"

Winn clenched his jaw, waiting to see exactly what Hoss remembered as he walked Hoss back toward town. He didn't want to have to glamour him, but he would if he needed to. Pa's theory had been that the best way to take down a Darkin was to know what made them tick and learn how to use it against them, so he'd trained Winn to cast a glamour, and a few other things he preferred not to think on too much.

"Where's the boys?"

Winn gazed at Hoss through the corner of his eye. "You were hiding up in the rocks waiting for the stage, weren't you?"

Hoss stumbled slightly. Winn caught him by the upper arm and kept him walking.

"The stage—"

"That mountain lion must have had its fill 'fore it got to you."

Hoss looked at him, his bloodshot eyes narrowing with suspicion. "There weren't no mountai—" Winn locked gazes with Hoss, and the man went blessedly mute.

Winn carefully modulated his voice, keeping it low, slow, and even, letting the power well up from his gut and resonate in his throat as the glamour took over. "A large mountain lion attacked you and your gang before the stage with the Black Gulch bankroll came through. You were knocked unconscious after your gun backfired and slammed your head up against the rocks. And because it was so traumatic you're never going to hold up that stage again."

". . . backfired . . . traumatic . . . never again . . ." Hoss repeated softly, his eyes glazed.

Throwing a glamour over the man made a kind of sickening feeling slosh about in the pit of Winn's stomach. He didn't like resorting to Darkin tricks, hadn't even when he was a Hunter. But it was better this way, he assured himself. Better for Hoss. Better for the town. There was no need for these folks to be afraid of vampires, or even know they existed.

The walk back into town was slow going and damn hot. But thirty minutes later, Winn trudged up the sagging wooden steps of the Bodie jailhouse and led Hoss inside.

"Now you're going to sit down here for a bit till that sunstroke wears off you, you hear?" Truth was Winn was a might concerned the glamour might wear off before Hoss was fully functioning again, and he might relapse and remember everything. Winn needed to keep a close eye on him for a bit.

Hoss shook his head again. His eyes cleared as the glamour faded, and he dutifully sat down in the only ladderback chair on the front side of Winn's large, scarred desk.

Winn sat in his office chair and opened the left side

drawer of his desk, pulling out a brown glass bottle of whiskey and a shot glass.

"You mind if I have some of that?" Hoss eyed the bottle longingly and licked his cracked lips.

"Yep. I do." Clearly Hoss was back to normal and good to go.

Hoss scooted to the edge of his seat and closer to the bottle. "But I'm mighty parched."

Winn refrained from bodily just shoving Hoss out into the street and instead jerked his head toward the door. "Plenty of saloons in town. Go take your pick. Just make sure you tell Brewster to go take care of your boys up there first. No need for the buzzards to pick them clean."

Hoss got up from the chair, not needing further encouragement. The door swung shut behind the older man, and Winn kicked back a slug of the old Kentucky Red Eye, letting it sear a path down his gullet and chase away the chill in his stomach. He thought twice about taking another shot. If the vampires were coming, he'd have to have his wits about him for certain.

Winn set the shot glass on his desk, then leaned forward and scrubbed his hands over his face. He pulled on the hard waxed ends of his mustache.

It had been bad enough that his little brother Colt was bent on stirring up demons, but now there were vampires to contend with, and who knew what else might be dredged up by Colt's danged obsession with the Book of Legend.

Pa had hid his piece for good reason. The three brothers who had started the Legion of Hunters—Cadel, Haydn, and Elwin—had hacked the Book apart for good reason. And as far as Winn was concerned, he had one damn good reason for keeping himself out of hunting.

If that was even possible. He rubbed at the tight rope of scars across his thigh. Perhaps he'd been deluding himself for the last ten years. Ever since he'd had the run-in with

that demon who'd nearly drowned Colt, and got an axe imbedded in his own leg for his troubles, he'd realized he wasn't cut out to be a Hunter. There was too much at risk. He poured another jigger of whiskey into the glass and swirled the tawny liquid around.

It reminded him of the contessa's eyes, so clear and pure a color they were almost translucent amber. They were very unusual. Very pretty. But where there were Darkin, Hunters died. Where there were Darkin, the loved ones of Hunters died.

Years ago, his mother's blue eyes had gone wide with shock, her hand shaking and slick red with her lifeblood as she pulled it away from the spot the bullet had struck. Winn's legs wouldn't move. He couldn't even speak. The demon he'd meant to shoot had laughed, then turned into a black smudge in the air. The bullet had passed straight through it. His mother had sunk to her knees and fallen forward in the dirt, her honey-colored hair coming loose from the twist she always kept it in.

Time had seemed insanely slow as he stumbled toward her, falling beside her. "Mama?" He'd turned her over, but it was too late. Her eyes were open, but they were hollow. All the life in them was gone.

His stomach roiled at the memory, bile rising up in the back of his throat. Winn struggled to bring his shaking hand under control. He slammed the glass on the desktop, making the whiskey slosh over the rim. He cupped the back of his head with his hands and closed his eyes, breathing out in a slow, steady stream to calm his raging heartbeat.

His pa had spouted off the platitudes of it not being his fault. He hadn't known what the demon could do and that it took special bullets to wound one. He'd meant to do the right thing. But the distance between what Winn had meant to do and what had actually happened was from Bodie to the moon. Winn had never stopped blaming himself. His

world was black and white. He'd killed his mother, and he'd only been twelve. Only he and Pa had known.

The disaster with the demon almost drowning Colt ten years ago, then hitting Winn with an axe that almost cost him his leg, had been the last straw. Much as Pa wanted him to be a Hunter, he wasn't fit for it. He wasn't about to be the reason he lost his brothers too.

That vampire was just going to have to find some other poor sap Hunter to help her.

Chapter 2

The heavy thud of boots on the worn wooden steps outside the jail two hours later was the first clue Winn had visitors.

He pulled the pistol from his hip holster, cocked it, and held it level to the top of his battered desk, far more wary than he had been when his day had started. His brow furrowed and his eyes grew dry as he refused to blink. The seconds seemed to stretch in the late afternoon heat.

The door flew open as it was kicked inward. Winn's shoulders relaxed when he recognized the silhouette. His little brother Colt formed a dark shadow in the doorway, the bright sunshine outlining him. A smaller silhouette—that of a woman whose backlit red hair turned to flame in the sunlight—was close on his heels. Colt and the woman looked as though they'd been dragged behind a stage, maybe even trampled by the horses. Their torn, dirty clothing was splattered with dried blood.

Winn's heart stopped beating for a second as he tried to ascertain if it was his brother's blood or someone else's. By the pissed look on Colt's face he guessed it might be a bit of both. But he was relieved his brother was still standing.

Colt pulled the woman in with him. The dirty blue

calico hung limp and ragged from her shoulders, and her hem was torn clear up to the thigh, exposing long, shapely legs in torn fishnet stockings. Colt had his hand manacled about her wrist, and she didn't seem to be resisting. Who the hell was she, and what had she done to his brother down in the mine while he searched for the Book?

Winn shoved his Stetson back to get a better view. "What happened?"

Colt threw him a dirty, accusatory look. "We found the damn door. We got in. We got the wooden box open. There was nothin' in it! Nothin' but this scrap of paper." He threw the yellowed bit of paper on Winn's desk. "And we nearly got killed for our troubles."

Winn picked it up, unfolding the aged, brittle parchment with care. His eyes narrowed as he angled the paper first one direction, then the other, looking at the odd words scribbled into a spiral, trying to make sense of it. "It's in code."

There'd always been the chance that Pa would have taken extra precautions when he'd hidden his part of the Book down in the depths of the Dark Rim Mine, but apparently he hadn't trusted Winn enough to be completely honest about the location of the Book, or what would have to be done to reach it.

Fire erupted behind Colt's eyes, and the air shivered with his palpable rage. "No shit, Winn. What'd you do with Pa's part of the Book?"

Winn's gaze lifted from the page, boring deep into Colt. He counted slowly from ten to one in his head to keep from cuffing the boy for his attitude. "I didn't do a damn thing with that Book. Pa just said to keep watch over the thing. I haven't seen it since he hid it down deep in that mine when we were kids."

Unspoken hostility eddied between the Jackson brothers, making the air crackle. "You're tellin' me somebody

else got to it first?" The accusation was there, hanging between them unspoken, and it cut Winn to the core that his brother thought he'd do anything to hurt him.

Winn's gaze shifted, landing squarely on the woman beside his brother. He hadn't seen her before, but he knew a Darkin when he saw one, even if the telltale scent of sulfur hadn't followed in her wake. Her eyes were unnaturally green, like fine, clear emeralds. An ethereal beauty, she was too perfect to be a mere mortal. Dollars to pesos, she was a succubus, a demon designed to tempt men into giving away their very souls in exchange for physical pleasure. Just the kind of thing Rathe would dredge up to tempt a womanizer like Winn's youngest brother. "Not someone, some*thing*."

Colt shifted his stance, stepping slightly in front of her. Damn. The hair on the back of Winn's neck pricked both with irritation that his brother would actually protect a Darkin rather than just kill it outright, and with the knowledge that she'd already gotten to Colt and Winn hadn't been there to stop it. "She's been with me the whole time."

He bet. "This the demon you summoned to help you out?"

Colt gave one quick nod.

Winn huffed out a disgruntled sigh and coolly assessed the succubus from head to toe. Damn demon. His fingers tightened on the butt of his pistol. He ought to just shoot her and send her right back to Hell on principle alone. But that was Colt's job. Not his. He wasn't a Hunter. Not anymore.

"You sure know how to pick 'em, I give you that," Winn muttered. He released his grip on the pistol.

"Point is, she don't know any more about this code or the location of the missing piece of the Book than we do."

Winn picked up the scrap again, turning the page side-

ways, then upside down. "It's written in a circular fashion. Starts at the center like a spiral and coils outward."

"Like a spring." The demon's voice snapped both men's attention to her. "It's like a lock, and you're holding the key to the spring in the lock."

"Huh," Winn said, the one word conveying a host of unspoken I-don't-give-a-damn-what-you-think messages loud and clear. The sooner his brother got rid of the demon, the better.

"So what do you think it says?" Colt pressed, the impatience giving his voice a raw edge as he leaned in on the desk, the demon standing slightly behind him. Baby brother always had been rash, impetuous, a ladies' man, and prone to taking stupid risks. The demon's presence confirmed it.

"Have no clue. You're gonna have to have Marley pick this one apart." Their friend Marley Turlock was a bit of a mad genius. He could figure out just about anything, and when he couldn't, he was brilliant enough to invent something that *could*. Only problem was that his inventions tended to fall into two distinct categories: brilliant and disastrous.

Colt's brows dipped down below the level of his brown Stetson forming the tip of a V between his blue eyes. "He's not a code breaker."

"He's not, but Balmora is."

Colt released his hold on the demon beside him and pushed his Stetson up at the brim with his index finger. "Balmora?"

"Some fancy-pants contraption he's been building for the British government." Colt wouldn't have heard of it before. Marley rarely talked about an experiment still in the development stages, especially when he was working on it

for a paying client. Winn had only seen it once, halfway completed.

Colt leaned in, planting both fists firmly on the scarred expanse of Winn's desk. Confidence radiated off of his little brother, that certainty that he knew exactly what he was doing and believed in it with all he was worth. For a moment Winn envied him.

"Come with us. If the Darkin have found Pa's piece of the Book and moved it, there's no telling how fast this is gonna unravel."

Winn shook his head, spreading his hands wide on the surface of his desk. The image of the vampire contessa's face flickered in his vision, superimposed on the inside of his eyelids when he blinked. He had a lot more to deal with than Colt could possibly imagine. Vampires didn't tend to travel around in small groups. He sincerely doubted it would just be the contessa and the royal envoy. By tonight there was going to be an entire contingent of vampires swarming down on Bodie, and he was the only thing standing between them and the population. "Can't. Got an important foreign dignitary showing up this evening."

Colt shoved away from the desk. "Can't be bothered with the supernatural when you've got such important matters to tend to, eh?"

Anger simmered below Winn's skin, making it tight over his wind-chapped cheeks. Colt didn't know half of the shit he'd been through or done—things so dark they still lurked in the recesses of his conscience, waiting to stab at him whenever he thought he was past such behavior.

"Don't start with me, boy. I was hunting before you were walking." *And killing before you could talk*, Winn added silently to himself. Hardly the kind of thing a child should have been expected to do. And yet his pa would

accept nothing less than Winn's total immersion in the Hunter life.

"Which is exactly why we need you to come along."

"He's right. Rathe is planning something," the demon said.

Winn glared at her. Rathe was an archdemon lord, and just hearing his name made Winn twitchy. He thought he was showing an amazing amount of restraint considering he hadn't shot her in the forehead already. Between that and not killing the vampire this morning, he briefly wondered if he had been out of the game long enough to have completely lost his touch. "And I'm supposed to trust you?"

Colt stiffened, his skin turning ruddy. Winn knew he'd struck a nerve. There was a hell of a lot more going on between his little brother and the demon than Colt had admitted. "We've got a deal. She's going to help me get the Book."

Deep down Winn's stomach shrank to the size of a walnut. He knew it. The demon had already got her hooks into Colt. His glare shifted to his little brother. "Dammit. Didn't I tell you not to give your soul for that Book?"

"I didn't. She wants our help."

Winn rolled his eyes and gave his head a small shake. When the hell was Colt gonna stop thinking with the head in his pants and start thinking with the one under his Stetson? "They all say that, brother."

"She wants to get away from Rathe. She wants to return to being human again." Colt looked so damn sincere, like he actually believed the tripe he was spouting off.

Winn glanced at the demon. "Is that true?"

She stepped around Colt, her lithe body built for seduction. Winn could hardly fault his brother. Colt might be a Hunter, but he was human. Things would have been much easier if he'd just summoned up some ugly sonofabitch with forked tongue and tail.

The creamy skin of her throat flexed with a heavy

swallow. It didn't take a lawman to know she was scared and desperate. Two things that were not a smart combination when going up against a powerhouse like Rathe. "No one has ever tried it before, but the way I see it, if anyone could find a way to break Rathe's hold on my soul, it would be the Chosen."

The word made Winn's insides curl, like paper to a flame. It seared his gut, burning hot and quick. The Chosen. Those stupid rumors were never going to die. It was like some damn religion among the Hunters. Well, he wasn't some hero. Hell, he barely considered himself civilized most of the time.

Colt grunted and scraped his scuffed brown boot over the gritty wooden floor. "Told you before, Lilly. We're not the Chosen."

So the demon even had a first name. The slight widening of her eyes in surprise was quickly narrowed as she balled up her fists. "You don't *think* you are. Big difference. Doesn't mean you're not."

Interesting. The fact that she was willing to go head-to-head with his brother meant he actually respected her. Respect for a Darkin wasn't exactly trust. But it was damn close. Whatever had happened down in the Dark Rim Mine had tested them both and forged a bond of trust between them. Winn wasn't about to trust Lilly, or the contessa, or anything else non-human, but he trusted Colt. And if Colt thought she was necessary to his plans, he'd support his brother—Chosen malarkey or not.

"Either way, don't matter," Winn said, clasping his hands over the back of his head. "You two need to get to Marley on the double. I'll see what I can do about tapping into a lead on the second part of the Book for you, but I'm not going on any fool's errand to fetch it back."

"You know we're going to need more than just Pa's part of the Book, don't you?"

Winn snorted. Maybe he'd given Colt too much credit. "Now she's really got you addled, boy. The parts were never meant to be brought together. That's why the Legion separated them in the first place. It's too damn dangerous."

Colt shook his head slowly, his eyes deadly serious. "That's where you're wrong. If what I think is happening is true, then we need to get those other pieces. Pa told me this might happen."

That got Winn's attention.

There was precious little his pa hadn't drilled into him about hunting. He was itching to know what Pa had told Colt, but he didn't dare ask in front of the demon. "We don't even know where the two other thirds of the Book are located."

"A lead is all we need."

Too bad even the vampires didn't know where the other third of the Book was located now. It would have made Colt's search easier. Winn stared at him long and hard. Damn, but his little brother's confidence was infectious. He didn't want to hunt, but could he really stand aside knowing Colt needed his help?

He knew his baby brother well enough to know Colt's course had already been set. Like a runaway locomotive on a straight stretch of track, there was no changing his direction. The best Winn could hope for was to remove as many obstacles in Colt's way as he could and pray it was enough to keep his brother alive.

"If I find anything, I'll send word through Marley," Winn said simply.

Relief softened the hard set of Colt's jaw. He might be stubborn, but he knew he needed help. Deep down in Winn's chest a warm, solid feeling unfurled. He knew

backing his brother was the right thing to do, even if it meant putting his lot in with a bunch of vampires and going along in a scheme to bring the pieces of the Book back together.

Colt's mouth lifted into a smile. "Thanks, Winn."

"You'd best go on," he answered back.

His little brother and the demon he'd come to rely on left the jail in the quickly dwindling afternoon light. He didn't have time to ruminate too much on his decision to go search for the second lost piece of the Book of Legend. The vampires would be there come nightfall, and he needed to be prepared.

Winn pulled open the bottom drawer of his desk and pulled out a worn wooden box with a slider lid. The lid rasped as he shoved it open, revealing the specially crafted silver bullets and salt-packed shotgun shells he rarely used. His fingers caressed the smooth silver, the familiar zing of anticipation firing his blood.

He might have walked away from being a Hunter, but it was something that never left you. The memories still haunted him. The knowledge of the things he'd done in the name of protecting mankind still burdened his conscience and stained his soul. Once a Hunter, forever a Hunter. It was like a brand. There was no amount of scrubbing or whitewashing that could hide what he truly was at his core.

Winn slid the lid shut and set the box atop the desk. His brain went on automatic, like he was an automaton, just going through the motions without thought or rationale as to why he was performing the actions of packing. His rifle and back sling, his special ammunitions and packages of salt. His bowie knife and whetstone to sharpen the blade.

By sundown everything was ready for Winn to leave at a moment's notice, but the churning in his gut left him unsettled. Winn sat back in his office chair and waited, scrap-

ing the bowie against the surface of the stone, finding the hissing grind of it comforting.

Four hours passed. Firelight from the potbellied stove flickered along the walls, casting the jail cell bars into sharp stripes of shadow. Winn kept pacing. The ticking clock seemed overly loud to his ears and was keeping time with his heartbeat. He hadn't bothered to light a lantern when dark fell. Vampires had excellent night vision.

The clock struck ten. A whiff of sulfur tainted the air, and Winn stopped his in tracks, stiffening. A knock rattled the door. Polite vampires? That surprised him. They could have just as easily pushed the door off its hinges and strutted right in, or, judging by the contessa's disappearing act this afternoon, vaporized themselves into the room.

He hesitated for just a moment, taking in a deep, fortifying breath. There was no way of knowing exactly how many vampires she'd brought with her.

Winn pulled the jail door inward with a long, mournful creak. Before him stood the contessa, her dark hair, dress, and small hat blending in with the night around her. Only one vampire stood beside her, a young man with pale skin and streaky blond hair. The highly polished brass buttons that ran on either side of his black uniform glinted in the firelight. He was broad of shoulder and a good six inches taller than the contessa, but they shared the same unusual coloration of their eyes. One didn't often see a pretty boy like that on the frontier.

"Good evening, Mr. Jackson," she said, her voice warm and rich.

He nodded once in acknowledgment.

The contessa touched the arm of the vampire beside her. "This is His Imperial Majesty's envoy, Enric."

Enric bowed slightly from the waist, but never took his gaze off of Winn or his gun holster.

Winn's glance darted to the shadows, making sure there weren't others waiting in the wings. Finding none, he opened the door further. "Won't you come in?" The distinct rotten-egg stench of sulfur emitted by nearly all Darkin was barely perceptible, but still tweaked his nose, making him hold his breath slightly as they passed.

He shut the door behind them and offered the contessa the one chair he had, dusting the seat of it off since Hoss had been the last to sit on it. He figured the envoy was vampire enough to stand for a bit.

Her blue-black skirts rustled as she sat stiffly and primly on the edge of the chair. The envoy stood, feet spread, hands clasped behind his lower back, in military fashion. Clearly neither of them planned on staying long. Good. He wasn't in the mood to drag this out either.

He settled into the spot behind his desk, giving him some kind of barrier between him and the vampires. The contessa's gaze slid about the room, taking in the rough frontier conditions of his jail, making him feel like he was being looked down upon. Winn bristled. She stared pointedly at his hat, and Winn got uncomfortable enough to remove his favorite black Stetson, setting it on the top of his desk.

Her gaze connected with his, assessing him in the same manner she had assessed the Bodie jail that had defined his life for the past five years. "The American West is indeed a wild place." She paused, a frown drawing the dark wings of her brows together, as if choosing her next words with care. "Are you satisfied being a peacekeeper among your people?"

"Are you asking if I miss hunting?"

She gave a nearly imperceptible shrug of her shoulders. "It never hurts to know the people one hopes to work with in dangerous times."

Winn leaned forward in his chair. "So why don't we just

stop the square dancing, and you tell me why you really want me to come with you so badly."

"His Imperial—"

"I didn't ask what His Majesty wanted," Winn interrupted, growing impatient with the faux politeness being passed around the table. He wanted to know what stake she had in all this. "I asked about you." That would tell him everything he needed to know.

Alexa eyed him, trying to read his thoughts, and found them effectively blocked. How was that possible? In all her centuries as a vampire she'd never run into a mortal that she could not access or read. He had to be strong, very strong, and well-trained.

But they were treading on territory too close to home for her taste. "Have you any children, Mr. Jackson?"

Winchester snorted. "No. Haven't really ever led the kind of life that was conducive to having children."

She sighed, irritation lacing her exhale. "Have you ever lost someone close to you, someone who you loved more than life itself?"

Sorrow glistened for an instant in his brilliant blue eyes, then was ruthlessly shuttered away. He'd lost someone dear to him, and likely in a brutal fashion.

"I can see you have," she said simply.

"What does that have to do with your wanting me to tag along to the vampire motherland and help recover the missing piece of the Book?"

Alexa gripped her hands tighter, making the black kid leather squeak slightly. "Mr. Jackson, over the past several hundred years I've watched everyone dear to me, all my mortal family and friends, die. I've even watched some of

those I've transformed, my own children by gift, perish at the hands of Hunters like yourself."

"I don't hunt anymore," he practically growled.

She briefly nodded in acknowledgment. "Regardless, you don't forget."

His bottom lip flattened into a hard line beneath his dark mustache.

"I refuse to stand by and watch my children by gift, and the other members of my kind, be wiped out by an archdemon lord intent on erasing their food supply from existence."

Winn flinched and swallowed hard.

"Rathe is bent on controlling everything he can to amuse his sadistic self, and he cares not what the casualties may be among the Darkin," she added. She leaned forward, her hand curling around his, and found it callused and warm, even through the thin barrier of her glove. "If you could go back and prevent the loss of the person you loved, wouldn't you do everything you could, no matter who or what you had to partner with?"

Winn quickly pulled his hand from her grasp. "So this is personal to you."

She locked gazes with him. "In ways you cannot possibly imagine."

"Bringing the Book back together is a bad idea. A concentration of power like that is too much temptation for any being—Darkin or mortal."

"It is why we were instructed to seek your help," the envoy interjected. "His Majesty believes that the Chosen can withstand the full power of the Book once it is reunited and bring about the prophecy. We have an airship waiting."

Winn glanced out the window, his eyes mirroring the dark depth of the desert sky at night. He was arrogant, boorish, and still a Hunter to the core no matter what he'd

done for the last decade. Alexa tamped down her personal responses to the man who set her off in all the wrong ways.

Their hopes all rested with Winchester Jackson and his brothers. If the Chosen couldn't help them defeat Rathe, then they were outmatched before the battle could even begin. No matter how she personally felt about Mr. Jackson, it was her duty to get him back to His Majesty and assist however she could to help him recover the second piece of the Book of Legend. She took in a fortifying breath, even though her useless lungs didn't require air.

"Will you come with us, Mr. Jackson?"

Chapter 3

Slouched back in his chair, Winchester Jackson stared into the middle distance, brooding, in stoic silence. But his body betrayed his agitation.

Although he sat perfectly still and appeared composed, Alexa could hear the rapid, rhythmic susurrus of his blood coursing through his veins and the slightly elevated throb of his heartbeat.

My gods, but he was enticing. Alexa pushed back the overwhelming desire to taste him. A man as rugged and strong as this would have an intoxicating vitality that would make a vampire positively drunk.

You sound like a man with his first taste of vodka. Enric's amused tone annoyed her.

Hush, Enric.

Mr. Jackson pulled at the ends of his handlebar mustache, making them curl in a dark smile. The moment his gaze flicked back and locked with hers, she saw that he'd made his decision.

"Before I'd agree to step aboard your ship, I'd need to set some conditions."

They both knew he was in no position to set conditions

or dictate the parameters of what could and could not be done on board her ship, but she humored him. "Naturally."

"First. I get a secured cabin, with a locked door, to myself for the duration of the journey."

I thought you were being overly cautious to prepare such things ahead of time, but it seems you've anticipated him well. Enric's voice echoed in her head.

"Second. No vampire feeds in my presence."

Alexa gave him a regal nod. Her people fed whenever the need arose. Whenever. Wherever. If he wanted to eat in the isolation of his room, she certainly wouldn't stop him. But the request irritated her all the same. Didn't he realize his presence was just as intrusive, just as galling to her and her children as their existence was to him? Even if he didn't think himself a Hunter, he still was one down to the worn tips of his very American boots.

"Third. I want your solemn oath that if a single mortal under my protection is harmed by a vampire, I have the right to use any means at my disposal to retaliate."

Alexa hesitated. The smell of sweat and horse, dirt and whiskey permeated his skin and made her glad she didn't need to breathe. Her gumline throbbed, her fangs attempting to engage and slip down from the soft folds of her gum tissue. She kept them scrupulously in check.

He is ruthless, uncouth, and uncultured, Enric reminded her. *Everything distained by our kind. Do not forget that, Alexa.*

I am aware, she shot back mentally, not needing the reminder. They had a name for Hunters like this in her corner of the world:

Slayers.

Slayers killed without compunction or thought, without plan or intellect. To kill and keep from being killed were their only immediate goals. They were primitive and dangerous.

She wanted to refuse Mr. Jackson, but at what cost?

Vlad wants Mr. Jackson at any cost, Enric reminded her, growing impatient. *If the Slayer won't come willingly, we will kidnap him as planned.*

Alexa shot Enric a small frown. *Having a willing Slayer aboard will be far safer than an abducted one bent on revenge.*

Alexa reminded herself of her duty and stiffened her spine and returned her steady gaze across the cluttered desk to meet Mr. Jackson's dark blue eyes. "Agreed." *Reluctantly.* "Anything else?"

"Yes. I want to stop somewhere before we go. I have an inventor friend I think can help us."

"Certain—"

"And I want your promise that no matter what happens, you'll bring me home when this is all over. Dead or alive."

Alexa looked at the imperial envoy, Enric. *You notice he didn't mention undead.* Enric's voice, laced with amusement, filtered through her thoughts.

I certainly did. Can you read his thoughts?

No. They're blocked. He frowned slightly. *It poses a risk to have a trained Hunter aboard who can shield himself like this.*

Alexa's mouth flattened into a determined line. *We are at far greater risk from Rathe and the other Darkin aligned with him. We must recover our piece of the Book at any cost.*

You are right.

She caught Winn's hard stare and offered her hand. "Agreed."

Winn took it and shook it twice. His grip was firm but not punishing. He was a man who meant what he said and said what he meant. Perhaps there was no reason she needed to read his mind when his emotions were so boldly displayed on his features and his words were so plain.

Relieved that they hadn't had to forcibly kidnap him,

Alexa's shoulders relaxed. This had gone more easily than she'd imagined, although she suspected that Winchester Jackson wasn't an "easy" man. He was far more complex and deep than he let on. But Alexa had had hundreds of years to learn how to deal with complicated, difficult men. For now she'd enjoy her victory. She offered him a small smile. "We shall depart within the hour. Will that give you sufficient time to pack?"

"I already did."

His response took her aback, making an uncomfortable tingle skitter up the back of her bare neck. If he'd planned to go with them all along, why did he act so hesitant, and why all the conditions?

It didn't matter, she firmly reminded herself. Vlad would be pleased she'd accomplished her diplomatic mission regardless. And the sooner she got away from Mr. Winchester Jackson, the safer she'd feel.

A slight scuffling noise and the uneasy shuffle of horse hooves caught her attention. Alexa cocked her head to listen, her preternatural hearing particularly acute.

Mr. Jackson's nostrils flared slightly. His gaze flicked to the door, and his eyes narrowed. "We've got company. Your people?"

"No." Enric raised a brow. "There's someone outside." The clack of Mr. Jackson's cocking his rifle caused her gaze to dart back to the Slayer. In just the brief second she'd looked away, he'd settled his Stetson on his head and grabbed a long black oilcloth duster and his rifle from an iron nail on the rough wall. She didn't miss the gun belt and holster strapped to his thigh that disappeared behind the oilcloth or the glint of the bowie knife handle in the top of his boot.

"Just past the cell block on the left is the back door to get to the outhouse. Get her out of here. Now," Mr. Jackson

said low and deep. He hunkered down behind his desk and leveled his rifle, taking aim at the door.

The telltale odor of sulfur might be faint to Mr. Jackson, but now that she noticed it, Alexa didn't know how she'd ignored it before. There were Darkin outside. How many, she didn't know. But they must be here for him.

His Imperial Majesty said Jackson was key to defeating Rathe. Surely the other side, under Rathe's command, was just as eager to keep him from reaching Europe as the vampires were to get him there. Enric grabbed her by the elbow and tried to steer her toward the door at the back of the Bodie jail. Alexa yanked her arm from his grip. *I'm staying.*

With all due respect, my lady, my job is to protect you.

She glared at Enric. *And my job is to protect him.*

Enric frowned. *Very well. We will both stand and fight.*

Today had been filled with enough weird encounters with Darkin that Winn wasn't exactly sure what to make of the ones coming his way now.

A loose board on the rickety porch right in front of the door creaked. Winn slipped his finger over the trigger of his shotgun. No use taking chances. The knob on the front door rotated, then stopped. The back door clicked shut.

There was a muffled curse and a hiss, then the sound of running feet that doubled around the back of the jail.

Winn shot up out of his stance and rushed the front door, yanking it open only to find darkness. There was no one to be seen. "Damn," Winn muttered.

A heavy blow near the back of his neck sent a spurt of stars into his vision. Winn wheeled around, trying to use the butt of his rifle on his attacker. He grunted, landing one blow, but the man was too fast, or invisible.

The stench of sulfur cut through the night air, sharp and

pungent, burning in his nose and eyes, but Winn couldn't see the creature's face until he stepped into the pool of light coming through the doorway.

Winn went momentarily rigid as he saw the face of Hoss Dalton.

"What the hell—"

A fist like a sledgehammer slammed hard against his jaw, making Winn stumble back. Didn't matter what the bastard looked like, he had a hard right hook, and no way could Hoss hit that hard. Winn bent low and grabbed up his rifle, firing it point blank in the belly of the Darkin while he could still see the bastard.

The creature stumbled back screaming, its voice fading to a thin wail almost like a steam whistle as the silver in Marley's special bullets dissolved the Darkin into a column of acrid black smoke.

"That's one down," he muttered. Winn didn't waste a second. He dashed inside, grabbed his black knapsack, slapped his rifle holster and gun on his back, and ran out the back door. Enric and the contessa were fighting with two more Darkin that looked like members of Dalton's gang. Damn shifters. They must have gotten to the bodies and taken the skins before the mortician reached them.

Bits of flashing light were still sparking in his vision, but he could see the vampires and shifters were equally matched. If he'd been a normal Hunter, he would have sat back, poured himself a shot of whiskey, and watched the show, but nothing about this was normal. He'd already given his word to help the vampires, and even if he wasn't a Hunter any longer, Winn was still a man of his word.

He squinted, trying hard to aim at the shifters in the dark, but the vampires moved so damned fast he couldn't get a clean shot. He settled for winging one of the shifters and letting the silver do the rest.

Winn shut one eye, set his sights, and shot. The sound of the gun firing made all the Darkin, shifter and vampire alike, pause for one second. The creature he'd shot bucked forward, one hand clawing at its back. It twisted, its eyes fully black now, and not anything close to human, while it dissolved into a thick twist of dark sulfuric smoke.

The vampires took off running, the last shifter taking off after them.

Winn cursed under his breath. He was clearly out of practice in this game. He'd forgotten how fast Darkin could move. He ran back around the front of the jail and grabbed the horse at the closest hitching post, kicking him into a gallop after the contessa, Enric, and the shifter.

Beneath the dark, starlit sky, a moon, cleaved in half as it waxed toward full, hovered over Bodie. It illuminated the pale surface of the desert enough that he could see their bodies, dark and moving in the night.

The horse huffed beneath him, hooves pounding out a solid rhythm and kicking up spurts of dirt as they galloped toward his target. Damn vampires. He knew they could move fast as a bolt of lightning under the right circumstances, but he hadn't thought they could make it this far in the time it had taken him to get a damn horse.

The night smelled of dirty oil from the creosote bushes, and wood smoke from the fires in Bodie. A faint tint of sulfur in the air, from the supernaturals ahead of him, confirmed the Darkin presence.

Silver moonlight washed the desert in light and shadow, turning it surreal and painting haunted faces on the rocks where there were blank slates in the daylight.

Winn pulled the reins, moving the horse in a wide arc so he could intercept the quickly moving supernaturals. He pulled his rifle from the holster on his back and pulled down the lever, preparing to shoot. The vampires ran straight at

him, then split apart at the last moment, giving him a clear opening at the shifter.

Winn fired.

The shifter jerked to a stop, peering down at his chest before his whole body began to shake and convulse, exploding into a fireball, then a twisted column of smoke.

Both the contessa and Enric walked toward him, neither of them breathing hard, because they didn't need to, but both looking far more worn than they had in his office. "You two okay?"

Enric gave him a stiff nod. A dark, deep set of scratch marks across his cheekbone marred his pretty face. "Was that the last of the four of them?"

"Four?" Winn knew of only three. Damn. There was still one on the loose.

A haughty laugh, deep and vile, interrupted them. All three of them turned in unison as a man dressed like a dapper plantation owner in a long, gray coat, hat, and gloves approached. He clapped, his gloves muffling the sound. Despite the dust of the desert his clothes were spotless perfection.

"Very well done. Very well, indeed." His smooth Southern drawl had an unctuous quality to it that crawled beneath Winn's skin.

"Who the hell are you?" Winn growled, his horse sidestepping beneath him as it sensed the agitation eddying in the air.

"Dr. Adder Morpheus, at your service."

Hardly. Winn caught the distinct odor of sulfur about the man. He was Darkin, Winn would bet his gun on it.

"A pleasure to make your acquaintance, Lady Drossenburg. I've heard so much about you."

The contessa nodded briefly, her gaze flicking to Enric. Something was going on between the two vampires, Winn could tell. He wasn't sure exactly what it was, but with

every glance and change in facial expression, he knew they were somehow communicating and leaving him and the doctor out of the damn conversation.

"What is your business, Dr. Morpheus?" the contessa asked, her voice steady and controlled, without a flick of emotion.

"I'm afraid I must insist on Mr. Jackson's company. You see, my employer doesn't want him anywhere near your charming influence."

Both the contessa and the envoy tensed, their fangs descending with an audible *flick*. "We are taking Mr. Jackson with us, with or without your employer's consent, sir," she said firmly.

Winn had had enough.

"There ain't a need to be so damn polite about all this," he growled. "Look here, Morpheus. I ain't goin' with you." Winn shifted his gaze to the vampires. "We done now? I thought we had a ship to catch."

"Not so fast, Mr. Jackson," Dr. Morpheus said, his voice dropping a notch with expectation. "Rathe has plans for you." The man began to swell, his belly growing. The buttons on his acid green vest popped off and flew in all directions.

The sound of ripping fabric filled the air. Beneath Winn the horse whinnied and shied backward, the white of its eyes visible. Winn tightened his hold on the reins. "What the hell—" he breathed.

Morpheus continued to swell, his grotesquely distended stomach shiny in the moonlight. He let out a blood-curdling yell as his abdomen split open from waist to breastbone and thousands of small, shining objects poured out of him onto the desert sand.

Winn wasn't about to stick around long enough to find out what they were. "Run!" he yelled. He wheeled his horse around and kicked it into a full gallop.

He glanced back and saw Morpheus standing, fully

whole once more, watching them with a satisfied smirk right below his pencil-thin black mustache. For a moment Winn thought it a trick of the light. The desert sand seemed to shimmer and move, though it wasn't midday and there was no heat wave; the tide seemed to be following them in a ripple across the valley.

"What do you make of that?" he yelled at Enric.

"The ground is moving."

"Impossible," the contessa shot back.

Winn narrowed his eyes. "That ain't the ground. There's something moving on top of it." The unnatural silvery sheen kept advancing.

"Come on. The ship is just on the other side of this mountain." The contessa motioned them forward with a sweep of her hand. Winn urged his horse to follow, but the animal had to trot to keep up with the rapid pace of the vampires. As they crested the mountain range they looked down upon a most unusual sight.

An enormous silver dirigible, nearly two hundred feet long, sat upon the floor of the desolate desert valley, illuminated by the moonlight. On the pale surface he could easily see the sigil marking the side of the vessel, a red castle turret with a crenellated top in the Norman fashion, bracketed on either side by black bat wings. It fairly screamed vampires. "Hardly subtle," he muttered to himself.

At the base of the ship, beneath the large curve of the air balloon, rested a three-story gondola crafted with polished teakwood, brass, and glass. In a word, expensive. Clearly they were a well-funded group, which explained why they thought they could buy just about damn near anything they wanted—including him. Well, they had a surprise coming. He had his own reasons for joining up with these Darkin. He pushed forward, the loose rock and dirt on the downward side of the hills forcing him to move slower or risk breaking the horse's leg or getting thrown.

Behind them the silver moving tide crested the face of the mountain. The horse shied, tossing its head and whinnying in distress as mechanical spiders the size of a tin cup moved in a clacking swarm over the rocks directly behind them. "Move!" Winn yelled.

The vampires darted down the uneven slope, and Winn did his best to follow without injuring the horse. While the spiders were close, the vampires and the horse were faster.

The massive dirigible was even larger up close. Enormous creases marked the rigid frame latticework of ribs beneath the silver fabric skin of the ship. It looked sturdy enough, but could it actually fly? The ship shuddered and hissed, a column of white steam erupting from near the rudders. He glanced back at the advancing silvery tide of spiders, with their glowing, beady red eyes. Looked like they didn't have much choice.

"Get aboard! They have already set the fires to high to accommodate liftoff." The contessa's voice startled Winn. He glanced down at her upturned face. Damn, but she moved quiet-like. He was going to have to be more aware. Being away from hunting for so long had left his senses dulled. He didn't wait to be told twice. He swung down off the horse and slapped the creature's backside, letting it run off into the night. It'd have a better chance of escaping the spiders and getting back to Bodie if he turned it free.

Winn jogged up the thick wooden gangplank that had been extended from the first deck of the airship to the ground as he followed the vampires.

"Enric, see that those things are kept off the ship," she instructed as she kicked a mechanical spider off the gangplank. "And bring Mr. Jackson up to the captain as soon as possible." She turned and disappeared through a door with a stained-glass window in it that bore the same castle-tower-and-bat-wing emblem as on the dirigible's balloon.

If she thought he was some trained lapdog that was

gonna come running every time she snapped her little fingers together, she'd better think again.

Enric swore as he hauled up the gangplank. "We're not going to get off the ground in time. Those things are everywhere."

The swarm of spiders was indeed covering the ship, weighing it down. The clicking of their millions of sharp, metallic legs caused an almost constant hissing sound, like a sleet storm against a metal roof. They skidded off the smooth wood of the gondola but clung to the gangplank and the ropes. The airship rose slowly into the air. Too slowly. But at least no more of the things could climb aboard.

Winn stomped one with his boot. A thin, greenish liquid squirted out, and the wood beneath it began to smolder, sending up wisps of acrid smoke. "Damn things are filled with acid. Don't squash them!" he yelled at Enric.

He and Enric worked side-by-side trying to brush the spiders off the ship through the railings of the gondola with their feet. A few got close enough to crawl up Winn's pants, their needle-like appendages gouging into his legs. "Ow. Those damn things are sharp," he snapped as he kicked them off and swore in Latin, English, and French. "There's got to be something we could do to get rid of them." But there were too many of them.

"I have an idea," Enric said. A swirl of smoke appeared at Enric's feet, forming a large, banded steam trunk and a pair of iron tongs Winn had seen farriers use to dig red-hot horseshoes out of the coals at the stables.

"Start throwing them in here!" Enric said. He lifted the lid.

Winn snatched up the tongs and started grabbing and tossing as many spiders as he could into the trunk. Enric's vampire reflexes were fast enough that he could open and shut the trunk quickly and keep the spiders contained. The wind tore at Winn's hat, threatening to rip it off his head as

the ship rose higher and higher. He was moving so fast he almost missed seeing the several harried faces of identically uniformed crewmen that seemed to appear here and there as they scurried about ridding the ship of spiders.

Winn glanced around and didn't see any more. "What are you going to do with them?" he asked Enric.

The vampire smiled back, showing off his fangs. "What we usually do to a nuisance. Get rid of them."

Winn watched as Enric tossed the trunk over the edge of the airship. It hurtled down, spinning end over end until it crashed on the desert floor.

Adrenaline pumped hard and fast in his system, causing every sense to be on edge as Winn moved. He didn't trust Darkin, especially not vampires. And now that the spiders were gone, his neck felt exposed. Winn pulled the collar of his duster up to cover it as a precaution. No sense in taking chances on a ship full of vampires.

Enric opened the same door the contessa had entered, and close up Winn could see the stained glass was as fine as anything made by Tiffany & Co. "Let's get you to the bridge. I know the captain and the contessa are waiting."

They walked quickly along a narrow hall to the base of a set of stairs, then climbed up to the second deck. It appeared to be nothing more than an endless set of long hallways punctuated at regular intervals with doors.

"Sleeping quarters?" Winn asked out of curiosity.

"*Da.*"

"Everybody on the same deck, or are crew and passengers separated?" Winn asked. He mentally counted the doors and figured there were two, maybe as many as four bunks to a room, so he could estimate the total number of vampires on the ship.

"There is only one sleeping deck, but since most of us need only a few hours at most, we rotate in shifts."

Great. That blew any kind of calculations to hell.

Enric barely paused enough for Winn to get his bearings before he continued on with the abbreviated tour. "The bridge is located on the top deck."

"So are you and the contessa both from Transylvania?"

"*Da*. The entire royal court is there."

"You connected to the vampires here in the States?"

"We have diplomatic relations with them."

They traveled up another set of stairs to the top deck. The top level of the dirigible looked modern, like the rest of the ship, but far more plush, like an expensive hotel lobby, surrounded by windows that looked out into the night sky.

Huge potted palms, with their long, feathery green boughs, broke up the large open space, making the heavily stuffed and elegantly carved chairs and settees grouped together in clusters seem more inviting. Underfoot a thick, Oriental carpet muffled their steps. He didn't miss the vampire's crest in rich burgundy and gold bracketed by the ominous black wings. At the far end of the room, a roaring fire crackled and sparked in the grate of a marble fireplace. It seemed tranquil in comparison to their fight with the shifters and spiders.

Granted, the stone cherubs holding the ornately scrolled columns aloft had fangs, but knowing this was a vampire ship didn't make it any less impressive.

"How long have you known the contessa?"

Enric stared at him for a moment. His lips twitched. "About four hundred years. I was a stable boy in the count's household, and she offered me the chance to become a child by gift for my service."

Winn's gut heated a bit. Enric probably knew her better than anyone. "Why does the count let his wife serve in politics?"

"Her ladyship is a widow and isn't one to let any man tell her what she may or may not do."

Enric gave him an amused glance and gestured to an ornately carved set of wooden sliding doors. "These lead to our dining area."

"Dining room? The couches out here don't work well enough for you?" Winn jibed.

Enric raised one brow. "No, it's much better when we just line our victims up in the dining chairs and ask them to lean to one side." He hissed and bared his fangs, causing Winn to stiffen, then Enric chuckled. "Truly, you'll have to do better if you wish to wound me, Hunter."

"And you'll have to do better than that to scare me," Winn retorted.

A spiral of smoky particles beside Enric twisted into the solid, petite form of the contessa. "Gentlemen, manners." The cold edge to her voice left no doubt she disapproved of their exchange. "Do not bare your fangs again at our guest unless you are invited to."

The blond vampire gave her a sheepish look and bowed his head. "Yes, my lady."

"You are excused," she said simply with an upward tilt of her chin.

Enric stalked off back the way they had come.

The contessa turned her sharp gaze on Winn. "Before we go on any further, Mr. Jackson, let's clarify some rules of my own."

Winn braced his feet apart and crossed his arms. He felt the sway of the floor and was grateful he couldn't observe the ground dropping away beneath them. The faint throb of large engines was more a sensation than a sound. Now that they were airborne, she had the advantage, and they both knew it. "I thought we'd already done that."

"Well, you certainly let me know what you wanted. But it's time you learned what *I* want." Her sleek, dark brows pinched with disapproval, and she nibbled away at her bottom lip. An image of kissing that exact spot flared to life

in his mind and caused his gut to twist with awareness of her very lush female form.

"Do you always wear your hat indoors?"

Winn lifted his chin and snatched the Stetson off his head, heat pricking his neck beneath his shirt collar, making it itch. He hated how easily she made him feel as if he wasn't worthy enough to be scraped from her boots. "I thought you *wanted* me to go with you."

She turned away from him and looked out through the dark windows that rimmed the observation deck. The airship rose higher into the intense midnight blue of the sky. Her gloved hands gripped the smooth teak railing. "I am tolerating your presence on this ship for a simple reason." She glanced at him, and sincerity mixed with distrust shone in her eyes. "I feel you could make a difference."

Winn let that soak in for a second. She needed him, but didn't like him. "No offense, Lady Drossenburg, but as long as we're being honest with one another, I find the fact that you're a vampire revolting." He resolutely settled the Stetson back on his head.

She glanced at him, her dark brow arched with bemusement, but not anger. "No offense taken, since I find the fact that you are a Hunter equally revolting." She turned away from him again, her slender back straight as she stared out into the depths of the dark, star-strewn sky.

A long pause stretched out between them, as if she were waiting to see who would fall into the gap and speak first. Winn figured it would have to be her since he didn't have anything more to say.

The broad expanse of glass acted like a mirror, reflecting the curves and elegant lines of her profile. Flawless skin, the color of cream, stretched over high cheekbones and a straight, small aquiline nose. Her lips were a touch too full, but they somehow balanced the thick, long fringe of

lashes that curved upward, nearly touching her brow. Winn realized he was staring a second before she caught him.

"Mr. Jackson, I realize you are not comfortable with us, but if you plan on being difficult I will be forced to isolate you to your rooms for the duration of our trip."

Winn was sorely tempted to tell her to go ahead and try, but experience tempered his tongue. There were far more vampires aboard this ship, and while they wouldn't kill him, because they needed him, they didn't have to be nice about how they got him to wherever they were headed.

She turned and looked at him, the unusual color of her eyes drawing him in. The contessa might be a vampire, but she was also a mighty fine-looking woman. Her glossy curls curved around the small shells of her ears, and each slight tilt of her head made the blood-drop ruby earrings at her lobes dance with movement, drawing his eye to the long column of her neck.

Unlike some homespun frontier woman, there was a natural polish to her that seemed to make her glow with confidence, and an air of superiority which clung to her like a second skin. The way she held up her chin and straightened her spine, the subtle movements of her hands, all spoke of someone used to ordering and being obeyed. She was as intoxicating as a bottle of Kentucky's finest redeye.

"Our captain is awaiting instruction as to your first destination," she told him briskly, pushing away from the rail and walking quickly past him. Winn silently fell into step behind her, down through the wide-open observation deck to a narrow hallway that ran along the edge of the dining room. A dark, sweet floral perfume followed in her wake, but he couldn't place it. No hint of sulfur. It was a clever trick, but he must never forget that under that creamy skin, behind that sometimes radiant smile, she was a Darkin. A vampire. Someone who, with little provocation, would terminate his life in the blink of her long lashes.

The corridor terminated at a dark, polished wood door with a brass porthole in it.

She stood back and waited for him to enter. Winn felt a bit odd about that. It was true, he'd never taken the time to get to know a vampire before. When he'd been an active Hunter, it had always been kill or be killed. Vampires in his experience weren't much for polite conversation. But her uppity manner was annoying all the same, as if he didn't even measure up to the heel on her highly polished little boots.

Winn put his hand on the warm smoothness of the wooden door. "You know I might not be so inclined to be defensive if you vampires weren't acting so high and mighty."

Her shoulders stiffened slightly at the insult. "Good evening, Mr. Jackson." She spun on her heel, but before she could walk away, Winn put his arm out on the opposite wall, barring her exit.

There was barely room for both of them in the confines of the narrow hallway. The wild scents of desert, sun, sagebrush, leather, and male invaded Alexa's space as she turned and stared hard at him. Her imposing glare usually sufficed in getting others to do as she wished.

Even through the fabric of his duster, she could tell his arm was thick and well-muscled. Winchester Jackson was not a man easily dismissed. And yet, by the gods, she wanted to. From the moment he'd leveled a gun at her, and chosen to think first and shoot later, she'd been intrigued by him. That, coupled with the fact that he seemed to have developed an aversion to hunting, and was part of the legendary Chosen, made her far too interested in him for her own well-being.

"It's two A.M. That's hardly evening anymore."

It wasn't his words, which were prosaic enough, that slipped under her carefully maintained exterior. It was the

dark, smoky tone; it was the way the words sounded like pillow talk between lovers. It was the heat in his eyes, and the sound of his elevated heartbeat. Sparks snapped along her nerve endings. Alexa was profoundly grateful she didn't have a bothersome pulse to contend with. Like his pulse, clearly visible at the base of his strong, brown throat, hers would have given her away.

Her gaze snapped to meet his, and she felt herself falling into the blue of his eyes, so dark they matched the midnight sky. Part of being a good diplomat was knowing when to fall back from negotiation. "Of course. Then I'll wish you good morning, Mr. Jackson."

"Not so fast. Once I've talked to this captain of yours, I'd like to know where my bunk will be. Your kind might not need much rest, but I do."

"Oh, don't make the assumption we do not sleep," she replied. "We just sleep like the dead."

His sculpted, firm bottom lip smoothed slightly at her humor, but it was hard to tell with his mustache if it was the beginning of a smile. The tension that eddied in invisible currents between them began to ease just a little.

He might not like that she was Darkin, or vampire, but he wasn't averse to her personally; she could tell that without being able to read his thoughts. "I'll be back in fifteen minutes. Is that enough time for you to talk to the captain?"

He gave a nod, but a spark still lingered in his eyes.

"You want to tell me why Doc Morpheus and those shifters were after us tonight?" he asked, his voice low.

"Oh, they weren't after me, Mr. Jackson. They were after you. Rumors are circulating among the Darkin that the Book of Legend may be reunited, possibly by the Chosen." She waited for him to deny it, and when he didn't, Alexa slipped below the level of his arm and walked away. The swish of her taffeta skirts sounded loud to her own ears, but didn't drown out the rush of ichor under her skin.

While vampires might not have a pulse, the immortal ichor, sustained by the life force they withdrew from blood, still ran hot and fast through their veins—and it was certainly doing so now. She held a hand to her heated cheek. Certainly vampire skin was still several degrees cooler than that of a live mortal, but for her it was nearly a blush.

The snick of the door shutting at the end of the hallway indicated he'd entered the bridge. Only then did Alexa hazard a quick glance behind her. He stood there watching her, his gaze intense and assessing. Alexa stifled a gasp, but not quickly enough to stop the rapid intake of breath. He'd deliberately opened the door slightly and let it swing shut and waited for her reaction.

She swung about, mortified that he'd caught her, and balled her fists at her sides, then marched around the corner, where she promptly sagged against the wall. *Insufferable Hunter.* Alexa found she was just as angry with him for tricking her as she was with herself for being affected by him. Why on earth did she react to him in this manner? The feelings were dangerous. Just like the man.

Chapter 4

Alexa didn't see Mr. Jackson again until the sun had already turned the horizon a brilliant apricot over the reddish rock rim of the mountains. Her position on the observation deck, located on the prow, gave her a one-hundred-and-eighty-degree vantage point to the fiery view of the sunrise.

It was so different from the court's location in the Carpathian mountains. Just seeing the rugged beauty of the landscape made her feel, dare she say it? Alive.

She'd deliberately sent Enric back to the bridge to guide the Hunter to his cabin. Under different circumstances she would've escorted a special guest to his quarters personally. But the less time she spent in Mr. Jackson's company, the better.

Over the centuries she'd met hundreds of handsome men. Men of power and prestige. Men who'd satisfied her in many ways. Some she'd cared for. Others had professed their love for her. She was intimately aware of the power of physical attraction. And gods only knew, had acted on it with wild abandon many, many times. But there was something . . . different about Mr. Jackson. Oh, he was a hand-

some man with those stormy blue eyes and the well hidden smile that made the corners of his eyes crinkle delightfully.

Yes, he was tall. And strong. And appealing on a man-woman level. But there was something else—a hard-to-put-her-finger-on danger that emanated from the lawman like a strong aphrodisiac. The wildness of him, she reminded herself, pressing her fist against the giant window and the spectacular view of the rising sun.

Jackson was layered. Tightly layered, and he challenged her on every level.

The lawman was intriguing.

Fascinating.

Unattainable.

Because no matter how much he attracted her, no matter how captivating he might be, he was here for one purpose, and one purpose only: to help her find and recover the stolen piece of the Book of Legend and stop Rathe.

Alexa knew herself well enough to know a temptation when she saw one. Besides, feeding from him would be the ultimate in bad taste as the host of a vampire-phobic guest. But that didn't mean she hadn't thought about it. The image of her teeth scraping over his skin elicited a shiver that danced over her.

The thick, hardy, *thump bump* of his pulse announced his presence before she saw him. He strolled into the observation deck, proud as could be, his battered black duster skimming his long legs as he wove between the groups of chairs and settees. She'd seen the type far too many times—Hunters, drunk with their own self-worth, obsessed with carrying out the order of the Legion no matter what the cost. Winchester Jackson might claim he had abandoned hunting, but the essence of a Hunter clung to him, acrid and permeating as smoke.

He lightly brushed an errant palm frond from his path with the back of his hand. Alexa turned slowly, watching

his panther-like approach. Oh, he was dangerous to a woman on so many levels it made her dizzy. After her unexpected reaction last night, she decided to peel apart her behavior and resolved to be more objective and scientific in assessing his strengths and weaknesses.

In the morning light his freshly shaved jaw looked smooth, his nose slightly crooked, as if it had been broken a time or two, and his sculpted mouth was firm and unsmiling beneath the imposing mustache. He'd changed into the fresh white shirt, pinstriped black vest, and black pants Enric had instructed the porter to provide him. And while the more sophisticated clothing made him appear more civilized, good tailoring only emphasized his raw, latent power.

He doffed the black Stetson and bowed slightly, amusement flashing in his gaze as if he could read her mind. Which, she reminded herself, he couldn't. "Good morning, Lady Drossenburg."

She gave him a slight nod in acknowledgment. "Yes. Good morning. Again," she murmured faintly, but turned away to gaze out the windows so he wouldn't catch her assessing him too keenly.

A strange sight caught her attention as the sky brightened, turning a turquoise blue at the lip of the horizon. Down below, on the edge of a ridge, sat the most peculiar building she'd ever seen. Strange appendages equipped with hooks, enormous metal pincers, and large lenses stuck out of the building, moving at odd intervals, rather like legs and antennae. The structure resembled an insect. "What is that strange building down there? Not a house, surely?"

Mr. Jackson joined her at the window. Alexa felt the heat of his body so close to hers. Her senses filled with the sound of his blood pumping strongly through his veins, and the heady fragrance of his clean skin. She shifted slightly—not that it helped—and gazed down at the strange little house.

"House, laboratory, workshop. Our first stop. Marley's place."

"Marley?"

"Yep. Best inventor this side of the Atlantic."

Alexa turned with a raised brow. "Surely you don't mean Sir Marley *Turlock*?"

His face broke into a cat-ate-the-cream grin. "The one and only. Only out here he don't go by 'sir' much."

A bubble of excitement mixed with anticipation welled up inside of her. Alexa hurried out the side door of the observation lounge onto the open-aired deck encircling the gondola and leaned over the rail to get a better look at the inventor's home. She heard the heavy falls of Mr. Jackson's boots against the teak decking as he followed her.

While such scientific occupations were not considered appropriate for nobility, let alone vampiric nobility, she was somewhat of an amateur inventor herself. Accounts of Sir Turlock's work were legendary within scientific circles. Alexa glanced at Mr. Jackson. "I should very much like to meet him."

His dark brow arched, a glint of surprise flitting through his eyes. He smoothed his mustache with a finger. "I don't know if that'd be the best idea. Marley's a bit touchy when it comes to Darkin."

She nibbled a bit on her bottom lip. "He doesn't have to know."

The Hunter snorted and placed his hands on his lean hips. "Lady, he probably knows already. The bat wings on the emblem of your ship are kind of a dead giveaway, and Marley's likely been watching us since first daylight."

"But if you made the introduction . . ." she suggested hopefully.

"But nothing. I can't guarantee Marley won't shoot you on sight, and I'm pretty sure that wouldn't please His Vampire Majesty much."

"Why don't you let me be concerned with what pleases His Imperial Majesty." This was an opportunity she couldn't afford to miss. No one had heard of Sir Turlock since the unfortunate electrical experiment that had turned his hair prematurely white, injured a few people, and wiped out the entire fish population in a lake in North Umbria.

Mr. Jackson cracked his neck to the side and rolled his rather large shoulders. "It's your funeral."

"Those are very overrated," she murmured, gazing down at the strange little house.

The dirigible neared the bluff. *Zip. Ping.* The unusual noise caught her attention. A small ball sailed past them and burst into flame. "He's shooting at us!"

Mr. Jackson simply shrugged. "Told you he don't care much for supernaturals."

"Can't you reason with him?"

"He won't hear me at this distance, even if I shouted."

She extended her hand, and a dark swirl of smoke turned into the solid physical shape of what looked like the horn off an Edison phonograph, only with a straight tube instead of a bent one. "Would this help?"

"How's it work?"

She smiled and flipped a few switches on the side of the horn. "It's my own invention. Try speaking through the narrow end."

Winn didn't see the harm. He'd done far worse testing out Marley's inventions, which tended to be fantastic successes or horrible failures, with little in between. He held up the small round end to his mouth and spoke. "Marley . . . Marley . . . Marley . . ." The sound came so loud it echoed off the hills. Winn pulled it back and looked at it. "I'll be. It works." The astonishment in his voice earned him a sour look from the contessa.

Another missile sailed past and, with a *ping*, exploded against the hull. "Good. Get him to stop shooting before he damages us," she ordered.

Winn lifted up the horn and bellowed. "Damn it, Marley! Stop your shootin', it's me, Winn . . . Winn . . . Winn . . ." The words vibrated his arms so hard they tingled. The volley of projectiles from Marley's direction stopped.

One enormous lens on the roof swiveled into position, lifting to look at them. Winn waved his hat, knowing Marley could see them. A few moments later, Marley flashed the word SAFE in Morse code via a large communication mirror.

"He knows it's me. He gave us the go-ahead to land," he said. She gave him one quick nod, then closed her eyes as if concentrating.

He waited until her lashes fluttered and her eyes had opened again and the ship began to drop down toward the bluff before he questioned her. "What are you doing?"

"Beg your pardon?"

He rolled his hand in a small circle. "You're doing something when you close your eyes. What is it?"

The contessa gave him a mild look. "Talking to my crew."

"Talking—*Mind*-talking?" He'd heard of the strange and improbable ability, but Winn wasn't sure he bought into it. He had a hard enough time communicating sometimes even when he spoke clearly and concisely, but deep down he had known something had been going on between her and Enric, and now he knew he'd been right.

The contessa gave him an indulgent smile, as if he were a simpleton. "Vampires are capable of far more than communicating telepathically, Mr. Jackson. It appears your education on my species is lacking."

That poked a sore spot. Hard.

Winn knew not all Hunters were educated the same, but it was because information in the different parts of the Book scattered across the globe varied considerably, not because he was ignorant.

"Perhaps you'd like to educate me," he volleyed back. The dilating of her pupils indicated that she hadn't missed his double entendre. Winn wondered what he'd do if she took him up on his offer. Foolish as hell to give in to the churning emotions and needs inside him. She was a vampire. He was a Hunter. They weren't just different people; they were different beings.

He handed her the speaking amplification device. Her eyes narrowed, making the whiskey color of them more intense. She poofed it once again into the smoky particle it had come from.

Last night had been an experiment. He'd wanted to see how she'd react when he turned on a little of the famous Jackson-family charm. It had rattled her for sure. Which meant anytime he needed information or wanted to goad a reaction out of her, he now had a secret weapon in his arsenal. He just had to remind himself to keep a mental distance.

She turned and leaned a hip against the rail to look up at him. She was a good head shorter and had to turn her face up, like a sunflower seeking the sun. In the early morning light her skin was pale and as fine-grained as a baby's. Winn had to shove his hands into his pockets to prevent himself from reaching out to sample her skin and discover if it was as soft as it looked.

Her lips curved in a small smile as if she knew exactly what he was thinking. "Are you going to take me with you to meet Sir Turlock?"

Winn schooled his features, not liking that she so easily read him. He wondered fleetingly if he hadn't been vigilant enough and she could read his mind. He hoped like hell not. While mind reading was part of the glamouring

process he knew about, the whole idea that they could telepathically communicate with one another was something new and different. "I'm not going to stop you, but I'm not going to be responsible for his reaction either. I warned you."

Her lips pressed together into a firm, stubborn line, but given the fullness of them, it only made it look more like she was puckering up for a kiss. His skin contracted. Winn quickly looked away and focused on Marley's place instead. It annoyed him that he reacted to her. Clearly it'd been too long since he'd sought out some female company. She was a vampire. Just a damn vampire, and she'd suck him bone dry just as soon as kiss him. He'd do well to remember that.

A breeze, still cool with morning dew, blew across the deck, heavily scented of wet earth and the last sweetness of night-blooming cactus flowers. Birds zipped about, twittering and chirping morning songs. With quick efficiency the crew unfurled a wooden-rung rope ladder over the side of the airship. The rungs clacked as they hit one another, tumbling end over end to reach the ground. The contessa marched over to the swinging ladder, her military-like efficiency firmly back in place. Posture regal, she glanced over her shoulder. "Are you ready?"

"Perhaps you ought to let me go first. Just so I can prepare him a mite."

She folded her hands in front of her, but Winn didn't miss the curious mix of anger and disappointment in her eyes. "Very well. Can you please inform us by the mirror when you are ready for me to join you?"

Winn tugged at the brim of his Stetson. "Yes, ma'am." He caught himself and bristled. His pa might have imbued him with hunting, but his ma had driven manners deeper still.

He muttered to himself while he swung down the ladder,

rung after rung. He jumped the last few feet, his boots kicking up a small cloud of pale dust. The sun was fully risen now, a brilliant ball of white light in a blue sky, but the air wasn't hot. Not yet.

Just in front of Marley's place sat Tempus, his brother Colt's mechanical horse. It looked like some bizarre frozen beast, the black-and-white cowhide covering over its copper body both protecting it from the elements and making it eerily realistic. Only the solid silver eyes and brass hooves completely gave it away. Why had Colt left it here? He never went anywhere without Tempus, unless something drastic had happened.

The door of Marley's home swung open and out came a man a full foot shorter than Winn, his brown eyes magnified into outlandish proportions by the elaborate brass goggles on his face. No one knew for sure exactly how old Marley was, but his hair was tufts of white cotton surrounding his head. Yet, his brows were still as dark as his eyes, and his face didn't have a wrinkle on it.

There were rumors among the Hunters in the Western territories that things had gone bad during one of Marley's experiments, and that had brought on the change in his hair color. But Marley's past didn't matter much to Winn. Hands down, nobody, but nobody could outmatch Marley for a mind and sheer ingenuity.

"Winchester!" He wiped his hands on his stained leather apron and approached Winn hand outstretched, a large smile on his face. "To what do I owe the pleasure of seeing two of you Jacksons in one week?"

"Family business." Winn took Marley's hand and gave it a proper shake.

Marley's dark brows rose above the level of his goggles. "My word, does that mean you've begun hunting again?"

"Not exactly. I'm trying to help out Colt."

Marley lifted the goggles away from his eyes, perching

them on his forehead so that he looked like a demented double-horned unicorn. "So, you two have patched things up, as they say?"

"Close enough." Winn glanced at the dirigible hanging overhead. "I've got a job to do. Was Balmora able to help Colt decode that slip of paper he found in Pa's box?"

Marley nodded, his eyes gleaming with satisfaction. "She did an exemplary job unraveling that code."

"Well, what did it say?"

"The inscription said something regarding needing the entire Book to seal the Gates, and then there was a riddle: At the height of the mountains, where legends are reborn from the ashes, is the eye through which we must pass to sew the tapestry of our Chosen destiny."

"What the hell is that supposed to mean?"

"I really don't know. Colt couldn't make sense of it either. He's taken it to Remington in Tombstone to see if perhaps your brother can understand the instructions your father left."

Winn hitched his thumb at Tempus. "So why'd he leave his horse? He don't go anywhere without that thing."

"He left Tempus at the train station with the request that I ship it back to you in Bodie for safekeeping until he returned. He thought the train would be a faster means to reach Remington."

"So now it's a race?"

Marley's face turned deadly serious. "A race of great significance. If my calculations are correct, we have only until the next new moon before there will be an attempt made to open the Gates of Nyx permanently, and Colt agrees, which makes time of the essence."

"Damn," Winn growled, swiping his Stetson off his head and plowing his fingers through his hair. His gut twisted into a Gordian knot just thinking of the odds stacked against them. "Three weeks?"

Marley nodded. "You might want to stop there if you can and find out what they've discovered. Your brothers may need your assistance. And you could deliver Tempus back to Colt."

Winn swore under his breath. "You think whatever they've decoded might make a difference?"

Marley picked one of the tools out of his heavy belt and twisted the top of it absently. "Considering how well-guarded it was, it certainly has potential."

Winn glanced back over his shoulder in the direction of the airship that loomed like a large balloon over Marley's home, casting the yard in an enormous shadow. "I only stopped by because I'm leaving on a trip. I suppose I could go to Tombstone, find out what Pa meant, and deliver Tempus, then leave."

"By airship you could be there in a trice." Marley's eyes lit up with a curious gleam. He tucked his tool back in his belt and clasped his hands together. "A trip? Where are you going, if I may be so bold as to inquire?"

"Europe."

Winn was surprised Marley didn't even flinch at the surprising news. "Any chance you might be passing by London?" he asked simply.

Winn quirked a brow. "Why?"

"I have some rather special plans I'd like hand-delivered to Her Majesty, without interference. If you ascertain my meaning."

Winn shrugged. "I could try."

"Lovely, lovely," Marley said as he waved him toward the building. Winn followed him into the dark recesses of the house, if it could really be called a house. It was more like a laboratory gone berserk.

Piles of papers and books teetered in stacks. Glassware, wire, and bits of metal were heaped upon nearly every available surface. An entire wall housed nothing but differ-

ent clocks of all sorts. In short, it was a pack rat's paradise. And the faint odor of ammonia and dust permeated the air.

"This job wouldn't possibly have anything to do with the Drossenburg vampire court, would it?" Marley asked. He shut the door behind them, causing dust motes to swirl in the shafts of sunlight that leaked in past the heavy velvet draperies.

"Told them that emblem on their dirigible was a dead giveaway."

Marley shook his head as he pushed through a pile of old papers. "What is the world coming to? How is it that you come to be working with vampires, and your brother has partnered up with a succubus?"

Winn shook his head and pulled on the waxed end of his mustache. "Beats me, Marley. That's a mystery as much to me as anybody. All I know is they want my help in recovering the second part of the Book. They say it's been stolen."

Marley's eyes narrowed. He folded his arms over his chest, the corners of his mouth hardening in disapproval. "You'd better be careful, Winchester. Vampires always have their own agenda. You know what they say—"

"Yeah. Never trust a Darkin."

"Precisely."

"Say, you know something about the Darkin they've got over in Europe. You got anything that I might find useful?"

Marley's eyes sparked with manic delight as he grabbed hold of Winn's arm and pulled him down the hallway. "Of course, old chap. Right this way."

They approached a door Winn was certain led to just another bedroom, but when Marley opened it the smells of dank earth and mustiness eddied out. Marley grabbed an oil lamp from a nail on the wall and lit it, leading Winn down a rough wooden staircase. In any normal house this would

have been the basement or root cellar, but in Marley's place it was an armory.

Winn tried to take it all in. The swords and pikes, shields and steel traps, an entire wall of different guns and gizmos. "Jumpin' Jehoshaphat, Marley, what the hell are you doing with all this stuff? Starting your own war?"

The clatter of gears and wheels turning preceded the crackle and bluish light of an arc lamp that brilliantly lit up the room as bright as the broad daylight outside. "Oh, these are remnants, mostly," Marley murmured, surveying the stacks of spikes, guns, and other dangerous-looking implements that Winn had never even seen before. "Now where did I put it?"

Marley dug through a stack of what looked like crazy bows and arrows to Winn. "Ah, here it is!" Marley pulled out a heavy crossbow with a circular bolt holder on top that looked an awful lot like the bullet chamber of a revolver to Winn. It had a crank where the handle joined the top of the bow and a series of intricate pulleys and wheels.

Winn whistled long and low. "That's some crossbow, Marley."

"It's an Amanarath. Should slay anything Darkin when the proper silver or jade-tipped bolts are used. The windlasses and special clockworks allow it to re-tension the bow quickly. And *this* little bit," he said as he tapped the crank, "is my personal favorite."

Winn took the crossbow from his friend, holding it up and sighting down the shaft. It had heft and was exquisitely balanced for a bow. "What's it do?"

"It automatically reloads the bolts, allowing you to shoot multiple bolts very quickly."

"You mean like a Gatling gun?"

Marley's mouth widened into a pleased smile. "Precisely."

"Damn." Winn hefted the solid weight of the weapon in his hand. "That's brilliant."

Marley's smile widened even further. "Why thank you. It's a bit of my own vision on the bow originally used by the Van Helsings."

"The Van who's?"

The brilliance of his eyes faded slightly, and Marley shook his head. "Famous Hunters from the European branch of the Legion. It's a very different world over there."

"As good as this is, one weapon ain't going to do the job. Got anything else?"

Marley tapped his finger to his lips. "Where are you going, precisely?"

"Transylvania. Going to meet His Vampiric Imperial Majesty, Vladimir the Fifth."

Marley's brown eyes widened, and his face turned a bit ashen. "Oh! Well, in that case, you'll also want this."

Winn slung the crossbow over his back, adjusting the strap around his chest while Marley dug through another stack of weapons comprised of various shapes and sizes of glass bulbs, tubes, and wires. He pulled out a small brass gun outfitted with a large glass jar in the base.

He handed it to Winn, and it felt so insubstantial that Winn wasn't certain it would make it through a single use. "What the hell is this?"

"Repeating water gun."

Win bit back a laugh. He was going to fight the Darkin with a liquid-shooting pistol? "Water?"

Marley lifted up on his toes, pulling a brown bottle off the shelf that seemed to hold all manner of ammunition. "Holy water."

Almost as useless. "That stuff don't kill vampires, Marley."

"I know, but it's hell on werewolves and useful against demons. It'll scald them like acid."

Winn wasn't planning on interacting with werewolves, but he shrugged and took the proffered bottle. Overhead

the boards creaked. Both of them looked up as a bit of dirt filtered down through the cracks in the floorboards. A red light on Marley's belt began to flash. "Darkin!" His whisper was harsh. He grabbed a silver-tipped pike pole and started for the stairs.

"Now hold up a minute, Marley." Winn grabbed him by the shirt. "It might be those vampires I'm working with. Let's not be too hasty. In fact, the Contessa Drossenburg is a big admirer of your work. Even called you *Sir* Turlock."

Marley turned, the tip of the pike dropping to the floor, and stared at Winn, a perplexed look on his face. "She knew me?"

Winn shrugged. "She knew about you, at least. Was all hot 'n' bothered to meet you in person."

Marley swallowed hard. "Really? How do you know it's not a Darkin ploy to murder me?"

Winn frowned. He didn't. The contessa had certainly seemed genuine enough in her interest. "Well, they ain't tried to kill me yet, so that's some indication they've got other purposes in mind. Why don't you let me go up the stairs first."

Marley nodded. "I think that would be for the best. You're the Hunter, after all."

Winn winced. This was all temporary. Once he'd gotten the second part of the Book, he had no intention of staying in the life. He'd go back to being sheriff of Bodie.

He pulled the crossbow off his back, preparing it to fire, and eased past Marley. With swift silent steps he took the stairs two at a time and approached the front room of Marley's house with caution. There, standing among the flotsam and jetsam of Marley's quarters, was the contessa, looking like an exquisite marble statue in the midst of a catastrophic mess. Her eyes glowed with pleasure as her fingers traced with obvious admiration over the glass apparatus Marley had set up on a table.

Winn pulled down the bow, slipped the strap back over his shoulder, and slung it onto his back. "Thought you were going to wait for my signal."

Her gaze connected with his, and she lifted her chin a slight bit. "You were taking too long."

Winn crossed his arms and leaned his shoulder into the doorjamb. "And now you're my wet nurse?" His gaze deliberately dipped lower to her well-rounded bosom.

She lifted her brow, her gaze raking over him in equal measure. "Hardly." She folded her hands together, her giddy excitement replaced by detached coolness. "Where is Sir Turlock?"

"He'll be along shortly." Winn twisted his head and yelled over his shoulder. "Hey, Sir Marley. You got a visitor." Winn tensed, not knowing if Marley was going to come running with his pike pole or his manners.

As he turned his body, Alexa thought she noticed the distinct outline of an Amanarath crossbow on Mr. Jackson's back. Her ichor chilled. Those only had one purpose—to kill Darkin outright with the first shot. Was that what he'd come to do: collect weapons strong enough to kill her and her crew?

The quick shuffling footsteps behind the hulking Hunter drew her attention. A man much shorter than Mr. Jackson appeared from behind him. He looked slightly different from the ambrotype she'd seen of Sir Turlock. Then his hair had been thick and dark, not shockingly white. But the face and the intelligence in those brown eyes could not be mistaken. This was indeed Sir Turlock.

She dipped low into a curtsey worthy of the highest vampire court. He hesitated, then responded by bowing at the waist in the traditional fashion, which made the

enormous multi-lensed goggles perched on his forehead bob precariously. Mr. Jackson seemed slightly stunned.

"My Lady Drossenburg, I presume," Marley murmured, his voice tight.

"*Da.* And you are Sir Turlock, world-class inventor. A pleasure to make your acquaintance. I am a great admirer of your work."

His intelligent brown eyes flecked with gold narrowed, as his hand came to rest on the special weapon at his hip. "But you are a vampire."

"And an amateur inventor, sir. One does not have to be favored by the inventions to appreciate their genius."

Marley's chest lifted slightly, the worried crease between his enormous eyes easing. "You are escorting Winchester to His Imperial Majesty?"

She inclined her head. "*Da,* the honor is mine."

Mr. Jackson pushed off the wall and rolled his shoulders, suddenly anxious. "In fact, we really should be on our way."

"Did you get everything you needed?" she asked, determination keeping her voice smooth and even. And her gaze away from the formidable weapon he carried so casually across his back.

"Enough."

She settled her gaze on Sir Turlock. "Would you mind if I wrote to you? I have so many questions I would love to ask you."

Sir Turlock fidgeted. "I—I suppose. If they are scientific inquiries."

Mr. Jackson started walking toward the door and gently gripped her upper arm as he walked by, wheeling her around. "Say your good-byes. We've got one more stop to make."

She resisted his tug and turned back to the shy inventor. "It was a pleasure to have met you, Sir Turlock. Thank you."

He gave her a nod, but she heard the thoughts flicker through his head—*Polite for a vampire . . . oddest day of*

my life . . . who would have thought they were really the Chosen . . . but if the vampires believe it, then surely . . .

Mr. Jackson's grip about her upper arm was firm and no-nonsense, and she had to practically trot to keep up with him. They headed out the door to stand next to a monstrous machine stationed outside Sir Turlock's home.

"Are you always so discourteous?" she snapped.

He dropped his hold on her arm as if burned. "Only when we've got a time limit and have to get somewhere in a hurry. I got to get this horse loaded and take it down to my brother in Tombstone before we can leave."

"May I ask what the rush is that I couldn't spend a few minutes talking to Sir Turlock?"

"We've got three weeks. Actually less than that now."

"Until what?"

"Until the dark moon. That's when Marley and Colt think Rathe will attempt to open the Gates of Nyx."

If Alexa had possessed any blood in her system, it would have all drained out of her face. The Gates of Nyx were the largest portal between the human realm and the Darkin one. If Darkin came pouring in and took over, eliminating humans and subjugating them, without a source for new vampires and food to sustain themselves, the reign of the vampire would come to a swift end. Her ichor cooled to a sluggish consistency that made her feel suddenly weak. "Are you certain?"

"You think I'd make up something like that?" The hard planes of his face and the determination like white-hot blue flame in his eyes left no room for doubt. He meant every word. If they didn't retrieve the second part of the Book and reunite the pieces, they would be doomed. All of them.

Chapter 5

The heat waves in the air outside made the plants in Marley's yard appear to dance. Even the mechanical cacti she'd spied here and there cleverly hidden amongst the real prickly native plants seemed to sway.

Behind Alexa and Mr. Jackson the door to Marley's home creaked open. They turned in unison to look at him. The inventor threw Alexa a pointed look, clearly still not comfortable in her presence. "Winchester, might I have one more word with you?"

Alexa resisted the urge to huff like a commoner and instead lifted her chin with as much regal air as she could muster. "I shall inform the captain to lower the dirigible enough for us to load your machine," she said, her voice cool.

Intrigued by the mechanical horse sitting close to the door, she considered walking up to the machine and running her hands over every inch of it while the men talked. It was clearly a Turlock original.

But to do so might be seen as an insult to Sir Turlock. Inventors didn't like having their work touched without issuing an invitation. She promised herself she'd inspect it

thoroughly in the privacy of her ship; for now she had to make do with observing it from a distance.

The man was a genius, and while she'd love to spend hours questioning him, Alexa knew time and his obvious distrust made that happy event impossible. She thought, rather wistfully, that in another time and place they might have been friends of a sort.

But this was here and now.

"If wishes were mechanical horses . . ." she murmured with a small regretful smile.

While she waited for Mr. Jackson's return, Alexa gave orders. If Mr. Jackson was as confident as he seemed about their deadline, then every moment spent not traveling was a clock ticking toward their demise.

She reached out to His Majesty's envoy. *Enric. Ready the ship for our next destination. There is no time to lose.*

What is the matter, my lady? The concern in his voice echoed in her head.

Vlad has been deceived. This is not merely a mission to recover the missing piece of the Book. The time for the Chosen to act will soon be upon us. We need to help Mr. Jackson load one of Sir Turlock's inventions onto the ship as quickly as possible. Instruct the captain to bring the ship down to ground level.

Yes, my lady.

The port valves gave off a loud hiss of steam as the dirigible descended toward the edge of the bluff, like a ship coming in to dock at port. The crew worked efficiently, lowering the gangplank to connect the ground with the back end of the ship's cargo hold by the time Mr. Jackson had come outside to join her. He was alone.

"At least he didn't shoot me," she said dryly, as Mr. Jackson came up beside her. Each time she was with him she was surprised at his great physical presence. Not just his impressive height, but the breadth of his shoulders, and the

way he carried himself. Assured. Confident. And handsome, gods help her. Her physical reaction to Winchester Jackson was palpable.

"We'll leave as soon as Sir Turlock's invention is loaded," she said crisply.

He eyed her critically, but a sly smile curved his mouth. "How'd you know Marley made it?"

Alexa made a derisive noise. "Even an amateur inventor can tell the hallmarks of a master craftsman. Is it the only one of its kind or are there others?"

"That's the only one—so far."

"Walk it across the gangplank. Enric will be waiting inside to guide you to where you may secure it." She indicated the back of the dirigible. "Ask him and the crew for whatever you require to secure it properly. We do not want it damaged in flight."

He touched the brim of his hat with his finger, then turned and walked back to the mechanical horse. He mounted it, turning the backward-facing ear forward. The whirr of gears and click of clockwork coming from the mechanical horse intrigued her even more.

How had Sir Turlock engineered it? Were there pistons inside? Springs activated with clockwork mechanisms? Alexa couldn't wait to get on board where she'd have the time and privacy to inspect it minutely.

She crossed the dusty yard to follow Mr. Jackson. He certainly made a fine specimen atop a horse, especially a mechanical Turlock original, but he was still a far cry from the European Hunters who had taken so many of her kind over the centuries.

For a moment she doubted Vlad's plan. Perhaps the Chosen weren't up to the task of recovering the lost pieces of the Book of Legend.

* * *

Winn hadn't missed the wistful edge to her voice. She liked Tempus. Most Darkin wouldn't, since it was a machine they could neither manipulate nor control with their powers, but she apparently had some penchant for Marley and his machines.

He trotted Tempus right up to the edge of the gangplank and took a long second look at the drop off the edge of the bluff on either side and kept going up the gangplank.

Marley, who'd designed the beast for Colt, said the GGD—or, as he'd originally called it, the Giddyup God Dammit switch—was a double precaution against horse thieves. Unless a person knew to flip the ear to forward facing, the pressure plate beneath the saddle wasn't enough to engage the clockwork mechanics of the beast. It took both the switch and the weight of a rider depressing the pressure plate to get the machine to move.

The contessa's second-in-command, Enric, waited at the top of the gangplank. The sun gilded his blond hair, and his fine aristocratic features made him appear more angel than vampire. Ha. That was laughable. Winn didn't doubt for a moment every vampire on the ship was capable of killing. Winn tipped up the edge of his Stetson. "Where do you want me to park this thing?"

Enric led him up another ramp to the cargo deck. Large metal rings were bolted into the wooden floor, and cargo nets crafted from thick, brownish hemp rope were draped over piles of wooden crates and oddly assorted items, including what looked like enormous folded canvas umbrellas with stiff metal framing, keeping them secure. "You can tie it up in here." Enric indicated a space off to one side of the cargo hold beside what looked like doors in the bottom of the ship.

"Those lead anywhere?" Winn asked.

"Down," Enric answered simply, but the humor in his voice was evident.

Winn reined Tempus into position, then flipped Tempus's GGD switch to the backward-facing spot that immobilized the horse, locking him into place. The ticking and whirring slowed and eventually stilled altogether as Tempus froze. Winn grabbed a set of rope cargo nets from the hooks along the wall and draped them over Tempus, using the rings in the floor to secure the nets tightly over the machine's broad back.

Standing back to review his work, Winn dusted off his hands, then crossed his arms. The ship gave a sudden jolt beneath his feet, making him stumble and his stomach pitch uncomfortably. He certainly hoped he'd get used to the sensation, or it was going to be one long, miserable flight to Transylvania.

The cargo doors closed with a clang, throwing the cargo bay into nearly pitch darkness, save for the small oil lamp Enric held. "The Lady Drossenburg has asked that you join her on the observation deck." Winn followed Enric up the stairs in the middle of the ship to the topmost deck.

The contessa turned to him, beckoning him to join her with a crook of her finger. Winn bristled but joined her at the rail; his fingers dug in reflexively as the ship lifted away from the edge of the bluff.

"How long have you been friends with Sir Turlock?"

Just how much should he tell her? He certainly didn't trust her, and if his own instincts weren't enough, Marley had advised against giving her too much information. But as long as she stuck to small talk, he supposed it couldn't hurt. "Long as he's been around these parts."

"How long has that been?"

Winn shrugged. "Can't really say. He was here before I moved to Bodie."

* * *

She glanced at him briefly, then returned to gaze at Sir Turlock's home. "You ride a horse well."

Mr. Jackson looked slightly taken aback by the compliment. "Don't everybody?"

She sniffed. "Not where I come from. Only those in higher society can afford to ride good horseflesh."

"Guess you have to learn out here."

She looked out over the desert and sighed. There was so much room, such freedom everywhere you looked. It was breathtaking after the crowded cities of Europe and the confines of the court.

"Your country is a large place. I guess I can understand why everyone would need the skill. My captain has informed me we shall reach Tombstone just after noon."

"That mind-talk must come in real handy," he mused.

It would have, if she could have read his mind. "Mr. Jackson, may I ask you a personal question?"

He stiffened slightly, but nodded.

"Most mortals are very open with their thoughts, allowing us to read them easily and conform to their deepest fantasies when we feed upon them." He flinched at the words. "But you are different. I cannot read you, Mr. Jackson. Why is that?"

He brushed a finger over his dark mustache, letting it follow the curve at the end that intrigued her. "Maybe there's more to American Hunters than you think, my lady."

Alexa caught a whiff of the cedar scent of male pride tainting the air. Even without being able to read his mind she could tell he was sensitive about his colonial roots. Peasant, nobleman, it wouldn't matter if Rathe got ahold of the Gates and opened them wide.

"I think perhaps, Mr. Jackson, it has more to do with you than with the Hunters of your country." She inclined her head in a little bow, tucking behind her ear the strands

of her hair that came loose in the wind as the dirigible lifted and picked up speed.

She turned away from him and looked down upon the odd house of Sir Turlock shrinking in the distance, a little pang of yearning squeezing her chest. She would have liked more time. Just a little. There were very few in the vampire court who would approve of her predilection to craft the ideas that swarmed about in her head. Even fewer who would understand it. For centuries she'd felt more of a butterfly among ravens, both capable of flight, but not at all alike.

"What are the Hunters in Europe like?"

The raw curiosity in his voice made her glance back at him. He was squinting hard now against the brightness of the light. "Here. Try these." She held out her hand and focused, letting the power run and hum through her veins to call the particles together. A pair of dark-lensed brass goggles formed in her palm, and she handed them to him.

"Thank you." He gently took the goggles from her hand and took off his hat. His dark hair was slicked back against his scalp, neat, and tightly under control just like the rest of him. He snapped the goggles into place, and they obscured his piercing blue eyes, making it easier for her to think.

"You didn't answer my question," he said smoothly as he leaned against the rail and settled his hat back on his head.

Alexa stared back out at the brilliant blue sky, but she could feel the heat of his gaze still upon her as surely as if he'd reached out and touched her instead. "They are more . . . reserved." It was the best word she could think of. They simply didn't emit the raw, primal power he did.

"You mean they got better manners."

She sighed, out of pure frustration. "They are more aware of the rules of society. You Americans have thrown

all that out the door. Everyone is equal. Everyone is the same in the eyes of your government, *da?*"

"Yeah. I suppose."

"Well, it isn't like that in Europe, Mr. Jackson. Even among the Hunters there is a sense of knowing one's place. And *everyone* has a place. The Hunters there are more like an invisible extension of the military, known but not acknowledged."

"Huh. Seems like a waste of time to me."

"How is order and civility a waste of time?"

"Because when it's you up against a demon and he don't give a damn if you or your kin lives or dies, do you think there's time to wait for orders from some higher-up?" The brutality in his voice rattled her spine. She could never forget he'd turn on her in a second if he thought he was in danger. His hand absently ran back and forth over the middle of his left thigh.

"I suppose it is a different life."

He snorted. "You tellin' me Hunters over there have nice little orchestrated battles with Darkin?"

She raised a brow, slightly surprised. "No. There are treaties in place. They don't fight the Darkin in most of Europe. They have learned to live in harmony with them."

Winn was shocked. She could have thrown a feather at him and tipped him right over the rail of the airship. "You telling me they all live *together?*"

She gave a shrug of her dainty shoulders. "I wouldn't say together. More like coexisting. As I said, there are many levels of society in Europe, Mr. Jackson. The Darkin are simply one of them."

Winn pulled off his hat and scratched his head. Damn.

He was out of his depth. "So you aren't asking me over as a Hunter. More like a Pinkerton."

"A tinker? Hardly."

"Pink-er-ton."

She tilted her head, curiosity in her eyes. "Please explain."

"They're hired security and detectives. Look into crimes, find stolen things, track down criminals, that sort of thing."

"*Da*. A Pinkerton."

The land spread out beneath them in hues of brown and tan with fingers of green in the arroyos between the reddish rocks. The sun beat down, and Winn replaced his hat, enjoying the breeze caused by the motion of the airship. He could smell the heavy floral scent that clung to her and tried to identify it. Lilies? Maybe. Roses? No. Whatever it was, the tantalizing fragrance heated his blood and made him painfully aware that she was a desirable woman.

And a Darkin, he reminded himself as he stared out at the ground moving rapidly beneath them. The shadow of the dirigible skated across the surface of the ground, up and down hills and valleys in a fascinating dance of shadow and light.

"This is the most amazing place I've ever seen," she murmured.

The wistful sound hit Winn straight in the chest. "Yeah, but as beautiful as the land is, it can kill you in a heartbeat if you don't respect it."

Her gaze connected with his, and awareness flared deep in his gut. The contessa wasn't just any vampire. She was something far more, just as exotic and beautiful as the desert, and just as deadly. But Winn couldn't ignore the pull to know about her.

"Since you asked me a personal question, may I ask you one as well?"

Her full lips lifted into a subtle smile. "*Quid pro quo*?"

Winn rubbed the back of his neck. "Yeah, I suppose."

"What do you wish to know?"

"How'd you become a vampire?"

Humor danced in her eyes as she looked at him. "What a silly question. I was born one, of course. And into one of the oldest vampire families, I might add."

Winn about choked on the apple-sized lump that suddenly seemed lodged in his throat. "Born? Vampires are born?" He coughed hard against the uncomfortable thickness. "I thought you had to get bit."

She gave a shrug of her shoulder. "That happens, and those are children by gift, but for the most part we are born, the same as you mortals. We are living vampires, with heartbeat and breath the same as you. Living vampires only fully transition into the undead after their first blood meal."

"The vampires I've run across don't have beating hearts. Holy water and stakes don't work on the undead."

"The truly undead are not as impacted by things like sun, salt, stakes or holy water. But the living younglings are much more susceptible."

"That explains an awful lot about the confusing accounts we got of things working on some vampires and not others," he said softly as he glanced at the smooth column of her neck. There was no movement of a heartbeat beneath the fine-grained skin, or any indication that blood moved through her veins. It was a bit unnerving. "The black blood you vampires have, that happen after you transition too?"

"*Da*. It is the blood of the undead. There's no life force in it, which is why we must feed on the living."

"What happens if you feed on somebody who just died?"

"Dead man's blood is poisonous, Mr. Jackson." She

shuddered delicately and rubbed her upper arms. "We do not touch it."

"I suppose the inventing thing isn't something you're supposed to do either."

The contessa gave him a sharp look. "It is . . . undignified." She looked away from him, her finger tapping on the rail. "But that does not mean my curiosity for Sir Turlock's inventions is any less."

"I saw you eyeing Tempus."

She sighed. "I admire a well-crafted invention. It's a brilliant piece of work."

"You want to look it over?"

Lady Drossenburg glanced at him through the dark fan of her lashes. "Yes."

He walked with her through the maze of halls and staircases back down into the bowels of the ship. In the half-light thrown by the lantern, Tempus appeared out of the gloom, his black-and-white cowhide making him look more like a real animal than a machine. Winn carefully pulled back the cargo netting enough that he could unlace the cowhide cover and get to the panel in Tempus's side. He wasn't as familiar with the machine as his brother Colt. Living horses were more his thing.

"There's a button here somewhere Marley uses to open Tempus up."

The contessa bent double, her fingers sliding slowly and gently across the copper skin that formed the outer layer of the clockwork horse. "Here. There's a slight ridge to it." She pressed the small square indentation. With a click, the hatch to the undercarriage of Tempus opened.

She hunkered down, practically crouching beneath the horse, heedless of the dust and grime on the floor, and held the lantern closer, then gasped. Winn noticed that glint in her eye that Marley often got when talking about his

creations. "This is absolutely marvelous," she whispered. "Look at how he's enabled the gears to shift. That's ingenious."

He'd never seen a vampire like this before—one so absorbed in the moment that she forgot herself and seemed almost human. "This is one of his better inventions."

The contessa spared him a brief glance. "You are very lucky, you know. There are many who would love to have Sir Turlock's genius at their beck and call."

"Oh, I wouldn't say he's a servant or anything. He's more a partner. And, well, sometimes, we're the lab rats. Especially when he's got something new he wants to try out and hasn't got the quirks worked out of it yet."

"Then you're even luckier." Lady Drossenburg straightened, dusting off her skirts and smoothing out the rumples. "Thank you for letting me look at this."

Winn simply nodded. He hadn't done anything except walk down with her and unlace the covering on his brother's horse. What she admired was all Marley's doing, not his.

There actually hadn't been much that he'd done that could be admired. He put everything back the way it had been, then resecured the cargo netting. They walked back in a companionable silence through the ship to the observation deck. Winn just figured she was busy mulling over what she'd seen.

The airship rocked slightly, pushed by a great gust of wind, forcing Winchester to steady himself. He gripped the rail, looking out across the desert. A dark, thick cloud of dust was billowing, growing taller as the wind whipped up the dry, loose soil. "Dust storm is coming," he said, pointing to it. "Sometimes they blow in on the front edge of a monsoon."

The contessa looked at it with interest. "I've never seen such a thing."

Particles began to fill the air, and Winn was even more grateful for the goggles as the grit abraded his skin. The thick, swirling cloud grew taller, approaching like a brown wall across the desert. "Sure that stuff ain't gonna clog up the engines?" Winn shouted over the rising rush of wind.

She frowned, not at all pleased by the thought, and materialized her own pair of goggles, slipping them over her head. "It might. We've never flown through a dust storm before, or a monsoon."

"We'd better get inside. Now." The tone of his voice left no doubt this was something serious.

They dashed into the safety of the gondola to escape the wind tearing at their clothes. Through the windows, the approaching brown wall, rising well over a hundred feet above the desert, looked even more ominous as it darkened the sky. Winn had seen these storms tear whole houses away. He sent up a prayer that the fabric and ribs of the dirigible were strong enough to withstand the coming storm.

Chapter 6

The airship shook, the engines whining loudly and sputtering slightly as the blast of wind-whipped sand hit them. "I sure hope those engines hold out," Winn said over the hissing sound of sand scouring the fabric of the dirigible and the wood and glass of the gondola. The shuddering of the ship grew worse, making Winn's teeth vibrate. "I ain't exactly ready to die yet."

For a moment it seemed they were suspended in the murk, unable to see more than ten feet in any direction. Bits of paper, dried tumbleweeds, even an old shoe went sailing past as the ship powered forward, determined to stay in the sky despite the forceful strength of the dust storm.

The ship dipped hard and fast, causing Lady Drossenburg to stumble. Winn caught her about the waist and held her for a moment, bracing his feet wide against the erratic sway of the ship. She was soft under his hands, far more woman than monster.

"Dying isn't so bad," she murmured. "You could always try becoming undead."

Winn pulled away from her, giving himself a mental shake. That would teach him for thinking of her as anything

other than Darkin. "Thanks for the offer, but I'm not interested."

His agitation increased. They were in real danger. If a monsoon were pushing the sand ahead of it, they were about to get pounded by wind and driving rain. The ship struggled to maintain its position and actually started going sideways.

Grime on the windows turned to dark, tear-like streaks as fat raindrops began pelting the ship, the sky ominously dark ahead of them. Winn ground his teeth together and glanced at the contessa. "You better hold on to something," he muttered. The fury of a monsoon could be terrifying and destructive.

CRAAAACK. A flare of light lit the sky, brilliant white like flash powder.

BOOM! The thunder shook the ship hard enough that a jagged line zipped along the wide pane of glass at the front edge of the gondola as it cracked. More lightning tore across the sky followed by thunder, in bursts so fast it looked and sounded like gunfire on a battlefield. Winn and the contessa covered their ears and crouched low to the carpeted floor of the gondola.

Torrents flowed from the sky, rain hitting the airship in massive sheets. Amid the earsplitting thunder, the high whine of the engines stopped, their sudden silence constricting Winn's chest like a vise. The ship pitched violently downward, furniture starting to slide toward them.

Winn grabbed the contessa, wrapping himself around her so she wouldn't get hit. "We're going down!" she yelled over the noise of the lashing rain and booming thunder.

"In that case, you better hope it's quick," he yelled back, his heart beating hard in his chest, his stomach crawling up into his throat as they began to free-fall.

Winn had never intended to die like this—well, at least not surrounded by Darkin he was working with. He realized

with a start there was still more he wanted to do. Things he'd been putting off while playing it safe. He wanted to see more than just the four unpainted walls of his office in Bodie. Wanted to . . . live up to the legacy left to him. But deep down festered the doubt that he ever could.

A sputtering cough and fitful stop and start of the engines gave him a small burst of hope, but then they quit again.

"We're not going to survive, are we?" she murmured against his chest.

"Give your crew a chance," he replied, even while he was thinking that without the engines they didn't have a prayer.

A sputter and cough and one engine started up enough to slow their descent. A minute later the second massive engine sputtered to life, the whine smoothing out until the ship once again flew level. The rain still lashed at the airship, buffeting it about, but at least they were still airborne.

Then, like all monsoons, as quickly as it had released its fury, it moved on. They emerged out of the violent tumult into a clear blue sky, scoured clean by the storm.

Off in the distance Winn spotted their target. "There's Tombstone." A blast of dry heat, smelling of horse, dust, and the oily scent of creosote, tightened the skin on his face as he opened the door to the outer deck to look over the railing as they neared the town. Far below, the grid-like layout of the growing town was evident. So were the ant-like mounds of tailings from the various mines that surrounded the town.

In moments they were overhead, descending slowly over the main street. A mixture of screams, whinnies, and the galloping of spooked horses filled the air. Winn saw one of the crew cast over an anchor. The thunderous crash of wood splintering as the anchor cleaved through a roof indicated his aim had been off.

"It looks like you are making quite an impression on the locals."

She glanced at him, humor dancing in her eyes. "We always do."

Citizens and animals scattered beneath the looming shadow of the ship. Winn pulled at his mustache. He didn't like spooking folks, and he was certain the massive ship, all two hundred feet of it hanging over their heads, was doing just that.

"Prepare the ladder," the contessa told a nearby crew member. Still wiping grit from his face, the man raced off to do her bidding.

"You're used to people following your orders, aren't you?"

"Why wouldn't I be? I was born to lead."

Winn stuffed down an irritated grunt. She'd better not presume that, since he was there, she could boss *him* around. He wasn't about to be told what or how to do things by a skirt-wearing vampire, no matter how beautiful she was.

He was only with her to find that missing piece of the Book and get it back here before the moon went dark and all Hell broke loose.

She was a means to an end. Nothing more.

"You might need these." She held out two more pairs of the dark glass goggles to Winchester.

"We're just going to drop off Tempus."

Lady Drossenburg gave him a knowing smile. "Humor me. Not all your brothers are as clever as you in hiding their thoughts."

Winn grumbled, irritated that she'd looked into his brothers' heads at all, but took the goggles and stuffed them into the pocket of his duster. Never hurt to be prepared.

The little half door, built into the railing of the deck, was swung open and latched into position so Winn could descend. He grabbed hold of the railing and eased his boot down on

the swinging rungs of the ladder. Once he had his footing, he took it at a quicker pace, eager to see his brothers.

He glanced down and recognized the two smaller figures who appeared from beneath the wooden awning that shaded the walkway.

"About time you made it out," Winn shouted down to his younger brothers. "I was beginning to wonder if Marley had told me wrong about you coming here."

They were both armed, but holstered their weapons once they recognized him. "What in tarnation are you doing on a vampire dirigible, Winn?" Colt called out. A large animal that looked suspiciously like a mountain lion paced behind them, but they paid no attention to it.

Winchester made it farther down the ladder and hopped the last few feet to the ground. The dust billowed up in a cloud around his boots as he pulled the dark goggles down to rest around his neck. "Was made an offer I couldn't refuse."

Remington stood gussied up like some city-slick lawyer in his fancy pinstriped pants, long black jacket, and red paisley vest. His middle brother gave him a narrow-eyed look, glancing upward at the dirigible. "You in trouble?"

Winn couldn't resist smiling at him. If there were two people he loved more than anything in this world, it was his little brothers, even if they were always spoiling for a fight. "No. Not yet. Seems the vampire royalty in Europe thinks they could use our help in tracking down a missing third of the Book. The contessa says they sent her here to request our assistance."

"Who *they*? Vampires? They want *our* help?" Disbelief tinted Colt's tone. In his denim jeans, battered brown duster, and matching Stetson and boots, Colt looked even more disreputable next to Remington.

Winn shrugged. "Simple matter of survival. If Rathe wipes out humanity, their food supply disappears."

Remington grimaced, his hands reflexively gripping his guns. "Hardly seems like the best of reasons for us to forge an alliance with them," he muttered, more to himself than his brothers.

People peeked out from behind their doors, and drapes moved in windows. Across the street the tinny sound of a piano started up again. As odd as the dirigible was, just like in Bodie, nothing could get the hardy souls of Tombstone ruffled for long. A gust of hot wind blew, kicking up dust along the mostly deserted street and making the rope ladder sway and clatter against the hull of the dirigible.

"Considering how little time we've got, if Marley's calculations are correct, I don't see much of an option. If we want to discover where all the pieces of the Book have been hidden, we'll have to split up," Winn pointed out. "You two any closer to decoding Pa's message?"

Colt caught Remington's gaze for just an instant, then turned his attention back to Winn. "Remy thinks it's got something to do with either the Weaver's Needle in the Superstition Mountains or a place called the Eye of the Needle outside of Phoenix, close to McDowell."

Winn rolled the sharp, waxed end of his mustache between his fingers, and frowned in concentration. "Phoenix." He paused for an instant. "I could get you there in about an hour."

Raw-arr. From behind them the mountain lion growled, and Winchester gave it a pointed look. "What is that? And what is it doing here?"

"You mean *who* is that," Remington corrected him.

Winchester nodded with understanding. "Shifter?"

"China McGee," Colt and Remington said in unison.

China? Winn's eyes widened slightly in recognition, and his gaze darted to Colt. He at least had the decency not to let his jaw drop. "Not the same one who—" He waved his hand. "Never mind. I don't want to know."

Remington tried to hide his amused smile, and Colt punched their middle brother in the arm. That was the thing about brothers. They never let you forget anything, especially if it was embarrassing, and Colt's first run-in with China had been a whopper, leaving him buck naked and tied to a bed. How could Winn and Remy ever forget something like that?

"It wasn't my fault," Colt growled.

Raw-arr. The mountain lion growled again in retort.

"She begs to differ." Remington holstered his guns and flipped his long jacket back over them. "Despite that, she's agreed to go with me down to follow the clue Pa's friend Diego left about the map in Mexico."

Colt gazed up at the dirigible and frowned. "You sure the contessa would be all right with extra company?"

Winn smiled. Colt was going to be surprised. "We already have Tempus on board. Thought we might drop it off for you. We're flying to Europe."

"And now Phoenix is on the way to Europe?"

"It could be. Are you up for it?"

Colt nodded. "Let me go and fetch Lilly down here from Remy's office and we can get going."

Winn scowled. He thought once they'd taken the riddle to Marley and decoded it, Colt would have sent her back to Hell. "You still hanging on to that demon?"

Colt pulled back his shoulders a bit and set his jaw. "She's with me until we find Pa's part of the Book."

Damn, that boy was stubborn. Colt had long ago passed the point of taking anyone's advice but his own. "Just watch yourself," Winn said simply. He wanted to watch Colt's back every step of the way, but that was proving impossible. Not if he was going to be protecting his own from a dirigible full of vampires.

The tension gone, Colt jibed back, "Look who's talking.

You better consider wearing extra starch in your collars. You might need it, considering the company you're keeping."

That was true. Funny how things seemed to twist upon themselves like that. Winn smiled. "Fair enough, little brother. Go fetch your demon and let's be on our way."

Colt took the steps two at a time back up to Remington's office. Winn waited until the door closed behind his little brother, then speared Remy with a glance, and jerked his head up toward the second-story office window. "What do you think of the demon he's with?"

"Nice enough looking."

Beside Remington, the shape-shifter in cougar form chuffed and growled deep and low, the tip of her tail twitching.

"Wasn't what I meant and you know it. Do you think Colt is in danger?"

"Well, on one hand, I think he's as safe as he lets himself be. He's got good hunting instincts, and he seems to have struck a fair bargain with the demon."

There was no such thing. Winn frowned.

"On the other hand," Remington continued, "he seems agitated around Miss Arliss, and I'm not sure if it's because he's so damn attracted to her or because he doesn't trust her."

"Can't you ever give a straight answer, boy?"

Remington's lips curved with amusement. "Attorney, remember?"

Winn tugged on the left side of his mustache. "Well, I don't trust her. Not yet."

Remington snorted. "You've *never* trusted a Darkin."

"With good reason." The rope-like scars the demon had left on his left thigh ached every day and twice as much when the damn weather changed. It'd been a small price to pay to save Colt's life, but was a lesson he'd never forget.

"At least give her a chance."

"I will. But that doesn't mean I won't have a backup plan in place."

Remington's eyes narrowed slightly, and Winn could almost hear the gears grinding and spinning inside Remy's head as he thought. Finally he spoke. "China, you can change into just about any animal shape you want, can't you?"

She instantly shifted, her blond mountain lion fur retreating, her body blurring completely like a watercolor washed over with a wet brush, until she was a woman with long blond hair down to nearly her waist. The fringe on her pale brown leather jacket swung slightly as she stood up, bracing her legs apart. Tight brown buckskin pants hugged her long, lean legs and fit over her cowboy boots.

"Human too, if I'm in the mood," she grumbled in reply as she crossed her arms over her ample chest.

Winn could see why both Remy and Colt had been attracted to the shifter. Her unusually attractive looks were topped off by a pair of intelligent gray eyes. "Do you think you could hitch a ride up the ladder and check things out to make sure the vampires aren't just setting a trap for my brothers?" he asked.

China shrugged. "I could," she said, then made a show of inspecting her nails on her long, slim fingers. "But I don't see what's in it for me."

"How about two hundred dollars?" Remington offered.

"And half of whatever we find off Diego's map?" she countered.

"Half of everything but the Book."

China reached out her hand. "Shake on it, Jackson."

Remington grabbed her hand. Winn noticed the sparks that charged between them, but kept his mouth shut. He had enough on his plate to worry about. Remington was smart enough to sort that out for himself.

China glanced at Winn and gave him a very cat-like

self-satisfied smile. "Seems I'll be going along for a ride on your vampire's dirigible as well."

"She's not *my* vampire."

Remy chuckled.

"That funny to you, boy?" Winn shot back.

"Yeah. Never seen you so agitated about a woman before."

"You haven't met her," Winn grumbled.

"Uppity?"

"Yep."

"Know-it-all?"

"Yep."

"Sounds like a typical vampire to me."

Winn ignored Remington's last statement and focused on China. "Look, I want you to wait until Colt and that demon are at least halfway up the ladder before you try to get on board the airship."

China nodded. "That's easy enough."

"Can you change into something inconspicuous?"

China sighed in exasperation. "Would a mouse do?"

Winn gave her a smile. "Perfect. Colt won't suspect a thing. Much better if he doesn't see you."

"Can't handle being looked after by his big brothers?" she jibed.

"Yep," Winn and Remy said in unison.

Winn glanced at Remy. "Let me know what she finds out as soon as you can. I don't want to drop him off in Phoenix with that demon if there's any problem."

Remy nodded.

Colt and Lilly came out the double glass doors and stepped out from under the shaded walkway into the bright Arizona sunshine. Winchester didn't miss the long, lingering gaze Remington gave Lilly or the deep, throaty growl that rumbled around China's pursed lips, even though she'd transformed back into her human female form.

Good thing they were leaving. Ten minutes more and those boys would be at each other's throats pissed off because each thought the other was eyeing his woman. Good thing Winn didn't have any such issues with the contessa. She was cold and businesslike as could be. Better yet—other than business, he had no claim to her.

Winn snapped the dark goggles back into place, adjusting them on his face. He dug deep in the pockets of his duster and fished out two pairs of similar goggles, handing one to Colt and the other to Lilly. Damn. The contessa had been right. He was going to need to proceed with greater caution around her. "You'll want those once we get up in the air. The sun seems even brighter up there, and there's some dust."

Lilly and Colt dutifully pulled the goggles on, and Colt pulled his hat down good and firm on his head. Winchester started up the rope ladder and left Colt and Lilly to follow.

He knew the moment they started climbing because the rope grew steadier with the extra weight at the bottom and didn't twist about so much. Winn reached the opening in the railing surrounding the polished teak deck of the dirigible's gondola platform and found himself nose to toe with the contessa's highly polished black boots.

"Did you need the extra goggles?"

Winn ground his teeth. "Yep. He'll be up shortly with his demon."

"His demon? I thought Hunters weren't allowed to possess Darkin."

"He don't own her. He just . . ." Just what? He didn't know exactly what Lilly was to Colt. His partner in crime? His helper? Clearly there was more going on between them than it had first appeared, but Winn had been so fixated on his own challenges with the vampires, he had figured Colt

was big enough to figure that part out himself. "He's working with her to find the first part of the Book."

The contessa's lips lifted in a subtle, knowing smile that fisted through his chest. "Another of the Chosen working with a Darkin. It seems the world is changing, *da*?"

"It'll change a hell of a lot more if we don't find the pieces of the Book and keep Rathe from getting his hands on them."

All the humor dropped from her face. "Rathe will do anything to open the Gates of Nyx. We must not fail, or both humans and vampires will be wiped from existence."

"Or tortured and enslaved. That's more his style."

"You've met Rathe?"

Winchester thought about the vertical, slit-like pupils in the demon's yellow eyes and how those same eyes had lit with pleasure the second Winn had fired the shot that had blown clear through the demon lord like smoke, while his mother had taken the bullet to the chest. He yanked his tinted goggles down around his neck. "Yeah, I know the bastard."

"Then you realize how important this mission is."

"Lady, if I didn't, I sure as hell wouldn't be on a dirigible full of vampires."

Chapter 7

A small, feminine hand gripped the teak platform at Winchester's feet. He leaned over to offer Lilly his hand. "Hold on and I'll help you up."

With his assistance she clambered up onto the deck beside him. Her cheeks were flushed, making her red hair and her unnaturally brilliant green eyes seem even brighter. Even with her being Darkin, he could see why Colt was enamored with her.

"Hello? Anybody still up there?"

Speaking of the devil. Winchester leaned over the rail and grinned down at Colt. "What's taking you so long, little brother? You're holding up the circus."

His brother was still grumbling as he boosted himself onto the deck of the gondola, landing with his nose almost on top of Winn's boots. Winn looked down at him with a genuinely amused smile. "Took you long enough," he chided.

Colt pulled the goggles down to his chest. "If you wanted me up here faster, you could have helped."

Winn couldn't help goading him just a bit more. "And risk making you look bad in front of these lovely ladies? Not a chance."

Colt glanced at Lilly and the contessa.

"Another Mr. Jackson, I presume?" Lady Drossenburg asked. Her Eastern European accent made "Jackson" sound more like "Yakson," but that sultry, accented purr was growing on Winn. He liked the way it rolled deep in her throat, which made him contemplate what other kinds of sounds she might make when aroused. *Stop it,* he firmly told himself.

Colt sprang to his feet, dusted his hands on his denim pants, then gallantly took her kidskin-gloved hand and brushed it European style with an air kiss. "Contessa."

"Mr. Jackson," she murmured, her amber eyes twinkling with amusement at Colt's enthusiastic flair as he lifted his head and gave her his most charming, devilish grin.

"Youngest, and the most handsome of all the Jacksons, at your service, Your Ladyship . . ."

Winn's gut curdled as he recognized the patented Colt Jackson charm flip on like a switch. Didn't the boy realize he was dealing with a blood-drinking vampire? His gaze flicked to Lilly. Her mouth was a firm, flat line, and from the way she glared at Colt he guessed she wasn't amused by his flirtatious nature.

Winn unceremoniously took the vampire's gloved hand out of Colt's on the pretext of giving a belated introduction. "Lady Alexandra Porter, Contessa Drossenburg"—his tone was tinged with a ripple of irritation—"my *little* brother, Colt Jackson." Judging by the stiffening of Colt's shoulders, he didn't miss Winn's emphasis on "little," as if it somehow referred to his stature and not just the age difference between them.

"So this is the contessa."

The woman gave Colt an indulgent smile. Damn it. She'd never smiled at *him* that way, Winn thought, with a fresh surge of annoyance. "It seems we are to transport you to Phoenix, along with your charming companion." Her

voice was like warm, rustling silk, smooth but husky and inviting at the same time. For *Colt.*

Winn forced himself not to scowl at her. The woman was annoying as hell, and he had no idea if she really was charmed by Colt's performance, or if she was just acting that way because she sensed he was annoyed. No. Not annoyed. That would imply he gave a damn about her. He didn't.

He cared about his brother, who was standing between two Darkin as if he were at a church social. For a moment Winn didn't know who was the bigger fool. Him for standing there not doing anything about it, or his brother for encouraging both Darkin to pay attention to him in such a manner.

"Yes, we're much obliged, ma'am, um, Lady Drossenburg," Colt corrected himself. His faked insecurity might be endearing to the ladies, but all it did was annoy the hell out of Winn.

Her full, dusky mauve lips curved into a sensual comehither smile. "It is my pleasure to help the Chosen."

Alexa noted the succubus's reaction out of the corner of her eye. The red-haired beauty didn't like the attention the younger Mr. Jackson was paying to her and was uncomfortable. It showed in the stubborn tilt of her chin and the mutinous fire in her green eyes. Her chest, above the brilliant copper and gold brocade of her underbust corset, rose and fell in fast rhythm with her rapid pulse. Alexa could hear the demon's heart beating hard beneath the low-cut dark green gown she wore, but it was drowned out and muddled by the two other deeper beats of the men's hearts. The woman yanked the goggles resting on her forehead off completely.

Alexa turned on her heel and walked regally toward the

stained glass doors of the upper deck's observation lounge. In negotiations with unknown parties, she had learned it was always good to hold one's tongue and allow the other party to be the first to capitulate.

Yep. No doubt about it, she's a vampire, all right. Cocky, insufferable bloodsuckers. The younger Jackson's thoughts came through loud and clear, unlike his brother's. But the one thing they both seemed to have in common was a dislike for her and her kind. He took her reserved manner for hubris. He was wrong. It was merely experience. Their bias would only be natural, as they had been raised as Slayers, but that didn't mean she had to put up with it on *her* ship.

Alexa's head snapped around, her eyes narrowing in warning as if he'd said the words out loud rather than merely thought them. She looked down her nose at him, amplifying the power around her until it crackled in the air so he would know she meant business. "Fair warning, sir, this ship is filled with vampires. And we can hear your thoughts as clearly as if you'd spoken them out loud." It was better to educate him now than to let the situation get out of hand and risk his possibly engaging one of her crew.

His Adam's apple bobbed reflexively with a hard swallow. Good. He was smart enough to know his place. Perhaps there was a chance he would be smart enough to recover the first part of the Book as well.

Apparently, and foolishly, he was not in the least intimidated by her censure, and gave her an unrepentant sultry smile. "Yes, your ladyship."

Naughty boy. Just from his mannerisms alone she could tell he was a man who liked to play with women the way he played at cards, bluffing and reserving his hand until the moment winner took all. At one time, when she'd been far younger, she'd enjoyed such diversions. But now, with centuries of experience behind her, his older brother's steadfastness and no-nonsense character appealed to her far more.

She gave Colt a curt nod and turned back, heading for the double doors bearing the Drossenburg coat of arms. Winchester opened the door to let the ladies enter the interior observation deck of the dirigible first.

"Mind your manners, boy. No sense in offending the vampires before we know if they can help us find one of the missing parts of the Book," Winn whispered harshly to Colt.

The contessa smiled to herself. Vampire hearing was excellent, and there was nothing they could have whispered that she wouldn't have heard. But his words perplexed her. Did they truly think that her kind even knew where the Book was located? True, they had known for centuries, but that was before it had been stolen from the imperial library.

The succubus walked along beside Alexa looking at the ship as if everything fascinated her, but held her hands together in a tightly woven knot as if she were afraid she might break something if she touched it. If Alexa had a guess, she'd say the succubus had been of the peasant classes before being turned. She was beautiful, but her every mannerism spoke of one who had endured hardships and uncertainty while very young. The young woman stopped to stare at a beautiful painting in an elaborate gilt frame of the Drossenburg's main castle in the Carpathian mountains. Colt came up beside her, placing a hand at the small of her back just above the dark green bustle of her gown. Perhaps now was the most opportune moment to speak with Winchester while the others were momentarily occupied.

"Mr. Jackson?"

The men turned toward her in unison. They certainly were a striking pair, both dark-haired and muscular, with piercing blue eyes and an indefinable air of wildness about them that was both dangerous and appealing. But it was the elder who fascinated her more. "Might I have a word with you, Winchester?" she amended.

Winn touched his fingers to the brim of his hat. "My lady." He stepped toward her, then turned back to his brother, pointing a stern finger at him. "Stay out here and out of trouble until I get back."

Colt snorted, clearly ignoring him. From the tense set of his shoulders and the scowl on his face, Alexa could tell Winn didn't care for his younger brother's casual attitude and dismissive behavior.

He fell into step beside her. "You wanted something?"

"Since we are accommodating dropping your brother and his companion—"

Winn cut her off. "She's not his companion. She's Darkin. Name is Lilly Arliss."

Alexa's gaze flicked to the pair standing at the painting, then she looked back at Winchester. Darkness swirled behind his angry gaze. He didn't like the Darkin succubus being with his brother, that much would be obvious to any female. But was it because he saw the easy relationship building between them, or because he felt a duty to protect his sibling? Without reading his thoughts it was impossible to tell for sure. Alexa carefully modulated her tone. "Could you please determine exactly where would be best for the captain to land our ship safely for them to disembark?"

"I'll need some maps."

She inclined her head. "Of course. Our chart room is on the bottom deck. I shall show you."

His presence behind her as they traveled down the stairs from the observation deck to the base of the gondola spiked the air with a combination of brooding male and the wild outdoors. He grumbled beneath his breath, "reckless . . . cocky . . . going to get himself killed."

The constant *whop, whop, whop* of the steering props and the hiss and hum of the steam turbines crowded out his mutterings.

My lady? The younger Mr. Jackson and two ladies seem

to be having an argument in the observation lounge. Should I intervene? Enric told her in thought.

Alexa frowned. She felt as if she were forever taking care of and managing the details of others, both at court and on this ship. She sighed. *Separate them only if necessary; otherwise do not interfere.* She was sent to check on the companion of the younger Mr. Jackson by his elder brothers.

Yes, my lady.

The air grew stifling near the engines. Normally it wasn't an issue, but the very air here in the American desert was oven-like to begin with during the daylight hours, making the situation worse. She turned, steering them down another long hallway that ended in a dark wooden door with a brass porthole in it.

As she opened the door she was greeted by the musty, mellower scents of leather and paper, ink and wax. The noises of the engine room grew noticeably fainter as the heavy door closed behind them.

Alexa spread her gloved hands out wide. "Our chart room."

"Do you have many charts of North America?"

"A few." She stepped sideways around the massive table that took up the bulk of the room, careful that her bustle did not topple anything from its surface. The far wall was covered in open cubbyhole bins where the charts lay curled up and nesting like grubs in a honeycomb.

She plucked four charts and set them out side by side on the table. "These should be the ones we have for North America."

Mr. Jackson took the first one and spread it out, holding each edge to keep it from rolling back on itself. His large hands were rough, tanned, and strong. Not at all the hands of a dignitary or noble in His Majesty's court. A small shiver rolled down her spine, as she thought of how they might feel against her skin.

"This one covers from the East Coast to the Mississippi River." Carefully he rolled it back up and handed it to her. Alexa held the paper, still warm from his touch, in her hand before she turned and placed it back in its cubbyhole.

The Hunter opened another chart. "This is better."

She leaned in over his large, outstretched arm to get a better look. He turned to talk to her, putting his face inches from her own. At this proximity she could see the flecks of paler blue that danced in the depths of his ocean-like eyes, and her limbs felt lighter, as if she were buoyant and swimming in those eyes.

Alexa abruptly pulled back. "You'll need an Atherscope to chart our course properly." More than Hunters, she feared the sea. Looking into his eyes had been the closest she'd ever come to drowning willingly.

Mr. Jackson straightened and ran his finger along the inside edge of his shirt collar. "Is it hot in here, or is it just my imagination?"

She felt it too. "The temperature is warmest here near the engine rooms." But she'd been in and out of this chart room enough times to know that it wasn't the engines that spiked the temperature but the spark of something this Hunter set off in her. It got worse when he removed his hat, then his jacket, tie, and collar. He rolled up the sleeves of his white shirt, exposing muscular forearms dusted in dark hair.

Alexa squeezed her hands together tightly, trying to control her reactions, and turned away from him to search for the Atherscope among the other materials stacked along the edges of the room. The room was cluttered. She was going to have to talk to Enric about that.

At the thought of him his voice intruded once more. *My lady, the blond woman arguing with the younger Mr. Jackson was apparently a Miss McGee.*

Follow her.

There was a moment's hesitation. *I can't, my lady. She has just changed into a raven and flown away.*

Interesting. It looked like the Jacksons had their hands full of Darkin. *Very well, Enric. When you get the chance and the chart room is not in use, can you please see it is organized. It is a mess in here.*

Yes, my lady.

Alexa spied the Atherscope, and as she reached for it, her hand connected with Mr. Jackson's far darker one. An arc of awareness sparked along her skin, tightening her stomach and making it flip-flop in a most distracting manner. Alexa gazed up at him and lightly ran her tongue over her lips, finding them suddenly very dry. "Have you used one of these?"

He gave her a smile that coiled her insides into a knot. "No, but I've seen them. Perhaps you can explain it to me."

She cupped the glass instrument in her hand. Inside, the small cogs, weights, balances, and magnets teetered and swayed with the movement. Alexa placed it on the map over Tombstone. "We place it over our starting point and we roll it forward to the destination." He pointed to Phoenix on the map, and she stretched her arm across, forcing her to bend slightly, her bustle taking up most of the space between the wall and the map table. "It should give us both a bearing and a distance."

He leaned in beside her, and Alexa could feel the warmth radiating off his body. His breath stirred the hairs on her neck so that they tickled her skin. "Can it calculate wind resistance or pressure?"

She didn't dare turn to answer him with his face so close to hers. "*Da.* If you lift it like so." She pulled the Atherscope up and found her back pressed almost against his chest in the confined space of the room. She swallowed hard. "You can see the small balances within, shifting. For every tick mark there will be an increase in pressure, but

that is only an estimate. It can vary greatly with the temperature."

He placed his hand beneath hers, the roughness of it lightly abrading her skin. "May I?"

Alexa smoothly slid the Atherscope into his outstretched hand. The ichor in her veins was pumping hard. She'd never been this close to a Hunter without fearing for her health.

He looked through the Atherscope and wrote down several numbers, then handed her the slip of paper. "This should get your captain to our destination, if your Atherscope is correct in its calculations."

"I'll take this to the captain so we can be on our way." Alexa had to brush by him to reach the door, and the contact of her sliding over him made her legs tremble. If she could not gain control of herself better than this, it was going to be a most long and exhausting trip home.

A few minutes later, the chart room door creaked, but Winn kept his gaze focused on his growing stack of notes, maps, and charts spread all over the table. Whoever was coming through that door wasn't a threat, and he had bigger fish to fry. It was hot in here, so close to the boiler room, and if that hadn't been enough, the outside temperatures in the air above the desert were blistering as well. That had to be the reason he'd been so uncomfortable when the contessa was in the chart room; too much body heat and ambient heat in one small, windowless room.

The door swung open cautiously, and Colt sidled inside the small room. "Am I interrupting?"

Winn looked up at him and held back a smile. A sense of déjà vu filled him, but Colt had been much younger when he'd come upon Winn poring over hunting maps

with Pa. "Of course you are. You always do. Sit down anyway."

Colt ran a finger along the inside edge of his own shirt collar. "Doesn't your neck feel a little exposed?"

Winn grinned at him. He knew exactly what Colt was thinking. "She's not that kind of vampire."

Colt snorted. "What, she's the kind that don't drink blood?"

Winn shook his head. He'd already gotten a promise out of her not to feed in his presence, and while he didn't exactly trust her, he didn't fear her either. "I don't have time to explain it all to you. Look, I've got an idea where Pa might have stashed his pages. If my calculations are right, Waltz's mine should be somewhere close to this military road, practically in sight of it." He'd done his best to narrow it down with the clues Remington had unraveled. Any head start he could give Colt would keep him safer.

"You really think Pa stashed the pages in the Lost Dutchman's Gold Mine?"

"Why not? Waltz was a Hunter from the old country. Chances are he's got it hidden well enough that nobody would find it if they didn't know the Hunter lore."

Colt's eyes narrowed as he stared at the spot Winn had circled on the map. "How do you know that's not some wild goose chase?"

"You have any better ideas based on the clue he left us?"

Colt shook his head.

"Good. Then listen up, little brother. This ain't going to be easy."

Chapter 8

Alexa wasn't sure exactly what to make of the Darkin who traveled with the youngest of the Jackson brothers. The succubus sat as far away from the windows as she could get. Certainly she was beautiful. What succubus wouldn't be? But underneath Alexa sensed a frightened little girl, used to plying a trade to get her way, one afraid of authority or those of higher rank. And guessing by how she'd positioned herself in the spacious room, she didn't like heights much either.

Lilly's heart beat far too fast. Alexa could hear the fluttering, rapid beat like the quick ticking of a pocket watch in her sensitive ears. The girl's booted foot bounced as she perched on the edge of a very comfortable settee covered in deep, plush burgundy velvet, one of several cushiony chairs and sofas scattered about the large and luxurious observation deck of the airship.

Unaware that she was being observed, the demon closed her eyes and breathed out slowly, and managed to control it enough to qualify as somewhat normal. But when she opened her eyes once more, they widened with surprise when she observed her hostess standing silently nearby.

The demon let out a nervous giggle, which she covered

with a cough. Alexa's skirts swirled around her ankles as she crossed the room. She lifted her bustle to sit beside the young woman, and inspected the succubus who'd already managed to ensnare a Hunter's trust—a truly spectacular feat.

The demon exuded sensual charm. Her lithe grace, glorious tumble of fiery curls, even the bright keenness in her gem-like green eyes, were calculated to enslave a man's will and bend it to her every whim. For a brief moment a pang of envy pierced Alexa's breast. It had been a very long time since a man had looked at her the way Colt Jackson eyed Lilly Arliss. So long, that to Alexa it seemed more like a dream than a real memory.

Count Drossenburg had been the most charming of men. Suave, noble, and elegant. Everything he did was calculated to the nth degree, and he had been a brilliant strategist. But, unfortunately, not brilliant enough to escape the Inquisition. They'd captured him on his way home from a business trip to Paris. His Imperial Majesty had forbade her to go to her husband, although Alexa had begged and pleaded. For six agonizing months she'd heard in her head every painful moan and tortured scream he'd made, every plea for mercy. Until one day, Ivan's cries had stopped, chilling her to the bone with the throbbing, empty silence. If she'd had a heart, it would've broken.

She'd not let another touch her heart since. But this Darkin understood the male nature of these Hunters. Likely knew some of their secrets as well. She would befriend this demon. Certainly it was not something vampires often did, preferring not to mix with the lower, more mindless classes of Darkin. But for Miss Arliss's knowledge and insight, Alexa decided she would make an exception.

Alexa did her best to start up a banal conversation with the succubus and even ordered tea to soothe the woman's frayed nerves. There was so little time she had to get the

information she so desperately needed, Alexa thought. Embarrassment and normal social proprieties must wait. "You are a supernatural like me, are you not, Miss Arliss?"

Miss Arliss nodded as she reluctantly placed the tea cake on the little plate provided, licked the trace of powdered sugar from her lips, and took a sip of the fragrant tea. She relaxed.

"What do you know of the Chosen, Miss Arliss?"

"Only what I've discovered by reading their archives and from Darkin lore."

Alexa leaned slightly forward in her seat, trying not to appear too rabid for the information. Her raven-colored taffeta skirts and bustle rustled slightly with the movement. "And what do you know of the oldest, in particular? Does he have any weaknesses I should know of?"

"A few."

The vampire ichor in her veins pulsed. "Would you mind if I summoned some key members of my crew to hear as well? Anything we can learn to protect them during our mission could make the difference." Winchester Jackson was already proving to be an enigma. In six hundred years she had never before run into a human who couldn't be glamoured or who was able to effectively block the vampiric ability to read human thoughts.

Miss Arliss squirmed on the settee and glanced about the elegant room, as if looking for another way out besides the door to the outer deck. "If you wish," she answered simply.

Within a moment six vampires materialized beside Alexa in a curl of dark particles like smoke. They clustered behind the settee. Her children all shared the same whiskey-colored eyes as her, but unlike hers, those eyes were filled with avid male interest. Miss Arliss smiled, and her shoulders dropped, releasing the tension there. Having a host of Alexa's sons about her improved the situation, as the suc-

cubus was drawn into her natural role in the universe and instantly began to charm them.

Lilly batted her lashes slowly at them, letting a subtle, coy grin spread across her lips. They leaned forward ever so slightly, and every male eye was fixated on her, or perhaps it was the low cut of her gown. As long as she had their attention either way, Alexa didn't care.

"Go on, Miss Arliss. May I call you Lilly?" Alexa said smoothly.

"Certainly." Lilly smiled, tilting her head at a coquettish angle. Her gaze flicked briefly to Alexa. "Winchester Jackson is the oldest of the Chosen. Born and bred into the life of a Hunter. One of the most ruthless and skilled we've seen in centuries. But his biggest weakness is his brothers. He'd do anything to protect them. Even give up hunting."

"And is that why he's become the sheriff of some little hamlet in the wilds of America?" Alexa pushed.

"Yes. When his youngest brother Colt was fourteen, he was nearly drowned by a demon. Winchester stopped the attack, but not before being gravely injured in his left thigh. He nearly died."

"Hunters die all the time," Alexa said blithely.

"Or are changed into Darkin," one of her sons murmured. Alexa gently patted his hand for silence. "Not now, Michael. Let Miss Arliss finish her story." Michael had been a Hunter, and he knew the role well, but they would talk of it later when the demon was gone.

"It was enough to make him decide to leave hunting and turn his back on his legacy."

"And you think he did this to protect his brothers?"

Lilly nodded. "The loved ones of Hunters never live long."

Michael snorted.

"What can we do to protect them, and the eldest Mr.

Jackson?" Alexa brushed a thumb across the smooth edge of her china cup.

"Nothing. They're the Chosen. They're marked. Rathe wants their shrunken heads to swing as fobs on his watch chain."

Alexa's spine stiffened. Rathe was an archdemon lord. One of the most powerful of all Darkin and easily able to match the might of His Vampiric Imperial Majesty. He wasn't just a demon; he was a fallen archangel, twisted and vicious to the core, who had laid a bounty on the European vampire court's head. The moment Emperor Vladimir had broken ranks with the Darkin by calling for the vampires to locate and help the Chosen reunite the Book of Legend, he'd made an enemy of Rathe.

Alexa lifted her chin. "How well do you know Rathe?"

Lilly's brilliant green eyes betrayed nothing, but the vein in her throat pulsed hard. She knew Rathe well enough to be terrified of him.

"Are you going to turn Colt over to him?" Certainly the question was beyond blunt, but Alexa didn't see the point in dancing about the Maypole in this matter. If the succubus was indeed going to betray one of the Chosen, Alexa would have to eliminate her.

"No."

A spark of recognition and fire lit Lilly's eyes. The Chosen were as much her ticket to something she dearly wanted as they were to ensuring the vampire court's victory against Rathe and the Darkin who had joined him in his crusade to open the Gates of Nyx and eliminate humanity.

Alexa left Lilly discussing the particulars of the Chosen with her crewmen. The attention distracted Miss Arliss enough to soothe her apparent fear of flying. Too bad it did

nothing to appease the uneasiness building like a maelstrom in the pit of Alexa's stomach.

"How do you feel the Hunters in our homeland will respond to Mr. Jackson?" she asked Michael as he accompanied her to the bridge. Of any of her children by gift, Michael would know. He'd been a Hunter until his entire family had been turned into werewolves and he'd willingly become a vampire with the House of Drossenburg to escape the fate of being forced to hunt his family down. His smooth brown hair curved about his collar and swept over his forehead, making him look far more boyish than his one hundred and fifty years.

"He's a Slayer. It is only natural that they will shun him, perhaps even seek to take the Book from him and claim the glory of stopping Rathe for themselves among the Legion."

"It is quite an honor."

"Yes, my lady."

"An honor worth killing for," she mused. "Have we had word on how the British Hunters are faring in their quest to locate our portion of the Book for Queen Victoria?"

Michael cleared his throat. "Yes, my lady. The report from the castle is that they have met with resistance from the French Hunters and are taking the long route through Germany to reach the castle."

"Of course they would. The French Hunters are an enclave unto themselves, and Queen Victoria has strong familial ties in Germany, making her Hunters welcome there."

They reached the bridge, and Michael opened the door for her. Alexa hesitated as a thought coursed through her mind. "Michael, you don't think the British Hunters would have made an alliance with the Austro-Hungarian empire to get the Book for themselves, do you?" Considering he'd once been one of their numbers, he would be the most reliable source of information on the subject.

"I could see it being a possibility. Their leader is very keen to stay in the Queen's good graces. Whomever holds the complete Book would hold the fate of the world in his or her hands, and the British are most eager to extend their empire by any means, natural or supernatural."

It was simply too far a distance to Castle Barranoch to communicate effectively with Count Vernay via her thoughts, and it opened up the potential for any vampire to overhear their conversation. "Dispatch a message immediately to Count Vernay and alert him that we may be double-crossed if the British join forces with the Austro-Hungarian Hunters. We must ensure that the Chosen are the ones who hold the Book."

Chapter 9

The airship came to rest in a barren, tan stretch of dirt and rock. In the distance was a cluster of buildings veiled in the layers of dust hanging in the hot, still, creosote-scented air. Other than a few houses, the only building was the old fort, constructed out of the same reddish tan stone that littered the landscape and rose up in mountains around the little wilderness outpost. Half tumbled down, it blended in so well that it was hard to discern it from the desert. Alexa shivered at the thought of ever having to live in such a desolate, inhospitable place.

Lilly seemed giddy at the sight of the dilapidated settlement, as she walked down the gangplank to join Colt. Truly these Americans had very different ways of seeing the world, the contessa thought.

The air stirred with the scent of leather and male, and her skin prickled with heated awareness. Alexa didn't need to look to know Winchester was standing directly behind her.

"Do you think they'll succeed in finding the first part of the Book?" she asked as the crew pulled up the gangplank and readied the ship for departure.

"If anyone has tenacity in this family, it's Colt. He'll

find it or die trying," Winn answered flatly, but she could also hear a tinge of disapproval in his tone as they watched his brother walk with Lilly toward the speck of civilization in the distance.

Alexa glanced at him. "His tenacity displeases you?"

"Nope. Wouldn't be a Jackson if he didn't have that in him."

"Ah," she said, with a knowing smile. The clank and thud of the gangplank being raised and the roaring sound of engines told her the ship was ready for departure. Her captain was nothing if not efficient. She'd allotted him thirty minutes. They were lifting off in ten."You wish to protect him."

Winchester blew out a harsh puff of breath that ruffled his mustache. "Cain't always be around to save that boy. He's going to have to do this one on his own."

She knew precisely how he felt. Since she and Count Drossenburg had not been married long enough before his death to produce children of their own, all her children had been by gift. And each time one of them left the court, she worried that he or she would not return. Alexa wasn't sure what compelled her to touch Winchester; she only meant to offer him her sympathetic support. Her hand looked very small against his muscular arm clad in his rough oilskin duster. Even through several layers of fabric she could feel the tantalizing heat of his skin. "If he is anything like his brother, he will do well."

The ground dropped away from beneath the hull, and she wrapped her other gloved hand around the railing to steady herself.

He gazed down at her hand on his arm, and when he looked up the raw intensity of his gaze, filled with male awareness, rippled like a surge of hot water through her veins. The ship rocked slightly, the air filling with the hum

and shush of the steam turbines and whopping sound of the props as they pushed up farther into the endless blue of the desert sky.

Perhaps it was the rapid climb in elevation that was making her feel light-headed, Alexa thought. Surely she could not find this rough, rugged, common Hunter appealing. But the ichor pumping hard and thick in her veins told a different story.

Something about Mr. Winchester Jackson had flipped a switch inside her, making her intimately aware of him in ways that she'd never been of another being, vampire or human. The inventor in her wanted to explore and test the flood of new sensations, trying to divine the cause. The intellect in her shouted she should withdraw and avoid him in no uncertain terms. Curiosity won.

Winn knew that look. The contessa was intrigued by him, like any red-blooded, mortal woman. The wind teased dark tendrils of her hair across her cheek and her full mauve lips. He resisted the urge to wrap his hands about her waist and pull her closer. For a moment he questioned if she was trying to throw a glamour on him, but then she wasn't speaking, so that couldn't be the reason he felt compelled to bring her closer.

The contessa broke the spell weaving between them first. She shifted her gaze and withdrew her hand, and clamped it beside her other on the rail, looking out at the land that spread beneath them. "The world looks very different from up here, doesn't it?"

Wasn't that the truth? Up here, flying among the heavens, the contessa didn't look like some child of the night. She looked like an elegant, proper lady—a beautiful one.

Winn swallowed hard, trying to bring his response to her

under control and realign his thoughts. There were no gray spaces. It was black and white. She was Darkin. He was a Hunter. Black. White. And he'd do well to remember that.

He focused instead on the shifting colors and shapes of the landscape below them. He'd never gone any farther than the Mississippi River, and the change in scenery fascinated him, tempting the adventurous part of his nature that'd he'd ruthlessly suppressed for the past ten years.

Adventure was dangerous. Hunting was deadly.

"I don't know about you, Mr. Jackson, but I am going to retire for a bit to refresh myself before dinner."

The thought of vampires and dinner made him immediately tense.

Her expressive eyes twinkled as she asked, "Will you join me this evening?"

His gaze flicked to hers. He was starving, but he wasn't about to be part of the meal. "I don't think that's possible," he said gruffly.

She laughed, and the sound was husky and sensual. "You won't eat braised beef and vegetables, with an apple tart for dessert? I promise you my ship's chef is most accomplished."

Winn scratched the back of his neck in confused agitation. "I thought—well—"

"I know what you thought, Mr. Jackson, but I am determined to prove an amiable host to you on our journey."

His throat swelled with embarrassment, making it hard to swallow properly. Winn cleared his throat against the sensation. He removed his hat and placed it over his chest. "My apologies for jumping to conclusions, my lady."

She dipped down into an elegant curtsey and looked up at him through her lashes in a most seductive manner. "Dinner is at seven. I shall see you there in the dining room then."

Winn watched her walk away, the rustle of her skirts making his skin suddenly too warm. He ran his finger along the inside edge of his collar. He was on this journey to an unknown foreign country alone. Jumpin' Jehoshaphat, he'd never even been off of American soil. He stared down at the lights that marked the cities far below. Between them stretched miles and miles of darkness. Winn got the uncomfortable sensation that every mile closer to the home of the vampire court weakened his hunting abilities, which were rusty to begin with.

He knew what to fight here in the States. He knew the Darkin that roamed here. But over there, over there was one big unknown for which he was clearly unprepared. Winn patted down the large hidden pocket in his duster and found Marley's water shooting device still safely stored there.

He bent his arms on the rail, staring out at the stars on the horizon, brilliant against the blue-black sky. Marley had said Russian werewolves were different, when he'd called him back inside and given him the letter he wanted hand-delivered to Queen Victoria. Winn had seen shape-shifters, but not the kind that only turned to wolves. He'd seen demons aplenty and a rare vampire now and again. But what else waited out there to cause him to screw up and make a mistake? And that's really all it would take. Just one mistake, like the colossal one he'd made with that yellow-eyed demon before he'd known better, and he could die, or worse yet lose the piece of the Book to Rathe's minions.

He heard the clock above the fireplace mantel inside strike the half hour. Winn glanced at it and decided he probably needed to clean up for dinner himself.

He entered the observation deck and took the stairs down to the second deck and found his cabin. Winn opened the door and sucked in a surprised breath. There on the bed was an elegant black-and-white tuxedo with a long,

split-tailed evening jacket. He closed the door behind him and touched the fabric. It was finer than anything he'd ever worn.

Winn rolled his shoulders and eyed himself critically in the looking glass poised above the ceramic washbasin on the stand in his room. He looked like he'd been out in the desert for two or three days. His stubble always grew in fast and dark, and the dust storm had left his skin gritty and streaked with dirt. Beside the white washbowl, rimmed in gold, was a fluffy white towel, a tin of shaving soap with a bristle brush, and an ivory-handled straight razor. Curls of steam eddied above a pitcher. Perhaps it was time for a shave.

"Am I late?" Despite hearing his heartbeat before she saw him, Alexa was still startled by his voice. It had a gravelly edge to it, a rumbling sort of sound—one that made her ichor surge just a little harder and faster than normal through her veins.

"Not at all." She turned from the window and gazed at him. His tanned cheeks were smooth and clean, almost touchable. The stark black of the tuxedo complimented his slicked-back jet hair and mustache and made the blue of his eyes that much more intense. "You look quite handsome when you're civilized."

He chuckled, his gaze both assessing and appreciative. "I bet you tell that to all the men you invite for dinner."

It was a barb, but delivered with such charm and bedevilment that Alexa easily dismissed it. It was only natural that he should be uneasy in her presence during their first meal together, she reasoned. He truly had no idea what to expect. For all he knew vampires could act like the wild cannibals reported to exist in the deepest, darkest jungles of Africa. But of the two of them in the room, he was by far

the more wild and untamed. He was barely thirty. She was
more than ten times that in both age and experience.

The crew had truly outdone themselves. The long table
was set with crisp white linen, and the crystal goblets
sparkled beneath the blue flames of the gas lamps overhead.
Each piece of silver and china proudly bore the Drossenburg crest. Alexa chose not to focus on it. The crest that followed her every waking moment was a reminder that she
was a contessa by marriage, and while noble, was not free
to make her own choices. The title came with certain expectations and certain procedures. But just for tonight, Alexa
planned to break some of those rules.

"Shall we be seated?"

Mr. Jackson rounded the far side of the table, keeping it
between them, even though his eyes followed her every
movement with more than just casual interest. At the head of
the table, he pulled the cherrywood and burgundy velvet
chair out for her. Alexa's skin warmed at the simple courtesy.
Perhaps he was not as barbaric as he attempted to appear.

She'd given strict instructions that no one was to disturb
them this evening, not even to bring in the courses. They
were to transport them instead, leaving her utterly alone
with her guest.

Winn stared down the length of the table at the contessa.
Her hair was upswept in a complicated creation of curls and
twists, leaving her elegant neck and her collarbone and the
tops of her creamy shoulders tantalizingly bare just above a
swath of red silk. A whiff of onions tweaked his nose, and
he looked down to see a steaming bowl of soup had materialized unannounced in front of him.

Winn found himself at a loss as to which of the spoons
he should use. He'd never found a need for more than one,

and certainly not three. And there were just as many forks. Which should he use? A prickle of sweat began to itch his neck beneath the stiff starched rim of his boiled collar.

"Do you approve of our first course, Mr. Jackson?"

Winn glanced up and saw her lightly tap the spoon to the farthest right of his place setting. He picked it up and waited for her to take the first bite, then followed suit. Hunting had taught him a lot, but never anything about the ways of high society. Who needed to know which spoon was used for soup when it was a properly packed shotgun shell that was going to save your ass?

He shifted uncomfortably in his chair and took a bite of the onion soup. "It's tasty."

He could tell she tried to suppress her smile. She took another bite, then lightly patted her lips with her napkin. "You seem surprised."

"Wasn't anything I expected, that's for sure."

Her laugh was husky and genuine, wrapping around him and making him even more aware of how very feminine she was. Winn was out of his element. How did one make fancy dinner conversation? It wasn't as if he could talk about work at the jail, or hunting. Ma had taught him enough to know those weren't appropriate topics at the dinner table. The sudden memory of her pierced him, turning his stomach with regret. He put down his spoon and pushed the bowl away from him.

"Is something wrong with your soup?"

"Little rich for my blood," he murmured.

One of the crystal goblets to his right began to fill with red liquid out of thin air. "That's a mighty fancy trick."

"Materializing objects is not a trick, Mr. Jackson, it is a power we work to achieve."

He took the glass and sniffed the contents, making sure it was wine. The pleasantly tart flavor of grape swirled in

his mouth, but he nearly choked when he saw what the contessa had in her own glass. She held her own goblet to her lush mouth, but the red liquid was too bright, too viscous, to be wine.

"That a special vintage?" he asked, suspicion lacing his tone. She pulled the glass away from her lips and nodded.

"Anything I'd want to try?"

The contessa arched a brow and shrugged. "I'm not in the habit of telling men such as yourself what you can and cannot do."

Winn was momentarily distracted by the disappearance of his soup bowl and its replacement by a dinner plate filled with braised beef, tender asparagus, and roasted red potatoes. It smelled better than anything he'd eaten in months. The back of his mouth ached and watered. His stomach growled. He didn't bother trying to figure out which fork he was supposed to use to be proper; he just grabbed one and tucked in.

"It's good to see a man with an appetite," she said softly.

Winn glanced up at her as he chewed a bit of beef so tender he could cut it with his fork. He swallowed. "You say that like it hasn't happened in a while."

She sipped at her wineglass thoughtfully. "Perhaps because it has been a long time. I've been a widow now nearly two hundred years."

Winn choked and launched into a coughing fit. "Two—two hundred years?"

She wove her hands together and rested her chin on them. Her gaze danced with amusement. "Does that surprise you?"

"A little," he muttered. "You don't look a day older than one-fifty—one-sixty at most." He knew she had to be an old vampire to have the powers she did, but there was no way a man looking at her could have guessed her age. The

smooth unblemished complexion, glossy hair, thick fringe of lashes about her eyes, and lush figure hinted at someone likely in her twenties, if that. "Not that I mean any disrespect," he added quickly, then started eating again. Perhaps if he was eating she wouldn't expect any more conversation from him.

She gifted him with a generous smile that fisted straight through his chest and squeezed his heart hard, and for a second Winn forgot how to swallow.

"No offense taken. In fact, it pleases me enormously."

"That I can't guess your age or that you surprised me?"

"Both. You aren't like any other Hunters of my acquaintance."

"And that's a good thing?"

"Absolutely." A flicker of anger flared deep in her eyes then disappeared as quickly as it had appeared.

"You don't like Hunters much."

"Before meeting you, no. You see, Mr. Jackson, Hunters killed the count, my mother and father, my brothers and sisters. My cousin, the emperor, is really all I have left of my original family."

"Hard to forget those who've done you wrong, isn't it?"

"Which is why I find you so refreshing, Mr. Jackson. The Hunters in Europe will smile at you while they stab you in the back. They are well versed in the arts of politics and intrigue. While they profess to live as equals among us, they can never be truly trusted."

The fork slipped from Winn's grasp and clattered on the plate. "Sorry," he muttered, feeling every inch a sodbuster sitting with royalty, rather than an accomplished lawman.

"You are everything you appear to be, Mr. Jackson, and you say precisely what you think. That is what I like best about you. I will always know where I stand with you, whether enemy or ally."

Her words were simple enough but wormed their way

down into the deepest parts of him, pricking his conscience and bruising his honor. She was wrong. There were dark parts of him that never came to the surface, were never allowed to. He'd done things he was horribly ashamed of. How could she accept him so completely when he didn't even accept himself? "I can honestly say, Lady Drossenburg, you're not like any vampire I've ever met before either."

She leaned forward slightly, the light from above causing a slight shadow along the velvety upper swell of her pale breasts. Her long, tapered finger lightly brushed her full lips, making Winn think seriously about what it might be like to kiss her. With her finger she traced around the edge of her crystal goblet, making it sing. The vibration of it went straight through him. "True, but then how many noble vampires from the House of Drossenburg have you had dinner with?"

A smile tugged at the corner of Winn's mouth, and he couldn't stop it. "Only one."

"And how many noble vampires from the House of Drossenburg have you danced with?"

Her question took him aback. He didn't dance. Climb trees, scale the rock face of a cliff, or crawl through a forest on his belly, he'd done, but not dance. The promising start of his smile flattened. "None."

"Well, clearly we shall have to remedy that immediately." She rose, elegant and fluid, from her chair, and Winn automatically stood out of courtesy.

As she walked by, the tantalizing scent of sweet female filled his nose and the satin of her dress made soft slithering sounds, bringing to mind the sound of sheets moving on a bed. Winn discarded the thought with annoyance. He'd been far too long without a woman. That was all.

The contessa glanced over her bare shoulder at him, her amber eyes half hidden behind luxurious sable lashes. "You will dance with me, won't you, Mr. Jackson?" The words

were simple. Easy. Something any female could have said. But her husky tone slipped like smoke through his defenses, making him far too aware of just how truly female she was.

Winn's pulse sped up, and he tried to ignore the distinct pressure building in his groin. She might be a vampire, but Lady Drossenburg was much, much more than *just* a vampire. How could he tell her no without appearing impossibly rude? he told himself. Besides, he could certainly find her attractive without trusting her. The two didn't have to go together like meat and potatoes.

He followed her out the double doors of the dining room and found that the furniture and potted palms of the observation deck had been pushed aside, and the carpets rolled away, leaving a smooth expanse of dark wooden flooring.

At the corner on a high table stood a phonograph. The contessa scooped up the train of her red satin skirt and draped it over her arm and nodded at the phonograph. Winn watched in wonder as it began to spin, the needle lifting of its own accord onto the wax cylinder. Strains of music filled the room, and Winn stepped toward her, grasping her right hand in his left and settling his right hand upon her slender waist.

"You'll have to show me what to do," he said, and was horrified by how lust-filled his voice sounded to his own ears. The contessa simply smiled, her teeth white and even against the dusky color of her full lips.

"It is easy enough. First let the music fill you. Then step to the side and allow your other foot to follow. Then repeat to the other side."

He took a deep breath, letting it fill his chest, and felt the music causing him to sway, then stepped as she suggested. Outside the windows of the observation deck the night was a midnight swath of blue velvet studded with

diamond stars. He wasn't sure if any of her crew was watching them from hidden locations, but he doubted it.

Beneath his hand the curve of her hip slid against the silk of her gown, causing a friction that made it hard to focus as she swayed and turned with him, alone on the dance floor. Her breasts brushed now and again against his chest. Winn wasn't sure how long he could endure the torment. The suit was beginning to chafe, especially the pants.

She gazed up at him, her eyes soft and sensual. "See? You have an untapped natural ability, Mr. Jackson," she murmured.

He gazed down deeply into her eyes, nearly getting lost in the rich golden color, and stopped dancing. For a moment he just held her in the circle of his arms. "Winchester," he said softly.

"Pardon?"

Winn lightly wrapped one of her dark curls around his finger. It was silken to the touch and made him envision threading his fingers through a mass of curls tumbling down her bare back. "You ought to call me Winchester, or Winn. After all, there are three of us who are Mr. Jackson. I'd hate to think you meant one of my brothers instead of me."

Her eyes twinkled with merriment, and she lightly bit her bottom lip. "Then you shall also call me by my given name."

Winn shook his head. "Oh, I don't know that your crew would be very happy if I stopped using your title."

"Then what do you propose? We have clearly gone beyond formal titles."

Winn bent his finger, tucking it under her chin and lifting her face a fraction closer to his. He'd never been this close to a vampire without fearing for his life, but in this moment he found himself fearing a loss of his control far more. "Would you mind if I called you Tessa?"

Her gaze shifted, lingering on his mouth for a moment,

then reconnected with his, full of heat and intent. "Tessa it shall be."

Winn knew what a woman looked like when she wanted to be kissed. And while every male instinct in him shouted to grab her, kiss her hard, and indulge in the feel of her, Winn was experienced enough to know that just because you wanted to do something, didn't mean you should.

Instead he brushed the satin softness of her cheek with his fingertips. The pad of his thumb lightly grazed her sensual bottom lip. He drew in a sharp breath and found it saturated with the exotic floral fragrance that cloaked her skin. It reached in and coiled about his senses. It intensified the feel of her soft curves beneath his hand, and the heat which radiated off her. His pulse grew so loud he could hear the rushing thump of it filling his ears. For a moment it was just the two of them alone flying among the stars.

He leaned down slowly, and kissed her gently at first, taking his time as he sampled the soft suppleness of her lips. But the contessa was not about to let him set the pace. The moist, warm tip of her tongue slid against the seam of his mouth, and he granted her access, kissing her deeply. She stood on her toes, pressing her lithe body firmly against his. Her eager response shattered his control. A growl of need vibrated deep in his chest.

Her lips curved into a smile against his mouth. "You have an untamed wildness about you," she murmured between sensual, lingering kisses. "I like it."

God help him, he liked the very feminine feel and smell of her. But try as he might to lose himself in the moment, Winn couldn't ignore a lifetime of training. There at the edge of her bottom lip were the slightly longer canines that had descended.

Reality hit him hard upside the head like the butt end of a rifle, making his ears ring. What was he thinking? No matter how exquisite she felt in his arms, she was a vam-

pire. With one flick of her fangs she could end his life. And while her fangs had yet to fully emerge, there was a fine line between lust and bloodlust. He pulled back, far too aware of exactly where this was headed, and grasped her hands in his. He brushed a kiss over the back of each of her hands.

"You are a temptation, Tessa, but this is not the time, nor the place. We have a mission, and despite what you may think of my station, I am underneath it all a gentleman." *And a Hunter*, he added silently.

He gave her a deep bow from the waist and retreated to his cabin, where he locked and barred the door.

Chapter 10

Weak sunlight pouring through the porthole of his cabin woke Winn. He opened the round brass porthole and found himself staring at the most unusual sight. Down below was the bustle and hum of a large city surrounded by water. The sun was coming up in the east, so he knew they could only have made it as far as the East Coast. On closer inspection, he recognized the outline of the newly completed Brooklyn Bridge from drawings he'd seen in the newspaper.

Tall, boxy buildings, crammed cheek to jowl, rose into the sky along wide, bricked avenues. The clatter of horse hooves and cart wheels and the hum of voices grew fainter as they rose into the sky.

Winn pulled on a clean shirt and buttoned it quickly, running his hand through his hair to smooth it. If they were already in New York, they must have made a stop to resupply before crossing the Atlantic.

He took the stairs two at a time up to the topmost deck. The observation lounge was back the way it had been before last night's dance.

The contessa stood alone, observing the city and the ocean as the dirigible rose higher.

"Did we stop already?"

"Yes. There were certain supplies needed before we made the crossing."

Winn tensed, wondering if any of them had been people. She turned her gaze, connecting with his. "Before you ask. Yes, some of my children did feed. One thing you must understand about vampires, Winchester, is that while they may be undead, they still have strong urges and desires, as real and passionate as any living mortal. They will be far more focused when we reach our destination if I let them satisfy themselves before we embark on the rest of our journey."

Winn's ears grew distinctly warmer and his heart beat a little faster. He wasn't used to talking about such matters with proper ladies, but since she'd brought up the subject . . .

"And is that what happened between us last night? Was that just an urge?"

Her eyes hardened into glittering amber. "Perhaps you are unaware, but there is more than one reason a vampire's fangs might descend."

"Who said I was talking about your fangs?"

Alexa stared hard at him, challenging his ludicrous question. They both knew he'd left abruptly as soon as he noticed her fangs had been exposed. She'd seen his eyes narrow and grow troubled. But she truly couldn't have helped it. Before he'd even kissed her they'd begun to throb behind the soft tissues of her upper gumline, begging for release. Kissing him had only made it worse. "When vampires are aroused, their fangs are often released."

For a second, confusion swirled with indignation in the blue of his eyes, then clarity dawned, and his eyes widened slightly. A sly smile lifted the corner of his mouth, reminding her with bone-liquefying intensity precisely why she hadn't been able to hold them back with him.

"Is that what happened." He sounded far too pleased

with himself. "So if I do this"—he ran his fingertips lightly across her cheek and down the length of her neck—"is that enough to make them descend?"

Sparks arced through her from the contact, tightening her breasts and quickening the pulse of her ichor. "It's a start." She knew better than to bait him, but she couldn't seem to stop herself.

His gaze grew determined, sucking her in and making the very air between them vibrate with the tension. "Hmm, what about this?" Winchester leaned in and followed the path of his fingers with the firm, sensual press of his mouth against her skin in a series of quick kisses.

The tickle of his mustache sent tremors up and down her spine. "Show me your teeth."

Her request made him pull back a fraction. "Pardon?"

"Bite me."

One of his brows quirked upward. "That's certainly a first. Never had a vampire ask me to bite them before."

He nuzzled beside her ear, inhaling deeply. "Why is it you don't smell like sulfur like other Darkin? You smell instead like a flower garden at midnight." He brushed his lips over skin in a silken slide along her neck that turned her knees to the consistency of aspic.

"It's jasmine—" She gasped as his teeth scraped her sensitive flesh, making her ichor flow faster and harder through her veins. "We only emit the characteristic Darkin marker when we are preparing to kill or in imminent danger. Otherwise I just smell of jasmine."

"Ummm. I like it."

Not half as much as she did, she was sure. The pressure to release her fangs was causing a substantial ache both to her gums and much lower. It had been a long time since she'd taken a lover. How could she even consider it? He was a Hunter, after all. He nipped at her collarbone, then soothed the spot with a soft laving of his tongue.

Alexa couldn't hold them back. Her fangs came out in full force, and she knew from experience her bloodlust wouldn't be far behind. Sexual satisfaction was intensified a hundredfold when paired with feeding, for both the vampire and his or her chosen partner. But it was yet one more reason she couldn't take Winchester Jackson as a lover, even if he made her crave it.

He pulled back, and his gaze was seductive. "Well, I'll be. You were right, Tessa. There they are."

She was shocked when he pulled her hard against him and slanted his mouth hard against hers, the tip of his tongue tentatively caressing one of her fangs. Alexa's knees threatened to buckle. The fangs were tied so closely to her most intimate places on her body that she felt the slick, warm caress between her thighs.

She gasped at the intense sensation. If she did not restrain him, or at the very least herself, the temptation to feed from the virile offering, pumping so richly through his veins with a pulse like a siren's song, would overcome her. So Alexa did the only thing she could. She feigned indifference, even though it was the furthest thing from the truth.

"And is your curiosity now satisfied, Mr. Jackson?"

Winn's skin prickled as confusion tore through him at the sudden shift in her demeanor to nearly that of an ice princess. He didn't care for women who played games. Damn. He'd let himself get so caught up in her allure, he'd forgotten for a moment that she wasn't just a woman, she was a vampire. Winn released his hold on her, fixing his gaze on the sharp ivory points pressing against her bee-stung, rosy bottom lip. "It was very educational, Lady Drossenburg. Thank you." The air cooled even further, turning frigid between them.

She straightened the edge of her dress that he'd pulled

aside when he'd bitten at her neck like a damn vampire. No wonder it had gotten her aroused. The contessa inclined her head politely. "My pleasure, Mr. Jackson. If you will excuse me, I will see to the necessities of our departure."

Winn watched her walk away, stiff as a board, her skirts slithering over the floor in a train of dark purple taffeta the color of a bad bruise. He wanted to kick something. Hard. Instead Winn pulled back his fist and slammed it into the wall. His knuckles screamed in protest. He rubbed his throbbing hand with his opposite palm. Next time he'd know better than to trust his libido. Hell, who was he kidding? There wasn't going to be a next time, or for that matter an ever again.

Hunters had strict rules of engagement for good reason: to save their asses. And rule number three was ironclad.

A Hunter didn't involve himself with a Darkin lover. Ever. It clouded one's judgment.

Winn growled, angry at himself and just as pissed at Colt for falling into the same damn trap. Maybe his little brother was smarter than he was; maybe he'd gotten rid of that demon by now. He hoped.

Winn watched the city fall away as they drifted purposefully out over the ocean. Soon there was nothing more to see than endless blue. It became monotonous, rather like the life of a Hunter. He sequestered himself in his cabin, cleaning and checking his weapons for the remainder of the day.

Once upon a time he'd been naïve enough to believe he could simply walk away from the life and be someone normal. Now Winn knew better. Hunting wasn't going to let go of him. Not now, not ever. Unless Rathe managed to open the Gates of Nyx. If he did, then none of them had much longer. With that morbid thought, Winn went back to polishing his weapons.

As the sky beyond the porthole darkened there was a knock at his door. He didn't bother answering it. It wasn't

until he smelled the tantalizing fragrance of roast chicken that he bothered to open the door. A dinner tray covered with a linen napkin sat waiting for him. A quick glance up and down the beautifully wood-paneled hallway showed it was empty. Taking the tray into his cabin, he kicked the door shut.

He ate dinner, then washed up and got between the soft cotton sheets. The bed was too soft, the gaslights too bright. He switched off the lights, allowing a stream of silvery moonlight to fill the small cabin. He tossed and turned, brooding in his bed until he couldn't keep his eyes open any longer, and somewhere over the empty openness of the Atlantic, he fell into a deep, dreamless sleep.

He awoke with his head throbbing and his joints aching like he'd been on an all-night bender down at the Golden Goose Saloon with a miner determined to celebrate his good fortune with everyone in the place.

From the pale daylight he could tell it was morning. He washed his face, but didn't bother scraping the stubble from it. What was the point in appearing respectable? He'd gone and proved to himself yesterday he wasn't. What Hunter went and kissed a vampire?

Winn glanced at the fancy-pants suit he'd worn dancing with the contessa and decided against putting on any of the clothes her crew had neatly placed in the drawers of his dresser. Instead he pulled on his familiar clothes and gathered up his weapons. His duster and hat gave him a sense of security. Winn knew who he was and who he wasn't. The weight of his rifle and the crossbow on his back, the pistol and water repeater holstered on either hip, and his bowie knife in his boot comforted him. Besides, he wasn't about to leave them behind for anyone to help themselves or sabotage him.

He marched up the stairs to the observation deck. Through the windows it looked as if they were lost in the clouds. White and grayish mist obscured everything, and Winn couldn't even tell if they were still above the endless ocean or not.

Just beyond the windows, he caught sight of the contessa pacing the rail. Her long-sleeved, dark blue gown sported a rather large bustle, had an underskirt and accents at the hems and cuffs of pleated purple, and twin rows of large, gold buttons marched down her chest to the bottom of her military-style jacket. Winn decided to join her and find out exactly how long it was going to be before they reached their destination.

"Good morning, Tessa."

She turned, her eyes narrowing a fraction as she lifted her chin. Drops of moisture clung to her upswept dark hair like little diamonds. "Did you sleep well?"

Winn shrugged. "Pretty deep, but good." Why did she want to know?

"Enric was concerned when you didn't wake the second day."

A chill skated through him that had nothing to do with the dampness in the air that clung to his lashes and wet his skin. "Second day? How long was I asleep?"

"This is your fourth day aboard the ship."

How was that possible? Her brow furrowed slightly before she turned away from him to stare at the nothingness of swirling white on the other side of the rail. A prickling sensation at the back of his neck told Winn she knew more than she was telling him. Winn moved as quickly and silently as he could, placing a hand on either side of the railing, effectively trapping her between him and the rail. "What are you not telling me, Tessa?" he growled into her ear.

She stiffened in front of him, her posture defensive,

making her shoulder blades poke him in the chest. "Enric added some herbs to your roast chicken to help you sleep."

Winn cursed in four different languages. That explained the pounding in his head. "You drugged me?"

"It was for your own benefit."

Winn lost his patience. He leaned forward and grabbed her determined little chin in his hand, forcing her to twist around and look him in the eye. "Don't you *ever* do that to me again. I'll decide what's best for me. Got it?"

She nodded, but her eyes were mutinous. He'd been rougher than he'd meant to be. He let go of her, releasing his hold on the rail and stepping back.

"You should be giving me your thanks instead of haranguing me," she muttered, an angry edge to her tone. "The voyage over the ocean was hardly smooth. You're better off having slept through it."

"Don't matter. I'm not afraid of the hard stuff, Tessa, but I hate not being able to control my own decisions."

Before them the misty gray veil of clouds parted, revealing a sight that shocked Winn's mind and ensnared his imagination. The pale stone walls of a castle stood stark and defiant on a rocky perch. A lone tower, capped in a sloped, black slate spire, pierced the sky. Even from this distance he could easily make out the image of the Drossenburg family crest on the flag, bat wings and all, in the field of bloody red.

The wet, green scent of the surrounding thick evergreen forests filled the air, along with the smells of mold and decay, earth, straw, and wood smoke. Thick swirls of mist eddied between the trunks of the trees, making the entire valley seem both mythical and foreboding.

"So that's home," Winn said, cracking his knuckles.

"For a vampire, it's the highest royal court." There was a note of pride in her voice.

"There's more than one?"

The contessa rolled her eyes. "Are you certain you're a Hunter?" The implication that she thought him an idiot didn't need to be said for Winn to hear it loud and clear.

The truth of the matter was that he and his fellow Hunters in the States were at a disadvantage when it came to vampires. Pa's portion of the Book, which they'd been trained by, held precious little information about vampires. It was part of the reason Hunters in the States were so wary of them.

Each portion of the Book was rumored to hold the secrets most useful to disposing of the Darkin most common in the region. He imagined the vampires had a pretty damn good reason for guarding the second portion of the Book, since it likely held all kinds of information about how to dispatch their kind.

"We don't have many vampires. Demons and shapeshifters are more common out West."

She stared out at the stark castle, sticking up almost like a fang from the dark jaws of the forest. "*Da*, with all that sunlight I can well imagine why vampires might avoid your desert territories."

Winn pulled the brim of his Stetson down tighter, keeping the wind from tugging it off his head. "Are all the vampires in the royal court older, like you?"

Her generous mouth firmed into a taut line. "You'll see."

Chapter 11

The closer they got to the castle, the more imposing it became. It wasn't so much a fairytale castle as a fortress that took up the entire top of the hill. The pale stones topped by crenellated battlements looked like something medieval. Only the tall tower with its elegant spire seemed even remotely fanciful. A solemn road, bordered on each side by a low stone wall, wove up to the wooden portcullis.

As fast as the mists had parted, they folded back in again, obscuring everything but the battlements that they were closest to. Crewmen threw tethering ropes down to uniformed guards below as the dirigible lowered gently toward a landing platform cleverly concealed by the crenellated stone of the battlements.

The behemoth of a ship angled into position, hovering over the castle and swaying like a ship at sea in the slight wind blowing through the valley. A familiar clatter indicated the lowering of the rope ladder.

So this was it then. Winn's heartbeat increased in anticipation of what was to come.

Salvation or ruin.

He felt the pressure of responsibility and prayed that

he and his brothers would triumph, despite the over-whelming odds against them.

If Rathe won, all of mankind would be wiped from the face of the earth. Winn's petty human frailties—lust, desire, pride—were nothing more than a drop in the ocean in the face of this monumental challenge.

Rathe would not be content simply to let the Darkin overrun the surface of the planet. He'd enslave mankind, making anything humanity thought they knew of misery look like a stay at some fancy-pants resort at the seashore. Rathe had the power to twist minds, rend hearts, and steal souls.

"Shall we?" The contessa motioned to the opening in the deck rail where they could descend.

He tipped his Stetson. "Ladies first." She gave him a brief bow of her head in return, then her chin tilted up a degree, and her shoulders dropped as she whisked past him, her movements so elegant and regal her boots barely made a sound on the teak decking. In a split second she had changed from the curious, sensual woman he'd danced with to a consummate diplomat, with no expression upon her face.

But even her formality couldn't change the glossy dark-ness of the curls that blew in lazy little twists about her throat where he'd kissed her or the heady fragrance of jas-mine that drifted in her wake. Winn ruthlessly shoved his observations aside. It was time to focus on the matter at hand rather than the subtle curve of her cheek or fullness of her lush mouth.

A substantial military escort, in two ridiculously straight lines, faced forward, awaited them when they reached the battlements below. They were smartly attired in the same crisp black uniforms as her men on board, their gold but-tons polished bright. The high collars looked as uncomfort-able as hell and reminded Winn of the clothing worn by

Chinese railroad workers. Only a lot fancier. Black angled hats, reminiscent of the Civil War veteran kepis and embroidered with the flashy gold and red Drossenburg crest, hid the men's eyes with a spit-polished brim.

The highest-ranking officer bowed to brush a brief kiss to the back of the contessa's gloved hand. "Welcome home, my lady." Winn didn't miss the curious glance cast in his direction by the captain. "I see your mission was successful."

"*Da.* Mr. Jackson, may I present to you Herr Trouchlin, general of His Imperial Majesty's personal guard."

Winn tugged at the edge of his Stetson brim, and the captain gave a quick, efficient bow and clicked his heels together before dismissing him entirely to focus on the contessa.

"Has His Majesty been informed of our arrival?" She fell into step beside the general as they turned in unison and strode purposefully along the battlement, leaving Winn to follow in their wake. He tried hard not to step on the train of her skirt or look too long at the sway of her bustle.

"Certainly. He is awaiting you and your guest in the throne room."

Winn's Hunter instincts returned automatically as he subtly scanned his surroundings. Possible exits, means of escape, hiding places. Anywhere an enemy might lurk.

Lesson number four: always have an exit strategy.

The castle was well fortified. The walls were made of five-foot-thick, solid stone blocks, fitted together so tightly, he'd be surprised if he could fit a knife blade between them. It was a sixty-foot drop to the ground, which was unforgiving rock. To the north, a damn steep slope led to a fast-running river; to the east lay a picturesque little village; south the cold, gray face of the mountain backed the castle. A single road, rimmed by the small stone walls with a sheer drop on either edge, wound up the western hill, ending at well-fortified wooden gates.

All in all, a good place to be if one wanted to be protected, and a bitch of a place to break out of if one wanted to escape.

They passed through an arched door in the battlement tower and entered the castle proper. As they traveled down several wide stone staircases and a convoluted maze of hallways, Winn noted all the extravagant medieval tapestries and thick carpets that hushed their steps. He didn't know much about artwork, but even he could tell that the massive paintings in gilt frames, and the rows of white marble statues, most of them missing arms or heads, were older than dirt. Probably worth a large fortune as well. The place oozed wealth and excess.

Soon enough they arrived at the heart of the castle. The giant central room, with its high-arching vaulted ceiling, was surprisingly light and airy. Heavily carved double doors, crafted from a dark wood and ten feet tall, were flanked by more expressionless, uniformed guards.

The contessa's gaze raked over him, and Winn got the distinct impression she was assessing if he were suitable to present to the emperor. He gave her a steady look in return.

If she thought he'd be intimidated by meeting such an exalted person, she didn't know him at all. Where he came from, all men were considered equal. Although some were a little more equal than others, Winn thought, following her across the white marble floor.

"Please remove your hat and do not speak unless spoken to," she said.

"I'm from America, not the moon, Contessa," Winn murmured softly, removing his hat. "My mama brought me up right. Don't you worry, I know how to comport myself."

He brushed his fingers through his flattened hair, but it did nothing to smooth down the prickly sensation racing through his system. At their approach the doors were pulled open, and he took a deep breath, letting it out slowly.

A long stretch of room, punctuated with enormous stained glass windows, proclaimed that once it had been the sanctuary of the castle. The large chamber was filled with people—or rather vampires. On either side of the vivid red carpet running the length of the room, they sat in gilded chairs. All heads turned as one to observe the slow stately progression Winn and the contessa made toward the prominent dais.

Every Hunter instinct in Winn went on high alert as his gaze slid over the vampires gathered there. Holy hell. He'd never seen so many vampires gathered in one place before, and his hands itched to hold a weapon.

Vampires holding court in an old church. The irony wasn't lost on him.

In the nave, where the four parts of the chapel met in a central point, sat a man. As they approached he turned dark eyes to silently watch their progress. Winn took the time to assess Alexa's emperor.

His Vampiric Emperor Vladimir the Fifth was an imposing figure, taller than most, with thick, dark hair worn long and tucked behind his ears. His sharp, dark eyes looked as black as his thick, well-shaped beard, and his importance was underscored by the heavily embroidered embellishments of seed pearls, rubies, and gold thread upon his mink-edged black robes. For a vampire reputed to be hundreds of years old, he looked like a younger man in his prime. His throne, crafted of highly polished wood, set upon a raised dais, gave him the advantage of looking down on everyone else.

Winn leaned in slightly to the contessa as they walked. "I see the family resemblance in that flinty stare of his. Is everybody in your family this imposing?" he whispered. She said nothing in reply, her back ramrod straight and her face impassive. Had he not been such a keen observer he would have thought she was just blatantly ignoring him,

but instead the tension around her eyes indicated intense concentration. Was she silently communicating with everyone in the room?

"It's rude to talk about a person when they can't hear you," he muttered under his breath just loud enough for her ears only.

Her gaze flicked to his, and she raised a brow.

Yeah, sweetheart. Winn shot her a small smile before she faced forward again. *I might not be able to hear you, but I know what that look indicates. A private chat with your emperor.*

A buzz of whispered conversation grew louder as they approached the throne, giving Winn the distinct impression he had a target slapped on his back. He looked at the crowds gathered on either side out of the corners of his eyes. There were pointed glares and disdainful glances. The men were richly dressed in velvets, silks, and golden brocades, but a century out of fashion, at least. The contessa seemed the only one who dressed fashionably as a modern-day Victorian woman of means.

At the foot of the dais she dropped into a deep curtsey, her skirts spreading out about her. The general fell to one knee beside her, head bowed. Winn's fingers dug into the rim of his Stetson. He bowed from the waist, rather stiffly, not exactly sure if it would pass muster. It wasn't as if he met royalty every day, Darkin or otherwise.

"Welcome home, Lady Drossenburg," the emperor said. There was a distinct note of fondness in his voice. "I see you've accomplished what I've asked of you."

The contessa rose from her curtsey, gripping her hands in front of her, her index finger fidgeting with the large ruby ring on her right hand. The nervous gesture was not lost on him. She was just as intimidated by the emperor as everyone else in the room. "Your Imperial Majesty, may I

present to you Mr. Winchester Jackson, eldest of the Chosen." Her gaze shifted in Winn's direction.

Alexa saw him stiffen slightly at the title, and she resisted the urge to smirk. It would not be proper, especially in front of the vampiric court, to openly comment about Mr. Jackson's lack of faith in his own title in the presence of His Imperial Majesty. If Mr. Jackson was uncomfortable with it, that was certainly not her problem. She'd done as Vlad had asked. She'd brought him one of the Chosen to find their piece of the Book. And now she could be done with Mr. Jackson and the unsettling desires he produced in her.

Deep down, Alexa was growing less and less certain Mr. Jackson's presence alone would be what gained them back the missing piece of the Book. Certainly the Hunter was powerful enough, but he lacked the basics to navigate their Darkin/human/Hunter politics. But Vlad had been insistent that it be one of the Chosen and not the European Hunters who assist them.

Vladimir was ensuring unification and support among their kind with this very public display of welcoming the American Hunter into his court, and she would not undermine him. But later, when the two of them were not surrounded by the rest of the court, she would tell him what she truly thought of Winchester Jackson. Well, perhaps not all of it, but the parts that mattered most.

Among the mass of vampires, Winchester certainly stood out. Not just because his skin was a healthy, *alive*, golden brown when everyone else's was milky pale. But also because of his rugged appearance. The host of weapons he had holstered to his large frame were at odds with the intelligence that sparkled in his blue eyes and the rough stubbled

edge of his strong jaw. What Winchester Jackson was, was a contradiction.

"Welcome to my court, Mr. Jackson," the emperor said clearly.

Alexa suppressed a smile as she watched Vlad try to infiltrate the Hunter's mind and fail, just as she had. It made her feel a measure more secure in her own abilities. If the emperor himself could not penetrate Winchester's mind, then she was not as affected by him as she thought.

Vladimir's dark eyes flicked to hers for an instant. *Can you read his thoughts?*

No, Your Imperial Majesty. He has been taught how to conceal them from our kind.

Interesting. This is more promising than I had hoped.

"Mr. Jackson, you are aware of our interest in recovering the second part of the Book of Legend, which has been stolen from us?" the emperor said, his tone confident.

"I am, but I got one problem with the plan."

The emperor raised a dark brow. "And what is your objection?"

"I need to use it before you can have it back."

"For what?"

"To seal the Gates of Nyx." A buzz, like a slapped nest of bees, grew louder as the vampires in the room talked to one another both out loud and in their heads. Alexa wished she could shut it out.

"It appears the time for the prophecy is at hand, Your Imperial Majesty," she said loudly enough for Vlad to hear her clearly. His onyx gaze snapped to hers. For the last six hundred years they'd guarded the piece of the Book, using its contents to reinforce their position as the most superior of the Darkin. If they did not support the winning side, that reign would quickly be coming to an end.

"So it is true, just as the oracle foretold?" he asked smoothly.

"Yes. The three shall become one, but never whole," she recited from memory.

"Who took the piece of the Book?" Winchester's voice was strong and commanding and caused a shiver to race from the base of her skull down her spine. All eyes in the room turned toward the Hunter in their midst. Even surrounded on all sides by hundreds of vampires, confidence radiated out from him. Inwardly Alexa tensed. While she was proud of him, she also feared a backlash from the others who might perceive him as far too bold in his demand and dictate to the emperor.

The emperor eyed him speculatively, but apparently approved of his question. The tension in Alexa's chest eased.

"We believe it was the *Oboroten*," Valdimir answered.

Winchester frowned. "What?"

"Russian werewolves," Alexa said, not bothering to conceal the contempt in her tone. "They, along with most of the Darkin, have sided with Rathe in his bid to uncover all the pieces of the Book."

Winn pulled at the brim of his hat in his hands. "Surely the lot of you could take on a few overgrown furballs. Why'd you really go to all the trouble to fetch me?"

His Imperial Majesty leaned forward, lacing his hands together and steepling his index fingers so that their tips touched his mouth. "It was foretold long ago that the Chosen would decide the fate of this world."

Winchester shifted his weight from one booted foot to the other, and glanced briefly around the room, his bottom lip coming up and over the bottom edge of his mustache and smoothing it out before he locked his gaze back on Vladimir. "You're puttin' a powerful lot of hope in one prophecy." The challenging tone of his voice caused a ripple of reaction among the crowd.

"Are you not up to the task?" Vlad challenged.

The Hunter's jaw flexed, and Alexa's sensitive hearing

picked up the grinding of his teeth. "Oh, I can get the Book back," he shot back, "but I might have to do some damage. You up for that?"

"If it will stop Rathe, you may do as you please." The emperor's eyes sparked with appreciation. Vlad's voice echoed in her brain. *He'll do just fine. Take him to see Kostick. He's in the dungeons.*

An uncomfortable pressure clamped down inside her chest. *Whatever for?*

He let the Oboroten *take the Book from the imperial library, and paid dearly for it, I'm afraid. The wolves left him to the villagers, who attempted to burn him alive.*

Alexa gasped. A vampire as old as Kostick would never burn completely; he'd just suffer endless pain. *But why did you put in him in the dungeons? Surely—*

It was necessary, Alexa. Not only is he recovering from his injuries away from the light, but he's gone mad. It was not safe to keep him among the courtiers.

"Lady Drossenburg," the emperor said slowly, out loud. Alexa's stomach twisted uncomfortably. She knew that tone of voice from Vlad. He was about to proclaim something, damn the insufferable man.

"You shall accompany the Chosen one on his mission to recover our missing piece of the Book of Legend."

Every cell in her body wanted to rebel, knowing the temptation it set firmly in her path. She had thought once she'd gotten him here, she would be free of the far too attractive Hunter. "But sire—"

He held up a finger, silencing her. "Take him to Kostick."

She bent her head and deeply curtsied again, knowing she had no further recourse. The emperor's word was law. "Of course, Your Majesty."

Vladimir rose from his throne. Instantly his personal guard surrounded him. He walked down the dais and out of the throne room to his private chambers without so

much as a backward glance. The instant the door shut behind the monarch, the chatter started. There was outrage and anxiety, and the combination of so much noise both in her ears and in her head was almost more than she could bear. She grabbed firmly onto Winchester's duster sleeve and wheeled him about, marching out of the throne room with far less grace than she had entered it.

"Where are we going?" Winchester shoved his black cowboy hat back on his head, his eyes sparkling with purpose.

"To the dungeons."

"Whoa there. Nobody said anything about dungeons." He dug his heels in, forcing her to look back at him. "Who's Kostick?"

"One of the oldest vampires in the court. He's been protector and prophet. He was the one who prophesied the Chosen more than seven hundred years ago. Now come on."

Winchester shook his head as he fell into step with her. She liked the way he matched the length of her stride, and gods help her, she liked that he was broad and strong and a reassuring physical presence in this time of uncertainty. Of course, she reminded herself, his frail human form would be no match for the Darkin he was going to encounter on his perilous journey. But for now she drew from his strength as they moved through the castle.

The castle was enormous, constantly being added to over the centuries, with a labyrinth of corridors and hundreds of chambers. It took them half an hour to reach their destination. Time Alexa would never get back, since she could just as easily have transported herself there in the blink of an eye.

Eventually, they arrived at a simple wooden door bound with thick black iron bands. "And you keep this geezer in the dungeon? What kind of people are these friends of yours?"

She glared at him and opened the door. The air smelled stale and fetid, and she produced a scented handkerchief and pressed it to her nose. "He was tortured and maimed by the werewolves. He's gone mad." Lifting her skirts she started descending the worn stone stairs lit with only a flicker of a torch burning in the iron sconce in the wall.

"Jumpin' Jehoshaphat." His deep voice echoed in the close confines of the spiral stairwell. "You tellin' me the closest lead we got to finding this missing part of the Book in the next week is some half-dead vampire more than a few pickles short of a barrel?"

She stopped pressing forward for a moment and gazed at him in confusion. "If that means what I think it means, then *da,* he's old and likely insane."

They circled down a spiraling staircase that grew darker with each step. Alexa knew this area of the castle well. Until the Darkin of her country had made alliances with the Hunters, they had hidden here like vermin, forced to go out only at night and subsist on what nourishment they could find.

"Damn, it's like a crypt in here," Winchester said, a distinct tone of discomfort in his voice.

"It *is* a crypt in here," Alexa said dryly. Her eyes were far more sensitive than his. She grabbed another torch from a bracket on the wall and lit it with a flare of materialized flame. "Better?"

The flickering light of the flames highlighted the strong edge of his jaw and made slashing shadows beneath his brows and cheekbones. "If this is the vampire idea of how to help your wounded, remind me never to get hurt around you."

"Surely you aren't scared of the dark," she teased.

"Just don't like dark closed-in spaces like this. I'm a wide-open, fresh-air-spaces kind of man."

He'd never make a decent vampire, she thought with

amusement. She pointed down a dank row of cells, each with a half-moon-shaped arch filled with bars. "This way."

Alexa actually smelled Kostick before she saw him. The cell had been made as comfortable as possible, but being that it was in the castle's massive dungeon, that had been an almost fruitless effort. Seeping water stained the stones with black and green slime, and while the bed was a thick mattress, rather than a plain straw pallet, there was still evidence of rats in the cell. She could see their beady little eyes in the recesses beneath his bed and hear their skittering feet upon the stone. She handed the torch to Winchester and put both her hands on the bars.

"Kostick! Kostick, awaken. It is I, Alexandra."

"What in the sam hill is all that jibberish?" Winchester muttered.

Alexa scowled at him. "What are you talking about?"

"That." He pointed and slowly moved the torch to illuminate each of the three walls. Where the walls were dry, they were covered in the scrawl of various sigils and pictures, made in charcoal or, she thought, with a sick sliding in her gut, dried ichor. The frightening images and cryptic bits of phrases looked like the ravings of a madman written in his own fluids.

Mr. Jackson stared hard at the walls, and his eyes narrowed. "Tessa, I hate to crush your hopes, but if this is the fella who's supposed to help us, I'm afraid we're out of luck."

The pile of blankets on the mattress shifted at the sound of Jackson's voice. A balding head, the hair no more than wisps upon the grimy and scabby scalp, poked out and swiveled toward them.

Alexa gasped at the gruesome sight, then clapped a hand over her own mouth to hold back the bile surging up in the back of her throat.

Half of Kostick's face had been burned away, the

charred remains housing an eye socket, but no eye. His remaining eye was white with cataract. White teeth and a fang were visible through the blackened husk of what had once been lips. Clearly he could not talk to them physically. He shifted the covers off of himself and limped toward them. The loose nightshirt he wore shifted on his frame, revealing a blackened shoulder and chest and one blackened leg. Half of him had been badly burned nearly to the bone. When Vlad had said he needed to recover, he'd never hinted it was this bad.

Who are you? The voice of the vampire poured into her mind.

"I am Alexandra, the Contessa Drossenburg, from His Imperial Majesty's court," she answered out loud, so Winchester would at least hear part of the conversation. "We need to know where the Book has been taken."

Kostick shuddered, flinching away from them and sidestepping back to his pallet.

Alexa swallowed hard. Kostick was far worse than she'd ever anticipated. "We know the *Oboroten* took it. But do you know where?"

Those thieving bastards! It is because of those werewolves I was captured and burned by the villagers! Kostick communicated.

"What's he saying?"

She speared Winchester with an irritated glance. If they were going to make any progress whatsoever, she had to focus on getting the information out of Kostick, not acting as the interpreter for a Hunter. "The Russian werewolves ambushed Kostick and left him to be burned at the stake by villagers."

"I thought you said you had peaceful relations with the folks around here," Winchester challenged.

"We have. The werewolves have been raiding the village, and as a consequence the villagers no longer trust us

either. All Darkin are the same to them. Monsters. Sound familiar?"

She turned her attention back to the ancient vampire. "Where have they taken the Book, Kostick? Help us find it. It is important," Alexa urged.

The vampire scrambled to the far wall, his fingers searching, counting the number of cracks and interpreting the shapes of the individual rock blocks. *Here! Here is where it lies!*

Alexa leaned in, peering at the scrawled gibberish on the wall. "He says that is our clue."

Winchester leaned in over her shoulder, taking a closer look. The masculine scent of him and the pounding rush of his pulse made her squirm with sudden discomfort and yearning.

"What the hell does *Herve* mean?"

She glanced at him, which brought their faces dangerously close. "See the outline of a wolf beneath it?"

He shrugged. "Still don't make sense."

"St. Herve?"

"Never heard of him."

Alexa threw up her hands in disgust and groaned. "St. Herve of Brittany. He was said to be blind and led about by a wolf he tamed."

"Nice story. Does it have a point?"

She turned back to Kostick and grasped the bars of his cell. *Kostick, have they taken it to Brittany, to the chapel of St. Herve?*

Kostick frowned. *Herve was a werewolf. They'll take it where they feel safest, among their own.*

But why not take it directly to Rathe?

Kostic swiveled his opaque white eye in Winchester's direction. *They think to capture him with it, to ingratiate themselves further with Rathe. They don't just want our*

piece of the Book. They want to hasten the opening of the Gates of Nyx. They will try it at Cleder, in Brittany.

"The Russian werewolves have taken our piece of the Book to Brittany. There was once a chapel in Cleder, before the Revolution, that held the cradle of St. Herve. He thinks they've taken it there."

Winchester's face broke into a smile, and he tipped his hat back. "Well, that ain't so hard. Seems like a pretty direct trip, especially with your airship and all."

Alexa speared him with a hard glance. "Mr. Jackson, I am aware that you know very little about how things are done here, but let me assure you a trip to Brittany is anything but simple for us vampires. Within the border of France we are hunted ruthlessly, just as we are in your country."

"You mean to tell me there are no Darkin in France?"

"No. Yes. Of course there are Darkin in France. There are Darkin everywhere! But they do not venture out into society as we do here."

A foul whiff of sulfur tweaked Winn's nose as a curl of dark smoke swirled beside the contessa, turning into one of the uniformed guards from the throne room. Winn jumped back, a little unsettled by the sudden appearance of the vampire. Didn't they get tired of poofing from place to place all the time?

"Lady Drossenburg!" The guard clicked his heels together and bowed.

"What is it?"

"An attack on the castle. His Imperial Majesty has instructed you to leave with the American immediately."

"An attack? That's absurd!"

The guard scowled, his expression of utmost seriousness. "Things have changed for the worse while you've

been away, my lady. The villagers have been convinced by the Hunters and the church that the end of the world is coming unless we are eliminated. They've been told we hold a key to preventing the end of the world."

"Of course. Make the vampires the scapegoats for the end of the world. Never mind the other Darkin in their midst," Alexa muttered. Their logic was twisted and completely irrational. Darkin were threatening them. But there was no time to educate them as to why the vampires weren't the same as all the other "monsters" they sought to eradicate, nor to explain that they no longer possessed the piece of the Book.

"They've become increasingly unsettled in the past month, but until now it's only been minor skirmishes. Until they burned Kostick last week."

Her face warped slightly, brows protruding outward as they had when she'd killed Hoss's gang. The taint of sulfur in the air grew stronger. Alexa's hands curled into tight fists at her sides as the tips of her fangs peeped over her bottom lip. Winn backed up a pace at the rapid change in her. "This is intolerable," she growled.

The messenger bowed his head slightly. "My lady, if we wish to spare the Chosen, we must get him out of here now."

She whipped around to face the messenger. Her fists released, her brow smoothed out again, and her fangs retracted. "Of course." She locked her gaze on Winn, all her composure regained. "Come, Mr. Jackson. We have our destination."

Chapter 12

They didn't make it past the throne room before the sound of the wooden gates in the outer bailey being split open by the tumultuous mob reached them. The roar of the mob grew louder as Winn and the contessa raced across the polished marble floor to the battlement tower steps.

"Sounds like a mighty large crowd," Winn muttered, grabbing her arm as her shoe caught in the uneven stones and she stumbled.

She shot him a grateful glance, then frowned. "I don't understand. We haven't been attacked like this in over two hundred years. The Hunters must have whipped them into a proper fury." Panicked vampires filled the lofty chamber outside the throne room in a confused mass, their shouts and cries echoing into a frenzied noise. They pushed and shoved at each other, trying to get enough room to dematerialize. So many of them did all at once that a thick, black, smoky haze filled the air. Winn had never seen anything like it.

"If Rathe has his way and opens the Gates, we're all going to suffer," Winn muttered darkly.

A startled gasp escaped her at the scraping, crunching noises on the doors. Then came a solid *BOOM* that echoed

through the chamber, rattling the crystal in the chandeliers overhead. "Oh gods! The villagers are right outside the door, and they're using a battering ram." Fear and anger spilled over into her voice. "Run!" Alexa yelled, tugging at the edge of his duster.

Her mouth pulled into a determined line as she hiked up her voluminous skirts and started to sprint for the stone staircase leading up the edge of the room to the battlement tower. Winn was right on her heels. The way her bustle thrashed about, he was hoping it wasn't going to tear off and cause him to stumble. They were halfway up the stairs when the large doors leading into the great hall burst open with a resounding crash. A flood of angry villagers armed with rush torches, burning slabs of wood, and farm implements poured inside. They stabbed at any vampire they could reach.

Screams pierced the air and mixed with hisses and growls as vampires fought back, their faces warping into fearsome visages with crimson eyes and protruding brows. Dark, slick vampire blood spilled across the floor, swirling with the red blood of villagers who were having their throats ripped open. Winn fought against his ingrained instincts to turn back and join in the fray. He hesitated a step, torn. Duty burned deep, but intellect reined it in.

"Come on!" Alexa urged as she grabbed his hand. "Nothing can stop them now. We must get to the ship!" They increased their speed, taking the ancient, worn stone stairs two at a time, arms and legs pumping hard. Alexa glanced down at the fray below. "Insufferable villagers. They would have died out without us. And this is how they repay us?"

"This ain't the time to reason with them. Move!"

"We saved them from starvation many times. Vlad has always seen to their safety and protection."

"Yeah, I can see why you'd want to protect your livestock," he grumbled. "You callin' His Imperial Majesty Vlad now?"

She glanced over her shoulder as they exited through the large, arched stone doorway to the narrow battlement walkway that topped the walls. "He's my cousin. Before I called him Your Imperial Majesty, I called him Vlad."

Between the large stone crenellations, Winn caught a glimpse of more angry villagers filling the road below. A shot pinged, and some chips of stone flew off one of the crenellations by him. Damn. They even had guns.

"You better hope he made it out too. You best get movin'."

Focused, shoulders pulled back and stiff, she marched across the battlements toward the ladder they'd used to descend from the airship. "You go first," she ordered.

Winn speared her with a glare. "Not damn likely. Get going if you want to make it off this rock in one piece. You need to tell the captain where we've got to go next."

"Fine." She narrowed her eyes in annoyance and started quickly climbing the wooden rungs. He hustled her up the rope ladder, coming up behind her in such a hurry that his hands brushed her ankles as he climbed. She glared at him. "This is hardly the time."

"It was an accident," he growled, pissed off that she thought of him as unable to control or focus himself. He'd been hunting long enough to know how to be professional when the situation demanded it, and had manners enough to carry him through when the situation didn't demand it.

Winn was halfway up when the airship began to move, making the ladder sway dangerously close to the tall, slate-topped tower of the castle. A shot zipped past him and splintered the bottom of the gondola directly over their heads. Winn felt the heat as another shot grazed past his ear. He shifted his hold, wrapping the rope of the ladder around his left arm and swinging the crossbow from his

back to his right hand. The thing was a damn sight heavier when he had to hold it single-handed, but he wanted to be ready to shoot if necessary.

The ship rose quickly, which was a damn good thing. The mob had spilled out onto the battlements and were shooting and throwing whatever they could at the ship. Handheld sickles, stones, even shoes were thrown at them. Winn fired off a shot at the man with the rifle, winging him in the shoulder. He didn't want to kill the idiot, simply keep himself from getting shot.

The wind, moist and cool, buffeted him, making his duster flap loudly. The castle grew smaller. Far below, the mob, piled onto the road leading to the front gates, looked like a seething mass of ants, all with little lights strapped to them, clambering over one another to enter the castle.

Winn glanced up. It was still a long climb, and his hands were aching and growing numb in the cold. The slap of his duster around his legs obscured the sound of the wind blowing around his precarious perch on the wildly swinging ladder. His hair blew across his face and stung his skin. For a moment the contessa's billowing skirts and petticoats obscured his vision. But his handhold and footing were sure, and Winn didn't waste any time. He kept climbing as fast as Alexa's progress above him allowed.

Did she have the strength to hold on as they moved through the air at a dizzying speed? Hell, yes. She was a vampire. She was probably stronger than he was physically. "Can you go any faster?" he yelled into the wind, then spat a froth of white petticoat from his mouth.

"Just keep up," she called back to him. Why the hell had she stayed with him in the castle and why was she climbing with him now? At any time she could have just zapped herself back to the decks of the dirigible in a cloud of smoke and left him to catch up. Then a thought hit him square between the eyes.

All this time he'd thought he'd been protecting her back, but maybe she'd really been sticking to him like pitch because she thought *she* needed to protect *him*. Annoyance crackled along his nerves. He was a trained Hunter, perfectly capable of taking care of his damn self.

The airship flew over the mountain, and he assumed they were headed west toward France. Maybe they weren't. It wasn't as if there were map lines drawn across the landscape. It all looked like mist-shrouded forests and spectacular snow-capped mountains to him. His scarred thigh throbbed with every beat of his heart as he climbed. Her skirts disappeared over the edge of the gondola's deck just about the time the clouds gave up being congenial and opened up, spitting rain. By the time he reached the deck he was soaked to the skin and as annoyed as a wet cat.

Or perhaps the weather had little to do with his annoyance. She didn't need him, and it stung. The contessa wasn't the "weaker sex." She wasn't weaker at *anything*. It was hard for Winn to accept that she wasn't the damsel in distress so much as a mistress of her domain. He wasn't sure just how to deal with a woman who didn't need him.

He let out a groan as he hoisted himself up on the deck, exhausted and chilled to the marrow of his bones. The contessa was waiting for him with a thick Turkish towel. "Does trouble follow you everywhere?" she asked loudly over the beating rain and howling wind as she wrapped it about his shoulders.

"This ain't nothing, Tessa," Winn said between chattering teeth as he followed her through the stained glass double doors into the observation deck. "You should see my little brother, Colt, in action." He used the corner of the soft towel to wipe his face. The cessation of the wind made his ears ring, and the warmth of the room, with its leaping fire in the hearth, made his wet skin tingle. The smell of jasmine was

heavy and decadent and intensified by the sudden heat after the chill of their climb.

She seemed oblivious to the wet fabric of her gown clinging to her equally wet skin. Her smart chignon had escaped most of its anchors, and her dark hair tumbled in glossy, wet ringlets about her back and chest and clung to her pale skin. She looked magnificent. Alluring. Vulnerable.

Winn reminded himself that this was not a woman who would be, or could be, vulnerable. She was a vampire. An old and strong vampire. But for the fact that she needed his skills, he would already have been a snack for her.

Her lips curved into a small smile as she looked up at him. Could she read what he was thinking? He hoped to hell not.

"The youngest of the Chosen." It was a statement. She knew who they were. Knew their history. Knew why they'd been put on this earth. Or at least she thought she did, listening to that half-crisped madman in the dungeon.

Winn removed his dripping hat and rubbed the towel over his head. "Yeah. If you believe in that sort of thing." He might not like it, but facts were facts.

"You don't believe in the prophecy?"

Winn shrugged. "All I know about the whole thing is somebody way back when said three brothers from the Legion of Hunters would save the world, and I ain't positive it's us."

"Well, you met Kostick, the vampire who made the prophecy."

Winn grunted and shook his head. "Yeah, well, after having met him, I've got even less confidence in his predictions."

He walked over to the marble fireplace and stood by the blue flames, resting his forearm on the mantel and gazing into the flickering light as if he could somehow divine his future in its ever-shifting depths.

"Here. Drink this; it'll warm you up." She offered him a fine, bone china, gold-rimmed cup on a fragile saucer. Swirls of steam rose from the fragrant tea. Seeing delicate china in his large, rough hands made him feel clumsy as a newborn colt as the cup rattled on the translucent saucer.

He eyed the brew dubiously. "What's in it?"

She raised a dark brow. "Tea with lemon and honey. Now drink."

Winn sniffed it just to be sure, and smelling nothing off, took a tentative sip. The hot, sweet/tart liquid raced a burning path down his throat straight to his belly. Instantly the warmth radiated out to his limbs and he felt better.

Water was still dripping in a steady rhythm from the rim of his Stetson. He tossed the hat onto a nearby marble-topped coffee table to dry out. "That hat ain't never going to be the same," he muttered into his cup, then took another fortifying sip.

He slid a glance in her direction. She looked disheveled but not soaked through like him. "Don't suppose you have any whisky I could add to spice this up a mite?"

Her generous lips curved up into a smile. "Would vodka work?"

"I can give it a try."

"I hope Vlad escaped," she murmured as she materialized a flask and poured some into his teacup.

Winn fixed his gaze on her until she looked up at him. Her eyes were a swirl of gold and pale browns. "You're worried about him, aren't you?" His chest tightened waiting for her response.

She lifted one dainty shoulder in a half shrug. "He *is* our leader and my cousin; of course I'm worried about him."

They both knew it wasn't what he'd meant by the question. He wanted to reach out and touch her, but it wasn't the proper thing to do. "I'm sure he's fine," he said, his voice huskier with emotion than he intended.

An earsplitting crack of thunder tore through the sky as a streak of white-hot light nearly blinded them. Winn almost dropped the china cup and saucer in surprise when the contessa bumped into him, her hands gripping his shirt. The sound rattled the airship, but it was the contessa who rattled Winn's insides. Maybe going through the monsoon had shaken her confidence in the airship's capability to fly during a lightning storm.

"That was close. Too close," she murmured. She gazed up at him and, realizing how she clung to him, abruptly removed her hands and smoothed her skirts. "We must have flown into the oncoming storm. I'll check with the captain to see if we can skirt around it."

A storm was certainly coming, Winn thought, and it had nothing to do with the atmosphere outside. Sooner or later he was going to have to confront the fact that she stirred him in ways that just weren't right. Not for a Hunter, at least. But for the moment he shoved the thoughts back down into the deep recesses of his mind where they belonged. He had an important job to do, and that was all he could be focused on.

CRRRACK! BOOOM! The lights flickered momentarily, accompanied by the hissing of the pelting rain against the fabric sides of the airship. The ship swerved, the lightning switching from directly ahead of them to off the port bow. But through the windows of the observation deck Winn saw they were headed toward an even larger mountain range.

"We should be out of the storm soon. We'll simply travel north a little farther and make a short stop at Castle Barranoch for weapons and reinforcements. The skies over the Alps between Bavaria and the western edge of the Austrian Empire can be unpredictable."

Her voice caused an arc of awareness to skate over his skin. Damn, she moved quiet-like. "You ever consider that

maybe airships ain't the best way to get around?" He never forgot they were floating a mile above the earth with nothing but air to cushion them if the damned airship should fall. Winn looked forward to once again being on terra firma. Marley might trust things he couldn't see or understand, like physics and electrical forces, but Winn liked the tangible.

The Darkin that troubled him most were the ones who could vanish and reappear or were sometimes invisible altogether. If he could see it, he could at least shoot at it. If it was insubstantial and indefinable like the tension swirling between him and the contessa, he had very little chance of getting it under control.

"Airships are perfectly safe as long as you don't catch them on fire," she said firmly, sounding more like she was trying to convince herself than him.

He wasn't buying it. "Uh huh. Yeah, tell that to the lightning storm after it turns this thing into a flaming lantern."

The slash of rain against the windows lessened. "You don't care for complications, do you?" She gazed at him, her eyes assessing, as if she were trying to figure him out.

Winn let out a mirthless chuckle. "Name me one man who does."

Her mouth curled into a kissable pout. Winn resisted. "Complications," she told him mildly, "are simply part of life."

"Not for everybody, Tessa. Some folks live simple. They breathe in. They breathe out. They till the soil and watch their crops and children grow. Then they get old—"

"And they die," she finished for him. "But we each have our role to play, and that is not your role; surely you know this."

"What makes you so all-fired sure we're even the Chosen?"

"Kostick—"

"Screw Kostick. If all you're holding onto is something one old vampire spouted off a couple centuries ago, there's reams of that in practically every history book. So what else have you got?"

Alexa massaged her chest, right over her stone-cold heart. It no longer beat in the traditional sense, but it still served as a touchstone to her deepest feelings. "Haven't you ever been sure of something, down to your toes?"

Winchester's mouth flattened. "Yeah. Sure of mistakes I've made that I don't intend to repeat."

"I meant, a—How do you say it inelegantly in America? A gut feeling?"

"All the time. It's part of being a Hunter."

"Well, it's part of being a vampire as well."

He stared hard at her, the intensity of his gaze stripping away her ability to think clearly. She needed him to trust her if they were to outwit the werewolves, rather than always feeling she needed to look over her shoulder to see if he held the Amanarath pointed at her.

Unable to bear the directness of his gaze when she couldn't read his mind, she looked out the large windows. Outside the ship the storm clouds broke, their angry gray masses giving way to lighter, whiter clouds. Day was giving way to twilight, lining the clouds in a hazy, golden glow.

"From the moment I saw you from the steam stage, I knew there was something different about you." She caught his gaze to see if he truly understood all she meant.

He gave her a lazy, disarming grin. "Is that so?"

"Do you think I would have just asked anyone about the Chosen?"

He pulled at the end of his mustache and stepped closer, into her personal space. His body nearly brushing hers caused a shiver to ripple through her. "I suppose not."

Alexa wove her hands together. "You are destined for great things, Winchester Jackson, whether you wish it or not."

He narrowed his eyes and indicated her with his chin. "What about you?"

With her finger she twisted the large ruby ring on her right hand, all too aware of what it signified. She had no business being so attracted to him. None whatsoever. It was time, past time, to tell him the truth.

She lifted her chin and met his blue gaze directly. "I am Vlad's future queen."

He frowned, his massive shoulders hunching, his eyes turning stormy and dark. "You could have mentioned that sooner." Irritation laced his tone. "Congratulations."

She twisted the ring around her finger. "It is a purely political match."

He glanced at her, one brow raised. "I thought you said he was your cousin."

"He is."

"Well, *that* ain't right."

She shrugged. "Within the nobility of vampiric society it does not matter, not when we live for so many centuries. The only thing considered important is to keep the noble family lines pure. Vlad only offered for my hand because he believes it will cement his position as emperor in these uncertain times. Count Drossenburg was second in line for the throne."

Winn grunted. "So when are you going to get married?"

"A date has not been set." Alexa wasn't even sure if she wanted to be queen. For several centuries she'd had the time to contemplate what she really wanted after the count's passing, and while she had been born into nobility, she couldn't escape the gut-deep certainty that she was meant for something different.

The first day she'd glimpsed the vast interior of the American continent had been the first time she'd felt lighter in ages, as if an invisible burden had been suddenly lifted, if only for a brief moment. Every moment she spent with Winchester was like a sip of fresh air to a suffocating woman. She dropped her head and studied the ring. The deep red of the ruby was bracketed by ornate silver bat wings, their points serving as the prongs on the stone.

He ran his fingers through his hair, slicking it back. "Sounds like you aren't exactly sure."

She gave him a knowing gaze from beneath her lashes. "Let us say I've found reasons to reconsider Vlad's offer."

Winchester's face slackened, his pupils dilating, as he lightly grasped her arms. "Sounds like a foolish decision to me." The strain in his voice spoke of a man with a careful leash on his control.

She closed the gap between them and laid her palms upon his broad chest. Even through his clothing she could feel the flex of his muscles and the hard, throbbing beat of his heart. "Completely reckless," she whispered.

He leaned down, putting their mouths close enough that she could nearly taste him on her lips. "I don't do reckless, Tessa."

"You could have fooled me."

The clearing of a throat caused her to stiffen immediately and pull away from his hold. "How long have you been here, Enric?" she demanded, not turning.

"I only just arrived, my lady," he lied easily.

Alex turned to face him, her eyes narrowing. *Don't bother lying to me.*

My loyalty is first to the house of Drossenburg. I shall not say a word to His Imperial Majesty.

There is nothing to report.

As you say, my lady. He inclined his head. "The captain

has asked to see you, my lady. Our change in direction means we shall have to take another route to reach Brittany."

"Very well." She gave a last longing look at the Hunter.

Winchester muttered under his breath and headed out the double doors, Enric on his heels. Winn gripped the rail in his hands and stared out into the roiling storm clouds as twilight fell. It was that time between night and day, that moment when it was neither. Was he a Hunter and a solid, dependable man, or was he not? He ought to know better. He ought to *be* better. She was an engaged woman. Vampire—he corrected himself. A royal vampire at that.

Enric looked at him inquisitively. "Just what are your intentions toward the contessa?"

"My intention is to find that missing part of the Book and keep our heads on our shoulders in the process," he said between gritted teeth.

"Don't be daft. You know she is attracted to you."

Winn glared at Enric and his glib mouth. "Don't matter. You know as well as I do she ain't available. 'Sides, Hunters and vampires don't mix like that."

Enric shrugged and joined him at the rail. "I wouldn't say that. Sometimes it happens. Michael used to be a Hunter. Often Hunters facing the certainty of death realize they have another option and become children by gift."

Winn frowned, his lips pressing into a hard line. "Yep, I'm sure it happens. But not to me. And I ain't almost dead, yet."

Enric sighed. "Being undead isn't so different, you know. We may not have a heartbeat, but we certainly still have feelings."

Winn grunted and stared down into the thick tangle of forest beneath them, just as impenetrable and dark as his conscience. "Who said Hunters have feelings?" He slipped

the flight goggles from around his neck and slid them into place.

Enric straightened. "A few days ago I would have accepted that. But I've seen the way you watch her. You're fighting a losing battle, Mr. Jackson. You just don't know it y—"

A high-pitched wail rent the air, forcing Winn to cover his ears or lose his eardrums. "What the hell is that?"

Enric grabbed hold of Winn's arms and pointed. "Arrows!"

The hundreds of infinitesimally small dots grew larger like a swarm of bees until Winn could see their sharpened tips and shivering shafts flying straight toward the massive balloon right above them. He scanned the woods below trying in vain to see where they'd come from and who the shooters were, but he could see nothing but thick forest.

"They're trying to crash the ship before we can reach Castle Barranoch!" Enric yelled over the noise as the arrows grew closer and their high wailing pitch increased. He leaned backward over the rail of the deck, nearly tipping over and out into the air as he attempted to catch the attention of the crew member on the deck below them. "Incoming! Take evasive action!"

"Who?" Winn said as he gripped the rail so hard his knuckles turned white.

"Werewolves, fae, some kind of Darkin that wants to stop us," Enric snapped.

The barrage of arrows pierced the balloon, creating a great hissing and flapping sound as the hot air began to escape out of the ruptured fabric.

The ship pitched and began to lose altitude rapidly, causing the pit of Winn's stomach to dip uncomfortably. "We're going to crash, aren't we?" Winn asked as the wind picked up the faster they descended. The moisture from the

clouds caused rivulets to form along the dark outer surface of his flight goggles and made his face wet.

"What can I do to help?" Winn yelled over the increasing noise.

"Nothing. Just try to stay alive."

Knowing he was worthless to the harried crew burned like acid. He was out of his league both here on the ship and in this country, and with the woman who filled his thoughts constantly.

Enric gave him a quick, precise nod. "You better hold on to something, Hunter." And with that he disappeared in a dark swirl of smoke—like mist that dissipated on the air.

The door behind Winn opened suddenly. "What in the name of the gods are you doing out here?" the contessa barked. "Get inside!"

Winn didn't normally take orders from a vampire, but in this case he thought it was wise to make an exception. He dashed in the open door and snagged her as he went by, pulling her along in his wake.

"Let go of me!" She pried at his fingers, far stronger than he'd anticipated.

He pulled her up against him. "I'm betting the rest of the crew has already vanished off this thing. You aren't leaving me alone on this sinking ship, lady."

"I had no intention. My job is to accompany you no matter what the obstacles, and I have yet to fail on a mission. I've got a glider ready for us, but we can't wait any longer."

"Well, why didn't you say so?"

She gave him a sour look, muttering under her breath something terribly unflattering about Hunters.

Winn released her and followed her down the two sets of stairs to the cargo hold. The thick canvas wings that had looked like some odd, giant umbrella when he'd last seen them were now stretched taut and fastened to a small, egg-

shaped wooden pod, big enough for one. It sat suspended only a foot or two above the floor of the cargo hold by an enormous hook.

"Get in!"

Winn didn't waste unnecessary words on questioning how, why, or what they were going to do. As fast as the ship was going down, they'd be lucky to launch the glider before they were smashed to bits in the forest and jagged rocks below. He suspected from glancing at the charts in the chart room that they were somewhere over Germany, or maybe France or Austria, but it was impossible to know for sure.

He clambered into the swinging pod and secured the thick strapping about his waist. He was a big man, and it was a tight squeeze. While there was precious little room in the pod, he managed to shuck off his Stetson, his pack, and his rifle and stow them in the open space within the narrow nose of the pod. The whirr and chug of the props losing the ability to spin and seizing up grew louder.

"Ready?" she yelled over the din.

He gave her a thumbs-up. She turned, putting her petite hands on a large lever in the wall of the cargo hold. Winn suspected that it would open the panels beneath the glider.

"Wait! How are you—"

She squeezed the release at the top of the lever and pulled down hard. The bottom of the airship's cargo hold tumbled away into open air, leaving the glider swinging by only the hook above an expanse of sky. Winn gripped the edge of the glider tightly, all words shriveling to dust in his throat. He had no idea how she planned to reach the glider now that there was no floor except for the narrow section where she stood.

The wind whipped her dark hair into streamers about her face as she crouched near the precarious edge. Surely she couldn't . . .

Like a tightly wound spring finally released, she leapt

from the floor onto the front of the pod. The hook holding the contraption gave an ominous moan.

Her eyes widened with terror as her boots scrabbled for purchase on the smooth exterior of the pod. Winn grabbed hold of her wrists and pulled her up, his arms burning with the effort. She squeezed into the pod atop of him, her backside brushing all the way down his chest as she slid into position. An ear-splitting crack startled them both as the hook gave way, pulling the ring out of the pod completely and jettisoning them into flight.

To her credit the contessa didn't scream. She squirmed herself into his lap, her round bottom pressing firmly down on his groin, and strapped herself in for the ride.

The glider shot out of the cargo hold of the falling airship, a mechanical bird soaring through the gray mounds of misted clouds.

"How do you control this thing?" Winn yelled over the deafening rush of wind. His mouth was very close to her ear, and the scent of night-blooming flowers and the spicy female scent that was purely her teased his nose.

"You don't! The best we can do is guide it. I designed it to be a glider, not an airship."

"Then how do we land it?"

"From the looks of things I would say the trees will take care of that before we ever hit the ground."

Winn glanced back at the airship, its shape considerably sadder now that half of it was deflated. The rigid structure had crumpled in parts from the rapid descent. He looked over the nose of the small craft. The thick forest showed no hint of a forgiving opening where they might land the glider. Perhaps they'd fallen from the proverbial frying pan into the fire.

The trees were getting closer. "Who do you think shot us down?"

"Given we're in the midst of Bavaria, most likely Hunters. But then it could be the werewolves or the *Sidhe* as well."

"She? What the hell are those?"

"Dark fae. They've chosen to side with Rathe, so we find ourselves in negotiations with them more frequently."

"You call a volley of arrows taking down an entire airship negotiations?"

"Hostile negotiations," she amended.

Great. He was likely going to crash in these dark woods with no one to rely on but a bunch of vampires who were on hostile terms with the other Darkin in the area. Winn was beginning to seriously reconsider why he'd ever left the good ol' United States in the first place.

"Brace yourself," she warned.

Chapter 13

The only place Winn could put his hands was on the front edge of the pod, which required him to extend his arms around the contessa, placing his fingers on either side of hers.

The soft swell of her left breast brushed against the inside edge of his forearm, and Winn tensed, aware of the temptation. It was one thing to be working with a supernatural, and something else entirely to be so physically aware of one. One he ached to touch. It was unacceptable that he was consumed with the notion of kissing a vampire, and worse still that he wanted a promised woman.

Far below, Winn caught a glimpse of something moving beneath the trees. The swift, dark forms merged and separated, following their progression as the pod dipped lower. The glider skimmed the tops of the trees, shushing as the fir boughs brushed the bottom of the pod, releasing their sharp evergreen scent. There was nothing below them but trees; not a house, not a curl of smoke to be seen, and daylight was fading fast.

A shift in the wind caused the pod to dip slightly to the left, catching a canvas wing in the trees and tipping them over. Winn pulled the contessa back into his chest and

tucked his head down, using his arms to spare them both the worst of the beating from the tree branches as they tumbled downward toward the forest floor.

A violent jerk stopped the glider's motion. The apparatus hung by the framework of one shredded canvas wing to a thick tree branch.

"I think you can let go of me now." Her voice sounded muffled from beneath the protection of his arms.

Her hair tickled his nose and smelled of jasmine. Maybe he didn't want to let go of her. Winn released her, and she pulled away as far as the small confines of the pod would allow. She glanced over her shoulder, bringing her mouth perilously close to his. Her eyes were bright, filled with intensity, her hair a riot of dark, tumbled curls. Winn imagined she'd look much the same in bed. Damn.

"You sure about that?"

She shivered slightly. "No."

The branch creaked as she shifted her position. It was still easily a twenty-foot drop to the ground, and Winn didn't fancy getting any broken bones this far from nowhere, out in hostile territory. "I don't think this branch is going to support us for much longer, and that's a mighty big drop."

She arched a brow at him. "I've jumped far worse."

He'd been shocked at just how far she'd jumped to reach the pod. "Can all vampires jump like that?"

"The older ones. Our combined weight is too much for the branch," she said as she wriggled out of the pod, in the process rubbing up against him with her bottom and making him ache uncomfortably. The tree branch swayed dangerously.

"If I jump, then you'll have more time to climb down safely." She scooted out onto the front of the pod. Winn could tell she was calculating the distance. She tipped her head up, the tip of her pink tongue brushing her upper lip,

and awareness of what it was like to kiss her flashed fresh through his mind.

"Don't. We'll climb down together."

She smiled at him. "You're sweet to worry for me, but it isn't necessary. Wind is from the west," she murmured, and with that she leapt into thin air.

Branches cracked and snapped as Alexa tore through them on her way to the forest floor. Fortunately the drop wasn't too great. She landed in a crouch on the ground, letting her knees absorb the shock of her fall. She slowly rose and glanced up at Winchester, still suspended in the ruined glider. From this distance he reminded her of a Christmas ornament in a very tall tree.

"Are you going to join me?" she urged. The sooner they left this area the better.

"Not like that, I'm not," he replied as he carefully maneuvered his way out of the pod, loading his pack and the holstered rifle onto his back and grabbing his hat. Hunters. They were nothing without their toys.

She sniffed the wind, trying to scent out their distance from the Castle Barranoch. It lay on the edge of the border with France. The moldering smell of ancient stone and fresh blood reached her, but it was tainted with the feral scent of wet wolf. The castle was fifteen miles to the northeast, and the wolves were no more than a few miles away, between them and the protection of the castle. She swore heartily in Russian under her breath. For herself she wasn't afraid. She was stronger and smarter than any werewolf. But the Hunter was merely human, with all the frailties that entailed.

"Insufferable creatures," she muttered to herself. When they later retrieved the wreckage of the airship, she had no doubt that it would be *Sidhe* bolts recovered. No one

else but the dark fae who lingered in the Black Forest could shoot that distance accurately, which was bad news. It meant the *Sidhe* and the Russian werewolves had formed an alliance in her absence. While the werewolves had brute strength, the *Sidhe* had more powers. It was a formidable combination. Now that the *Sidhe* had brought down their airship, the werewolves were closing in for the kill.

Where are you? Are you harmed? Enric's insistent voice, edged with worry, penetrated her mind.

The Hunter and I are fine, for the moment. How far are you from Castle Barranoch?

We transported there, per your instructions.

Excellent. Remain there until I arrive. Inform Count Vernay that we have landed and need an escort through the forest. There are werewolves on the ground, and I suspect Sidhe *in the forests. We shall be arriving shortly.*

His Majesty is not going to be pleased his airship was wrecked.

Pfft. He can have another built. He'll be more worried if we allow these werewolves to kill the Chosen.

She kept a close eye on Winn's progress down the tree. A crackle in the underbrush caused her to tense. Alexa sniffed the air, her gumline beginning to throb. The wolves were still a few miles away; this was a different scent altogether. Gunpowder, oil, and leather.

From the bushes sprang five men, all armed and pointing their weapons at her. Helsing crossbows, loaded with silver-tipped arrows that could pin her to a tree in less time than it would take to transport herself away from the clearing. Each of them had a scabbard at his side, the handgrip of their swords easy for her to see even in the gathering gloom.

"I think we have us a lone vampire, men, and one worth

ransoming from the look of it," said the blond man, German by the sound of him, a glitter of avarice in his eyes.

Alexa hissed at them. Damn Hunters. "Where is your honor? Do you not have treaties with His Vampiric Imperial Majesty?"

"What that old vamp doesn't know won't bother him," the blond Hunter sneered. "Take her." Two of his comrades lowered their crossbows, shifting them to their backs, then pulled out their swords and started forward.

There was a crack just above her, and Winn dropped from the tree between her and the Hunters. He sprang up, armed and ready to fight, the Amanarath stretched and loaded.

"Not so fast, boys," Winn said slowly in German. "This vampire happens to be off limits."

The blond Hunter stepped forward, brandishing a blade with a twist and flourish of his wrist, making the metal flash.

"Drop it." Winn held the Amanarath poised and pointed right at the Hunter's chest.

"Identify yourself," the Hunter demanded.

"You first. I'm gettin' a mighty itchy trigger finger. Takes a lot of thought to control it. Might hit every one of you before I get my control back."

"I'm Lieutenant Victor Van der Hoff, a Hunter with the Saxe-Coburg regiment of the Legion. And this vampire is in our custody."

"Is she now? How do I know you aren't just making that up?"

Van der Hoff quickly unfastened the buttons of his shirt, pulling it aside. A tattoo of the triple cross, bracketed by a lion, palm tree, and raven at the points, was inscribed over his heart. He was definitely a Hunter. No one else would want a tattoo that ugly. "Satisfied?"

Winn nodded and lowered the crossbow slightly from

his shoulder. "I'm Winchester Jackson, part of the Legion out in the Western territories of America."

"A Slayer?" one of the others behind Van der Hoff said, a note of derision in his tone. Two of the others snickered as if it were some kind of a joke.

Winchester frowned. He didn't know what they meant, but he knew he didn't like it. Choosing to ignore them, he locked gazes with Van der Hoff. "Our airship went down. We're trying to get to Castle Barranoch."

Van der Hoff jerked his chin in the contessa's direction. "What about the vampire?"

Winn's hands tensed on the Amanarath, ready to aim and fire in an instant if it became necessary. "She's my guide."

One of the Hunters in Van der Hoff's party gave Alexa a lewd appraisal. "To what?" he interjected.

Van der Hoff glared at the other member of his hunting party. "Hold your tongue, Werner. I'll ask the questions." He turned back to Winn and switched to speaking English. "What are you looking for? Perhaps we can help you, and you can give her to us in exchange."

Winn raised the barrel of the Amanarath an inch from Van der Hoff's face. "No deal."

Van der Hoff smiled, but it didn't reach his pale green eyes. They remained as unyielding and cold as deep lake ice. "All right. No harm, no foul, Slayer. But you can't possibly want to protect that Darkin."

For a moment the irony did sink in. Here he was protecting a Darkin, and a vampire at that, from other Hunters. Pa would have risen out of the grave and kicked his ass if he'd known. But this wasn't a normal situation. He needed her help. "My bow begs to differ with you."

A bloodcurdling howl tore through the night, and all of them turned to peer at the dark maw of the forest.

"Werewolves!" Alexa shouted as she ran up and grabbed Winn's arm, almost causing him to misfire the bow. "We're running out of time!"

"Correction," Winn said as the shadows burst from the trees. "We're outta time."

The twenty or so wolves were far larger than any Winn had seen before. They were the size of grizzly bears, and while most of them were gray, there were a few brown, white, and black wolves among them as well. With coordinated movement they circled him, the contessa, and the small band of German Hunters.

"Insufferable weres," the contessa muttered, her voice turning more guttural and growl-like as her face shifted and changed.

By now it didn't shock Winn as much, even though the sight of her in her fighting mode still disturbed him. She hissed, and the wolves came to a stop. They were close enough in their formation that Winn could see no easy gap for him and the contessa to get through.

He changed his target for the crossbow, grateful Marley had offered it. Winn's mind quickly calculated his options. With only fifteen shots in his rifle he would have been out of ammo before dispatching all of the wolves. He had that pathetic water shooter, but he didn't trust it to do more than slow the wolves down. And it wouldn't do anything to the Hunters. If he ran out of bolts, he could likely take out the other Hunters with his rifle butt first, backed up by his fists if necessary.

"Kill only if necessary," the contessa warned under her breath.

Winn nestled the crossbow against his shoulder, ready to let it release. "They attack, then it's all necessary."

"Hold your bloodthirst, Slayer." Van der Hoff's voice itself was irritating right now.

Winn wanted to tell the Hunter to go screw himself. This was no time to be some pasty, yellow-bellied mama's boy. It was kill or be killed. That's how it always went in these kinds of situations. Negotiation was done by whoever had the least dead. Period. "This ain't bloodthirst. It's survival, and I swear I'll kill every damn one of them if I have to."

The wolves glanced at one another, ears twitching as if they talked to one another the way the contessa did with the other vampires. The hair on the back of Winn's neck prickled up like an agitated porcupine.

A few of the wolves growled low and belly-deep, their black lips curling up to reveal razor sharp, yellowed teeth. It was a veritable Mexican standoff with the furries on one side, and the Hunters and vampire on the other. "They don't look like they're here for a tea party, Van der Hoff. What do you wanna do here?" Winn prompted. His finger was getting itchy to pull the trigger on the bow as tension pulled at the muscles in his neck and shoulders.

"Hold," Van der Hoff ordered.

"You don't even know what they want." Winn's thigh burned with the tension of the muscles beneath his skin.

"Does it matter? They're Darkin."

Winn's mood darkened further. He didn't see a good way out of this. He edged closer to the contessa. "I thought you said there were treaties for this sort of thing."

"That's the problem with treaties. They get broken all the time, and usually when it's most inconvenient," she said with annoyance.

"What the hell do they want?" Winn asked. "They're just holding back."

"Why don't you ask them?" the contessa growled through her fangs.

A loud howl broke the standoff. Winn didn't wait another second. His Hunter training kicked into gear, taking

over both his body and his mind, making his movements as automatic as breathing. He shot down three of the were-wolves in quick succession. The *thwang* of the crossbow jolted up his arm with each rapid release of the bolts. *Thunk. Thunk, thunk.* Three of them fell. The others kept coming, a blur of movement.

Winn cranked the bolts into place and shot off three more. The contessa leaped forward into the fray, fangs at the ready. For an instant Winn's heart forgot to beat as he watched a bolt graze past her, shearing off a lock of her hair. An inch closer and he would have hit her square in the head. She tore every werewolf within reach with her bare hands, sending fur, muscle, and skin flying as she ripped away limbs.

His heartbeat returned twice as hard, and Winn turned away from the grisly sight to glance in the direction of Van der Hoff and his men. The Hunter hacked and slashed at anything with fur that came within striking distance. Winn's chest burned. His blood was pumping hard. The fighting had turned hand to hand now, wolves and men in mixed battle. Winn swung his crossbow to his back and pulled the bowie knife from his boot.

A great gray wolf coiled his back legs a split second before he launched into the air, seeming to sail toward Winn in slow motion. The dinner plate–sized paws con-nected like a solid punch to the solar plexus, knocking the wind from him and leaving him gasping as he fell back-ward into the fir needles of the forest floor. But he didn't need to breathe to act. Winn pulled hard and fast, slashing the blade of his bowie across the exposed throat of the wolf looming over him.

Hot blood splattered Winn's face, and the weight of the enormous dead wolf crushed down, smothering him. Winn's lungs burned as he scrabbled to lift the huge beast off of himself. Cries of anguish and pain from Van der Hoff's

men were followed by sickening crunching sounds and abrupt silence.

"Winchester!"

Winn managed to shift the weight enough to crawl out from beneath the wolf carcass. The contessa was surrounded. He scrambled up, hacking a bloody path to her. He and the contessa stood back-to-back against the ten remaining werewolves.

The growls of the largest wolf shifted and warped into words Winn could comprehend, stunning him. "Slayer, cease your resistance. Rathe wants you taken alive, but he didn't say unharmed. Put down your weapons. Come with us now, and we will let the vampire live."

Winn twisted the handle of the bowie in his extended hand, still brandishing it against the werewolves. Tessa was snugged up tight against his back, her derrière brushing the backs of his thighs. "Let me get this straight. You expect me to just give in and come quietly?"

"Yes."

Winn let out a brittle, caustic bark of laughter. "Clearly you've never met an American Hunter before. We don't quit, and we sure as hell don't give in."

"Are you certain about this, Winn?" Her voice shook slightly. "There is nothing wrong with admitting a defeat when one is outnumbered at the hands of the enemy."

"It ain't their hands I'm worried about. I ain't letting Rathe use me like bait for my brothers."

"I see. Very well."

"You sound kind of hopeless—like we ain't got any options."

She gave a mirthless laugh. "We don't."

"Don't give up yet. Nobody's told you how ingenious American Hunters are." He pulled Marley's water shooter from his holster and pumped it up hard and fast. "Here's a

little gift, courtesy of my friend Marley," he shouted at the wolves. Under pressure, the stream of holy water shot surprisingly far. The wolves howled in anguish as they dropped to the ground in surprise, rubbing their faces against the dirt and only succeeding in peeling away more of their bubbling, crisping flesh.

"Hot damn. It worked!" He didn't wait to find out how things turned out. He grabbed Alexa and ran like hell.

Chapter 14

Winn and Alexa ran blindly through the forest, away from the Russian werewolves and the slain Bavarian Hunters. The cold air knifed through his lungs each time he inhaled and came out in white gusts as his sides bellowed in and out. In contrast, Alexa flew over the ground, her limbs nearly a blur. 'Course, she didn't have more than fifty pounds of weapons strapped to her back either, Winn thought.

He ground to a halt and bent double, his hands resting on his thighs, as he struggled to breathe. Alexa stopped. Bits of twigs and leaves were tangled in her hair. Her face was paler than usual in the filtered moonlight, but he realized that she had a fine layer of dust on her skin.

"You've got a bit of something . . . just there," he said, indicating the corner of her mouth. It was red, dark, gory matter, and he didn't want to think on it too much, nor wipe it away himself. Certainly it had been a battle, which was never pretty, no matter who was fighting, but to see her in full-out fighting mode still came as a shock to his system. He also became aware of the sticky blood on his own face and wiped it as clean as he could with his shirttail.

His mind couldn't reconcile that the incredibly beautiful woman who was so soft and pliant beneath his hands was the same vampire who could tear apart another being with such horrifying efficiency. She was like some twisted female version of the ancient two-faced god Janus. Two very different beings in the same sensuous package, and he hadn't the faintest idea how to separate them. One he was definitely attracted to and the other he inherently found repulsive.

Her features had returned to normal. She rubbed at her mouth with her sleeve. Hardly ladylike, but then he suspected there weren't many ladies who had to battle werewolves with just their bare hands and teeth, either. "Sorry," she murmured and looked away as if embarrassed.

"Nothing to be sorry for. A fight is a fight."

Her face crumpled. She fisted her hands and hit the nearest tree. "How could I have been so blind? Stupid, Alexa, absolutely idiotic of you." Her chest lifted with a heavy sigh, her gaze connecting with his. "Now that they have the piece of the Book, they want you as well. It was a mistake to bring you here."

"There was no way you could have known."

She shrugged and leaned up against a tree, her head tilting back to look up at the small bit of starry night peeking through the dark branches overhead. "I've lost my bearings. I don't even know in which direction Castle Barranoch lies. The stink of those werewolves still fills my nose and has completely eroded my sense of smell."

Winn straightened up against the protest of his screaming muscles and gave the misty forest air a tentative sniff. Wood smoke and the smell of roasting meat perked him up. He scanned the trees, looking for the telltale glow of a campfire. There in the distance he saw the slight shift of the light and the faint wisps of smoke. Winn pointed. "Where

there's smoke, there's fire. That's got to be a camp. Perhaps they'll know where the castle is."

The contessa swiveled, looking in the direction he'd indicated. "How could I have missed that?" She shook her head, holding the heel of her hand to her temple. "They must have hit me with wolfsbane powder." She rubbed her sleeve over her face.

He would have mistaken it for just the dust had she not been acting so strange. "Are you all right, Tessa?" Winn grasped her upper arm to steady her as she swayed.

"I will be," she assured him. "Perhaps I just need to eat." Winn stiffened slightly, but didn't remove his hand. While he still didn't trust her completely, he certainly knew her well enough by now to know she didn't mean to eat *him*.

"I don't know if going to the camp is the best idea," she continued. Her pupils were beginning to dilate, even in the dark of night. His eyes narrowed as he scanned her face. Her smooth skin was growing even more waxen and paler than that of a normal vampire.

"Why?"

"There are a lot of things in these woods besides just the Darkin."

Winn huffed out an irritated breath that ruffled the edges of his mustache. Her cryptic responses were setting him on edge. Every minute they didn't get closer to the Book, they were lowering their odds in the fight against Rathe. "Like what?"

"Fae. Elves. Dragons. Trolls. Gypsies."

Winn scanned the thick forest, remaining vigilant for any sign the werewolves were still following them, as they walked toward the source of the smoke and light. "Well, out of those, I'm thinking only one uses a campfire, and right now gypsies are the least of our worries."

He held on to her, his arm about her waist supporting her as they went, but she faltered, leaning up against him.

"Just give me a moment," she said as she began to sag, then crumple, her knees giving way beneath her. Winn caught her before she hit the forest floor and scooped her up into his arms.

"You're definitely not all right." She didn't respond. Her dark head lay heavy against his chest, her body limp. The heavy floral fragrance of her now mixed with far earthier scents of fir and the musty odor of sodden decaying leaves that clung to her clothing. Panic welled up, swelling in his throat. He didn't know what was wrong with her, and he didn't know the first thing about resuscitating a vampire.

She looked so damn delicate, her face smooth and slumberous, he had thought she'd be light as a pillow. But she was heavier in his arms than he'd anticipated. Not that he minded. Her curves fit perfectly against him, and he enjoyed the weight of her head resting against his chest. But he couldn't carry her all night.

The comforting smell of wood smoke grew stronger the closer they got to the camp. They might be gypsies, or they might be just common folk. Either way he bet they knew of the castle and the quickest route to get there.

He listened harder and picked out the faint sounds of shared conversation, the strum of a mandolin accompanied by the wheezing melody of a squeeze-box, shuffling horse hooves, and the clink of pottery being used to eat an evening meal. Winn adjusted the weight of the contessa in his arms and peered through the trees.

The gypsies had created a small camp from wagons, their arched tops and small window frames and doors painted in garish colors. There were no more than twenty people gathered around the larger bonfire at the center. They ate and joked with one another, passing a leather flask and pouring what looked like red wine into their mouths. His throat ached, and he swallowed against the dryness. At

this point Winn only hazarded a guess. He'd seen enough in the past few days to make him question everything he thought he knew and then some. It might be wine. It might be something else.

"Don't move if you wish to live." The deep, guttural voice was slightly slurred, speaking a Latin-based language that Winn could understand well enough. It was backed by the sharp point of a cold metallic object jabbed up against Winn's ribs. Damn.

He grunted, unable to turn to see his assailant, his arms and shoulder sockets burning as the contessa's deadweight seemed to get heavier with every passing second.

"Who are you?" the stranger asked, prodding the metal deeper into Winn's back. A knife, definitely.

Winn did his best to speak in Latin, but it was rusty. "I'm American. You've got me at a disadvantage," Winn said with absolute calmness. One thing he'd learned as a lawman was that calm, cool heads usually prevented additional problems. "I'd like to introduce myself, but I'm afraid my arms are occupied."

The stranger, who came up barely to his shoulder, bent around him, staring at the contessa. "You do that to her?" the roundish man, more dark hair than visible skin, demanded in clear Latin. His head was wrapped in a colorful blue silk scarf, a gold hoop dangling from one ear pirate-like.

"Why would I be carrying her if I did this?" Winn muttered, losing a fraction of his cool as his arms began to lose feeling. The knife was still jammed into his ribs, keeping him from setting her down. "Look, I'm not here to harm anybody. I just need directions and some help for my friend. We're trying to get to Castle Barranoch."

Winn sighed in relief when the point of the blade eased back. He readjusted his hold on Alexa.

The shorter man still brandished his knife, the blade glinting along its sharp double edge. His eyes were wary. Clearly he didn't trust Winn, but then if a stranger had shown up in the middle of nowhere at his camp uninvited out in the desert back home, splattered in blood, he wouldn't have trusted the fella either. Winn could have taken him in a fair fight, but not with both hands full of unconscious female.

"You bring her to Mama Zinka. She will fix."

Winn was urged at knifepoint into the gypsy camp. The laughing and conversation came to an abrupt stop the moment he entered the edge of the firelight. Suspicious dark eyes surveyed him, lingering on his black Stetson and the array of weapons he still had strapped to his back. Smoke scented with roasted venison writhed up from the flames, twisting in gray curls into the dark night sky. His stomach took the inopportune moment to grumble loudly.

The womenfolk tucked their barefoot young ones behind their skirts, and the menfolk rose up as a unit, almost as if they were all programmed automatons with some kind of sensory gauge that had been tripped. Winn nodded at them, unable to offer a hand to shake and not understanding the flow of quick, sharp words that they spoke to one another. But from the furtive glances, they didn't look happy to see him, that much was for damn sure.

Three men, including the one wearing the blue head scarf who'd brought him to camp, bracketed him on either side and from behind, while they marched him up to the door of one of the brightly painted wagons that stood off from the rest.

"Mama Zinka," the blue-scarf man said, jerking his thumb at the wagon with a series of yellow stars painted over the bright blue door. Light filtered from beneath it, and Winn saw movement. The man rapped at the door.

It was opened by possibly the oldest woman Winn had ever seen. While the bits of hair that poked out from beneath the fringed silk scarf tied about her head were as white as Marley's, her face was tanned and had the wrinkled texture of a peeled apple that had been set out in the sun to shrivel. Her back was humped beneath the black sack-like dress she wore. Unlike those of the rest of the gypsies in the camp her eyes weren't dark, but instead a pale green, made all the more intense and eerie by the weathered color of her skin.

She glanced at the man, Winn, and the contessa and waved them into her cart with her gnarled hands. Winn didn't bother with the small three-step ladder placed at the bottom of the wagon. He just hauled himself and the contessa up in one step that made him grunt with the effort.

The exterior appearance of the wagon was deceptive. Instead of mustiness and body odor, it smelled of cloves, sandalwood, and the sweetness of beeswax candles. He'd expected to not be able to stand up, let alone turn around inside. But the instant he was through the narrow door that scraped his shoulders as he entered, the wagon opened up, not into just one large space but into a central room filled with wooden cupboards and a large wooden table and a black iron stove. Doors to two other rooms stood off to either side. Brightly polished copper pots hung from black iron hooks in the ceiling, and the curved wooden walls were painted like windows, draped with curtains.

Mama Zinka used a weathered fingertip to push his gaping jaw up and then tugged at the sleeve of his duster and indicated a bed set into the wall, half-hidden by deep purple velvet curtains edged in gold tassels. "Put her here," the old woman instructed in English.

Winn was surprised, but gently he laid Alexa down in

the bed, then gaped anew at the strange vast interior of the wagon. "How is this possible?"

Mama Zinka smiled wide, showing off all three of her teeth. "There are some secrets Mama shares with no one. That is one of them. Now we look at your mistress."

"She's . . ." Winn stopped himself from saying she wasn't his mistress. What was she exactly? His ally? Certainly, for now at least. His partner? Of a sort. But beyond his pa, his brothers, and Marley, he'd trusted very few people enough to partner up with them on a hunt. His lover? Not yet. Maybe not at all. Should be not ever, but then Winn couldn't help but feel somewhat tethered to her by some invisible connection. It tugged low and insistent in his gut and made his heart beat harder when her gaze caught his or she brushed against him.

He said none of what he was thinking, merely stated, "She's been feeling weak. Said something about being hit with powdered wolfsbane."

The old woman's eyes grew shrewd and narrow. She turned to Alexa's supine form and gently lifted her upper lip, then pressed down on the pink gum just above Alexa's incisors. A longer feeding canine pressed out through the soft tissue and instantly retracted the moment the old woman moved her finger away. "She's a vampire," she said simply. Winn was grateful there was no rancor in her tone. "How long has she been sleeping?"

"About forty minutes."

The old gypsy grunted. Her lips moved, rubbing over one another in her nearly toothless mouth as she turned to a wall full of small, cork-stoppered bottles and fingered through them with her arthritic, bent fingers. "What she needs is vervain and mint tea."

The tension twisting Winn's belly into a sickening knot eased some. At least someone knew what to do, and for

that he was profoundly grateful. She took two of the small glass bottles, pulled out the stoppers, and took out pinches of dried green herbs, placing them into a chipped pottery cup.

"You lucky she's vampire. Had your lady been human, she'd be dead. Wolfsbane is a powerful poison that can go right through the skin." The old gypsy whispered to the contents of the cup as she poured boiling water from the spigot of an odd teapot over the herbs and stirred them counterclockwise with a silver spoon. The fragrant steam drifting up from the cup smelled both minty and lemon-like at the same time as it steeped.

"What's it do?" Winn asked, curiosity getting the better of him as he leaned against a nearby wall, out of the way, but close enough to prevent any physical harm from coming to Tessa. He folded his arms, watching every move the old woman made.

Her green eyes pinned him with a stern, penetrating gaze. "It helps." She carefully washed the powdery sub-stance from Alexa's face with a clean rag dipped into a bowl of water she poured from the kettle, then spooned a bit of the golden-colored liquid between her parted lips.

Winn held his breath and waited. He shoved away the bitter taste at the back of his mouth and doubts about what would happen if it didn't work. Alexa lay so perfectly still, almost death-like as the old woman continued spooning the tea between her full, unmoving lips. His gaze skimmed over the curve of the contessa's cheek, down to the smooth expanse of her neck just below her ear where he'd kissed her. Hell, she didn't even have a pulse, and while that was normal, her being a vampire and all, it still unnerved him.

Winn stared hard at the old woman, willing her potion to work, and work fast. His throat closed as he waited for a sign of life. "I need her," he murmured, almost absently,

hardly aware of what he was saying. Yes, he needed her. Needed her to be "alive" and viable and capable of escorting him where he needed to go. But he realized as the words slipped from his lips that he needed Alexa on a different level altogether. She was a world of possibility untapped. He wanted that chance. . . . "She has to wake," he finished simply, even though his thoughts were anything but simple.

"Patience," the old gypsy admonished him, as she handed him a wet cloth to wipe his own face and hands. "Wash yourself. Wipe your clothes. Get rid of any of the powder that lingers."

He did as he was told, but with each passing second an icy chill slipped farther through Winn's veins, aching as it went until it turned him numb. He closed his eyes. Visions of her gaze sparking with intelligence, of the allure of her lips when they curved into a subtle, seductive smile, and of the way the wind stirred the hair across the pale silk of her nape skated across the insides of his eyelids.

The rustle of fabric caused Winn to snap his eyes open. She'd either moved or Mama Zinka had moved her. He stared unblinking at her just to be sure which it had been. Alexa's long, tapered fingers twitched slightly and her lashes fluttered, but her eyes didn't open.

Was it his imagination? His heart beat hard and thick in his ears. No. She was responding to the draught Mama Zinka had given her. He gripped the edge of the bed, leaning close to her. "Come on, Tessa," he whispered fervently. She still didn't open her eyes.

"Takes time," the old woman muttered knowingly. "You very lucky she's already undead. Saves me time having to raise her from the dead." .

He threw a glance at the old gypsy, who had a pipe now in her mouth and was sucking hard on the stem, her cheeks

caving in as she attempted to light it. Surely she didn't mean she could have created the living dead from Alexa? His gut twisted in upon itself at the thought.

Winn grabbed one of Alexa's hands, rubbing and patting it between his. He didn't know if she was as cold and numb as he felt, but it gave him something else to focus on besides her slow progress.

Chapter 15

The problem with wolfsbane was that it acted as a powerful paralytic in vampires. Werewolves, who were immune to it in that manner, knew it. The entire time she'd been in the gypsy camp she'd been unable to do so much as blink an eye or twiddle her thumb, but she'd been fully cognizant of what was going on around her.

From the odd mixture of herbs, the whicker of horses and the scent of the wine they favored, she'd been able to tell they were in a gypsy camp. The colloquial speech and heavy Romany accents, which slipped now and again into Latin, only confirmed her supposition. She struggled against the heaviness encasing her limbs like hardened wax. Her eyelids were the first things she could finally move. She opened them to find Winn sitting at her bedside, worry creasing his brow and casting shadows beneath his eyes.

The instant her gaze connected with his, he seemed to relax, the blue of his eyes lightening a degree. "You're awake," he said softly, but the relief in those two words confirmed she hadn't imagined what she'd heard him say while she'd been paralyzed. *I need her.*

With effort, Alexa found she could turn her head and

shift her limbs. They ached and were heavy, but at least she had control of them now. She tried to sit up, and Winn's strong arm wrapped around her back, helping her. She attempted a smile but found her lips were still not responding well. She stretched her face, opening her mouth wide and pursing her lips to regain feeling. Then she gave Winn a barely manageable smile. "If you hadn't brought me here, I would have remained frozen."

"Frozen?" He quirked one brow. "Nearly dead is more like it."

Alexa didn't argue the point with him. Undead was as nearly dead as one could be, after all, but she didn't want to have to explain that she'd heard everything he'd said. Mama Zinka patted her hand, and Alexa turned to the old woman and bowed her head and chose her next words very carefully. "You are very kind."

Mama Zinka smiled in return and motioned Alexa to come and sit beside the large, scarred wooden table. "It's not often I get to meet a vampire this close to the border. Now that you are feeling more yourself, I will read your future." Winn helped Alexa to a chair opposite the old gypsy across the table, and Mama Zinka held out her hand. Alexa hesitated. She knew the future. Kostick had foretold centuries ago how her future would unfold.

It would take all three of the Chosen to keep the Gates of Nyx closed. To seal the Gates, one would have to make the ultimate sacrifice, giving up his own life to spare them all, and the Chosen would never be whole again. Just the thought that it might be Winn made her stomach shrivel into an uncomfortable knot.

But there was more of the prophecy. And the knowledge inside her grew, swelling and heavy, making her chest ache. Kostick had also prophesied that Alexa would be the downfall of the Chosen, a traitor to her own kind, and would ultimately find herself destroyed by her heart's desire. This

aspect of her future he'd told Alexa alone. The knowledge weighed heavy on her.

Until she had met Winchester Jackson, the Chosen were to her merely some future mortals of mythological proportions. Until the Chosen had surfaced, the vampires had had no reason to separate themselves from other Darkin to survive. And it was becoming abundantly clear to Alexa that Winchester Jackson was more than capable of destroying her if she did anything so foolish as to fall in love with him.

Alexa turned back to the elderly gypsy. It would be the height of poor manners to deny her request, especially when she'd been so helpful and kind to them as outsiders. She held out her right hand.

Mama Zinka ran her fingers over the ruby ring, a glint in her eye. "And I will take this as payment for helping you." Alexa pulled her hand back, clenching it tightly. The ring was certainly not hers to give. It belonged to Vlad—to the vampire royal family, actually. The weight of a heavy masculine hand pressed upon her shoulder.

"Give her the ring, Tessa." He said it with such calmness and authority that her hand seemed to open of its own volition. And there it was. The moment of choice. Two paths lay open before her. To rage against the prophecy, or to throw caution to the wind and let the fates take their pound of flesh and ounce of bone.

Alexa stared for a moment at the large ruby. It represented many things. Her duty to her family, the court, and her emperor. Her life as a noble. Her tangible link to her life as a vampire. And all of it was going to come abruptly crashing to an end if they didn't get the Book. The heat of Winchester's hand penetrated her clothing, making her very aware of the man beside her and the danger he presented to her. With trembling fingers, she pulled the ring off and offered it to the gypsy.

The moment the old woman plucked the ring from

Alexa's palm, Alexa felt somehow lighter, as if an invisible weight had been lifted from her back. But Winchester's hand on her shoulder still remained. He gave her a light squeeze of reassurance, then pulled back and rested his shoulder against the wall of the wagon. In his severe black clothes, he looked so at odds with the bright colors and flamboyant interior of Mama Zinka's wagon.

The gypsy took Alexa's palm in her soft, weathered hands once more, and Alexa turned her gaze back to the old woman.

"Now we will see your future." She ran her fingers along the lines that stretched in spider-web fashion across Alexa's palm. She moved her mouth as if chewing on something and uttered a series of ahhs, ohhs, and umms. While part of Alexa thought it mostly theatrics, the gypsy had been right about the vervain and mint. She might know other arcane arts as well.

The woman's pale green eyes gazed deeply into hers. "What is it you seek?"

"Something valuable that has been taken from us." There was no point in telling her more. Either she was authentic and would know, or she was a charlatan who was good with herbal remedies whose predictions wouldn't support Kostick's prophecy at all.

The gypsy grasped Alexa's hand. A slight tingling started in her palm and spiraled up her arm and into her chest, then grew quite hot. Alexa stiffened. To find someone of true power was an astonishing thing. The gypsy held Alexa's hand between her own soft, knobby fingers. "The object you seek is hidden away from the wolves, with the bones, deep in the earth. An empire of the dead guards its secrets. The skull with tears of blood is the door you seek."

Alexa tried to reach into the gypsy's mind and read her thoughts. The gypsy leveled her with a pale green stare. *Go*

back, vampire. I know you are here, and I will tell you all I know.

Alexa sucked in a startled breath. Perhaps she was losing her touch. First Winchester and now this gypsy had foiled her skills. Fortunately for her and Winn, Van der Hoff had been easy to read. He had wanted the Book. Correct that: Her Majesty the Queen of England wanted it and would use all means necessary to ensure that the English Empire remained at the height of its glory.

"Where are the bones?"

The gypsy closed her unusual eyes and took in a deep breath, holding it. The very air about her vibrated with the hum of power that flowed around and through her. Slowly she opened her eyes. "Paris."

"Paris?" Winn said, standing straight. He turned, his gaze piercing Alexa. "I thought you said it was in Brittany."

"Maybe I was wrong. Maybe Kostick just meant that it was the werewolves that took it and maybe he was using Herve as a link to them and to France."

Winn grunted. "Didn't make much sense to me. In Hunter lore the youngest brother Haydn was said to have taken the Book to the farthest reaches of the known world. He took it to the Byzantine Empire."

"And it ended up in Transylvania."

"Last time I looked at a map, Transylvania isn't exactly the same as France."

"Ah, but the wolves took it from Transylvania," Mama Zinka said, her mouth twisting into a wry grin. "And on their way to Brittany, our people took it back. We put it into the hands where it belonged." She gave a meaningful look at Alexa.

The gypsy released Alexa's hand. She jerked her small pointy chin in Winn's direction. "It is your turn." With a wave of her weathered hands she beckoned him to her.

Winchester put up his hands, but it was no defense

against the agile little gypsy who stood up and grabbed one of them, pulling him down to sit at the table beside Alexa. Like she had done with Alexa, she held his hand between her two far smaller ones.

Alexa scooted back, watching the moment unfold. Winchester was a large man, and he positively dwarfed the little gypsy, who looked like a wizened little monkey holding a lion's paw, but she held him captive nonetheless.

The old woman closed her eyes, drawing the power to her again. It raised the hairs on Alexa's skin. When Mama Zinka opened her eyes, they were glassy and unfocused as she spoke in a wheezy monotone.

"You will find what you have lost, but it will not be what you think. In the end, one will sacrifice to save them all."

She slumped forward, and Winn caught her before she hit the table. He shook her lightly. "Mama Zinka?"

She raised her head slowly, rubbing and blinking her eyes like a sleepy toddler. "Did I fall asleep again?"

Alexa and Winchester looked at one another, unsure if this was a consummate con artist at work or a true mystic.

"You just drifted off for a bit," Alexa said. It wasn't a lie. She had drifted off after her prediction.

Winn began to speak. "Than—"

Alexa cut him off with a swift kick to the shin. There were two things one did not do in a gypsy camp. One was to thank them, as it was considered a grave insult. The other was to refuse their hospitality if it was offered. He glared at her and she glared back at him, telling him with her eyes to follow her lead and keep his mouth closed.

The old gypsy waved her hand. "You must be hungry. We should go to the campfire, and Boris will find us something to eat."

Alexa aided the gypsy as she rose from her chair with difficulty. The old woman gave her a nearly toothless smile. "My children, grandchildren, and great-grandchildren

will want to meet you. But do not tell them you are vampire. They will not understand as Mama Zinka does that there are Darkin we do not have to fear. Come, I will feed you and introduce you to them."

A twinge hit Alexa just below the sternum. Not sadness, but more of an empty ache. She really had no family to speak of other than her more distant relations. Certainly she had her children by gift, but they, like all other adults, came into their own once they were no longer fledglings and went out to make their own lives. What she lacked was a true partner. An equal to share her burdens and joys with.

She glanced under her lashes at Winchester. He would have been nearly perfect if not for two glaring problems. First, he was a Hunter, so destroying Darkin was part and parcel of the very fabric of his being; second, she knew once they found the Book he'd return to America and she'd stay in the court—and marry Vlad, and avoid ever giving her heart to anyone to keep from being destroyed.

The thought itself left an unpalatable taste in her mouth. Being offered the position of queen should have elated her. She liked Vlad. She just didn't . . . she just didn't love him. In fact, it had been so long since something other than mild interest had touched her that being around Winchester was a heady aphrodisiac. He was more dangerous to her than any being she'd ever met.

The old woman led them outside, where everyone waited. She led them to a long table and pushed them both onto worn wooden chairs. Firelight danced red and gold against the overhanging branches, as someone played a mandolin, and a big-eyed child giggled nearby. The old woman introduced Alexa and Winn to one and all as enormous platters of roast venison and mugs of strong red wine were placed before them.

Alexa tamped down the urge to pass on the overcooked

meat and put a piece of the venison on her plate along with a piece of the dark, thick rye bread. She nibbled at it, watching the gypsies with a keen eye.

More than once she caught Winchester staring at her intently, not with the caustic or haughty look of a seasoned Hunter, but with the hungry, curious gaze of a man that made her stomach flip and tighten.

All through dinner, Winchester was very aware of every movement she made, of the heady floral scent of jasmine that clung to her skin and hair. The golden firelight played over her skin so fine, so smooth it could have been crafted of porcelain, but he knew from touching it how extraordinarily soft it was beneath his fingers. Everything about her was exquisite, refined, and feminine. Far too refined for the likes of him.

She looked pale, nearly ethereal. Not at all a confirmed killer who could wipe out the population of this little camp in less time than it took him to wolf down a steak dinner.

She seemed to sense his regard, and her amber gaze flicked up to meet his. Mingled in the depths of her eyes were attraction and worry. He felt the pull as well. A warring of lust with duty. As much as he fancied the contessa, they were bound to go their separate ways, and he refused to make a target of her when he deserved the bull's-eye on his own back.

Winn tried to turn his attention back to his meal. The meat was flavorful and tender, the bread coarse against his tongue, but filling, and the wine sweet and strong enough to make him relax, giving everything about him a softer focus. It wasn't the whiskey Ames served down at the Golden Goose, but it was damn fine. But all of it—the food, the wine, the company—couldn't keep him from

turning over and over in his mind the cryptic message Mama Zinka had given him.

It was bad enough to be stuck this far from home without his brothers or another soul he could trust. The contessa was the closest thing he had to an ally in these strange lands.

He leaned in, making it appear to anyone else watching them that he was whispering something sweet and seductive in her ear. "How long do we have to do this before we can slip away?" he asked softly.

She shivered, and Winn was instantly aware of the change in the texture of her skin as it contracted. "Anxious to get to Paris?" she teased.

"We're measuring our progress in hours, not days or weeks. We need to find the piece of the Book."

She nodded and pulled back, locking her gaze with his. It had to be getting close to midnight. "We should wait until morning. Until we have daylight, this is the safest place we'll find in the woods until we reach the castle. Count Vernay's escort for us must have gone to the site of the airship wreckage and lost our trail."

During the dinner of roast venison and root vegetables, Mama Zinka had fallen asleep. She slumped against Winn's shoulder, snoring none too softly, but no one seemed to take notice, as if this were perfectly normal.

Boris, the gypsy who'd first found them, approached the rough table where they sat. He nodded toward a small wagon that stood apart from the others. "Mama Zinka said you should have her second wagon for the night."

Alexa smiled politely. "We are most honored," she said smoothly, dipping her head lightly in a small nod. No one could say Winn was a slow learner. From the earlier kick in the shin, he'd deduced that one didn't refuse gypsy hospitality.

Boris waved them to follow him. They walked across

the camp to the little wagon painted a vivid red. It was a bit smaller than the others, nearly the size of a buckboard back home.

Unless Mama Zinka's second wagon was as spacious as her first, Winchester was fairly certain there was only going to be room enough for one bed. He flicked his gaze toward the contessa. Perhaps he ought to offer to sleep underneath the wagon. He'd done far worse when out hunting with his pa than sleep on the hard ground for a night.

"I'll just stay out here," he muttered.

The contessa speared him with a look that brooked no argument. "The wagon will be fine for *both of us*," she insisted. Boris looked from one of them to the other, his expression puzzled, then shook his blue-scarfed head.

Winn waited until the stout man was out of earshot before he spoke again. "I'm not certain me and you both being in that little wagon is the best idea, Tessa."

"You don't have to think. You just have to do it."

"Give me one good reason why."

"How about the only reason these people helped us is because they believed you and I were together. These people are superstitious. A woman alone in the woods would have been automatically suspected of being Darkin. If they discovered I was a vampire alone, they would have celebrated my passing, not revived me. Not to mention that there's more than one of the men who was eyeing me with speculation through dinner."

Winn had noticed. And just thinking about it made his blood boil. If men had eyed a proper woman like that back in America, her brothers and father would have had something to say about it, most likely from the end of a shotgun.

"I saw them."

"Then you understand why the safest thing is for us to spend the next few hours in this wagon *together*."

He wasn't at all certain of the safety of it. Every

moment he spent with her, she wormed her way a little deeper under his skin. Hell, he was beginning to enjoy being around her.

There'd been powerful little female company around their home growing up once Ma had died, and even less once he was out on the road hunting. Pa had said any woman paired up with a Hunter was bound to meet a miserable end.

"I hadn't realized how badly you loathed the idea," she said tartly. She'd mistaken his silence for dislike.

"It ain't that."

"Then what is it?" she demanded, her mouth firming into a hard little pout.

He stepped closer, putting his hand on the wagon behind her. His chest was close enough to her that he couldn't even feel a current of air slip between them. She inhaled sharply and stared up at him, both defiant and glorious. Winn let his mouth curve up into one of those legendary, devastating Jackson smiles his ma had passed down to each of her boys.

"You know if we go in there together, you aren't going to be able to keep your hands off me."

Chapter 16

Alexa gave an outraged gasp at Winchester's audacity and firmly fisted her hands at her sides to keep from slapping him. She swore silently to herself in Russian, Hungarian, and French. He was as arrogant as any male vampire. "You, sir, overestimate the power of your charms."

The light of challenge ignited in his eyes as he leaned in farther, the scent of male and leather invading her space and teasing her excellent preternatural sense of smell.

"Oh, I highly doubt that," he said in a soft rumble that set off sparks along her nerves and tightened the coil of awareness spiraling through her yet another notch, perhaps two. The intensity of his focus on her, like a hungry animal sensing its prey, made Alexa squirm. Then he came closer.

The firm ridge of his sensual mouth skimmed over her cheek and below the lobe of her ear, the bristles of his beard lightly abrading her skin, making it even more sensitive.

She could deny it all she wanted, but the animal magnetism of Winchester Jackson was far more addictive than all the power, prestige, and wealth of the vampire nobility she'd been surrounded by her entire life.

Alexa couldn't seem to stop herself, against her better

judgment. The warm touch of his mouth as he nibbled and kissed along the column of her neck sent ripples of desire coursing through her, making the ichor beneath her skin flow like heated honey. And when he came back up, his mouth at her cheek, she turned and deliberately held them a whisper away from a kiss. "Maybe you just can't resist me," she whispered, her lips brushing enticingly against his.

Winchester growled, the sound of it vibrating straight through her. He was lethal animal magnetism, and she was doomed. He crushed his mouth to hers in a kiss that demanded everything of her. Like a forest fire it roared through her, all heat and intensity, and left nothing but fragile ash and smoldering coals behind. The slick sensual slide of his tongue tasting her made her recall exactly what a heartbeat felt like; the sensation moved through every cell of her body like one gigantic pulse, beating from the very center of her being.

It had been a long, long time since she'd responded to a man with such intensity. His hands slid possessively down her spine, and pulled her flush up against the hard planes of his chest. Alexa clung to him, her every sense heightened. The pinpoints of starlight between the fragrant evergreen trees seemed brighter. She could hear the crackle of the fire in the glade nearby and the rush of his hot blood pumping hard and fast through his veins. Becoming bold, she rocked her hips against the growing ridge pressed against her belly.

He broke their kiss just long enough to nip at the ridge of her collarbone. A zing of electric spark ran from the spot his mouth claimed and seared straight to the tips of her breasts, making them ache against the confines of her corset. Alexa could no longer hold back the fangs that pulsed and throbbed just above her normal teeth and let them release with a slight moan.

* * *

He'd been taking a risk right from the start being around her. Now Winn knew without a doubt he was in uncharted territory. It was mattering less and less to his ramped-up libido that she was a vampire. He didn't even give a damn about kissing her with her fangs out. The dividing line between what was right and what was easy was getting blurry.

His fingers dug deeper into her hips, making the dress a damn nuisance. Every fiber of his being seemed to hum and burn with an intensity he'd never experienced before. She was womanly soft beneath his hands, and her hips cradled him to perfection. If the little wagon had been a temptation before, it was deadly serious now. Just based on the silky texture and fragrance of the skin in the soft spot at the nape of her neck, he could imagine exactly how smooth and sexy the other dips and hollows of her lush body might be.

But the insistent, nagging little voice in the back of his head demanding that he stop and think about what he was doing sounded an awful lot like his pa, and that was damn hard to ignore completely, even if his hands were full of willing female. *Walk away from her, boy. She's nothing but trouble, even wrapped in a pretty package.*

And if that weren't enough to stop him cold, his ma's voice made the point. *You don't have anything to offer a woman like this.*

Winchester sobered up quick as a preacher on Sunday and pulled away from Alexa's drugging kiss. God help him, but the woman had lips like laudanum. She could wipe every thought from his mind, every good intention, and years of training, with just a touch, and leave him in a sensual fog that dulled his senses and blunted his reflexes.

He pulled back and looked down into her face. Her eyes, hazy with desire, were half shuttered behind a fringe of

sable lashes. Damn, she was beautiful. An image of her waking up beside him, her hair dark spirals across the pillow, tugged at his gut and made him ache for just one more taste. The flavor of her, sweet and potent, was still on his tongue.

He was going to hate himself for this later, but it had to be done. "That convincing enough for the locals?" he asked smoothly, not betraying a hint of the inner turmoil she brought out in him.

The seductive softness in her eyes instantly hardened, making him feel instantly like a cad. "Very." She turned away stiffly and lifted the hem of her gown.

Winn tried, and failed miserably, not to notice the natural movement of her hips and the curve of her spine as she climbed into the little red wagon. Saints preserve him, he still wanted her with a carnal longing that made no logical sense. This was getting complicated, right quick.

She's just a means to recover the Book; remember that, boy. Winn blew out a harsh breath and rubbed his hand over the back of his neck. He might as well accept that he wasn't going to get any sleep. Staying in the confined little wagon with her and a warm bed was going to be torture, and he was already pained enough as it was.

He'd barely climbed into the close quarters of the little red gypsy wagon and shut the door when all hell broke loose in the camp. The screams of men and women caused the hairs on Winn's scalp to prick. He spun around, one hand on his gun, the other on the ornate door handle.

"Don't!" The contessa jumped up from the edge of the bed. "The werewolves have found us! How?"

"They're goddamn persistent. That's h—" He spun around aiming his pistol as a noise in the back of the room alerted him to the presence of someone breeching the small wagon. His finger tensed on the trigger as a panel in the wall opened. "What the—"

Boris peered in at them. "Out this way! Quickly!"

Winn all but shoved the contessa through the opening into Boris's waiting arms, then tried to pull himself through, only to find the crossbow wouldn't fit strapped to his back. The acrid stench of burning hair and flesh was accompanied by a cacophony of chaos. Guttural screams cut off into gurgling; the tear of rending fabric and the pop and crack of wood and bone made his stomach twist into a hard, uncomfortable knot. He yanked the bow off, scrambled through the opening, and pulled the crossbow to him.

Instinct took over, and he turned to go back and defend those being attacked by the werewolves. He wouldn't be much against a pack of grizzly-sized wolves in a rabid frenzy, but it might slow them down enough for the contessa and a few others to escape. With one glance he saw more than he ever wanted to.

Broken bodies torn in half, wolves stripping the flesh off of the dead, the poor, sightless eyes of Mama Zinka as she lay limp in a crumpled heap at the base of her wagon. Fury caused his muscles to spasm in his arms and face.

Boris grabbed his arm with a punishing grip to stay him. Winn thought it odd he wasn't rushing to help his people, but then maybe that was the sacrifice he'd been instructed to make.

"It's too late. There are too many of them. Nothing we can do. Run!" Boris urged. He darted off into the woods.

There was no time to think, only to act. If he didn't get ahold of the piece of the Book of Legend, that grisly sight would become the norm rather than exception as the Darkin were encouraged to scour humanity from the face of the earth. He gently pushed Alexa ahead of him, and they followed.

A heavy mist clung to the ground, making it nearly impossible to see where they were going. Winn kept his focus locked on Boris and the contessa, making sure the pair

stayed ahead of him so he could defend them against whatever might come at them from behind.

After an hour the trees finally grew thinner, allowing the intermittent moonlight to turn the drifting mist opaque. Their dark trunks became fewer and more spread apart, then the animal path they followed opened up into the edge of a crumbling church graveyard. The headstones teetered and slanted, having sunk with age and neglect. A stone angel dark with age had been weathered so black tears seemed to streak its cheeks. The church itself was no more than a moldering heap of crumbled stone.

The chilly night air caused his labored breath to cloud. He stayed close on Alexa's heels, relying on her far superior vampire eyesight in the dark of the night as they pushed forward. In the far distance the screams and growls had stopped, replaced by sickening howls.

Winn berated himself for running. But it had been the right thing to do, hadn't it? He no longer trusted his instincts. Not after what had happened with the demon and his mother, and then a different demon and Colt. Between the two incidences he'd been convinced he wasn't cut out to be a Hunter, let alone to fulfill some prophecy.

Alexa's face was streaked with dirt, and there were small tears in her gown from the undergrowth and branches they'd run through. Her face was drawn and tight, a mixture of focus and fear.

Boris darted in between the headstones, not bothering to glance back to see if they followed. Winn listened for any indication the wolves were coming, but the night had become starkly silent, as if the woods themselves held their breath. A chorus of blood-chilling howls cut through the cold air and shrunk Winn's skin a whole size.

The gypsy came to an abrupt stop. "There!" he said, pointing at the ground. It was so damn dark Winn nearly fell in as his feet hit the edge of freshly turned earth.

Through the swirling mist, a freshly dug grave yawned. Six feet down, a large man lay inside a lidless casket. The musty smell of recently turned cemetery earth made Winn shudder with suppressed memories.

"Get in!" Boris yelled.

Winn glared at him. "That coffin is already occupied."

"And you'll need your own if you don't get in now!"

Everything in Winn raged against the idea of going into that small, narrow space with nothing but walls of soil and a small patch of dark night sky.

Ever since he'd watched them lower his mother down into a grave, he'd been unable to stomach small, dark spaces. It should have been him in that casket, not her, and he always felt like the grim reaper, or worse yet a demon, was only a step or two behind him waiting to rectify the situation.

"I ain't getting in there. Those werewolves will be able to sniff me out."

"Not over the stench of Yakov," countered Boris. "Trust me. Even when he was alive you always could tell where he was and wanted to walk upwind of him. Now that he's dead, they won't be able to even tell you're there."

The howling grew louder as the wolves tracked their path to the churchyard.

Winn's skin crawled with revulsion as he dug his hands into the earthen walls and slid down to the open coffin. He climbed in beside the corpse in the confining wooden box, but still sat up, unable to stomach the idea of being sealed in the coffin.

Alexa leaned over the edge of the grave. "Lie down and we'll cover you up."

"What the hell are you going to do?"

"Evade and attack."

"Then I'm coming back up there with you."

"No! They want *you*."

Winn had thought the idea foul to begin with, but the

sickly odor of decay and heavy dose of body odor that reeked of rotten cheese emitting from Yakov brought up the bile to the back of his throat. Winn had to cup his hand over his mouth to keep from vomiting. They could hear the breaking of brush as the howls grew louder.

He tried not to take too deep a breath as he stared up at Alexa. "I can't do this."

"Yes, you can," Alexa insisted. "Be still. We haven't time to argue."

Winn fought against every instinct and lay on top of Yakov's stiff form in the coffin. Boris appeared at the edge with a shovel in each hand and used the wooden handle of one to tip the coffin lid down over Winn with a slam.

Full-blown panic set in that moment, stealing his ability to breathe the instant he heard the patter of dirt as they heaped it over the lid. Winn's heart slammed hard against his ribs. He blew out a steady, slow breath, trying to calm himself. Breathing hard and fast was just going to get him killed.

There was no way there'd be enough air for him to survive, as putrid as Yakov was. The thought of dying in this coffin with Yakov sent his brain into a fever, making his ears buzz and his skin too hot. Winn beat against the wood, not giving a damn if he was heard. He couldn't stay in the box a moment longer—with all due respect to the dearly departed Yakov. "Get me the hell out of here, now!"

The hard thump of a boot hitting the lid and dirt above him drove the panic deeper. "If you want to live, you must hush, Hunter."

The howls grew closer.

Winn didn't give a damn. He was getting out of that box no matter if he had to claw his way through to the surface. He shoved Yakov aside and began trying to shove the lid upward, even an inch.

It didn't budge.

Desperate, he began scratching at the wood of the lid with his fingernails, not caring if it shredded his fingertips. "I'm getting out of this damn box if it's the last thing I do."

That would rather defeat the purpose, as we'd just have to put you right back in one if you gets killed. The contessa's voice echoed in his skull, making Winn freeze for a moment. What the hell and damnation was that?

It's me, Winchester. Your mental barriers aren't as strong when you're panicked.

"Goddamn right they're not," he yelled, his frustration mounting.

I want you to close your eyes and count to five hundred.

"I can't! Get me out, now!"

Five hundred. Silently. And I will dig you out myself. The werewolves are almost here.

Winn squeezed his eyes shut tightly and visualized a row of whiskey bottles, all lined up. With each bottle, he'd count as he visualized downing the contents. Damn, but he felt mighty parched.

One hundred. There was snuffling and scratching overhead. The thunder of dozens of paws running and then stopping as they passed overhead, just six feet above him. Sweat popped out on his forehead, chilling his skin even as the temperature in the box grew warmer. His throat seemed to swell shut, and Winn couldn't tell if he could even swallow his own spit.

Two hundred. The pack howled, one after another. He was trapped, without any hope of escape. Perhaps he wasn't leaving this coffin after all. A horrific screech rent the air, a sound that sent a chill rippling down his spine. There were howls and the thunder of feet, the sound of a battle. Winn beat at the lid and began scraping away with his knife.

Three hundred. The air was thickening, and his head

beginning to pound in rhythm to his heartbeat. The sounds above him came to an abrupt halt. What if Boris and the contessa had both been taken by the wolves? What if there were no one to dig him out? Panic became outright terror, making his skin burn and his lungs feel as if they might burst.

Four hundred. Stars began to pop and burst before his tightly shut eyes, and he resorted to holding his nose and breathing through his mouth as he counted silently.

Five hundred. Above the coffin the dirt was scratched and scraped away from the lid. Winn shoved upward with every ounce of strength he had.

A rush of cool night air greeted him as the lid was pulled back, and he scrambled up out of the coffin and climbed side by side with Alexa out of the grave. Once they reached the top he lay on his back for a moment sucking in great gulps of fresh air, his pulse so hard and loud he could hear the roar of it and nothing else in his ears. Slowly his heartbeat lost its frenetic pace.

He opened his eyes and stared up at the contessa. "You're alive."

Her lips twitched with humor. "No, I'm not, but I am here."

Winn sat up and glanced around. "Where are the were-wolves?"

"The dogs have been dealt with." He tried not to look too closely at her hands or the dark splotches on her gown. She wrinkled her aristocratic nose and pulled a handkerchief out to cover it so she could breathe easier. "We need to walk up the river."

Winn staggered upright, his limbs weak. Fear beat the crap outta a man, that was for sure. Those dark, cramped spaces had the ability to reduce him to a cowering twelve-year-old in mere seconds. It wasn't something he was proud

of—in fact he hated it about himself. But he'd yet to find a way of staving off the paralyzing fear of claustrophobia.

The mists cleared enough that Winn could see the slender, shining ribbon of moonlit water near the horizon. "River. Cover our tracks. Good idea," Winn muttered, his head still a bit fuzzy from his fast heartbeat.

"I was thinking to wash off Yakov's odor but, *da*, it will cover our tracks as well."

"Where's Boris?"

The contessa frowned and pointed up a tree. The stout little man scrambled down through the branches. He jumped down, then quickly brushed away the few leaves that clung to him. He cast a wary glance at the contessa. Obviously after what'd he seen her do, he was now aware of what she was and wouldn't protect her again.

Winn dusted off his Stetson and gave it a sniff before shrugging and pulling it back on his head. "So now where to, Tessa?"

Boris did his best to ignore the contessa and instead focused on Winn. "I will ferry you across the Danube, but no farther. Past this river we are not welcome. The Castle Barranoch is just beyond it."

Winn deliberately put himself between Alexa and Boris as they tramped the distance to the river's edge in stony silence. The mists grew thicker and the ground wetter, becoming a mushy, soft mud studded with thick sedge grasses as they neared the water. Overhead the moonlight broke through the quickly shifting clouds, making it easier to see and walk through the chilly, dark night scented with the murky smell of marsh water. From the depths of the forest behind them came the hooting of an owl. Crickets chirped. But there was no sign of more werewolves.

Alexa narrowed her gaze, her stare strong enough to bore a hole through Boris's back. Agitation tightened the edge of her full mouth and gave her regal chin a stubborn jut,

but the way she nibbled her bottom lip with her teeth told him there was more at stake. Something had her worried.

He leaned close and brushed an errant dark curl away from her cheek, causing her to startle and look at him as if he'd just suddenly appeared out of thin air.

Winn put his mouth next to the delicate shell of her ear. "You don't trust him, do you?" he whispered.

She shook her head. "It's the skiff. I don't cross water well, and I doubt it's going to be stable. Be on your guard. I don't want to fall in."

Winn relaxed slightly. For a moment he'd been concerned that she'd seen something in Boris he hadn't. Perhaps, like cats, vampires weren't fond of water.

A small skiff, its front snubbed and flat, with only a single long pole for power and steering, was tied at the bank, bobbing with the movement of the swiftly flowing water. The blue paint on the skiff was chipped and faded, and it was barely big enough to hold two, let alone three. They climbed in, and Alexa sucked in an uneasy breath and reached for the edges of the boat as it rocked. Boris gave an impatient grunt and used the long pole to lift the tie and set them adrift.

Under the moon's fickle light Winn got the impression he was crossing the River Styx. The only thing that destroyed the illusion was Boris's gold earring glinting in the moonlight. And as stout as he was, he hardly looked like the specter Charon, who ferried folks into Hades.

Halfway across the water Boris brought the boat to a virtual standstill by jamming the pole deep into the riverbed. The silver liquid of the river flowed about the bow. The boat tipped slightly against the current, river water splashing against the side and splattering over Alexa's skirts. Her face, already pale in the moonlight, turned drawn and waxen and

a bit green. Her knuckles whitened as she gripped the edges of the skiff and pinched her lips tightly closed.

"Why are we stopping?" Winn growled. The water crossing wasn't agreeing with Alexa, and he needed to get her to shore as soon as possible.

Boris rubbed his thumb against two of his fingers as if rubbing a coin between them. "There's the matter of payment, Hunter."

Winn glared at the man. "Don't anybody help out around here just for the hell of it?"

Boris looked at him incredulously, his avaricious gaze drifting to the Amanarath on Winn's back. "Give me the crossbow, and we'll call it a fair trade. My help and not killing the vampire for your bow."

Winn grumbled. "Marley's gonna have my hide for this," he muttered as he pulled the bow over his shoulder and handed it to the gypsy. Being without it sort of made him feel like he was standing in his underbritches, but what else was he to do? Marley would just have to understand that sacrifices had to be made in order to get the piece of the Book they needed.

Boris slung the crossbow over his shoulder, and it was large enough on his back that it made him look as if he had small metallic frames for wings sprouting out of either shoulder blade.

"Get moving," Winn growled. He was quickly running out of patience with the gypsy.

Boris laughed, but instead of a hale and hearty rumble it came out low and haughty, making Winn's gut coil tightly with revulsion. It sounded too close to the demon that haunted his nightmares. He shifted his position, making sure to place himself between the man and Alexa.

The gypsy's face began to sink inward, the skin sucking close to the bone as his body stretched upward, growing

taller. His short, curly dark hair began to lengthen, turning flaxen, and the tips of his ears extended. He was a goddamn shifter!

"Those dogs never even anticipated our plan. We will rule as we were meant to, once I deliver you to Rathe. And now, Slayer, you will come with me or die."

Chapter 17

"Watch out, he's *Sidhe*!" Alexa shouted as she jolted up, forgetting their precarious position in the unstable skiff. The boat rocked violently, and her sudden change in position tipped Winn over the edge into the icy water.

All the breath left his body in a rush. He kicked up to the surface, gasping, and grabbed hold of his hat floating by in the water, jamming it back on his head, and ignored the pole floating down river.

"You double-crossed the werewolves? But why?" The contessa's voice drifted over the water.

"It's no more than you vampires have done. There is no loyalty among the Darkin now. First to Rathe with the prize takes all. And you are no longer useful in protecting our prize."

Alexa screamed as the pale, long-haired creature reached for her. She struggled to evade his hands and keep her balance, causing her arms to flail like pinwheels spinning backward. Winn started swimming hard, arm over arm, for the boat, kicking for all he was worth toward the skiff drifting down the river faster than he could swim.

A loud bang brought his head up from the surface of the water with a start. The blond creature shrieked, clasping his

hands to his chest, his mouth open wide as he cried out and keeled back into the silver, rippling surface of the water.

Alexa sat down in a flurry of dark skirts and white petticoats. As Winn neared the boat he could see she was shaking. In her hand was a strange little gun. He knew it was pointless to try and climb in. Chances were good he'd only succeed in tipping her out into the frigid water with him. One of them might as well be dry. Besides, without a pole to push them to the bank, they'd just drift downstream.

His limbs were growing numb now as they adjusted to the temperature of the water. Winn grabbed the edge of the skiff and found himself face to barrel with the odd little gun she held.

"How about you point that peashooter in the opposite direction and let me push us to shore," he said through gritted teeth.

Alexa blinked, then slowly lowered the gun. Then like the first blush of dawn her face lit up, and she leaned down to kiss him soundly.

That warmed Winn down to his toes and made him feel as though he could push the little skiff across the Atlantic if need be. She pulled back and stared at him, her eyes filled with a mixture of exhaustion and relief.

"I was so worried you'd drowned!"

Winn grunted. "Drowned, no. Nearly froze to death, yes. Are you all right?"

"I'm fine."

He kicked hard, and his feet came in contact with the bottom of the river. He shoved the skiff up against the shore, then slogged his way out of the water and offered her a hand out of the rocking boat, afraid he'd get her cold and wet if he did more.

Her hand was soft and dry against his chilled skin. No matter how tough she acted, she still looked as dainty and

aristocratic as a woman could be. It was easy for Winn to see a crown upon her head. Hell, she was born to be a vampire queen, while he was—well, he was born to serve. Plain. Simple. Cut and dried. No matter how she affected him, he wasn't ever going to be able to change that.

As they walked across the dark, deserted field of over-grown, thigh-high grass, a thick mist that smelled of mud and rotting vegetation crept off the river. The mist chilled Winn to the bone and slicked the grass with a heavy coating of dew that soaked through Alexa's skirts. Winn felt for the waterproof oilskin packet containing Marley's letter to the queen. Good. It was still in his pocket, safe and sound. He cleared his throat. "What the hell was that thing in the boat?"

"A *Sidhe*—dark fae. He must have killed Boris after he'd left us in the wagon, then taken on his form to lead us here into his trap once the werewolves had done the dirty work of getting rid of the gypsy camp for him."

"They're shifters?"

"Fae. Far different. The shifters can only change their form; the fae not only change form, but have other powers and are more dangerous, and apparently have dangerous allies, too."

"Those the same Darkin that shot the arrows that brought the airship down?"

She nodded, her features grim. "Make no mistake, if the *Sidhe* and the *Oboroten* are competing with one another to capture you, as it appears they have, we have a fight on our hands. Neither will stop, nor any other Darkin, to get you before we can uncover where the piece of the Book is hidden. Rathe will accept nothing less."

Winn stared at her. He was so damn cold, his bones ached, but her words put the fire in him. "Nobody is likely to want me dead until I have the Book in my hand." They

had no time to waste. He walked faster, ignoring the cold cling of his clothes to his skin. She hurried along beside him, matching him step for step. "Where'd you get that little gun you used on it?"

The contessa gave him a sly smile. "Sir Turlock isn't the only inventor of your acquaintance." She patted the weapon.

"You sayin' you made that thing?" She was full of surprises.

"A creation of my own design, *da*. It's a cyanide shotgun. Kills anything with living flesh. Shots are packed with cyanide salts."

Ingenious. "So vampires are immune. Kind of like the werewolves using wolfsbane on you."

"Precisely."

He grinned at her in approval. "Why didn't you use it sooner?"

"I hadn't tried it before, because I wasn't confident it would work."

Winn muttered darkly. "Next time don't wait so long. You about gave me a heart attack, woman."

"Me? Weren't you the one taking a moonlit swim?"

He grunted and pulled at his mustache, trying to get it to re-form points before it dried completely. "Hardly my choice."

"No matter, we need to get you out of those wet clothes soon."

Winn's stomach did a backflip and he warmed all over, as the idea of his shucking his clothing, and hers as well, entered his mind.

"Mr. Jackson, are you listening to me?"

Winn shook his head, refocusing his gaze on her beautiful, upturned face. He was shaking, freezing really, in the cold night air. "How far to the castle?"

"We should be there soon."

In the dark Winn couldn't tell if Castle Barranoch was

indeed there in the distance or not. Without any light save the moon, it all looked black on black to him. Her vampire eyesight had to be far better than his own.

"You didn't have to do that," the contessa said softly as they walked through the thickening grasses. A scent of wheat drifted up, and Winn realized they were walking through a field of green grain.

"What?"

"Give up your crossbow."

Winchester shrugged. "You gave up your ring. It was only fair. 'Sides, if I'd known I was giving it to a shifter—"

"*Sidhe.*"

"She, fae, shifter, whatever, I wouldn't have given him the damn bow in the first place."

"You looked good with the Amanarath."

He paused at the compliment and gave her a long look. "It wasn't mine to give. Marley just loaned it to me."

"The ring I gave Mama Zinka was not mine to offer either. It belonged to Vladimir." Her gaze locked with his, and he realized for the first time that far more had been attached to that bit of jewelry for her than a betrothal promise. There were shadows of the past in those eyes, secrets she'd yet to reveal to him.

"You really gonna get hitched to the emperor?"

She broke eye contact and stared into the distance, then jerked her chin north. "There's Castle Barranoch. If we hurry we can make it there before daybreak."

"You didn't answer me, Tessa." She moved to step away, and he grasped her by the arm, his hold gentle but implacable.

Her face turned up toward his. "If we get through this, and get back the piece of the Book we seek, I will answer you then."

They walked on through the field that seemed to spread out for miles in the river valley. Winn's skin prickled in

warning, and he stopped striding forward through the swish of wet wheatgrass, eyeing the dark hunch of the castle looming ahead of them, its turrets and peaks sharp, black, teeth-like points against the clouds.

Something at Castle Barranoch wasn't right. It seemed too quiet for early morning. There were no sounds of animals or people, no smoke or scent of baking bread that indicated it might be occupied. But then again, these were vampires. Maybe they were just turning in for the night.

Winn gritted his teeth, unable to shake the churning in the pit of his stomach. "You sure your crew is waiting for us?" he asked, caution underscoring his tone.

The contessa closed her eyes and focused. "I can't reach Enric or the others." She frowned. "They aren't answering."

"Is there a chance they might have left?"

Alexa turned her head toward the horizon. Predawn light edged it in a paler blue, but the stars and moon still dominated the patches of sky between the clouds overhead. "They were told to wait for us here until we arrived. They wouldn't have defied direct orders."

He pulled the shotgun from the holster on his back with one smooth motion and yanked down on the lever, cocking it so it was ready to fire. "What exactly did you tell them?"

The contessa locked her gaze with his. "Only to come to Castle Barranoch directly and wait for us. Enric was to tell Count Vernay we required an escort through the forest."

"You mean the one that never came?"

Alexa nibbled on her bottom lip and nodded.

Around them the tall wheatgrass began to rustle as if a great wind swept through it, but there wasn't even a light breeze. Dark, menacing forms appeared from the grass, the moonlight glinting off their sharply honed weapons. Alexa gasped and huddled closer to Winn.

"Welcome to Castle Barranoch, my Lady Drossenburg and Mr. Jackson. We've been waiting for you." Goggles

with tinted lenses obscured the tall man's eyes. His thick, dark hair swept back over his head, but was neatly trimmed, not touching the collar of his pristine scarlet military jacket with extensive amounts of gold braid. Winn's first guess was British military.

"Who are you?" Winn asked calmly, shifting his center of gravity and making sure Tessa was well clear of any bullet he might have to fire.

The man fidgeted as if he were clicking his heels together—impossible in the long grass—and bowed. "William Wallace Frobisher, lieutenant in Her Majesty's Hunter Service."

Winn didn't remove his finger from the trigger. And he made no effort to hide the fact that he was prepared to fire if need be. "Hunter Service? What in the blazes is that?"

Frobisher's dark brow rose above the edge of his goggles, and a supercilious sneer curled his lip. "You Slayers are so regressive it's almost amusing, rather like watching the apes at the royal menagerie." He made a show of stripping the pristine white gloves from his hands one finger at a time. "The Royal Hunter Service is a select branch siphoned off of the ranks of the Legion for special training. We are the most elite Hunters in the world."

Winn's eyes narrowed with instant dislike. He thought the vampires had been haughty? This Frobisher fella plumb put them to shame. And he hated not being able to see the man's eyes. "The goggles included as part of the assignment?" he gibed.

Frobisher's mouth flattened into a cruel slash across his face. "I was injured during a scientific experiment. The goggles are a necessary inconvenience."

Next to Winn, Alexa stiffened, drawing in a quick sharp breath. "You're *that* Frobisher," she murmured.

The lieutenant's head snapped in her direction, like a pit viper sensing out the heat of its prey. "You know of the North Umbria disaster?"

Alexa merely nodded demurely in response to his question. Who didn't? It was the reason Sir Marley Turlock had been dismissed from Queen Victoria's cabinet, and had disappeared from public life. Not only had the experiment turned Sir Turlock's hair stark white, it was said to have nearly been blinding in its intensity. Frobisher must not have heeded the warnings to avert his gaze.

Winn glanced at her and back at Frobisher as if trying to assess what was going through her head. She would have loved to tell him, but didn't dare speak it out loud. Among the Darkin, Frobisher had a reputation as the most cruel, vindictive, and power-hungry of Her Majesty's Hunters. He didn't go after just an offending Darkin; he went after everyone they knew, their family, and the community that harbored them. He found ways and means of skirting around such petty things as international treaties.

"So, if you're an elite Hunter, why do your men still have their weapons trained on us?" Winn asked, his tone distinctly more adversarial.

"We have commandeered Castle Barranoch and will be incarcerating the Lady Drossenburg along with her minions until such time as we receive the piece of the Book of Legend the vampires have been withholding from Her Majesty."

"Ain't you a little out of your jurisdiction?"

"Mr. Jackson, the British Empire spans the globe. My jurisdiction is wherever Her Majesty wishes it to be." He motioned to his men with a flick of his hand. "Seize them."

With weapons still drawn, Frobisher's men advanced, grabbing hold of Alexa. Incensed by the audacity of Fro-

bisher, she tried wresting her arm from the burly guards who grabbed her, but found two of them were stronger than she was, which shocked her. Their gloves had to be lined or woven with silver. Another guard held a gun to Winchester's head as two more stripped him of his weapons and forced his hands atop his head.

"Not exactly the kind of reception one Hunter expects from another," Winn muttered darkly.

"But then you're not a Hunter, are you, Mr. Jackson? You're a Slayer."

Alexa's fangs throbbed, aching to be released out of anger, but she forcibly calmed herself and focused her simmering rage on Frobisher. "Where is your honor, sir? We have a treaty, and it expressly forbids taking political prisoners."

As a unit they began to march toward the castle, through the wheat field, the burgeoning dawn now turning the bowl of the sky a delft blue. Frobisher didn't even face her as he spoke. "There is nothing personal in this. I am simply following orders."

Winn grunted. "Well, you see, that's the difference between you Hunters in your fancy uniforms and us frontier types. We don't follow orders blindly 'cause we've got minds of our own."

Frobisher's shoulders tensed slightly, but he didn't acknowledge Winchester's slight. "Unlike your American Slayer, slavering at your heels like a trained dog, I do not jump just because a vampire noble speaks."

Years of tactical and political negotiation skills surged forward, suppressing Alexa's anger and making her more focused. Now was not the time to lose composure. "What are your plans for us, Mr. Frobisher?" she asked as they stepped from the wheat fields onto the dirt road leading to the castle. It loomed large ahead of them, the overlapping

stones looking like the scales of a great sleeping dragon in the growing light.

"You are to be held with the others, until such time as His Royal Imperial Highness Vladimir the Fifth returns the Book."

His words pierced her calm façade, making it hard to think. "Others?" she asked as nonchalantly as she could.

"Your minions are caged and awaiting us within the castle."

Caged? Like animals? That explained why she couldn't reach Enric, Count Vernay, or any of the others. If Frobisher had locked them into metal coffins, they would not be able to hear her or communicate amongst themselves. It was a monstrous thing to do to a vampire.

Winn's eyes blazed with red-hot fury, and the line of his jaw jumped as he ground his teeth. She tried to throw him a quelling glare and attempted to reach him with her mind. *I have this under control. Please do not make it any worse.*

Me? How am I gonna make it worse? They've taken us prisoner and snatched every weapon I've got, he shot back, not even aware that he was communicating with her, a sign that he'd let down his guard with her. Alexa shook off her surprise and returned her gaze to Frobisher's broad back.

Morning sunlight peeked over the mountains on the horizon, turning the sky golden with streaks of pale orange and casting the wet fields on either side of the road in shimmering green. Had she not spent the night running from werewolves, being attacked and nearly drowned by a *Sidhe* soldier, and now captured by the most unprincipled of Her Majesty's Hunters, it would have been a stunning end to her day. As it was she was surrounded on all sides by well-armed English Hunters, Winchester was weapon-less, and she had a very strong desire to plunge a dagger into Frobisher's back at the first opportunity.

"As the ambassador of His Imperial Majesty and a Hunter, can we expect better or similar treatment to that given my minions?" she said with as little emotion as possible.

Frobisher huffed. "As a vampire and a Slayer you're lucky I haven't already knocked you unconscious and dragged you back to the castle."

"You ain't as smart as you think you are." The mocking edge of Winn's tone suggested that even with his hands on his head he didn't fear Frobisher. He was either a supreme fool or knew exactly the kind of man he was dealing with and didn't give a damn. Considering he'd been a Western lawman, Alexa was betting on the latter rather than the former, but either way agitating the man was counterproductive to her own civil negotiations.

"You hear me, Frobisher? Holding us ain't gonna get you nothing," Winn called out.

Frobisher's shoulders and neck tensed, but he didn't turn to acknowledge Winchester; he just kept their little party steadily marching forward to Castle Barranoch.

"'Course, you want to sit on that lily-white ass of yours and not do nothing about getting the Book back from those furries, that's your choice," Winn muttered loud enough for Frobisher and his men to hear. "But if you was an American Hunter, we'd say it was just 'cause you didn't still have the balls your mama gave you."

That ticked Frobisher off. He whipped around and slammed a fist into Winn's jaw that snapped Winn's head sideways and sent him stumbling back a step into the men behind him. Frobisher's men pushed Winn forward to meet their commander.

Winn rubbed his jaw with his hand, but what Alexa saw in his eyes scared her far more than Frobisher's puffed-up chest and raised chin. Frobisher might not know it, but he

had just unlatched the lid on Pandora's box. She suspected that while an honorable man, Winchester Jackson was not opposed to fighting dirty when the situation demanded it.

Winn's eyes sparked with challenge, the tension between the two men charging the air with enough energy that Alexa could feel the crackle of it raising the small, downy hairs on her skin. "You hit me because you're too temperamental to take an insult like a man or 'cause the truth hurts?"

Frobisher drew himself up. "We know the werewolves no longer have it. Tell me where the bloody Book is." He said it with such deadly calm it chilled Alexa to the marrow of her bones. Then everything happened too fast.

With a loud click, a blade snapped from beneath the cuff of Frobisher's sleeve into his hand. She was unprepared when he snatched her, throwing her off balance so that she fell heavily against him, the edge of the blade against her throat. "And perhaps I'll let your vampire live."

Two things filtered into Alexa's stunned mind. First, Frobisher was truly an idiot if he thought she couldn't protect herself; second, Winchester hesitated. His gaze flicked to hers, and in those eyes she glimpsed a tortured man. Something about this situation touched more than a nerve in him; it raked across a scar that marred his soul. His jaw worked as if he were chewing over his words carefully before he spoke.

"We don't have the Book. The gypsies have taken it. All we have is clues," he said slowly. "You let her go, I'll give the Book to you once we use it to close the Gates of Nyx."

Alexa gasped in outrage. He'd promised to return the Book to Vladimir. Winchester's gaze connected with hers. *Trust me.* The sound of his voice in her head kept her silent. The edge of the blade came away from her skin, but stayed less than an inch from her neck.

"You'll give it to me once you obtain it, because Her

Majesty will be the one to close those Gates, Slayer. Not the lowly likes of you."

"But he's part of the Chosen," Alexa said, her voice resolute.

Frobisher growled, shaking her, his spittle hitting her skin. "Why, because your precious vampire prophecy said so? I can't imagine a less worthy choice. If anyone is going to receive the honor of closing those gates, it should be someone of royal blood with the right to rule."

Winn didn't even flinch at the insult; he just kept his gaze level and steady and ignored the weapons trained on them both. "Let us go, and I can get you what you want."

Chapter 18

Lieutenant William Wallace Frobisher smiled. If one could call the sneer that curled his mouth into a grotesque approximation of satisfaction a smile. It was made more sinister by the fact that tinted goggles he never seemed to remove obscured his eyes, making it impossible to see if the humor reached them or was merely a social convenience.

"You will go and get the Book for me. Excellent choice," the lieutenant said as he withdrew the knife from Alexa's throat and touched a button at his wrist to retract the blade. It slid silently back into its hidden sheath beneath the edge of his red coat sleeve.

Alexa spun away from him, moving close to Winn's side. Despite her proximity, and the withdrawal of the blade, his heart was still beating hard beneath his damp clothing. The sight of the blade pressing a firm line against the smooth column of Alexa's neck had jellied his mind and set his pulse to galloping. He had offered up the first thing that had come to mind.

Ironic, really, that Frobisher's lack of faith in the prophecy of the Chosen only increased Winn's own. Her Majesty might think she should be the one to close the

Gates, but no little old grandmother, queen or not, was up to facing Rathe and his Darkin horde. She had to be smarter and far more reasonable than Frobisher. When the time came, he'd deliver Marley's message and talk to her about his plans for the Book.

They stood in the morning shadow of the castle. It stretched over the road, beyond the bailey walls and over the moat bridge like dark tenacious fingers.

"Where is the Book?" Frobisher asked as he motioned for his men to stand down with a wave of his hand and a nod.

"First I want the assurance that you will release my minions," Alexa said bluntly, her hands clasped before her. Despite the dirt and disheveled hair, Alexa exuded regal command, her shoulders tilted back, her spine straight. The glint in her eye indicated that like the dark gray stone castle looming before them, she would not be moved.

Morning light gilded the dew-drenched wheat fields around the road to the castle. Mists rose as the sunlight warmed the earth, but it did nothing to alleviate the perceptible chill between Frobisher and Alexa.

Winn had to admire her gumption. She was no simpering female. The Lady Alexandra had more guts than many of the Hunters he'd fought side by side with over the years. Even when threatened, she'd remained cool, calm, and collected. His estimation of her increased exponentially.

"Very well. They shall be released . . . as soon as you return with the Book."

Her eyes flashed golden fire. It had become a game of chess, each waiting to see who would call "checkmate" first.

"My patience grows thin, Contessa," Frobisher said as he caressed the handle of the sword sheathed at his side. "I repeat. Where is the Book?"

Tessa lifted her chin defiantly, and Winn thought she'd never looked more beautiful. Not a vampire, but an avenging angel haloed by the rays of the sun. "Paris," she said simply.

Frobisher tapped his sword. "A group of my men will be happy to accompany you. I shall even provide you a coach." He made eye contact with three of the burly and most hardened-looking of his scarlet-coated guard. "You three ready a carriage and two horses. Simpson, you'll drive. Hardgrieve and Wexler, you'll ride guard." The three broke off from the main group and walked toward the castle's high, arched-stone gate, the points of the portcullis making it look like a wide open maw with dark, pointed teeth.

"And my weapons?" Winn pressed. He wasn't about to see his pa's rifle disappear into the hands of these Hunters.

Frobisher's jaw ticked once, twice, three times before he spoke. "Of course." He nodded, and his men returned Winn's rifle, his bowie knife, and his pistol. Just having them back made him feel more secure, but he missed Marley's Amanarath that had slipped beneath the waters of the river with the *Sidhe*.

"Come. The sooner you leave, the sooner you can recover the Book and put it in proper hands." Frobisher turned on his heel, his highly polished knee-high boots thumping loudly as he strode with confidence across the planks of the drawbridge. He disappeared beneath the great stone arch that led into Castle Barranoch's bailey.

His fifteen other men marched alongside them as they crossed over the drawbridge and into the grounds of the castle. Winn looked over the edge of the drawbridge. The water in the moat looked slate gray in the morning light and was probably as cold as the chill still in the air.

They crossed beneath the arched entry into the bailey. Winn estimated the walls around the castle had to be fifteen feet thick. Outside the vampire emperor's castle, Winn had never been in a place so damn big made from so much stone. Just by the look of it, he could tell the castle had withstood the ravages of war and time, for the stones had been

worn smooth beneath his feet. The age of it permeated the very air with the weight of its history.

"How old is this place?" he murmured to Alexa as she walked beside him.

"About seven hundred years, give or take."

Winn whistled long and low. Hell, these stones had been there before Leonardo da Vinci had invented the first Hunter weapons, back as far as the damn Romans. It could certainly make a man whose country had barely one hundred years under its belt feel a bit insecure. He could suddenly understand Frobisher's haughtiness a mite better. One didn't grow up hanging out around this stuff without a little pride rubbing off. But it didn't impress Winn enough to make him like Frobisher. He doubted anything could. The man was nearly as arrogant as regular vampires, and deep down it irritated him, like a cat getting its fur rubbed up the wrong way.

Inside the castle there were twenty iron caskets lined up in row upon row. Alexa gasped. She could hear the scraping of nails against the metal, the rasping of words, even though she couldn't make them out. She whirled on Frobisher. "How dare you, sir! This is no better than torture and you know it."

His lips twitched. "They all seemed willing enough when they found out it was this or risk losing you."

Alexa winced. The fact that they would sacrifice themselves for her, when she was so very willing to leave them all for Winn, struck her deeply.

"My lady, do not let this Hunter cause you guilt," said a deep, rasping voice from the dim recesses of the hall. A small blue light pierced through the darkness. Alexa stepped closer, Winn following a step behind. There, pinned by six huge magnets against the stone wall, she found her long-time friend and ally Count Vernay suspended a foot off the ground.

His damaged body had long ago been partially replaced by mechanical construct. He was part vampire, part machine, and all loyal. But it was these metallic body parts that held him immobile against the forces of the magnets. The lens of his one mechanical eye closed tighter, the metal iris flexing over the blue glow.

"Count!" She rushed to him, placing her hand against the skin of his cheek. The flesh half of his mouth smiled, while his metallic half of a jaw and lips stayed firmly in place.

"Have you been harmed?"

He let out a great, brittle guffaw. "These pathetic excuses for Hunters could hardly harm me more than was done back in 1812." His clothing was rumpled and stained, nothing like the way she'd last seen him.

Alexa knew he referred to the unfortunate battle that had changed him. "And the others?"

Vernay's bushy dark brows pinched together in the center of his balding head. "The Hunters seem bent on destroying them if their demands are not met. I tried to warn you, but by the time your crew arrived, it was too late."

Alexa nodded. "I am sorry to have failed you."

Vernay looked at Winn. "Is this the Chosen?"

"Winchester Jackson, sir," Winchester said with a quick nod of his head and a tug on the brim of his Stetson.

Vernay flexed a beefy hand. "As you can see I'm in no condition to welcome you properly to Castle Barranoch, but you are welcome nonetheless."

"Clearly that ain't your fault," Winn muttered in reply, throwing a glare in Frobisher's direction.

Alexa's throat swelled shut. She hated to think that she had anything to do with what her friends and children by gift suffered. "What can we do?" she asked, her voice tight.

She glanced at Winn. He slipped his much larger hand over hers.

"Don't you worry. We're going to find that missing piece. And when we do, we'll make sure they get freed. I promise," Winn said.

An hour and a fresh change of clothes later, Alexa and Winn were in a fancy carriage bound for Paris. The roads were narrow, rutted, and muddy, making Alexa bump against him as they rode over the worst patches. That he didn't mind so much. The feel of her soft feminine form was distracting but pleasant. And it had the added benefit of taking the edge off his building irritation with Frobisher's men, who rode on either side of the carriage, as an armed escort.

Winn slouched down in the well-padded leather seat. "Don't know what the hell Frobisher thought he needed them for. He damn well locked the doors when we climbed in. We ain't passengers. We're prisoners."

Alexa shrugged. "Prisoners. Passengers. It's all semantics as long as we get where we're going."

He focused on her feminine profile. The end of her nose tipped up slightly, and her full lips were dusky mauve.

Winn tried to ignore the stirring she caused in his blood and focused instead on thinking his question very hard in hopes she'd be able to hear him. *What do we do once we get there?*

She snapped around and stared at him, the dark curls about her temples swinging with the movement. *Are you talking to me on purpose?*

'Course I am. Why would I waste an advantage over those herders? He glanced briefly out the window.

It's just that . . .

What?

Well, communication like this is usually a very personal thing done only with those you trust, even among vampires.

Winn said nothing. He'd let her draw her own conclusions. Fact was, Darkin or not, she'd proven herself more reliable than half the men he'd worked with and a damn sight more concerned with his survival than anyone else on this continent.

So what's the plan when we get there? he asked again.

Her eyes narrowed. *I don't know. But one thing is certain. We'll have to evade these Hunters or they will take the Book back to Frobisher before you can use it to close the Gates of Nyx.*

Well, that damn sure ain't gonna happen. If anybody is going to hand off the Book to the queen, it'd be me. And granny ain't getting it until I'm done with it.

But you told Frobisher—

I told him what he wanted to hear to get us the hell out of there.

What about my people?

We'll find a way to get them out. One way or another.

Gradually, their guards relaxed, moving farther ahead to talk to the driver. They passed little hamlets; the whitewashed houses with thick thatched roofs had smoke curling out of chimneys. The fields were either the dark brown of newly turned earth or the achingly bright green of new shoots. Occasionally there were groups of woolly sheep with long tails, moving randomly about like puffs of clouds, and rows and rows of vineyards that made the rolling land look like it was a woven tapestry. Unlike a train, they were going slowly enough for him to take it all in.

"It's kind of pretty out here," Winn murmured, trying hard to take his mind off of how sore he was getting, cooped up in a carriage with no room to stretch out his legs. "Don't look nothing like Bodie. Don't look nothing like Missouri, either."

The contessa turned and looked at him, her eyes soft. In the confines of the carriage the jasmine scent of her filled the space, making every breath he took laced with a taste of her. "Is that where you were born?"

Winn nodded. "Hell of a lot flatter than this place." He paused for a moment, his drive to know everything about her picking away at his brain. "What about you? Were you born in Transylvania?"

"No. Krakow, when it was part of the Russian Empire. It is a very large city. And flat too." She smiled at him and glanced out the window. "Your home in the American wilderness is beautiful too, just different than this place."

"I thought vampires didn't like sunshine."

She locked gazes with him. "Nor are we famed for our love of open spaces, but then I'm a bit different from the other vampires at court. I've never quite blended in."

Winn's large hand swallowed up hers, and he gave her fingers a reassuring squeeze. "You ain't the only one who feels out of place, Tessa."

"Well, here perhaps."

"Nope. Even at home."

She blinked, her long lashes fanning for a moment over her cheeks. "Why is that? You have brothers."

Winn shrugged. "Don't mean we're all cut from the same cloth."

"But you're all Hunters."

He tried to smile, but it ended up a more sad, half-tilting of his lips. "I'm not a Hunter. Not anymore. If I had been, I would have been able to tell that Boris was something unnatural. I would have known how to defeat those werewolves. I may be the Chosen, but I'm a sad specimen of Hunter. Shouldn't be one at all."

Winn leaned his head back against the cushions and stared up at the diamond pattern of golden threads woven

through the red brocade lining the interior of the opulent traveling coach.

"Why is that?" she coaxed softly.

"I've done things I'm not proud of."

Alexa turned to fully face him and laid her free hand upon him, sending a ripple of awareness up his arm. "We all have."

Her sensual fragrance was driving him insane. Winn turned his head and looked at her. He'd certainly been wrong about her. Hell, in just a short span of time he'd come to think of her as an equal. He valued her bravery, her judgment, her keen intelligence, and her refined manners. She was beautiful, not in some flowery way, but in a lush, carnal fashion that made him think of what her curves would look like beneath silk sheets.

Beneath him.

She moved in closer, the soft swell of her breast over the edge of her bodice pressing against his arm, making him rock hard.

"Why do you hold yourself back?" she whispered. She caressed his cheek with her smooth, gentle fingers. Winn moved enough to be able to bring the tips of her fingers in contact with his mouth and lightly kissed them.

How could he possibly explain that every time he'd let someone get close to him, he or she eventually paid a terrible price? And while all the situations and people had been different, there'd been just one consistency—him. His mother, Colt, his pa. All of them at one time or another had suffered because of him. "Trust me, Tessa, you're better off not linking your train to my engine. We ain't even on the same track."

He should have known by now she wasn't one for taking suggestions. She leaned into him, her soft breasts pressing against his chest. Alexa's eyes narrowed slightly, her mouth forming an all too kissable pout.

"Your mouth says no, Mr. Jackson, but your eyes say *da*." His heart beat loudly in his ears as she slowly closed the space between them, her lips touching his in a slow, sensual kiss that burned. Winn put his hands on her shoulders to push her back, but the contact started a warm fizzing sensation in his blood that quickly turned to a heated rush, burning away all sense of what was right and what was wrong.

The instant her slick tongue slid against his in invitation to deepen the kiss, all hell broke loose inside him, opening the gate to temptation. He used his hold on her shoulders to pull her into his lap, then let his hands travel down the arch of her back to knead the soft curve of her hip as pure male need took over.

She wriggled on his lap, but her voluminous skirts, petticoats, and bustle made truly enjoying her assets almost impossible in the confines of the carriage. But between the two of them he thought they could find a way to manage. Her hands fisted in his hair, and her kisses turned demanding. The smell of her, spicy and floral at the same time, filled his senses, making him wonder whether her most secretive places tasted as sweet. The buzzing sensation in his system almost canceled out the sharp, swift nip at his lip. But he didn't miss the slow, lazy lap of her tongue against the cut.

He pulled back from their kiss, his breathing harsh and fast. "You just tasted my blood."

Winn tore his gaze away from her, looking at the scenery outside the windows as it changed from rural to the outskirts of a city. He tried to gain his bearings while his heart thumped loud and hard against his ribs.

"You have no idea how good you taste."

He could hardly fault her when he'd been thinking the same damn thing, albeit in a different manner. He turned and stared at her. Her eyes were luminous.

"Maybe this ain't the time and place for us to try that out right now, seeing how it's only fair if I get to taste you in return."

Her skin flushed with pleasure. "Is that a promise I can hold you to?"

"Yes, ma'am," he said, his tone husky with need. He pulled her in for one more kiss and broke it reluctantly.

"We must be getting close to Paris," she murmured.

More carriages, and carts, horses, people, and steam cars began to crowd the road, a mess of noise and dust. The acrid stench of smoke and refuse blended with the good scents of roasting meat and fresh laundry being dried outside. Paris was a contradiction, just like him. Just like the contessa. A compassionate vampire. He never would have believed it if he hadn't met her himself. "We ought to focus on interpreting the clues Mama Zinka gave us."

Alexa sighed, sliding from his lap and settling back into the carriage seat beside him. "Very well."

"Tell me again where Mama Zinka claims the Book is."

"She said the Book was deep with the bones and guarded by an empire of the dead," Alexa muttered. She stared at the stone walls that formed the boundaries around Paris. "What does it mean?"

"Don't like it. Sounds to me like we're going to be battling the living dead. And she did mention them."

Alexa nibbled at the fingernail on her index finger. "It can't be that. The Hunters would have wiped out a large contingent of zombies ages ago. Parisian Hunters are most vigilant about hunting down Darkin within the city."

"What about a cemetery? Plenty of bones there," Winn grumbled. A full-body chill threaded through him at the idea of even going close to a graveyard again after having gotten so personal with Yakov in his casket. The next time he saw a damn cemetery he wanted to be good and dead.

Her face lit with clarity. "The catacombs! Of course."

"Catacombs?" Winn's neck itched with agitation, and he tugged at the end of his mustache, making the waxed tip of it stick out sharply.

"Since Roman times the limestone used to build the city has been cut from its heart. Beneath Paris there run miles of quarry tunnels turned ossuary for the overflowing cemeteries of the city. It is an empire of the dead."

Winn ground his teeth. The last place he wanted to go was back under the earth with even more dead people, reduced to bones or not. Their carriage slowed, caught up by the snarl of traffic into the city.

"What we need to do is lose Frobisher's men," Winn muttered.

Alexa turned to him, a saucy smile on her lips. "I think I may have a way." Her eyes rolled to white, before her lashes fluttered shut and she slumped to the seat.

Winn shook her lightly. "Alexa?"

No response. Was she unconscious? Hell, he couldn't exactly feel her pulse to tell. "Alexa?"

One eye opened a crack. *Call the guards*, her voice echoed in his head. Her eye shut again. Winchester smiled to himself. She was certainly a clever little minx.

He leaned over, pressing his face against the carriage window, and motioned furiously to the guard. He slammed his fist on the roof to alert the driver in the box above them. The carriage veered out of traffic to the edge of the cobblestone street and slowed to a stop. The heavy padlocks on the door were unlocked, and the chain made a chinking sound as metal links slid through the handles on the outside of the carriage.

Simpson—or was it Wexler?—opened the door and poked his head into the carriage. "Oy, what's the problem?"

"She passed out cold. Just slumped over. You idiots haven't carried any wolfsbane in here, have you?"

The guard's brow furrowed. "No. Well, least not that I

know. Now the governor, he might use that kind of thing. Has a host of stuff what he uses to control them nasty Darkin."

Winn stared hard at the guard. "Focus, man. She needs help."

"Oh no. Can't have you leave the carriage until we reach what place you've got the Book. Frobisher's orders."

"She's the only one who knows where the Book is located. If we don't revive her, then I'm not going to be able to locate the Book, and I think that's probably a bigger priority for your lieutenant than keepin' us in some carriage, don't you?"

The guard licked his nearly nonexistent lips, his gaze darting from Winn to Alexa a few times as he considered his options. Finally he gave a reluctant jerk of his head. "Right enough, captain. What we gonna' do? Don't know nothing about helping Darkin."

"First of all, help me get her out. Perhaps she just needs some fresh air. It was hot as hell in this box."

He looked puzzled. "But vampires don't breathe."

"It's not for the oxygen, you idgit. It's to cool her off. With as many layers as she's wearing it's a miracle she didn't pass out sooner than this."

The guard blushed slightly. He took hold of her booted ankles, and Winn hooked his hands beneath her arms at the shoulder joint. Before they were even down the first step, Alexa sprang into action.

She slipped from Winn's light grasp and kicked the guard square on the chin. His head snapped back, and he slipped to the ground with a thud, unconscious. There was just enough time for Winn to grab the man's sidearms and Alexa to pull out the small cyanide gun from her skirts before they darted into traffic. The city became a blur of sound and color as they dodged the carts and a rearing

horse, startled as they made a beeline into the alley. The other two guards were off their horses, abandoning the carriage and yelling and chasing after them.

"This way!" Alexa barreled down the alley, which stank of urine and refuse at full speed, and Winn had to pump his arms and legs hard to keep up with her. Vampires could flat-out move. A trapping net, created from heavy hemp ropes and weighted with three small metal balls, went sailing past Winn's shoulder and thumped against a brick wall. He glanced back to see the guards discard their net launcher and pull out their guns.

"Go. Go. Go!" he yelled. Bullets pinged against a nearby wall, sending stinging bits of brick flying. Winn raised up his arm, trying to protect her from the worst of the shrapnel, pushing her around the corner ahead of him.

They circled the city block, zigzagging across traffic three times into different alleys. There was no time to gaze at the trees that lined the cobblestone streets in their gay, spring green, or to admire the sparkle of early evening sun on the ripples of the Seine, both things that he should have been doing in Paris with a beautiful woman.

Instead, sweat trickled down his neck, and his heart was beating so hard, he could barely hear over his own pulse. They pressed their backs against the cool bricks, and Winn glanced at her. Dark curls had dampened and curled, framing the edges of her face, and her eyes were bright.

"This ain't exactly how I'd envisioned sightseeing in Paris," he said with a touch of humor. He gently brushed a few chips of brick off of her smooth skin, the familiar tingling when he touched her zipping up his arm, straight to his chest, then lower.

Her glorious mouth broadened into a smile, and she laughed, the sound of it easing the raw tension that coiled

in his gut, helping him to focus. "Life with you is never boring, is it?" she teased.

Winn bit down on his tongue and held back his response. Since giving up hunting his life had become as dull as the sandstone that surrounded Bodie. He'd convinced himself that safe was better than dead, but maybe that wasn't the case. While the thought of having two trained Hunters after him and the contessa didn't make him happy, it certainly did make him feel alive.

"We need to get back toward the edge of the city. That's where the entrance to the catacombs will be," she said. The little tinge of excitement in her voice was infectious.

Winn nodded.

"Have we lost them yet?" she asked.

He peered around the corner and saw a flash of red. He wasn't sure if it was a lady's fancy walking dress or a split-second glimpse of the uniform Frobisher's men wore, but he sure as hell wasn't taking chances. They needed to find a better place to hide. Fast.

"If we get out of this alive, remind me never to trust another Hunter," he muttered.

She gave him a sad smile. "I told you Hunters here were not like you. They are more a military group, obeying only one leader who is tenacious, like an English bulldog."

Scanning the tops of the buildings, Winn spotted a spire about one block over. Perhaps they had a good place to hide after all. "I've got an idea."

Alexa slipped her small hand in his, and they hurried toward the church. Winn tried hard not to look at her. It hurt to. Once they found the Book, she'd go back to Transylvania and become Vladimir's bride, and he'd go back and try to help his brothers save the world. Noble, but hardly a happy ending. Hell, maybe he didn't deserve a happy ending after everything he'd done. He gave her hand a squeeze to reassure himself she was there, even though

he felt her slipping further and further away from him emotionally the closer they came to getting the Book.

He pulled her along up the steps and yanked open the door of the church. "In here!"

The dimly lit interior of the church was a world away from the noise and bustle of the city streets. The air was cool and scented with lingering traces of spicy incense and the heavy sweetness of beeswax candles.

The sound of his harsh breathing echoed off the stone walls, and he pressed his hand against the stitch in his side. While he was used to fighting hand-to-hand, he'd never been much of a runner. Alexa looked completely composed, save for the heightened color of her skin and the sparkle to her eyes.

"How did you know?" she asked, her voice low and quiet as befitted their location.

"You mean that you wouldn't burn up the minute you stepped on holy ground?"

She nodded.

"Your throne room is in an old church sanctuary, ain't it?"

She smiled at him, and the twinkle in her eyes intensified, nearly stealing away what little breath he had left. "You're far more observant and clever than you let on, aren't you?"

Winn tipped his hat at her. "Back home it's adapt or die."

Alexa glanced past the font of holy water, through the double doors that led to the sanctuary. "European Hunters are far less observant. They won't think to look for us in here."

"That's what I was counting on. We'll let them stew for an hour."

"Frobisher is not going to be pleased with them." She sounded delighted.

Winn smiled, although there was no humor in being pursued in a foreign city by determined soldiers. Deep down he felt bad, knowing they were fellow Hunters with a hell of a lot of pain coming their way, not because they were bad men, but because they had a bastard for a leader. "He don't look like the forgivin' sort."

"He's not."

"How do we get to those catacombs you were talking about?"

Alexa bit her lip and stared at the smooth stones on the floor, then tapped at her chin and frowned. "The closest entrance will be just south of *Barrière d'Enfer*, near the old city wall."

He glanced cautiously out of the church doors, looking for any sign of the scarlet coats of the guards. "Looks like we're clear. Time's running out. Let's go."

Alexa held out her hand and materialized a black parasol to help them better hide from detection out in the open. They stole quickly out of the church and down the residential section. Overhead the elegant little balconies were draped with pots of blooming lilies. They approached the entrance of the catacombs with caution. Winn kept glancing over their shoulders. There was no reason to draw attention to themselves or lead Frobisher's men directly to the catacombs if they could help it. Alexa stayed in the perpetual shade of her parasol and picked up her pace, her skirts swishing about her ankles while she approached a plain wrought iron door in the tan stone wall just south of the *Barrière d'Enfer*.

Winchester glanced at the unimposing door. It didn't look dangerous. But then looks could be deceiving. Evening shadows fell across the gate, making it appear more sinister. "Are you really going in there?"

Alexa pulled open the door and gave him an arch

glance. "Do you have any better ideas for retrieving the piece of the Book?"

Winn scowled. He didn't like it. Going underground made him distinctly uncomfortable. Going underground into an ossuary filled with the bones of millions of the dead, well, that bordered on entering a casket of one's own. But neither could he stay near the door waiting and make them a target for Frobisher's men. Either way he'd be closer to a casket than he'd like.

The spiral staircase just inside the entrance circled downward like a drill bit into the rock for more than fifty feet before emptying out into a narrow tunnel almost the width of a grave for a man Winn's size. Smoking oil lamps periodically lit the way, casting pools of yellowish light. Wet gravel crunched beneath their feet and voices echoed in the tunnels ahead of them. Winn tensed. There was no way Frobisher's men could have made it there ahead of them unless they'd used another entrance. He slid his rifle from the long holster on his back. "Someone else is down here," he muttered.

"Of course they are. It's considered a point of macabre fascination. People tour these tunnels all the time. Put that thing away before we scare an innocent."

Winn grunted. "Don't mean they ain't dangerous."

"All the better reason to find what we need and get out of here as soon as possible," she retorted.

"What do you think she meant by the skull with tears of blood?" he muttered. "Bones don't bleed."

"They could be paint, or they could be dried blood, or even a jewel fashioned like a tear."

"Great. That narrows it down."

After about sixty feet the tunnel opened up into a large room cut from the rock; its walls were crafted out of human remains. The bones, heaped in orderly, almost artful stacks, formed walls out of the rounded ends of long

bones, punctuated in patterns here and there with rows of jawless skulls. It was both macabre and fascinating, and made him all too aware of his own fleeting mortality, but Winn didn't have time to stare. He was looking for the skull with the blood tears.

A chill swept through Winn that had nothing to do with the temperature of the catacombs. These had been people. Thousands, possibly millions of people at one time.

A metal gate, red with rust, shut off one of the darkened passages. "Do you think they will have hidden it behind one of these gates?"

"It's possible. The quarry tunnels run for miles."

There were still faint echoes of other voices, but they grew dimmer as Winn and Alexa moved deeper into the catacombs, their lantern the only light. The dampness grew worse. A constant rain of water droplets dripped from the skull-infused ceiling. The bones had taken on a slick, glazed look from the coating of liquefied limestone. Starts of stalactites could be seen forming, like a twisted version of a cathedral ceiling with elegant points.

"Jumpin' Jehoshaphat. We ain't never going to find that skull down here," he said as he gazed up at the skulls. "There's got to be a million people down here."

"Six."

"There're more than six people in here!"

"Six *million*, give or take a few. They emptied out all the cemeteries within the city for the last several centuries and brought the bones here."

Winn pulled off his hat and swiped the back of his hand over his brow. The humid air saturated his shirt, making him sweat. "That old gypsy could have been a little more specific about her directions," he muttered. They'd wasted an entire day traveling in the coach, and the gritty dryness in his eyes, despite the humidity of the tunnels, was from being bone weary. "We don't have time to play hide-and-

seek. Frobisher's men are likely to show up any moment and Rathe's got every intention of beating us to the Gates and opening them."

"But he can't without the pieces of the Book, nor can you close them without the pieces. Isn't that correct?"

"Partially. He'll find a way to open them with or without the Book. But what's in those pages is the only thing we can use to stop him." Winn scanned every skull in the ceiling and those within the walls, searching for the elusive marker Mama Zinka had indicated.

The grit from above filtered down as a crack zigzagged through the damp stones in the vault above them with a scream-like noise that made the hair on the back of Winn's neck lift. "Move!" He grabbed her arm and began to run. Fetid water splashed up from the puddles beneath their feet, and Alexa stumbled trying to keep up, her sodden skirts tangling about her legs. *Crack!* A loud groan echoed from behind them. The stone vault gave way, the sand, soil, and stones from above sinking in to fill the narrow tunnel behind them, forcing them to rush forward.

They were trapped within the tunnel.

Chapter 19

Winchester frantically dug at the fallen stones blocking the tunnel with his fingers, nearly ripping his nails from their beds. Alexa knew panic when she saw it. He'd harm himself by trying to get out, when they needed to keep moving forward.

"It's no use," Alexa said simply, trying to be the voice of calm and reason.

He glared at her, his skin paler and his lips taut beneath the dark edge of his mustache. "If you want to just clear off a place and lay yourself out and wait, that's fine, but I got no intention of staying in this crypt. I'll get out of this place if I have to chew my way out."

She smothered a hopeless laugh.

"Something funny to you about all this?"

"Chew. Would you really even try that?"

Winn growled and dug harder at the stones.

"You're wasting time. We're better off trying to find another exit."

He turned, his eyes narrowing. "Are there other exits?"

"There are all kinds of entrances to these catacombs. Some were sealed up long ago, but surely we can find something."

"Without a map? You might as well try to navigate the Sonoran Desert by the cactus."

She sighed. "Without proper tools we'll never get through that debris." Alexa didn't remember much of how the catacombs wound their way through the earth, but she had enough sense of direction, even here beneath the surface, to know they needed to keep heading down the tunnel if they wanted to find an exit.

Winn swore under his breath, then spun on his heel and marched past her. "Well, come on, then. No use staying down here in these tunnels longer than we have to."

The light from their torch flickered, drawing strange ghastly shapes on the uneven tunnel walls as they walked farther into the catacombs.

"Only thing worse than being under the ground is knowing you can't get out."

Small, beady red eyes darted in the darkness, flashing as they reflected the torchlight. Rats. He hated the damn things. They were always in the horse or chicken feed. He muttered a few choice curses as he kept plodding forward.

"Winchester?" The tinny edge to her voice made him glance away from the small dots of color. "Are those rats?"

"Yep."

Alexa skittered back a step. "Rats don't have red eyes."

Winn paused only for a second. Damn. She was right. And there wasn't any squeaking. The click of a hundred little metal legs against the stone froze his blood.

"Mechanical spiders. Go! Go! Go!" Alexa grabbed up her skirts, and they sprinted down the dark passageway, taking whatever turns they could to lose the creatures.

The clicking sound grew fainter and fainter. Winn's lungs seared as he gasped in great draws of damp air. "I think we lost them."

"For now."

"I think we got less time than we'd thought to get the hell out of these catacombs."

"Winchester, look!" The contessa pointed to one of the skulls lined up in a row in the bone wall behind them. Winn shifted the light from the torch, and the dark, blood-red stones, shaped like tears, sparkled on the skull's smooth off-white cheek.

"Look underneath it."

She bent in half trying to peer beneath the jawless skull. "I can't see anything there."

He moved beside her, bringing the torch closer. At this proximity Alexa could see the outline of his upper lip. The Hunter certainly knew how to kiss. The memory of their last kiss both fired and infuriated her. How could he so easily elicit passion from her when it was merely an exercise for him?

"There's nothing there."

"Let me see."

Alexa huffed. Why would he not believe her?

Winchester reached into the cavern of the skull's mouth, making it look like the skull was eating his hand. "There's a raised bit in here." His voice shimmered with excitement.

"Can you pull it?"

He grunted. His forearm bulged with the effort. "Nope."

"Push it?"

He tried and shook his head.

"What about twisting it?"

"Like a knob?"

She nodded.

"My hand's too big." He pulled his hand out from beneath the skull. Alexa didn't wait for an invitation; their time was growing absurdly short with each passing hour. "Move aside," she ordered. If he didn't like it, that was unfortunate. She had been born to lead.

She slipped her hand into the opening and found the

small circular piece that fit neatly in the palm of her hand. Twisting it like a knob on one of Sir Turlock's mechanical marvels, she heard the distinct click followed by the grinding movement of gears.

The wall of bones seemed to crack open and shift backward. The seams had been so well hidden by the edges of the bones, one could not see them until the wall was opened. A wash of cooler air, dry and stagnant, blew across them.

She stepped forward and was stopped by his grip on her upper arm. "Let me go first. If this was put in place by Hunters, it's likely booby-trapped."

While the act of chivalry from an uncultured Slayer was commendable, Alexa still pulled her arm from his grasp, causing him to lock gazes with her. "After six hundred years, I think I know how to spot a Hunter's trap," she said archly.

"Maybe you do. But maybe you don't know as much as you think you do." The clicks were growing more rapid.

Winchester pulled her up hard against him, as an iron spike dropped down from the ceiling where she'd been standing. Alexa looked over her shoulder at the spike and shuddered. "Your point seems abundantly clear."

He had the temerity to grin at her. "It's a good sign. Means we're getting close. Let's find out where they've hidden the piece of the Book."

Alexa stayed right behind Winchester. They slowly skirted the piece of wall that had shifted inward. The light of the oil lamp flickered and swayed along the roughly hewn rock walls. This section still bore the marks of the ancient tools that had carved away the limestone from the quarry when she'd been but a girl.

A grinding sound startled both of them. The piece of wall began to shift back into place. "No!" Winn dropped the oil lamp. It shattered as he darted to the moving rock and tried to hold it back with his hands, to no avail.

Pitch darkness swallowed them whole.

* * *

The roar of his pulse kicked up another notch. Ever since they'd descended down the staircase, Alexa had tried without success to shut out the shushing sound of his blood, but the increasing tattoo of it made it almost impossible to ignore. She turned, glancing at him, able to see the ripple of heat coming off his skin, outlining his muscular form beneath his clothing. Being a vampire did have its advantages, but being able to see him clearly in the dark right now wasn't one of them. All it did was send her bloodlust to a dangerous tipping point.

"You're not scared of the dark, are you?"

"No."

She thought about how he'd panicked in the casket while Boris had climbed the tree and she had transported when the werewolves had come barreling through the graveyard. Realization hit her. It wasn't the dark. It was the tight, confining space that triggered his deliciously rushing heartbeat.

"Just because it's dark doesn't mean this section isn't vast. It could go on for miles and miles," she said, hoping to reassure him.

"Ain't going to help if we can't see it," he ground out.

Alexa sighed and drew down into the center of her being just behind her solar plexus, pulling the energy together to manifest a new oil lamp. The weight of it settled firm and cool in her hand, and she lifted the glass to blow on the wick and light it.

The flicker of light grew and illuminated the sculpted planes of Winchester's face, pale and drawn. "All you had to do was ask," she said, then handed him the lamp. "Is that such a hard thing?"

He blew out, making his mustache flicker with movement. "You have no idea." Alexa's own lips began to tingle

as she remembered just how his mouth felt slanted against hers.

Winchester held the lamp high, illuminating the tunnel. But the light only stretched so far, ending in a black, gaping maw ahead of them. "Well, we ain't getting out the way we came in."

"If my sense of direction is correct, then this tunnel should lead us almost beneath the church of *Saint-Germain-des-Prés*," she murmured, her voice echoing off the rough limestone walls.

There were no walls of stacked bones in this section of the catacombs. It had been intentionally sealed and protected by the ossuary. Surely this tunnel would lead them to where Mama Zinka claimed they'd find the missing piece of the Book of Legend.

They turned a corner and found the tunnel branched into three. "Which one do we take?" she asked.

Winchester searched the pale stone, looking for any clue they'd missed. Above each tunnel entrance, carved into the stone, was one of three small images. A lion's head, a palm tree, and a raven. The signs of the three brothers of the Legion of Hunters who'd hacked the Book apart in the first place: Cadel, Elwin, and Haydn.

"That way." He pointed at the tunnel with the raven above it.

The contessa searched his face and glanced at each of the tunnels. "How can you tell?"

He pointed up at the insignias.

"Of course. Haydn. He brought our piece of the Book to the Byzantine Empire."

Winn stopped in his tracks and stared hard at her. "*Our* piece?"

She frowned, putting her hands on her hips. "Well, we have been guarding it for six hundred years. So, yes, I've come to think of it as ours."

"It belongs to the Legion."

"It belongs to whoever can keep hold of it," she challenged.

He stiffened and rolled his shoulders back. "You know I'm going to take it back with me."

"Of course. And then you'll return it, as you promised His Imperial Majesty."

Winn gave a harsh, grating laugh. "That's if I survive."

"What do you mean?"

"I ain't stupid, sweetheart. When you spouted off that prophecy I noticed that the Chosen don't all survive. If that's part of the deal, then I'll go along with it, but it's going to be me who takes the fall, not one of my little brothers."

Her lips thinned, as if she wanted to say something but purposely held it back.

The internal clock in Winchester's head still ticked away the minutes. Their time to find the Book and return with it grew shorter and shorter. He grabbed hold of her bare hand, instantly aware of the spark that arced between them when skin touched skin. "Come on, we've got to find that piece of the Book and a way out of here."

They tramped down the darkened tunnel, aware of the steady plink and plunk of water that dripped down through the limestone. No wonder the catacombs were unstable, Winn thought. The ground above them was being held up by a sponge of rock that was growing more porous and flimsy all the time, and whole sections of Paris blithely went about their business completely unaware they could sink to their deaths if the ground collapsed beneath them.

Without warning the tunnel abruptly ended at a locked and rusted iron gate. Winn lifted his lamp to get some kind of view of what lay on the other side and found himself staring at a stone sarcophagus. It was like being in the tomb of an ancient Egyptian pharaoh. Those ambrotypes of his

friend Marcus's explorations and digs in search of errant mummies would have come in handy about now.

Winn rattled the gate, getting a fine powdery coating of red rust on his hands and down the front of his black pants for his trouble. "We've got to get this gate open."

"All you had to do was ask." Alexa evaporated in a swirl of smoke-like particles and appeared on the other side of the iron bars. She tinkered with the complicated latch on the other side of the door. Her brow furrowed. "It's stuck. We need something that can break it loose."

Winchester cursed under his breath. "Move."

She took a step back.

"Farther."

She took two more steps back. Winn pulled out his revolver from his hip holster and held it at almost point-blank range to the lock and fired. The shot rang out, echoing loudly in the chamber, and spiked the air with the smell of gunpowder and hot metal.

Winchester kicked open the gate and stepped into the small vaulted room, holding the oil lamp aloft. The stone of the massive sarcophagus was a gray marble and totally different than the surrounding limestone. Atop it was carved the figure of a man with long, flowing hair and a copious beard, his eyes closed, a kind of crown around his head. His chain-mail armor and long tunic made him look a bit like how Winn expected King Arthur might have appeared. An ancient metal shield, depicting a raven, wings outstretched, rested atop his stone midsection.

Alexa stepped closer, inspecting the reposing statue. "Is that Haydn?"

Winn pulled at the end of his mustache. It could be. No one knew for sure where they had buried him. "Don't know." A ragged crack ran along the hardened wax seal that caked the seam between the lid and the base of the sarcophagus. Small chunks of the hardened wax lay in the dirt.

"Whoever it is, someone's been to visit lately. The seal's been broken. There's no dust on the bits of wax on the floor."

Winn crouched down to examine the stone more closely. All along the sides of the sarcophagus were images in intricately carved relief. There were demons with forked tails and horns battling three knights on the ground while harpies dive-bombed from the air. Each knight held a book in his hands. There was another image of a sword hacking the center of the book. Winn ran his fingers reverently along the images. Each one was part of the stories of the Legion that his father had told him and his brothers so often when they were children he'd memorized them.

But there were other images. Disturbing images that clamped down on his gut and made him break out in a cold and clammy sweat. One showed a man in what looked like a cowboy hat atop a mechanical horse, a piece of the Book held aloft in his hand as he battled a giant scorpion. Another showed a man in modern jodhpurs and boots and a cowboy hat, a machete held high over his head as he fought back an enormous jaguar the size of a horse against the stepped sides of a temple. And then there was the one of what looked like a cowboy with a crossbow hanging from an airship. What the hell?

"The prophecy is far older than you realize." Her voice seemed awkward and unnatural in the eerie stillness of what could only be the tomb of the youngest brother, Haydn.

Winn turned his gaze at her. "You said Kostick—"

"Kostick was not the first. Just the best known."

Winn stood up, his legs feeling a bit wobbly. "Others?"

"Since the time of the brothers."

"You know about Legion lore?"

She nodded and looked away from him. "It always pays to know one's enemies."

He deliberately stepped closer to her, the energy sparking in the air between them like a living thing. "And is that how you feel about me? Am I your enemy?"

Her amber gaze, sure and strong, connected to his. "No. Not anymore."

Winn sensed there was something she still held back. "But?"

"But, there were things Kostick told me that he told no one else."

He grasped her by the arms and forced her to meet his gaze by tipping up her chin. "Tell me."

She swallowed hard, and he watched the movement beneath her flawless skin. "He said I'm to be the destruction of the Chosen. And that I'll be a traitor to my own kind."

"Nice story, but not necessarily the truth."

She glared at him. "How can you say that?"

"Because we all make choices, Tessa. You get to decide if this is your fate or not. Same as me."

Her eyes welled dangerously with unshed tears. Damn. What had he said wrong? He'd been trying to encourage her, but apparently he'd mucked it up somehow. The tears spilled a shining trail down her cheeks, and he inwardly cringed, as if she'd dealt him a physical blow.

"Ain't worth crying over," he murmured softly, pulling her into his chest. Hell, if there was something to cry over, it would be the fact they were trapped like rats in this deep, dark hole with nothing but bones and a stone sarcophagus for company.

Alexa sniffled. Gods, did she wish she could believe him, but she'd held back the most important part of

Kostick's prophecy from him. *You shall be destroyed by your heart's desire.*

Even as he held his strong arms around her, deep within her chest her stone-cold heart fractured a bit. She had never thought to see the day when a Hunter would comfort a Darkin. He rubbed a reassuring hand back and forth over her upper arm. "We'll stick together and find the Book and a way out."

She pulled back and stared up into the deep blue of his eyes. "And then what?"

Winn sat down on the floor, bringing her down to sit with him, his arm around her. "Fate is a fickle mistress. We aren't going to wait on her. We'll decide what we do next when we get there."

She nodded, suddenly quite mortified at her bout of feminine hysterics, so out of character for her. How long had it been since she'd cried? Ivan's death. Two hundred years worth of pain and sorrow bottled inside her could only be contained for so long. Alexa nestled against Winchester's side, absorbing the comfort he offered her. Even trapped within the catacombs, he offered her hope that they'd escape with the Book and prevent the ending of their world. Her eyes grew heavy, her body relaxing. Perhaps she was better off following Winchester's suggestion and focusing herself on the task at hand and leaving what-ifs for when they arrived in the moment.

Beneath her cheek his breathing became deeper, more rhythmic. Alexa realized he had fallen asleep. It was a wonder he hadn't collapsed sooner. By her calculations it was well past midnight and they'd had a most trying day.

Normally she didn't sleep well, but with Winchester's arm around her, his strong body beside hers, a few moments of rest could do no harm. Alexa let herself drift off as she listened to his slow, steady heartbeat.

Images of fire raining down from the sky and smolder-

ing ruins infiltrated Alexa's dreams. She knew it was a dream because she could neither speak nor move, only watch the tableau unfold before her. Outside the city burned. The lick of red flames left the stones of the old Roman city wall and church smoldering and blackened, but still standing. Holy ground remained the only protection left against the tumult that reigned in the streets of *Caer Guricon*.

It was not the English from the East who burned their city, nor Viking invaders. It was something far worse.

"We must separate the book. It is the only way." The knight turned from the nightmare outside the window to look at his two younger brothers, Elwin and Haydn. Both wore dour expressions through the soot streaked on their faces, their tunics tattered and singed, their once proud breast plates now dented and scratched. For six long days since the Gates of Nyx had cracked open on the solstice, shaking the very earth with great rolling waves, they had battled the demons, the children of the night, the monsters dredged up from the very pits of Hell itself. Now there was nothing left of the city save the church and the rubble of the walls and Roman ruins that had once surrounded it.

"That is madness, Cadel. Without the information inside, how can we hope to defeat them?"

Cadel turned away from Elwin, staring again out at the flames that ate the city whole, unable to block the terrified screams of its people. "That is the point. If they take the Book, all of the Book, our cause is lost forever. Only by separating it can we have a prayer of its survival. Of the survival of mankind against these devils."

"It's impossible. We've already lost over four hundred men. What hope do we have?"

"If we take the oldest catacomb passage beneath the church we could reach the wood."

"Run? What kind of honor is there in that?"

Cadel stiffened at the blatant insult. He spun, his honed reflexes giving him the advantage over his slightly younger brother. He grabbed fistfuls of Haydn's tunic and heaved him up to his toes. "We are avowed Hunters. We are bound to no lord, no country and no king, save He who reigns in Heaven. We leave not as cowards, but as means to preserve and save humanity itself."

"But surely the Book is not worth—"

"Have you no idea how important the Book of Legend is? With it, the hosts of Hell could fully open the Gates of Nyx forever. Look how much suffering has happened when it was only cracked open for mere minutes. The whole Kingdom of Mercia and of Powys must have felt the earth's upheaval."

"But how will we pass the knowledge on? How can we hope to train a new legion of Hunters without the Book complete?"

"We will each take a third of the Book and scatter it to the corners of the earth, farthest from this place. From these portions we will train new Hunters as best we may."

Elwin sighed, beating his thigh with his fist, the chain mail clinking. "I think he's right. There's no other way now."

"But when will the Book be brought back together?"

Cadel opened the Book, placing the leather binding down upon the tabletop. "My hope is never," he said as he heaved a heavy swing of his sword, cleaving the Book into two parts. He handed the first third to Elwin, then flipped the Book open again and aimed his sword.

"But the prophecy of the Chosen—"

Thwack. Cadel took a second third of the Book and held it out to Haydn. "Today is not that day. We have closed the Gate. The Book will be made whole once more only when the Gates falter once more. Until then our course is clear. We must battle those that have entered our world and pre-serve our knowledge to train the next Legion of Hunters.

Take your portion of the Book and guard it with your life. Tell no one, save your heirs, of the Book."

Haydn linked Cadel's forearm in his own, a greeting and also a good-bye. "So be it. I shall go east to the borders of Hungary."

"And I shall travel south to the Kingdom of Navarre."

Deep down Cadel knew he'd never see either of his brothers again. "God preserve you both."

Elwin nodded. "And you, brother."

The graze of a rough finger over her cheek woke Alexa. "Rise and shine, my lady." The sleepy rumble of Winchester's voice was soothing after the disturbing dream about the brothers who had separated the Book.

Alexa pulled back and yawned, stretching her arms. "You slept well?"

"As well as one can in a catacomb when you're not dead," he archly replied.

"So where do you think the Book is hidden?" she asked.

"Funny you should ask that. I had this strange dream." Winn glanced at her, and an arc of recognition passed between them. Both of them gazed at the same instant at the stone sarcophagus.

"Do you think we can shift the lid?" Alexa asked.

"If a group of gypsies could do it, certainly together we can."

She gave him a tremulous smile of gratitude.

"We'll push on three. Ready?"

Alexa put the heels of her hands on the edge of the heavy stone lid and dug her feet into the gritty dirt of the rock floor. "Ready."

"One. Two. Three." Winn sucked in a deep breath and shoved at the same time she did. The lid scraped, making a grating sound like a metal sword being drawn against a rock wall that put her nerves on edge. Without the hardened

wax seal to hold it in place, the lid slipped from its mooring, sitting crooked on the coffin.

Within the thick, stone sarcophagus lay the shrunken, desiccated remains of a knight in his helmet, gauntlets, and chain mail. The fabric hauberk he had once worn had long since disintegrated, leaving only a film of colored dust against the intricately woven metal rings. He held his massive broadsword in his skeletal fingers, and just above his hands sat a large, heavy square object wrapped in oil-cloth and tied with modern twine.

Winchester let out a gasp. "The Book!" With a shaking hand he reached for the package atop the corpse's chest.

A skeletal hand grasped Winchester's wrist in a firm grip. The head rotated, its empty eye sockets locked on Winchester.

"Who dares disturb me?" a dust-dry voice crackled. Clearly someone had placed an enchantment on the knight's remains. Alexa wasn't sure what to do next. Without knowing who'd cast the enchantment, it could be nearly impossible to break it.

"I'm a Hunter, trying to close the Gates of Nyx."

"You are of the Chosen?" the skeleton said, his grip still implacable.

Winchester's gaze connected with hers, and Alexa gave him the barest of nods. *You know you are. Tell him,* she told him with her thoughts.

What if it's not enough?

We'll deal with that once we get there.

He gave her a nod in return and turned back to meet the knight's sightless gaze. "I am eldest of the Chosen."

"What do you wear upon your chest?"

Winchester's brow furrowed in confusion. He glanced down at himself for a second, then at her.

Alexa thought about the first time she'd seen Winchester and the gleam of sunlight upon his sheriff's badge. *A*

star. Tell him you wear a star. Alexa didn't know why it seemed right to her but it did.

Winchester turned to the skeleton once more. "I wear a star."

"Welcome home, Chosen of the Legion." The skeleton released his grip and returned his skeletal fingers to his sword.

Alexa held her tongue while Winchester lifted the package from the chest of the skeleton. What if it wasn't the piece of the Book? What if this had been an elaborate ruse to lock them away and allow Rathe to open the Gates unchallenged?

Winchester's hands shook as he tried to untie the string that held the oilcloth closed. Alexa couldn't help herself; she reached in and helped him. The instant their fingers touched, a zing of energy arced between them, zipping throughout her body to each and every cell.

"Here goes everything," he murmured. Winchester peeled back the edge of the oilcloth.

The familiar sight of the glass case edged in gold and locked with an elaborate raven lock sent a rush of relief coursing through her. Within the case lay a thick chunk of illuminated pages on old vellum.

"These are Haydn's pages. He got the middle of the Book," Winchester murmured, his eyes wide with wonder.

Alexa had seen it several times over the centuries when she'd gone to see Kostick, but the power of the Book never seemed to diminish, nor fail to astound her. The fine lettering and brilliant colors and gold detailed illustrations of the illuminated manuscript glowed in the lamp's light.

"You've done it!"

Winchester locked gazes with her, serious and sensual at the same time. "*We've* done it, Tessa."

"Now all we have to do is find a way to get out of here."

"Didn't you say we were likely beneath a church?"

"*Da, Saint-Germain-des-Prés.*"

"Then there has to be a way out of this crypt."

"You mean a stone head marker in the floor of the church?"

Winchester nodded and held the oil lamp up higher, searching for seams in the ceiling overhead. Finding the Book was fantastic, but it was only the first step. They had to get out of here, and more important he had to get this piece back to the United States and join it together with sections found by his brothers. *If* they had found them.

For a moment he contemplated that Colt and Remington might be going through the same trials and tribulations, perhaps worse than he'd endured, and his joy at finding the Book crumpled a bit. He didn't want either of those boys to experience the pangs of loss and pain he had, and yet stuck down in this pit, there was nothing he could do to protect them from it. Each of them had a mission to complete, and the stakes were too high for them to fail.

Despite an exhaustive search of the stone ceiling of the crypt they failed to locate the seams of a head marker. Winchester lowered the oil lamp. The room seemed— literally—like a dead end.

He did one last search of the chamber. On one wall, carved into the stone, loomed the same image from Haydn's shield. Winchester had thought it just decorative, but perhaps it wasn't. He glanced at the contessa. "Here, hold this." He handed her the piece of the Book carefully rewrapped in the oilcloth.

She stared at him for a moment. "Are you sure?"

He grunted. "Of course I'm sure." Winchester moved closer to the raven carved into the wall. The bird itself seemed solid as he ran his fingers over it. It wasn't until he reached the round edge of the shield-like image that his

sensitive fingers found what his eyes couldn't. "This whole thing is a trigger," he said. He glanced back at her.

"For what?"

Winn shrugged. In their current predicament did it matter? He put his palms flat against the surface of the raven and tried to twist the emblem to the right. Nothing happened. He tried turning it to the left. Winn shouted with frustration. "There's something here, but I can't figure it out. You'd think with all the lore my pa fed me he might have mentioned some specific instructions for these kinds of situations."

"What did he tell you?"

Winn grunted. "It don't really apply."

"Humor me and tell me anyway."

"If you can't go over, under, or around it, go *through* it." His face brightened. He leaned his shoulder against the emblem and pushed hard, growling at the effort. A series of clicks echoed behind the seal.

"Push it!" Alexa said.

Winn put his shoulder against the raven and pushed hard with all his might. The entire emblem shifted in by several inches, then began to roll away within the wall.

Chapter 20

"A secret tunnel." A snap and fizz of excitement sparked along her nerves. Perhaps they had a way out of the crypt holding the remains of the Hunter Haydn after all.

"Never underestimate a Hunter," Winchester said. He grasped her about the waist, making her all too aware of how his hands felt upon her. His muscles stretched the fabric of his coat taut as he swung her up to perch on the edge of the round tunnel that had been revealed by the shifting stone shield. Alexa handed him back the precious piece of the Book he'd taken from Hadyn's sarcophagus. She was surprised she had no sense of hesitation. The Book was important to them both, and she knew it belonged in Winn's capable hands. "Wish me luck," she said.

He cupped her cheek, drawing her face down to his. His kiss was strong and potent, leaving her tingling from head to toe. But more than that, it left Alexa breathless, because in that kiss she tasted acceptance and faith. Two things that were worth more than vaults of gold or any ruby ring or fancy title. Without realizing it, he'd just given her the most precious gift she'd ever received, and it left her speechless.

He broke their kiss and tenderly swept back the curls that framed her face. "Be careful, Tessa." He kissed her on

the tip of her nose. Still in a daze, Alexa twisted herself to her knees and began crawling through the tunnel.

The curved walls of it had been carved from the limestone, and her movements stirred up the fine dust that seemed to coat everything. He grunted, and she heard him scrabble into the tunnel. She glanced back behind her and saw Winchester close on her heels.

"Can you see anything yet?" he asked, a tremor in his voice. The tunnel was far smaller for him than for her, his broad shoulders brushing either wall as he moved. It must seem tight and confining to him.

She turned again and peered into the darkness. The opening of the tunnel appeared, a circle of light ahead the size of a small coin. "Just keep moving. There's an opening ahead."

He muttered curses in four different languages, and Alexa stifled the urge to comment. Winchester was far more educated than many of the European Hunters. He was also kinder, more concerned with the outcome than with following orders to curry favor. The sound of his strong, even breaths and the echo of his pulse in her ears made her heart twist just a bit more. Now that they had the Book in hand, what would become of them?

Did she even want to go back to the court? She knew without a doubt if she married Vlad it would only be to satisfy the expectations of others, not for any happiness of her own. Even struggling on her hands and knees in the catacombs, her dress torn and dirty, her hair a disaster, a warm glow infused her. And deep down Alexa knew it had to do with Winchester.

The warmth of his body blotted out the scents of earth and mildew with those of leather and male, tinted still with evergreens from the woods. Alexa inhaled deeply. Even though she didn't need the oxygen, she wanted to inhale the scent of him and imprint him on her memory.

Every bit of him, so she would never forget how extraordinary he was. The thought of being without him triggered an acute pain that started in her throat, then grew and swelled until it filled her chest. She gasped as the realization hit her.

She was in love with Winchester Jackson.

Somehow her dream of escaping the social rules that had bound her so tightly all these years had transformed into something more. Now being free from the rigid society of noble vampires wasn't enough. She wanted more. She wanted to breathe in the fresh air and marvel at the wide, limitless blue skies of his home. She wanted him.

"Are we there yet?" he rumbled. The timbre of his voice rolled over her, eliciting a shiver of longing. Of wanting. Gods help her, of love.

She slowed. "Nearly." Perhaps it wasn't the best time to ask, but when would be? "Winchester?"

"Yeah?"

"What do you want in life?"

"You mean other than to keep breathing another day?"

"Surely you want more than that. What will you do once you've closed the Gates?"

"You mean *if* I close the Gates?"

"*When*."

He chuckled. "See, that's what I like about you, Tessa. Always focused. I don't know. I guess I'll just keep being the sheriff of Bodie."

"And that fulfills you?"

"Never had a chance to think about that." His voice echoed in the close confines of the dark tunnel. The light up ahead was becoming large. He'd be glad of that, she knew. She loved the sound of his deep-pitched voice, loved his confidence. There were many things she loved about Winchester Jackson. Here was a man who knew who he was and his place in the world. "Always been tied to duty

and family in one way or another," he told her quietly. "Pa taught us those come first. Don't really matter what I want."

Want me, she thought, the ache in her chest unfamiliar. "Why not? Don't you deserve happiness?"

The long pause before he spoke again told her more than his words ever could. "Are we close to getting out of this hole?"

"Yes! I can see steps!"

"Don't stop now!"

Alexa crawled the last few feet of the tunnel with renewed purpose. Winchester was right on her heels. The tunnel opened into a small stairwell carved from the rocks. She straightened and waited for Winn to do the same. The stairs ahead were steep and narrow.

She stood, bracing her hands against the small of her back and stretching. It certainly wasn't the ladylike thing to do, but with Winn she didn't care. She knew he accepted her just as she was, fangs and all.

He straightened beside her, dusting off his hands.

"Where did you put the Book?"

He hitched a thumb over his shoulder. "Strapped it to my back using the holster leathers for my rifle."

Not only was he handsome and rugged, strong and honorable, he was smart as well. Alexa smiled at him.

"So that Book is truly more precious to you than even your own life?"

He looked her in the eye, his gaze serious and unflinching. "You're damn right it is. I've got a whole world counting on me to make sure they don't end up enslaved to a sadistic archdemon lord."

Alexa tapped her finger against her lips. "You have a point."

"Let me go first in case it's booby-trapped."

"I have a better chance of surviving a tra—"

"Wait here." His tone was adamant. He eased past her in the narrow confines of the stairwell.

"You don't command me, Winchester Jackson. I shall *follow*." Very closely. Should anything happen to him, Alexa knew she would not survive it.

"Stay close and walk where I walk."

"*Da*." She fell into step behind him.

The steep stairs led to an old wooden door, dark with age and bound with thick, black iron bands. It rattled as Winn tugged on it. Locked. Alexa huffed an exasperated sigh.

"You didn't expect them to leave the entrance to the crypt open to just anyone, did you?" he chided.

"Just once, can't something about this entire endeavor be simple?"

"Then it wouldn't be an adventure, would it?"

She gently pushed him aside. "Give me a moment and let me see what I can do." She shimmered into a cloud of smoky particles, and the door rattled on the other side, then creaked open.

"That didn't take too lo—" Winn drew back abruptly when the face he saw was not Alexa's but one wizened with age. After everything he'd seen and done, he didn't hesitate. He grabbed a fistful of the man's shirt, pulled the bowie from his boot, and held the tip of the knife right beneath the man's chin. "Where is she?"

The elderly man stammered. "Th-the lady is right here." The door swung open wider.

"Let go of the father," Alexa said calmly. Winn relaxed his hold on the man's shirt, which he belatedly realized wasn't a shirt at all but the long flowing robes of a priest. "Forgive him, Father. We have been pursued by the worst of Englishmen."

The old man nodded, never questioning her, his eyes glassy.

"You glamoured him?"

Alexa gave him a slow smile. "Better than holding a knife to his throat. Besides, once we've escaped he'll have no memory of either of us. It's better this way."

Winn nodded. He was learning when one worked with a vampire there were no hard-and-fast rules. The priest locked the door behind them, and they followed him through a warren of passages beneath the church to the sanctuary above.

Alexa grasped the man's weathered hand in her own, looking deeply into his eyes. "You have found there are rats down in the cellar and need to tell them to wall off the door."

"Rats . . . wall off the door," he repeated.

They walked out of the front doors of the church into the brilliant morning sunshine. The puffy clouds dotting the cerulean sky seemed surreal after the depths and darkness of the catacombs, but the fresh air felt divine on Alexa's skin.

"We need to get out of the open and find an airship to get us out of here and back to the States," Winn said, as he pulled his hat down tighter on his brow.

"That should be easy enough. We'll just pop down to the market the next street over and pick one out," she said mildly.

He looked at her, quirking a brow. "You really think it's that easy?"

Alexa rolled her eyes. Sometimes men were dense as stone. "No! Of course not. We don't have the resources or the connections to buy an airship that can carry us that distance."

"What about His Imperial Royal Majestic Highness? Doesn't he have an extra airship he could send?" he said sarcastically.

Alexa stared at him and folded her arms. She had had just about enough of his misplaced jealousy of Vlad. There was only one man she wanted—him.

"The one that went down in the forest was the only one he had," he answered himself glumly.

She gave one curt nod.

"Damn." He pulled at the end of his mustache. Mud and powder-fine rock dust clung to his hat and black duster, making him look almost ghost-like. Once they found an airship, the next things they needed were a change of clothing and some sustenance. The taste of his blood on her tongue had nearly sent her into a frenzy, but she'd hidden it from him well. Overhead a light breeze rustled the leaves of the chestnut trees that lined the street. It could have been pleasant if they weren't being chased and Winchester hadn't been muttering like a madman to himself.

Winn ran his hand over the back of his neck while he scanned the city streets looking for any hint of Frobisher's men. *Think. Think,* Winn told himself. If he were a lawman in these parts, where would he go to find something you couldn't normally get? He stopped in his tracks, his face hardening with determination. "We need to find a saloon."

"I hardly think now is the time for a drink."

He flicked his gaze to hers. "If what I've crawled through in the last few days isn't enough to make a man drink, I don't know what would be, but liquor ain't what I'm after. I want a bandit."

"Bandit?"

"Somebody on the wrong side of the law."

Understanding made the golden flecks in her eyes pulsate with excitement. "A pirate."

Winn shrugged. "Whatever gets us there."

"There should be pirates in the absinthe houses of *Montmartre*."

An hour later they had entered the most disreputable part of the city. Winn looked at the dingy sign that read King's Men in French. It hung from a rusted chain on one side. The other side's chain had rusted through, and the placard had been shot a time or two, leaving gaping, splintered holes in the forehead of the king's image on the sign.

"A remnant of the Revolution," Alexa said under her breath.

If they'd been back home, Winn would have expected raucous laughter and perhaps the tinkling sound of the piano that sat in the corner of the Golden Goose. But this place was far different. It had an eerie stillness to it.

He opened the door to find a low-ceilinged room, barely lit by the fire in the massive stone fireplace against one wall and the windows created from multiple panes of small bits of diamond-shaped glass so grimy they looked like they hadn't been cleaned in a century, perhaps two. The ancient beams overhead were blackened with smoke and age, and the air smelled of sour, cheap wine, dark hops, tobacco, and the fire.

A few men sat at old, scarred tables, cradling pewter tankards. All eyes turned to stare at the contessa. Frenchmen were appreciative of a beautiful woman, despite her dirty and slightly disheveled appearance. Winn cursed silently under his breath. He should have known better than to bring a lady into a place like this. It was like waving a gold nugget beneath the nose of a hardscrabble miner.

An older man, his wide middle wrapped in a filthy apron, ambled toward them, eyes gleaming with anticipation. But his manner turned suspicious the moment he took in Winn's

cowboy hat and boots. Then he turned his attention fully back to Alexa. "What can I help you with, *mademoiselle*?" he asked in French, dismissing Winn entirely. He might be speaking a different language, but that didn't mean Winn didn't understand the slight or his words.

She leaned in, and rather than back away as instinct dictated, Winn decided he'd watch her. He'd always been so careful to avoid being glamoured that he'd never actually paid close attention to the process when performed by a vampire. Of course, he'd always been trying to defend people against becoming a vampire's next meal as well.

Alexa's eyes widened ever so slightly, her voice growing husky and deep while she allowed the glamour to form. He could feel the power of it resonating through her, and it made a hungry shiver race through him. "Perhaps you can help us," she said slowly.

The barman's eyes lost their sparkle of greed and became glassy and unfocused in response to her voice. "We are seeking an airship. Do you know of a captain?"

"*Oui, chérie*," the man said, his voice low, almost a whisper. Winn cast a glare at the others in the small tavern, brushing back the edge of his duster and moving his hand to rest on the butt of his holstered pistol, just to be sure they hadn't taken too much interest in their business. The few eyes looking their direction hastily looked away.

"Tell me," she breathed. Winn felt himself leaning toward her. While he wasn't nearly as affected by the glamour as the barman, he knew she was impacting him more than if he'd been on guard, blocking her.

The difference was there was no fear, only intense curiosity and a fierce sense of pride that she would undertake this to get the Book back to the States.

"Le Renaud has an airship."

"Tell me where I can find him."

The barman's head turned, and his arm rose slowly to

point to an open door off the main keeping room. "In there, my lady."

Alexa didn't waste time. She turned on her heel and strode across the room before Winn could even check to see what lay on the other side and if it might be a threat.

Wait! he thought hard.

She stopped for an instant and turned, her amber gaze connecting with his. *He's merely a pirate: I think I can deal with him.*

How can you be so sure?

Unlike you, most people when glamoured can't hide the truth. Had Le Renaud been anything other than a pirate the barkeeper would have revealed it to me.

Unless he didn't know any different. Then you'd only be getting his version of the truth.

Her brows pulled together slightly. "True."

Winn stepped ahead of her a pace and entered the small room first, his hand on the hilt of his rifle, ready to draw and fire if need be. The pungent odors of sea brine, machine oil, and wet wool swirled in the air. There was only one table pushed up against the wall beneath the dirty window.

In a pool of watery sunlight sat a slight man. He was nearly lost in the folds of a long, threadbare blue military jacket, fifty years out of date, the brass buttons tarnished deep brown. An oversized, broad-brimmed black hat with tattered, drooping feathers sat upon his head and shaded his face. The man had both small, booted feet propped up on the table, crossed at the ankle. *He's too damn small to be much of a threat,* Winn thought. "Le Renaud?" he asked.

The pirate took a long draw from the pewter tankard in his hand, then belched. "Go away. I'm busy," he answered in French. The voice was far richer and a shade higher than Winn had anticipated.

"You're a woman!" In his surprise the words slipped out in English.

Click. The pirate leveled the barrel of a cocked pistol chest level at Alexa and Winn. "I said I'm busy," she repeated in English.

Alexa walked straight up to the pirate, heedless of the loaded gun pointed at her heart, and Winn's chest contracted, but he found himself rooted to the spot, still too stunned to speak. God, but she was magnificent, if a bit foolhardy. Of course, unless that shot was silver it wouldn't do much to a vampire of her power besides piss her off, so she had less to fear than a mortal like himself with a gun pointed at his heart.

"We wish to hire your ship," Alexa said, standing firmly on the other side of the table from the woman, her back ramrod straight, the curves of her form outlined in golden sunlight. Le Renaud took another drink, pretending to ignore Alexa's comment, then tipped the empty tankard to the side, peering into its dry depths. "Damn. Empty again."

Winn watched in fascination as Alexa pulled up the edge of her skirts, exposing a trim, booted ankle and a length of silky calf. Surely she didn't think to offer herself! He took a step forward.

The tip of the pistol swiveled in his direction. "Stay where you are, sir." The heavy French accent made her *s*'s sound slippery. The pirate regarded him for a moment, her eyes widening slightly, then her lashes half lowering with appreciation. Winn stood his ground.

The sound of tearing fabric captured his attention. Alexa pulled out a strip of cloth sewn with gold coins and tossed it on the table with a heavy clinking sound in front of Le Renaud. "This should help."

With that sewn in the lining of her skirts, no wonder she'd been terrified of ending up in the water. She would have been dragged under for certain; which in turn made Winn wonder precisely what else she had hidden in the folds of her skirts.

Le Renaud pulled her scuffed boots off the table and sat up straight, pushing the brim of her wide hat up with an index finger. Her face was round, and a deceptive dimple in her left cheek made her appear far more cherubic than any normal pirate should have. Winn could tell from the way her body angled forward and fingers twitched she wanted the gold, but her eyes narrowed with suspicion. "Maybe I have a ship and maybe I don't. It depends." Her gaze flicked back to him, assessing.

"On what?" Winn stepped forward to stand beside Alexa across the worn sticky table from the pirate.

Le Renaud's hazel eyes shifted back and forth between Alexa and Winn. "Who you are."

"We're not government agents."

Le Renaud guffawed and leaned back, swinging her feet back on the tabletop. "I could tell that just by the smell of you. But neither are you French."

Her grubby fingers pulled the coin-sewn cloth closer, and she brushed one of the coins against her lips. "What's the cargo?"

"Us," Winn answered simply.

"And the destination?"

"The United States, by way of London. I have a letter to deliver."

The pirate's lips buzzed as she made a disgusted noise and pretended to inspect the crust of dirt around her nail beds. "That would cost you at least double."

Alexa grumbled and bent over, lifting the edge of her skirt yet again. *Rip. Clink, clink, clink.* Another strip of fabric loaded with gold coins hit the tabletop. "Now do you have a ship?"

"Yes, but only because you are traveling with him," Le Renaud said as she grabbed the small pile of coins, blew a kiss at Winn, and nodded. "Meet me at the *Parc de Vincennes* outside the eastern edge of the city in two hours. We'll be ready to leave then."

Chapter 21

Every one of Winn's senses was heightened and on edge. While the sky pirate had picked a lovely open park to land, it left them terribly exposed, especially this close to the outskirts of Paris.

Wind whispered in the trees, insistent little voices that he didn't like and couldn't understand. People rode their horses or strolled along the many paths that crisscrossed the park's wide swaths of green grass. The rhythmic splash of ornamental fountains produced a soothing atmosphere. The perfect place for a picnic with Alexa, a spot he would've picked if he were trying to woo her, if he hadn't been rushing to try and save the world. The thought rankled.

He tried so damn hard to be normal.

And just like the flick of a lucifer to a rough surface it had all gone up in flames in mere seconds and he'd been back in the Hunter life. Wooing a woman wasn't going to happen. Hell, even having a normal relationship with one wasn't possible. Not with what he did, the kinds of things he fought against. It was just too damn dangerous for those around him on every level. He was like a lodestone for mayhem, destruction, and death.

He glanced away from the increasingly cloudy skies and

gazed at Alexa. She stood, hand shading her eyes, looking over the people populating the lawns and shaded areas of the park. Somehow she had changed her clothing and looked immaculate, from the neat, glossy coil of dark hair at her nape, to the froth of white petticoat peeking beneath the hem of her gown, while he looked like a desert rat fresh from rooting around in the sandy earth. She wasn't just any woman.

As a Darkin she knew the risks of what he did, and what team he played for. She knew he was capable of killing, and yet, he knew that much about her too. If there was any female he could have paired up with who would be able to withstand the dangers of being married to a Hunter, it was Alexa.

She caught him watching her. "I don't like how she was looking at you." Alexa's mouth was pinched, her eyes hard.

"Who?"

"The pirate. She looked at you the way a woman looks at a cream-filled pastry."

"Ain't no different than every man looks at you," he fired back, amused and touched by her jealousy.

Her glare turned withering in its intensity. "That's different."

Winn snorted. "Sure it is." He'd argue with her on the point, but the truth of the matter was he needed his focus. The sky pirate garnered about as much interest from him as a horse did as a form of transportation. He didn't admire the animal's hide or the shape of its damned ears. The pirate was merely a means to an end.

It was having his brain filled with all things Alexa that was Winn's problem. He didn't have the luxury of thinking about her silken skin, or the sweet-smelling fragrance of her hair—*Stop it. It ain't going to happen, boy. Just let it go*, he told himself firmly.

"We're taking a chance waiting out in the open like this. Frobisher's men might still be searching for us," he said.

Alexa nibbled on her lip for a moment, fixated on rearranging her skirts. God, he wanted to kiss her, right there where her teeth had turned her lip more rosy. "No doubt they are, but Paris is large, and they'll be looking for us in the city, not the outskirts. Besides, it's so open here, we'd see them long before they got close enough to do any harm."

"That was very impressive, by the way." Winn couldn't help himself. Every time he tried to bring his brain back to focusing on the task at hand, the mere suggestion of her kisses knocked reason on its backside.

She glanced up at him, her dark curls bouncing with the movement. For a long time Winn had wondered what her dark hair would look like unbound and draped over her shoulder, a silken curtain for her bare breasts. He rearranged his duster to conceal his rising interest.

She raised a brow. "What's impressive?"

"The things you manage to hide in your skirts. First a cyanide gun, then a treasury. Have anything else of interest hidden there?" he teased, trying to lighten the monotony of waiting on the pirate.

Her mouth twisted into a saucy smile, and she raised one brow. "I think we might be able to find something you'd be interested in."

Her words were a match to kerosene, making his skin burn in a flash and causing Winn to be very aware of how the play of light made her flesh luminous. He knew precisely the texture of it in the hollows, and the vivid memory of it made him harder just thinking about it. But despite anything they'd shared, she belonged to someone else, until she said different, and he'd do best to remember it. He turned abruptly away from her, focusing instead on the leaden sky. "See anything yet?" Her eyesight was a damn

sight better than his own. She'd see a dirigible long before he could.

His drastic change in demeanor dampened her expression. Obviously hurt, her eyes shuttered. His gut twisted hard in response. Damn. The thought of her being with someone else made him crazy, and yet, neither could he have her. A flirtation was one thing, lust-fueled desire another, but deep down Winn knew he didn't want either of those from her. He damn well wanted more.

The blue skies of the morning had given way to clouds. They rolled in, thick and charcoal gray, a sign of rain. After so many years in the desert, Winn could detect the heaviness of moisture in the air, waiting to fall.

At first he thought it was merely a trick of the light and rubbed his eyes with the back of his hand. There, skimming the tops of the heavy gray clouds, like misty seas, was an old-fashioned wooden ship, complete with unfurled sails and an enormous rudder. Unlike the vampire's airship, this air vessel reminded Winchester more of a wooden sailing ship from centuries before. Only the enormous propellers perched on either side of the ship's stern and the long wide strips of brass just below the deck gave it away as something other than a hallucination.

"What is that?" she asked, shading her eyes with her hand.

"Our ship." None in the park had glanced up to see what they saw. But they certainly would once it got closer. They'd have to board and get back in the air fast. Damned fast. But it would be a while before it was close enough for them to board.

She glanced at him and burst out laughing. "I can only imagine the shocked looks of your town folk when the sheriff arrives in a galleon in the midst of the desert."

Winn grimaced. "Too much attention for my taste." He scanned the picnickers, and people strolling the paths, before glancing back at her.

Her eyes turned keen, sparkling with the need to know all the answers. "Why is it you prefer to operate behind the curtains?"

He tugged at the edge of his mustache. "When you live life in the shadows, the spotlight's a shade too bright for comfort."

The contessa rubbed her hands together, her fingers worrying the bit of lighter skin where the emperor's band had been. Winn's heart contracted a bit. Was she thinking about him, about the wealth and power he could offer her? He'd been a fool to think she'd ever consider some random American Hunter over one of the most powerful vampires on the planet.

She locked gazes with him, her eyes almost a caramel color as the amber in them deepened. "We are more alike than you realize." Alexa took what looked like, but wasn't, a fortifying deep breath, which revealed the depth of her anxiety, and she stared hard at him.

"I'm not going back."

Her pronouncement shocked him so, it took a moment for him to respond. "What are yo—"

Alexa moved so fast there was barely room between one breath and the next before she was right next to him, her hands spread wide on his chest, her face tilted up to his. And then he found it hard to breathe at all. The scent of her skin, that exotic dark floral fragrance that coiled about his senses, invaded his brain, turning it to mush.

"I want to come with you. Back to America."

He was certain she could feel the stuttered beat of his heart as it stopped for a second, then started back up again with the force of a mule kick, threatening to break his ribs. Disbelief crept in, its tenacious tentacles wrapping around and smothering the little leap of joy he didn't dare to indulge. "You want to come back with me?"

She stood on her tiptoes, pressing her very female

curves against him, bringing her mouth closer to his. It was everything he could do to hold himself back from closing the gap and sampling her lips. "*Da*," she breathed, then touched her luscious mouth to his in a kiss both soft and warm that stripped away his ability to form a coherent thought. It took a moment for his brain to reengage once her lips left his.

"What about Vladimir?"

She held his face between her dainty hands, and her eyes bored into his very soul. "I'm not interested in Vladimir. I want you."

"And what of your minions, your children, your fantastic palaces and—"

She cut him off with the crush of her mouth against his in a searing kiss.

For a moment the world seemed to tilt on its axis, spinning off kilter as it changed the center of the universe to the woman against him. Winn couldn't resist and wrapped his arms around her, afraid the moment might shatter into a million small pieces he'd never be able to fit back together.

She felt so damn right against him. A perfect fit, as if she'd been fashioned just for him. Her kiss became more demanding, and her fangs lengthened against his lips. The gentle, erotic scrape of her teeth as they grew longer and harder echoed his own reaction to her. Knowing that he aroused her made something inside him snap.

He wanted her. Not just as a woman, but her.

The way she taunted him. The way she smiled. The sashay of her hips in those damn bustled skirts. Her damn uppity, refined manners and all.

But how could he possibly make it happen? Sure, she might find it a lark to go to America for a bit. But sooner or later the harshness of frontier life would take its toll on someone so cultured and elegant.

Remington had always been the one with the gift of

words and a sly way with women. Colt had both a wicked sense of humor and a devil-may-care recklessness that attracted females like bees to honey. But Winn knew he was just the responsible, solid one. Boring. Plain. Predictable. And good with a gun. *What could she possibly see in you?* the little devil inside him whispered in his ear, even as the delectable slide of her lips against his proved she damn well saw something she liked.

Her fingers sank into his skin, demanding more, and it boosted his need another notch, making his skin feel too damn tight all over. Winn couldn't hold back a groan in response to her kiss.

Only the chuffing air and the whopping sound of the propellers on the airship drew them apart, even though they still gazed longingly at one another. This flair of heat between them was far from over, and now they both knew it.

"Ahoy below!"

They looked up to see Le Renaud leaning over the edge of the hovering airship.

"Ain't you gonna land this thing?" Winn shouted over the propeller noise. A rung and rope ladder unfurled over the side in response.

The pirate cupped her hand around her mouth. "No time! Climb aboard."

He nodded to Alexa. "Ladies first."

"I think you may just want to inspect the contents of my skirts more closely," she said, her tone husky and inviting.

"Damn straight I do," he growled back. "But it'll have to wait."

Le Renaud glanced back over the side, frowned, then waved them upward as she tapped her boot with impatience. "Hurry up! The winds are shifting. A storm is coming in."

They climbed the rope ladder, and as Winn neared the hull of the ship he could tell from the roundish white marks

and small points of bleached barnacles it had once been a true sea vessel. Just how damn old was this thing? He hoped it could make it to the States in one piece.

He made it onto the decks, sanded smooth from use. Le Renaud swept her hat from her head and gave a small bow from the waist, which let her loose linen shirt gape open enough to reveal ample cleavage. Her dark curly hair, no longer queued behind her nape, fell over her shoulders, looking even darker against the faded blue of her worn military coat. Now that she was standing, Winn could see she was shorter than even Alexa, the top of her hat barely coming to his shoulder. "Welcome aboard the *Circe*."

Winn pulled at the brim of his hat. "Captain." That made the pirate smile, revealing the deep dimple in her cheek. He noticed she had yet to recognize Alexa. Winn slipped his arm possessively around Alexa's waist and pulled her up close beside him, leaving no shadow of doubt that they were together.

"This is quite a ship," he murmured. "Looks—"

"Old," finished Alexa for him.

"I was going to say original," Winn said under his breath. The women glared at each other, and an uncomfortable prickle worked its way up his back. He scanned the decks and noticed that all the ship hands were like the captain—female. That surprised him. What would they do in battle? He was just about to ask about the curious situation when Alexa spoke out.

"Are you certain this hulk can hold together long enough to get us to America?" Alexa asked with asperity, as she folded her arms over her chest.

Le Renaud lifted her chin and tugged her hat firmly back on her head, making the sad, wilted feathers bob. "She'll hold right enough. Might look a bit old-fashioned, but that's just because I've got a soft spot for the romance

of the seas." She threw a saucy glance at Winn, which he studiously tried to ignore.

Alexa persisted in being vexed. "But it's an airship."

The pirate locked gazes with her. "Don't matter if she sails the seas or the skies, she's wicked fast and near impossible to catch." She obviously loved her ship.

Winn cleared his throat, causing both women to turn toward him. "I thought pirates tried not to be obvious. Kind of hard not to be noticed in a ship like this, with such an unusual crew."

"Didn't know sneaky and male was what you were looking for," the pirate countered. "In my experience sneaky is nice, but fast is better. And these women, they're the most loyal crew I've ever worked with. Besides"—she looked Winn up and down, her gaze assessing and very female—"who are you hiding from?"

"We all have our secrets, Captain."

A small smile curled her lips, deepening the dimple, and she gave Winn a slight nod of acknowledgment. "America's a vast place. Where exactly are we headed?"

"California," Winn said without further explanation.

Le Renaud's eyes widened with appreciation. "Gold country."

Sure, in some parts, he supposed. Winn nodded. "The sooner we get there, the sooner you can find out for yourself."

The pirate captain began shouting orders to her crew. Beneath their feet the ship shuddered, then began to rise into the misty gray clouds, the whopping of the propellers turning to a low hum as they spun faster.

A hatch in the deck opened up, and out popped the head of a crew member clad in a goggled leather hood. She pulled back the hood to reveal damp copper curls and a face that looked so like Marley's that it shocked him. "Captain, we need more water!"

"Bring out the wings!" Le Renaud shouted. Levers on deck were pulled, and with the clank of gears, a huge brass apparatus that looked like bat wings, with long ribs and thin metal sheeting stretched between them, extended from the sides of the ship. Alexa leaned over the edge of the ship, her eyes assessing.

Despite her attitude toward the captain, Winn knew Alexa well enough by now to know that the ins and outs of how the airship worked would fascinate her agile mind. Inventor's heat, they called it—the fevered state the brain reached when an inventor like Marley or Alexa became absorbed by some new idea. He knew the feeling, not because he was in the midst of invention but because of the fevered state she'd created in him. Now was certainly not the time or place, but soon enough he was going to get her alone.

Alexa stared at the wings, trying to take in all the details so she could sketch it down later. "Those are the strips alongside the ship," she murmured, looking at the wings, which connected to the front of the boat in a fan-like manner. They rose and fell slowly through the misty air, the thin metal gathering moisture as they rose higher through the clouds, the ground falling away into a patchwork of roads and country lanes, then fields and farms. Alexa turned back to the captain. "Surely those aren't what keep us afloat."

The captain recognized Alexa's fascination, and her prickly demeanor softened slightly; the topic of the ship diverted her attention away from Winchester. "They don't provide the lift, but they do help us float in a manner of speaking. The metal sheeting catches the smallest amount of moisture in the air, and as the wings rise, they channel the water into the holding tanks through those ports at the base of the wings."

Alexa frowned. She could see the small brass catch basin at the base of the wings. "For steam power."

The captain nodded with approval, then glanced at the closed hatch, where the crew member had now disappeared. "Octavia, our engineer, is in charge of replenishing the metal sodium bars in our chemical thermal engines."

"The sodium reacts with the water and heats it," Alexa said, impressed. She sensed the heat of Winchester's gaze lingering on her, and glanced at him to find his intense blue eyes riveted to her as if he mentally were undressing her right there on the ship's deck. Alexa bit her lip and looked away, profoundly glad vampires didn't blush.

She cleared her throat and gazed at the captain. "But what of the hydrogen byproduct? And how do you keep the sodium from reacting to the air?"

Pleased with her own ingenuity, Le Renaud's smile widened. "We store the metal bars in barrels of mineral oil. It's crude but efficient. The hydrogen is funneled into the large air bladder installed in the ballast holds of the ship during its conversion. It's what provides the lift we need to stay airborne."

A cool, constant breeze caressed Alexa's face as they rose higher into the air. Alexa tapped her finger against the side of the ship trying to imagine it all below her feet, including a possible cabin with a bed, which made tingles race across her skin. She studiously tried to ignore Winchester, but the needs of her body warred with the intellectual pursuits of her mind. "And the steam it produces does what?" she asked the captain.

"It drives the propellers for direction and speed. Ingenious, no?"

Indeed it was. She damn well wished she'd thought of it. So much more elegant than the gas-fueled steam engines on Vladimir's airship. The gentle swish of the metal wings as they cut through the air, their metallic surface streaked

with shining beads of moisture, was accompanied by the hum of the propellers.

Alexa found she had a new respect for the dingy old ship. It was truly an invention worthy of the likes of Sir Marley Turlock.

"And what of the sails?" Alexa persisted, possessed to know every detail so she could record it later, even though Winchester was a constant distraction when this close, with his broad shoulders and sensual smile.

"When the winds are right, they relieve the engines; and when the winds aren't right, they look pretty."

Alexa reluctantly gave the captain a smile. She couldn't help herself. She appreciated both the extraordinary mechanics of Le Renaud's ship as well as the fact that they shared a mutual appreciation for things as beautiful as they were functional. "I would love to see your engines, if I may, Captain."

Le Renaud bent her head. "It would be my pleasure to accompany you and Mr. Jackson below decks."

Winchester cleared his throat. "We've got a long journey ahead of us. Perhaps there may be another time to see the engines after we've settled in?"

Alexa turned and found him focused solely on her, his gaze so intense and heated, it neared a physical caress. A delicious shiver skated over her skin, causing her breasts to grow heavy and sensitive.

Trust me. His simple words made her mind spin with the possibilities.

All thoughts of the engine and potential inventions fled her mind. She glanced back at the captain. "I am a bit tired." She yawned and hid it lightly with her hand just to add legitimacy to the show.

Le Renaud waved her hand with a flourish and gave a small bow. "Another time then. Let me show you your

quarters. Follow me." They couldn't move fast enough for Alexa's taste.

They crossed the decks toward the forecastle of the ship, and tramped down a set of stairs to below deck. Unlike the metal wings, chemical reactor engine, and propellers, this part of the ship had not been updated. It smelled musty, a blend of old wood and lemon oil. The dimly lit wooden hall was so narrow Winchester found he had to turn his shoulders sideways to walk through it without getting himself wedged. The entire time Alexa admired the breadth of his shoulders and thought about what it might be like to have his strong arms wrapped around her.

Le Renaud walked ahead of them, and toward the end of the hall she pointed at a single door. "Here's your berth." She turned her gaze toward Winchester. "Please let me know if *you* need anything."

Alexa stiffened, a red burning anger welling up in her throat at the pirate's unspoken offer to Winn. She kept herself from tearing the captain into little tiny bits. Alexa caught herself. Anger? No. Jealousy. Since when had she ever been jealous because of a man? Never. But then, no man before Winn had made her feel unstable on her own feet. And while she had come to love Ivan in the two centuries they were together as man and wife, their attraction to one another paled in comparison to the white-hot reaction Winchester inspired in her. Unable to pass them in the hall until they entered the room, Le Renaud waited.

Well, she knew how to show the pirate how futile her offers were. Alexa curved her hand around the rough surface of Winchester's strong jaw, reveling in the feel of it, and lifted up on her toes, placing a soft, sensual kiss on his mouth. The touch of his firm, sculpted lips coupled with the rasp of his shadow of a beard ricocheted through her, making her stomach flip and increasing the steady throb

building at the apex of her thighs. His mustache had grown longer, and it now tickled her cheeks.

Winchester pulled back, his eyes bright and hot with need. "Excuse us," he muttered to the captain as he opened the door of their cabin, swept Alexa inside, and quickly shut the door behind them.

The small, well-lit room barely allowed them to stand side by side. Most of the miniscule cabin was taken up by the bed built into the wall, for which Alexa was immensely grateful.

If Alexa had had a heartbeat, it would have been in her throat. As it was her ichor simply swelled and rushed, making every inch of her achingly aware of the very virile man who was staring at her with hungry eyes. His heartbeat, hard and strong, seemed to fill the room and echo the building pulse of need the kiss had started in her.

"Is this a damn game to you?" he growled, looking every inch uncivilized and wild. The porcelain bowl and pitcher on the washstand beside Winn rattled as he brushed past it when he stepped toward her.

"She certainly wanted it to be."

"And what about you, Tessa. What do you want?" Raw sexual intensity radiated off of him in a heat wave that warmed her skin. Alexa fought back the urge to back up a step at the untamed wild power of him, and yet it thrilled her. Instead she lifted her chin a notch and dropped her lashes a fraction. Here in this little room there were no social expectations. No nobles watching over her shoulder, no other Darkin to report her actions.

She'd contemplated for far too many hours exactly what it might feel like to let herself fly free with this man, to feel his hands upon her like a lover. The hairs on her body lifted as a shiver started on her scalp then shimmied down her spine, making her skin heat and her breasts grow taut.

Alexa reached up and pulled the pins from her hair, letting the thick, dark coils and curls of it fall down her back.

His eyes widened slightly, and he swallowed hard. Winn reached forward with a shaking hand and raked his fingers through her hair. "So damn beautiful," he murmured. "I've always wondered what you looked like with your hair down."

"I thought you wondered what I had hidden in my skirts," she teased. She leaned into him so that her sensitive breasts pressed into his chest, finding relief in the rasp of them against him as he brushed his mouth with hers.

A sexy half smile curved his bottom lip, and he wrapped his hands around her waist and pulled her hips toward him. "That too," he growled as he pressed his erection against her.

"You asked me what I want." Alexa rocked herself against the hard ridge cradled against her thigh and right hip, trying to ease the growing ache to feel him. "I want you," she said boldly, grabbing the edges of his jacket and shoving the garment off of him. His eyes grew fever bright in response. "So stop being a gentleman and get this damn corset off of me."

Chapter 22

Winn crushed his mouth down on hers, his tongue sweeping in to tangle with hers in a sensual slide. His stubbled chin abraded her sensitive skin. An unbridled groan of appreciation echoed in Alexa's chest as their kiss intensified. Deep within she contracted with wanting and melted with desire and desperate need, making her body a taut string ready to be plucked by his fingers. The confines of the small cabin made it difficult to maneuver as their arms and hands became a blur. They blindly tried to undress one another in a frenzied rush.

His pack and weapons were hastily discarded. Buttons flew and ricocheted against the wooden walls as she tore at his vest, rucked the shirt out of his pants, and ripped it off of him. He'd managed to undo more than half of the little buttons at the top of her gown, but it wasn't nearly enough, and her corset needed to be done away with. Alexa pulled away from his mind-bending kiss. "This is madness," she panted.

Winn stiffened, his gaze suddenly tortured. "You're not asking me to stop, are you?"

"Gods, no. But there's just too many damn clothes!" She snapped her fingers, and both his and her clothing

evaporated into nothing but smoke, leaving her scandalously and tantalizingly bare against him.

Alexa gasped at the sensation, reveling in the searing heat of his skin and the firm rigid planes of his glorious body. His arms, chest, and back were far more muscular, more scarred than she'd anticipated through his clothing, attesting to his hard, physical life, rather than one of leisure. The dark dusting of hair upon his chest teased her breasts and arrowed down to the hard silken length of his penis, which jutted out proudly.

She grasped it, exploring him with her hands. Winchester shuddered and groaned, tilting his head back and closing his eyes. "My God, are you trying to kill me?"

Alexa gave a throaty laugh. "Rest assured, if you do die, I'll bring you back again so we can repeat the process." Behind the folds of her soft gum tissue, her fangs throbbed and ached for release, echoing the very real needs at the core of her.

Winn growled, lifting her up off her feet, the length of her naked body pressed from mouth to knee against his. As he held her there with one arm wrapped around her waist, his other hot hand cupped the globe of her breast, teasing the nipple into an even tighter bud with the rough pad of his thumb.

"Ummm, more. Just there," Alexa sighed. She felt him smile against her skin, the scratchy surface of his cheek making her skin even more sensitive.

He bent his head, and his mustache brushed the sensitive nub, causing sparks to fly before her eyes, but when he sucked at the hardened peak, then grazed it lightly with his teeth, shocks of pleasure rippled outward, causing Alexa to arch. She made an incoherent sound deep in her throat that dissolved into panting. Every sound seemed louder, from the thud of his heart to the whisper of his lashes against her skin. Every sensation amplified a hundredfold as her world

coalesced into a single focal point of the man who held her like a precious bit of porcelain in his arms.

"Not fair," she murmured.

"I think it's completely fair. You've only tortured me for several days," he chuckled.

She squirmed in his arms, forcing him to let her down. The long, sensual slide of her slick skin against his only escalated her desire, turning her body into one throbbing beat that matched his roaring pulse. Alexa gazed up into his chiseled face. "When have I tortured you?"

"Every time you walked in front of me, with those damn skirts swaying. When we had to crawl through the tunnel, and I had that exquisite bottom of yours in front of me but couldn't touch it." He reached down and cupped her rear in his hands to illustrate his point.

"Umm, what else?" Alexa said as she went up on her tiptoes to make it easier for him. His fingers traced the seam along her bottom until they encountered the warm liquid core of her, slick with need.

He groaned, closing his eyes.

"You were saying?"

"Every breath I've had to take, saturated with the scent of you."

He slipped a finger into her, and Alexa trembled at the sensation of him touching her swollen flesh in the slow, rhythmic motion, making her feel suddenly hollow and ache for the feel of all of him. "You do rather breathe a lot," she murmured. "And with every beat of your heart you've tortured me as well." Her bloodlust, so closely tied to her physical desire, raged beneath her senses, carefully controlled but begging for satisfaction.

He opened his eyes a crack and kissed her, his tongue sliding in and out against hers in a mimic of his clever fingers, laving her fangs. Each suck and pull at her fang might

as well have been at the small bud hidden within her folds, for she felt them both equally.

She broke apart from him, unable to keep the red haze from seeping into her vision. "See, you're doing it right now."

"How?"

"Do you have any idea how sensitive fangs are?"

His mouth tipped up in a lopsided, cocky grin. "I do now." And to prove his point he kissed her thoroughly, paying special attention to her fangs. Alexa shuddered under the onslaught, desperate to quell the throbbing ache that demanded she take him.

He pulled back and gazed at her, adoration in his eyes, making Alexa's heart swell. Men had always looked at her, but none had made her feel she was precious to them—not for her title, or what she owned, or even for what she could give them, but simply for being her.

"I've been nothing but a gentleman," he teased.

Alexa grasped the hard silken length of him in her hand, her finger sliding up and over the glistening tip. "Is that so?"

Winn thought he might disgrace himself right then and there, with her soft hand stroking from base to head, making him buck. "Unless you say different," he amended quickly, sucking in a breath, then blowing it out slowly.

She was exquisite. Her supple body and skin were smoother and hotter than any shot of whiskey, inflaming him to the point he thought his brain might actually fry.

He realized with a jolt that the jasmine scent of her, so dark and mysterious, was not some artificial scent applied to her skin or some expensive soap or cream, but her own

natural arousal, which made him inhale even more deeply. "You are like no one else I've ever seen."

She pushed against him, far stronger than he'd anticipated, as fragile and graceful as her long limbs were. The edge of the bunk caught against the back of his knees, causing him to topple to the blue wool blankets.

Alexa climbed over him, a knee on either side, and straddled him, pressing the wet heat of her against his penis. "And when have you ever seen a vampire like this?" she asked with a saucy toss of her head and a roll of her hips, her creamy breasts, with their pale pink pearls at the tips, thrust out for his touch.

He hissed at the silken slide of her. The tease worked in reverse, ratcheting her own need further and causing her mouth to part. He reached up and stroked her smooth cheek, his eyes lingering on the rosy, bee-stung lips swollen from their ardent kisses, the twin white points of her fangs. "It's not because you're a vampire," he said as he lightly touched one of the fangs with the tip of his finger, "it's because you're you."

He lost all ability to think the moment she took hold and slid the tip of him into her heated folds. Her body closed around his with a slick heat that seared away all pain, all worry, all honor or duty. Only the two of them existed in this little corner of paradise. The throbbing ache that had been building in his groin now consumed his entire body. Each pulse washed through him like one enormous heartbeat even in his fingers and toes.

She rocked her hips, indulging in the slow slide of him. Winn grasped the delicious curves of her, letting the heels of his hands rest against the flair of her hips. They matched their rhythm to one another, a dance of desire, neither wanting to finish. But the song became more frenetic.

"Winn," she groaned. "Will you let me?"

She ground against him. The pleasure overrode the fear and rendered his judgment useless. He knew she wanted to feed from him, and Pa forgive him, he wanted her to. "Taste me," he begged, wanting to pleasure her as much as she had him.

She leaned into him, her slick breasts rubbing against his chest as she moved with him inside of her. Alexa nuzzled his neck, her soft, warm tongue licking a hot path, before she sank her fangs into him, slowly, completely, just as he had sunk himself to the hilt into her. Pleasure, pure and potent, flooded his system like a flow of heated honey, viscous and thick, making his heart pound and sparks dance before his eyes. Her in him and him in her created a circle of living, sparkling energy and ecstasy. He felt the flow between them, the exchange of more than just pleasure, but of soul. Winn cried out as her body shuddered and arched above him, driving him over the edge of the blessed abyss with her.

For the first time Alexa knew utter bliss. Her fangs retracted, and she kissed his neck, laving the twin indentions in his skin so they would heal faster.

She'd never fed like that from a mortal in the midst of sex, where there was more than blood or carnal lust involved, but actual devotion as well. It was both a heady and humbling experience. While he hadn't said he loved her, he'd given himself to her in every way possible. His life force, strong and powerful, circulated in her veins like a sparkling aphrodisiac. She collapsed, utterly boneless upon him, their sweat-slicked skin fusing together, his warm breath in her hair as he stroked her skin gently with the tips of his fingers. He rolled them side by side, holding her in his arms. Her skin was tender from the burn of his whiskers, but it made her feel alive. So very alive.

Alexa gazed up into his face. The blue of his eyes was soft and distant like an endless, tranquil sea. "Why did you let me feed?" she asked softly.

He touched her lips with his fingers, slowly caressing the bottom one. "I would do anything for you." He kissed her tenderly.

Warmth unfurled inside Alexa's chest, infusing her entire body, but not the heat of bloodlust or even something so mundane as passion. It was more than that. It was the surety that she loved this man without reserve and would follow him to the Gates of Nyx itself to stand by his side.

Her fingers plied lazy circles through the whirls of his chest hair. "So why is it I couldn't read your thoughts when we first met?"

He tugged her hand, moving it down the sheet until it met the firm ridge of his slick erection. "Can you tell what I'm thinking now?"

Alexa nipped him on the shoulder, and his pupils dilated. "I was being serious."

Winn's chest rose in a heavy sigh. "My pa taught me how to block Darkin when I was very young." She edged closer, letting her bare breasts press against his side. "What else did he teach you?"

"I was loading shotgun shells for him by the time I was three, and shooting my own shotgun by the time I was five." His fingertips lightly traced down the narrow channel on her back, following her spine, then slid back up again.

"How old were you when you first killed a Darkin?"

"Six."

So young. "You never even had a childhood, then."

"Nope."

"And the rest of your family, were they trained as well?"

"Everyone but my mother. She was innocent." He stiffened slightly beneath her, but her body recognized the same paralyzing fear that had frozen her solid when she'd

realized Ivan's tortured screams had stopped because he was irrevocably gone.

"What happened?" she asked softly.

"It was an accident. Least that's what Pa kept sayin'."

"But you didn't believe him."

His gaze connected with hers. Pain and anguish swirled in those dark blue depths, along with a heavy dose of self-loathing. "I shot her. I killed her. My mother died because of me. I was aiming for a demon, and he vanished, leaving her to take the bullet."

She didn't argue. It would have been pointless. Just from the look on his face, she could tell that no one could convince him he hadn't been responsible for her death. "How old were you?"

His gaze became unfocused as he looked away. "Twelve."

Alexa gently brushed at the thick fall of nearly black hair that hung heavy over his brow. "No matter what has happened in the past, Winn, you can only go forward."

He nodded, but it was stiff and slow, an automatic reaction, not agreement. He leaned into the touch of her hand, seeking solace. "You can't take something like that back. Not ever."

"Do your brothers know?"

Winn slowly shook his head. "And they ain't ever gonna know. It was mine and Pa's secret."

A small shimmer of hope sparkled in her chest. He'd trusted her enough to share something he hadn't even told his brothers. "You're still a good man, Winn. No matter what you've done."

"The measure of a man is his actions."

"Who else would take on what you have to try and save the world?"

His mouth tipped up at the corner in a heart-stopping half smile that made her want to kiss him hard and feel his touch on every inch of her skin all over again. "You're

something else, you know that?" He tenderly brushed his fingers through her tousled hair.

"I love you," she said as she kissed him. "Truly, deeply."

His eyes darkened a shade, the pupils growing slightly larger. There was not a thing about him she would change. Not now. Not ever. Just as he was—scars, sordid history, questionable occupation and all—she loved him.

"People who love me have a tendency to wind up dead."

She gave him a teasing smile. "Well, we've already solved that little problem then, haven't we?"

His bottom lip trembled a bit, and his eyes softened with memories. "I suppose we have."

A heavy thump jolted the ship so hard that it almost knocked her off the bed. Winn's strong arm anchored her firmly to his side. He bolted upright and peered out the porthole by their bunk. "Damn. Looks like Frobisher's found us."

"Let me see." Alexa scrambled up, holding the coverlet to her nude body as she strained to look out the porthole as well.

There beside them was a dirigible, with the flag of England emblazoned on her side in big and bold red, white, and blue. There was no mistaking the man who gripped the rails. From the angle of his shoulders and the glint of his goggles, Alexa would never forget him.

There was a crackle of static, then a loud voice echoed across the decks of Le Renaud's ship, rattling the wooden walls of their cabin. "Surrender the Slayer and vampire to us, or I will knock your ship from the sky."

Chapter 23

Winn stared out the porthole at Frobisher's dirigible. "That bastard's sure persistent," he muttered.

He glanced at Alexa, clothed in nothing but a white sheet, her hair a mussed, delectable dark cloud about her head. Danger was at their door, and the cabin was still saturated with the scent of her and their lovemaking. He would have liked time to stand still, returning to the point an hour ago when nothing but the two of them existed in the world. But that wasn't going to happen. Not now.

"If you were working for Queen Victoria, you'd likely be persistent as well," Alexa said dryly, smoothing back her tangled hair.

"I got bigger fish to gut than Frobisher." Winn gritted his teeth as a memory of Rathe's yellow eyes and mocking slash of a smile stabbed at him. Frobisher was a gnat on his ass. It was Rathe that posed the danger. "Get dressed."

She raised one dark brow. "You're not seriously thinking of going with him?"

How could the woman look both regal and shocked when she was bare naked? "You got a better plan to keep these people from being scuttled at five thousand feet?" He was the only man onboard, and while Winn presumed they

knew what they were about, every male fiber of his being resisted standing back to find out what they knew about defending themselves.

The smell of gunpowder and burning wood wafted through the cracks of the walls. High-pitched screams were mingled with the thump of running feet on the upper deck and the squeal of cannons being rolled into place.

"I could come up with something if I had more time."

"Time is the one thing we don't got," Winn said as he looked for his clothes. His fuzzy brain actually remembered that what she hadn't shredded of his clothing, she'd vanished into a cloud of particles. "Where'd you put my pants?"

A deafening explosion rattled the ship and was immediately followed by the high shrill whistle of a cannonball. The ship jolted with the hit, knocking them back on the bed. Winn tried his best to brace himself so he didn't crush her.

"I see he don't play fair either," he growled as he stood, pulling her to her feet and admiring her naked body and hating that they had no more time. They needed to dress quickly.

"Or give time for a lady to properly don a corset, so I'm afraid this shall have to do." Alexa snapped her fingers and materialized them both fresh clothes.

Winn looked at his familiar duster, the clean black pants, crisp white shirt, and blue and black paisley vest complete with gold pocket watch. It was nicer than anything he could have pulled on out of a tangled pile of clothing from the floor. "And my hat." His Stetson appeared on the bed beside him, and Winn snatched it up and shoved it on his head. "Thanks." He grabbed his weapons and the pack with the Book and Marley's note. "Ready?"

Alexa sat up, her long, silky limbs now swathed in rust bombazine, her hair coiled back into the familiar intricate

twist at her nape, just above the high, black lace-trimmed collar of the gown. She adjusted her bustle and nodded. They hurried out of the cabin, and, just as they reached the deck, more explosions sounded from the direction of the dirigible.

The shots fired across the deck, shattering the aft mast. With a great, creaking groan the wood splintered like a falling tree. A tangle of rigging and sails began to topple toward the deck, causing the crew to scatter and scream. Winn shoved Alexa up against the wall of the ship's forecastle, shielding her from the falling debris.

"Return fire!" Le Renaud yelled over the chaos. Rifle fire from the *Circe* was punctuated by two chuffs from atop both the forecastle and the aftcastle. Winn watched two deadly metal-tipped harpoons arc over the airspace between the two ships. But his heart sank as he saw them both come short of piercing the dirigible's balloon.

He grabbed Alexa's hand and kept low, avoiding getting shot as they skirted the debris on deck and headed straight up the stairs of the aftcastle to the captain. Winn gripped the captain's shoulder. "I thought you said this ship was fast."

Le Renaud glared at him, but her eyes were troubled. "It is when they haven't just shot our engine out from underneath us! Our engineer is working on it now."

"Use whatever steam's in the pipes to run the propellers and jettison your hydrogen!" Alexa urged. "I know the capabilities of a class A dirigible. They're quick, but difficult to maneuver quickly. This vessel is more nimble. We might escape them if we can descend fast enough."

Le Renaud nodded her head once, her eyes growing bright again. "It might just work." She leaned over the railing of the aftcastle and shouted down at her crew. "Raise the sails! Dive!"

Winn was astounded by the pace of the crew. They fairly

flew over the decks and hauled on ropes to roll up the sails. "You'd better hold on!" the captain said as she gripped the railing with white-knuckled hands.

He pulled Alexa close, took off his hat and stuffed it in his shirt, and wrapped his arm around the railing. The *Circe* creaked and let out a tremendous belch of hydrogen, then began to tip precariously. The entire deck shifted as the nose of the ship dipped downward, and they began to plunge through the air.

A funny swooping sensation hit Winn in the groin as they went into a free fall. Air whistled by, and the clouds became streaks of white as they dove. Winn held onto the railing by one hand with a death grip, and Alexa with the other. They broke through the cloud cover to see an iron gray sheet of sea churning below them. Alexa cried out, and he held her tighter.

"Hold on the air bladder! Release the sails!" Le Renaud yelled. The crew released the sails, and for a moment they flapped wildly before they swelled upward, catching the wind like wings. The ship jerked upward, sending them all sprawling to the deck. It wasn't rising, but its descent was instantly slowed.

They gradually leveled out, coming to rest with a splash on the water. Alexa grabbed hold of Winn hard around the middle. "Easy there, Tessa. We made it," he said softly, rubbing his hand in soothing circles over her back.

She pulled back and looked up at him with terrified eyes, her skin looking a little greenish. "Yes, but now we're stranded at sea, which is even worse."

"Ship incoming, Captain!" One of the crew pointed to the silver bullet breaking through the clouds and headed in their direction, and damned if they weren't sitting ducks.

"It can't be." Alexa bit her lip in frustration and thought.

Winchester wrapped his arm around her. "It was a good plan."

"Just not good enough," she retorted. Winn realized that far from being frightened she was angry.

"Captain Le Renaud, isn't there any way we can get this ship underway?" Her tone was short and irritated.

The captain shook her head. "We've used all our steam reserves. Until Octavia can patch our water basin, our engines can't run. We're at the mercy of the winds to reach land."

The shadow of the dirigible grew larger over the water, making it look like a giant monster awaited them in the deep waters, when really the threat was from above them.

"Get me something white," Winn said harshly. "I don't want him sinking this ship before you can get to land." Everything in him hated to surrender, but there was no choice. With the exception of him, the ship was populated by women. Frobisher was single-minded in his pursuit and had already proven he didn't give a damn about the ship or its crew as long as he got what he wanted. A crew member handed him a white bit of sheeting.

"Do what you must, and I'll be by your side," Alexa said.

Winn glared at her. "I'm not letting him get his hands on you again. You'll stay here."

Alexa glared back. "No, I won't." Her face began to warp, brows protruding slightly; her eyes turned a glaring red as her fangs appeared. "I'm just as capable of fighting him as you are."

Winn couldn't deny that she was absolutely right. As a fighting vampire she could be formidable. "If it were only you, I'd agree"—he glanced back at the crew of the ship—"but ask yourself, do you want the rest of them risking their lives for us?"

"We could defend them," she retorted.

"We could get them accidently killed," he volleyed back. Alexa let out a growl of frustration, her brows and

fangs receding but her eyes remaining crimson. "Fine. We'll go with him. Together."

"Captain Le Renaud, we will give ourselves up for you and for the sake of your crew. Flee if you are able."

The captain nodded, her pixie face serious and brows drawn tightly together as she stared at Alexa's fangs. "Wave the flag," she said, her tone somber.

Winn waved the white cloth and hoped the lieutenant was a reasonable enough man to know they meant to go willingly, before he took it out on Le Renaud's ship.

The dirigible, far more enormous than the ship, hovered over them like a bird of prey, not more than twenty feet above the ship's remaining standing mast.

"Prepare to be boarded," a booming voice called down to them. They must have used an amplification device similar to Alexa's invention, because after having met Frobisher, Winn sincerely doubted the man was capable of such imposing volume.

A rope ladder unfurled down the edge of the dirigible's gondola and landed with a smack on the *Circe*'s deck. Two men, accompanied by the lieutenant, lowered themselves. They stood at attention as their commander stepped forward, his face almost nose to nose with Winn's. The invasion of his personal space didn't sit well with Winn, but unlike his little brother Colt, he'd mastered his temper enough to know how to hold it back when need be.

"We meet again, Mr. Jackson. I understand you evaded my men in Paris. But you'd be amazed how easily a little torture can induce people to loosen their tongues. The priest and barman were most cooperative once we broke through the glamour the contessa placed on them. I can assume you are aboard this ship because you have located the Book?"

Winn ground his teeth and ignored the urge to punch him in the gut. It was a damn shame the same rules that

applied to American Hunters didn't apply to the Brits as well. He would have beat a fellow Hunter to a pulp for things Frobisher had already done.

"You seem to have forgotten our engagement with Her Majesty. Her Highness Queen Victoria doesn't appreciate being kept waiting."

The lieutenant's goggles caught the light, glinting as he stood with his hands behind his back, chest and chin lifted, master of the ship. An Amanarath crossbow was held by each of his men. "Well, it seems the Slayer and the contessa aren't nearly as clever as they believed." His voice had an odd resonance to it, as if there were an echo, slightly deeper, right beneath his regular voice. "You should have known you couldn't evade me."

"It was worth the try." Winn glanced at the dirigible hanging overhead. "You know your queen is not capable of closing the Gates of Nyx."

"Bind him." Frobisher's mouth screwed into a wry smile as one of his men put his crossbow aside and did his bidding. Winn didn't fight, knowing what was at stake. "Where is the Book, Slayer?"

Winn jerked his head toward the pack on his back. "I got it." The truth was, other than when he'd made love to Alexa, he'd never had the Book out of reach.

Alexa stepped up beside him, her chin lifted and her eyes fierce. "And there is no reason we should give it to you, Hunter. You're out of your jurisdiction, and if you try to take it, I assure you I'll bring a full diplomatic redress directly from one queen to another."

The English Hunter raised his hand as if to slap Alexa, and she glared at him defiantly and hissed, her fangs bared. Some of the crew gasped in surprise. He stood his ground. "You're not a queen, yet. If you don't mind your manners, *Contessa* Drossenburg, you'll end up satisfying my curios-

ity about whether vampires can fly when I toss you over the side of my ship."

That damn bastard. Winchester strained so hard against his bonds, the ropes cut into the flesh of his wrists, making them burn.

"How dare you threaten her. You're nothing more than a fancy errand boy. She's nobility."

Frobisher turned, his mouth twisted with malicious satisfaction. "I'm disappointed in you, Mr. Jackson. I wasn't aware that Slayers were so softhearted toward Darkin. Clearly another failing of your countrymen."

Unable to rip him apart, Winn settled for spitting at him. The lieutenant pulled a pristine white handkerchief from his breast pocket and swiped away the glistening trail of spittle on his cheek. "Why Her Majesty cares whether you live or die is quite beyond me. You're no better than they are, Slayer." He jerked his head in Alexa's direction. He spun on the heel of his highly polished boots and stomped back toward the ladder.

Without warning the *Circe* suddenly jerked, her propellers beginning to whop loudly as she started moving faster over the water. A fine spray of seawater began to course up along the ship's sides, and their speed steadily increased.

"Stop this instant!" Frobisher shouted, but no one on Le Renaud's crew heeded his order. He headed for the closest crew member yarding on the lines to the sails, grabbed her hard by the shoulder and swung her about, pulling back his fist, ready to strike her.

Winn barreled forward with a yell and butted the lieutenant aside with his shoulder, sending the man skittering backward on his backside. He glanced back at Alexa. She'd already disarmed both of Frobisher's men and held her cyanide gun on them. Four of Le Renaud's crew gathered

around her to assist in holding the men at bay using their own Amanarath crossbows against them.

The lieutenant rose from the deck and in a slow, smooth move, removed his goggles.

Shock like an electric current rippled through Winn's body.

He'd thought things couldn't get any worse. He'd been dead wrong.

Frobisher's eyes changed from a pale, almost colorless blue to yellow with vertical slits—a demon's eyes.

"Surprised?" Rathe said with undisguised satisfaction. In an instant Winn recognized the sound of the Darkin's voice echoing beneath Frobisher's as the ship lifted off the water and began to climb steadily into the blue sky and away from the English dirigible.

"Rathe."

"Winchester Cyrus Jackson. How nice it is to see you again."

The rope-like scar across Winn's left thigh throbbed, growing taut. There'd been only two times he'd gone up against a demon face-to-face, and both had been disastrous.

"You may now give the Book to me."

"Never had any intention of giving it to the queen, did you?"

"Oh, Frobisher did. He's still in here, you know, screaming to get out now that he realizes his partnership with me isn't going exactly the way he'd planned. But I find I am enjoying this body very much, and I'm loathe to give it up. After all, so many people trust him so implicitly."

"He gave himself over to you willingly?" Winn asked smoothly, playing for time. His mind spun. There were only so many options. He could grab Alexa and dive off the side of the ship. Out of the corner of his eye he could see the ocean falling farther and farther away as they rose higher

into the sky. By now the drop was getting too dangerous. He could throw his pack to Alexa and she could dematerialize, but wherever she went, Rathe could easily follow, and then she'd have to fight him on her own without his help. As they entered the clouds, a ghostly fog swept over the ship, chilling Winn's heated skin with droplets of moisture and making it difficult to see the crew as they bound the lieutenant's men in chains.

"Since he wanted revenge on Sir Marley Turlock for the loss of his eyesight." The yellow eyes sparkled with malevolent appreciation. "Of course, not every Hunter is satisfied with his lot in life. Many become Darkin once they tire of the fight."

Rathe in his Frobisher bodysuit leaned forward, putting his booted foot up on the rail and resting his forearm atop his bent knee. "Are you growing tired, Winchester?"

Winn glanced at the crossbow Frobisher's man had left propped against the railing for an instant, then locked gazes back with the yellow-eyed demon. Winn shrugged. "Still got plenty of fight in me."

Frobisher's sneer collapsed into a firm, angry line. "Give me the Book."

"*No.*"

The dark vertical pupils widened from slits and took over the yellow of the demon's eyes—a predator ready to pounce. "Now!" he yelled.

All hell broke loose. With a snarl and a yell Frobisher's two men shifted into a large, black wolf and a tall, pointed-eared fae, lunging at Le Renaud's crew. To their credit the surprised women fought back.

The demon's hands moved so fast Winn couldn't follow their movement. He only knew that the instant he saw the Amanarath raised up in Alexa's direction was the same instant he heard the twang of multiple bolts being released. There was no time to think. Winn jumped and dove in front

of her. Hot pain pierced his shoulder as the bolt tore through flesh and nicked bone. Alexa cried out and crouched down beside him, undoing the bindings at his wrists.

"Why did you do that?" she muttered, her voice shaking.

"Silver-tipped bolt would hurt me"—he sucked in a harsh breath—"kill you."

Her eyes turned luminous, golden, like liquid sunlight as she cradled his cheek in her small palm. He glanced up to see both the werewolf and the fae bleeding out on the deck, each struck through the heart with bolts from their own crossbows, fired by the crew. They turned them now upon the archdemon. "Hold your fire!" Winn yelled. "The bolts won't kill him."

Rathe let out a malicious, vile Frobisher laugh that wasn't wholly human, the echoing of his voice overlaid with Rathe's. "Foolish Hunter. Did you really think you could stop me from taking the Book from you once you retrieved it from holy ground?"

Winchester's heart stopped for a beat. Holy hell. Rathe was right. Without Winn's help in removing the Book from Haydn's sarcophagus, Rathe would have had to find another means to extract it from hallowed ground. But Winn, being the fool-headed, take-charge idiot he was, had just had to go and get it. Had to beat Frobisher to the punch. And Rathe had counted on it.

"So you see, now I have you, *and* I have the Book."

"Like hell you do. You're going to have to pry it out of my cold, dead hands."

"Your offer is acceptable," Rathe replied with sick delight. He advanced, but Winn was ready.

With practiced ease he flipped the rifle from his back one-handed, jerked it to cock it, and fired. Frobisher stumbled backward, his chest beginning to bleed, but then kept

coming. Alexa jumped forward to attack him, her fangs bared and face warped into a mask of vampiric fury.

She swiped at Rathe's falsely human face, raking four deep gashes in his cheeks with her fingernails. He hit her hard with a fist to the side of the head, sending her down to the deck. Winn bent low and ran forward, knocking the demon up against the railing of the airship.

While Rathe's powers were limited by the shell he was in, Frobisher was a damn sight stronger than Winn had anticipated. Frobisher threw two quick punches to Winn's solar plexus, making him double over. But growing up on the frontier and dealing with drunken miners and rough-shod gamblers meant he'd learned a fair bit about fighting, the dirtier the better.

Winn jerked his head up hard, coming up right beneath the lieutenant's jaw with the top of his skull, resulting in a satisfying crunch and groan. At the same time, he reached for the bowie in his boot. Winn spun out of range of Frobisher's fists and sliced at the man's belly, trying to gut him with his knife.

Frobisher dodged the blade but came close enough to Alexa to grab her by the hair on the back of her scalp, hauling her against him as a shield. The crew behind Winn gasped, their feet shuffling forward.

"Let her go. This is just you and me," Winn growled.

Frobisher let out a maniacal laugh that made Winn's skin crawl and his wounded shoulder throb like hell. "She has every bit as much to do with this as you have."

"Let her go, and I let you live."

The yellow eyes of the demon flickered. "Frobisher's scared. Too bad I don't give a damn. Do your worst, little Slayer. Let's see what you can dish out before I kill you and pry the Book from your cold, dead hands. That was the bargain, wasn't it?"

Winn shifted, placing the balance of his weight on his

left foot. He gauged the distance, then snapped up his leg and kicked out hard, the heel of his boot snapping Frobisher's head back with a crack.

Frobisher stumbled backward and hit the railing, but as he tumbled, one of his flailing hands grabbed hold of the back of Alexa's dress and dragged her with him over the edge into open air. Eyes wide with terror, she screamed.

"Alexa!"

Chapter 24

Winn sprinted forward, and his fingers touched Alexa's for a mere instant before she slipped beyond his grasp. His stomach dropped as she and Frobisher fell faster and faster.

A great dark cloud billowed out of Frobisher's open, screaming mouth as his frightened eyes turned from demon yellow back to ice blue when Rathe vacated his body. His limbs flailed, clutching nothing but air.

The dense black cloud surrounded Alexa, obscuring her as she and Frobisher fell into the nothingness below. Even after the swirling clouds swallowed them, Winn still heard their cries.

He slumped to the deck, every inch of him exhausted and throbbing with a potent mixture of disbelief, sorrow, and anger. He expected her to poof onto the deck of the ship. But she didn't. Each second slipped by, increasing the cold, numbing sensation that closed in around him, like the fog that surrounded the ship. She wasn't coming back because she couldn't. She was gone. And he'd let Rathe take her to her demise.

The crew were cautious in approaching him. They stood about in a semicircle with somber faces and idle hands. Le Renaud was the first to speak. She knelt beside him, her

hair streaking darkly across the dried blood on her cheek. "You need to get that wound tended to."

She squatted down beside him and began peeling back the bloodied part of his jacket and shirt. "Pierot, get me some water, salve, and bandages," she ordered tersely.

"Aye, Captain!" A blond crew member went skittering below decks to fetch the supplies.

"I'm fine," Winn grunted.

Le Renaud raised a dark brow, her dimple deepening as she flattened her lips into a firm line. "Aye. I can see that. Blood being on the outside's completely normal."

Pierot came back with a bowl of water and a small wooden chest filled with the supplies the captain had ordered. She began to help peel away Winn's shirt. Le Renaud gave her a piercing look. "I can handle it from here." Pierot cast her glance downward and gave a quick nod.

The captain began to wash away the blood that was beginning to crust on Winn's skin and took out a pot of salve and used the glistening ointment to pack the wound. "What can we do to help you?"

"Have you got any whiskey?" Winn said morosely, knowing the alcohol would only dull his pain, but never erase it.

She bandaged the wound with clean linens and pulled his shirt and jacket back into place. "Let me see what I can find." She looked him in the eye and placed a hand on his good shoulder, giving it a squeeze. "I'm sorry you lost her."

Up until that moment he'd held back the pain. With her words it washed over him in a numbing tide. In one fell swoop he'd lost the chance to rid himself of the demon that had plagued him his entire life and save the woman he loved. But that didn't mean the battle was over. He had to get the Book back to Bodie and join his brothers in stopping Rathe from opening the Gates.

The captain got to her feet. When she moved, he spied

Alexa's cyanide gun on the deck. It must have fallen from its hidden place in her skirts when she'd gone overboard. With a shaking hand he grabbed it and held it. The only thing he had left of his brave, inventive vampire. Duty alone dragged him to a standing position.

He eyed the captain. "How far can this thing fly in its current condition?"

"Turlock was able to get it running again, but we'll need more supplies to fix it properly for an Atlantic crossing."

"Who?"

"Our engineer, Octavia Turlock." Winn had thought the woman had more than just a passing resemblance to his friend. Her presence reminded him that he hadn't opened the missive from Marley for the queen, but perhaps he should.

Through the fog on the water, Winn could make out a rim of land, stark white against the edge of the water. "Where are we stopping to get supplies?"

"London. Those are the cliffs of Dover ahead of us. We should make English soil in an hour at most."

Winn pulled at the edges of his mustache. His heart and soul were a gaping wound. And he'd get to them—as soon as the Book was united and the Gates closed. Until then he had to put Alexa and everything she was out of his mind.

He wanted to crawl into a dark hole and grieve. His chest felt restricted by a viselike band of pain.

Focus. "Good," he said grimly. "I've got a call to make."

Alexa didn't know which end was up. One moment she'd been in free fall off the edge of the *Circe,* seeing Winn's agonized face, frantically trying to grab his hand only to feel the sliding, desperate touch of his fingers against hers. The next she'd been caught in a moving cloud of suffocating, oily darkness that threatened to crawl up her

nose and down her throat. She could see and hear nothing, and her equilibrium was beyond hope. She tried to scream, but no sound emerged.

Don't worry, Alexandra Minunet Porter, I have plans for you. The voice in her head made her flesh crawl with revulsion. A demon only used all of a person's name when he or she wished to bind one into servitude.

Release me! her mind screamed.

Release the bait? Rathe's harsh, soulless cackling rang inside her head.

Her feet finally found purchase on something solid, and the oily smokiness around her began to dissipate, turning into the form of the archdemon lord Rathe. She didn't recognize the room, but from the large, glass-like, obsidian throne upon a raised dais, she had an idea this was Rathe's private domain.

The expanse of black marble beneath her feet seemed to float on a lake of molten lava. The red-orange glow of it reflected in the highly polished surfaces of the floor and the throne. While she could see the walls crafted of black volcanic rock, there seemed to be no ceiling, which disappeared hundreds of feet above her into stygian darkness.

"Welcome to my home," Rathe said as he smoothed his immaculate, long-tailed dress coat and sat upon his throne, looking every inch the dapper gentleman out for an evening's pleasure. The only difference was that his snowy white cravat made the tightly stretched, waxy skin on his emaciated face look even more pale and dead, and accented the yellow of his eyes. His dark hair was slicked back, and rubies sparkled like drops of blood at his wrists and in the pin in his cravat. His mouth was a deep, dark slash in his face, just below his blade-like nose.

Alexa's mind raced, trying to think of a means of escape. Winn would move Heaven and Hell to find her. *If*

he believed she was alive. "You think to draw Mr. Jackson here?"

Rathe's chuckle was mirthless, cold, cruel, and slyly calculating. "No, my dear. We are going to pay him a little visit once he is out of range of help from the meddling Hunters in Queen Victoria's court. And then, I will retrieve the piece of the Book of Legend from him. On the night of the dark moon I will open the Gates of Nyx and usher in a new world order. *Mine*."

Alexa lifted her chin. "And what about me?" No matter what Rathe threatened, no matter what Rathe did to her, she couldn't allow Winn to sacrifice his third of the Book. The fate of the world depended on the Chosen's uniting the pieces of the Book, so they could seal the Gates.

His pupils widened like a cat on the prowl. "Yes, what about you, vampire? It's not often that my children are so disobedient and difficult. Perhaps you should be disciplined."

A cold wash of dread sluiced through Alexa's system. In six hundred years she'd seen a lot of Rathe's handiwork, and all of it chilled her to the marrow of her bones. While there were as many archdemon lords as there were archangels, among the Darkin, Rathe had a well-deserved reputation for being the most sadistic and malevolent.

She'd personally seen him take the heads of his most prized conquests, only to discover later he'd done so merely to decorate his watch chain. Shrinking and gilding the heads, he kept his enemies sentient so he could impose additional pain and anguish on them whenever he suffered from ennui.

From across the throne room she saw his watch chain, gleaming and golden, heavy with living fobs. She placed a gloved hand about her throat as her stomach rolled at the sight. She dragged her gaze back to Rathe's ghastly face.

"Do you blame us for rebelling?" She used her smoothest, most sensual tone. Cool. Unafraid. Regal. Alexa felt none of those things. There were few times in her six hundred years of existence that she'd felt bone-deep, abject fear. Today was one of those days. "Vampires have to eat," she reminded him smoothly. "If you rid the earth of the humans, what shall we feast upon?"

Rathe leaned forward slightly as if her words intrigued him. "And is that what Mr. Jackson was to you, a traveling snack?"

Alexa did her best to keep her reactions in check, every tick, every swallow, so as not to betray herself or Winn. "I was ordered to assist him in relocating our piece of the Book." In years of negotiations, she'd found sticking as closely to the facts as possible earned the best results. She had indeed been ordered by Vladimir to assist Winn, but nothing had been said about falling in love with him.

Deep down in the region of her stone-cold heart, a pang of yearning took her by surprise. For while she had told Winn she loved him, she had never heard the same from him.

"Ah yes, dear Vladimir. I shall have to see that he is burned thoroughly once I've opened the Gates, to pay for leading this little rebellion."

Alexa couldn't stop the shudder that shook her. After seeing what fire had done to Kostick, she could only imagine the horrid suffering that awaited Vlad if the Chosen should fail.

"What if I can help you get the Book?" There was a slim chance that she could help Winn if she could escape. But with her here in Rathe's control, she knew beyond a doubt that he'd use her as an advantage over Winn, jeopardizing their chances at closing the Gates. Winn was so responsible, so utterly devoted to doing the right thing no matter what

the odds, that she knew he'd falter only if her existence or that of his brothers was at stake.

Rathe rubbed his fingers and thumb together. "You wish to make a deal with me?"

Everything in Alexa rebelled against the idea, and she held back the bile surging hard in the back of her throat. "I am a diplomat. Bargaining is what I do."

"Well, you've already proven you won't give me the Book, but you could still be of use to me. What is it you want?"

"I want you to promise that you'll free those imprisoned at Castle Barranoch and won't seek retribution on the vampire court, or on Winchester Jackson."

"That's a high price. What are you willing to give me in exchange?"

Alexa's stomach swished uncomfortably. What did she possibly have that Rathe could want? He didn't care for influence in the vampire court. Couldn't be bothered to consider her servitude of worth. But he liked power. All kinds of power.

"My immortality."

Rathe rolled the little gold fobs on his watch chain as he contemplated the offer. One squeaked in pain, but Alexa averted her gaze. It was all she could do to stand here and bear Rathe's penetrating gaze. Alexa knew the Darkin lord. He wanted power, all of it he could get. If she gave him her Darkin powers, it would add to his own, and in doing so she would become a mere mortal. She'd be helpless against him; worse, she would be a traitor to her own kind, turning her back on the Darkin realm. Heavy burdens for her to bear, but it was a small price to pay if it ensured the safety of the court and of Winn.

Rathe sat forward slightly. "I counter your offer."

Alexa lifted her chin a notch. Negotiations were her specialty, and she'd expected this. "What do you propose?"

"You are an old and powerful vampire so your offer has merit. But I want more."

"What?"

"Once you've given me your immortality, you will accompany me to see the Slayer. *If* he chooses you over the Book, then and only then will I free you."

It was a horrible choice.

"And whether he chooses me or not, you will swear to spare the court, my minons, and him?"

Rathe frowned. "I so swear."

Her chest swelled. Rathe's oath was as unbreakable as were the ancient gods'. Once made, he could not take it back. If she could protect Winn, then he would at least have a chance. She took a moment to pretend to consider the offer. "I accept your terms."

"Excellent." Rathe opened his mouth wide, and the sickening black smoke that stank of sulfur roiled out, coiling about her like a constricting snake. It blocked her ability to see and hear and pressed upon her with such force that it cracked her bones. She cried out in pain as she felt her body being pulled and stretched. The smoke filled her nose and throat, burning, stripping them raw. She'd never dreamed that losing her immortality would cause such unbearable agony. Somewhere in the haze of pain she blessedly lost consciousness.

Alexa woke to find herself curled up in a heap on the cold, black marble floor. Every inch of her body ached, and she couldn't suppress a groan. Then she found her lungs burning as they starved for a breath of oxygen. A loud rushing filled her ears, and Alexa realized with horror that it was her own pulse she heard.

She was truly mortal again.

She leveraged herself up to a sitting position. As bad as

she felt she had to look like hell. She looked at her reflection in the polished floor. Alexa drew back in surprise when instead of her own features she saw another woman's face, with honey blond hair upswept in a simple twist, her blue eyes so like Winn's it caused her chest to constrict with longing. Her clothes were homespun frontier clothing: a rough, brown calico skirt topped with an ivory button-up blouse and a worn, stained apron.

Alexa reached out to the image. She glanced at her hands to find they weren't her own. Instead of elegant fingers with long, neat nails, these were ruddy, rough, with traces of dirt ground into the cuticles. She pulled back her hands, ashamed of them.

"Who is she?" she murmured, only to find to her shock that her voice was no longer her own either, but the other woman's. Alexa grasped her throat gently with her hand. "What have you done to me?"

Rathe smiled, if the deep dark gash in his face revealing black gums and rows of sharp teeth could be called a smile. He steepled his fingers to the bottom of his mouth. "Patience, Lady Drossenburg. You'll find out soon enough."

The spires of London and the face of Big Ben pierced through the dense, low-hanging fog. "Welcome to London," Le Renaud said, an edge of distaste to her voice. The feathers on her broad hat drooped in the moisture-heavy fog and matched Winn's own deflated state.

All Winn saw was another big, dirty city. Too busy, too complicated. The crazy mix of anger, pain, and sorrow left no room for more sensory input, and it made his head, body, and heart ache.

While he knew what he had to do, he had no heart for it. Not anymore. A future bereft of Alexa was hardly a future at all.

Focus.

On the other side of him Octavia Turlock sighed. "I always love seeing that clock," she said softly. Her accent was definitely British. She looked far different without her leather hood and goggles on. Pretty even. The top of her coppery curls barely reached his shoulder. She had a wide, expressive mouth and big, blue eyes and looked so much like his old friend Marley that it gave Winn a start every time he looked at her. But from what he understood, the Turlocks were a large family with connections to the Crown. Other than that, Marley never spoke of them. They'd parted ways when he'd left in disgrace.

Around Octavia's neck hung a simple chain with an oval gold locket. It didn't match her rough work pants, man's shirt, and leather apron and tool belt hanging heavy around her slim hips. She looked awfully young to be the engineer on any ship, let alone old enough to be consorting with a bunch of sky pirates.

"You sound like someone else I know," Winn said absently. He began to wonder if there were more things Marley had never mentioned about his past.

She turned her curious big blue eyes upon him. "Who's that?"

"A good friend named Marley Turlock. You don't happen to know him, do you?"

Octavia gasped and blinked, her hand covering the surprised O of her mouth. "You know him?" Seagulls whirled and cried about the ship as they came closer to the water of the wide river bisecting the city.

Winn gave one nod.

"Where is he? How is he? What does he look like?" She shot off the questions in rapid fire, grasping his arm in her excitement.

Winn held up a hand. "Whoa now. One question at a

time." It was clear enough from her enthusiasm she knew Marley; the question was how. A cousin, perhaps, or a niece?

"You a relation of his?"

Octavia nodded. "I'm his daughter."

That revelation took the starch right out of Winn's knees. He sucked in a breath. "His daughter?"

Octavia bit her lip. "I've never met him."

A squirming discomfort took up residence in Winn's gut. "Does he know about you?"

Octavia stared out at Big Ben. "I don't know. My mum told me about him, but he left England before I was even born." She fiddled with the locket on the chain at her neck, opening it. Inside were two miniature ambrotypes. One of them had a crack across the glass, making it hard to see the image.

"That's my mum," Octavia said, pointing to the image of a flame-haired woman. "And that is my father." Winn looked closer. The man in the image had a head full of dark hair, but there was no mistaking those huge, dark eyes and the stubborn tilt of the chin. It was a younger Marley.

"I'll be damned," Winn breathed. He glanced down at Octavia's face. "You look an awful lot like your pa." And then the thought hit him. She looked a lot like Balmora too. But then so did her mother. Dear God. Marley had fashioned the decoder automaton to look like his wife! No wonder he was so obsessed with it.

A broad smile lit up her face, and she bounced up to the balls of her feet. "Do you know where he lives?"

"Yes, ma'am. You get this ship fixed enough to fly to America, and I can take you right to him," Winn said, then thought better of it. Maybe there was a reason Marley didn't want to see his daughter. Winn stiffened. Too damn bad. If she was his child, he had a duty by her.

Octavia's eyes glistened with welling tears. "Really? You could take me to him?"

Winn gave her a nod and a light pat on the shoulder. "It all depends on how fast you can fix this ship. Is there anything I can do to help?"

"No. We'll need thieves for that," murmured the captain. She glanced at him, bracing her hands on the railing as she looked out across the city.

"Thieves?"

Octavia snickered. "There's hardly a legitimate market a pirate can go to, to obtain pieces for an exothermic chemical sodium engine."

"For something like that you need the Forty Elephants," the captain said as she stood up and glanced at the sails. "Turlock, make sure we're able to land in the Thames."

Octavia bobbed her head. "Yes, Captain." She darted off to the open hatch that led to the engine room.

"Forty Elephants?" Winn asked, bemused. He'd heard of elephants, but never actually seen one, except in pictures from the exotic lands of India.

"They're thieves. Best gang in London at picking up things you want pinched. All women," Le Renaud said with a touch of pride.

"I take it you fashioned your crew after them."

Le Renaud gave him a sly smile, her dimple flashing. "Now whatever gave you that idea, Mr. Jackson?"

"How long will the repairs take?"

"If we find everything we need quickly, and Octavia is fast, which you've now given her reason to be, we could be ready to leave by morning."

Winn straightened. That gave him time to send a coded message to Marley by Morse code, perhaps find out how his brothers were faring, and perhaps drop off Marley's message to the queen. Then he could get himself good and drunk so he could get rid of the growing darkness inside that seemed to be swallowing him alive, leaving nothing

but a gaping hole. Goddamn, he missed Alexa. His eyes burned, and his chest ached as if bruised.

The picture of her wide, frightened eyes, the memory of that last touch as she fell into oblivion, were going to haunt him for the rest of his life. But she was gone, and there was nothing he could do about it now. It was too late.

Winn's eyes narrowed as they neared the river. The muddy stench of it filled his nose. Those he loved ended up dead. It was a goddamn curse.

He gripped the railing, the truth he'd only now realized almost unbearable in its painful weight. He loved her. He loved Alexa, and it didn't matter if she was a vampire, or nobility, or . . . dead.

The ship splashed down easily upon the water of the river, but Winn didn't care. Anger, red and seething hot, began to boil beneath the pain. Right then and there Winn made a vow to himself. He'd see that Rathe paid if it was the last thing he did. For his mother. For Alexa.

Chapter 25

The note Marley had asked him to deliver to Queen Victoria, what seemed like a lifetime ago, scraped against Winn's fingers as he shoved his hand in the pocket of his duster. Marley had packed it in oilcloth to protect it. There was a risk going to see the queen. Maybe Frobisher *hadn't* lied. Maybe the queen *did* want to close the Gates herself to cement the global reign of her empire.

Need, want and *should* were three different things.

She'd *need* all three pieces of the Book to do the job.

Not gonna happen.

She *wanted* to do the job herself. But Her Royal Majesty was hardly capable of battling Darkin. No matter how large and powerful her army. Closing the Gates of Nyx was a job exclusively for the Chosen.

Should he and his brothers capitulate, give the British queen the complete Book, and help her close the Gates? Hell no.

First, the Jacksons had been entrusted on their honor to accomplish this task, and complete it they would. No matter what.

Second, Americans were familiar with going up against

monarchy. It was in his blood. Winn's lips twitched at the thought.

Time was running short. But dressed the way he was dressed, and being an American, he knew better than to march up to the front door and demand an audience with the British queen, not that he even had a clue where to find her.

Winn glanced at Captain Le Renaud gazing out over the rail of the ship as they negotiated their way around the other boats on the river. Her plumed hat hid her features, but her dark curls twisted and the large lapels of her faded military coat flapped in the breeze coming off the water. "What are the chances that your thieves might be able to sneak me in to see the queen and help me send off a message in Morse code?"

She turned and looked up at him, her eyes full of mischief and a touch of pride. "I think it could be arranged. They aren't the best pickpockets, blackmailers, and shoplifters in London without reason. What do you have in mind?"

Winchester withdrew the letter from his pocket. "To give her this."

"Do you want an audience?"

Winn didn't know. Marley hadn't said, and Winn had been a little too busy to read the unopened letter. Things had been too dangerous to care what was scrawled there. While he didn't feel right invading his friend's privacy, now wasn't the time to worry about manners. Since Marley hadn't been privy to the events that had brought Winn here today, the letter might contain something that instead of helping them, could now harm them.

Before he blithely handed over the letter he had to know the contents.

He pried open the flap of the oilcloth and removed the heavy vellum and attempted to decipher Marley's horrible handwriting. Hell. Where had Marley learned to

scribble? The words were illegible! Odd swoops and curls, and straight lines in the middle of what might be words, but could possibly be very small drawings of his inventions.

This missive could possibly change the course of the world, and Winn couldn't read the damned thing. He turned it every which way and muttered, "Damn it, Marley," under his breath.

Le Renaud put out her grubby hand to take the missive and offered, "May I—?"

"I got it." Winn didn't know what the hell was in the thing. As it was he was violating a trust by reading a letter from Marley to the queen of England. It wasn't for anyone else's eyes, although another pair of eyes trying to untangle the swirls and strokes would probably be useful.

On the banks of the river, London was a beehive of activity, and the place stunk to high heaven. Coal-fire smoke, rotting fish, and piss combined in a smell that made his country-boy's eyes sting.

He couldn't wait to get home.

After he read this letter.

After he delivered it to the queen.

After he contacted Marley.

After he closed the Gates of Nyx.

Then he'd go home to mourn the loss of his beautiful Alexa and the dream of building a normal life with her.

Le Renaud leaned against the wall of the aftcastle, putting her booted foot up against the wall. "Read then," she told him.

Winn tilted the page. After a few minutes he concluded that the squiggles weren't some secret blueprint for a new engine design. They were all words. *Illegible* words, but words nonetheless. It was a start.

He made out the words *Balmora, delivery* and *exchange,* but that was about all. He tried half a dozen times to pick out more than a small handful of words, to no avail.

Finally, because they couldn't stand there all day in the stinking river aboard a pirate airship, he refolded the missive and tucked it back in the envelope. He handed the note to the captain. "It's important. Put it right in the queen's hand. Then see this message is delivered to Marley Turlock. Here's the station you'll have it sent to."

Le Renaud nodded. "I'll see to it." She pushed off of the wall and with a fast stride crossed the deck, shouting orders. "Make ready the boats!"

"Aye, Captain." Several of the crew began pulling ropes to lower a skiff down into the water beside the ship and flung the rope ladder over to meet it.

The twisting sensation in Winn's gut hadn't lessened. If anything, it had gotten worse. He grazed his fingers over Alexa's gun in his holster. Rathe would return for the Book. It was only a matter of time. Winn knew he needed more than firepower if he was going to fight him off. He needed a plan.

Winn headed for the hatch that led to the engine room. For his plan to work he needed someone with more ingenuity than he possessed. Someone with a mad genius for chemicals.

He navigated the narrow hall until he came upon a door with a porthole. One glance told him he'd found the right place. The engine took up the bulk of the room, but the other half contained an inventor's wide wooden workbench covered in bits and scraps of glass, copper wire, tubes, and assorted tools. It all looked very familiar. Marley would be right at home here. Winn pushed open the door.

Octavia fiddled with the metal patch she'd welded to the side of the enormous water tank that formed the bulk of the engine, her tongue between her teeth as she worked.

He cleared his throat, and she looked up. "Was there something else you needed before I go into London for parts, Mr. Jackson?"

"Can you booby-trap a book?"

She cocked her head and screwed up her face in thought. "It depends on what I have for supplies."

Winn pulled Alexa's gun from his holster and held it out to Octavia. "Can you do something with this?"

Octavia's eyes sparkled with curiosity as she took it from him gingerly, turning it this way and that in her slender, dirty hands. "What kind of gun is this?"

"A cyanide shotgun. The contessa invented it. The shells contain cyanide salts."

"Cyanide salts?"

He nodded.

She caressed it as she inspected every inch. He'd seen the same spark in Alexa's eyes when she'd seen Tempus, and it made his heart ache.

"What result were you hoping for?" she asked.

"It has to protect this." He pulled the Book bound in oilcloth from his pack and set it down on the wide wooden workbench between them.

Octavia reverently placed Alexa's cyanide gun down on the workbench, then narrowed her eyes in concentration as she unlaced the binding and opened the oilcloth. "Liquid is out of the question; it would damage the pages."

Winn let her mind work, glad she was talking out loud so he could follow along.

"We could sprinkle the pages with the salts. If there's enough moisture on the hands or in the air, it would cause the salts to be absorbed easily through the skin. Although ingestion is the best method—if you're trying to kill someone." Octavia eyed him speculatively. "Who do you wish to prevent from getting his or her hands on this? And the end result of the booby trap?" When Winn remained silent, she asked shortly, "Do you want to deter someone from picking up the Book? Do you want to injure them? Do you want to kill them? It makes a difference in dosage, you know."

"Any of the above. All of the above." He wanted Rathe dead. Anything short of that yet causing him pain was good enough for Winn, too.

"What manner of person?"

He knew she meant male or female so she could adjust the potion for weight and body mass. "An archdemon."

Octavia raised a brow. "Demons?" Her tone implied disbelief. Of course she would think it mad. She was a woman of science and mechanics, not a Hunter.

"They're around. Everywhere. Ask your father, when you get the chance."

Octavia shrugged. "The crew has been talking about the strange creatures that came aboard ship and how the Lady Drossenburg was a vampire. Personally, it doesn't surprise me. I always knew there were things out there we couldn't explain with just science. Let me get my gloves." She rummaged through a wooden trunk beneath the bench and pulled on stained leather gloves. "They'll protect my hands, but make it difficult for intricate work. Could you open the gun for me and pop out a cartridge?"

Winn knew better than to touch the salts within. Alexa had been able to handle the ammunition only because she was a vampire. Anything with living flesh, including an archdemon, would be susceptible to the cyanide; a demon more so to the salt, which would scald and blister his skin like fire, causing it to peel off of him, before it burned deeper.

Winn opened the ammunition chamber and withdrew one of the brass shells. The glass top showed it was filled with white pellets. He handed it to Octavia.

Excitement flared in her eyes. "Fascinating. Rat-shot converted to accommodate cyanide salts. Ingenious."

She laid the cartridge on top of a flap of the oilcloth holding the Book and broke open the glass at the end with a fast tap of a wrench. "Stand back. And don't breathe, if

you can help it. In fact it might be best if you stood outside the engine room."

Winn didn't like leaving the Book where he couldn't reach it, but he retreated to the hallway and closed the door, then he watched through the porthole as Octavia pulled her leather goggled hood over her head.

She smashed the small white pellets into a fine powder, which she then picked up in pinches between her gloved fingers and sprinkled on the pages of the Book. Once she'd used it all she swept the brass end of the cartridge into a trash container and proceeded to fold the oilcloth around the Book.

She removed her goggled hood and gloves and grinned at Winchester, motioning him back into the engine room. "There. All done."

A faint odor of bitter almond he hadn't smelled before lingered in the air. "Can I touch it?"

"The outer edge of the oilcloth, yes. The inside, no. Not without heavy-duty gloves. And whatever you do, don't lick your fingers after you've turned the pages."

Winn didn't like that he'd had to make the pages untouchable, but what choice did he have? Rathe was bound to come for the Book sooner or later, and he had to have some advantage over him.

"Thank you. You're as clever as your father," Winn said softly.

Octavia beamed at him, blushing to the roots of her hair. "If that's all, Mr. Jackson, I'm going to go get parts to fix the ship so we can be on our way as soon as the captain gives the word."

Winn tipped his hat at her and let her pass, then carefully tucked the Book back into his pack. Now, no matter when Rathe came, he'd be ready.

The crew left in groups using a small skiff that ferried back and forth to the shore, leaving him alone on the

anchored ship with one of the crossbows on his back. The evening air smelled of coal smoke and horses, wet cobblestones, and muddy river water that lapped gently against the hull.

From the deck Winn watched the brilliant white light of the arc lamps light up the Thames Embankment. He'd heard of them, but never seen one: tall, moonlit towers constructed of open-framed piping, stretching more than one hundred feet into the sky, causing pools of light nearly as bright as sunlight upon the streets below. Elsewhere in the city gaslights flickered on.

But all of it—the noise, the lights, the smells—made his battered soul long for the quiet of the open desert where a man could feel the stillness and solitude.

What he wouldn't have given to hold Alexa in his arms for a night. To have her sleep beside him soft and warm, her head cradled on his chest. To wake up with her kiss upon his lips and her fragrance on his pillow. But that was never going to happen. She was gone. And he'd never had the chance to tell her the truth.

He loved her.

A ripple of wind washed across the surface of the water, stirring his hair. The stench of sulfur followed. He whipped around searching for the source of it, all senses suddenly on high alert.

"I can fix your pain, you know." Rathe's voice caused Winn's gut to curl up and twist with a slimy, painful feeling, like a slug sprinkled with salt.

Winn grunted as he turned to see the demon standing against the railing twenty feet away. "Kind of hard to believe you'd give a damn about my pain or anyone else's." Winn put one hand protectively on the strap of his pack where the Book rested. The other he placed on the butt of the pistol in his holster. It was loaded with Marley's special silver bullets capable of killing almost anything Darkin.

Anything but a ghost or archdemon. "I don't want anything you've got to offer."

"Oh, but I assure you, you do." A filmy image of Winn's mother appeared directly in front of Rathe, dressed as she'd been the day she died. Her brown calico skirts fluttered around her feet in the breeze, but it was her sweet, loving smile that cleaved him in half. She reached out a slender, work-worn hand. "Winchester."

Her soft, wheat-colored hair glimmered in the arc lighting; her well-remembered blue eyes were filled with love.

He'd never thought he'd hear her sweet voice again, and doing so now made his chest ache and his eyes sting.

His arms ached to hold her, and his feet moved forward instinctively. *Mama.*

No, she wasn't.

He pulled himself up short with every fiber of his being.

She wasn't real. None of it was real. He hardened himself against the blatant trick. It struck too deep on the heels of losing Alexa.

"Give me the Book and I let her live again," Rathe said, a gravelly edge to his voice.

"Winn, please listen to me. I love you," she begged. Her voice only underscored the point; it wasn't quite right, not like he remembered. Sweat prickled his brow and his upper lip beneath his mustache, but he kept the tremor welling up from deep in his core from reaching his hands. Every worthless feeling. Every agonizing second of that day he remembered with clarity, and it burned like constantly dripping acid in his veins. He'd do anything to take back what had happened that day.

Anything but believe Rathe's lies.

There was nothing the demon could offer him to make him give up the Book. He'd sacrifice anything and everything to save the world, even if it was his worst nightmare come true.

"Nice try. But I know you better than that. She's not my mother."

Winn grabbed the crossbow from his back and fired. *Thunk.* The silver-tipped bolt hit the Darkin standing in front of Rathe and flew straight through her shoulder, striking Rathe in the chest.

Her eyes widened with surprise and pain for a moment, and then she slowly slumped to the deck, a bright red spot blooming on the white expanse of her blouse. Behind her Rathe screamed in reaction to the bolt. Grabbing at the bolt with both hands, he struggled weakly to rip it from his body. Black ooze dripped from the hole in his chest.

Winn kept his attention on the agony on his nemesis's face, while his fingers tensed on the trigger as he readied to fire again. Then the filmy image of his mother at Rathe's feet began to dissolve into another form altogether.

His mother's warm honey-hued hair turned darker— first mahogany, then finally to raven black. Her face too morphed, the cheekbones growing more prominent, the nose more aquiline, and the eyes going from vivid blue to a tawny amber color that was imprinted upon his memory like none other.

"Alexa!" Winn's numb fingers dropped the crossbow in his haste to reach her. Without hesitation, he rushed to her side, kneeling beside her. Gently he scooped her into his lap. She was real and solid in his arms. No apparition, not a ghost. He buried his face against her hair, deeply inhaling the sweet, dark spice. Beneath his hand he felt a faint *throb-throb-throb.*

"What the hell?" She had a goddamn pulse!

Rathe chuckled, and Winchester glared up at him, shocked he was still there. The demon clutched at his chest and pulled the bolt, letting it fall to the deck of the ship mired in dark, thick ooze. "I see your aim hasn't gotten any better," Rathe said, his tone mocking and caustic.

Rage boiled up inside of Winn. He tensed, ready to leap up and throttle the demon with his bare hands if necessary, but everything stopped the moment he heard Alexa struggle to suck in a breath. She coughed, bright red blood tainting her lips.

"You're alive!" A mixture of relief and torment flooded his system. Dear God. What had he done?

Her whiskey eyes were hazed with pain, but her tone was pure contessa as she murmured, "For the moment."

Winn used a handful of her skirts to try and staunch the blood saturating her bodice. "Ssh. Don't try to talk."

She winced as he put pressure on the wound. "I bargained with the only thing I had to spare you. My immortality for your survival. He's agreed not to harm you. The rest of Kostick's prophecy is complete."

He needed help, goddamit. Where was everyone? "What do you mean, the rest?"

"I never told you. I told no one. Kostick said that I'd be destroyed by my heart's desire." She coughed, the blood on her lips an alarmingly bright red.

Winchester cursed in Greek, Latin, French, German, and Italian. Never had he felt so damn helpless, not even when he'd held his mother in his arms as her life's blood slipped away. His whole body shook with fear and despair.

He was going to lose her again. And there wasn't a damn thing he could do about it.

"Give me the Book, and you can keep her alive," Rathe said as he cupped a thin, grayish hand to his chest and paced the deck.

Winn had anticipated the Book would be the only thing to keep Rathe's interest. His eyes narrowed. He didn't want to give Rathe the Book. Everything within him, all the years of training beat into him told him not to, but one thing swayed his decision. He'd lost Alexa once, and it had

crushed his will to live. He didn't think he could survive losing her again.

"Heal her first. Then I'll give you the Book."

"Do I look like I was born in the last millennium? Put the Book down between us. Back away, and I'll heal her."

"Swear to it."

Winn knew the archdemon's oath was binding, just as it had been for the gods of the ancients. A Darkin could swindle his or her way through trickery out of a bargain made, but an oath was unbreakable.

"I swear to heal her before I take the Book."

Winn pulled the pack from his back and took out the precious parcel. He slid it across the worn boards of the deck toward Rathe.

Alexa bucked in his lap. She gasped and writhed as black smoke issued from the hole in her chest. Winn held her close, then met her eyes briefly before easing her down on the deck to free his hands.

His gaze flicked upward to see Rathe advancing on the oilcloth-covered Book. *Open it*, he thought hard. *You want to see it. Hold it. Touch it. Feel its magic.*

The pupils in Rathe's yellow eyes widened with anticipation, the black almost wholly swallowing the malevolent yellow. He snatched up the Book and clawed at the oilcloth, eager to strip it away. A garbled, revolting laugh of triumph crackled in his throat past his black gums and pointed teeth as he held the ancient manuscript's vellum pages in his hands.

Suddenly his hands began to smoke, filling the air with the hideous stench of burning flesh and sulfur. Rathe refused to let go, even though his mouth was a rictus of pain as he began to roar, the smoke almost obliterating his hands as they blackened and charred. "What have you done!" he howled.

"Just a little present from me to you."

Winn snatched up the crossbow he'd abandoned on the deck and shot twice more in rapid succession. Rathe dropped the Book and staggered back, staring at the silver-tipped bolts embedded in his chest. He screamed in agony and turned into a twist of oily smoke that shot into the night sky.

"Winn?" Alexa's cracked voice sounded like an angel's singing to Winn. He carefully pulled her back into his arms.

"Alexa." He breathed her name like a prayer and held her, trying to absorb every sensation he could. He gently brushed the dark curls from her face and gazed down into her eyes.

She opened her mouth slightly and brushed her tongue over her dry lips. "You shot me," she murmured.

Winn didn't know whether to laugh or cry. She was alive. Whole. And that was all that mattered. The earth could have opened up and swallowed him, and he'd still be content knowing she was safe once more. "I'm sorry."

Her brow puckered. "Do you have any idea how much that hurts?"

He chuckled and rolled his injured shoulder. He knew exactly how it felt. It stung like hell. "You aren't going all soft on me, are you?"

"What if I was?"

He glanced at the bloody hole in her shirt and saw smooth unblemished skin beneath it. He wanted to kiss that patch of creamy skin and then continue onward from there. His gaze connected with her golden one. He was never going to get tired of looking at her. "I'd say I'll have to keep an extra close eye on you out in the wilds of the frontier."

"Damn."

Winn quirked a brow, questioning her.

"I was hoping you were planning to keep your hands"—she leaned up, wound her arms about his neck, and kissed him—"and your mouth on me."

Winn couldn't stop himself from smiling. "You know I think I could manage that once this whole nasty business of closing the Gates of Nyx is over."

He looked deeply into her eyes, trying to talk to her with his mind. He didn't know with her vampire powers gone if he even could, but the look in her eyes told him everything he needed to know. Vampire or not, Alexa would follow him to the ends of the earth and beyond.

They were stronger together than apart. "Are you certain you want to come to America? I can't offer you anything like the luxury you're accustomed to. It's rough and rugged, and there's snakes—"

Her nimble fingers brushed across his lips, silencing him. "It's where you are, and that's enough for me." She swept his hair off his forehead, a smile curving her full lips, making him crazy to kiss her again. "I'm not a vampire, or a contessa any longer. I'm just your Tessa."

He kissed the tips of her fingers. "All I ever wanted was you."

She bit her lip and gazed up at him, her eyes full of appreciation and desire. "Promise?"

"You have this Hunter's promise," he whispered, his voice tight with longing, "and my love."

"Do you think we have a chance to stop Rathe?"

"We do, if we do it together."

Her eyes turned bright, full of fierce determination. "Then let's go slay a demon."

He chuckled and kissed her. "You're starting to sound like a Hunter, Tessa."

"You have to be careful of the company you keep. It can be a terrible influence, you know."

The odd whisper of metal against metal drew Winn's gaze away from her for an instant. A mechanical bird, each silvery feather a meticulous and artistic impersonation of

the real thing, perched on the rail of the deck and stared at Winn with glowing blue eyes. "What the—"

Alexa twisted, her eyes narrowing. "It's a clockwork carrier pigeon. A Turlock original, by the look of it."

A miniature door in the creature's breast slid open, revealing a small letter sealed with red wax. The bird bent, grabbed the missive, and held it in its shining copper beak, the door in its chest closing with a *clink*.

Winn reached out. A moment after he took the letter, the bird chirped once, then flapped its wings and rose into the air, darting like a silver bullet into the sky.

Small, neat handwriting slanted over the front surface of the pristine white paper. *Mr. Winchester Jackson*. The red wax on the back bore the oblong seal of the crown atop a shield surrounded by a belt bearing a Latin phrase.

Alexa sat up with a hiss of breath, her eyes widening. "That's the seal of Her Royal Highness Queen Victoria."

Carefully Winn broke the hard wax and opened the letter to find it was merely a single sheet wrapped around another sealed note, this one addressed to Sir Marley Turlock.

"Well, what does it say?" Alexa said, her tone underscoring her impatience. She leaned in closer, her breast brushing against his forearm, making him momentarily forget all about letters, mechanical birds, inventors, or royalty.

His whole world narrowed down to focus on Alexa. Just Alexa.

"Winn?"

"Yeah."

"The letter?"

He glanced down, smoothing the paper in his hand. "She thanked us for our service to the Crown. Apparently Frobisher's been using the Royal Hunters for his own purposes for some time, and she wasn't sure how to rein him in short of an all-out battle."

Alexa sighed and rolled her eyes. "Surely that's not all."

Winn shrugged. "Your people have been released at Castle Barranoch. She asked me to deliver the enclosed message to Marley. Something about supporting a critical mission."

"Are you going to open it?"

He cracked a smile. "You know me; I'm not the type to go looking for trouble. We'll have enough once we get back to Bodie and have to close the Gates."

Her full lips tilted up in a way that made all his aches, scars, and pains, old and new, fade away completely. "You don't have to look for trouble. It seems to find you."

He pulled her close, taking extra care with her injured shoulder, fully aware that, despite her mortal state, she was still just as full of fire as she'd been the day he'd met her. She was strong and smart, beautiful and inventive, his Tessa. In short—the perfect woman for a Hunter like him. "And will you be right there beside me when it comes around?" he asked softly.

Her gaze, full of acceptance and admiration, fixed on his. "There's no place else I'd rather be."

a playground that opened onto Marlboro Pike Road. It was thirty-five minutes to National Airport.

After letting the engine warm up Karl parked the motorcycle where he would need it for his getaway. Back inside the Winnebago he removed the Redeye from its case, installed the cylindrical battery and checked the voltage. The missile was ready. Finally, Karl brought out the CIKOP-34F radio in its Sony housing. The radio had multi-channel reception, which allowed him to access three channels at once. He tuned in Andrews Air Force Base approach, tower and ground control frequencies. It was eight-thirty. The General Secretary had one more hour to live.

CHAPTER

34

ELIOT INGERMAN ARRIVED AT THE SECURITY command post at Andrews Air Force Base at seven-thirty. The command post was a small room on top of the terminal that had a good view of the runway and arrivals area. Ingerman could see the Russian leader's special limousine, flown over from Moscow, along with a rank of government cars. Reporters and cameramen were setting up near a roped-off area, and at the periphery were the ubiquitous television vans with their dish antennae pointed at some distant relay station. Everything looked normal for such an event, calm and under control.

And then Paul Stafford called from Glenway Hospital. His wife had regained consciousness and corroborated what Paul had told them before: Karl Alexander was in Washington and had kidnapped Joanna.

Ingerman remained deliberately calm.

"That's very interesting, Mr. Stafford," he said. "Particularly since we confirmed last night that Karl Alexander is at a training camp in the Soviet Union."

"Confirmed? How? Did anybody see him?"

"I assume someone talked to him—"

"Not unless it was a local call. He's here and I'm betting he has a Redeye and is going to use it on the Russian—"

"I'm also informed that a Redeye missile has no chance of success against the Soviet air-defense screen."

"According to whom? The same guy who talked to my brother last night?"

Stafford's certainty worried Ingerman more than he wanted to admit.

"Your wife," he said. "Is it possible to talk to her?"

There was a pause. "Are you saying you don't believe me?"

372

"I'm not saying anything beyond the obvious and that is that Karl Alexander can't be two places at once. It would help if I could talk to your wife."

"Then you better talk to the doctor."

The doctor refused to let Ingerman talk to Joanna Stafford directly but agreed to relay one question and one answer. Ingerman wanted to know if Joanna was positive that her husband's twin brother was in Washington. The answer was a definite yes. Ingerman asked to talk to Paul again.

"He's gone," the doctor said,

"Gone where?" Ingerman demanded.

"I have no idea. Mr. Stafford is not my patient, his wife is. If you'll excuse me . . ."

It was Ingerman's worst nightmare come to life: two pieces of absolutely critical and absolutely contradictory evidence. He had a half hour to decide whether to switch to the Dulles option, with all the attendant publicity that would involve. Of course, an attempt on the Russian leader's life, no matter how easily defeated, would mean worse publicity. He cursed softly and Colonel Coswell looked over.

"That was Stafford?"

Ingerman explained the situation but Coswell seemed unconcerned. "The Russkies say the Redeye is non-deliverable. You should hear the old air marshal—he acts like he'd welcome an attack just to show what Soviet counter-measures can do."

Ingerman's stomach was churning. He had no intention of letting the Russians prove they could fend off an attack that the U.S. wasn't able to prevent.

"We've got no choice," he said. "We're going to have to go to Dulles and I'm going to have to explain it to the President."

He moved to the phone.

"You serious?" Coswell asked.

"What else can we do? Flip a coin to see if Karl Alexander is in Russia or out there on Interstate 495? I'd rather deal with the Dulles repercussions than chance an attack. Unless I'm overruled."

Coswell turned a weather eye to the runway as Ingerman picked up the phone and asked the Comlink operator to connect him to the White House.

"You know," Coswell said, "this runway is almost ten thousand feet long and the winds are less than seven knots. That's not too much of a tailwind component for an Ilyushin 62."

Ingerman frowned and told the operator to hold the line. "What are you suggesting?"

"If there *is* anybody out there with a missile, they're going to be positioned for aircraft landing on Runway 19. Seems to me the simplest solution would be to switch directions. Have them land on Runway 01."

Ingerman looked out the window.

"Where's that?"

"Right there. It's the same piece of concrete but each end has its own runway designation."

"You mean switch the direction they'll land?"

"Right."

Ingerman replaced the phone.

"We can do that?"

"It's not recommended. You land with the wind behind you and it takes longer to come to a stop and wears out the brakes. But we've got ninety-seven-hundred feet of concrete here and with winds less than seven knots an Ilyushin shouldn't have much problem. If there's some guy out there in the bushes, we leave him with his thumb up his ass watching the wrong side of the sky."

The more he thought about it, the more Ingerman liked the idea. It seemed simple and foolproof. And it avoided any negative political repercussions.

"Okay," Ingerman said, "let's see if we can clear it with the Russians."

The plan was simple but not, as Ingerman imagined, foolproof. The emergency vehicles at Andrews, the crash trucks, were routinely positioned one-third of the way from the approach-end of the runway. When the runway designation was changed, the crash trucks were notified of the change over the ground control frequency, one of several channels that Karl was monitoring. He was adjusting the mirror at the rim of the sunroof when the call came through:

"Attention all ground vehicles, Andrews active runway is now changed to Runway Zero One. Repeat: Active runway designation is now Zero One. Confirm by station."

When Karl realized what they were saying, he sat down at the dinette table and turned down the volume on the other two channels. One by one, each unit acknowledged the change.

"Crash 3, positioning Zero One."

"Crash 4, on the way to Zero One."

"Crash 5, uh, I don't know what the winds are like for you guys but from where I sit, they're still from the south."

"Winds are two one zero at five," the ground controller confirmed. "Be advised that Summit One will be landing downwind."

An unidentified low voice growled, "Ain't that just like a Russian."

Karl jumped up. It was almost nine o'clock. He had barely half an hour to change his position to the launch site south of Andrews, a housing development called Linwood Acres. He shoved the motorcycle back inside the Winnebago, covered the Redeye with a blanket and took off.

Why? The question dogged him as he manuevered the cumbersome motor home down streets that suddenly seemed clogged with traffic and stop lights. Why had they changed runways? Airplanes always landed into the wind. Always. It didn't make any sense for them to change the procedure, not unless they knew.

The thought that the mission might be blown was too much to accept. But if it were, something must have gone wrong in Moscow. It hadn't come from him. The only loose end he'd left was his brother, and even if Paul escaped the jail in Berlin, he knew nothing of the Redeye mission.

A less ominous possibility occurred. Perhaps the Americans were doing this as a precaution—a last-minute change in plans to avoid just such an attempt as this, however unlikely . . . As he approached his destination Karl became mired in a traffic jam. With time critical, he was suddenly bumper-to-bumper on a country road that led to a small suburban neighborhood tucked into the woods.

Then he saw what was causing the delay. Up ahead a number of cars were turning into the Piscataway Golf Course. A sign at the entrance announced: "Memorial Day Tournament." It was the damned holiday. He made a mental note to take the opposite direction when he left.

After he passed the golf course the road became clear. Oddly enough, it was clear in both directions; he would have expected an equal number of cars coming the opposite way. A moment later he saw why. A police car was blocking the road.

Karl felt in his jacket pocket for the Smith & Wesson. He had two shots left and there were two officers standing at the car. As he stopped, one of the policemen stepped over to the Winnebago.

"Are you a resident, sir?"

"What's going on?"

"Only residents of Millsford and Linwood Acres beyond this point. I've got to see a driver's license or some proof of address to let you through."

Karl thought quickly, remembering a street name from his earlier reconnaissance.

"I'm visiting the Wilsons on Arrowhead Drive."

"Well, you'll have to call and get them to come meet you. Or have a cup of coffee somewhere and we'll be out of here around nine-thirty."

"What's it all about?"

"Who knows? They just want the road closed. But if you want my guess, it's the Russians. They got their head honcho coming in to Andrews today."

Karl turned the Winnebago around, trying to remain cool, trying to consider his options. The land at this end of the Air Force Base was rural and wooded. Could he park the motor home and hike through the hills? He doubted that there was enough time. Then he remembered the Kawasaki. It was made for off-road use. He'd be conspicuous as hell with the Redeye over his shoulder, but if he stayed clear of roads and houses and kept to the woods, he might make it. Unless he was spotted by the helicopters, which were now flying patterns over the approach area.

And then the Piscataway Golf Course appeared and gave him a better solution. He remembered from studying maps of the area how a triangular wedge of the course extended next to the approach path. Without a second thought he turned in, parked and ran to the clubhouse. Five minutes later he was back at the Winnebago with a golf cart and a set of clubs.

He dumped the clubs unceremoniously to the floor, got out a knife and sliced the leather dividers at the mouth of

the golf bag. The longest part of the Redeye, the barrel, fitted easily down the bag, but the handgrip and eyepiece were too bulky and the overall length too great to completely hide the unit. He slipped off his jacket and draped it around the remaining portion of the missile. It might not look exactly like golf clubs but at least it didn't look like a Redeye missile. Particularly not to the helicopters overhead.

He put the golf bag into the back of the cart and headed to the eighth hole, just another sportsman out for a little exercise with the oddest set of clubs on the fairways.

Paul and Annie drove to Andrews for the second time in twenty-four hours. Paul was determined to prove that Karl Alexander was real. His brother was too much of a threat to go free—to Joanna and himself as well as to the target of his assassination. Who knew when Karl might impersonate him again or for what purpose? The only way was to stop him.

Annie sat beside him, leaning forward in her seat. "You know," she said, "in a way I hope they don't believe you. I think I can get to Karl, make him come over to our side—"

"I already tried that."

"You threatened to expose him. You didn't offer him a new life."

"Is that what you're going to do?"

"I want to get him amnesty if he'll come over."

"What about me? Maybe I'll go over to the Russians." She looked up quickly, realized he was being sarcastic. "You still don't understand the significance of the gift you've got."

"It's not a gift, believe me."

They arrived at the Chevron Station, where they had arranged to meet Hugh Roark. The CIA man was leaning against a Ford Taurus dressed in slacks and a lightweight beige sport coat over an open-necked shirt. By contrast, Paul hadn't shaved, slept or changed clothes in over two days. Annie didn't look too much better. Her eyes were less hollow than his but her dress was badly wrinkled and the leather boots seemed to sag around her calves.

Hugh spread a map on the top of the car and showed them the areas he thought they should check. He seemed to be the only one except for Annie who believed that Karl

Alexander existed. At one point he glanced at the Alfa and asked if it had a radio. Paul shook his head.

"The mobile phone was in the Audi."

"Then I'll take the highways here—337, 4, I-95, Westphalia and the Suitland, as well as this industrial park. You cover these two neighborhoods and this shopping center."

Hugh wanted to know if Joanna had specifically meant a Winnebago or was she speaking of motor homes in general? Paul wasn't sure so they decided to check all motor homes.

As they left, Annie called to Hugh, "If you find him, remember our deal."

Hugh barely nodded and took off in his Taurus.

"What deal was that?" Paul asked.

"Hugh agreed he'd try to take Karl alive."

"Too bad you didn't ask Karl if he'd take Hugh alive."

Annie opened her mouth to respond, then thought better of it. They spent ten minutes checking a shopping center and found three motor homes, none of which showed any sign of Karl or a Redeye missile. They then drove the streets of a local neighborhood. At one point they spotted an actual Winnebago parked on the street, but the curtains were drawn making it difficult to see inside. A man came to the door of the adjoining house and called to ask what they wanted. It turned out to be his Winnebago and, no, he hadn't seen any other motor homes in the neighborhood that morning.

They ended up at the same 7-11 where they had stopped the day before. It was nine-fifteen. Looking at the map, Paul wondered about the areas they had checked, the ones left for Hugh. Annie was scanning the sky.

"Where will the plane appear?"

"That direction." Paul pointed. "He'll come right across there. Look through the fence and you can see the runway."

The fence was on the other side of the road. Beyond it, in the distance, a row of air force jets was visible in front of a huge hangar. Low in the sky two helicopters were circling over the approach path the same way they had when Air Force One landed.

The approach path.

Paul turned back to look in the direction he had pointed out to Annie. The sky was empty.

"I'll be damned," he said.

"What?"

"He did believe me. Son of a bitch, he believed me, after all."

"What are you talking about?"

"Look out there, beyond the base. What's in the sky?"

"Just a helicopter. It's not a plane."

"Two helicopters. They always fly security over the approach path. Remember yesterday?" Paul turned to the car. "Come on."

"But this is the—" She stopped as the import of his words became clear. She slid in beside him. "They changed runways?"

"You got it. They're going for a downwind landing."

The tires squealed as Paul accelerated out of the parking lot. Annie grabbed for the dashboard. "If they did switch runways," she yelled, "what makes you think Karl knows?"

"If he doesn't, Hugh's got him all to himself."

Annie struggled to keep the wind from whipping the map off her lap as she gave Paul directions and tried to pinpoint the area beneath the approach path. It took ten minutes to reach the other side of Andrews. When they passed the golf course, Annie called out, "We're close now."

And then they were at the roadblock. When the officer saw Paul, he did a double-take, then looked the car up and down and slowly smiled.

"Well, sir," he said, "it's a lot smaller but it still ain't going to get through."

A rush of questions revealed that Karl had been turned back in a Winnebago not more than ten minutes earlier.

"There's a motor home at the golf course," Annie said. "I saw a couple of them."

In fact there were four motor homes, two of them Winnebagos. They started looking through windows, and in the second Winnebago they found a motorcycle and pile of golf clubs on the floor.

They went to the clubhouse, an open, airy building of varnished white pine, where the pro shop was busy selling golf balls, sun visors and bags of tees. The tournament didn't start until noon but the place was already full of both serious golfers and families out for a picnic.

Paul pushed his way to the rental desk. "Have you seen a man who looks like me?"

The kid behind the counter wore a green blazer with the club insignia. He grinned at Paul and said. "Well, it was either you or your twin brother."

"My brother," Paul said. "Did he rent a cart?"

"Just a little while ago."

"What color?"

"White, like all of them."

"Which way did he go?"

"Couldn't tell you."

"I need a cart."

"Excuse me," said a man wearing checked pants. "But I was here first."

"This is urgent—"

"Sure, but get in line."

"Look, this is a matter of life and death—"

Annie jumped in then. "His brother is on medication. He took the wrong bottle this morning. He's got digitalin instead of insulin and if he uses it he'll have a seizure."

"Oh, well, sure, miss."

The man stepped aside, and a few minutes later Paul and Annie were navigating the fairways as fast as the cart would go. They took a shortcut between the fourth and eighth holes directly to the eastern border of the course. As they arrived, a couple who had just teed off was leaving. Nearby was an empty cart.

"Did you see who left this?" Paul called.

"I think it's broken," the lady answered. "It was here when we came."

They were at the eastern boundary, the beginning of the area beneath the approach path to Runway 01. The gently rolling hills beyond the rough were lightly wooded and offered Karl plenty of opportunity for concealment.

Paul checked his watch. It was 9:30. As they entered the woods Annie suggested they split up. "We'll double the chance of finding him."

Paul shook his head. "Too dangerous. He's got my gun, remember?"

"I've got this." Annie pulled a Deutonics automatic from her purse. Paul looked at her in surprise.

"You know how to use it?"

She gave him a scathing look and said, "Just yell if you see him."

They split up and began the search.

* * *

The golf bag, with its shoulder straps and heavy construction, made a good carrying case for the Redeye. Karl's first objective was to find a vantage point from which the missile would have a clear view of the aircraft. The ideal position was a water tower directly beneath the approach path. It rose from a hill and commanded a view of both the golf course and Andrews, but with the helicopters patrolling the area Karl decided it was too risky to station himself there. The tower was painted a red-and-white checkered pattern and drew attention to itself.

He finally found a clearing near the crest of a neighboring hill, a location that allowed him to remain sheltered by the woods until the last moment. With the missile lying against the golf bag, he used earphones to monitor the approaching target. The Soviets were running slightly behind schedule; it wasn't until 9:30 that the Ilyushin made contact with the control tower.

Karl stepped clear of the trees and took a position with his back to the incoming aircraft. The Redeye rested on his right shoulder, pointing high, waiting for the Ilyushin to enter his field of view. Because he wasn't on the crest of a hill the airport was hidden from view, but by using the water tower as a reference point Karl knew he was positioned directly beneath the approach path.

Through the earphones he heard the Soviet pilot report his position in heavily accented English.

"Summit One is now entering downwind for landing Runway Zero One."

"Roger Summit One, winds two two zero at six, altimeter three zero one four."

Karl flicked off the safety with his right thumb and bent his head to the eyepiece. There was a faint whine as the Redeye's gyroscope came up to speed.

From his left, a woman's voice said, "Karl Alexander."

He froze, then raised his head from the eyepiece and turned to find a woman with unkempt blonde hair pointing a gun at him.

"Don't be afraid," she said. "I'm not going to hurt you. I need your help and you need mine."

"Who are you?"

"My name is Anne Helms. I'm a research scientist with

the Central Intelligence Agency and I know all about you and Paul."

"Paul!"

"Listen to me. It's over. What you're doing now is useless. If you kill him another leader will take his place, maybe liberal, maybe conservative, it doesn't matter. In the end you'll accomplish nothing. Only your own death because they know—the CIA, the Russians, everyone. You're blown, Karl. It's all over, but I can help. I can offer you a new life..."

She moved toward him slowly, speaking quietly but intensely, the gun always pointed at his chest. He gauged the time it would take him to lower his right hand and get the Smith & Wesson from his pocket. Too long.

In the earphone he heard the Soviet pilot report turning the base leg. The woman was still talking...

"Karl, listen to me. I can offer you asylum. Come over to our side and nobody will hurt you. You can do something bigger and better than anything you've ever thought of. What you and your brother share is a priceless gift, a mental identity of such accuracy—"

"How do you know this?"

"I know about the dreams. I know you share an affinity so rare that it could be years before another case comes along, if ever. You and Paul are worth more than any political leader, do you understand that? You have a gift and I can save it. I want both of you to join my research program, you and Paul—"

"Did Paul send you?"

"He's here, he's with me."

So Joanna had lied. Paul was free, or had escaped. Over the earphones he heard the Soviet pilot, "Summit One is turning final."

"Roger Summit One. Cleared to land Runway Zero One."

The woman was still talking, faster now. "I'm *trying* to save your life, Karl. I'm not going to shoot you. If you go ahead with your plan I can't protect you. If you stop, I can save you."

Karl's eyes were on the gun in her hand, judging the threat, judging the distance. If only he wasn't weighed down with the damn missile, if his hands were free...

"Karl, please, you've got to trust me. Here."

And so saying, she tossed the gun aside.

Karl realized then: the wild hair, the wrinkled clothes, the strange expression—the woman was crazy. He reached into his pocket and took out the Smith & Wesson.

"I'm not here to stop you," Annie said, extending her hands. "I'm offering you a new life."

The sound of the approaching jet reached them. It was time. Karl raised the gun and shot her once, dead-center, in the forehead.

Paul heard the shot from the other side of the hill. He called Annie's name and began running. The low whine of the approaching jet grew in volume as he got to the crest of the hill and paused. Karl must be close, but where?

Through the woods, twenty feet down the slope, the trees cleared. Karl would need an open space to fire the missile. Paul ran toward the opening, jumping over fallen branches and stumbling over half-buried logs. A shadow washed over the land as the Ilyushin thundered overhead and Paul burst into the clearing. Karl stood not ten feet away, the Redeye resting on his shoulder, his head tilted to the eyepiece. At his feet lay the still form of Annie Helms, her blonde hair matted and stained with blood...

Karl hadn't heard his brother's arrival. When the Ilyushin swept into view, he positioned the aircraft in the ranging ring while his left thumb uncaged the gyro and engaged the guidance system. A high-pitched acquisition signal announced that the infra-red sensor had locked onto the jet's exhaust. Raising the launcher slightly to place the Ilyushin in the target dish, Karl pulled the trigger...

As Paul rushed headlong toward him, Karl's every movement seemed magnified. He saw the tension in the arms, saw Karl's final adjustment of the launcher, saw the finger tighten on the trigger... he threw himself forward in a flying tackle that caught Karl from behind. The two men crashed to the ground, and as they did the missile vaulted from its launch tube with a muffled whomp.

Paul's impact deflected the muzzle of the launcher and altered the heading of the emerging missile. The booster charge sent the Redeye twenty feet into the air, where it seemed to hang for a moment before the main engine ignited. The steering fins snapped open, but the infra-red sensor had lost its target. The Redeye surged blindly

forward at treetop level as its gyroscope attempted to recover the original heading. For a moment it veered wildly, then the sensor picked up the target, now at the very periphery of the missile's ability to correct course. With the Ilyushin's four closely positioned jet engines a bright bullseye, the Redeye began its swift upward trajectory.

In Aero-flot *Plamenny* a flashing red light and intermittent warning tone brought the air defense officer bolt upright in his seat. The Wildfire DeTect system had picked up a high-temperature heat source. The ADO hated these alerts. The DeTect system was so sensitive that even such innocent objects as fireworks and flares often created false alarms. But they were in the United States now and the possibility of a missile . . .

A quick glance at the blue panel-light reassured him that the DeCoy system was engaged. Unaware of Marina's sabotage, the officer turned his attention to the DeTect display screen and noted that the relative bearing of the heat source was 176 degrees, almost directly behind then.

"Hot flash," he called out.

"Identification?" from the co-pilot. But the ADO could not tell him. The heat source had vanished.

Paul's interference, crashing into Karl, had given the Redeye an erroneous trajectory that betrayed it. No sooner had the sensor picked up the Ilyushin's engines than the descending jet disappeared behind the water tower. The missile was sensitive only to heat; it had no radar to warn of intervening obstacles. Its exhaust trail described a quick corkscrew as it searched blindly for its target, and then slammed into the water tower. There was an explosion, followed by a cascade of water that sparkled like a Niagara Falls bursting from mid-air. The tumbling cataract momentarily drowned the sound of the disappearing jet. When it was over, the tower stood jagged and gaping, with water dripping slowly down its legs.

The two brothers were still on the ground. Now, as they turned toward one another, Karl was the first to speak.

"*You* . . ."

He reached for the Smith & Wesson but the gun lay on the ground between them and Paul was already moving toward it. By the time Karl lunged forward, Paul had the

revolver in his hand. Karl froze. Paul got slowly to his feet and Karl followed. Keeping the gun trained on his brother, Paul moved to Annie's crumpled body and confirmed what he already knew.

"Go ahead," Karl said calmly. "Shoot me."

Paul's hands trembled as he tried to control his anger.

"Do it, Paul. Kill me like I killed her, like I killed your wife, like I could have killed you when I had the chance. Go ahead. Kill me, damn you."

Part of Paul badly wanted to pull the trigger, but another made him hesitate ... to shoot any man in cold blood ... and here a man in his own image ...

Karl sensed the hesitation.

"You can't do it, can you? And do you know why? Because in killing me, you would become like me."

"I'm not like you—"

"Oh, I think you are. Deep down, Paul, we are the same. Brothers. You will kill ..." He began walking toward him.

"Don't, Karl—"

"You think I'll make it easy for you? No, we've come full circle now. You are the killer and I am the victim."

"You're no victim."

"I will not be a prisoner, you see? So you will make the final choice after all."

Paul understood what Karl was doing—forcing on him the burden of execution ... and betting that he would not accept it. Karl continued to advance, eyes fixed on him. Paul stepped back.

"No closer."

Karl extended his hand.

"Use the gun or give it to me."

Paul pulled back the hammer with a click.

"Put your hands on your head, Karl. *Your* choice, not mine."

A moment of doubt. Karl stared at the gun. An eyebrow twitched. "Then become me."

He grabbed for the gun, and Paul had no choice.

He pulled the trigger ...

EPILOGUE

IT TOOK WEEKS FOR JOANNA TO RECOVER FULLy from the accident. During that time Paul was tender and attentive, almost as if he were making up for his earlier coldness. When she was well enough he took a two-week vacation and they went to the cabin in Maine. It was a time of renewal and of healing for both of them. There were no more recriminations about either Jason's death or her affair with Luis de Cuevo.

Three weeks after their return to Washington, Joanna missed her period. She lay in bed that night, watching Paul get undressed, wondering if she should tell him now or wait until the doctor confirmed what she suspected—that she was pregnant. Paul stood at the dresser, shirtless, staring into the mirror. Joanna felt she knew what he was thinking. He was haunted by his brother's death, she knew, unable to free himself of the notion that Karl's blood was on his hands. There were times since they had been reunited when he became distant and distracted, even in the middle of a conversation, and on occasion the half-glimpsed image of himself reflected in a store window or mirror would startle him. When he came to bed, Joanna decided, she would tell him about the possible pregnancy. Maybe it would take his mind off the past, focus his thoughts on the future.

"Hey," she called. "You're doing it again."

He turned and gave her a quick smile.

"Sorry."

"Come on, come to bed."

He came to the bed, sat down and took her hands in his.

"I keep thinking about him—"

"I know."

"He could have run. I don't think I could have shot him

in the back. If he wasn't threatening me I doubt if I could have done it. But he came at me—"

"He didn't think you'd pull the trigger."

Paul shook his head. "I think he knew. I think he did it to prove we were the same in *every* way. Both killers—"

"You're not a killer, don't even think that."

"I think he was trying to turn me into him."

"*That's* creepy."

"If it had happened the other way—if he had grown up in this country, with mother and father, and a normal family life—would he have been me and would I have turned out to be him? Was it all a trick of fate, an accident of upbringing?"

Joanna shook her head. "No, no, no," she said softly but firmly.

"You're sure?"

"I'm positive. There was something missing in Karl, and it can't just be blamed on an accident or geography. If he had grown up in America he might not have been a killer but he'd never have been you. I forget the psychological term for it, but I don't think he was ever capable of feeling real love or even sympathy for anyone else. Loyalty, duty, yes. But—"

"But if I'd been brought up the way he was—"

"You would have been you, regardless. If anything I bet you'd have gone the opposite way, to compensate. Maybe you'd have become a doctor or priest..."

Paul ran his eye over her body, outlined in relief beneath the sheets.

"Not a priest, I hope."

Joanna put her arms around his neck and put her forehead against his.

"No matter how or where or what, you'd still be you—the man I want. Now."

He pulled her close and kissed her. Their need for each other surged into quick passion. Of late there had been an extra intensity to their lovemaking. She was grateful for it, and wondered if it was because they'd come so close to death that this most elemental affirmation of life had taken on a new and powerful dimension.

Paul moved to kiss her breasts but Joanna restrained him, still embarrassed by the angry red scar that disfigured her body.

"Turn out the lights," she whispered.

Paul got up and crossed the room. He stepped out of his pants and reached for the light on the dresser. A neat stack of coins caught his attention: quarters on the bottom, then nickels, pennies and dimes. With a frown, he pushed the stack over, then turned off the light and crossed the darkened room to Joanna.

ABOUT THE AUTHOR

RICHARD AELLEN is the recipient of a
National Endowment for the Arts grant, a
Writers Guild of America Fellowship and has
been, among other things, a naval reconnaissance specialist, a ferry pilot, a photographer
and a film editor. He makes his home in New
York City, where he is at work on a new
novel.

THRILLERS

Gripping suspense...explosive action...dynamic characters...international settings...these are the elements that make for great thrillers. Books guaranteed to keep you riveted to your seat.

Robert Ludlum

☐	26256	THE AQUITAINE PROGRESSION	$5.95
☐	26011	THE BOURNE IDENTITY	$5.95
☐	26322	THE BOURNE SUPREMACY	$5.95
☐	26094	THE CHANCELLOR MANUSCRIPT	$5.95
☐	28209	THE GEMINI CONTENDERS	$5.95
☐	26019	THE HOLCROFT COVENANT	$5.95
☐	27800	THE ICARUS AGENDA	$5.95
☐	25899	THE MATERESE CIRCLE	$5.95
☐	27960	THE MATLOCK PAPER	$5.95
☐	26430	THE OSTERMAN WEEKEND	$5.95
☐	25270	THE PARSIFAL MOSAIC	$5.95
☐	28063	THE RHINEMANN EXCHANGE	$5.95
☐	27109	THE ROAD TO GANDOLOFO	$5.95
☐	27146	THE SCARLATTI INHERITANCE	$5.95
☐	28179	TREVAYNE	$5.95

Frederick Forsyth:

☐	05361	THE NEGOTIATOR (Hardcover)	$19.95
☐	26630	DAY OF THE JACKAL	$4.95
☐	26490	THE DEVIL'S ALTERNATIE	$4.95
☐	26846	THE DOGS OF WAR	$4.95
☐	25113	THE FOURTH PROTOCOL	$4.95
☐	27673	NO COMEBACKS	$4.95
☐	27198	THE ODESSA FILE	$4.95

DON'T MISS
THESE CURRENT
Bantam Bestsellers

☐	27814	**THIS FAR FROM PARADISE** Philip Shelby	$4.95
☐	27811	**DOCTORS** Erich Segal	$5.95
☐	28179	**TREVAYNE** Robert Ludlum	$5.95
☐	27807	**PARTNERS** John Martel	$4.95
☐	28058	**EVA LUNA** Isabel Allende	$4.95
☐	27597	**THE BONFIRE OF THE VANITIES** Tom Wolfe	$5.95
☐	27456	**TIME AND TIDE** Thomas Fleming	$4.95
☐	27510	**THE BUTCHER'S THEATER** Jonathan Kellerman	$4.95
☐	27800	**THE ICARUS AGENDA** Robert Ludlum	$5.95
☐	27891	**PEOPLE LIKE US** Dominick Dunne	$4.95
☐	27953	**TO BE THE BEST** Barbara Taylor Bradford	$5.95
☐	26554	**HOLD THE DREAM** Barbara Taylor Bradford	$5.95
☐	26253	**VOICE OF THE HEART** Barbara Taylor Bradford	$5.95
☐	26888	**THE PRINCE OF TIDES** Pat Conroy	$4.95
☐	26892	**THE GREAT SANTINI** Pat Conroy	$4.95
☐	26574	**SACRED SINS** Nora Roberts	$3.95
☐	27018	**DESTINY** Sally Beauman	$4.95

Buy them at your local bookstore or use this page to order.

Bantam Books, Dept. FB, 414 East Golf Road, Des Plaines, IL 60016

Please send me the items I have checked above. I am enclosing $_____
(please add $2.00 to cover postage and handling). Send check or money
order, no cash or C.O.D.s please.

Mr/Ms _____

Address _____

City/State _____ Zip _____

FB–11/89

Please allow four to six weeks for delivery.
Prices and availability subject to change without notice.

Special Offer
Buy a Bantam Book
for only 50¢.

Now you can have Bantam's catalog filled with hundreds of titles plus take advantage of our unique and exciting bonus book offer. A special offer which gives you the opportunity to purchase a Bantam book for only 50¢. Here's how!

By ordering any five books at the regular price per order, you can also choose any other single book listed (up to a $5.95 value) for just 50¢. Some restrictions do apply, but for further details why not send for Bantam's catalog of titles today!

Just send us your name and address and we will send you a catalog!

Now there are two great ways to catch up with your favorite thrillers

ONCE A KILLER

The red-and-white barrier was raised, a red light turned to green and they drove a hundred yards to the American side. Paul felt much better now that they were back in the American zone. They agreed that Karl would call tomorrow after talking with his superiors.

They turned into a multilevel parking garage at the KaDeWe, drove to the third level, and parked.

"Until tomorrow, then," Karl said.

He offered his hand. As Paul took it the rear door opened and the car rocked as someone sat down.

"I'm sorry," Karl said, tightening his grip, leaning over and pinning Paul against his seat.

Paul instantly threw himself forward and up and might have been able to break free except for the seatbelt he hadn't yet had a chance to unfasten. From behind, an arm came around his neck and a white cloth covered his mouth. He kicked and twisted. When he gasped for air he could tell that it wasn't chloroform they were using, it was something less smelly and more powerful.

A strange dizziness took him, and then darkness. . . .

RED EYE

*This edition contains the complete text
of the original hardcover edition.*
NOT ONE WORD HAS BEEN OMITTED.

REDEYE
*A Bantam Book / published by arrangement with
Donald I. Fine, Inc.*

PRINTING HISTORY
Donald I. Fine edition published September 1988

Bantam edition / December 1989

*Bantam Books are published by Bantam Books, a division
of Bantam Doubleday Dell Publishing Group, Inc. Its trademark, consisting of the words "Bantam Books" and the
portrayal of a rooster, is Registered in U.S. Patent and
Trademark Office and in other countries. Marca Registrada.
Bantam Books, 666 Fifth Avenue, New York, New York 10103.*

For M.N. at R.H.M.

CHAPTER

1

THE WOMAN HE DREAMED OF KILLING WAS
not his wife. Her name was Lisle Beaumier and she was a
stranger. He knew the details of her apartment even
before she ushered him inside. He knew that in the
kitchen there was a row of copper pots hanging diagonally
above the stove and that the bedroom contained a twin
bed covered in Chinese brocade and in the bathroom
there was a claw-footed tub with a shower head attached
by a hose that lay like a pink snake curled in the bottom
of the tub. All these things Paul Stafford knew as he
kissed Lisle Beaumier and planned to kill her. He was
prepared.

Paul had no reason to dream of death. The night was
quiet and warm with only a faint breeze to disturb the
curtains shrouding his open bedroom window. From the
back yard came the chirp of crickets and soft rustle of
leaves against a rusty drainpipe. It was April. Above the
distant rooftops the peak of the Washington Monument
was visible, its white spire pointing like a finger to a
three-quarter moon that bathed the city in moonlight.
Lying in bed, Paul groaned and turned restlessly, fighting
the images that forced themselves into his mind, making
him an unwilling participant, a perilous seducer, a cold-
blooded killer.

The girl in the dream was provocative and alluring and
knew it. She had honey-blonde hair, jade-green eyes and
lips that surged naturally forward in a seductive pout. As
soon as the door clicked shut behind them, she pressed
against him, reckless and more than a little drunk. He
kissed her and let his hands slide down her back. When he
pulled her hips against his, she murmured in anticipation.
Her tongue came dancing into his mouth.

1

Curiously, Paul was aware of the dream even as it aroused and repelled him. He was caught, just as he had been in other dreams, unable to wake up before the final terrible moment. He could feel her breasts beneath the sheer fabric, could smell the perfume that enveloped them, could hear the little animal sounds she made as her hands slid down his body. Imperative fingers unzipped his pants and pulled him free.

"El Rancho Grande," she laughed, echoing the refrain of the floor show they had seen earlier.

He wanted to tear the dress away and shove himself against her but it couldn't be done that way. The death had to appear accidental. Instead, he forced himself to step back while he slid out of his clothes. Shirt, tie, pants, underwear—he dropped them all in a pile, careful that nothing should fall from a pocket.

Eager to please, Lisle Beaumier followed. She pulled the dress over her head and tossed it aside, then stepped out of her slip, revealing full breasts with tiny flat nipples, rosy with passion. The black bikini panties with lace trim slid quickly to the floor and she stood before him, confident in her nudity. He picked her up and carried her to the bathroom. She gasped with surprise when he placed her in the tub.

"I want to see you wet," he said, turning on the water.

"I am wet. See?"

She ran a finger between her legs and offered it to him. The water curled across their feet, a little too hot. He adjusted the temperature, then asked if she had any bubble bath, knowing from an earlier, surreptitious visit that she did. He poured the powder into the bath and sat facing her as bubbles rose around them. He let his fingers enter her, enter the taut, silken folds of flesh as her fingers pinched and stroked and fondled, bringing him closer and closer to the climax they could never share.

With legs wrapped around one another they pressed close, twisting and thrusting. Lisle's forehead glistened with sweat. She held his waist and rocked back and forth on his fingers, panting with dry lips and a glazed expression until she could stand no more. She pulled away and got to her knees.

"Come, come to bed."

But he couldn't let that happen. Much as he ached to bury himself in her, there must be no indication that Lisle Beaumier was anything but alone tonight. And so, reluctantly, he stood up and stepped out of the tub onto the rug. It was time to finish.

"Wait," he said when she started to follow him. "I must kiss you dry."

"You better hurry."

She stood with suds sliding down her stomach while his lips followed a towel across her body. He began at the neck then moved to each breast and down to her navel across her glistening abdomen to the delicate pink lips nestled behind warm pubic hair. He moved his feet slightly each time so that when the time came to act, his feet would be dry. Lisle watched with a benevolent smile until he was crouched in front of her. The tang of her arousal was still on his tongue when he gathered his feet and lunged upward.

She started to say something as the heel of his hand slammed into her chin, snapping her teeth shut and breaking her neck with a muffled crack. She fell backward against the wall and collapsed beneath the bubbles. When he lifted the body her head rolled back, revealed a tongue nearly severed—

Paul sat up quickly. His heart was pounding, his breathing deep and ragged; the pajamas tangled around his body damp with sweat. Because he was alone, it took him a moment to realize that he was still home and not on assignment tracking a story in some foreign land. Then he remembered the argument with his wife. Joanna had gone downstairs to watch television, nursing her grievance with a late-night movie and a drink. She hadn't come back.

Paul untangled his legs from the sheets, got up and went into the bathroom. He splashed cold water on his face, tilted his head back and breathed deeply. Tiny rivulets ran down his neck and slid down his chest until absorbed by the cotton fabric. The image of the woman swam before him, the woman he'd killed. He could still hear the quick intake of breath as his hand caught her chin, still smell the faint aroma of her perfume. The nightmares had come before but it had never been a woman he killed. Always before it had been a man.

Paul went downstairs. Joanna was asleep on the couch, bathed in the sullen light of the television. She'd pulled an afghan comforter over her as a blanket, leaving her bare feet sticking out from beneath its tasseled hem. One hand lay sandwiched between her cheek and a maroon throw cushion. Her thin lips were parted slightly, giving her mouth a fullness normally absent except in anger or love-making. Asleep, she looked even younger than her twenty-eight years. A bottle of Remy Martin had overturned beside the couch, leaving a small stain on the rug.

Paul picked up the bottle and placed it on the coffee table. He considered carrying Joanna up to bed but decided against it. Waking her might rekindle the argument they'd had earlier. Paul had been reviewing copies of Rockland-Birdwell inspection reports on a laser component for the Star Wars program when Joanna had come in. She had picked a report at random and inspected it. Her hands were narrow, with long, delicate fingers marred only by her habit of biting her nails.

"What story is this?"

"SDI. Rockland-Birdwell is faking progress reports. Changing test criteria so the components pass and they stay on schedule." Paul leaned back in his chair. "The question is, did they do it to fool the Department of Defense or did the DOD do it to make SDI look more formidable to the Russians?"

He was referring to the upcoming Mutual Defense Treaty, which involved a trade of "defense technologies" —the American laser-based Star Wars program and the Russian's secret RF wave transmitter, popularly called the Nevsky Project. The subject didn't interest Joanna. She slid her hand across Paul's shoulders and toyed with the hair on his neck.

"Are you coming to bed?"

She wore a pale blue silk chemise that matched her eyes and she stood close enough for her hip to touch his shoulder.

"I want to see what I've got here first."

Joanna dropped her hand.

"Paul . . . I want another child."

He kept working. After a moment she said, "Aren't you going to answer me?"

"Did you ask a question?"

"I said I want another child."

"We already had a child."

And he died, Paul thought.

"The house feels empty. I feel empty. I want another child—"

"No."

"Paul—"

"I don't want to go through it again."

"*You* go through it?"

"I don't want us to go through it."

She moved in front of him and stood holding her elbow, keeping her voice calm with an effort.

"Paul, what happened was an accident. You know that, don't you?"

"It's the way I feel."

He turned his attention to the reports.

"You were the one who wanted a family," Joanna said. "I wasn't even thinking about it when we met."

"Then nothing's changed."

"Everything's changed. We started a family. You said you wanted four children."

"Not anymore."

"When did this—when did you decide this?"

A strand of long dark hair had gotten into the side of her mouth. She flipped it aside.

"I've been thinking about it for a while."

"For how long?"

Since Jason died, he wanted to say. Since the morning after the funeral when I woke up and saw you sleeping, as peacefully and innocently as if nothing had happened.

But it had happened. Sixteen months ago Joanna had taken Jason and driven down to visit her parents in Charlottesville. They lived in a large, rambling country house on a hill overlooking the town. Jo had gone shopping, leaving Jason with her mother, who was preparing food for a Christmas luncheon, and her father, who was in the basement refinishing the floor. When Jo left, Jason was in the basement, helping his grandfather. At some point he went upstairs, and from that point on each of the adults thought he was with the other. Nobody noticed when he went outside. Nobody heard him fall through the thin coating of ice that covered the swimming pool. By the time they found him, it was too late.

Joanna knew what Paul was thinking.

"It's not fair," she said softly. "I didn't kill him."

"But you couldn't protect him and neither could I. Neither one of us could."

"You think it's my fault, don't you?"

No, he thought, as the same recurring rationalizations came twisting and turning through his mind. Nobody's fault. Forgive and forget. Forget that you took him to Charlottesville, forget that your parents were so damned oblivious that they let him die not fifty feet from the house, forget that I wasn't there that weekend, forget that we had a son at all.

He suppressed his anger and said, "No."

"Is it mom and dad? Is that who you blame?"

"I don't blame anybody."

"Yes you do."

He turned on her then, staring at her while he spoke in a hard voice.

"He's not here, okay? He's not here, not a part of the world anymore. Nothing he might have done will happen now; nobody will know him—friends he would have had, a wife, children . . ."

Joanna's eyes filled with tears; she put her hands over her ears and left the room without waiting for him to finish.

Paul felt a momentary urge to follow her but it faded quickly at the memory of his last glimpse of Jason . . . He had carried his bag of toys to the car and watched as he and Jo drove away, Jason with his Macy's Snoopy from the Thanksgiving Day parade pushed against the window, waving its paw goodbye. The look of trust in the boy's eyes wouldn't leave him. There were no excuses in raising children. None at all . . .

Now, as he watched Joanna sleeping, Paul tried to rekindle the feeling they'd once shared. He imagined making love to her while she slept. Her beauty still attracted him, her physical presence still aroused him, but he wanted her now without commitment. He imagined her body responding instinctively while she remained asleep, the white skin flushed with pink, her hips moving to his rhythm, her legs straining beneath him.

Paul knelt to kiss her. His knee touched a cold spot, the spilled brandy, and images from the nightmare returned, thoughts of death and mutilation. Joanna became a stranger to him, a pale woman with cameo features floating in a sea of black hair spreading across the pillow like ink on water. Images of death, decay crowded his brain. From past experience he knew he wouldn't be free until he purged the nightmare from his memory.

He went upstairs to his office, took out a yellow tablet and began to write. The nightmares were rare, but when they came he used them as the basis for mystery stories that he sent to Black Cat Mystery Magazine. The money wasn't much but Paul enjoyed seeing his name listed as an author of creative fiction. Somehow it seemed more impressive than a reporter's byline.

He wrote quickly, using both sides of the paper, and threw the finished sheets into an open drawer. Two hours later, when the world outside had turned gray and three-dimensional, a voice behind him said, "Have you been working all night?"

He turned with a start. Joanna stood in the doorway, the afghan comforter wrapped around her like a cloak. She looked tired. Paul got up and went to her. She leaned into his embrace and he buried his face in her hair. They stood silently for a moment.

"Have you?" she asked again, her voice muffled by the afghan.

"I had a nightmare."

She paused. "The kind where you kill someone?"

"I almost woke you up."

"I'm glad you didn't," she said. She had never had a nightmare in her life.

"It was a woman this time."

"Me?" she asked, showing a spark of interest.

"No, nothing like you. Besides, her name was Lisle Beaumier."

"You know her name?"

"I always know their names."

"How did you kill her?"

"Broke her neck." He didn't mention the seduction that preceded the killing.

"Broke her neck," Joanna repeated glumly, almost as if that was to be expected. She wasn't a morning person. As she left the room she said, "I'm going to make coffee. I feel like hell."

At breakfast they treated each other with the diffidence of exhausted boxers. Paul checked the Washington *Post* and compared the coverage to that of his own paper, the Washington *Herald*. The *Post* was a better paper but Paul felt no envy. The *Herald*, which was still trying to build its credibility and prestige, went out of its way to accommodate him. He was a star at the *Herald*. At the *Post* he'd be just another award-winning journalist.

Joanna gave a satisfied grunt. She had the Arts & Leisure section spread out on the kitchen table.

"Thank God it got in. See? They ran the story on Luis."

The article concerned Luis de Cuevo, the Brazilian artist whose show was opening tonight at the Gallerie L'Enfant. Joanna was assistant curator at the gallery and had been working with Cuevo, setting up the show. Paul glanced at the story and noted that the accompanying photograph wasn't contrasty enough and that Cuevo's work didn't show up well. It was all planes and angles and geometric forms. Cuevo himself stared haughtily at the camera like some sort of imitation conquistador. It wasn't a world that interested Paul and he doubted that Joanna's interest would last. Since he'd met her, she'd been involved in famine relief, architectural preservation, sailing, the theater, and now art.

"Will you come to the opening?" Joanna asked.

"What time is it?"

"Five-thirty until eight. We'll have free champagne. Maybe I can seduce you."

If it was a veiled reference to their sporadic sex life, Paul couldn't tell. Recently whenever they made love he sensed a kind of desperation that had never been there before. Joanna's need forced him outside himself and made it difficult to feel close to her.

She was still in her bathrobe when she accompanied him into the attached garage. The door opened at the touch of a button, grinding and clattering as it worked its way into the ceiling. The damp, musty air stirred slightly and light poured in revealing the two cars: Paul's Audi and Joanna's Alfa Romeo.

She stood on her tiptoes and kissed him hard and then bit his lower lip. He jerked back. There was a faint taste of blood, like a tin spoon, along the inside of his mouth. She stared at him.

"It's easy to hurt each other," she said. "Not hurting each other is hard."

She went back to the kitchen before he could answer. The slight quaver in her voice defused his irritation and he felt a sudden tenderness. She was still unpredictable, aggressive and tender in a way that made her the most attractive woman he had ever known.

Half a block away a man sat in a darkened room watching a video monitor. The monitor showed the front of Paul's house. Beside it another monitor was trained on the back of the house. As the Audi turned onto the street the man noted the time on a page filled with previous departures and arrivals. He picked up a walkie-talkie and spoke tonelessly.

"Decker Six, Decker One."

The responding voice was equally dry, flat.

"Decker Six, go."

"Alpha departure."

"Copy alpha departure."

"You got it."

"Lucky us."

The man replaced the walkie-talkie, stood up, stretched, then sat down again and opened a paperback novel.

Half a world away an overweight police inspector stepped off an antiquated elevator and made his way to an apartment where a group of spectators stood craning their necks for a peek inside, like pigeons searching for breadcrumbs.

"*Allez, allez,*" the inspector said as he waved them aside.

Inside the apartment he was met by a uniformed officer who led him to the bathroom where the body of a young woman lay curled in the bathtub, one arm draped awkwardly over the edge. The victim was naked, her skin wet and slightly furrowed, as if she'd been too long in the shower. A photographer with a fancy camera was taking pictures.

"The water was on when they found her," the officer was saying. "That's how the concierge knew something was wrong. No hot water this morning."

"An accident, I suppose?"

"Broke her neck when she fell. See the bruise on the

chin?" He shook his head sadly. "Such a waste of a pretty girl."

"Do we have a name?"

"Lisle Beaumier. Nobody special."

The electronic flash went off, momentarily blinding the two policemen before the white-coated attendants arrived and took the body away.

CHAPTER

2

PAUL STAFFORD DIDN'T HAVE MUCH OF AN
office at the *Herald*, but then, he didn't spend much time
there. The office was more of a status symbol, separating
him from the ranks of reporters who sat at desks in the city
room beyond the glass wall. Paul rated an office because of
his title: investigations editor. Twice a week he met with
the paper's three investigative reporters and offered counsel and advice. Once a week he met with Managing Editor
Bernie Stern and defended his counsel and advice. The
rest of the time he devoted to his own stories.

On the day that the CIA men showed up, Paul was in
his office talking with a young photographer named Dicky
Lazarus. Because Paul shot his own photographs he was
sometimes sought out by those who wanted to straddle the
worlds of words and pictures. Dicky had been trying to get
pictures of Angelo Vespucci, a notorious mobster who was
testifying before a Senate subcommittee. Twice he'd been
roughed up by Vespucci's bodyguards, and Paul had offered
to show him the "Stafford Switch." They were about to
leave, first for lunch, then Vespucci, when the girl at the
reception desk called to say that two men from the Central
Intelligence Agency were here to see him.

Paul glanced at Dicky, who seemed impressed.

"We'll have to wait on lunch," Paul said.

"Is this an ongoing?"

Dicky was new enough to Washington to be excited by a
visit from the CIA but smart enough not to show it.

"An in-depth report on homosexuality in the CIA," Paul
told him.

"Really?"

"These two guys share a houseboat on the Potomac."

Dicky whistled. "Explosive."

11

Within minutes the entire building was alive with rumors: Paul was doing an exposé of the CIA, Paul was being arrested as a spy, Paul was actually a CIA agent, Paul had taken unauthorized photos of a secret military base. In the city room outside the window, heads began peering over the maze of cubicles as news of the CIA men spread.

Paul picked up two motor-driven Nikon cameras from the desk, handed them to Dicky.

"You keep this stuff," he said. "I'll call you when we're done."

"You're sure you don't want a witness?"

Paul shook his head. "You look too tempting. They might make a pass at you."

The look on Dicky's face showed how little he liked that idea. He was an east-coast kid given to hip jargon and a faintly punk look: pleated gray pants, checkered suspenders, a blue tee-shirt and oversize lavender sportcoat with sleeves rolled to the elbows. It was no wonder Vespucci's men tossed him before he got within a hundred yards of the guy.

Outside the window the CIA men were visible coming toward them. One looked heavier than the other but they were both clean-shaven and neat in a way that made their conservative suits look like military uniforms. Like soldiers in civilian clothes, thought Paul. Or Secret Service men without sunglasses. He wondered if this was something to do with the Rockland-Birdwell SDI story.

Dicky slid out the door as the CIA men approached. Paul reached into his pocket and touched the shutter release of his Ricoh FF-90. The FF-90 was a small, fully automated camera that Paul used for grab shots. There was a faint click followed by a tiny whine as the electronic flash began charging. Outside the door Dicky paused to give the CIA men a look of distasteful appraisal as they entered the office.

"Mr. Stafford?" said the older man. "My name is Hugh Roark, senior investigator, Central Intelligence Agency. This is my assistant, Maurice Singer."

Singer closed the door to the office before acknowledging the introduction with a nod. He was thin and pale with an expression as blank as a store-window mannequin. Roark, on the other hand, had an easygoing manner and disarming smile that was at odds with his calculating, restless eyes. Both men flipped open identification cards and tucked them away just as quickly.

"Have a seat," Paul said.

Hugh Roark immediately took the single upholstered chair while Maurice pulled over one of the two molded plastic chairs along the wall.

"What can I do for you?"

"We have a problem that only—"

Paul lifted the Ricoh from his pocket and casually took a picture. The flash stopped Hugh in mid-sentence and caused Maurice to bounce up from his chair as if spring-loaded.

"Very clever. Now give me the camera."

"I beg your pardon?"

"The camera or the film, I don't care which."

Hugh said, "Easy, Maurice."

"He's got our picture."

Paul said, "I won't publish it without your permission."

"You won't publish it at all. That film leaves here in my pocket."

"Sit down, Maurice," Hugh Roark said quietly. The younger man turned toward his boss. "What happens if we end up on his hit list?"

Paul said, "Side view's good." And then snapped another picture.

Hugh saw it coming and managed to get a hand in front of his face but Maurice was taken by surprise. He turned to Paul with a murderous glare, but Hugh stood up and put a cautionary hand on his partner's arm.

"Easy," he said, then turned to Paul. "Mr. Stafford, whether you know it or not, there are times when taking photographs of field agents can be construed as a threat to national security. We could go to court and force you to turn over your film."

"If it was wartime you could," Paul said, "and if you were both engaged in covert operations. But this isn't wartime and the Washington *Herald* isn't a battlefield and I don't think that talking to a photojournalist constitutes any sort of covert operation."

"Then let me put it this way. We came here to talk in good faith. If you continue this kind of harassment we can come back with a subpoena and a U.S. marshal. It's up to you."

"Okay, no more pictures."

Paul slid the Ricoh back into his pocket, laid his hands flat on the desk and waited. He'd had his fun, now he just wanted to know what the two men wanted. What was it Maurice had said? Something about a hit list?

The two CIA men sat down and Hugh pulled out a metal rectangle slightly larger than the size of a domino.

"You don't mind if we tape-record the conversation, do you?"

"What for?"

"It saves time taking notes."

He placed the device on the edge of the desk.

"That's a tape recorder?"

"One of our own design. Ninety-six minutes on a permanent micro-filament. You don't mind, do you?"

It was a rhetorical question, Paul knew. If they wanted to tape the conversation, they could do it with or without his knowledge or permission.

"Suit yourself."

"First of all," Hugh said, "let's make sure we're talking to the right man. You're the author of five stories in the Black Cat Mystery Magazine, is that right?"

Paul grinned. "What is this? What are you guys pulling?"

"It's a simple question."

"I've got two Pulitzer Prizes—photo and journalism, both—and Langley sent you out to talk about a few pulp stories in Black Cat?"

"Are you that author?"

They were actually serious, Paul realized.

"I wrote the stories. What about it?"

Hugh pulled out a notebook and glanced at it. "Your first story was 'Ace High, All Die,' in which a man named Dan Kelso was murdered by drowning, is that correct?"

"I just told you I wrote the stories."

"Bear with us, please, Mr. Stafford. I want to lay a factual groundwork before addressing the substantive issues of the case."

"Case? What case?"

Hugh gave him the benevolent-uncle smile. "Please, if we can finish reviewing the stories I'll explain in a moment. Now your second story was, let's see . . ."

"'Death Sport,'" Maurice said impatiently. "Jurgen Manheim."

Maurice kept his eyes on Paul so there could be no mistake: he had the facts memorized. Hugh's smile faded slightly but he took the interruption in stride.

"Yes, that's correct. As the author, I assume you remember what death you devised for Jurgen Manheim?"

"A fake suicide. Shot in the head."

"Exactly. Then a year and a half later came 'Twist of Fate,' in which a man named Maxwell Durning fell while mountain climbing and broke his neck. Nine months later, in 'Odd Corpse Out' you have a victim named Jim Wilson executed gangland style and his body placed in the trunk of his car. Two years after that, a man named Frank Schrader is poisoned in 'The Grief Merchants.' " Hugh raised his eyes from the notebook. "Is that an accurate summary of the stories published to date?"

"You didn't summarize the stories, you summarized the murders." The nightmares, he wanted to say. You summarized the nightmares that prompted the stories.

"It's the murders that interest us, Mr. Stafford." Hugh's eyes scanned Paul's face for any change of expression. "I think you know why."

"I have no idea why."

"Those were real people, Mr. Stafford. And you either killed them or you know who did."

Paul laughed. "What is this? Did Buddy put you up to this?"

"I wouldn't laugh if I were you," Maurice said.

"What should I do—confess? Colonel Mustard with a candlestick in the dining room? Come on, guys, deliver the punchline. Whose idea is it? Where're the balloons? Where's the funny card?"

"It's not a joke, Mr. Stafford. Two of those who died were our people—agency employees—and the other three were assets. Provided us with confidential information about Soviet and Warsaw Pact activities."

"Oh, sure, sure."

"I'm trying to be honest with you, Mr. Stafford. We could do this differently, you know."

"Like *terminate* me?"

Maurice snorted. "This is getting us nowhere."

"Are you going to help us, Mr. Stafford? Or should we let it be known that you're a security risk and under investigation for murder? As you know, Washington is a

small town. People might not be so free about talking if
they didn't trust you."

What the hell were they telling him? That he killed
people by dreaming about them? Ridiculous. And then he
had another thought. He was doing an investigative piece,
an expose of defense contract misappropriations. There
had already been offers to buy him off and at least one
indirect threat. It wasn't the first time he'd been pressured
and it struck him that maybe this was part of the deal. A
way to make him think he was implicated in murder so
he'd lay off the investigation. But to make him believe that
characters in his stories were real? And he was somehow
responsible for their deaths? It seemed a farfetched way to
pressure him.

Paul stood up. "If you want to charge me with killing
fictional characters, go ahead. My guess is you end up in
the funny farm before I end up in court. Meanwhile, I've
got work to do . . ."

Hugh took a small piece of paper from the notebook and
handed it to Paul. It was an obituary notice from a French
newspaper. Paul was fluent in a number of languages but
even without French, the name was like a slap in the face:

> BEAUMIER, Lisle Jeanette, age 27 years,
> beloved daughter of Helen and Jacob
> Beaumier, 14 Rue Tilsitt . . .

Paul sat down quickly. A week earlier he'd typed the
Lisle Beaumier story and sent it to Black Cat. He hadn't
even gotten a response, but these men had obviously read
it. Read it and then what? Recognized Beaumier's name
from an obituary? He checked the date, knowing what
he'd find. The girl had died on the night of the dream.
Weird, indeed.

When Paul looked up, Hugh was watching him. "I'm
glad to see we finally have your full attention."

"Lisle Beaumier . . . is real?"

"Was real. She was having an affair with Terenti Vlasik,
the Russian ambassador to France. She was also reporting
to our Paris station. Lisle Beaumier was working for us."

"A spy?"

Hugh shrugged. "You weren't aware of the obituary?"

Paul glanced at the clipping again. It made no sense. None of this did. He shook his head slowly.

"Then how did you know?" Hugh asked.

"And why did you publish your knowledge?" Maurice added. He was leaning forward, elbows resting on the chair, the fingers of his right hand toying nervously with a rubber band.

Paul felt as he had after the accident, when he first heard the news about Jason . . . the sick sensation in his stomach, the feeling of disorientation, of life being out of control, of everything being a mistake.

"All of them?" he said slowly. "You're saying they were all real, all those people?"

"The names are real, you know that. You *must* know that."

"No."

"Let's not play games," Maurice said "The names and the circumstances of death are recorded exactly as they occurred. All but one was made to look like an accident— something only the murderer could know. Which means that either you're the murderer or you know who is."

"I didn't murder anybody—"

"Then how do you know their names? How do you know the way they were killed?"

"All I know is what you've told me. How do I know this thing is real?"

Paul flicked the clipping toward Maurice, who grabbed it as it fluttered through the air.

"How do I know your I.D.s are real? How do I know anything you've told me is real? I don't know anything about any murders and I don't know anything about you. For all I know, you're making this all up. How do I know? I never saw you before in my life."

Hugh took out a business card. "Call this number."

"What's that going to show me? Some anonymous voice on the other end says, 'Yeah, sure, this is the CIA. Sure, they're our guys. Sure, you can believe anything they say, including some cock-and-bull story about agents dying from mystery stories.' I can get an unlisted phone number and say the same thing." Paul picked up the phone and imitated a secretary. " 'Good morning, Central Intelligence Agency.' " He slammed the phone down. "You can be anything over the phone. I do it all the time working on stories."

He stopped, aware that he was talking too much and too vehemently. His visitors regarded him silently. Paul stood up, moved over to the door and opened it.

"Try Bob Woodward at the *Post*. See if he believes you."

Before he left, Hugh placed his card on the desk. "My number's on the back in case you change your mind."

When they were gone, Paul sat staring at the door until Dicky popped his head in.

"Are they?"

"What?"

"You know—sword swallowers?"

Dicky opened his mouth and poked a finger at his throat.

Ignoring him, Paul picked up the phone and called Stuart Meeker, the editor of Black Cat Mystery Magazine. Whoever the men were and whatever they were after, Stuart had let them see his story and Paul wanted to know why.

"Hey," Dicky said. "Are we going, or what?"

"Wait a minute."

"I'll be in layout," he whispered loudly.

Black Cat was published in Boston. After an initial bit of confusion about whether Stu had left for lunch or not, the editor came to the phone and apologized for not having called as soon as he read Paul's story.

"Like it a lot," he said. "We'll run it sometime in the fall."

"By that time half the world will already have read it."

"What's this? You're saying somebody else is publishing it?"

"I'm saying somebody else is reading it. I just had a visit from two men who saw the story and you've got the only copy outside of my desk."

"*Two* men?"

"What's going on, Stuart?"

"I guess one of them was Mr. Johnson, huh?"

"Who's Mr. Johnson?"

"He's a collector. He loves your stuff. Bought all our past issues with Paul Stafford stories and he wanted a first peek at anything new. A very wealthy fellow, Paul. A little eccentric, maybe, but willing to pay in real live dollar bills. I thought I'd humor him and maybe he'd get interested in some of our other authors. Does he want your autograph?"

"How much did he pay to see the story?"

"Oh, I don't know . . . twenty, not more than a hundred. Something like that."

"Meaning what? A hundred?"

"You've got to realize, Paul, that with the postal rate and printer's costs going up, we've really been squeezed. I didn't see any harm—"

"A hundred bucks for a peek?"

"Actually, for the original manuscript. We made a Xerox for the office. Like I say, he's a collector. He's got the original of *Treasure of the Sierra Madre*, so you're in good company."

Treasure of the Sierra Madre, my ass, Paul thought. But he admired the detail. Details made deceptions convincing. He knew. He'd used plenty of phony ploys backed with convincing details in pursuit of a good story.

"What's his full name?"

"Bob. Bob Johnson. He's a real fan."

Dicky Lazarus was standing in the doorway, pointing to his watch. Paul said goodbye and hung up.

"We got to get going," Dicky said, "if we're going to catch Vespucci."

Paul wrote Lisle Beaumier's name on a piece of paper and told Dicky to take it to Kathy Craven in research.

"Tell her to look for an obit in *Le Matin*. This date." He wrote it all down.

"Paul, it's almost one o'clock. '*Uno heura*,' as they say at the Miami *Herald*. Vespucci's going to be gone by the time we get there."

"We'll make it. Get the car. I'll meet you downstairs. Go, go."

Dicky left quickly and Paul made another call, this time to Ron Farquar, a case officer at the FBI. They'd first met when Paul funneled some information Ron's way during the Tongsun Park investigation. Since then they'd traded favors. I.O.U. city, Paul thought as he waited to be patched through.

"Farquar."

"Paul Stafford, Ron. I need a favor."

"If I can."

"Two names: Hugh Roark and Maurice Singer. My understanding is they're CIA. I need confirmation."

"You digging something on the CIA, Paul?" The idea intrigued him.

"You'll be the first to know. How about the names?"

"Not so easy. We've got a reciprocal—they keep off our grass, we keep off theirs."

"Confirmation of employment, that's all. I want to know if I'm dealing with real spooks or someone playing a game with fake I.D.s. Can you do me?"

"Twenty-four hours."

"I'll check back. How're the kids?"

"Teeth, Cub Scouts, ballet lessons and He-Man. How's the wife?"

"Art patrons and champagne. They're opening a new exhibit tonight. She's okay."

"That's 'Roark'—R-O-A-R-K—and 'Singer' like it sounds?"

"Yeah. Roark about sixty, Singer maybe half that, hard to tell, a bloodless type."

"Invisible ink in his veins."

"Maybe. I'd like to know ASAP."

"Doesn't everybody."

By the time he hung up, Paul had half-convinced himself that Hugh Roark and Maurice Singer were fakes.

CHAPTER

3

IT WAS THE FIRST TIME THAT JOANNA HAD gone to bed with a man she didn't love. Luis de Cuevo was talented and handsome and made no secret of his desire for her, but Joanna didn't love him and he didn't love her and she told herself, if Paul hadn't broken his promise it never would have happened.

He was supposed to meet her at the gallery for the opening of Luis' show. The event had been well attended, although not a packed house. They'd had a brief moment of panic when the caterer called saying that the delivery truck had broken down, but they found a replacement and the hors d'oeuvres arrived in time. A violinist in a Victorian evening gown had been Joanna's idea and was a great success. Everything had gone well and she'd had just enough champagne to begin looking forward to seeing Paul and getting over the tension of the morning when the phone call came.

"Something came up," Paul told her. "I can't make it tonight."

"Where are you?"

"Still at the office. Checking obituaries for you'll never guess who."

"Can't it wait until tomorrow?" she asked, not liking the undertone of irritation and supplication in her voice.

"*It* can, but I can't. Besides, smiling at pretentious art patrons gives me lip cramps."

"We'll be here until eight-thirty."

"Look, it's important, okay?"

As if that explained everything. Important. Everything that Paul did was important.

She knew that work was good for him, that it kept him from dwelling too much on what happened to Jason, but she also knew that it had become a thing between them. Paul was traveling more and working more evenings at the *Herald*, leaving her alone, and lonely, with only a snifter of brandy to ease the pain of her own memories. Most of the time she kept the pain to herself, tried to show a warm, happy facade, hoping and needing to lure him back to the intimacy they'd enjoyed before. But it wasn't working. Witness this very morning. Part of him was missing now. There were times when she felt he stared at her as if she was a stranger, and when he watched her undress it was without warmth. Their lovemaking had become sporadic, perfunctory.

From the phone came an angry chirping sound. Joanna was still holding the receiver. She replaced it and glanced around to find Luis watching her. He stood at a punch bowl, surrounded by admirers. When he caught her glance he excused himself and picked his way through the crowd, deflecting the attentions of those who would intercept him until he stood beside her.

"Your husband?"

"He's not coming, it seems."

Luis nodded, as if this was to be expected. When he spoke again it was in a lower, more intimate tone.

"A few of us are going out for drinks afterward. I would like you to join us."

And that's how it started. Or continued. They had already spent ten days working together, hanging the show, and Joanna was well aware that Luis found her attractive. He was self-centered and egotistical, but the simple fact that he *wanted* her was . . . a comfort, a reassurance. After Paul's call, all the loneliness, regret and guilt of the past months seemed to rise up inside her. And so she'd left with him, ostensibly for a quick drink with his friends.

The friends turned out to be a chubby art historian and her husband, both from George Washington University, and an expatriate Brazilian poet with an Israeli girlfriend. After a half hour of touching, then rubbing his leg along hers, Luis separated her from the others and took her to his hotel room. They exchanged their first embrace in the taxi, and by the time they arrived at his hotel, the hair around her neck was damp from his kisses.

Once inside, Luis lifted the mirror above the dresser

and brought it to a chair next to the bed. He put his arm around her waist and struck a haughty pose.

"You see? We fit well together."

He's trying to be clever, she thought. Luis, with his narrow face, prominent cheekbones, high forehead and thin hair swept backward as if blown by the wind was so different from Paul. He wore a black tuxedo that looked elegant next to her mauve silk dress with its paint-splashed pattern of turquoise blue, yellow, green and black.

Watching the mirror, Luis slipped his coat off and tossed it to the dresser. He pulled off the bow tie and said, with a smile, "You do the rest."

He kept his eyes on the mirror as she removed each stud from the shirt. He was sure of himself now, no need to rush. It probably happened all the time, she thought. He probably took a lover every time he opened a show. For him, it was routine. For her...? Hardly routine. She hadn't planned the evening to turn out this way. She hadn't planned for *anything* to turn out as it had.

She finished removing his studs, hesitated. Luis pulled off his shirt and tossed it to the floor. He wore no tee-shirt, his chest was flat and brown with a thin ridge of curly dark hair. He slid his arms around her and pressed her face against his chest. The smell of his body, cologne mixed with perspiration, was so *foreign*...

I must be going crazy, she thought.

Luis lifted her face, brushed his lips against her cheeks, then kissed her hard. Before undressing her, he removed her earrings. He did it gently, twisting the loops as if he'd designed them and knew every curve. He let his hands glide over her body, moving from her shoulders, down her stomach to her thighs. He lifted her dress, gathering it as he did so that all she had to do was raise her arms for it to slide free. As he knelt to remove her pantyhose he let his hand slide between her legs, brushing his fingers against her.

She shivered and closed her eyes. As he undressed her, he whispered how beautiful she was, how rich her hair, how smooth her skin, how perfect her breasts, how much he *wanted* her. Naked now, she allowed the sensations to spread like fire whenever he touched her. It had been so long since she'd felt wanted this way... It was like an affirmation of her womanhood, of her passion and grief and her *right* to the terrible, needing coalescence of body and spirit that had been missing for so long.

It was after midnight when Paul got home. The house was empty but that didn't surprise him. Joanna often stayed out late after an opening, sometimes until dawn. She liked to sit in smoke-filled bars with clutches of artists and intellectuals and discuss esoterica like the death symbols in Eric Fischl's work or the merits of Neo-Futurism. Paul had little patience with such talk and rarely went with her. He frankly looked forward to the day when Joanna lost interest in the whole phony art scene and moved on to something less pretentious and self-indulgent.

He went to his desk, flicked on the light and picked up the phone. He'd had a busy day. After leaving the *Herald* he and Dicky Lazarus had gone to the Sumac Club and set up the Vespucci ambush. When the mobster came out, Dicky went in low, pushing between the barrel-chested bodyguards, who promptly shoved him aside, creating an opening for Paul. By the time the guards grabbed him, Paul had gotten three shots and switched cameras. The film that the guards tore from his Nikon was blank. The second camera lay nestled under his arm beneath his coat. It was kid games, really, but it gave him a sense of satisfaction all the same.

When he got back to his office some time after six he found two messages on his desk, one from Kathy Craven and one from Ron Farquar. Kathy had left two copies of Lisle Beaumier's obituary, one from *Le Matin* and one from *France Soir*. Ron's message was equally succinct: both subject identifications confirmed.

The messages stunned him. Until that moment he hadn't realized how much he'd convinced himself that the CIA men were imposters and their story a fake. Now he knew: the story was real, the deaths were real, the people were real—and so were his dreams. But how?

Paul went to the research department on the second floor. Half of the room was divided by 4x8 sheets of plywood, a temporary condition necessitated by the new computer installations. All the files and records were bunched together in rows on the one side of the room, leaving little space for tables. Luckily, only three people were working in the room. He recognized Pam Markowitz but the other two were strangers. A lot of new people had joined the staff recently, mostly college graduates—"C and E's," the veterans called them. Cheap and eager.

Pam briefed him on the temporary layout and gave him a computer terminal. Paul started with the obituaries, checking the time periods that coincided with when he remembered dreaming the stories. It was a long process. He knew the publication dates but his memory of the dream dates was hazy. The other problem was that he had no idea of which city in which country the victims might have died. Roark had said that two of the victims were CIA agents. He discounted Jurgen Manheim and concentrated on the other four: Dan Kelso, Max Durning, Jim Wilson and Frank Schrader. He began checking U.S. obituaries, giving himself a five-week envelope around the estimated time he had the dreams.

After an hour the only thing he had to show for his trouble was a building headache. Here he was, looking for fictional people in a real world. Kelso, Durning, Wilson, Schrader—they were creatures of his imagination, the stuff of dreams and nightmares. He had no idea who they were. In the stories they died early and quickly. Usually they were bad guys with lots of enemies, to make the job of determining the killer more difficult.

At one point he thought he had Jim Wilson. The name cropped up in the L.A. *Times* at about the time Paul would have dreamed it. A Hollywood talent scout named Jim Wilson died in Beverly Hills when he backed his Mercedes into a swimming pool and drowned. The date was about right but the details were wrong. In Paul's dream, Wilson's throat had been slashed and his body stuffed into the trunk of his car. Aside from the name, the only other similarity was the car. Each man owned a Mercedes.

At which point Paul went to the lounge, got a ham sandwich from the machine and called Joanna to tell her he wasn't coming. Ten minutes later he was back at work. This time he checked the German press for the name Jurgen Manheim and scored a bull's-eye. An obit in *Berliner Zeitung* reported that Manheim, a fifty-nine-year-old resident of West Berlin, died of a self-inflicted gunshot wound. It was eerie to see the man's name in print, as well as the details of the dream: the same gunshot to the right temple. In the story he wrote afterward he made Manheim left-handed to provide a clue for his police inspector. He doubted that the real Manheim was left-handed. He doubted that anyone knew it was a murder. If it was a murder.

Paul felt his mind turn into a hall of mirrors. Every time he looked at a set of facts from one angle, another set of facts became an impossibility. A fifty-nine-year-old German had died and he'd dreamed it, just as it happened. Or had his dream made it happen? He remembered these old bull-session arguments in college about the nature of reality. Was the world a subjective perception or an objective phenomenon? If you weren't there to perceive it did the world exist? Or did it exist only because you perceived it?

He became aware of the conversation at the other end of the room. A girl in jeans and a khaki shirt was complaining to Pam about the fluorescent lights. A study had shown that fluorescents produced a flicker that caused headaches.

"See those things," the girl pointed at the ceiling. "It's like being bombarded with radiation. They should have flicker filters over them."

A tight feeling of claustrophobia came over Paul as he listened to the girl argue her inane ideas. He got up and went outside. The night was warm and the sidewalks were busy. He walked quickly and then began jogging. Without destination, he sought motion. He ran faster and faster, dodging pedestrians and dashing between cars. He narrowly missed a couple stepping out of a restaurant and the man shouted after him. Paul swerved from the sidewalk and ran full bore along the side of the road, feet pounding, breathing in loud gasps, until he collapsed in Franklin Park and lay on the lawn staring at the stars, the smell of fresh grass all around.

During the Vietnam War Paul had served for two years as a helicopter pilot. He remembered his flight training and how, the first time he had been given all three flight controls, the machine seemed to take on a life of its own, turning and bouncing and sliding all over the sky. It was as if the controls reversed their function at his touch so that every attempt to correct a condition caused the machine to gyrate even more wildly out of control. He felt the same way now. The more he learned about his dreams, the less sense the world made.

Paul watched the stars for a while, and then as the dampness from the grass began to make itself felt he got up and went back to the *Herald* Building. Pam was at her desk reading a book. Everyone else had gone.

"You left the terminal on," she reminded him.

"I'm not done."

Pam grew bored with her book and offered to help. Paul gave her a list of the names before remembering she was one of the few who read his stories in *Black Cat*. She looked puzzled when she read the names.

"These names are familiar," she said. "Who are these guys?"

"Confidential."

"Kelso . . . Manheim . . ." Suddenly it hit her. "Wait a minute, these are names from those mystery stories. The ones you write for that magazine."

"You've got a good memory."

She frowned and Paul held up his hand. "Don't ask."

"This isn't an assigned piece, is it?"

"I'm logging the terminal time 'personal.' "

"These *are* names from your story, aren't they? Or are they real people?"

Paul told her that he'd received libel threats from the relatives of people whose names were the same as the ones he used. He was checking the other names to see if there was a potential of other suits. Satisfied, she set to work and fifteen minutes later came up with a new Jim Wilson, this time in a story by Newsweek titled "Americans at Risk Overseas." The article detailed the increasing number of kidnappings and killings of Americans by terrorist groups. Pam pointed to a paragraph that read:

> In Karamursel, American James S. Wilson was found dead in the trunk of his Mercedes-Benz. His throat had been cut and the body left with a message calling for the expulsion of all U.S. military bases in Turkey. Wilson was an employee of the USAFSS.

"What's the USAFSS?" Pam asked.

"U.S. Air Force Security Service. They run a signals intercept station at Karamursel."

Pam was impressed. She gave a low whistle and said, "Our *Herald* reporters know *everything*."

The truth was that Paul had covered the Turkish invasion of Cyprus in '75. The resulting American arms embargo made the Turks mad enough to shut down the Karamursel intercept station for something over a year. It had been big news for a day or two and made a lot of intelligence officers mad who didn't give a damn about Cyprus as long as their eavesdropping stations were secure.

"They can't sue you for this one," Pam was saying. "Jim Wilson's a common name and this one died in Turkey while all your stories are in the States, right?"

Paul agreed that there was probably no threat of libel action. He wondered if Wilson was one of the agents that Hugh Roark mentioned—or was he merely an "asset"? He went back to the computer, but by this time his eyes ached and he had a roaring headache. Flicker-filters, he thought, remembering what the girl had said.

Now, sitting at his desk at home, he still had the headache. It wasn't the kind of headache aspirin could cure; he needed answers. He took Hugh Roark's card from his pocket, placed it beside the phone and dialed the number. One ring and a woman's toneless voice answered.

"Six seven five one," she said.

"This is Paul Stafford. I want to talk to Hugh Roark."

"Paul Stafford," she repeated. "One moment, Mr. Stafford."

There was a faint click on the line. Paul imagined the tape rolling in a listening room the size of a sound studio.

"Is it an emergency, Mr. Stafford?" Her voice sounded as if it was pieced together from computer tones.

"Call and ask him."

"We're patching through now. In case of a disconnect, what number are you calling from?"

Paul gave her the number and she put him on hold. Prerecorded classical music flooded the line; Prokofiev's *Peter and the Wolf*. Paul wondered what they'd do if he hung up. Probably send the marines over. He smiled, thinking that Joanna would call this another example of his knee-jerk rejection of authority. The music stopped abruptly and Hugh Roark's voice came on the line.

"Mr. Stafford?"

"You said to call if I wanted to talk. Okay, I want to talk."

"Are you in any danger?"

"Why should I be?"

"It's after midnight, Mr. Stafford. I'm just doing a situation assessment. Are you in danger?"

"Not that I know of." Situation assessment . . . the officialese always offended him.

"And you're willing to cooperate with us?"

"I'm willing to trade some answers. I'll tell you what I know and you tell me what you know and maybe we can both figure out what's going on."

"I can't promise any deals. Not over the phone like this. We have to talk first."

"The sooner, the better."

They made arrangements to meet the next day at a restaurant near DuPont Circle. After they hung up Paul took a shower and went to bed. By the time Joanna got home, he was asleep. He felt her climb beneath the sheets but it wasn't until the bed began to shudder that he realized she was crying.

"Jo?"

No answer. He reached over and turned on the light. Joanna lay on her back staring at the ceiling, her dark hair tangled and wet with tears.

"What happened?"

He touched her cheek but she turned away. There was a crescent discoloration on her neck, the mark of a lover.

The world glided to a stop. Staring at the mark of another man's passion, Paul felt a deep emptiness, not unfamiliar, that had been with him a long time now.

"Who was it?" he asked, surprised that his voice sounded so calm. Joanna turned and hugged him, hard.

"Hold me, Paul," she whispered. "Hold me, please hold me."

He put his arms around her, aware of the smell of cologne in her hair, on her skin.

"I love you," she said in a low voice. She repeated it like a chant or incantation. "I love you I love you I love you."

Paul remained silent. He could feel conflicting emotions leap and whirl as his perceptions of Joanna shifted. She was lover and betrayer, wife and enemy, giver of joy, bringer of pain, a stranger, a woman's body surging and trembling against him.

He became aroused. When Joanna realized it she pulled up her nightgown and guided him to her. She was still wet. He entered without preliminaries, quick and angry.

Joanna locked her legs around his waist, grabbed his buttocks and pulled him close, her fingernails digging deep into his flesh. The pain spurred him on. They watched each other's eyes as they made love, staring like enemies, teeth clenched, bodies slamming until they bruised. Slowly, Joanna's expression changed. Her eyes dilated, her mouth parted and she whimpered each time they met, faster and faster until she exploded with a cry and held him close.

Her climax was a cue for his release, but this time Paul felt the opposite sensation, a dying away of passion, a moving away from intimacy. He became still. Joanna sensed what was wrong. Keeping him inside, she changed positions, sitting astride him, her hands braced against his shoulders. She began moving, seeking his rhythm, willing his climax. Paul closed his eyes and matched her movements, searching for the lost tempo. They met again and again, the rhythm increasing and decreasing and increasing until they were both flushed and glistening with sweat and the sheets lay tangled on the floor. Finally Joanna pushed free and moved to take him in her mouth.

"Don't," he said.

"You didn't come."

"It doesn't matter."

She stared up, her chin on his stomach. She moved down again but he held her tight.

"You'll taste *him*."

She froze and then rolled away to the side of the bed, sat there with her back to him, shoulders rising and falling as she regained her breath. When she spoke her voice was empty, tinged with bitterness.

"You're a withholder, Paul. You hold everything back. Even this."

He said nothing. Anything more might end it for them, end the marriage right there. And no matter what he felt, or didn't feel, he knew he didn't want that.

CHAPTER

4

KARL ALEXANDER SAT JAPANESE-STYLE BESIDE
three other instructors from the Eichwalde Combat School.
They wore the traditional white karate *gi*, each with a
black belt, as did their opponents. The men were partici-
pants in the annual Armed Forces Karate Tournament,
held at a military base near Potsdam, twenty miles outside
Berlin. It was an event that Karl had won five times
previously and was favored to win again. Only one person
doubted his ability to win and that was Karl himself.

Mizu no kokoro, he thought, recalling the karate maxim
"A mind like water." *Mizu no kokoro*. He repeated the
phrase mentally in an effort to rid himself of the dark
thoughts and terrible memories that drifted through his
mind ever since the latest mission. He had killed a woman, and it was a woman whose memory had returned to
haunt him. Not Lisle Beaumier, but another woman,
someone whose very name he had repressed, whom he
hadn't thought about in thirty years, never wanted to think
about again. He swept the name and the bitter memories
aside. Now was the tournament. Now he needed clarity of
thought and concentration of will. *Mizu no kokoro*

The contestants on either side of Karl were from various
branches of East Germany's Armed Forces. They sat outside an eight-meter-square area that had been marked
with yellow tape on the polished wood floor of the gymnasium. This was the contest area. Beyond it was an official's
table with a time keeper and recorder, while the four
judges were stationed at each corner. The bleachers were
sparsely filled with other armed forces personnel. From
windows high up near the ceiling came narrow bands of
sunlight that struck the dark floor and turned it a glowing
amber.

31

The first part of the tournament were *katas*, formal exercises composed of a number of karate movements and executed by a single individual in fixed sequence. An air force man was performing now, hands and feet flashing, bare feet squeaking against the hardwood floor as he battled imaginary attackers. Karl could tell that the man was attempting a complicated pattern beyond his abilities. He would not score well. Karl, on the other hand, had chosen the Heian Number 4, a comparatively simple *kata* but one he knew intimately and could perform perfectly even when distracted, as he was now.

What was on his mind was that he'd lost control on his last mission. Not during the killing of Lisle Beaumier, but afterward, with the Algerian girl. He had lost control and that was dangerous. As a member of the Staatsicherheidienst—the Stasis—East Germany's equivalent of the KGB, he couldn't afford to make mistakes. He had been activated as an assassin in 1981 after the Bulgarians bungled the assassination attempt on the Polish Pope. Having demonstrated their ineptitude and very nearly implicated the KGB, the Bulgarian Durzhavna Sigurnost was replaced by East Germany's Stasis as Moscow Center's preferred agency for "wet" work. Karl had killed six times since then, but Lisle Beaumier had been the first woman. And her death unlocked long-buried memories of his childhood and of the woman who had dominated his early years, the woman whose name still made his stomach tighten with fear. Tante Inge.

He saw her again, rising like a specter in his memory, dressed in her scavenged clothing, layered like a gypsy queen, the bitter mocking lips turned inward, her hair an unnatural henna red, her eyes mirroring the unpredictable moods that seized and shook her like a tree before an autumn wind. It was her eyes that terrified him, trying to read their expression, hoping she wasn't angry, afraid that if she was happy it was only a prelude to some new cruelty. Her eyes mirrored her passions, alternately glazed with tears of self-pity or sparkling with alcoholic euphoria or smoldering with perverted sexuality that made his childhood a nightmare.

"Meeow kitty," she would call him to her bed. "Put me to sleep. Put me to sleep like a kitty cat."

Karl knew what she meant. He would have to crawl beneath the covers and lick her most secret places. Sometimes she would rub chocolate on herself as an added inducement.

"I have a chocolate mouse tonight," she would tell him. "Be a little kitty and eat my chocolate mouse."

Childhood memories... The tawdry apartment was his prison and Tante Inge was his jailor. He had been been kept indoors, fed and pampered and coddled and shampooed like a show dog. He remembered how she brought home candy and bathed him and touched a drop of cologne to his forehead as a prelude to turning him over to the furtive, heavy-lidded men who came to the apartment and used him like a woman, pushing his face against the rough sheets or forcing him onto their laps, thrusting into him as they fondled his genitals. And afterward, when all he wanted was to crawl beneath a blanket and hide, Tante Inge insisted on cleaning him with endless scrubbings and enemas of scalding water.

The only time he felt safe was at the mass graveyard in Treptow, where he imagined his mother lay buried. He had never known his mother. She had died in the streets, blown apart by an American bomb, and Karl would have died as well if Tante Inge hadn't rescued him. She'd told him the story many times, emphasizing her own courage and his subsequent ingratitude. And so he endured her until the day he'd run away and joined a gang of wild children living in the rubble of Berlin...

The sound of applause brought him back to the present. The air force man had finished his *kata*. Now it was Karl's turn. Quickly he emptied his mind of disruptive thoughts and imagined a white, luminescent screen, pure and clean and free of memories.

The loudspeaker announced him: "Oberstleutnant Karl Alexander, the Heian Number 4."

As Karl stood up, Heinrich Lammers, a new instructor at Eichwalde, wished him good luck. Karl's two other teammates, who knew him better, said nothing. Walking to the contest area, Karl was aware of the stiffness in his legs. He wished he had paid more attention to flexing his muscles while he was sitting.

He made the ritual bow to the officials, took his position. The Heian Number 4 involved twenty-seven movements; Karl would execute them in forty-three seconds. The movements would take him forward from his starting position, then diagonally to the right and left, reversing direction to a position behind the starting point and through a series of movements that concluded back at the original position. When done skillfully enough, the shadow opponents could be imagined as clearly as if they'd materialized out of thin air.

Karl took a deep breath and began. He stepped to his left, blocked an incoming blow with his left hand and countered with a knife-hand right and a front kick. He moved smoothly, never stopping except for that fraction of a second that marked the culmination of a strike or block. At those moments all physical and mental energy became focused at a single point, like the rawhide tip of a whip when it explodes in a loud crack.

The room, the spectators, the white-garbed contestants— all faded from Karl's consciousness as he moved into the *kata*. His mind fused with his body, his muscles became an extension of his will. He moved with the grace and energy of a young man although the lines around his eyes and the salt-and-pepper hair suggested a man in his forties. Rigorous physical training kept him lean and hard; when the mistake came, it was not his body that betrayed him but his mind. He lost his concentration.

Karl felt it as soon as it happened. He had just completed the thirteenth movement, a *riken-uchi*, or backfist strike. The next movement involved a 225-degree turn to the left, but even as he felt the sweep of air over his arm he knew that his center of gravity wasn't low enough. He overstepped the fourteenth position by six inches. To the casual observer the mistake was imperceptible, but Karl felt it and the judges would note it. A mistake on a simple *kata*, the Heian Number 4. Even if he performed the rest of the exercise correctly, he would finish six inches from his original position. The only alternative was to correct during one of the other movements, weakening its execution.

His momentum carried him through a left-and-right punch to the mid-section, and then he stopped. The silence grew loud as spectators sensed that something was wrong. Karl straightened, turned to the judging table and bowed.

"I apologize," he told the officials. "I cannot participate in the tournament."

Ignoring the buzz of surprise that rippled through the

audience and the whispered exclamations of his own teammates, he turned and left the gymnasium. In the locker room
he took off his *gi* and changed into civilian clothes. From
outside he could hear the announcement: Oberstleutnant
Karl Alexander, representing the Eichwalde Combat School,
had withdrawn from the tournament. The sound became
momentarily louder as the door opened and Heinrich
Lammers entered. He came quickly down the long row of
blue lockers and stood before Karl with a worried look.
Heinrich had blond hair and strong features that were too
broad for his round face.

"Are you ill?"

"It's poor form to leave the contest area," Karl said
cooly.

"But . . . are you all right?"

"As you can see."

Karl lay the heavy twill jacket on a bench, placed the
pants on top, then rolled the *gi* into a bundle. He ignored
Heinrich, who was too young, too eager and too much a
part of the new generation for Karl to feel comfortable
with him.

"It is a family matter?" Heinrich persisted. "Your wife,
your children, they are in good health, *ja*?"

Karl looked at him. "If they weren't, what would you do?"

"Anything I could do to help, Herr Oberstleutnant."

Heinrich came to attention as he spoke. Karl knew what
the young man wanted. He'd heard the rumors about
Karl—that his occasional absences, ostensibly to advise
combat schools in other Warsaw Pact countries, were
actually wet assignments for the KGB. Heinrich was eager
to do this type of work himself. He had already confided
his ambition to Karl, who professed ignorance and was
unresponsive.

Now Karl told him, "You can help most by winning your
match today."

"I will, sir. I'll win for both of us."

Karl could feel Heinrich's eager eyes on him as he
walked away and an unkind thought crossed his mind, that
the boy's opponent would foul and land an *oi-zuki* to
Heinrich's wide, pumpkin face.

He did not return to the training ground at Eichwalde
but drove instead toward the city. The road rose and fell as

it followed the Spree River past the rolling farmlands and pine forest that bordered Berlin. This was Karl's favorite route, one he normally drove at high speed, enjoying the feel and movement of his Mercedes 280 E. Today he drove slowly, unwilling to acknowledge that the appetites he'd begun to satisfy in Berlin's hedonistic Western Sector were no longer a game. It was no longer the pretense of violence he craved but the real thing. The experience with the Algerian girl had proved it.

Fassi, that was her name. She had come to his room at the Hotel Angleterre, the same room, according to the maid, in which the American writer, Ernest Hemingway, had once stayed. The Angleterre was known for its modest elegance and well-insulated rooms, which made it ideal for Karl's purpose. When he was on assignment he always stayed at expensive hotels, where privacy and the dollar were equally respected. His money was real and his documents were false and this was his protection.

Fassi arrived with an assortment of leather gear and a willingness to participate in bondage—for an extra fee, of course. Karl had specified a small woman, young and thin and limber, a *chicky girl*. Fassi was taller than he would have liked, but otherwise she fit his description exactly. She was angular and lithe, with small budlike breasts and narrow hips. Her full brown lips curved inward and became glistening pink where they framed strong white teeth. Her eyes were wide and expressive, but the impression of innocence was mitigated by the assurance with which she set down her purse and bag and surveyed the room. Her hardened expression didn't fit the adolescent body, but Karl was confident that he could reduce her to a frightened child quickly enough.

He gave her a moment to admire the room, which was decorated in pastels of lime and peach and gold and contained a double bed whose bedspread matched the floral design of the wallpaper, a coffee table flanked by two upholstered chairs, and a large dresser. After a few moments chatting she told him that her safety-word was "enough"—all other protests he could ignore. Karl pretended to agree and told her to go into the bathroom and remove her makeup. He wanted her looking fresh and young, just as he had been with Tante Inge. While she washed her face Karl inspected the devices in a shopping bag. He noticed with a professional's eye that the shopping bag was from Cartier. The little whore's employer paid attention to details.

Karl spread the leather goods on the bed, feeling as he always did the mixture of anxiety, fear and anticipation. He noticed, too, the faint buzzing sound he associated with these episodes. Barely discernible now, he knew the sound would increase in volume, reaching a crescendo at the moment of climax. The analytical part of his brain categorized these and other symptoms of what he considered an abnormality even as he accepted and indulged it. Karl did not delude himself. His safety lay in the recognition and control of his sickness.

Fassi had brought the items he asked for: an assortment of leather thongs, a ball gag, a combination headband-chinstrap studded with metal rings, handcuffs, and an enema bag. Karl tied two of the thongs to the metal rings on the headband. While he did this Fassi undressed. She hung her dress in the closet, placed her undergarments on a chair and approached him, thin and dark, ribs faintly visible under glistening walnut skin, the diminutive breasts topped by prominent dark nipples. She had shaved her pubic hair.

"You want me on the bed?"

"Put this on, first."

Karl handed her a white tee-shirt. She slid into it without comment. The tee-shirt was large but Karl had cut away the lower half, revealing her body from the navel down.

"Now this."

He tossed her the headband. She inspected the two thongs dangling from it and half-smiled in recognition.

"We are going to Auteuil this afternoon, *mon bête?*" she said, referring to the famous Paris racetrack.

"Put it on."

Fassi buckled the strap around her forehead and chin. The two thongs dangled like pigtails past her shoulders to her waist. He handed her the enema bag.

"Fill this with hot water and hang it up."

While she was in the bathroom Karl put out a "Do Not Disturb" sign and locked the door. He drew the drapes, turned on the lights, then cleared off the dresser and pulled it away from the wall. He took a roll of pink ribbon he'd bought at a gift shop and cut four long strips. These he placed on top of the dresser. By the time Fassi returned he was undressed and waiting. Lying across the top of the dresser, Karl instructed her to tie his hands and feet with the ribbon to each of the four legs. Humming softly, Fassi went about her work.

"Tighter," Karl told her. "Come on."

"These little things? They will never hold a big man like you."

"They're not meant to."

"Ah, you will be a brute today, *n'est-ce pas?*"

"Don't talk unless I tell you what to say."

She shrugged and continued about her business. When she was done, Karl lay across the dresser as if embracing it. The surface was hard against his chest and face, the edge cut into his thighs, awakening fierce memories and forgotten fears.

"Now bring the enema bag."

Silently she went to the bathroom and returned, the bag in one hand, the white nozzle attached to its orange hose in the other.

"Come at me with it," he instructed. "Tell me I've been a dirty boy and you're going to clean me."

She came toward him, the bottom of the white tee-shirt sliding back and forth across her stomach.

"You're a very dirty boy," she said in a sultry voice.

"Not seductively. You mean to hurt me. You're *going* to hurt me. You know it and you want me to know."

The girl assumed a severe expression and began again.

"You've been a very dirty boy," she said. This time her voice was hard, her attitude more what he remembered. A shudder ran through his body as the old hatred brought the taste of bile in the back of his mouth. The buzzing inside his head increased. He was growing hard.

"Keep repeating it. Tell me I'm dirty and you're going to get me clean. Come up slowly and try to do it."

She did as he asked. Karl strained against the bonds and pushed his cheek hard against the dresser. Eyes closed, he remembered the terror of childhood, the garish basement apartment with its heavily perfumed bedroom and Tante Inge coming toward him, just as the girl was coming toward him now.

His body tensed. "*Bitte, bitte*, Tante Inge. Please, no."

"A very dirty boy and you have to be punished."

He felt her coming closer and he strained against the bonds, remembering all the times he'd wanted to escape and been forced to endure. The dresser was sharp against his thighs and pressed uncomfortably against his erection. The smell of the bedroom rose in his memory, the smell of Tante Inge's perfume and of his own fear.

"Dirty boy has to be cleaned for his own good."

"I'll be good," he whispered, but the words were drowned by the angry buzzing that filled his ears. "Please, please, Tante Inge."

"Has to be cleaned right now—"

The nozzle touched him and all of the submerged fear and rage exploded as he ripped free of his bonds, rolled from the dresser and landed on his feet in a crouch. Fassi, taken by surprise, could only stare, her mouth a gaping pink O.

Karl grabbed her ankle and tumbled her to the floor. Before she could react he was on top of her. He shoved her arms beneath his knees, grabbed the enema bag and held the nozzle to her lips.

"*You* take it. Here, here!" Karl insisted.

She pulled her arms free, tried to push him away. There was fear and panic in her eyes, and angry desperation as she began to fight back. She scratched at his eyes, forcing him to drop the bag and grab her hands. He leaned forward, bent his arm and directed an elbow into her solar plexus, then lunged to the bed and got the ball gag. Fassi rolled to her side, legs drawn up, gasping for breath. Karl shoved her onto her stomach and sat on her narrow haunches as he shoved the ball into her mouth from behind. He moved quickly, never stopping, compelled to act, compelled to use the girl as he would an enemy, an object . . . as he would have used Tante Inge.

Pulling her arm back, he handcuffed her before flipping her over. Fassi was breathing in deep gasps now. Her eyes were fearful but wary, like a trapped animal. Karl wanted her emotions bared as completely as her body. Pushing beneath the flimsy tee-shirt, he sank his teeth into her skin. Fassi pulled away frantically, the force and suddenness of her movement making him lose his grip. She slid out from under him, kicking, trying to push free. Karl grabbed at her but her heel caught him in the temple. The blow brought tears to his eyes. Fassi scrambled to her feet. For a moment she stood over him, hands pinned behind her back, headband tight across her forehead, mouth distended by the ball gag. She looked from the door to the window, then ran for the door.

Karl rolled to his feet and went after her. This time she was ready for him. As she got to the door she kicked it once and then surprised him by turning and aiming a kick at his groin. His defense was instinctive; he caught her ankle in a cross-arm block, yanked upward and with a muffled cry she fell backward to the floor.

Her attack infuriated him. He had been through enough pain—more than enough. It was her time to endure and his time to punish. Instead she had tried to turn the tables, tried to hurt him.

Holding her ankles, he dragged her across the room. The rug scrunched the tee-shirt up around her armpits. Grabbing it, he lifted her and pushed her face down onto the dresser and took her, using her the same way he had been used as a boy, a sacrificial victim to the pain of his childhood, as if everything that he had endured could be transferred to her.

He felt no sympathy for the girl. She was an adult who chose to sell her body for sexual sport. If the trauma he inflicted was more than she bargained for, it was little enough compared to the hell of his childhood and no worse than what many a pimp had done before him.

Swept up in his contorted passions, Karl failed to notice when Fassi's eyes rolled back and she lost consciousness. Only after he climaxed and was lying with his cheek resting on her back did he become aware that she lay limp and had stopped breathing. In pulling her head back he had compressed her windpipe, cutting off her air. It took ten minutes of mouth-to-mouth resuscitation before she was breathing properly again, and during those minutes Karl realized the extent of his danger.

The episodes with prostitutes had started innocently enough as a reward for his first assassination. At first he limited these diversions to those times when he was far from home. Then he began going to West Berlin, seeking out the parlors that specialized in the types of sexual activity that attracted him. He kept this aspect of his life secret, telling himself that safety lay in controlling the impulses, not suppressing them.

But the accident with Fassi proved what he had suspected for some time—that the episodes were becoming increasingly violent and that instead of his controlling the dark needs inside him, they were coming to dominate him, overcoming his common sense, testing his strength of will and finding it lacking...

Karl left the road and drove through the neighborhood of Treptow. He stopped briefly to buy a red rose from a flower vendor, then continued to the Cemetery for Unknown Victims of Fascism. The cemetery wasn't large or well known. It consisted of a small field of well-tended grass surrounded by a two-foot-high stone wall. As a boy, Karl had helped build the wall, using the rubble from buildings shattered by the war. For this he had received a bowl of potato soup and half a slice of bread each day—a great deal at a time when many were starving.

But it wasn't for these memories that he'd come; it was for the memory of his mother, the stranger who had given him life and who linked him with unknown past generations, with aunts and uncles and grandparents and myriad ancestors lost to him but nonetheless real.

Karl walked slowly across the grass to the center of the field, where a statue stood, the only object to disturb the broad expanse of green grass. The statue, cast in bronze, was of a woman on her knees, head bowed, hands covering her face, hiding her features, leaving her identity unknown. As a boy he had come to the irrational conclusion that his mother had posed for the statue, and over the years, whenever he thought of his mother, it was this figure that came to mind.

He sat down with his back against the pedestal, tilted his head back and stared up at the hidden face framed by tufted white clouds that inched their way across the sky. The sound of children playing kickball on a nearby street came to him and their delighted laughter reminded Karl of what he had lost. He was a father with three children of his own, but his children were strangers to him. Too much was hidden—from them, from his wife, from the world at large.

"It can't go on," he said softly, twirling the rose idly between his fingers.

He sat for some minutes, breathing deeply, lost in thought. His fingers slowed and the rose became still. He saw clearly that the danger was inside him. Danger to his job, danger to his family, danger to his own personality. A choice had to be made. Either he resigned from the Stasis or he gave up the poisonous interludes with prostitutes. There was no middle way.

He closed his eyes and let his mind drift. He knew what the answer would be—what it had to be. Finally he got to his feet and stood in front of the statue, staring at the bronze hands that were as familiar as his own. A cloud passed over the sun, momentarily painting the grass a darker shade.

"Never again," he said quietly. "It stops now."

The resolution made him feel better. He drove home and found Magda baking May Day cookies while listening to the television. The two girls were still at school but Willy, their youngest, was in the back yard playing with a neighborhood boy.

Magda greeted him with a kiss, her upturned nose cool against his cheek, her hands held wide so as not to get dough on his clothes. There was a time, early in their marriage, when they delighted in each other's bodies. After the birth of their first child, however, Magda drew back from sexual experimentation and settled comfortably into a motherhood that Karl found excluded and comforted him at the same time. They were dutiful toward each other, nothing more.

"You're home early," Magda said. "Is Uncle Alex coming with us?"

Karl was suddenly alert. Alex Ikhnovsky was his mentor, a Russian KGB colonel who had been responsible for Karl's education and then his career in the Stasis.

"Coming with us where?"

"To Zinnowitz. Didn't he call you at the school?"

"No. Did you talk to him?"

"He called here just after you left. He said you invited him to come to Zinnowitz with us, which I don't mind but I wish you'd ask me first."

"I meant to," Karl said automatically.

The truth was that he hadn't talked to Uncle Alex in months and hadn't invited him along on their May Day holiday. The old Russian hated the beach. For him to invite himself along meant that something was wrong, something that he couldn't talk about on the phone but needed to discuss in person.

Karl was sorry he hadn't returned to the office, although when he thought about it he realized that Uncle Alex wouldn't call him there. Phone calls at Eichwalde were screened. Knowing the Russian as he did, Karl was certain that Ikhnovsky wanted to keep their meeting as casual and private as possible.

His thoughts were interrupted by Magda banging on the kitchen window. Outside in the back yard the two boys were fighting over a tree branch. They paused to look up.

"No sticks, Willy," Magda called out. "Put it down." The boys pretended not to hear and went back to their struggle. Magda banged on the window again, then turned to Karl.

"Make them stop that."

He opened the back door and yelled at the children. Both boys dropped the stick and turned to face him.

"Leave it alone," Karl ordered, trying not to sound severe but not succeeding too well. It annoyed him, these children who had everything and still weren't satisfied but had to make trouble.

He closed the door and stood for a moment watching Magda roll balls of dough and shove them onto a pie tin. He had come home early thinking to make love to her before the girls returned from school, but not now. He was worried about Uncle Alex, and he felt like a stranger in his own home.

He went to the garage, got out his tools and changed the oil in the Mercedes. He would not waste the afternoon.

CHAPTER

5

ONE HUNDRED MILES NORTH OF BERLIN, THE resort town of Zinnowitz sits on a low-lying peninsula thrust into the Baltic Sea. The town is bordered by hotels and guest houses facing an endless expanse of windswept dunes. One of them, the Apart-Hotel Nordsee, is a modern facility that offers, in addition to rooms and apartments, a tennis court, saltwater pool, sauna and sunbathing lawn. It was here that Alexander Ikhnovsky, former non-voting member of the Politburo and retired chairman of the KGB, came to meet Karl Alexander, the man he considered a son, the man who had taken the Russian's name as his own, the only man he could trust with his life.

"And God so loved the world He gave His only begotten son . . ."

The words came unbidden to his mind and caused him to smile. In his old age, bits and pieces of religious ceremony came washing up on the shores of his consciousness like nautical debris after a shipwreck. Ikhnovsky hadn't been to church in over sixty years, yet recently the sound of the wind in the birches took on the harmony of voices raised in liturgy, the smell of exotic pipe tobacco would startle him with the remembered aroma of incense, and the task before him called to mind God's sacrifice of His only son to save the world. Only Karl needn't be sacrificed. Not if everything went according to plan.

Ikhnovsky shifted uncomfortably. The rental car, an East German Trablant, was small and cramped, particularly for a man of his bulk. In his younger days he'd had enormous strength and energy. When he was seventeen he'd lifted a dead horse to free a fallen comrade. Another time, drunk and daring, he'd dangled one hundred feet in the air, holding onto a rope by his teeth. During the Krondstat

Rebellion he'd taken nine rebel bullets and had still been among the first wave to breach the ramparts of the fortress. "Iron Man Ikhnovsky," they had called him. But no longer. The years had thinned the once-massive limbs and caused the flesh around his neck to sag. Only his trunk retained its characteristic girth, as if all the flesh had shifted position, withdrawing to this one location.

Keeping one hand on the wheel, Ikhnovsky reached back and massaged his neck, which had become stiff. He thought longingly of Mischa, his driver during the many years the state had provided a limousine to whisk him back and forth to work. Now that he was retired he was no longer *nash*, one of the privileged few who had the General Secretary's ear. Not this General Secretary, anyway. Not the man who was willing to sign a Mutual Defense Treaty with the Americans and trade Russia's Nevsky Project for the so-called Star Wars technology. Trading a cannon for a bow and arrow—that was how General Gulst termed it.

Thinking of his fellow conspirators reminded him of their last meeting a few days ago in his dacha outside Moscow. He remembered their faces as they gathered, ostensibly to celebrate his birthday, actually to solidify their opposition to the Defense Treaty. There was Gulst, thick and stalwart, Likhacev with his disdainful smile, Pilayan with the self-righteous tilt to his chin.

Strange how different they were, each drawn to opposition for his own private reason: Gulst to protect the Nevsky Project, Likhacev to move himself closer to a position in the Politburo, Pilayan because of his fear of the Americans. None of it mattered to Ikhnovsky, who saw the threat of the Mutual Defense Treaty as cultural rather than physical.

The rich cultural heritage of the Soviet Union and the exhilarating frontiers of Marxism were being diluted by the West. Ikhnovsky knew how easily his country could become a pale imitation of America, like Canada or Western Europe. Another culture sapped by materialistic cravings, its people driven by superficial goals, eyes and ears assailed by garish advertising slogans and minds engulfed by television trivia.

Ikhnovsky recalled the day when his father had marched off to the Tsar's war and his mother had taken the family to church, where they sang and prayed for his father's safe return. *Gospodi pomuli*—even now the empty ritual phrases echoed in his mind. *Gospodi pomuli*. The prayers had availed nothing. It was not prayer that changed the course of history, but concerted action. The sort of action that was necessary now to save his country.

In his room at the Apart-Hotel Nordsee, Ikhnovsky changed his clothes, then went downstairs and asked to see the manager. Herr Oster, a portly man impeccably dressed with razor-edged sideburns and a rather flat face, hurried out to meet him. There was an air of officious subservience about Herr Oster that Ikhnovsky associated with the worst extravagances of the German character. Adopting an appropriate arrogance, Ikhnovsky presented Herr Oster with his briefcase, which he demanded be locked in the hotel safe.

"I shall place it there myself, Herr Ikhnovsky," the manager promised.

Watching the man strut away, his trousers tugging at his buttocks with each step, Ikhnovsky wondered what Herr Oster would say if he knew that inside the briefcase there was a map of a United States Military Ocean Terminal, a modified Sony radio housing a CIKOP-34F receiver with voice decryption capability, and fifty thousand American dollars?

Ikhnovsky left the building and went down to the beach, where he found Karl and his family. They were dressed in swimsuits in spite of the cool temperature and brisk wind. Sand peppered his ankles as he made his way toward them. Although he had little affinity for the sea, Ikhnovsky had changed into what he considered beach attire: a navy-blue sweater with white shorts belted high on the stomach. His legs were surprisingly thin for a man of his bulk, like those of a seagull marching across the beach. He wore leather shoes without socks, and already the sand was abrading his heel.

Karl greeted him warmly and Magda only slightly less so. The three children were dutifully polite. Bridget and Katrina actually curtsied, a gesture that struck Ikhnovsky as incongruous given the red spandex swimsuits they wore. Little Willy, the youngest, shook his hand solemnly and then raced back to his excavation in the sand. A handsome family, Ikhnovsky thought. The type of family he might have had if the years hadn't passed so quickly and the demands of trying to forge a new society hadn't been so all-consuming.

Without being told, Magda went to get another beach chair. It was early in the season and the beach was only moderately crowded. A number of people had rented rattan windbreaks, self-contained benches with backs that extended some six feet high. Others lay on towels and blankets scattered across the sand. A young couple walked arm-and-arm in the surf, a boy and his dog played tug-of-war with a towel, and from a distant radio came the melody of a popular tune.

"Sit down, uncle," Karl said, pointing to one of the two beach chairs. Once Magda was out of earshot, he gave the Russian a questioning look.

"So?"

"A crisis, Karl. We will speak of it later."

"But you—you are all right?"

Ikhnovsky shrugged. "A young man trapped in an old man's body. I am all right."

Magda returned and the two men shifted their conversation with ease that came from long practice. They spoke of the weather, of the children's progress in school, of Magda's volunteer work at the War Widows Home, of Ikhnovsky's health and of Berlin's recently relaxed border restrictions.

Ikhnovsky noted Karl's casual manner and approved. They hadn't spoken since the phone call a few days earlier, during which the Russian had been able to reveal nothing of the real purpose of his visit. He knew that Karl was curious, yet few would guess that beneath his casual pose, eyes half-closed, arms and legs draped carelessly over the chair, Karl was alert as a cat.

Magda was relating a humorous incident about a motorist who became lost in fog and drove into the sea the night before. Ikhnovsky put on a polite expression and listened without hearing. Magda had a milkmaid's freckled cheeks, blonde hair and blue eyes and a full figure that had once been voluptuous but now overflowed the edges of her two-piece bathing suit. Her interests were a traditional German hausfrau's: kitchen, church and children. She laughed easily and Ikhnovsky felt she was oblivious to Karl—to the complex personality beneath the simple facade.

Which was Karl's greatest asset, Ikhnovsky thought—that ability to function with such credibility in two different worlds. Most killers were lost and lonely men who lived without families and had few friends. They were social misfits whose secret passions knew no allegiance and this made them suspect. But Karl was different. He had grown up in the devastation of post-war Berlin, surrounded by death and dying, and despite the fact that he never spoke of the time before they met, Ikhnovsky suspected that Karl knew no difference between life and death. At some deeper level, the two states were the same to him. This was what enabled him to be a husband, a father and a killer, each with equal success.

On the beach the two daughters had joined their brother at their sand construction. They whispered among themselves and every so often turned to look toward Ikhnovsky. Finally Katrina got up and came to him, urged on by gestures from her sister. She stood awkwardly, rubbing a strand of wet hair against her cheek.

"Excuse me," she said. "Excuse me."

Magda reached over and put a hand on her daughter's shoulder while she finished describing the new addition to their house, then said, "What is it?"

"I have a question," Katrina said. She turned to Ikhnovsky. "Uncle Alex, Willy said something stupid. He says that in Russia you eat bears. Is that true?"

"Kati!" Magda said, but Ikhnovsky waved her objection away.

"No, no, no, she's right. We used to eat bears."

The little girl's eyes widened. "You did?"

"We ate field mice, too."

"Field mice!"

"Anything we could find. This was before the Revolution, when the Tsar took all the food for the soldiers and left the people to starve. So we had to eat whatever we could find. Shooting a bear would be lucky because a bear could feed a whole village."

"Oh." Katrina wrinkled her nose with distaste, then ran back to tell her brother and sister the terrible news.

"You shouldn't encourage her with such stories," Magda told him.

"All true, all true. We ate mice and pigeons during the Revolution."

Magda shuddered. "I think I would starve before I ate such things."

Karl said, "That's because you don't know what it's like to be hungry, Magda. Believe me, you would eat anything."

"A pigeon, perhaps, if I—"

"Anything."

For a moment, Karl fixed her with hard eyes empty of emotion. Then, as if someone had flicked a switch, the warmth came back. He smiled reassuringly. "I ate squirrels in the Tiergarden. Uncle Alex knows."

Magda looked uncomfortable. "You mean . . . after the war?"

"When else?" Karl stood up. "I'm going in."

He walked briskly down to where the surf tumbled and melted into the sand. The children ran after him, dancing in his footsteps and shrieking with excitement as he dove without hesitation into the sea. He swam with smooth, powerful strokes, shoulders glistening in the sun, his body lifting and falling on the incoming waves. How different he was, Ikhnovsky thought, from the dirty, half-starved little boy that he had first seen so many years ago.

"He never talks about those years," Magda said lightly.

She gave him an oblique look, inviting his confidence, but Ikhnovsky had no wish to confide in her.

"Terrible years," he said.

He closed his eyes and pretended to doze. The sun was warm where his face was sheltered from the breeze. Memories came unbidden . . . he saw again the old building on Liebnechstrasse in which the KGB offices had been located for many years after the war. The multi-story Italianate building was one of only a handful to escape the Russian shells and American bombs. It was surrounded by a wrought-iron fence, guarded twenty-four hours a day, with access strictly controlled. As *rezident* of the Berlin Section, Ikhnovsky had chosen the building precisely because it lent itself to tight security measures, and so it came as a particularly unpleasant surprise to discover an intruder.

Ikhnovsky had been on his way out when he heard the shots. He hurried downstairs and discovered a commotion in the yard. A janitor had discovered a boy in the basement. The boy had broken free, run out the back door and scaled the fence. By the time the soldiers arrived, the boy was on the other side, running across the snow-covered earth. The guards fired but the boy disappeared in the ruins of a neighboring building. The sergeant was certain the boy had been hit.

Ikhnovsky went with them and discovered a trail of blood in the snow. Following it through the debris and rubble of the bombed-out building, they found the boy sitting on the ground, his back against the wall, face contorted with pain. Although it was January, he wore only ragged pants and a frayed coat two sizes too large. His feet were wrapped in rags and were bleeding. His leg had been shattered by the bullet. The sergeant raised his rifle but Ikhnovsky placed a hand on the barrel, then picked his way through the debris. At his approach the boy pushed himself against the wall with the desperation of a wild animal. Ikhnovsky stopped in front of him.

"Does it hurt?"

In answer, a defiant stare. The Russian knelt and reached forward. Instantly the boy lashed out with a crude knife. Ikhnovsky parried the blow with a gloved hand but felt the blade cut his palm. He stood and kicked the boy's leg. Hard. The boy fainted. Ikhnovsky picked up the knife as the sergeant and guards came running forward.

"Should we call the police, sir, or shall I take care of the little Nazi privately?"

"Take him to the hospital."

"The hospital?"

"Have them fix his leg."

"Sir, he broke into a secured building and—"

The back of Ikhnovsky's hand connected with the sergeant's face.

"I will not give the same order twice," he said, then walked away without a backward glance.

An investigation of the basement revealed a crawl space behind the boiler where the boy had been living. The floor of the space was covered in newspapers and old rags, like a nest, and a window curtain blackened with soot had been hung to conceal the opening. It appeared that the intruder had been there for some time.

Ikhnovsky visited him in the hospital. The boy lay in a metal frame bed, his leg in traction. They had cleaned his face and brushed his hair but his eyes were still those of a wild animal's.

"They tell me your leg is going to mend."

The boy watched him warily, without speaking.

"How did you get inside the building?" Another pause. "Come on, nobody's going to hurt you now. How did you get in?"

"The coal chute."

"The door to the coal chute has a padlock."

"The frame is rusted loose. I got the whole thing free."

"You pulled the frame with the door attached?" The boy nodded. Ikhnovsky smiled to himself. The frame would be repaired immediately.

"You were living in the building. Why?"

"I was cold."

"You're from the rubble gang?"

Ikhnovsky didn't expect an answer and got none. Years after the war huge portions of the city still lay in ruins, inhabited by groups of homeless children known as rubble gangs. They became beggars, petty thieves, pickpockets and con artists. Their only loyalty was to other members of the gang and their only credo was survival at any cost.

"What's your name?"

The boy stared at him, his gray eyes blank. His thin cheeks and taut skin reminded Ikhnovsky of photographs he'd seen of victims of Nazi death camps.

"Come on, I want to talk to you. My name is Alexander Ikhnovsky. What are you called?"

"Karl."

"Karl what?"

"Karl Drei."

"Drei—three." Karl Three, the third in his gang by that name.

"How long were you living in the building, Karl?"

The boy shrugged.

"Days?"

He nodded.

"Weeks?"

The boy nodded again. In the building for weeks. A stowaway inside KGB headquarters in Berlin. A boy of what? Seven or eight? A boy had slipped through their security system and remained undetected for weeks? He knew what they would say at Moscow Center if they ever found out. And they would find out. Like anyone else in a position of power, Ikhnovsky had rivals who would be only too glad to see his reputation damaged.

"Can I sit here, Karl?"

The boy moved to the far side as the Russian sat down. Ikhnovsky took the boy's knife from his pocket. The blade had evidently been made from a piece of scrap metal. The shaft extended between two pieces of wood wrapped in electrical wire. "Where did you get this?"

"I made it."

"It's very sharp." Ikhnovsky held up his palm. "See what it did?" The boy tensed. "Yes, it's a good knife." Ikhnovsky held out the knife, handle first, to Karl. "Go ahead. You may need it when you get outside."

Karl took the knife and slipped it under his sheet.

"You're a clever boy, Karl. I could use a boy like you. How would you like a job?"

Taken by surprise, the boy's features softened, and for the first time Ikhnovsky could see behind the fear and desperation to the child hidden within.

"You would have enough to eat, your own room, warm clothes. In return you would be my eyes and ears on the street. A rubble boy is invisible. You can go places, see and hear things others would never be exposed to. How would you like that?"

"I would have food?"

"All you can eat."

"And shoes?"

"Shoes and wool socks to go with them."

"And I could sleep in the basement?"

"No, not there. But in my apartment, there's a cleaning closet behind the stairway. I'll have the landlady clear it out and it will be your bedroom."

Karl stared at him.

"When will I start?"

"You've already started. One of your jobs will be to test the security of all Soviet buildings—just like you did this time."

Ikhnovsky's subsequent report contained a stinging indictment of Major Bobkov, the security chief. After all, hadn't Ikhnovsky hired a rubble boy to penetrate the KGB building? And hadn't it taken the security force three weeks to discover this? What if the boy had been an enemy agent rather than one of his own people? Ikhnovsky recommended that a new security chief be sent, this time one who couldn't be fooled by a mere boy.

And so it began, a relationship based on expediency that became, in time, that of a father and son. Karl filled a void that Ikhnovsky hadn't known existed. At first this embarrassed him. He had, after all, hardened himself against emotionalism and sacrificed his personal life to building a new society. But after Karl began living beneath the stairway, the Russian found himself making excuses to avoid the drinking bouts of his peers in favor of a dinner at home with the boy, a quiet conversation and perhaps a game of chess.

For his part, Karl idolized and adored his mentor, so much so that there was never any doubt in his mind about what he would do when he grew up: he would join the KGB. The greatest disappointment of his young life was when he revealed this ambition to Ikhnovsky, who was forced to explain that only native-born Russians were allowed into the organization. But the East German intelligence agency would surely take him, Ikhnovsky would see to that.

Karl's life began on the day Alexander Ikhnovsky came to see him in the hospital. Of the time before they met, he never spoke. When Ikhnovsky sent him to grade school, he chose his mentor's first name as his own. He had been Karl Alexander ever since...

Now these memories warmed the old Russian as much as the sun and lulled him to a sleep where he dreamed of onion-spired churches and cheering crowds and clumsy wood toys carved by a man with bushy eyebrows and a thick brown beard. The man was his father but it was long ago, and the man seemed so young, so very young, so very long ago...

CHAPTER

6

KARL ALEXANDER TOOK THE LOOSE COINS from his pockets and arranged them in a neat stack upon the dresser. The currency was East German, the color and weight of aluminum, larger and lighter than its West German counterpart. Karl arranged them according to size, from largest to smallest, until they formed a graduated cone. It was a habit left over from his childhood, when a single *Pfennig* meant the difference between a crust of bread and starvation. The feel of the coins reassured him. Money was security. Money meant that he would never be enslaved by circumstance the way he had been as a child; the way he had been by Tante Inge.

Karl turned from the dresser and selected a coat from the closet. He had rented the largest and most expensive apartment at the Nordsee, one with two bedrooms and a living room with kitchenette. From the open doorway he could see Magda and the children sitting in front of the television. Willy was asleep on his mother's lap but the two girls lay on the floor, heads propped on their hands. His family gave Karl the same sense of security as did the stack of coins on the dresser.

Karl was not wealthy but he was privileged; there were many ways that a senior member of the Stasis could augment an otherwise modest salary. The anti-fascist barrier, known in the West as the Berlin Wall, was invisible to Karl. Merely by flashing his I.D. he could pass freely from one sector of the city to another. He was immune to his country's currency restrictions, and his car was never searched. A man with Karl's extensive underground connections in the West and a privileged position in the East would have to be a fool not to make money.

Magda said something and the two girls laughed. Karl

cocked his head to one side, listening, like a wolf alert to approaching game. At times it bothered him that the world of children was inexplicable to him. He knew nothing of their carefree manner and easy laughter, and on those occasions that he tried to join them, his attempts were forced and unnatural. Having had no childhood, he had no concept of a child's world. His only world had been Tante Inge.

Karl checked his appearance in the mirror, then said goodnight to Magda and the children and received a dutiful response from each. As he got into the elevator and pushed the button to the third floor, it occurred to him that he felt closer to Uncle Alex than he did to his own family.

He had been dismayed to see how old the Russian had become. Over the phone Ikhnovsky's voice had sounded strong and gruff—still the same voice that he remembered as a boy, the voice of a man who'd first appeared to him as a giant wearing a khaki greatcoat and a fur hat bearing the emblem of implacable military might, the red star. But this afternoon, when Uncle Alex played with the children, he was not so steady on his feet, and when he fell asleep in his chair his chin disappeared in the slack skin of his neck.

The elevator doors opened. As Karl stepped out a middle-aged man with a giggling young woman entered. The woman had dyed red hair and wore a tight-fitting black dress. She bumped into Karl, said, "Excuse me," and gave him a casual appraisal that made no secret of her approval. Karl paid no attention, but as he walked down the hall he found himself mentally replacing the lascivious look in the girl's eyes with one of pain and fear, just as he had done with the Algerian whore, Fassi. With an effort he pushed the image aside and concentrated on the immediate surroundings—the determinedly cheerful yellow walls, the fire extinguisher at the end of the hall, the muffled sound of a television.

He found Ikhnovsky's door and knocked. When the Russian appeared it was evident that he'd just taken a bath; his hair was damp and he wore crisp slacks with a pale silk shirt. Meeting now, they embraced again, this time with a warmth that underscored the limited significance of their earlier public greeting.

"Ah, Dreitsky, Dreitsky," the Russian said, using the nickname he'd given Karl as a boy. He held the younger man at arm's length, and Karl was surprised to see a sadness behind the joy in his eyes."

"Are you in trouble, Uncle Alex?"

"Soon enough, soon enough. Have you got the time, yes?" Ikhnovsky took Karl's wrist and turned it so that he could see the watch. It was a modern, digital design, but Karl knew he wasn't looking for the time. The watch was a Stasis design; if the digits flashed, it indicated the presence of a transmitter. Did Uncle Alex really think his room at the Nordsee might be bugged? He felt his senses sharpen. The Russian was not a man to harbor groundless fears.

Ikhnovsky grunted, reassured. He turned away, motioning impatiently to the television.

"Find us a good program, something to take our mind off our troubles."

Karl performed the ritual precaution, turning the volume up on a documentary about sailboat racing.

"Yes, good," Ikhnovsky called to him.

He was unscrewing the mouthpiece of the phone. Only after he removed the microphone and placed it on the table did he motion Karl to sit down.

"Come, come," he said, speaking in Russian. "Now we can talk."

They sat at a round formica table near a picture window that looked out over the sea. Below them the beach was bright with floodlights, but beyond it the water merged into darkness and only the white foam was visible, advancing on unseen waves like pale snakes sliding sideways through the night.

"Karl," Ikhnovsky began somberly, "what I have to say will jeopardize your career, the safety of your family, perhaps your life. If there was any other way . . . if I was young enough, if I could turn back the clock inside this old man's body and become like you, a man in his prime . . ."

He sighed. Karl watched and waited. He knew the old man's moods well enough not to try and hurry him. Ikhnovsky placed his hands on the table and shook his head.

"What the mind wills," he said, "this body can no

longer achieve; what the eye sees, these hands cannot grasp."

Karl slid his hands across the table. "Use these, Uncle."

Ikhnovsky smiled. "I know you have little interest in ideological concerns, Karl, but are you not aware that the socialist world has reached a dangerous crossroad? Our ideals are no longer closely held, our commitment has faded, and the great dream of the Revolution is dying. You are young, but I remember our vision of a new world, a vision that made us strong, so strong we could prevail even when we made mistakes. But this heritage is slipping away, and with it, the whole promise of the future."

Karl listened but the words had little effect. He knew the benefits of Marxism and the weakness of capitalism and the evils of imperialism, but he knew these things as dogma, as subjects that he learned in school. Karl was not an intellectual. Political concepts and abstract discussions mattered little until they led to action. He had only one allegiance—to Alexander Ikhnovsky, and only through him to the state he served.

"It's not nuclear weapons that will destroy us, Karl, it's cultural sabotage. Can you see that? No, no, I bore you. Very well, then. Let me show you something that may make an impression, even on your pragmatic soul."

Ikhnovsky crossed the room and lifted a briefcase to the bed. He unlocked it and pulled out a video-cassette.

"You've heard about the Nevsky Project, I assume?"

"The Soviet version of the American Star Wars program."

The Russian shook his head, waving the cassette in the air as he carried it to the videotape recorder.

"Wrong, wrong, wrong. That is what everyone thinks—that the two systems are compatible. And no wonder, since our illustrious General Secretary intends to trade the fruits of Soviet science for the so-called Star Wars program."

Karl knew what he meant. The General Secretary was flying to Washington at the end of the month to sign the Mutual Defense Treaty. The agreement provided for an exchange of defense technologies between the Soviet Union and United States, with scientists from each country working on both systems. The first system to be operational would be deployed for the benefit of both nations. The treaty had many critics, American as well as Russian.

Uncle Alex continued talking as he inserted the video-cassette.

"But I let you judge for yourself. See what the Nevsky Project is capable of. The Americans talk about their Star Wars and laser systems, still years in the future, seen only in Disneylands and Hollywood movies, while we—we *have* a system capable of erecting an electronic shield around every major city and military installation in the country."

The television screen flickered and the scene of sailboats was replaced by momentary hash that cleared as a title appeared: "Department of Research, Strategic Rocket Forces, Project N-181: Contents Classified *Top Secret*."

"You still have your sources, Uncle," Karl said with admiration.

"I am not alone, Karl. There are others."

The first scene showed what looked like a huge satellite dish over fifty feet in diameter with a long spiked pole extending from the center. The dish was housed inside a laboratory. Other scenes showed huge dynamos and multi-paneled control rooms. Men in white lab coats worked on machinery and occasionally one of them would catch sight of the camera and smile self-consciously.

"Very short frequency radio waves," Ikhnovsky explained in a voice that sounded as if he'd memorized certain facts. "Sixty gigahertz. A chip gun is what the scientists call it. It can destroy the microchip circuitry of a missile's guidance system. Watch. Watch this now."

Massive doors on one side of the building opened onto a broad field. The field overlooked a distant lake. Instinctively Karl noted the geography and tried to place it. He couldn't be sure, but it might be the Aral Sea.

The scene shifted to a launchpad where a missile sat pointed at the sky. In the corner of the screen white video numbers began a countdown from thirty seconds.

"The countdown is for activating the Nevsky signal," Ikhnovsky said. "The missile is launched first."

Karl nodded, said nothing. The tape reminded him of early German rocket tests he'd seen of the V-1 and V-2, except that here the quality was better. At five seconds the missile vaulted into the air. A slow-motion camera tracked it out over the lake. Moments later the countdown reached zero and the Nevsky transmitter was activated. Immediately the missile went out of control, began to tumble and then exploded. The camera followed a plume of smoking debris into the lake.

"And *that* is what the General Secretary wants to give the Americans," Ikhnovsky said with disgust. "The Nevsky Project, in exchange for what? Blueprints."

"A radio wave did that?"

"You see the possibilities? An electronic umbrella over every major city and military installation in the Soviet Union. Impervious to the advanced electronics of modern delivery systems."

Karl was impressed. The Nevsky Project had been kept secret and reports of its capabilities varied wildly. This was the first time he'd seen anything concrete.

"It's already operational?"

"As you see."

The tests continued, each with the same result.

"Then I don't understand," said Karl. "Why trade with the Americans if you have the Nevsky transmitters?"

The old man gave him a fierce look.

"If *we* have the Nevsky transmitter. Why speak as if it were separate from you? From the GDR? From the rest of the Warsaw Pact? This is *our* technology."

Karl nodded, thinking that Uncle Alex's patriotism seemed to become more extreme with age.

"We, then. Why don't we just deploy the Nevsky transmitters and forget the treaty?"

"The cost. Look there." Ikhnovsky indicated the last test, in which the missile escaped unharmed. "The power requirements for Nevsky wave-transmission are tremendous. As you see, the range in the tests is still limited. What we need are superconductors—technology that the Americans can provide."

"Forgive me, Uncle," Karl said, "but that sounds like a reason to sign this Mutual Defense Treaty. With a Nevsky transmitter using superconductors, both countries could deploy defensive screens without being vulnerable to the other."

"Without being vulnerable to missiles," Ikhnovsky corrected.

"You mean the danger is from manned aircraft?"

"I mean the danger from another Nevsky transmitter. Watch this now."

The screen had gone black but a new title announced the next set of tests. This time it was a Soviet T-54 tank that sat in the middle of the field. As Karl watched, two men brought a dog and lifted it into the tank, where it was harnessed in front of a video camera. The men left, closing the hatch after them. The scene shifted back to the tank's interior and the countdown numbers appeared. The dog waited, glancing up toward where the men had disappeared and occasionally pulling against its harness. When the countdown reached zero it let out a silent yelp, twisted violently and wrenched its head back, gnashing blindly at its shoulders. Then it collapsed and after a few quick convulsions lay still. The scene shifted and the technicians were shown pulling the dog's body from the tank. They held it up, smiling, like big-game hunters with a trophy.

Ikhnovsky stopped the tape.

"Sterile destruction," he said quietly. "That's what they call it. With more power a tank battalion could be stopped in its tracks. With enough power, the population of Tokyo or New York could be wiped out—and all without disturbing a single brick."

Karl, not usually impressed by new technologies, found himself talking in hushed tones.

"The effect is the same on humans?"

"All forms of animal life," the Russian said. "The electro-chemical impulses of the brain are just as susceptible to it as microchips."

Ikhnovsky removed the video-cassette, and the television returned to its normal program, a comedy about a man trying to learn to ski. "You see why the Nevsky project can't be allowed to fall into American hands?"

"Has the General Secretary seen these experiments?"

"Of course, he has. That's what makes his decision all the more criminal. To hand over to the Americans the weapon for our own destruction..." Ikhnovsky shook his head. "Can you imagine a transmitter orbiting the earth? Powered by the sun, making use of superconductors?"

"I thought you said it was cultural sabotage that worried you, Uncle."

"Cultural sabotage and physical destruction go hand in hand. The first prepares us for the second. I worry about both of them. That's why I've come to you. I want you to help save my country, Karl. Our country. The General Secretary has lost sight of what his mission is, what all his dealings with the United States are supposed to serve. He has become seduced by the wine of peace, corrupted by compromise, ready to sacrifice our heritage to economic expediency. He must be stopped."

"I'm not another Lenin, Uncle."

"Ignaty Grinevitsky," Uncle Alex said slowly.

Karl's smile died as he realized the full import of Ikhnovsky's words. Ignaty Grinevitsky was the man who assassinated the Russian Tsar, Alexander II. Every schoolboy knew that.

"But," added Ikhnovsky, "I don't ask you to sacrifice yourself, as happened to poor Grinevitsky."

"What do you ask, Uncle?"

The Russian pushed himself out of the chair and went to his briefcase, which was lying on the bed. He pulled out a manila envelope, drew from it a folded piece of paper and handed it to Karl, who spread it on the table without comment. It was a map of a shipping terminal. The legend and the building designations were in English, which Karl read without difficulty. He was trained to be fluent in both English and French, the languages of the Western occupation forces in Germany.

"Military Ocean Terminal Bayonne?"

Ikhnovsky nodded. "Bayonne, New Jersey, in New York harbor. I draw your attention to Warehouse E."

Karl ran a finger down the index until he found what he was looking for. Ikhnovsky, standing behind him, placed a hand on his shoulder.

"Before I tell you what is inside it, you must know two things, Karl. First, that this is not an official assignment. If you undertake it you will be given a two-weeks' leave of absence, ostensibly as an adviser to our KGB training facility in Yaroslavl. This will be a lie. You will disappear for thirteen days. When you return, you will be a hero, but you must never speak of it and no one can ever know."

"And the second thing?"

"If you fail, it will mean my death."

"Then you will live a long time, Uncle Alex," Karl said quietly. "What is in the warehouse?"

Ikhnovsky did not smile but Karl could see the satisfaction reflected in the old man's eyes.

"What *will* be in the warehouse three weeks from now is a shipment designated *QL 4416 H5*. The shipment is composed of Redeye shoulder-launched missiles on their way to the contra rebels in Nicaragua. One of the Redeyes will not reach its destination. Instead, you must steal it and shoot down a Soviet Ilyushin 62." He paused, then added, "I think you know who will be on the aircraft."

"The General Secretary?" Karl said.

Ikhnovsky nodded. Karl searched the old man's face; his intent was reflected in his eyes.

"Explain it to me."

"The Redeye shipment arrives by rail on the twenty-third. The ship, the *Coralis*, is a civilian vessel under long-term contract to Military Sealift Command, which will take the Redeyes to the rebels. It will arrive on the twenty-fifth. Between the arrival of the Redeye shipment and the *Coralis*, you must steal one of the Redeyes in such a manner that the theft cannot be detected."

"Steal an American missile? Why not use one of our own?"

"Because the attack must appear the work of an American patriot. A fanatic dedicated to destroying the Soviet Union."

"And who is this patriot?"

"I leave that up to you, Karl." Ikhnovsky patted his shoulder. "I leave too much up to you, I know."

"You challenge me."

"Because I have faith. I put my life in your hands." It was the most important argument for the mission he could put to Karl. More effective, Ikhnovsky knew, than talk of the glory of the Soviet Union.

Karl remembered something he had heard about the Redeye missile. "I thought the Americans replaced the Redeye with the Stinger."

"They did. That's why they're giving these to the Nicaraguan contras. That's why this shipment is unusual. The Bayonne terminal is not normally used for missile shipments and the security will not be as tight."

Karl began to consider the attack itself and its political ramifications. "The General Secretary . . . Are you sure?"

"Listen to me, listen carefully." Ikhnovsky came around

the table and sat opposite him. "I do not come here alone. There are forces in Moscow just as determined as I to rid us of the current leadership. They want to do this before the Mutual Defense Treaty is signed. They will fail in this attempt unless the General Secretary is destroyed and his so-called reformists discredited. We will do both, you and I, in one stroke. When the General Secretary's aircraft is shot down, the world will see the fallacy of even attempting détente with the Americans, and the reformists will be leaderless."

"But to shoot down his aircraft . . . there must be defensive systems. Countermeasures, electronic jamming, air-to-air missiles . . ."

Ikhnovsky waved his hand. "Yes, yes, of course. The Ilyushin is fully protected with sophisticated countermeasures. Nothing as primitive as a Redeye could succeed as long as the plane's infra-red defenses are engaged. But they will not be engaged. Only the display panel, which will indicate to the crew that the system is armed and operating properly."

"You can do that?"

"I told you, Dreitsky, I am not alone in this."

He returned to his briefcase and brought out two more items. His movements were quick and energetic now, like those of a young man. He was happier than Karl had seen him in years.

"I have everything you need." He handed Karl an expensive-looking Sony radio about the size of a walkie-talkie.

"Made by Sony, modified by our electronics expert. This will pick up all aviation frequencies as well as Alpha voice-encrypted Soviet air-to-air communications. I will show you how it works. You will also need this."

Ikhnovsky handed him a manila envelope and Karl pulled out a photocopy of a U.S. Army training manual. In large type across the front he read: *Operator Manual*: REDEYE Air Defense Guided Missile System XM41E2.

"You'd better memorize it," the Russian said. "The Americans would give you a rude welcome if they discovered this in your luggage."

Karl nodded absently, his mind on the political consequences of the Redeye plot. It was one thing to wage war against the enemies of the state, but this was not another assassination of a spy or a traitor. This was the head of the

Soviet state. He suppressed an urge to ask the names of the other conspirators. He had never questioned Uncle Ikhnovsky before. Besides, the information that the Russian brought was in itself enough proof that the conspiracy represented a significant portion of the Soviet hierarchy. Sensing his unease, Ikhnovsky said, "Something is wrong?"

Karl shook his head, smiled. "Just taking a deep breath, Uncle."

A distant look came to Ikhnovsky's eyes. "We are going to save the Socialist heritage, Karl. You and I, and a lovesick girl named Marina."

CHAPTER

7

"I WISH HE HAD CALLED ME AT MIDNIGHT," Maurice Singer told his partner. "I would have called him back two hours later just to change the rendezvous."

"And let him have control?" Hugh asked with a smile.

Both of them knew that Company doctrine specified the primary responsibility of a case officer was to maintain control of his asset. Maurice grunted. He had his own opinion of Company doctrine and of how to control men like Paul Stafford.

The two men were waiting at the Trio, a popular restaurant near Dupont Circle. They sat at an outdoor table next to a wrought-iron railing that separated the dining area from the sidewalk. After three months of intensive surveillance—expensive surveillance—finally there was some action on the Stafford case.

"You think he got instructions from our local *rezident*?" Maurice asked, referring to the KGB chief of the Soviet embassy.

"He's just as likely to get a bullet from them as instructions."

"Because he's blown?"

"Because he's blown the assassinations."

"He did it on purpose."

"Maybe."

"Why else?"

Hugh nursed his coffee and said nothing. Theoretically, he was training the younger man, but he half-suspected that Maurice was there to keep an eye on him. Hugh knew his own reputation well enough. Ever since the Iran debacle he was considered second-string material. Nobody had ever told him so, but nobody needed to. His subsequent assignments had proved it to him. It was only because he and Jock Lewis, the new deputy director of intelligence, were old friends that he'd been put on the Stafford case.

Hugh Roark had been dealt an odd hand. He'd joined the Company after World War II and served as a case officer first in post-war Vienna and later the Middle East. His instincts were good. He had a knack for recruiting and running agents, and in each station he quickly built a reliable, high-quality network. At one point it was widely assumed that he would someday inherit the position of deputy director of intelligence. But when Hugh returned to the States he discovered he had no patience for political maneuvering. His career reached a plateau, and for a number of years he remained a perennial candidate for great things. Then he had the misfortune to be named chief of station in Tehran two months before the Shah of Iran was deposed. When the CIA came under intense criticism for failing to predict that event, Hugh became a convenient scapegoat. Since then he'd been marking time, waiting for retirement. The Paul Stafford case was an intriguing exception to the routine jobs he'd been stuck with. What made it more intriguing was that his educated instincts told him that Paul Stafford was telling the truth. In this he was at odds with Maurice, who, as a poor judge of character, automatically suspected guilty motives in everyone.

"So what do we know?" Maurice asked rhetorically. "We know that before we caught Stafford's stories the deaths were all classified as accidents—all except the Wilson case. And with Wilson the death was designed to look local, not Soviet. To make a murder look like measles takes high-level talent, so the question is, why would Moscow waste it by having Stafford publish the truth in a mystery magazine?"

Maurice gave Hugh a sidelong glance, inviting him to respond. When the older man said nothing, Maurice delivered the answer himself.

"Unless they were testing us to find out how thorough our security office is. How about that?"

"Maybe," Hugh said. His eyes ranged over Maurice's shoulder, scanning the street, watching for Paul.

"But you don't think so?"

Hugh sighed. "If they were going to test, they'd use

something less damaging than assassinations. Remember how close the trail got to Moscow when the Bulgarians blew the job on the Pope? If we make murders out of these accidents and connect them to Moscow, the smell will make the Chernobyl meltdown look like a picnic. I can't see any way that Moscow wants those stories published."

"Then where's he getting the information if he's not getting it from them?"

"Maybe we'll find out."

Hugh nodded toward the street, where Paul Stafford was coming toward them. He wore what Hugh considered a typical journalist's outfit—jeans and an Oxford shirt with a herringbone jacket. When he caught sight of them, Paul changed direction and came directly to their table, stepping over the iron railing. Hugh thought he looked haggard. Probably up all night, trying to decide what to do, how much to tell.

"Different color every day?" Paul said, gesturing to the rubber band Maurice was twisting between his fingers. It took a moment, but when Maurice realized what he meant, he shrugged and said, "Whatever the morning paper is wrapped in."

"The *Herald*?"

"The *Post*."

"Yeah, they got the best rubber bands."

As an exercise in one-upmanship the exchange was a minor one, but for Hugh it added another detail to the emerging portrait of Paul Stafford, who had evidently noticed Maurice's habit the day before. An observant man, Stafford.

A smiling waitress appeared with coffee and menus. Paul ordered a slice of pie; Hugh and Maurice, on an expense account, ordered full lunches. When the waitress left, Hugh began the conversation by telling Paul he was surprised but pleased that he'd decided to cooperate.

"It's a two-way street," Paul told him. "I'll tell you what I know, you tell me what you know."

"I'd like to do that," Hugh said, "but I can't agree to conditions until I know the nature of the information you intend to provide, plus how deeply implicated you are."

"That's easy," said Paul. "But you won't like the answer."

"Try me." Hugh was smiling but his normally restless eyes were still now, alert and watching Paul closely.

Paul took a deep breath. When he spoke, his voice was flat. "I have nightmares. I dream about killing people and when it happens, I write stories about it. I don't expect you to believe it, but there it is. All of it."

The rubber band popped off Maurice's fingers and landed in the sidewalk. "Dreamed it? You mean like, made it up? Like it didn't happen?"

"I know it happened. Now I do. What I don't know is *why* I dreamed it."

"What does that mean?" Maurice demanded. "You came here to ask us the same question we're asking you?"

"You wanted to know what I have to do with the killings. I told you. What I want to know is the circumstances—particularly on Kelso, Durning and Schrader."

"Why them particularly?"

"Because I already know something about Manheim and Wilson. I know when and where they died, but I don't know if they were—what? Agents or assets? Aren't those your two categories?"

"Or enemies," said Maurice.

"Were they enemies?"

Hugh said, "They were both assets."

"In case you didn't know," Maurice added.

"I didn't. I got my information from the morgue. Files and research."

The waitress brought an apple pie. There was a slice of cheese draped over the top that Paul lifted with a fork and placed in an ash-tray. After the waitress had gone Paul explained how the dreams came sporadically but in vivid detail, including names. Maurice expressed his disbelief while Hugh watched silently, occasionally raising a question or making a comment to soften Maurice's abrasiveness. After repeating himself half a dozen times Paul asked about the other deaths, the ones he hadn't tracked down. Maurice became quiet and glanced at Hugh, who was absently stirring a bowl of vegetable soup long since grown cold.

"You make me feel like a man with one foot in the boat and one foot on the shore," Hugh said slowly. "On the one hand we know you weren't physically present when the killings took place—you weren't even in any of the same countries. On the other hand this story about dreaming up the details is something I just can't accept. If you'd give us something more to work with—"

Paul stood up. "I don't have anything more to work with. I've told you all I know and one way or the other I'm going to find out the rest. When I do, you guys will be the last to know."

He left without a backward glance. The two men stared after him and Maurice said, "Did he really think we were going to believe that?"

Hugh gave him a sharp look, then got up quickly. "Take care of the bill," he said.

Paul was already in his car when Hugh caught up to him. He leaned down and peered in the open window on the passenger's side.

"Wait a minute, Mr. Stafford. I have a proposition for you. Would you be willing to take a polygraph?"

"A lie detector?"

"If you can prove you're telling the truth I'll go along with you. Maybe we can help each other. But I've got to have something besides sweet dreams and fairytales before I put my ass on the line."

Paul stared at him a moment. "If I take the test, you tell me what you know?"

"If you *pass* the test."

Paul thought about it a moment, then nodded. "When and where?"

"I'll call you."

As the car pulled away, Hugh wondered what they were going to do if his instinct was right. What if Paul Stafford really was telling the truth?

The note was waiting for Paul when he got home that night. The house had been cleaned, the rug vacuumed, dirty clothes washed, the dishes put away. The note was on the dining room table beneath a saltshaker.

Dear Paul—
We are not this kind of people. I have to get away—I need time to think things out. I would say I'm sorry but you would say that's an excuse. If you need shirts, the laundry ticket is in the top drawer of my dresser. I'll call you in a few days. Believe it or not, I still love you.

—Jo

Paul felt a rush to anger. She had stayed in bed that morning when he left for work and he had never had a chance to tell her about the CIA men. Now, when he needed her as an alibi and as a witness, she was gone.

He crumpled the note and threw it across the room. It had taken him ten years to build a career and during that time his philosophy had been *run fast, run lean and run alone*. Not until he was near the top as a journalist did he figure he was ready for marriage and its commitment, and not until Joanna was he willing. Very willing. She was twenty-six, he was thirty-eight, and each ignited the other. They were smart and quick and bright and they lived with a sense of special dispensation, as though immune from the mundane considerations that burdened the rest of the world. They woke up gladly to each new day and mined it for all the exhilaration and laughter it could bring and then fell asleep in one another's arms, rocked by ebbing waves of passion, exhausted, full, content.

When Jason came they incorporated him into the vision they had of their lives. They planned to travel with him, expose him to foreign countries, to other races and religions; they would teach him foreign languages, make him part of a new, enlightened generation, a citizen of the world. He became an extension of their dreams, and with his death their world came tumbling down...

Paul poured himself a drink and wandered through the house, trying to guess Joanna's intentions by what she'd taken. He looked in her closet, her dresser, the bathroom. Some clothes were gone, some shoes, makeup and toiletries. And birth control pills. A glance inside the medicine cabinet showed him that. He felt a stab of jealousy at the thought of her with Cuevo. And then he thought of last night; of the marks on her body, the desperation of their lovemaking, the recriminations followed by the empty silence as they lay back-to-back, not touching. He saw her now as if through the wrong end of a telescope, distant, almost like a stranger. A stranger running away...

The next day Paul followed instructions from Hugh and arrived at a nondescript building on Sixteenth Street. He took an elevator to the seventh floor, to an office labeled "Barrington Associates." The receptionist, a middle-aged

woman in a cashmere dress, sat behind an L-shaped desk
reading a newspaper. She announced Paul on an intercom
and a moment later Hugh Roark appeared. Paul noticed
that he wore a coded blue identification badge. After
exchanging a brief greeting Hugh ushered him to an
interior room with off-white walls, a salmon rug and
simple upholstered furniture of white ash. Maurice was
waiting with two other people, all wearing blue badges.
Hugh made the introductions.

"This is Bob Gonzales, our technician, and Dr. Annie
Helms, with our office of medical services."

Paul shook hands with Gonzales, a middle-aged man
with a droopy Arab-looking moustache and a glistening,
peppermint smile. Then he turned to Annie Helms, a tall,
willowy woman in a beige suit. Her pale greenish eyes
regarded him from behind black-rimmed glasses and she
greeted him with a no-nonsense handshake. Except for her
teased blonde hair, she was all business.

"What kind of medical services do you provide?" Paul
asked.

"My branch is in charge of things like candidate profiles,
personality testing, character analysis—personnel services."

"Psychiatric testing?"

Behind the glasses Paul caught the quick blink of surprise, followed by a slight smile.

"I hope you have no objections."

"No, no, some of my best friends are blonde psychiatrists."

Her smile broadened slightly.

"I asked Dr. Helms to be here," said Hugh, "because
I've got to consider the possibility that you're telling the
truth. And if you are, well, we're going to have to look
in . . . in unusual directions for the answers."

"Meaning inside my head?"

Hugh spread his hands. "That's where you say you find
the murders."

"Or they find me."

"Shall we find out?"

The test itself took an hour. After Paul signed a consent
agreement Hugh reviewed the form and nature of the
questions, which were to be answered either "yes" or
"no." Bob Gonzales had him take off his coat and roll up
his sleeves so he could attach the machine. Gonzales
explained what he was doing as he went along, all very

friendly and reassuring, except that it did nothing to reduce Paul's feeling of being readied for the electric chair.

"This strap is called a pneumograph," Gonzales said. "It measures changes in your breathing. This device is just a standard cardiograph—have you ever had a cardiograph taken, Mr. Stafford? Nothing to it, really. And these are galvanic sensors that measure the skin's resistance to electric current."

"One-ten or two-twenty?"

"Heh, heh. No, nothing like that. We use one point five volts of direct current. You won't even feel it."

Once Paul was hooked up, Hugh asked the questions while Gonzales sat off to one side, monitoring the machine. Annie Helms and Maurice sat on a couch along one wall. Maurice was on good behavior today. He said nothing to Paul, but sat quietly, whispering occasional comments to Annie. Once the questions started she put up a hand to silence him and focused on Paul.

Hugh began with simple, obvious questions: "Are we in Washington, D.C.? Do you live in Arlington, Virginia? Is your name Paul Henry Stafford?" Then came more relevant questions: "Did you dream of the death of a man called Dan Kelso? Did you know that Dan Kelso was the name of an employee of the Central Intelligence Agency? Had you received any information about Dan Kelso prior to dreaming about him? Did you receive any information about the manner of Dan Kelso's death from any source other than your dream?"

Hugh asked each question in a calm, unemotional tone and paused before asking the next one. Interspersed with the relevant questions were more of the innocuous ones designed, Paul assumed, to provide a contrast in readings in case he was lying. They did each death in turn—Kelso, Manheim, Durning, Wilson, Schrader, Beaumier. Even though he was telling the truth, there was a tightness in his stomach that Paul associated with childhood visits to the dentist.

They ran through the questions once, took a ten-minute break, then ran through them again, asking the same questions in a different order and having Paul offer double responses. The double responses took twice as long because each question was asked twice with Paul answering first "yes" and then "no." Hugh assured him that this was standard procedure in sensitive cases because it gave them a direct comparison of high and low stress responses.

When it was over Bob Gonzales disconnected the polygraph and took his graphs and charts into another room to analyze them. Hugh and Maurice followed but Annie stayed behind. She handed Paul a medical form and asked him to fill it out.

"You mind if I get a drink first?" Paul said.

"There's a fountain down the hall. I'll show you."

"I can find it."

"You don't have a blue tag," she said. "Security."

"You have a lot of secrets in this building?"

"Well, some. Or so we like to think."

There was a soft, Southern lilt to her voice that Paul found appealing. Following her down the hall he found something else appealing: a fullness in her buttocks that was unexpected considering her narrow body. When they returned Annie sat quietly on the couch while he filled out the form. The first part detailed the state of his physical health; then came questions about mental illness. Had he ever undergone psychiatric treatment? Had he ever been institutionalized? Had he ever been diagnosed as having this or that condition? Had any of the following drugs ever been prescribed? Had he ever suffered from dizziness, hallucinations, hot flashes, cold flashes, blackouts, premonitions, visitations . . . ?

He had almost finished when Maurice came into the room. "Dr. Helms, we've got a readout."

He held open the door for her. After she left, Maurice stood with his arms crossed, eyeing Paul.

"You look unhappy," Paul said. "What's the matter, I passed the test?"

"There's a tiny percentage of the population that doesn't have guilt feelings, no matter what they've done."

"And you think I'm one of them."

"It's a more logical explanation than dreaming."

But when Hugh returned with Annie he said, "Bob gives you a clean bill of health, so instead of solving a mystery we've got a bigger one. Let's see if we can pool our resources and come up with something."

Hugh was carrying a briefcase, thin as a cigarette pack with a combination lock. He lifted it to the table, opened it and brought out a manila envelope. Now that he'd made the decision to trust Paul, he gave him the details in a brisk, businesslike manner.

"First case, Dan Kelso. He was one of ours, working out of the Hague. Officially he drowned when he fell from a ferry crossing the English Channel. Death listed as an accident. In your story, 'Ace High, All Die,' the killer strikes him in the stomach before throwing him overboard. A nice touch. The first breath he took would have filled his lungs with water. Second case, Jurgen Manheim, one of our assets, but unreliable. He was a black-marketeer who ran goods back and forth between East and West Berlin. We never completely accepted the suicide but never questioned it either. Manheim was an opportunist, expendable. Third case, Max Durning, another asset. Durning was one of Bertil Lindstrom's assistants. You're familiar with Lindstrom?"

"Swedish scientist. I think nominated for a couple of Nobel prizes, never got one."

"He's a physicist. Durning was one of his assistants. The Russians got a lever on him and had him delivering data from Lindstrom's research. We caught him, turned him and gave him something different to pass on to the Soviets. You remember a few years back, when the Russians lost some key scientists in an accidental explosion?"

"The Karpov Institute accident."

"It seems the formula had a flaw. Anyway, Durning's death was in retribution for the stuff we had him pass the Soviets. Durning died in the mountains on a hiking trip. Looked as if he fell down a ravine and broke his neck. Nobody questioned it, but in your story you've got a killer who snaps his neck with a blow to the jaw. The same way, in fact, Lisle Beaumier died."

Paul nodded. In his mind he saw the face of each victim, no longer imaginary, but a real person, killed before his eyes.

"Fourth case, Jim Wilson. You already know the details here. Wilson was a cryptographer who pretended to go over to the other side. I can't give you details on this one but you know about as much as we do about the killing. Except it wasn't right-wing Turks who did it. Fifth case, just last year: Frank Schrader, one of ours, died on vacation in Jamaica. An autopsy showed a heart attack. In your story, Schrader was popped with a spray gun of hydrogen cyanide." Hugh shook his head. "We should have caught that one. Hydrogen cyanide's an old KGB trick—leaves no trace and reads like cardiac arrest. Anyway, that's what we know. Now what about you? Can you tell us anything else? Anything more about the dreams, when or why they come?"

Paul shook his head. "I put all the details in the stories. As far as the dreams go there's no rhyme or reason. I've made time charts, tried to remember what I ate the night before—there's nothing."

"What about the killer? Do you ever get a name on him?"

"The killer? *I'm* the killer. In the dreams, it's always me."

"But you don't get a name, like you do on the victims?"

"Get a name? From where? It's not like turning on the television and watching J. R. Ewing kill his wife." Paul let out a deep breath. "It's as if I experience it, not watch it. While I'm dreaming I am the killer."

"Wait a minute," Maurice said. "Assuming he's telling the truth—"

"I thought we just proved that," Paul said.

"Okay, okay." Maurice had been standing against the wall, watching skeptically. Now he moved forward. "I was just thinking, what he said about the television. I read somewhere about a man living close to a radio transmitter and he actually heard the programs in his head. The frequencies resonated in—it was either a tooth or one of those little bones in his ear. Anyway, isn't it possible his house is in the path of some kind of transmitter from a surveillance setup? That he's picking up the murders like this man picked up radio signals?"

Paul shook his head. "I didn't even have my house when I dreamed of Dan Kelso. And when Durning died I was in El Salvador."

"Not only that," Hugh added. "There would have to be more than a transmitter. Somebody would have to be filming and broadcasting the murders. Not very likely."

"*Nothing's* likely," Maurice said. "But it's a lot more likely than dreaming things up out of thin air. We all know those stories weren't just coincidences. Even *he* knows that."

Maurice pointed to Paul, who said, "I'm not deaf and blind, Singer."

"Well, you don't think they're coincidences, do you?"

"No, I don't think they're coincidences."

"Okay then, that's my point."

There was a long silence, broken by Annie Helms' quiet voice. She had been sitting on the couch, studying Paul's medical report.

"You mentioned here that you sometimes have premonitions, Mr. Stafford."

"It's more like an instinct. Usually when I'm out on a story and things don't feel right."

"Can you give me an example?"

"Yes, but I don't see... Well, okay, there was the time in Afghanistan when I was with a rebel unit that was going out and I was set to go with them. We started in the morning and were crossing a stream at the edge of town when I got a very uneasy feeling. I decided to go back and do an interview with a convoy leader I'd been trying to get to and who had just showed up. That night the men didn't come back. It turned out they'd been ambushed, all killed. That kind of thing. You spend enough time in combat zones—starting back in Nam—and you begin to develop a sort of sixth sense. Sometimes it's strong, sometimes less so. And sometimes you act on it, sometimes you don't."

"But these premonitions are only feelings? Not like the images you have when dreaming?"

"Not the same thing at all. I don't know how to describe it exactly, but the whole experience is different. The premonitions are part of me that feels uncomfortable but the dreams—while I'm asleep it feels like I'm being... invaded. Almost as if someone's taking over my body..."

Maurice was trying to light a cigarette. Now he looked up. "What does that mean? You're a victim of some sort of demonic possession?"

"Please," Annie said, then returned her attention to Paul. "Mr. Stafford, you consider these dreams to be unpleasant, unwelcome occurrences, don't you?"

"They're sure not pleasant."

"And you prefer to forget them as soon as possible?"

"That's why I write them down. As soon as they're part of a story I can forget about them."

"I wonder if you'd mind doing the opposite. I wonder if you'd mind thinking back, going through each dream, detail by detail, so that we could see if there was something you perhaps overlooked."

She was leaning forward, legs crossed with both hands resting on the upraised knee. There was an eagerness in her eyes, an anticipation.

"I'm sorry," he said. "Once I write it down I put it out of my mind. When I read the stories now, there are things that seem brand-new—that's how much I've forgotten."

"Only consciously, Mr. Stafford. Subconsciously the mind is a repository for everything you've ever seen, heard, smelled, tasted or touched. Everything of significance, that is. Those things that make the strongest emotional impact are the easiest to retrieve. Your dreams certainly belong in that category."

"Are you talking about my mind or a computer?"

Maurice cleared his throat and gave Hugh an uneasy look. Hugh said, "What are you suggesting, doctor?"

"If Mr. Stafford will agree, I'd like to hypnotize him. By doing that we can return to each dream, relive it, and perhaps access details that are missing from the stories."

"You really think you can do that?" Maurice asked. It was evident by his tone what he thought the answer was.

"We can try, if Mr. Stafford is willing."

They all turned to look at Paul, but he kept his eyes on Annie Helms. "You'd be the one to do it?"

"Yes."

"Alone?"

"We'll establish whatever conditions make you most comfortable." She took off her glasses as if to emphasize her sincerity. "If you'd like it to be just the two of us, then that's how it will be."

She had a long, oval face, Paul noticed, and her greenish eyes reflected the room, bowed and distorted, with him in the center of it.

"Okay, doctor. You've got a deal."

CHAPTER

8

THEY MET THE NEXT DAY AT THE ELITE DINER,
a cafe that had been redone in the style of the 1950s.
Having lunch was Annie's idea, a way of getting acquainted
and building trust before she tried to hypnotize him.

"Hypnosis is a two-way street," she told him. "If you
don't want to be hypnotized, I can't make it happen.
You've got to want it."

A middle-aged waitress whose uniform included bobby
socks and a pillbox hat took their order. The pink and gold
flaked formica table was framed in chrome and the thick
padded seats were upholstered in turquoise vinyl. A huge
Wurlitzer jukebox glowed in one corner and the menus
were in the shape of a 1959 Cadillac.

While they ate, Annie explained that hypnosis was too
often misunderstood by the public. It wasn't a method of
controlling another person against his will. No one could
be hypnotized against his will or made to do things while
hypnotized that weren't in keeping with his basic character.

"It's only the conscious mind that's hypnotized," Annie
said, "not the subconscious mind. And the subject has to
be a willing participant."

"Is that a reassurance or a warning?" Paul asked.

"Both. From reading your file and watching you with
Mr. Roark and Mr. Singer, I'd say you're a man who likes
to be in control. But part of undergoing hypnosis involves
relinquishing control. If you're unable or unwilling to do
that . . ."

Mention of a file got Paul's attention.

"What file did you read?"

Annie was crumbling crackers and dropping them into
her soup. At the note of hostility in his voice, she glanced

up and said, "The agency file. You've been under investigation for three months, you know."

"No, I didn't know." He hadn't considered the possibility of a long-term investigation, but it made sense. They would put him under surveillance, hoping to discover a link to the murders, and only when that failed would they confront him directly. Paul's mind flashed back over the events of the previous three months, seeing them now from a new perspective, a third party's, a Peeping Tom's. Had they tapped the phone? Bugged the house? Had they been listening to every intimate conversation and argument?

"Maybe I shouldn't have mentioned it."

"I don't like to be spied on."

"Normally you wouldn't have been. But innocent men were murdered and the evidence indicated that you knew how and why. Given that, an investigation doesn't seem inappropriate."

"They weren't innocent men. He's an innocent man." Paul pointed at one customer, then at others. "That one, those two—they're innocent men. But your people were agents and assets, playing spook games. They weren't just garden-variety innocent men."

She nodded. "And your sympathies are with the innocent public rather than with those who protect them."

"The 'innocent public' doesn't need *protection*, it needs the truth—after that it can usually protect itself."

Annie changed the subject to Paul's family. She already knew some facts: that his father had been a German soldier who died before he was born; that his mother, Greta, had met and married a young American army officer, Ralph Stafford, who was stationed in Berlin after the war; that Ralph had brought his new wife and her son back to America, where the couple subsequently had three daughters; that Ralph had divorced Greta five years ago to marry a younger woman.

"A bimbo and a boat," said Paul. "That's what dad wanted after he retired from the army."

"It sounds as if you don't like your father."

"I don't respect him, that's all."

"Because he left your mother?"

"Because he ran a cowboy operation in Vietnam. He went over there to get a promotion, knew it all before he arrived. Of course, he'd tell a different story. He'd say if more commanders had been as aggressive as he was, we could have won the war. I guess we have what you might call 'basic philosophical differences.' "

Annie probed gently into his past, listening carefully as Paul told her about his experiences in Vietnam. For three years he flew Huey troop carriers in and out of jungle clearings no bigger than a back yard. He went to Vietnam naive and optimistic and came back angered by the false hopes raised by politicians and army generals every time they wanted more troops to throw into the morass. The only accurate information about the war seemed to come from journalists who went to the battlefield and reported what they saw. Paul had planned to make the military his career, but after his experience in Vietnam he decided to resign his commission and become a journalist.

"My first story was about fragging—soldiers killing incompetent officers. It caused a big scandal at the time. Dad never forgave me. He said I'd betrayed the army—which meant him. I told him I was sorry but I felt he and his buddies had betrayed their commands. That pretty well summed up our differences. I doubt if we've spoken a dozen words since."

"And your mother?" Annie asked.

"She was caught in between. Dad's whole life was the army but I was her son. She was German and remembered how Germany rationalized its way to war—not that she equated the U.S. with Nazi Germany. Anyway, she got an ulcer trying to keep the peace between us."

Paul picked up the sugar dispenser and held it over his glass of iced tea but nothing came out. The spout was clogged.

"Where is your mother now?"

"Isn't that in the file?"

"I'd like to hear it from you."

Paul cleared the spout with one prong of his fork, then added sugar to his ice tea.

"She lives in Fort Lauderdale," he said brusquely. "She keeps books for a country club and teaches German once a week at Broward Community College. Now ask me something that's not in the file."

"Are you close to her?"

"Sure. I'm the oldest, the only son, it's natural. What about you? Are you on good terms with your mother?"

If he thought the question would put her off, he was wrong. Annie was as forthcoming about her own history as she was curious about his. She had grown up in South Carolina, had a doctorate from Duke University, was divorced, had one child, a girl named Shelly. Paul's expression must have shown his surprise because she held up a finger and said, "I know, I don't look old enough to be a mother."

It wasn't that she didn't look old enough, it was that her flat stomach and full breasts seemed like strangers to the rigors of motherhood. Paul doubted if Annie Helms would appreciate this kind of appraisal, so he said nothing.

Annie called the waitress and ordered a vanilla milkshake for dessert. When it came, she removed the cherry and tipped the tall glass forward to bring the straw to her lips.

"Let me ask you something, Dr. Helms—"

"Annie."

"Annie, then. You said you graduated from Duke University, right?" She nodded, her cheeks hollow as she drew the liquid through the straw. "Isn't that where they give degrees in things like extrasensory perception?"

"The official designation is Paranormal Psychology."

"Is that the degree you have?"

"That's one of them. I'm also a board-certified psychiatrist, if that's a more reassuring credential."

"Then in your dual capacity as both a board-certified psychiatrist and paranormal psychologist let me ask you this: what do you think's causing these damn dreams?"

"I'd rather wait until we have a little more data before venturing an opinion."

He smiled. "Be brave and venture a wild guess."

Annie's head was bent low over her glass but her eyes remained on him.

"Don't worry," Paul said. "You won't scare me off."

From the bottom of the glass came a hollow slurping sound. Annie wiped her mouth with a napkin, pushed the glass aside and leaned forward to speak in a low, intense voice.

"I'll give you my best guess, which is also my best hope." She took off her glasses and looked directly at him. "I think you may be a receiver of some form of mental energy. I think that every so often, for whatever reason, your mind becomes sensitive to someone else's sensations, which you experience in your sleep as dreams."

She watched him, eyes showing her excitement.

Paul laughed uncomfortably. "You think I'm some kind of ESP freak?"

"In the broadest definition of extrasensory perception, yes."

"Oh, come on."

"What do *you* think?"

The question took him by surprise. Ever since he had discovered that the murders were real, Paul had been looking for a rational, a logical explanation. Whatever deep-seated suspicion he had along the lines Annie now suggested, he suppressed. He was a journalist, after all, a man of hard facts, not a member of some California mantra-of-the-month club. In his experience there was always a rational explanation for even the most bizarre occurrence if you looked long enough and dug deeply enough. Instincts he could believe in. Instincts and premonitions like the one that saved his life in Afghanistan. But the death dreams were different. There was no explanation for them except the one Annie suggested—the one he had rejected until this moment. His smile faded. "You think that's possible?"

"I know it's possible, Paul. I know it's happened before, but only under extraordinary circumstances. The most common incidents of telepathic communication are associated with death—usually the death of a loved one. The largest body of documented evidence comes from World War II. In one case a sailor's ship was torpedoed and his wife woke up dreaming of flames at the exact moment her husband died. In another, a soldier was killed and his mother woke up with a burning pain in the same place her son was shot. The cases go on and on, all involving death and the simultaneous dream by a loved one. So you see, your pattern fits the others except that *your* dreams are recurring."

"And I don't dream of just dying, I dream of killing."

"And you're not a loved one, in close harmony with someone else's emotional state."

She sat watching him with her glasses dangling from one finger, swinging them back and forth in a way that Paul found oddly appealing.

"So where does that leave us?" Paul asked.

Annie shrugged. "Let's go find out."

They returned to the CIA's Sixteenth Street building, to a small room with walls covered in a soundproof material that looked to Paul like a tightly woven rug. There were no windows. The furnishings were a small desk, three chairs and, of course, a couch. Annie had him remove his shoes and lie down. From a closet she took two pillows, which she gave him with instructions to make himself comfortable. Then she brought out a metal stand with a glass ball, about two inches in diameter, suspended from a chain.

"You're kidding," Paul said. "A crystal ball?"

"Would you rather concentrate on some other object?"

He made a wry face and shook his head. Annie positioned the ball above him, then took a tape recorder and placed it on the desk where she could reach it from her chair. She turned a switch that changed the lights from direct overhead to indirect baseboard lighting.

"It's easier on the eyes. You ready?"

"I guess."

Annie turned on the tape recorder and settled herself in a chair beside and slightly behind him. The room was quiet except for the hushed sound of air-conditioning. When Annie spoke, her voice had a husky, melodic lilt, gentle yet insistent.

"I want you to concentrate on the glass ball," she began. "Concentrate on the ball and listen to my voice. Let your mind empty of thoughts, let it become as clear as the glass; let your mind empty and concentrate only on my voice. Let your mind become clear; let your body grow heavy. Your hands, your arms, your legs, your feet, your whole body is growing heavy now."

As he listened to her voice he found it easier to relax than he'd anticipated. Annie directed his attention to each part of his body, describing how each muscle was relaxing, how each limb was becoming so heavy he couldn't move it. Her voice was like a flowing river bathing him in words, seeping into his consciousness, leading the way, subtly assuming control. As the tension drained from his body he realized how worried he'd been recently; worried about Joanna's disappearance and the dreams and the alien consciousness that seemed to take control of his mind during the nightmares.

Annie's words continued to caress him. "Now your eyelids are growing heavy, as if each eyelash is made of lead, they're so heavy that no matter how hard you try you can't keep your eyes open; no matter how hard you try, your eyes are closing; you can't keep them open; your eyes are closing now..."

Paul felt the drowsiness induced by her voice but even as his eyes closed he felt his rational mind rebel. Like the quick flex of muscle, resistance rose inside him and his will tensed to oppose her suggestion. Then he remembered what Annie had said at lunch. He could resist—he could feel it—but what was the point? He needed the information locked away in his subconscious and the key to opening that door lay in relinquishing control. He took a deep breath, let it out slowly and let her words take him.

"Your arms are heavy now. Your arms feel like they are made of lead. You want to raise your arms but you can't. Your arms are made of rock, part of the earth, immobile and so heavy you can't move them."

She led him once again to each part of his body, weighing it down, making it part of the earth, freeing it from his mind. He was immersed in darkness, the room bounded only by her voice, which came without pause, leading him, lifting and falling in a gentle rhythm, massaging him with sound, weaving an invisible cradle of words, strong, gentle, secure, taking him deep into himself, beyond the boundaries of conscious thought to the hidden, shadowed regions of his subconscious.

"Your eyes are closed but you can still see the glass ball floating in your mind, clear and white and transparent. I want you to imagine that the glass ball is your memory, and it's opening now, expanding to include you inside it. You're inside your memory now and it's stretching out, like a long white hallway with many doors, a long white hallway stretching back to the time of your birth. Can you see the hallway, Paul?"

Watching his face closely, Annie knew that this was a critical juncture. Paul Stafford had a strong personality, one that might reassert control if called on to respond actively. The trance might be broken, but Annie had no choice. She had access to the subconscious now, but the information had to be brought outside, into the open, and only Paul could do that by speaking to her.

"The long white hallway, Paul. You're standing at one end of the hallway, which is your memory. Can you see the hallway? Tell me if you see the hallway?"

His lips quivered, then parted as he spoke in a lethargic voice. "Yes."

Annie smiled and clenched her fist with excitement, but she kept her voice calm.

"Good. We're going to go back now, Paul. We're going to go down the hallway, backward in time. We're going back to the last nightmare, the last time you dreamed of death. You're going down the hallway, backward in time, to the last vivid dream, the last nightmare in which someone died. You're getting close to that dream now, you can see the face of the victim."

Paul's face twitched. It was an uncomfortable memory.

"All right, Paul, I want you to tell me where you are in this dream. Where are you?"

"An apartment."

"And where is the apartment?"

A pause, then, "Paris."

"Do you know the name of your victim?"

"Yes."

"What is the name of your victim?"

"Lisle Beaumier."

His answers came slowly and sometimes reluctantly. But one by one, they reviewed each of the murders. Annie avoided the actual details that caused Paul obvious discomfort and that she feared might break the trance. Instead she concentrated on Paul as the killer, on who he was, why he was there, what his name was. She was looking for clues to his identity, but in this she was disappointed. "Who are you now?" she would ask. His answer was always the same. "Paul Stafford." "And in this dream? Who are you in this dream?" "I am . . . me." "Why have you come to kill Jurgen Manheim?" "I don't know . . ."

It was frustrating. Paul had turned out to be a better subject than she'd anticipated but the only new details she uncovered had to do with the physical description of the sites of the murders. There was nothing new about the killer, whom Paul identified with so fully that his answer was always the same: the killer was him.

She wondered if Maurice Singer was right and the whole thing was an elaborate KGB ruse. If so, it seemed complicated beyond belief and without apparent purpose. Unless it was to assess how seriously the CIA was pursuing ESP research. The Russians had a long-standing interest in paranormal psychology and the KGB sponsored a number of research projects. Was it possible that Paul was fed details of KGB hits with the intention of becoming the subject of a CIA investigation whose details he could later report to Moscow? Maurice might think so, but Annie couldn't believe it. Or didn't want to believe it, she corrected herself. She was also well aware that there was an attractive quality about Paul Stafford that made her want to believe him. At the same time she was a professional, and knew the difference between an emotional response and intellectual judgment. Her faith in her abilities remained strong.

They had returned now to the first dream, in which Dan Kelso had drowned when thrown from a ferry crossing the English Channel. As with the other dreams, the new details that Paul remembered were inconsequential, like the name of the ferry and the color of Kelso's jacket. About his identity as a killer, the answer was still the same: it was him. Annie was about to end the session when a routine question brought an unexpected answer.

"And Dan Kelso was the first time you dreamed like this?"

"No."

The answer stunned her.

"You dreamed of killing someone else?"

"Not . . . not killing."

"But this kind of vivid dream? You've had it before?"

"Yes."

"In a different context than killing someone?"

"Yes."

Adrenaline made her light-headed; it took all of her self-control to keep her voice calm.

"All right, Paul, I want you to go back now, let yourself float backward to that earlier time, when you had this same kind of dream. You're floating backward and you see the details emerging. The earlier time is coming closer, becoming more clear. And now you're back, you're in that earlier dream, back before Dan Kelso, back in that earlier dream that has the same vivid quality as the others . . ."

Paul's face tensed and his arms moved, pulling close to
his chest as if seeking protection. He was actually shivering.

"Paul, tell me what you're dreaming. What is it?"

"Hurts."

"What hurts, Paul?"

"Leg. Shot in the leg."

"You shot someone in the leg?"

"No, shot me. Guards . . . I ran but . . . ah, my leg . . ."

"What guards? Who shot you, Paul?"

"Russian . . . Russian guards." He shivered again.

Annie's mind was racing to keep up. Shot by Russian
guards? How, why, where, when? She had a thousand
questions but forced herself to proceed calmly.

"Where are you, Paul? In the dream, do you know
where you are?"

"Yes."

"Where? Where are you?"

"Berlin."

"How old are you?"

"Eight . . . years old."

For a moment Annie was speechless. They had regressed
to Paul's childhood. Eight years old. Then she remembered something else: Paul's history. The information she'd
read in the file. Paul was five when the family left Germany.
When he was eight years old, they were stationed in Fort
Sheridan, Texas. Either he was lying or—

The apparent answer struck her like a physical blow.
The telepathic sensitivity wasn't new, he'd had it since
childhood. He was sensitive to other people's thoughts, to
their experiences, to incidents in their lives. To someone's
life in Germany when he was eight and living in Texas.

Paul groaned and Annie continued quickly.

"What else happens, Paul? After the Russian guards
shoot you, then what?"

"A man. A man reaching for me. Then kicks . . ."

He grunted with pain and a tremor passed through his
body. For a moment Annie was afraid she'd lost him, but
the trance held and he stopped shivering and relaxed.

"Was that the end of the dream, Paul?"

"Yes."

"And did you wake up?"

"I . . . don't know."

"But the dream stopped?"

"Yes."

"And was that the first time you had these vivid kind of dreams?"

He didn't answer. "Can you hear me, Paul?"

"Yes."

"Was that the very first time you dreamed like that? So vividly that it seemed as if someone else had taken over your life?"

A faint muscle spasm disturbed his features.

"Paul?"

"I . . . don't know."

"Listen to my voice, Paul. I am your guide. Let my voice fill your body, fill your mind; my voice is like a bubble, a soft bubble all around you, protecting you, leading you back, leading you back to the earliest dream, the first nightmare where you dreamed of something outside yourself. We're floating backward, backward to that earliest, very first dream . . . back and back and back . . . Now you see that first dream emerging from the mist; the details become clear and you're in the first dream. You're in that very first dream. Tell me what you see, Paul. What do you see?"

For a moment Annie thought he hadn't heard her. Then his hands flew up, pressing flat as if he was against a wall, and his face turned to one side. He cried out.

"Nein! Nein, Tante Inge!"

"Paul—?"

"Bitte! Bitte!"

And he came out of the trance, sat upright and looked around wildly.

"It's all right," Annie said quickly. She reached to touch his arm but he drew back.

"Paul," she said gently, "you're awake now. You're all right. You're back, back in Washington. Everything's all right."

He heard her voice dimly through fear and nausea. His breathing was ragged and the blood seemed to pound in his ears. His face was clammy with sweat. Annie kept talking and finally he remembered where he was and what was happening. He let out a deep breath and smiled weakly.

"What the hell was all that?"

"Do you remember what happened?"

"I remember pain and..." And what? How could he explain the nameless, terrifying horror, the paralyzing helplessness and the feeling of... humiliation. That was it. More than the pain was the humiliation. He shifted uncomfortably, aware of a queasy feeling in his stomach.

"What is it?" Annie asked.

"Nothing."

"Don't hold back, Paul. Tell me."

"I felt sick for a moment, okay? Now can we go on to something else—like what happened and why? What did you find out?"

Annie told him about the earlier dreams, the one with the Russian guards and the last with the violent reaction that had awakened him from the trance.

"You said something in German. Do you remember?"

"No."

"Listen. I'll play it back."

She rewound the tape and played the last portion for him. Paul had the uncanny sensation of listening to someone else speaking in his voice.

"I sound like a zombie," he said.

"Shhh. Here it comes."

He heard himself shouting. The hysteria embarrassed him but the words were clear.

"No, Aunt Inge." He repeated in English. "Please."

"What about your Aunt Inge?"

Paul looked puzzled. "I don't have an aunt by that name. Not that I know of."

"You must have known somebody by that name."

Somewhere deep in his memory the name had a familiar ring, but Paul couldn't place it.

"I don't know," he said. "I left Germany when I was five."

"Think hard." She was sitting on the edge of her chair, watching him.

Paul shook his head. "I've seen the family tree. There's nobody named *Inge*."

"Then we'll go back. It'll be easier this time, now that we know what we're looking for. Do you want to get a drink first?"

Paul stared at her. "Go back to that? No thanks."

He stood up. The back of his shirt was clammy and damp.

"Look," Annie said, "I know how you feel but we can't quit now. This afternoon was a breakthrough. Now we know that the assassinations weren't the first time you received impressions from someone else. You've been sensitive since you were a child, don't you see? So you don't have an Aunt Inge, but somebody did, and that's the person whose thoughts you picked up."

Paul was shaking his head.

"What?" Annie demanded.

"No, no, the whole thing's crazy."

"It's not crazy. This has happened before. Not with this kind of regularity but it's happened. I can show you case histories—people who suddenly know—know absolutely— that something has happened to a loved one. They *experience* it as if it happened to them."

"To a loved one, yes. Not to a *killer*."

"It's not just a killer. You're sensitive to—"

She stopped in mid-sentence. Until now she had thought of his sensitivity as non-discriminating, like a quiet pond whose surface might ripple from the vibration of a distant explosion. But what if his sensitivity were linked to one specific individual? Someone whose brainwaves and thought patterns were remarkably similar to his own? In that case, the childhood memories might be those of the killer when the killer was young.

"You might be right," Annie said, a new note of excite- ment edging into her voice. "That's all the more reason to go back. Childhood memories may give us more of a clue than the murders."

"No."

"Paul—"

"You don't understand. This is worse than your worst nightmare and it's all mixed up with feelings of humiliation and self-loathing and disgust and a kind of nauseating fear that you've never experienced—that I've never experi- enced before. There's no way I'm going to put myself through that again."

He turned away but Annie grabbed his arm.

"You *can't* stop now. Don't you see how important this is? You're the first case of telepathic communication that has a chance of being scientifically proved. We have got to find the person whose experiences you've apparently been receiving, even if it's painful."

"What if we go back and I experience something that pushes me over the edge? I mean, that changes me, makes me crazy? What the hell then?"

Annie gave him a professionally reassuring smile. "That won't happen." (Was she sure?)

"How do you know?"

"You have to trust me."

"Why? Because we're such great friends or because you wouldn't jeopardize a key element in the first scientifically proved case of mental telepathy?"

Her smile became conspiratorial.

"Let's say a little of each."

"I'll bet you've already got your bio ready for the article in the New England Journal of Medicine."

"It's important, Paul. It really is."

He nodded, knowing that sooner or later it had to be done. He had to find out whose thoughts, whose life was echoing inside his own.

"I'll let you know."

"When?"

"Call me tomorrow."

Driving to the *Herald*, Paul felt isolated, cut off. The world beyond the windshield was familiar but distant. He was a freak. He was, it seemed, part of somebody else. The experience under hypnosis had led him to another reality, someone else's reality; a small kernel of that alien consciousness stayed with him, dividing and somehow diminishing him. He felt compromised, soiled, as if he had something to hide. It was a damn unpleasant feeling.

His mood didn't improve when Bernie Stern, the managing editor, called him into his office to compliment him on the Rockland-Birdwell story and then told him they were going to delay publication for a month.

"Delay? I thought you wanted to run it next week."

Bernie rolled the stub of a cigar between his lips. He was a short, thickset man with a cottage-cheese complexion and white curly hair perpetually in need of washing. He affected the look of a hard-boiled "front-page" newsman by rolling his shirtsleeves and wearing a vest rather than a jacket.

"I thought we better have the raw data checked by an independent scientist."

"What's all this? You don't trust my sources?"

"If it's wrong, Rockland-Birdwell sues us, not your sources."

Bernie was chewing his cigar a little too vehemently. Something else was going on here.

"Meaning what? You talked to the Mayhues?"

"You cynical bastard," Bernie said.

The Mayhues owned the paper. It seemed as though the more successful the *Herald* became, the more conservative the Mayhues became.

"Independent contract, Bernie. You don't want it, I take it across the street."

"Hey, hey." Bernie looked hurt. "No need to get down and dirty. We're running it. Next month, after the Mutual Defense Treaty's been signed, that's all. You wouldn't want to weaken the U.S. bargaining position for a story that can just as easily wait a month."

"Sure," Paul said. "Forget the ethics, screw the Russians. Great way to run a paper."

He wandered off without waiting for a response. There were days that he enjoyed a mock battle with Bernie but today wasn't one of them.

At his desk Paul reviewed the transcripts of an interview with a naval engineer. When he reached the end of the page he could remember nothing. His mind was still on the hypnosis session and the words that Annie had played back, his own voice speaking to him from his childhood.

He got out his address book and dialed the number of the Umbrella Tree Country Club in Fort Lauderdale. A cheery-voiced receptionist answered and Paul asked for the accounting department, where his mother worked. Maybe his mother knew who *Tante Inge* was. At this point he was willing to try anything to avoid another ordeal like the one he'd just been through.

"Paul? Where are you? Are you here?"

"No, mom. Still in Washington."

"Are you coming down?"

"I don't know. Listen, mom, I've got a question for you. About the family. Did we ever have a relative named *Tante Inge?*"

A long silence.

"Mom. Are you there?"

Her voice, when it came, was a whisper so filled with anguish that Paul could hardly recognize it.

"*Ich bitte um Vergebung*," she moaned. "*Ich bitte um Vergebung*."

Forgive me.

"Mom?"

She kept repeating the words, more and more upset. Paul tried to interrupt but she paid no attention; her voice rose to a wail on the other end of the line.

"*Ich bitte um Vergebung*."

"*Mama*," but it was no use. She didn't hear him. Her voice reached a crescendo, the phone clattered to the floor. He could hear her sobbing but she wouldn't answer. He flicked the disconnect button, hoping to get an operator. Instead the line went dead.

He hung up and dialed the number again. When the receptionist answered, Paul tersely explained what had happened and told her to send someone to see that his mother was all right. It turned out that the assistant manager had already gone to help her. Paul waited on the phone for ten minutes, receiving occasional reports of what was happening. Finally a doctor came on the line.

"She was hysterical, Mr. Stafford, but I gave her a sedative and she'll be all right. We have someone to take her home."

"I don't want her left alone."

"No, of course not. I understand her daughter's been notified. A Mrs. . . . ."

"Steinberg."

"Yes. Mrs. Steinberg will be there so I don't want you to worry. The important thing is not to upset her again. If you can guard against that—"

"I had no intention of upsetting her."

"Yes, well, just so you understand the situation."

What Paul understood was that the name *Tante Inge* terrified his mother as much as it had him.

He drove home and grabbed his getaway bag, an Italian leather satchel filled with everything he needed for quick trips. By five o'clock he was on Piedmont's Flight 87 to Fort Lauderdale.

As was the CIA man following him.

CHAPTER

9

THE EVERGLADES WERE BURNING WHEN PAUL landed in Fort Lauderdale. It was dusk and the sun glowed a desperate orange through a gunmetal haze that hugged the western horizon. Paul rented a car, rolled up the windows and turned on the air-conditioning. Bugs accumulated on the windshield as he drove down endless freeways bordered by tall palms and identical shopping centers.

Before leaving Washington he had phoned his sister to see if his mother was all right.

"She's resting now," Ceci assured him. "But she won't tell me what happened. She says you know."

"I'll tell you when I get there."

Now as he pulled into the parking stall marked "Visitors," he wasn't sure what to tell her. Would she believe that he dreamed of deaths or that he was in some sort of telepathic contact with a killer? Would she believe that under hypnosis he'd experienced a trauma associated with the name *Tante Inge*, unfamiliar to him, but a name that made his mother hysterical? Would *anyone* believe it?

As it turned out, Ceci was so eager to get back home that she didn't press the issue.

"Bob called a few minutes ago," she said as she led him into the apartment. "The kids are driving him crazy. He had to leave work early to pick them up. We were afraid mom had a heart attack or something. Anyway, I'm glad you're here."

Ceci was tiny like her mother, but had soft round features more characteristic of dad's side of the family.

"How is she?" Paul asked.

"Asleep now. I really think she's all right, Paul. You

should have waited. You didn't have to come all the way down here."

Ceci began collecting her things. The apartment was a small one that mom had moved into after the divorce—a single bedroom with living room separated from a tiny kitchen by a narrow counter. A sliding glass door opened to an outdoor patio overlooking a man-made lake. Except for a white spinet piano in the corner, the furniture looked as if it had sprung to life from a Sears & Roebuck catalogue. Paul had never understood his mother's compulsion for economy, which resulted in undistinguished, ill-made goods that wore out twice as quickly as something only marginally more expensive.

He went to the bedroom and peered in. Mom lay curled on her side, her white hair adrift on the pillow, lips parted slightly, the sound of her breathing lost in the low hum of the air conditioner. On an end table next to the bed stood a familiar photograph of mom and dad on their wedding day. She held Ralph's arm and was gazing up at him while he stood tall and confident in his army uniform smiling at the camera. Their attitudes defined the relationship, Paul thought—mom dependent, dad carelessly confident.

"He gave me a new life," she once told Paul when he criticized his father.

Now he'd given her another new life, a lonely, empty one. But mom was still grateful and would allow no criticism of the man she married. Paul realized he was less generous. He tended to hold people to fairly strict standards, and as far as he was concerned his father had failed in his obligation to the marriage. Ironic, considering the state of his own marriage. Had he set impossible standards for Joanna?

He shut the door and returned to the living room. Ceci was on the phone, promising Bob she'd be right home to put the kids to bed. After she hung up she invited Paul to come over for a barbecue.

"As soon as you know your schedule," she said. "The kids would love to see you again."

She dug her car keys from the purse and added as an afterthought, "How's Joanna?"

"Still working at the gallery."

Ceci was in too much of a hurry to notice the tightness in his voice or that his answer was an evasion. After she'd gone Paul stood in the living room and thought more about Joanna. Suddenly he very much wanted to talk to her, to share his worry about his mother and his real fear that falling asleep would make his mind vulnerable to some unknown presence. He most wanted and needed her now not so much as a wife or lover but as a friend.

On the off-chance that she'd returned he called home. He got the answering machine. "This is Paul and Joanna Stafford. We're not available right now but if you leave your name and number we'll get right back to you."

Paul was about to hang up but changed his mind.

"Jo? Are you home? Listen, if you're there, pick up the phone. I'm at mom's place. I came down this evening and I need to talk to you so if you're there . . . or you get this message, give me a call." He stopped talking and listened. After seven seconds the voice-actuated tape shut off.

Frustrated, he felt an irrational anger. Where the hell was she? She said in her note that she'd call in a couple of days, so why hadn't she called? Why wasn't she around when something important was going on, when it counted?

He sat down and turned on the television. He was looking for something to put his mind on ice but the sitcoms annoyed him with their intrusive laugh tracks and the only movie, an over-earnest drama about teenage suicide, bored him. His mind kept returning to Joanna and to the magic of their first meeting . . .

She had been working with a relief agency helping victims of the famine in Ethiopia. Paul's first glimpse of her was in front of a Safeway store, carrying a sign and soliciting food. The sign had a photograph of an Ethiopian child, arms and legs thin as toothpicks, ribs like a birdcage and a stomach distended from malnutrition. The caption read, "Safeway Won't Feed This Child, Will You?" The photograph was one of his.

"Have you got a release for that?" Paul asked.

It wasn't much of an opening line but in the next five minutes Joanna managed to convince him to donate a dozen more photographs and two weeks later, when she and a team from the relief agency took the first planeload of food to Ethiopia, Paul went with them and covered the story. Their romance blossomed in the desert, and on the way back they spent two days together in Paris.

Joanna was a continual surprise. The first time they

made love she became a different person, strangely shy and reticent. Afterward she lay shivering in his arms. Thinking she was cold, Paul pulled the covers over them, but it made no difference. Holding her, he felt the texture of her skin, dimpled with goosebumps.

"I'm sorry," she said. "The more important it is, the more I'm afraid."

"Afraid of what?"

"Of you. You scare me."

She was dead serious.

"I won't hurt you."

"I don't mean physically."

"Then what?"

"That with you—if I let go with you I'll never come back"

"You'll come back. You'll still be you."

She touched his cheek, her pale blue eyes with tears now. "But I don't want to come back; that's what scares me."

Cautious in love and reckless in life, Joanna was different from any woman he'd ever known. He fell asleep thinking about her, and in restless dreams saw her standing naked on a diving board about to dive into a pool that held no water. Paul yelled a warning but Joanna just waved and smiled. He ran toward her but she paid no attention. She vaulted high into the air, jackknifed cleanly and descended to the pool, now filled with water. He saw her pale form flickering beneath the waves; then she broke the surface and swam easily away, laughing, as Paul stood stunned and shaken, staring after her.

The smell of coffee woke him up. He sat up and looked around. In the kitchen his mother was moving noiselessly, carefully taking silverware from the dishwasher and putting it in a drawer. She wore yellow slacks and a floral top. When she saw Paul she smiled.

"I tried not to wake you."

"What time is it?"

"Almost nine. I phoned the club and told them I wasn't coming in today. It isn't every day I have a visit from my son." She acted as if his visit were the most normal thing in the world.

Paul stood up and ran a hand through his hair. His neck was stiff from his night on the couch.

"There are fresh towels in the bathroom. And I'm making peach pancakes for breakfast. You still like pancakes, don't you?"

She kept puttering, paying no attention to his reactions. He went into the kitchen and stood watching her.

"Mom, are you all right?"

"I'm fine. Go ahead now. You get cleaned up. Go, go."

She turned him around and pushed him gently toward the bathroom. Whether she was trying to ignore what happened yesterday or simply wanted to delay discussing it, he couldn't tell. But he left her alone for a few minutes while he washed up. When he came back she was on the patio, setting places for breakfast.

"It's such a nice morning," she said. "I thought we'd eat out here. Sit, sit. I'll bring coffee."

She bustled off to the kitchen but Paul sensed the nervousness beneath all the activity. When she brought the coffee he took her wrist and insisted she sit down.

"We have to talk, mom."

"Paul, the batter's ready." She tugged against his grip like a trapped bird, eyes darting over his shoulder, as though seeking escape.

"We have to talk about this Tante Inge."

"*No.*" She yanked her arm free and stared at him, then turned and walked across the grass toward the lake. Paul followed. She sat down on one of the concrete white benches bordering the water and stared into the distance. Half a dozen ducks swam toward her, honking. Paul came up behind her and began massaging her shoulders. At first she tensed under his touch but after a few moments she relaxed. When she finally spoke her voice was flat.

"How did you find out?"

"I didn't find out. That's why I need to talk to you."

"You know her name."

"I had a dream. A bad dream, and Tante Inge's name came up."

She turned to look at up at him.

"But you were so young. How could you remember?"

"Who was she, mom? Who was Tante Inge?"

"*Not* your aunt. That was just . . ." She looked away.

"Just a name you called her. A name she wanted all the children to call her."

"Who was she?"

"Her name was Inge Heusner. She was Satan come to earth, a depraved thing who"—she shuddered—"who killed your brother."

Paul's hands stopped.

"My *brother?*"

"The two of you. Twins. Karl and Paul."

Paul's shock was complete. The world seemed to fall away as his senses turned inward; trees, lake and grass became mere pattern while sounds were attenuated, distant, as if he were swimming underwater. *A twin brother?* A brother named Karl? Annie's words came back to him: *emotionally close.* With a dizzying shift of perspective Paul realized that his brother was not dead. Somewhere in the world there was a shared consciousness, another part of himself. A twin. A brother . . .

He became aware of his mother's voice.

". . . sacrificed him. I gave Karl's life in exchange for yours."

"He's not dead," Paul said.

She turned to look at him, her eyes filled with hope, and horror.

"Not dead? What are you saying?"

"I know it. I know he's not dead."

"How? How can you know that?"

"Because I've had these dreams, mom. Dreams that aren't just dreams—they're real events, things that are happening—not to me but to *him.*"

"Dreams? No, you don't know what happened. You don't know . . ."

"Tell me, then."

She shook her head. "I *can't.*"

"Does dad know?"

"No one knows."

"But why? Why didn't you tell anyone?"

"I couldn't."

"Why not?"

"Because . . . because I *gave* him to her." She stood up. "It was my fault. I gave him to her and she . . . she took him to that place where they . . . they . . ."

Her lips moved but the words wouldn't come. Her

features were twisted, as if she were suffering some kind of seizure.

Paul got up and held her. "It's all right, it's all right," he said quickly. "Take a deep breath. Come on now, a deep breath. That's it."

When she was breathing normally he told her he was hungry and let the subject of Inge Heusner slip aside while they ate breakfast on the patio. She needed time to recover; he needed time to figure out an approach that wouldn't upset her.

The air grew warm and the sky took on a mid-morning haze. When they were finished she broke the leftover toast and fed it to the ducks. She called them each by name, admonishing one not to be so selfish, encouraging another to come and get its fair share.

He waited until she had finished and returned to the table, her face flushed, before he said softly, "We have to talk about her, mom. I have to know."

Her smile died and she looked away but in her eyes there was resignation now as well as sadness. After a moment she said, "Will you promise not to hate me?"

"You know better than that."

She nodded, accepting his promise without believing it. "Come, then. Come inside."

In the living room he waited while she went to the bedroom and returned a few minutes later with an old cigar box tied with twine. The cigar box was made of wood and the label was in German.

"In here is my shame," she said. "But first you must try to understand how it happened."

She closed her eyes and took a deep breath. When she spoke, her voice was low and tinged with a bitterness that Paul had never heard before.

"No one can imagine what it was like after the war, Paul. Berlin was—there was nothing left. All ruins. No street-cars, no sidewalks, only paths through the rubble. My mother and father had died in the bombing, and Erich— your father—was lost on the Eastern front. He never heard the news, his twin boys. So I was alone, a young mother with two babies. We lived in one room, a kitchen without water or electricity, but we were lucky. We had two wool blankets and the windows were unbroken.

"This was the first year of the occupation and there was

not enough to eat. The harvests had been ruined by the invasion, and people were starving. In November, before the ground froze, we watched the soldiers dig mass graves for all those who were expected to die during the winter. Every day I wrapped you and Karl in a blanket and waited outside the army base for them to bring out the garbage. The garbage was in special containers, metal barrels labeled 'Food For The Master Race.' The Russian soldiers thought this a fine joke. Food for the Master Race."

Her eyes narrowed at the memory and she paused, lost in thought. Paul had a sense of the strong will she must have had as a young woman.

"I remember," she said. "We beat the cans with sticks to drive out the rats. Then we took what was left."

"What about *her?*"

She looked away, took a deep breath. "Frau Heusner lived in the cellar of our building. She lived by begging. Each morning we watched her leave, dressed in rags and carrying a cane. Each evening she returned with food and occupation money and maybe a pair of shoes to barter or a coat to sell. Sometimes she came back with American cigarettes, and this amazed us all. In those days, one American cigarette was worth a month's salary, so everyone envied Frau Heusner and wondered how it was she was so successful in a city where so many beggars starved. Frau Heusner just laughed and said that God answered her prayers.

"One day I discovered her secret. I was in a new neighborhood looking for work when I saw Frau Heusner on the street. She was dressed in her usual rags but there was something new. She wore dark glasses and walked slowly, tapping the street with her cane as if she was blind. So that was her secret, I thought. She got extra sympathy by pretending to be blind.

"Later, I told her what I'd seen and was surprised at her reaction. She grew pale and asked if I'd told anyone else. When I said no, she swore me to secrecy, telling me she was afraid of being arrested. I thought it was funny because the police had so many serious problems that they wouldn't bother about somebody impersonating the blind. But Frau Heusner was very scared so I promised not to tell. I often wonder what would have happened if I *had* gone to the police, how many lives would have been saved. How many lives..." She stared vacantly at the wall, then looked up slowly. "When I look at you, I see him, too. It's always been that way."

Paul nodded, wanting her to continue but afraid to press the issue for fear that it would upset her again. "It must have been difficult," he said carefully.

"It got worse when winter came," she continued. "That's when you got sick, very sick, with fever and chills and even coughing blood. It was terrible to see. You were so young, helpless, and nothing I did was any help. So I went to the hospital and the doctor told me that you had pneumonia and you would die without antibiotics. There were no antibiotics in the Russian sector so I had to go to the American sector, but to do this you needed a special pass. It took all day, waiting in line, and when they issued the pass it was only for you and me. 'The other one's not sick,' they told me. They didn't care about the German people, whether we lived or died, you see? So it was only you and I who could go, and that's when I went to Frau Heusner. I was forced to, Paul. I couldn't let you die."

"And Frau Heusner took care of Karl?"

Mom nodded. "She had been kind to us. She used to bring things, little things, sometimes food, sometimes a piece of clothing—once she brought yarn and I knitted caps for the cold weather. Both you and Karl, matching caps. Frau Heusner joked about taking one of you with her when she went begging. She said the Russian soldiers had soft hearts for blind mothers and little babies. That's why I thought it would be all right, you see? To leave Karl...

"Of course, we were only going for the day, that's what I thought. I thought we would get the medicine and return, but when the doctor saw you, he put you in the hospital. They were afraid you would die, so they gave you oxygen and I stayed with you. It was six days before we went home. I went right away to Frau Heusner, but the police were there in her room waiting for her. The police told me what happened."

Mom bowed her head as if in prayer, then slowly untied the cigar box. Her fingers trembled. Finally he would know what was so terrible that his mother couldn't even speak the words to tell him.

The twine fell away and she lifted out a newspaper

clipping, yellowed with age. Without unfolding it she handed it to Paul.

"This is my sin," she said.

The paper was brittle and tiny pieces fell from the edges as Paul unfolded it. The clipping was undated and in German. The article was headlined, "Helpful Citizens Butchered in Pankow." Paul read on:

Police in the Pankow district discovered human remains in a blackmarket butcher shop located at 21 Uferallee. The shop is owned by Hans Furtz and his cousin, Rolf Jaspers. Both men have been arrested. An accomplice, Inge Heusner, is still at large.

The gruesome discovery came to light after police were contacted by Marie Naumann, 28 years old, of Weisensee. Naumann said that she came to the aid of a blind woman, later identified as Inge Heusner, who appeared to be having difficulty finding her way to Pankow, where she was to deliver a letter. Naumann offered to perform the errand for her but became suspicious when she glanced back and saw Heusner making her way down the street as if in full possession of her faculties. Police later confirmed that Heusner was not blind and had for some time been engaged in luring people from adjacent districts to the Pankow shop, where they were murdered.

Her suspicions aroused, Naumann went to the police, who in turn accompanied her to the butcher shop. One of the owners, Furtz, escaped by running out the back door but was later captured at home. Jaspers was apprehended on the premises. A search of the basement revealed two partly dismembered bodies.

Police said that the shop had been in operation for many months and that the actual number of victims may never be known. Apparently all victims were recruited from outside the district so as not to arouse suspicion. A chilling postscript to the incident was the message contained in the envelope Miss Naumann was to deliver to Furtz and Jaspers. In Inge Heusner's handwriting the message said: *This is the last one I will be sending today.*

Paul finished reading and looked up. His mother could only stare at him, as though waiting for judgment.

"Someone saw her there," she said, her voice hoarse and barely audible. "With Karl... But I kept hoping, I kept looking... Oh my God..."

The tears came, and Paul, in a daze himself, went to her. She shrank back into herself at his approach. He sat beside her, cradling her like a child, wanting to take her pain but not knowing how.

"It's all right," he said, an empty phrase, which brought no comfort.

She began whispering, over and over, like a litany, "*Ich bitte um Vergebung, ich bitte um Vergebung.*" Forgive me, forgive me.

But it wasn't his mother who needed the absolution, Paul was thinking. It was Karl, his twin brother... It was Karl who had killed six people and made Paul an unwilling accomplice. He would wait to tell his mother more. It would hardly ease the pain to discover this new horror, that her son Karl had somehow survived only to become a sadistic killer.

The memory of his dreams sickened him even more now... the possibility of it happening again made just the idea of sleep a terrible threat. It must not happen again. One way or another, Paul had to stop his brother from more killing.

But first, he had to find him.

CHAPTER

10

THE LOCAL AGENT'S NAME WAS TANZER. HE SAT in the cafeteria of Frankfurt Airport drinking coffee and paging through an Italian magazine filled with photos of naked women with glistening wet breasts sunning themselves at a seaside resort. In his pocket was a FAX copy of a photograph of the man he was to follow. The man's name was Paul Stafford.

The assignment had come at the last minute. His American case officer had contacted him before dawn, waking him from a restless sleep, and Tanzer had the distinct impression that he was not the first choice for the job. Tanzer had first worked for the Americans as part of an operation that uncovered a ring of high-technology bandits illegally shipping electronic equipment to the Soviet Union through Sweden. Since then there had been only routine assignments like this one, in which he merely made reports without knowing anything about the operation.

The public address system announced the arrival of Lufthansa Flight 465 from Miami. Tanzer finished his coffee, lukewarm by now, rolled the magazine and thrust it into his overcoat. He made his way to the customs area where he stood near a pillar at some distance from the crowd of people who gathered at the railing outside the opaque doors. How many of them, Tanzer wondered, were meeting friends from Miami? And did girls from Florida have bronze skin and bleached hair like the sand-spangled girls in the magazine?

He had no chance to find out; Stafford was among the first to enter the terminal. From the way he looked around to get his bearings, Tanzer guessed that his target had never been here before. Stafford carried a single overnight bag and his clothes were wrinkled from the long flight. As he walked away Tanzer checked the time and wrote it down in a dog-eared notebook, then followed Stafford to the Pan Am counter, where his quarry joined the ticket line. Leaving so soon, Tanzer wondered?

This made things more interesting. They were going somewhere. Tanzer was glad that he'd had the foresight to bring his passport. Already he was considering how he might pad the expense account. A trip outside Germany required authorization but this didn't bother him. He knew that he could plead lack of time and the Americans would pick up the bill. They always did. After all, unhappy agents made bad security risks.

Tanzer hoped that Stafford would buy a ticket to Italy. He had friends in Rome and he was in the mood to rent a car and chase Italian girls in short skirts riding motor-scooters. Instead, his quarry got in line to buy a ticket for the Berlin shuttle. The shuttles left hourly but the next one, the eleven-thirty, was all booked. Tanzer was in an adjoining line, close enough to hear the agent explain the situation and to watch Stafford buy a ticket for the twelve-thirty flight.

Tanzer was in a slow line, and his target had disappeared by the time he got his ticket. He worried that this was a ruse designed to lose him, but Stafford was waiting at the boarding gate when he got there. Security precautions were especially stringent for the Berlin shuttle. Only ticketed passengers were allowed into the waiting area, which was separated from the terminal by bulletproof glass walls. All luggage was x-rayed and inspected and entry to the area was carefully controlled. A security guard ran an electro-magnetic wand over Tanzer's body before passing him into the waiting room, where Stafford stood staring out the window at the plane.

The eleven-thirty passengers were in the process of boarding. Most of them were businessmen in shiny shoes and expensive ties. Tanzer sat down across the room from Stafford, pulled out his magazine and prepared to wait an hour. It was too bad they weren't going to Italy. Once, on the island of Capri he had made love to an Italian woman in a swimming pool who had slipped beneath the water to suck him off. Tanzer loved Italian women.

The passengers had finished boarding and the agent

behind the desk made an announcement over the loud-speaker, something about standby passengers. Tanzer was only half-listening.

". . . passenger Stafford and standby passenger Fuchs."

Tanzer looked up with alarm. Stafford and half a dozen others were being allowed to board the plane. Immediately he realized what must have happened: Stafford had put his name on a standby list when he arrived here at the boarding gate. With a quiet curse Tanzer put the magazine away and ran to the ticket agent.

"Wait, is there any more room?"

"The flight is full, sir."

The last person, a middle-aged lady with a huge plastic shopping bag, was at the entrance to the ramp.

"Excuse me, madam," Tanzer called after her. "I'll pay double the price for your ticket."

She shook her head with a frown, barely glancing at him, and kept walking. The agent shut the door behind her. He had lost Stafford.

Tanzer didn't want to give up the assignment, so he spent fifteen minutes trying to find another flight. He even called two charter companies, knowing full well that his American contact wouldn't approve such an expenditure but taking down all the information anyway as a way of demonstrating his resourcefulness. Then he called a special number and left a message. He waited another ten minutes by the pay phone before his contact returned the call. As he expected, the assignment was scrubbed. They would use somebody else in Berlin. Tanzer went to the bar, got a beer and spent the rest of the day considering his bad luck.

Paul was not aware that he was being watched. He hadn't noticed the man who followed him to Miami, and he hadn't noticed Tanzer in Frankfurt. He had put his name on the standby list at the suggestion of the ticket agent, and the fact that he had made the eleven-thirty shuttle was a matter of luck. Now he was too busy analyzing the difference between Germany and the United States to wonder if he was being watched.

Stereotypes, he thought, were often based in fact. The German propensity for order and efficiency was apparent at Berlin's Tegel Airport just as it had been in Frankfurt.

There was never any doubt of where to go or what to do. Everything was well laid out and well marked, with pictographs and arrows pointing the way to taxis, restrooms, police, currency exchange, buses, baggage—anything a traveler might need to know and always in the most rational place to look. The Germans were nothing if not well organized, and it was this organization that Paul was counting on to help him locate Inge Heusner and his newly discovered brother. Specifically, he was counting on the *anmeld*.

Anmeld was a German word that meant to register with the police. Each German citizen was required, within thirty days of moving to a new address, to stop at the local police station and notify them of his name, occupation, address, date he took occupancy and the number of people living in the dwelling. The *anmeld* was where Paul meant to start the search for his brother.

He took a taxi to the Hotel InterContinental just off the Kurfurstendamm on Budapesterstrasse. Like most of the new buildings in Berlin, the hotel saved its personality for the inside. The lobby featured marble floors with oriental rugs and walls that formed a backdrop for ferns that tumbled out of angled skylights. A sign welcomed attendees of the Fifth Annual Medical Technology Congress, and on the lawn outside, a large white circus tent had been erected as an exhibition space.

Paul stepped up to the front desk. "When do the elephants get here?"

The clerk, a somber balding man whose remaining hair was parted just above his left ear, stared at him with a blank smile.

"Bitte?"

"The circus tent," Paul nodded outside. "When do the elephants arrive?" The clerk turned slowly to look.

"Never mind," Paul said.

The man stared at the tent, blinked, then loosed a bark of laughter that ended as quickly as it began.

"Yes, good, good," he nodded to Paul.

As he filled out the registration form, the clerk kept glancing at the tent, pursing his lips and nodding with approval. Paul wondered how nightclub comics made out in Berlin.

In his room, he unpacked his getaway bag, an eclectic

collection of everything he needed for a quick assignment: two shirts, one a short-sleeve knit and the other a long-sleeve dress, a tie, dress slacks, shorts, three sets of underwear, tennis shoes and down vest. Hardware was a Sony micro-cassette recorder with a dozen micro-cassettes, the Ricoh FF-90 with six rolls of 1,000-speed Kodacolor, three sets of batteries, two Parker T-Ball jotters and a spiral notepad. Also a leather toilet kit, a gift that Joanna had bought in Ethiopia. She hadn't known it was elephant hide and he still remembered her quick tears when she found out. Her vulnerability to abstract tragedies had been one of the things that charmed him.

Paul pushed his thoughts of the past aside, kicked off his shoes, punched up the pillows and sat down on the bed with a phone book. A quick call to the mayor's office told him there was no central record repository in Berlin; each police district maintained its own registration. Records were available to authorized researchers, which included credentialed journalists. There would be no problem checking the twelve West Berlin districts.

"What about Pankow?" Paul asked. It was the district his mother was living in when she put Karl in Inge Heusner's care.

"Pankow is in the Eastern sector," the woman told him. "You will have to discuss with them their procedures."

Discussing procedures with East Berlin wasn't so easy. It took half a dozen calls to half a dozen offices to discover that only authorized personnel could check police records. There was a Bureau of Displaced Persons that might be able to locate Frau Heusner—if she was still alive and if Paul could afford to wait a few years for them to find out. What if Paul wanted to look through the records himself? Yes . . . it was impossible. He could make a request. Certain forms to be filled out, police background checks made, clearance from proper authorities . . . it could take some time. It could take a *long* time. Was there an address where Paul might like the application forms to be sent?

It was the "yes but no" game that every bureaucrat played. Paul was used to it. That's why he'd come in person rather than called or written from the States. Calling and writing got you front-door answers; what he needed was back-door solutions. He got out the *Herald* contact sheet and called Ray Tregerdemain.

Ray was a stringer working out of Berlin. Paul had met him a few years back at a Washington Press Association Awards ceremony. Tregerdemain's mother had died and he'd come back to the States for her funeral. On the return trip he stopped in Washington to see an old friend and somehow wrangled an invitation to the ceremony. He had spoken to Paul at some length, mistaking him for an overseas editor named Stanford. Later, Paul saw him at the *Herald* office and after that his byline began appearing on the odd Berlin story—the ones that weren't pulled straight from AP, UPI or Reuters.

An answering machine gave a John Philip Sousa introduction and then Ray Tregerdemain's recorded voice began explaining that he was on assignment but would get back to the caller right away. Halfway through the announcement another voice interrupted.

"This is Tregerdemain. I'm here, I'm here. Wait a minute and I'll—"

There was a yelp from the tape machine and the line cleared.

"Yes, yes? Hello?"

"Ray Tregerdemain?"

"That's right."

Paul introduced himself, referring to their earlier meeting. It took Tregerdemain a moment, but when he remembered his tone took on a new enthusiasm and he began speaking English.

"The WPA ceremony," he repeated. "Right, right. And I thought you were what's-his-name, that other guy—"

"Jerry Stanford."

"Stanford, sure. Hey, good to hear your voice, Paul. What's going on? You working a story in the embattled city or what?"

Paul explained briefly that he was trying to locate his brother, born Karl Weiss, who had disappeared in 1946. Ray seemed disappointed that the *Herald* wasn't doing a piece on Berlin but his interest picked up when he heard that Paul was looking for his twin brother.

"I need a way into East Berlin police records," Paul finished. "You have any ideas?"

"Yeah, lots of Westmarks."

"How many and to whom?"

There was a pause, then more slowly, "You're serious?"

"I'm serious about knowing the options. If bribes are one way to go, give me some idea of how much. That doesn't mean I've got the bucks to pull it off," he added, sensing that Ray might be as much opportunist as journalist.

"Okay, Paul, how's this . . . I'm in the middle of sixteen things so let me dump everything and meet you in an hour at the Journalisten-Club. How does that sound? Give me a chance to see what I can come up with, okay?"

They made the arrangements and Ray gave him directions. Paul made two overseas calls: one to tell the *Herald* that he would be out of the office until Monday, the other to his answering service to see if Joanna had called. She hadn't. The only message was from Annie Helms, wanting to set up a time for their next session. He considered calling her but decided against it. He figured it was best not to involve the CIA. At least not until he found Karl.

Hugh Roark had hoped to have a cup of coffee and call Annie Helms before facing Maurice, but the younger man spotted him in the hallway and came bounding after him.

"What's the word?"

"Not great."

"He slipped, right?"

They passed a file clerk, and Hugh waited until the man was out of earshot before responding. "The agent didn't know. It could have been an accident."

"An accident? How?"

The two men entered Hugh's office, which had been carpeted recently and still smelled of new rug. Hugh was sensitive to smells and it bothered him that in the new buildings you couldn't open the windows.

"You want some coffee?"

"No thanks. What happened?"

As he explained, Hugh opened his drawer, took out a handmade cup in the shape of a Chinese devil's face, and poured coffee from a silver thermos.

"Stafford landed in Frankfurt and took the Pan Am shuttle to Berlin. The eleven-thirty was full so he ticketed the twelve-thirty. The agent did the same, but apparently when Stafford checked in for the flight he signed up for the standby list."

"Apparently?"

"Our man didn't see him do it. He was back in the security line when Stafford reached the check-in counter."

"What about Berlin?"

"You know Berlin. Frankfurt contacted them but they wouldn't authorize a direct. By the time I got a back channel from Langley it was too late. The plane was on the ground."

Maurice waved his hand in disgust. "He's gone, he's gone."

"I'm not so sure."

"Come on, Hugh. He's playing Parcheesi in the Kremlin by now."

Hugh took off his coat and hung it on a hanger. Relax, he wanted to say. Don't make it personal. "We've got no proof," he reminded his partner. "If he wants to go over, we can't stop him."

"Then why tail him at all?"

"Because I don't think he's going over. I think he's after that relative he told Helms about. The aunt he remembered."

"It must be contagious," Maurice said.

Hugh ignored him and leaned to the intercom. "Gayle? I need Annie Helms in medical."

"You two have the same disease," Maurice persisted.

"What's that?" Hugh asked, knowing what was coming.

"Gullibility."

"What would you have done?"

"Arrested him, sweated him, turned him. If that didn't work . . ." Maurice shrugged. "He wouldn't be much of a threat in a wheelchair."

"Maybe you should have joined the Green Berets."

"Or the KGB, like our boy Stafford."

"He didn't do the killings," Hugh said.

"Then he knows who did."

"Not yet."

"Then why would he—"

"To find the killer," Hugh interrupted. "I think that's why he went to Germany. And that's why we're tailing him."

"To *warn* the killer."

"I don't think so."

Maurice opened his mouth to argue the point but the expression on Hugh's face changed his mind. He shrugged. "Okay, it's your call."

That's right, Hugh thought as he waited to talk to Annie Helms. It's my call. And my ass if I'm wrong.

CHAPTER

11

PAUL HAD TIME TO SPARE BEFORE MEETING
Ray Tregerdemain. Rather than sit in the hotel room, he
went outside and wandered away from the crowded
Budapesterstrasse into the adjoining neighborhood where
the streets were smaller and more of the pre-war buildings
were in evidence, broad brownstone apartments with cobblestone walks. Here, for the first time, he was struck by a
vague sense of the familiar.

After fifteen minutes of aimless wandering, he made his
way back and passed through an area of expensive restaurants, trendy nightclubs and a brightly lit casino. The
nightclub flanking the casino was named the Wyoming and
featured a sign that caught his attention. It was purple
neon, a bucking bronco in two positions, each one alternately
illuminated. Watching the sign, Paul was struck again by a
feeling of familiarity. He'd seen this sign before or one
very much like it. He was half-tempted to go inside but it
was getting late so he filed the Wyoming away for possible
future reference.

The feeling of déjà vu faded as he entered the crowded
Breitscheidplatz, where undistinguished concrete buildings sat like interlopers on streets whose history stretched
back five hundred years. The few pre-war buildings that
remained often stopped abruptly in a wall of plaster where
their neighbors had been destroyed in the war. It was a
city of architectural incongruity and it came as no surprise
that the Journalisten-Club was located above a Burger
King.

Paul signed the guest register and sat down to wait for
Ray. The place reminded him of a private men's club and
was divided into two areas, a lounge and a dining room,
both serviced by young waiters who probably wanted to

be reporters. Two couples were having an early dinner but most of the action was in the lounge, where groups of men and a few women sat in conversation, leaning toward one another, stabbing the air with cigarettes and nibbling nervously at peanuts and potato chips.

Ray Tregerdemain showed up ten minutes late. He was heavier than Paul remembered and it looked as if the weight was recent. Ray's shirt and coat seemed tight, as if left over from an earlier edition of his body. He was breathing heavily and looked around the room with a worried expression. When he saw Paul, he relaxed.

"Hey, there you are," he said in a voice that carried across the room. "Long time, no see."

Ray weaved through the crowd with a delicate grace that Paul wouldn't have thought possible considering his bulk.

"Didn't mean to keep you waiting," he said as the two men shook hands, "but the phone rang and one thing and another."

He sat down heavily. The exertion of climbing a single flight of stairs had sweat glistening on his forehead. He called to the waiter in a loud voice and, after a glance at what Paul was drinking, ordered scotch and water.

"Make it a double," he called after the waiter, then favored Paul with a conspiratorial smile. "You need a kick in the butt to take this place seriously. All the heavy hitters come out in the evening. That's Alex Sandor over there. Not his wife, though. 'Business associate.'" Ray kept up a running commentary until his drink arrived. Then he returned his attention to Paul and raised his glass. "As our American doughboys say, *Gut Kopf*."

He downed half the drink and set down the glass with a sigh of satisfaction and a shudder. Ray's warm, friendly smile was sabotaged by eyes that were bloodshot and bordered by skin that sagged like a hopeful bloodhound's. A lush, Paul thought. He wondered how much help Ray was going to be.

Becoming aware of Paul's scrutiny, Ray smiled sheepishly. "Journalist's lunch," he said, indicating the drink.

Paul nodded. "What about the *anmeld* records? You got any ideas?"

"One or two." Ray took out a soiled handkerchief and wiped his brow, hunching forward to stuff it back into his pocket. "First let me make sure I've got it straight. You're looking for your brother—twin brother, that is—who got lost in February of forty-six with some woman taking care of him. Name of brother was Karl, Karl... no, don't tell me. I've got a system." He squinted with the effort. "Weiss! Karl Weiss. Let's see, lost in forty-six with a caretaker woman some years his senior by the name of Inge Heusner! Name of district they disappeared from was Pankow! How's that?"

"How do I get access, Ray?"

Ray's attention had shifted to a man with silver-gray hair, a newcomer who was on his way to the dining room. Ray jumped to his feet.

"Herr Fricke," he called. "*Grüss Gott*. This is Paul Stafford, from the Washington *Herald*. The man who won a Pulitzer a few years ago."

"Ah," said Herr Fricke, turning with a polite smile.

"Paul, Herman Fricke, editor of *Berliner Zeitschrifte*."

Paul stood up and shook hands. It was evident that Herr Fricke had as little interest in meeting him as he did in meeting Fricke.

"Paul's working on a little *Kriegserleidnis* about post-war refugees and I'm doing what I can to fix him up with sources."

"Actually," Paul said, "the story's about the resurgent Nazi movement in Berlin."

Fricke's smile faded.

"There are no such groups—none that can be taken seriously by serious people. If you'll excuse me..." He moved on to the dining room. Ray took half a step after him. "He's joking," he called. Herr Fricke pretended not to hear. Ray turned to Paul. "Are you crazy? You'll ruin my reputation with these people."

"Have you got one left, Ray?"

Ray took a quick breath and blinked as if someone had thrown ice water in his face. For a moment Paul thought he might get angry. Then his gaze faltered and he looked away. "That's okay," he mumbled. "No harm, no sweat."

Ray sat down and reached for his drink. The glass was empty but he lifted it to his lips in a sort of reflex action. After a moment he said, "Is it that obvious?"

"What's obvious is that you're trading on my reputation. See and be seen at the Journalisten-Club, is that it?"

"You don't pull any punches, do you?"

"What is it, Ray? The work or the booze?"

Ray winced. "I'm not a basket case, Paul. Not yet, anyway."

"So what's the problem?"

"There are *no* problems, that's the problem. Nobody's interested in Berlin, nobody cares about the Wall, it's a dead issue. Oh, sure, occasionally some protester will go over and pee on the Wall and the *Grenzpolizei* will kick the beejesus out of him, but even then it's only worth a column in Berlin. The rest of the world's got its own problems. Meanwhile the East is busy turning itself into a communist Disneyland in exchange for tourists' dollars. Last summer things were so slow I worked for this Theissen Tourist Agency taking busloads of tourists to the Wall and reciting statistics about how many people were killed. After a while I got bored and started making the statistics up. *Ten people killed crossing the Wall here. Twenty people killed. A family with three children.* The next time it was six children and a dog. Then the youngest girl went back to get the dog and they shot her. A little girl named Heidi. I was a smash. The next day I get to the same spot and there's this couple from the day before with flowers they're going to leave in memory of Heidi." Ray shook his head. "I quit the next day. I couldn't stand it."

The waiter materialized, collected their glasses and asked if they wanted another. When Paul refused, Ray gave him a troubled look.

"You sure you aren't on an expense account?"

"Private business."

Ray turned to the waiter. "Make it a single."

After the waiter was gone Paul said, "Are you going to be any good to me, Ray? Because if not . . ."

"Okay, okay, there are a couple of ways to go. First, as an accredited journalist you can be working on a *Kriegserleidnis*. That's very common over here. Some noble German saved somebody's Jewish father or mother and now they're trying to find this savior to thank him. Even the East Germans will cooperate on something like that—as long as it's not an anti-communist slant. So in your case we make Inge Hausner an anti-fascist hero who saved some poor communist from the Nazis; some big boy in a baggy suit, Walter Ulbricht maybe, first leader of East Germany and hero of the Berlin Wall and all that . . ."

Paul was shaking his head. "A story like that wouldn't hold up if they investigated. Besides, I'm assuming she changed her name when she moved."

"Changed her name? Why?"

Paul took out his wallet and removed the folded newspaper clipping that his mother had given him.

"She was implicated in a murder conspiracy. That's why she disappeared in the first place."

He handed the clipping to Ray, who read it with growing interest. "Even better than a *Kriegserleidnis*. Except it doesn't say anything about your brother. How do you know he was with her?"

"My mother left him with her."

"Great, so how do you know he wasn't one of these human hamburgers? If you pardon my French."

Paul didn't want to talk about the nightmares or the killings, particularly with Ray Tregerdemain.

"I don't," he said. "But the *anmeld* records should tell us."

"Not if Inge Heusner became Kathy Nicekraut, which wasn't all that difficult back them. All she'd have had to do was walk into a refugee camp and say, 'Hi, I'm Kathy Nicekraut, one of the friendly *Deutschvolk* who got kicked out of Poland and I've been walking for a couple of months and lost my identity papers, sorry' . . ."

"*Inge* Nicekraut," Paul corrected.

"Why *Inge?*"

"I'm assuming she kept her first name but changed the last."

"How do you figure that?"

Paul shrugged. "Somebody once told me it's easier for people not to forget who's talking to them if they keep their first names." Actually, a low-level hood who'd acted as a source for him on a story had told him so.

The drink arrived and Ray busied himself nursing what he assumed would be the last drink he could charge off Paul. Around the room some of the groups had moved into the dining area while outside the window, streetlights were beginning to flicker into life.

"Question," Ray said. "How in the hell can you track down little Miss Inge if she changed her name?"

"Well, I know when she disappeared," Paul said, fingering the clipping. "So never mind the name, just check all records for the week of February ninth, a woman thirty-five to forty years old with a child between a year and two years old."

"Between a year and two years old? The kid was born the same day as you, wasn't he? You're twins, you said."

"She could have changed the birth date."

"She could have changed a lot of things. How do you know she didn't take off for Dresden or Leipzig? What makes you think she stayed in Berlin?"

"It's the logical place to start."

Ray shook his head sadly. "I should have ordered a double," he said. "You've got nothing, you know that? She might or might not have left Berlin; she might or might not have taken your brother with her; she probably changed one or all of her names and his names; she might have moved in with a friend or even slept on the streets for a couple of years—"

"I don't need you to tell me the odds, I need help. So we go with what we've got . . . Week of February ninth, a woman between thirty-five and forty with a child between age one and two."

Ray pulled back for a moment, like a turtle sinking into its shell. "Can we get another round?"

"Can I get an answer from you?"

"Ray Tregerdemain has more angles than a clubhouse politician. I've got a contact at Humboldt University. It's just hard to talk when my mouth is so dry."

Paul flagged the waiter and ordered another round. "Okay, what about Humboldt University? That's in the East, right?"

"As Adolf said, 'The destiny of the Fatherland lies in the East'—"

"Humboldt, Ray?"

"In the East, right. Has a great reputation, not exactly the party school it was in the twenties but academically still top of the line. Got some great professors. One of them's a buddy of mine, Julius Schiller. Julius is the kind who actually believes the key to one big happy world is communication. Has me come once a semester to give a little lecture on 'Journalism as Practiced in the West, or How Ethics Takes a Backseat to Entertainment.' I get them all jazzed up and afterward we go to the local Kneipe and argue over beer. That's an interesting thing about commie countries...the written word still matters so goddamn much. A typewriter's a gun and words are bullets."

"Meanwhile," said Paul, "how does your professor help us access *anmeld* records?"

"Not us, him. We let him do it. Julius happens to have a brother in the foreign office. One of the original commie kids who helped build the Berlin Wall. Still got cement under his fingernails. Anyway, he's a mucky-muck official and that makes life easy for Julius. He comes in handy in cases like this—no politics, just good old-fashioned fact-checking, research and red-tape cutting. Mr. Julius Schiller, brother of Comrade Rolf Schiller, Order of Stalin's Nosewart and all that? Yes, sir, step right up, take any old *anmeld* record you want, take it home with you if you like and remember to say 'hi' to your brother for me." Ray chuckled, coughed. "Human nature. They can put a wall around the city but they can't put a wall around human nature."

Paul was willing to pay for services rendered. He knew from experience how time-consuming checking records could be.

"All right," he said. "How do I meet him?"

"You meet him?" Ray looked surprised.

"I don't want a middleman, Ray, but I'll give you a finder's fee if he works out. And I'll need help on this side of the Wall. There're twelve districts over here and she might just as easily have moved west as east. I can use a researcher, if you want the work."

"I don't know, let me check my schedule." He pulled out the neck of his shirt and peered down at his stomach. "Nope, not too busy next week."

Paul half-smiled. Ray Tregerdemain might not be Woodward or Bernstein but Paul couldn't help liking him. They arranged that Ray would make contact with Julius Schiller and call Paul at the hotel by noon the next day. In the meantime Paul would make a list of districts in the West, dividing them into those he would cover and those Ray could handle.

"It really would make a good *Kriegserleidnis*, you know," Ray told him as they left the club. "Brothers torn apart by war reunited and all that."

"*No*, Ray. Don't even think of it."

"Up to you, but I hate to see a good story go to waste..."

The night had brought a change of character to the Kurfurstendamm, the main street that Berliners casually called the *Ku'damm*. The glass display cases that occupied prominent positions along the sidewalk were no longer the focus of attention for shoppers but had become illuminated islands streetwalkers posed against.

"Asphalt swallows," Ray said. "They've each got their own spot. I saw a fight once when some new kitty tried to take another's place. Better than professional wrestling, let me tell you."

Ray kept up a running commentary as they walked. He was meeting friends at the Europa Center casino, which was on the way back to the InterContinental. The drinks had boosted his natural energy and he walked briskly, head swiveling back and forth, a visual sniper taking potshots at the city.

Outside the gleaming arcadelike entry Ray hesitated, asked Paul if he wanted to come along.

"No thanks," Paul said. "I want to poke my head in there."

Ray followed his gaze to the Wyoming, where the neon bronco was kicking up its heels.

"You'll poke more than your head if you go in there."

A shriek of laughter obscured his words. Two couples had emerged from the casino, joking and stumbling against one another as they waited for their car. The men were obviously businessmen and the women just as obviously the evening's entertainment.

"They call him *die Schlange*!" the younger man said.

The girls tittered.

Paul started back toward the Wyoming but Ray took his arm.

"One more thing," he said. "How about a little advance on that finder's fee? I mean, I've got a couple checks coming in but you never know. The mail and everything. Fifty marks, say? You mind?"

Headlights swept across them as a long white limousine pulled into the driveway. Paul and Ray stepped up on the curb to clear the way.

"It'll come out of research," Paul told him.

"Fine, great. You're a lifesaver, old buddy."

As he got out the money Paul was only vaguely aware that the sounds of merriment had died away. It wasn't until Ray said, "Hello there, honey," that he looked up and saw one of the women, a waiflike oriental in a silk miniskirt, coming toward them. She was staring at Paul with fierce concentration.

"Hey, Kristy," the older man called.

Paul noticed that the back door of the limousine was open and that the other couple was staring out in mild surprise. He was aware of the older man standing on the other side of the car, his frowning image reflected in the polished surface of the roof, sparkling beneath dozens of tiny lights that bordered the awning. But only at the last moment did he realize that the girl's face had become a mask of fury.

And then she hit him.

CHAPTER

12

HER HAND EXPLODED ON HIS CHEEK. PAUL stepped back and raised an arm to protect himself. The girl, Kristy, came after him, flailing away with such fury that one of her blows knocked the money from his hands and Ray, who had just grabbed her arm, let go to run after the bills.

"Pervert bastard," Kristy was screaming. "You don't treat people that way, damn dirty pervert..."

She was so enraged that Paul had a hard time getting hold of one of her wrists. Meanwhile the doorman came running. He wore a maroon tuxedo with a matching top hat that tumbled to the ground when he grabbed the girl from behind. She struggled against him and he leaned back, lifting her from the ground. Instantly all the fight went out of her and she collapsed in sobs.

The doorman's concern was Paul. "Are you all right, sir?" His face was partially obscured by the girl's black hair.

Paul nodded. There was a ringing in his left ear from the first blow and his neck stung where the girl had scratched him but otherwise he was okay.

"I'm fine," he said, straightening his jacket. The doorman lowered the girl to the ground and took her by the arm. "We'll let the police take care of you, Miss Crazy." He recovered his hat and began leading the girl back to the casino. The white limousine had disappeared, its occupants not wanting to become involved in any trouble. Even the girl's companion had deserted her.

"Wait a minute," Paul said. "It's nothing serious. Why not let her go?"

"If I were you I should make a complaint." The doorman had the wide, flat face of a farmer and spoke with the moral certitude of a preacher. "You were not with the woman. I can attest to that."

"No, that's all right. I just want to talk to her."

"Eat shit," the girl said. She had stopped crying and stood glaring at Paul.

The doorman turned on her, took her by the shoulders and shook her. "You want the police?"

"I don't care," she mumbled.

"Let her go," Paul said.

Reluctantly the doorman let go of the girl but admonished her never to come there again. She was prohibited, *unerwünscht*.

As soon as she was free, the girl straightened her dress, watching Paul warily. Ray approached with a handful of bills. "How much did you have?"

"I don't know." The girl began to move away and Paul followed. "Wait, damn it, I want to talk to you—"

"Go *away*, I'm legal Berliner, you don't *touch* me."

She turned and began walking toward the Ku'damm. Paul and Ray caught up with her.

"You think you know me, don't you?" She ignored him and walked faster.

"I have to talk to you."

She turned to face him. "You leave me *alone*, I'm legal now."

"You're mistaking me for someone else," Paul said slowly. "I want to know who. I want to know when and where you met him—"

"It was *you*."

Ray stepped forward and said in a conciliatory voice, "Tell me, honey. You tell me what he did."

"What for?" she said with disgust. "You're probably a pervert, too."

Paul held up five bills. "Fifty marks to tell me—or him—what happened."

Ray whispered, "Just don't give her *my* fifty marks."

The girl insisted that they follow her to Breitscheidplatz, which was bright with lights from a film crew that was shooting a commercial at an outdoor cafe. Thick black cables snaked their way from a generating truck to an area bordered by a crowd that merged into mass silhouette. At the other end of the plaza stained-glass squares of the Kaiser Wilhelm carillon tower glowed translucent-blue against the night sky, and on the rooftops of surrounding buildings names of businesses marched in tall neon letters interspersed with gleaming company logos.

The girl stopped at a fountain where water tumbled from a marble dome over stone sculptures of figures embracing. She perched on the low wall that enclosed it, lit a cigarette and tossed the match into the water. When she spoke she addressed Ray rather than Paul. Listening to her, Paul found himself with conflicting emotions, excited by the concrete evidence that his brother existed, repelled by what Karl had done.

The girl told them that two years ago she had been brought from Thailand to work in a brothel. She arrived with fifteen other girls, all from Asia. They worked for three months and then returned home. The day before they left the girls were told that a very important man was coming, a man with specific tastes. He didn't like makeup or high heels or sexy clothing. They were to appear before him fresh, clean, like schoolgirls.

Most of the girls were excited. The great hope was always that an important man, a rich man, would take a special fancy to one of them and make her his mistress. This was called "going private." There were rumors that such things had happened before, that Asian women had been put up in apartments and given resident permits. So excitement ran high on the day that the man arrived. Of course, some of the girls felt naked without makeup and tried to sneak a light blush or a faint lip gloss, but Madam Tran, who ran the place, had a sharp eye and made them wash it off. There would be no makeup.

"Then *he* came," the girl said, pointing to Paul. "And nobody knows what kind of harm he has in his heart, so we are all smiling and each one he looked at until he chose me. 'You're so lucky,' my friend Lani told me when he pointed to me. But I'm not so lucky because he hurt me with the enema stick. I said 'no' because I don't like that preference. I told him, some other girls it's okay for that kind of thing. He should choose them but he wouldn't listen. Instead, he tied up my hands and feet, and then the boiling water came. He *hurt* me." She turned to Paul and pointed. "*He* did that. You *know* you did . . ."

Paul felt himself drawing away, trying to become detached the way he did when he was in the field. It was the only way he could listen to her story, which evoked memory of his dream, or whatever it was. "Where did this happen?" he asked quietly.

"You know very damn good where it was."

"Please tell me anyway."

"At Vanilla Rose Club, you pervert—"

"Ahh," Ray said. "The Vanilla Rose."

"You know it?"

"A specialty whorehouse supplied by a couple of ex-G.I.'s and run by a guy named Otto Wenzler. Very decadent *and* very expensive. Your brother's got to be living in the West. Visitors from the East can only bring in fifteen Eastmarks. Not enough to buy a watered Coke in a place like the Vanilla Rose."

While they spoke the girl busied herself with her hair, brushing it in swift businesslike strokes with a gold-flecked pink brush. Now she tucked the brush into her purse and asked for her fifty marks. Her eyes were already scanning the plaza, looking for her next client. Paul asked more questions about Karl—about himself as far as she was concerned—but the girl knew nothing more. He gave her the fifty marks and took a picture with the Ricoh—which surprised her and brought forth a string of over-the-shoulder obscenities as she walked away.

Paul stared after her. "She wouldn't believe it wasn't me," he said.

"You sure you haven't been to Berlin before?" Ray asked in a tone of mock skepticism.

Paul gave him a black look.

"Kidding, kidding," Ray said quickly.

Paul turned and began retracing their steps. Ray hurried after him and the two walked in silence. Finally Paul said, "The Vanilla Rose. Give me some background."

"Kind of an international consortium," Ray said, relieved to be on a neutral subject. "The G.I.'s get the girls in Asia—Thailand, Vietnam and the Philippines mostly—bring them over here on Interflug for a sixty percent savings off Pan Am."

"Interflug? They come in through the East?"

"You got it. That's where Otto Wenzler comes in. He's got contacts East and West, the original Berlin swami, knows all, hears all, sees all. Originally a street kid, came out of the rubble gangs but you'd never know it. Very pretentious fellow, very much involved in social functions—theater, opera, Berlin Philharmonic. Regular Tuxedo Joe, but you turn him over and up pops the majordomo of specialty whorehouses. Meaning very young girls. The kind who look like daddy's little daughter—none over five feet, hardly any tits, supposed to look thirteen although their passports say they're sixteen and their eyes say they're thirty. Anyway, they're all professionals, all presumed volunteers and they make more money in three months than they can make in three years back home so nobody complains. The kids are happy, daddy's happy, and Otto Wenzler's very rich."

They had arrived back at the casino. Paul gave Ray the advance he'd asked for and told him to call him at the hotel in the morning.

Ray stuffed the bills into his pants pocket and slapped Paul on the arm. "Don't worry," he said. "Now that we know he's real, we'll find him."

After Ray disappeared Paul had the doorman call a cab. As they waited, the man offered sympathy for the earlier incident.

"You were generous not to press charges, sir."

Paul shrugged.

The doorman stepped close and spoke in a low voice. A lacework of broken veins discolored his sunken cheeks and his watery blue eyes invited Paul's confidence.

"She was a foreigner, of course. They have no respect, these new ones. In the old days such a thing would never happen. But now? Too many *Ausländer, ja?*"

"Right," Paul said. "Give me a good old-fashioned German whore any day."

The doorman's complacent smile faded as a taxi arrived and Paul hopped in.

"The Vanilla Rose," he told the driver. "You know where that is?"

"Do I know where my mother lives?"

The cab shot forward, cutting off a Fiat that proceeded to tailgate them for the next three blocks, blinking its headlights.

The Vanilla Rose was located in Neukoln, a working-class district adjoining the Wall. On one side of the street were small neighborhood shops, most of them closed; on the other side, a canal with dark water glistening beneath overhanging trees. At first glance the Vanilla Rose seemed like a poor candidate for a bed of iniquity. No light came from the shuttered windows, but a porch light shone brightly over the entrance and a stained-glass rose worked into the mahogany door glowed with light from inside.

Paul looked for a bell, there was none. He opened the door and stepped into a small anteroom, dimly lit. Directly ahead there was a short hallway with a carpeted stairway at the end. From beyond an archway on the right, music, laughter and light spilled into the hall. There was another door on the left, and it was here that a Vietnamese woman wearing an elegant Bao Dai appeared. She was a type that Paul remembered from the war, her smooth skin stretched tight over a patrician face, thin lips made larger with red lipstick, flared eyebrows drawn in dark pencil like a raven's wings outstretched in flight.

"Madam Tran?" Paul asked.

He expected her to be surprised that he knew her name. Instead she surprised him.

"Good evening, Herr Alexander. Are you joining us for pleasure or are you here to see Herr Wenzler?"

"What?"

"Are you here on business or pleasure this evening?"

His surprise must have shown on his face. Madam Tran cocked her head to one side. "Is something wrong, Herr Alexander?"

"Nothing, nothing . . . I just—I'm fine."

"So. You are here to see Herr Wenzler?"

"Is he here?"

Again the quizzical look.

"Doesn't he know you're coming?"

"I'm pretty sure he doesn't."

"Let me call and see." She indicated a settee beneath the stairway. "Please."

Paul walked to the settee but rather than sit down he stepped into the parlor, where the air was thick with cigarette smoke and perfume. What unnerved him were the girls. Girls on the verge of puberty who looked as if they'd gathered for a slumber party. They wore pinafores and little chemises and skimpy teddies and knee socks and smocks.

He saw a girl on the couch who couldn't have been more than ten. Amber-skinned and blonde, she wore lacy panties and a rose silk camisole. Her slight build was a child's. Slender hips and legs, delicate shoulders and arms with barely a hint of breasts beneath the luminous folds of the camisole. The man next to her had taken off his jacket and loosened his tie. His shirt was partly unbuttoned and the top of his undershirt was visible. He had a florid face and receding hair and, as Paul watched, he lifted the girl and put her onto his lap. She squirmed, as if trying to get away. He leaned forward, encompassing her like a huge bear.

Without thinking Paul moved toward them. He knew where he was, he knew this was the Vanilla Rose, but the gross discrepancy between the man's heavy flaccid body and the girl's flawless delicacy repelled him. The girl was too young; she just couldn't know what she was doing . . .

As he crossed the room, another girl greeted him in an oriental wind-chime voice, but Paul ignored her. His attention was fixed on the blonde girl. By the time he reached the couch, his fists were clenched.

Twisting on the man's lap, the girl became aware of Paul and looked up. Instantly the impression of innocence was shattered. The girl had a lascivious yet elfish face. Her lipstick and eye makeup were matching shades of purple, her false eyelashes were silver. Close up, Paul could see that her hair was dyed and her skin did not have the childish purity that he had imagined.

"Hi, honey," she said. "You wish to wait for me?"

"Hey," the man protested, "not my little birdie. You're mine for the night, little birdie." He nuzzled her neck and the girl giggled.

Paul felt foolish—and sickened.

Madam Tran returned. "Herr Wenzler is at home," she said. "A reception of some sort; you will see."

She led him down a hall and ushered him out the back door. As Paul stepped past her, Madam Tran sniffed. "You smell like an American tonight, Herr Alexander."

He looked at her in surprise. His Berlin accent, he knew, was pure. Madam Tran smiled. "Mennen Aftershave. You didn't think I'd notice?"

She closed the door, leaving him at the edge of an irregularly shaped cobblestone plaza bordered by the backs of homes and apartment buildings. Two streetlights threw double shadows from a lone tree in the middle of the plaza. From open windows came suburban sounds: people eating dinner, a child crying, someone playing piano, the sound of radio and television. Strange juxtaposition, the Vanilla Rose next to these average, everyday homes. Paul wondered how he was supposed to know which one was Wenzler's.

His problem was resolved a moment later when a porch light blinked on near an atrium across the plaza and a man appeared in silhouette and called into the darkness.

"Herr Alexander?"

"Coming," Paul said.

At least he knew for certain his brother's last name now. Alexander. Karl Alexander. A madam and a whoremaster had established that much.

As he approached, details began to emerge. The harsh porch light glistened off coal-black hair and threw shadows over mannequinish features. The man stepped back, holding open the door for him. He was well-built, over twenty-five, dressed in a tuxedo. As Paul passed, he noted that the man was wearing a sapphire stud in one ear.

"We're having a reception for Ernesto Guianni," the man said, a slight hint of reproof in his voice. "If you don't mind, Otto asks that you use the servants' stairway."

So this was not Herr Wenzler. This was, what? The doorman? The aide-de-camp? The companion?

From down the hall came the sound of voices and wineglasses and laughter; a reception in full swing. Someone was playing the piano, and Paul heard the unmistakable voice of Ernesto Guianni raised in song. It was a Jekyll and Hyde situation . . . Wenzler hosting this reception for a famous opera singer while teen-age prostitutes writhed in mock passion less than a block away.

"This way, Herr Alexander."

His escort led Paul through a narrow door and up a circular staircase to the second floor, where they stepped out into a wide, thickly carpeted hallway. Track lighting focused pools of light on what looked like original artwork. Obviously Wenzler was involved in a lot more than the Vanilla Rose.

With his fingers trailing through the air, the man went to a carved oak door, knocked twice and entered. Otto Wenzler sat at a desk arranging a line of cocaine on an upturned mirror. He wore a tuxedo with a silver cummerbund. His blond hair hung pale and damp around his neck and everything around him, from the jeweled ring he wore on his little finger to the bronze statue on the desk, was meant to impress.

Wenzler glanced up and nodded. "Thank you, Helmut."

Not knowing how well he was supposed to know Helmut, Paul simply nodded a polite goodbye. As soon as they were alone, Wenzler said pleasantly, "I detest surprises, Karl. Particularly when I'm entertaining."

"I'm sorry," Paul said, wondering how long he could keep up this impersonation.

Wenzler blinked in surprise, moving his head in a nervous, staccato fashion.

"A red-letter day!" he said. "That's the first time I've ever heard you say you were sorry for anything. You must be getting old, Karl, coming here like this, taking such risks..."

He pulled a large gray envelope from the drawer and tossed it across the desk. "I suppose you want these."

With the eerie feeling that he had stepped out of his own clothes and into those of a stranger, Paul picked up the envelope.

"I'd offer you a line," Wenzler said, "but I know you confine your vices to a different arena."

Placing one end of a glass tube to his nose, Wenzler inhaled the cocaine, first one nostril, then the other. Paul barely noticed. He unwound the red twine holding the flap shut, reached inside and took out two passports, one a familiar American blue, the other the dark green of West Germany. Opening each in turn, he found two matching driver's licenses, American and German. The names on each were different but it wasn't the names that caught his eye, it was the face—his own face—pictured in photographs that he knew had never been taken. Not of him.

It was like looking into a tiny, wallet-sized mirror. The hair was a little shorter, combed differently, but other than that there was no difference. But studying the photo more closely, it seemed to him that there was something different about the eyes. Not their size or shape but their expression. Alien, not him.

He held in his hands the proof of his brother's existence. He was only vaguely aware that Otto was telling him about the performance that night; that it had been opening night and that the reception for Ernesto Guianni had lured even those of Berlin's social elite who normally snubbed him. After a moment, Otto stopped.

"What is it? Something wrong?"

Paul said, "This is my brother." The impersonation couldn't go on, he couldn't manage it. He'd have to take his chances on the truth.

"Who?"

"The man in the passport. It's not me, it's my brother."

Otto held up a cautionary hand. "Don't tell me, please. I only like to know secrets of the kind that make other people uncomfortable. Your secrets, Karl, are the kind that would make *me* uncomfortable."

"Mr. Wenzler, listen to me. I'm not the man you think I am. I'm not Karl, I'm Paul Stafford, his twin brother."

"Of course," Otto said with a sardonic grin. "And I'm the Queen of England with a frog up my ass."

He snickered and slid the drug paraphernalia back into a drawer. Paul stepped forward and held the passport photo next to his face.

"I'm serious. I'm not this man. I'm Paul Stafford—this man is my brother. I came to Berlin to find him and I need your help. Do you understand?"

Otto looked him carefully up and down. "You are not Karl Alexander?"

"My name is Paul Stafford. I'm an American. Here." Paul pulled out his wallet and flipped it open to display his driver's license and *Herald* I.D. card.

"Karl is my brother. We're twins but we were separated when we were young. I never knew I had a brother until a few days ago. Now I need to find him. I've got to know . . ."

A hooded look came into Wenzler's eyes.

"May I have those back, please?"

He reached for the passports but Paul moved away.

"In return for telling me how to get in touch with my brother."

"I believe you. You are not Karl. If you were, you would know better than to try and hold me up."

"Just a trade. My passports for your information."

"*Your* passports? Those belong to me."

"Not anymore—"

Wenzler reached into his desk and pulled out a pistol. A lady's gun, a 25-caliber chrome-plated Beretta, but it

could put holes in a man. "And now, whoever you are,"
Wenzler said, "I think you will give me the documents."
As Paul moved to hand over the passports the door opened
and a woman in a jeweled evening gown came into the
room.

"You have sixty seconds to come downstairs," she announced airily. "Ernesto is doing the aria from *La Traviata*."

The woman was about sixty, imperious and a little
drunk. Her dark hair was pulled tightly back and tucked
beneath a tiara. Otto hastily slid the gun inside his jacket.

"I shall be right there, my dear Helena."

"You know he won't sing without you there. *Wo ist
Liebling Otto?* he keeps asking. He thinks you're snubbing
him, but I told him that was just your way, sneaking off to
your little debaucheries."

At which point she turned to Paul, looked him up and
down. "You are a debaucherie, aren't you? Or are you a
servant?"

"Countess, if you please—" Wenzler began.

"A guest," Paul said. "And I'd love to hear Signore
Guianni sing the aria."

He moved toward her. Behind him, Wenzler called,
"Mr. Stafford, we have business . . ."

Paul turned at the door. "I think the countess is right.
Art before business." And he offered her his arm. "Sir
Cedric Stafford. Shall we?"

The woman touched her chin to her shoulder and
regarded him with amusement.

"We shall find out," she said. "Come along, Otto."

The countess took Paul's arm with ring-encrusted fingers and allowed him to lead her down the hallway.

"Are you really British?" she asked.

"Right now I am."

"Ahh, I knew it. Your teeth aren't bad enough to be
British. They breed wonderful dogs and horses but have
coal miners for dentists."

Paul decided that the countess wasn't as foolish or tipsy
as she appeared.

Wenzler caught up with them midway down the hall and
grabbed Paul's arm, stopping them.

"One moment, please. Excuse me, countess, but this
man has something of mine."

She raised an eyebrow. "Does he? How exciting. What is it?"

"This," Paul said.

He pulled out a passport, flipped it open and held it toward the countess so that she could see the photograph without reading the name. At the same time he leaned close to Wenzler.

"You be the judge," he went on. "Is that me or Herr Wenzler?"

Wenzler lunged at the passport but Paul pulled it away. "Let the lady judge."

"Don't be rude, Otto. It's our Sir Cedric's picture, no question. Now come on, Ernesto is waiting." She pushed between them, took each by the arm and led them to the top of a stairway that descended in two circular flights, mirror images of one another, one to the left and one to the right. Below, in a richly appointed foyer, a dozen people in formal evening clothes stood sipping champagne and waving jeweled wrists. A waiter in a pink jacket with a black carnation in the lapel offered drinks from a silver tray.

As they descended, Wenzler craned to see into the drawing room, looking, Paul guessed, for his partner Helmut. Rather than wait for the two of them to get together and figure out how to deal with him, Paul abruptly pulled away at the bottom of the stairs.

"I left the car in a no parking zone," he said. "Be right back."

Followed by the countess' protests and Wenzler's murderous glare, he ducked through the crowd to the front door. As he brushed past a surprised doorman he had one final glimpse of Wenzler pointing him out to the man called Helmut. Then he was on the street, running. At the end of the block he turned right, kept jogging and changing directions until he was sure that nobody was following. Then he went to a pay phone and called Wenzler.

"How's the party going?" he asked.

"You must be brothers," Wenzler said, ice in his voice. "You both take chances with your lives."

"Don't worry about it. If Karl wants his passports, tell him to get in touch with me. I'm in Room 317 at the InterContinental."

In the background Paul could hear the aria.

After that, matters moved with German efficiency. By the time he got back to the hotel a message was waiting: "Your brother will meet you at the Spree Bowl, Peoples Republic Plaza, GDR, at noon tomorrow."

Paul read the note twice. In his room he went to the window and looked out. The circus tent glowed a milky white in the yard below. Beyond it, the blackness of the Tiergarden and beyond the Tiergarden, East Berlin, dark and somber except for its modern television tower topped with a silver globe that hung like a metal moon over the divided city. The GDR. East Berlin. Where he would find Karl Alexander. A killer. His brother. His blood.

CHAPTER

13

THE PALAST DER REPUBLIK WAS A FIVE-STORY concrete and glass building situated where the baroque Hohenzollern palace once stood. Its primary function was as the home of the East German parliament, but for no apparent reason the ground floor also contained a disco, a nightclub and bowling alley, all of which overlooked the rock-embanked Spree River. The entrances were visible from the opposite side of the river, which was why Karl Alexander chose this spot to meet his brother. He sat in his car, monitoring the entrance to the Spree Bowl through binoculars.

Through the large picture windows, Karl could see the bowlers going through their slow-motion three-step and the spectators who sat off to one side drinking beer and eating pizza. A group of tourists passed, obscuring his vision. Karl lowered the binoculars and waited for them to take pictures of a slow-moving barge and its bare-chested bow helmsman. It was almost twelve . . .

Karl had been shaken by the phone call from Otto Wenzler. The man's obvious distress bothered him as much as the news itself. Otto wasn't the type to panic.

"I thought he was you," he kept repeating. "I was sure of it."

"Calm down, Otto."

"I prefer to be upset. I don't deal in dirty passports any longer, Karl. It's ridiculous for a man in my position. I do it only as a favor to you."

"Can you get me replacements?"

"Aren't you going to meet him?"

"If I do it's to recover the photos. The names are blown. I need replacements, all right?"

"By Wednesday? These are originals, you know. It's not so easy."

It was never so easy with Otto. Since difficult things cost more, everything with Otto was difficult. They had known each other since childhood, when both were members of the same rubble gang. Then Karl began his life with Uncle Alex and lost contact with Otto. Fifteen years later Otto's name appeared in a Stasis file; he was picked up trying to smuggle a professor and his wife into West Berlin. Karl offered him amnesty. All Otto had to do in exchange was to infiltrate other flight-helper groups and tip off the Stasis.

It was the beginning of a long-standing association whose emphasis shifted over the years from the political to the private. Karl's aid in smoothing the transit of the Vanilla Rose girls was just one of a number of business relationships. It was less risky than Otto supposed. The East German authorities had little interest in stopping a practice that proved that capitalism and degeneracy went together.

Because it was such short notice, Karl agreed to pay double the price for replacements. When he agreed so quickly Otto's curiosity was aroused.

"Just what kind of operation is this?"

"You know better than to ask."

"You mean I know better than to ask *you*?"

Karl spoke quietly and clearly. "Otto, if you so much as make an inquiry, someone will bury you in the Spree... Now tell me about this man. Could he have been an imposter?"

"I don't see how." Otto's tone was abrupt, showed his hurt. He didn't like threats. But he took this one from Karl.

"Plastic surgery?"

"No, no. He fooled everyone. Madam Tran, Helmut, me. Even when he told me, I didn't believe. If this man is not your brother, I'll kiss the cross and become a priest..."

His brother. Karl lay awake that night, his emotions running high. If Paul Stafford was an imposter, then he was in trouble. Only one organization had the skills and resources to perform a facial reconstruction so complete that it could fool Otto: the CIA. Had they discovered who was responsible for the assassinations and sent someone to capture or kill him? If so, why the elaborate deception? Why the oblique approach?

Unless it was the KGB.

The thought truly chilled him. What if the Redeye plot had been discovered? Uncle Alex betrayed? He had said that there were others involved. The map of the Bayonne Terminal, the cargo manifest and the Sony-disguised CIKOP-34F—all these had come from a source inside the KGB. And what about the girl, Marina? The one who was to sabotage the infra-red defense capability on the General Secretary's aircraft. Had she been caught? Broken?

No, Karl thought, if the KGB knew he'd already be dead.

Which brought him back to the possibility that the man Paul Stafford was actually his twin brother. The idea gave him a chill. He had to be careful. He had to make certain. If Paul Stafford *was* his brother, then the visit must be an innocent one, the timing accidental. But if he was an imposter . . . if he was an imposter he would soon be a dead one. And if he was his brother . . . Well, one thing was certain . . . whoever he was, Paul Stafford could not be allowed to interfere with the Redeye assignment.

Karl glanced at his watch. Five minutes after twelve. The man was late. He would give him another fifteen minutes and then he would call Otto.

Paul had actually gotten up early. He'd eaten a heavy German breakfast, pored over a map to the city and caught the eleven-thirty S-Bahn to the Friedrichstrasse station. The station was inside the Eastern sector but since the trains went only to the West, little effort had been spent in maintaining the place. The atmosphere was gloomy and not improved by the dour guards who roamed the long platforms in their rumpled gray uniforms or sat watching from crosswalks high above the tracks, profiled by grimy glass walls, cradling rifles in their arms. A worker's paradise, Paul thought. For guards.

The border formalities took longer than he expected. He had to stand in line before entering a narrow stall where a sad-eyed official sold him a one-day Cinderella visa—he had to be out of East Berlin by midnight or face arrest—and then join another line to exchange twenty-five Westmarks for an equal number of grossly inflated Eastmarks. By the time he reached the street he was running late.

He took a taxi down the Unter den Linden, surprised

that so many of the once-elegant buildings still showed bullet scars from the war. The famous tree-lined boulevard was made melancholy by the host of rooftop statues looking down from above, marooned in mid-air, searching for their lost city.

Paul's excitement rose as they approached the Palast der Republik. He hoped Karl would be waiting when he got there, but it didn't surprise him when he wasn't. He was probably a careful man, unlikely to show himself unless he felt safe. As he waited he wondered if the threat of CIA exposure would force Karl to stop the killings. He hated to think of his brother as an assassin, but the false passports and driver's licenses proved Karl was involved in clandestine activities, and any doubts he'd had about Karl's responsibility for the CIA killings were gone. There was only one explanation for his dreams—the one Annie Helms had proposed. He could imagine her excitement if she found out he had a twin brother, but whether or not he would tell her would depend on Karl . . .

The rumble of bowling balls and clatter of pins seemed an odd counterpoint to what had brought him here. Paul sipped his coffee, tried to control his impatience. It was possible Karl feared a trap and had decided not to meet him. But finally a waiter approached and told him that he had a phone call. Paul got up and went to the counter, where a red-haired girl handed him the phone.

"Hello?"

"Paul Stafford?"

It was like listening to an echo of his own voice.

"It's me. Are you Karl?"

"Yes. I prefer to meet you outside. You have no objection?"

"Anywhere you want—"

"All right, then. Leave the Spree Bowl, turn right and when you reach Rathaus-strasse, turn left. Keep walking on the left-hand side of the street. I will pick you up."

Paul gave the cashier two marks and went outside. It was almost twelve-thirty and the sidewalks were beginning to fill with businessmen and secretaries on their lunch breaks. One couple sat on a grassy embankment overlooking the river and ate sandwiches from a paper bag. A group of teen-agers in a parking lot performed skateboard tricks. There was no sign of Karl.

Paul followed the instructions, crossed the Spree and

headed toward the old town hall, the Rotes Rathaus. He'd gone a block and a half when a white Mercedes 280 E detached itself from the oncoming traffic and came quickly to a stop beside him. The driver leaned over and opened the door.

His hair is neater was Paul's first thought.

In the first moment of recognition, their eyes caught and Paul saw in Karl's face surprise, suspicion, pleasure, distrust and . . . fear? Or were these his own feelings? For a moment Karl's features seemed blurred by emotions, and then the moment passed, and Paul was staring at a man who looked exactly like him and not like a murderer at all.

"Get in," Karl said.

Paul slid inside and shut the door. Karl quickly drove off.

"Why all the precautions?"

"In case you were followed."

"By whom?"

No answer. Karl swerved quickly to the inside lane and turned left. Two more blocks he turned left again, down a side street blocked at the far end by a construction project. A tall crane loomed over a concrete foundation surrounded by steel girders and bordered by a chain-link fence, open to permit access to work trucks.

Barely slowing, Karl turned into the construction area. The car bumped up over the dirt-packed curb and headed for a gate on the opposite side, leaving a trail of dust in its wake. Workmen paused and a man in a hard hat got out of a rusty trailer and shouted after them. Karl paid no attention. A moment later they had regained the street on the opposite side of the project.

"More precautions?" Paul said.

"My work with the government makes such measures necessary. It is all right now."

"Just what is your work with the government?"

"I'm an instructor at the Eichwalde Combat School. Commando training, you would call it." Karl gave him a sidelong glance. "Otto said you were an American."

"I am."

"You speak German like a Berliner."

"I lived here until I was five. My mother and I still speak it."

"Your mother is alive . . . ?"

"*Our* mother is alive."

Karl looked startled.

Paul said, "You didn't know?"

"No."

"That's how I found out about you."

"I was told she was dead...killed by an American bomb."

"Told by whom? Tante Inge?"

Karl's reaction couldn't have been greater if Paul had tossed a live grenade on the floor. He turned toward him, the car swerved across the road and back again as he fought to bring it under control. He pulled over and stopped the car. His hands gripped the steering wheel so tightly that the muscles in his forearms bulged. When he turned to Paul his face was deadly pale.

"Who are you?"

"Doesn't the face tell you?"

"How could you know about her?"

"Tante Inge?"

Karl winced, and Paul thought, my God, he's more upset than mom was. He told him the story of their early separation, leaving out any mention of the CIA or of the dreams. At one point Karl became agitated and broke in:

"You're sure?" he demanded, "You're *sure* she was not my aunt?"

"According to mother she was a downstairs neighbor. All the kids called her *aunt*."

"Not my aunt," Karl muttered.

"You thought she really was?"

"I was a child. What could I know?"

"Where is she now?"

"She's dead."

Paul realized he had been trying somehow to reconcile the CIA killings with the man sitting beside him, this person made in his own image, this person linked so intimately to him, whether he liked it or not. Until the mention of Inge Heusner it had been nearly impossible. Now, seeing the change in his brother's expression, there could be no more doubts. Karl's eyes narrowed, his lips compressed, his clenched teeth accentuated the jaw. There was hatred there—hatred and a remorselessness that seemed to chill the air around them. Yes, Paul thought, he's capable of it, all right. He's capable of murder. His twin, from the same genes—he pushed *that* out of his mind.

Karl returned the conversation to the details of their separation. What seemed to bother him most of all was why their mother hadn't tried to find him.

"She did," Paul said. "She looked for months. She kept going to the police—"

"The police," Karl said derisively. "What could they do? We were hiding from the police—"

"She thought you were dead, Karl. Someone saw Frau Heusner take you into the shop. Mom thought they had . . ."

"Butchered me?"

Paul nodded.

Karl looked away, his expression seemed to soften. "Still," he said, "she should have said something later. To you. To her husband and her family."

"She was ashamed."

"Of me?"

"Of what she'd done. Of what she thought happened to you."

Karl nodded, but Paul sensed the answer didn't really satisfy him.

"And where is my . . . my mother?"

"She lives in Florida. A little house on a man-made lake. She and dad—my stepfather—are separated."

"All these years I thought she had been killed in the bombing," Karl said in a distant voice. "I used to dream about her. I never knew her face but I dreamed that she covered me with her body and saved my life." He gave Paul a sidelong glance. "But it was you she saved."

"What?"

"She took you to the hospital; she left me behind."

Stunned. He thought Karl would be happy to know about his mother. Instead, he blamed her. He had his own guilts, he realized, about being the one their mother had saved and his reaction was as much defensive as it was in defense of his mother when he said, "She was nineteen years old. You can't blame her for what happened—"

"*I* was fourteen months."

As if that settled the matter, Karl started the car and moved back onto the highway. Paul was about to argue that nobody could entirely protect another person, when he remembered hearing those same words before. Not from his lips but from Joanna's in response to something he had said. And what had he told her? That there were no excuses in raising children. The arrogance of it brought a quick sting of regret.

Karl was asking him something but Paul had missed it. "What?"

Karl gave him a curious glance. He had regained his composure. "How did you find Otto Wenzler?"

"A girl, a hooker," Paul said.

"What girl?"

"Her name was Kristy. From Thailand. She tried to beat me up last night. It seems that she once worked at the Vanilla Rose, and when she saw me on the street she thought I was you. It seems you play rough with the girls." An understatement, as he knew from the dream.

"And from this girl you learned about Otto?"

"No, from Otto I learned about Otto. When he realized his mistake—that I wasn't you—he got nasty and pulled a gun."

"Which you ignored?"

"We were interrupted. Fortunately."

"Yes, you seem to have fortune on your side."

"Not always," Paul said.

"When not?"

There was an eagerness to the question that made Paul uncomfortable.

"I guess I've had my share of disappointments."

"Oh. Disappointments."

Again the defensive feeling. "I suppose getting out of Germany was lucky," he said. "The army was a secure life, we had good housing, clothes, plenty to eat—all the good old American perks."

"When you were a child did you have a bedroom of your own?"

"Most of the time."

"And when you shut the door, would they leave you alone?"

"Who?"

"Your mother, your father, everyone."

"I guess..." A strange question. "What about you? Where did you live?"

"Berlin," he said and quickly switched the subject to

America, about which his curiosity seemed insatiable. Paul in turn wanted to find out more about Karl but sensed he'd better go easy. He was still a shock to Karl, and he was, after all, dealing with an explosive personality.

So as they drove on, Paul mostly answered questions about his childhood and career as a journalist. He showed his discomfort over Karl's questions about Joanna, how they'd met, why Paul hadn't married earlier. Karl was watching him closely now, and Paul realized why . . . he had discovered an area of uncertainty, an area where Paul felt defensive. He had zeroed right in on it. Paul had done the same thing in interviews, looking for a crack through which he could get at the person behind the persona.

Paul tried to get back the control of this bizarre meeting. "You know I came here to find out about you, about your life. You've been digging into me and my past—"

"So I am like you, then."

Not exactly, he thought, I'm not a killer. He asked if Karl was married.

"I have one wife and three children; two girls and a boy."

One wife and three children. As if they were objects, not people.

"Does your wife work?"

"Sometimes she teaches swimming for the Young Pioneers." All very matter-of-fact, as if Karl was reporting facts for a census taker. No matter how Paul tried to dig below the surface, Karl resisted. He either had no strong emotional ties to his family or he kept them well guarded.

They turned off the main highway and entered Treptow Park. Dappled sunlight filtered through the trees, flew up the hood and over the windshield. The road curved gently as it rose to the crest of the hill overlooking a lake with a small harbor dotted with sailboats and canoes. As they approached, an open-decked sightseeing boat began backing away from the pier.

They parked the car and went to an outdoor cafe where a youthful trio was singing folksongs in rudimentary English. Each table was sheltered by an orange umbrella that shuddered and flapped in the breeze. The place was alive with conversation, music and children playing at an adjacent playground.

"Do you have a picture of her?" Karl asked as soon as they were seated.

For a moment Paul thought he meant a picture of Joanna; then he realized Karl wanted to see his mother. He took out a photo of mom and Joanna and himself taken a few years ago. Karl inspected it.

"You can keep it if you want."

With barely a nod, Karl slid the photo into his coat pocket. A waiter appeared with menus and did a double-take.

"You must be twins," he announced.

"Why would you say that?" said Paul, straight-faced.

"Well, because otherwise—" The man finally realized Paul was joking, raised his eyebrows, puffed out his cheeks and laughed. "Otherwise I drank too much last night."

Karl ordered them both something called a *Berliner Weisse mit Schuss*, a bubbling local concoction of white beer with a dash of raspberry syrup. When it arrived Karl held up his mug for Paul's inspection.

"Cheap champagne," he said, and actually smiled. They drank. Later Paul would remember there had not been a toast.

CHAPTER

14

THE BEER AND THE WARM SUN RELAXED PAUL enough to make him aware of the strain he was under. Dealing with a physical duplicate of himself was more of a strain than he'd thought it would be. Especially when he allowed himself to think that this duplicate, his brother, was an assassin. He considered saving the question of CIA killings for another day but forced himself to push ahead. To know himself, to understand himself, he had to at least understand his brother.

His chance came when Karl became distracted by something behind him. Paul turned to look. A family had just sat down at a nearby table, a man and his wife and a couple of kids. One of the little boys was pointing toward them. When Paul turned, the mother slapped the child's arm gently and leaned down to whisper in his ear.

"Those people are looking at us," Karl said, tight-lipped.

Paul shrugged. "So what?"

"It doesn't bother you?"

"Why should it?"

"I am not entertainment."

Paul picked up on it: "You should tell them what you do for a living. They wouldn't think that was entertainment."

Karl had been toying with some coins on the table, stacking them in a neat cone according to size and running his fingers up and down the edges. Now his hand froze.

"You mean my teaching?"

"I mean Kelso, Manheim, Durning, Wilson, Schrader and Beaumier."

As he spoke the names it seemed to Paul that Karl's personality contracted, pulled away from the body leaving a shell with two empty eyes gazing at him.

"Whom do you work for?"

"I told you: The Washington *Herald*."

"You know what I mean."

"You mean do I work with the CIA? As of this moment, no. As of tomorrow, maybe. That could depend on you. I know what you do, Karl. I know you're some kind of contract killer, probably for the KGB . . . You're also my brother, more important—you're my mother's son. The CIA doesn't know about you yet. I might be convinced to let it stay that way. On one condition—no more killing."

Karl seemed not to be breathing. And Paul suddenly realized something else he'd pushed out of his mind: this man could decide to kill *him*.

"You say the CIA doesn't know," Karl finally said. "But you know. How is that?"

It was time for the truth. Paul took a deep breath and told him about the dreams, about the stories in Black Cat Magazine and about the CIA men coming to see him. Karl just looked at him. When he showed him a couple of back issues of Black Cat he'd brought along and told him to note the date, Karl said, "A man can have anything printed, with the help of the CIA. Why else would anyone publish such . . . dreams?"

"Nightmares. Names and particulars. It's not pleasant. But you know that—or maybe you don't. Maybe you like killing, I don't know."

Karl shook his head, sat back in his chair, and toyed with the coins. At least he's nervous, Paul thought. Which gave him some hope that maybe he could break through the defenses and get a look at the man underneath. He had to do that if he was ever going to begin to understand how a man made in his own image, whose genes and parents he shared, could commit murder. And to reassure himself that he was not that kind of man.

Karl followed Paul's glance and became aware of what he was doing, running his fingers over the stack of coins. He slipped them into his pocket, not pleased at this outward sign of his inner feelings. He was not prepared to deal with a brother who also knew about his wet assignments for the KGB. And he rebelled at accepting *dreams* as an explanation for this knowledge.

"If it's any help to you," Paul was saying, "I didn't believe it myself until mother told me about you."

"I would prefer to speak in English," Karl said.

"You're a man of many talents."

Hearing Karl now speak English gave Paul chills. The uncanny similarity between them was reinforced: this man, his brother, who spoke with his voice, now used the same words and sounds and meanings that he used.

Continuing in English, Karl leaned forward and said, "How do I know you are not with the CIA right now?"

A good question and Paul had no answer. "Can't you tell when I'm telling the truth?"

"Can you tell with me?"

Good question again. His answer wasn't, except it was true. "I hope so."

And I hope not, Karl thought. It made him uneasy to have this person, a double in appearance, sitting there, watching him, analyzing him . . .

"The CIA could have given you details of the killings before you wrote those stories."

"They didn't."

"It makes more sense than dreams."

"You made most of them look like accidents, remember?"

"The CIA is not stupid. They may guess what they cannot prove."

So now he finally admits it? Paul leaned forward. "Dan Kelso: you hit him in the stomach before you threw him overboard. Could they guess that? The girl, Lisle Beaumier— what was it you said? *'I want to lick you dry'*?"

Karl was on his feet, disbelief, even fear on his face.

"The dreams," Paul said quietly.

Karl nodded, forced to believe now.

"That's how I know about Tante Inge."

He sat down. "You said . . . I thought your mother told you."

"She did. But only after I had been hypnotized and remembered dreams I'd had as a child. Dreams about Tante Inge."

"You know what she did?"

"Not the details. But I know she scared hell out you, made you sick with fear—at least that's how I felt when I relived the experience."

Strangely, at mention of Tante Inge, Karl's self-control seemed to reassert itself. "Tante Inge," he said. "Would you like to know what happened when you and your mother—when *my* mother—abandoned me? Do you want to know? Come, then. Know everything, brother."

He stood up, went to the cashier and put a handful of bills on the counter, walked off. Paul caught up with him, and Karl set the fast pace, eyes straight ahead. As they walked he told Paul the story of his childhood. The words poured out in staccato fashion, so fast and drenched in bitterness that Paul could barely understand.

"She sold me, you understand? While you were in America going to school and watching movies and playing children's games Tante Inge was bringing men into my bed. She said that one of them might be my father, that we would test to see how much they loved me. There was a record she had—the song 'Lili Marlene'—and she played it over and over while the men came into the bed and used me for their pleasure. Played with my genitals. Smeared me with oil and butter, pushed their fingers into me, pushed themselves into me. Sometimes a woman was there, sometimes Tante Inge, all together. While you were eating ice cream I had to eat them. What came proved their love, that's what Tante Inge said. 'Drink your man's milk or no food tomorrow.' That was love. And the money she used for liquor and perfume. One of the men gave me a book, an illustrated version of the *Odyssey*. I was locked in the apartment, that book was my freedom. She took it from me, threw it away. An infraction of the rules. I was to have nothing."

He walked even faster, as though propelled by the flood of hated memories. Paul stayed half a step behind. It made it more difficult to catch Karl's words, but he sensed that during this outpouring Karl didn't want to—couldn't—meet his eye. Not until the end of his recital did Karl stop and turn to face him.

"So you understand now? The world turned its back on me. *I - made - my - self!*"

Karl paused, added, "And you have no right to judge."

They had come alongside a wide meadow with a soccer field on it. Abruptly Karl threw his jacket to the ground and started running. He headed across the meadow to the soccer field, turned right and followed the perimeter, running fast, arms pumping, head back.

Paul sat down on a bench, shaken by what he had just heard. The utter depravity of Karl's childhood sickened him even as it offered a measure of understanding of Karl's later ruthlessness. Understand, but not justify. Nothing would do that entirely, but Karl's childhood went a long way toward it. The child savaged by Tante Inge and her clients had become a killer. Karl's future had been traded for Paul's health, and now years later innocent people were paying the price. More than ever Paul felt he had to stop the killings, for Karl's sake as well as his own . .,.

Karl ran until he was exhausted, then stood doubled over with his hands resting on his knees as he fought to regain his breath. Paul took his coat to him. Karl straightened and took it.

"Come," Karl said, "I will take you back to West Berlin."

He was still breathing heavily. The two men began walking back toward the restaurant.

"You don't have to do that," Paul said. "Just drop me at the S-Bahn."

"It's not for you I'm going. My wife went shopping at the KaDeWe this afternoon. You know it? The big department store?"

"I passed it the other day."

"Magda goes once each month to the Western sector. We have dinner and attend the theater. If you will not mention our discussion this afternoon, you may meet her."

Paul hesitated. After what he'd heard, and already knew, he didn't altogether trust this brother. Noting his reaction, Karl smiled and said, "Unless you think I'm going to shoot you and dump your body in the Spree."

"I'd probably know it if you were."

Except he didn't believe that. He wasn't a mind reader. The only impressions he'd ever received from Karl were actual perceptions as Karl lived them. And even then it only happened when he was asleep and Karl was in a highly charged emotional state. He wished he *could* read Karl's mind, he would have felt considerably more secure.

When they returned to the restaurant Paul took out the Ricoh and asked a waiter to take a photo of the two of them. Karl objected. "I let no one take my picture."

"It's for our mother. I want to prove you're alive."

Karl's eyes hardened, and for a moment Paul was certain he would refuse. Then there was a subtle shift of expression and he gave in. The waiter had them stand at the entrance to the restaurant. He even had them strike an identical pose and insisted that Paul comb his hair back to match Karl's.

Before they left, Karl stopped at a concession stand and bought two packs of breath mints. Paul, wondering how he would ever be able to convince Karl to stop the killing, paid no attention to the nervous, smiling man behind the counter. As they walked to the car Karl offered Paul a pack of mints.

"Would you like one?" Paul took it and thought no more about it.

After the two men had gone, the man at the concession counter locked his shop and went to a pay phone. He took out a piece of paper and dialed the number written on it. The number was in West Berlin.

"Yes?" an unfamiliar voice answered.

"I have a message from K."

"Go ahead."

"He bought two packs of the mints."

"Two?"

"Yes."

"Is he leaving now?"

The little man peered around the booth toward the parking lot.

"Yes, he's just gone."

The line went dead. The concessions man fingered the twenty marks that he had received earlier that morning from the mysterious K. Twenty marks for a simple phone call. Too bad he couldn't duplicate the money in the same way that K seemed able to duplicate himself.

Smiling at this clever thought, the concessions man returned to his shop.

Paul returned to the CIA killings on the way back. At first, Karl seemed amused by his concern.

"They are all agents or spies or traitors. Why care about them?"

"Because I *know* when you kill. I have to live it *with* you. The crack of a spine breaking, the look on their faces, the last sound of a dying man. I feel like I'm doing it, you understand?"

"And what will you do if I refuse to stop?"

"Tell them."

"The CIA?"

"I won't be a party to murder, Karl."

Karl surprised him then. "I can understand that . . . I will talk to my superiors."

Paul should have felt relieved but despite Karl's last statement, his earlier reference to dumping Paul's body in the Spree River was not forgotten. He remained alert to every change in direction, and not until they approached the barrier on the eastern side of Checkpoint Charlie did he begin to relax.

While one of the East German *Grenzpolizei* stuck a mirror under the car another asked to see their papers. Karl flashed an identification card, and the guard, a husky young man who looked more like a farmer than a policeman, immediately straightened.

"Yes sir," he said. "And him?"

Karl handed him Paul's visa. The guard became uncomfortable. "Excuse me, sir, but this man came from the S-Bahn Friedrichstrasse station. He must return that way."

"He's returning with me."

The guard cleared his throat. "But the official regulation states—"

"If I have to get out of this car and call your superior," Karl interrupted coldly, "you will lose your job."

"One moment, sir." With a worried glance at the other *Grenzpolizist,* he ducked back inside the station.

Karl was obviously impatient at the delay, his index finger tapping nervously on the steering wheel. They sat beneath a covered plaza with stalls on either side, each facing a red-and-white-striped barrier. There was a fenced pedestrian crosswalk and beyond that no-man's-land, the wide strip of graded and raked earth that worked its jagged way round the western half of the city.

The young guard reappeared with an older man who was all crisp efficiency and accommodation. He leaned down and spoke to Karl. "Don't worry, sir. We'll take care of everything."

The red-and-white barrier was raised, a red light turned to green and they drove a hundred yards to the American side, where the U.S. Marines in full dress uniforms ignored them as they passed.

"You don't stop on this side?" Paul asked.

"Your American forces refuse to recognize a separate

Berlin so they don't consider this a border. Those guards serve only the military personnel of the occupation armies."

Paul nodded, feeling much better now that they were back in the American zone. They agreed that Karl would call tomorrow after talking with his superiors about a new assignment.

They turned into a multi-level parking garage at the KaDeWe, drove to the third level although there were a few parking places available on the second. Paul paid no attention. Why should he? He was on home territory again. He also paid no mind to the parking slot that Karl chose, bordered as it was on the driver's side by a wall and on the other side by a Volkswagen Camper.

"Until tomorrow, then," Karl said.

He offered his hand. As Paul took it the rear door opened and the car rocked as someone sat down.

"I'm sorry," Karl said, tightening his grip, leaning over and pinning Paul against his seat.

Paul instantly threw himself forward and up and might have been able to break free except for the seatbelt he hadn't yet had a chance to unfasten. From behind, an arm came around his neck and a white cloth covered his mouth.

He tried to shout but the sound was muffled and he knew it was no good. These were professionals, no one would hear. He kicked and twisted, trying to get his arms free. When he gasped for air he could tell that it wasn't chloroform they were using, it was something less smelly and more powerful.

A strange dizziness took him, and the last thing he heard, as if from a great distance, was Karl's voice, this time close to his ear, saying, "Go easy..."

And then darkness.

CHAPTER

15

THERE WAS NO WAY TO PREDICT AMERICANS, the desk clerk at the InterContinental decided. Some of them wanted to be treated like kings, while others were insulted if you didn't act as if they were your best friend. Take the man in 317, Paul Stafford. When he checked in, 317 insisted on joking about the exhibition tent on the lawn. A casual man with a sense of humor. And so today, when 317 came to check out, the clerk returned the humor with a reference to the elephants and what kind of a response did he get? 317 looked up with a frown and asked, "What do you mean?"

"Nothing, sir."

"You must have meant something."

"Yes, sir. I was referring to your humorous remark the other day concerning our exhibition tent."

317 glanced outside, then gave him an empty smile.

"Oh, right..."

No, wrong, the clerk decided. Obviously, 317 was in no mood for familiarity. Just no predicting, or pleasing, Americans...

There had been no choice, Karl told himself as he waited for the elevator. Too much had happened too fast. He needed time to think things out, check facts. He needed time but there was no time. In three days he would leave for America. In three weeks the General Secretary was scheduled to land at Andrews Air Force Base. He had to be ready and there was no time to negotiate with his new-found brother. Paul's existence jeopardized the Redeye mission. There had been no choice.

When the elevator arrived a group of businessmen

sporting name tags got out. Karl stepped inside, pushed
the button to the third floor and checked his appearance in
the mirror. The jacket, the jeans, shirt and shoes all fitted
perfectly. He'd washed his hair and combed it in a freer,
more casual style, and the disguise—if it could be called
that—was complete. "Paul Stafford" would now gather his
belongings, check out of the hotel and disappear.

Paul's room was like any other fancy hotel room, right
down to the two pieces of foil-wrapped chocolate, one
on each pillow, with little cards wishing each guest a
good night's sleep. Outside the glass door to the balcony
the top of the circus tent was visible. Karl pulled the
drapes and then remembered: he was Paul Stafford, not
an intruder. It was his room. No need to worry if anyone
saw him.

His first task was to recover his false documents Paul
had gotten. He began searching the dresser. The first
drawer contained a sightseeing guide, hotel postcards and
a room-service menu. The second was stuffed with tee-
shirts and underwear. As he started to run his hand along
the bottom of the drawer a movement in the mirror caused
him to freeze.

The door to an adjoining bedroom had opened and a
man stood watching.

"Looking for these?" the man said. He held up the two
passports.

Karl turned around. So his fine new brother had deceived him. Paul had said he had come alone and Karl had
believed him. The man in the doorway looked CIA—the
crew-cut hair, the clumsy American clothes—just like the
American civilians who flooded Berlin in the nineteen-
fifties.

"I told Maurice you were innocent," the man was
saying. "Annie Helms thought so too. It looks like he was
right and we were wrong."

Careful now, Karl thought. He wasn't blown—not yet.
This man thought he was Paul, now he really had to play
the part. What had Paul told him about the CIA? They
had come to him, suspicious. He met with them only a
few times. And this man was one of them. He wished he
had gotten more information from his brother.

"This is my room," he said coldly, buying time while he

searched his memory for anything else that might help him.

"But not your passports," Hugh Roark said. "And not your driver's licenses. We checked; they're stolen. And before the police get here I'd just like to know one thing— what were you going to use these for?"

Karl judged the distance between them. Twenty feet. If he could get a little closer...

"Those are jokes," Karl said easily. "Look, you can tell on the back..."

He came forward but the CIA man slid his hand beneath his coat and came out with a gun.

"Stop there, Paul. I don't trust you anymore."

I'm not Paul, Karl felt like shouting. Caught in a trap set for his brother... The police had been called, the man had said. If he was arrested they would find his real I.D. The entire Redeye mission would be threatened, maybe compromised. He decided to brazen it out. Hope for an opening... "This is ridiculous. I'm getting the manager—"

"Paul—"

"Those are jokes, I can prove it."

How, he had no idea as he moved to the door. At any moment he half-expected to hear a sharp explosion, feel the bullet tear into his back. Except an educated instinct told him that this was not a man who would shoot another in the back. He was, after all, a professional, and he thought he was dealing with a "civilian," even if a guilty one...

He kept talking, keeping his hands in full view. The CIA man didn't move. When he opened the door he knew why. Another man, younger, blocked his way. This man also had a gun in his hand, and a smug sort of smile on his face.

"Back you go, Paul," he said, shoving the gun toward Karl's solar plexus.

Karl's reaction was a reflex. He swiveled to one side, the barrel of the gun missed its mark and glanced off his chest. At the same time he kept his forward motion, stepped inside and clasped the man's gun arm close to his chest, slid the other around his neck. Pivoting from the waist in a *kubinage*, he tumbled the man into the room.

It happened as quickly and smoothly as a demonstration at the Combat School. Karl heard the grunt of surprise as the gunman hit the floor, and then a sharp report as the gun went off. The television screen shattered. The older CIA man went into a crouch as Karl stepped into the hall and slammed the door.

He moved quickly down the hall. A woman watched him uneasily, probably had heard the gunshot. Two police came around the corner, a man and a woman, and the look on their faces told Karl that they had heard the gunshot too. The man had drawn his gun.

Karl stopped, caught between the police and the room with the CIA. Until the door to room 315 opened and a florid-faced man peered out.

"What's all the noise—?"

"Get back inside," Karl snapped at him. "He's got a gun." And he pushed the man back and stepped in after him. Three other men were seated around a bed playing poker. Red, blue and white chips were stacked on the bed and beer cans littered the floor. Two of the men had taken off their coats and rolled up their sleeves; the third sat in his undershirt, stomach overflowing his belt.

"A gun?" one of them said, "Is that what—?"

The screen door was open. Karl climbed over the bed, scattered cards and poker chips and beer. Angry yelps followed him onto the balcony. Below, the angled top of the circus tent extended to within ten feet of the building.

Karl got up on the railing, crouched for a moment, then launched himself into the air. The tent's roof was supported by cables, and Karl aimed just to the side of one of them, hoping that the fabric wouldn't tear. Someone on the ground shouted and the world raced upward at him.

The impact wasn't too bad but his right ankle caught on the fabric as he slid. There was a twinge of pain and then he was rolling down into the trough as the tent dipped to take his weight.

He dropped to the ground next to people still staring at the sagging roof. It seemed some sort of reception was going on. Men and women posed in evening clothes, drinks in hand, cheese and crackers in the other. A table next to him was covered with glasses of white wine. Karl moved forward, felt a sharp pain and stumbled against the table. Glasses banged in a medley and overturned. The bartender looked at Karl in alarm.

"Did you fall, sir?"

"There's a man with a gun up there," Karl said. "I'm getting the police."

Ignoring the pain in his ankle, Karl moved inside the lobby. Behind him, he could hear the news spread: *a gun? who said a gun? what's going on?*

Karl walked as quickly as he could. With each step the pain in his ankle seemed to increase. Running was impossible. He needed a car, but first he had to cross the lobby without being spotted. Any moment he expected the elevator doors would open and the police or the CIA men would rush out. He forced himself to act nonchalant. Behind him, he could hear the men from the poker game yelling down at the crowd.

He reached the entrance and then was outside. Two vehicles were in the driveway: a taxi and a black limousine. The taxi's passenger was still counting out his fare. The limo was empty but the trunk was open and the chauffeur was unloading suitcases.

In the lobby someone yelled, "Stop him . . ."

Karl crossed to the limo. The driver's door was open and the keys were in the ignition. He slid inside and turned the key.

"Hey—"

The chauffeur came at him and when he realized the car was moving he grabbed a rear-door handle, running frantically as he tried to get his legs beneath him, then stumbled and fell. Karl was at the road now, yanked the wheel to the left and headed east on Budapesterstrasse. Two hundred feet ahead the road curved to follow the Tiergarden. Beyond was the Landwehrkan canal and side streets he could lose himself in—

Three pops in quick succession. In the rearview mirror he saw the younger CIA man in the middle of the street, legs spread, gun pointed at him. Just before Karl rounded the curve the man dropped to one knee, fired twice more. Matching holes appeared in the rear and front windows, and then he was around the corner and out of sight.

Karl smiled, and the smile froze on his face. Ahead of him three cars stopped in the middle of the road. A moving van trying to back into a driveway had blocked the road. What sidewalk remained was too narrow for the limousine. Karl yanked the parking brake. Tires screeched as the heavy machine swept one hundred eighty degrees in a bootleg turn. In moments he was headed in the opposite direction, back around the corner, back to the hotel. The CIA man was walking away when Karl reappeared. Startled, he turned around, dropped again to one knee and took aim. Karl turned directly toward him and slid low in his seat. He was protected by the engine now but couldn't see the road so he steered toward a distant building in line with where he knew the shooter was. Two more shots, and two more holes appeared in the windshield, one of them where his head had been.

As the wheel hit the curb Karl turned left to regain the road. He straightened up, but as he had anticipated, the CIA man had already dived to one side to avoid the car. He caught a glimpse of the man running in a low crouch across the lawn. In front of the hotel the policeman had moved into the street, where he stood like a sentinel with his hand raised, signaling Karl to stop as though he was a traffic cop. Karl sounded the horn and accelerated. *Move, damn you.* But the man held his ground. Karl swerved back and forth to unnerve him, sounding the horn all the way. There were no cars coming from the opposite direction and when the policeman didn't move, Karl waited until the last minute, then swerved to the other lane. He meant to pass close to the man, to scare him, but when at the last moment the man tried to leap aside, he picked the wrong way to go. The right fender struck him, threw him aside and sent his hat careening off the windshield. In the rearview mirror Karl saw him land heavily on the grass bordering the sidewalk.

And then he was past the hotel, in the clear. At Nurnbergerstrasse he turned left, after a block turned right, then left, then right again, back and forth until he was swallowed up in the vast labyrinth of the city.

He drove to the Yorkstrasse U-Bahn, where three subway lines crossed. After wiping his prints off the limousine he took the number 7 train southbound. On the subway he had time to inspect his ankle. It was already swollen, but not too badly, he thought. A good soaking and elastic bandages should suffice...

Now that it was over he felt limp, exhausted. Too many revelations, too much happening at once. He shut his eyes, breathed deeply, calming himself, clearing his mind. For a moment he thought of calling Uncle Alex but decided against it. The Redeye mission had not been compromised—the CIA men thought he was Paul and Paul was safely out of the way. Everything could proceed according to plan. In fact, he might be able to use Paul's identity to his own advantage. By the time Karl reached the Neukoln–Rathaus station, he at least felt in control of the situation.

Back in his own car, Karl considered whether or not to bypass Checkpoint Charlie and return through one of the three border stations at the western edge of the city. These exits served the highways that led to West Germany but it was a half-hour drive to the nearest one. Checkpoint Charlie was only minutes away. There hadn't been time to circulate Paul's picture, and if there was an alarm out the police would be looking for a stolen limousine rather than a Mercedes.

Checkpoint Charlie was a U.S. military facility and only military vehicles were required to stop. There were no barriers blocking his way, and when the white-belted American soldier in full-dress uniform saw Karl's East German license plate he ignored him. A moment later Karl was back on East German soil.

Whether his brother had tried to trick him or had been tricked by the CIA, he didn't know. It didn't matter. He had learned long ago that the difference between success and failure in a mission often hinged on his ability to adjust to unexpected circumstance and to turn a threat to an advantage. He touched his brother's passport, resting securely in his pocket. Brother Paul's unexpected appearance had already become an advantage.

In the United States, news that Paul Stafford had been involved in a car theft and hit-and-run was considered of minor importance on a day that included a hijacking and an attack on an American warship in the Suez Canal. It got only a one-column mention on the back page of major American newspapers and no air time at all on network television. The Washington *Post*, an exception, did run a headline on the second page: "Herald Reporter Accused in Car Theft."

At the *Herald* Bernie Stern found himself fielding questions about Paul for which he had no answers. Everyone wanted to know what Paul was doing in Germany, why he'd stolen a limousine and whether or not he was back in the States.

"He's not working a story," Bernie told them. "He hasn't canceled his weekly meetings. I don't know what he's doing. I know nothing."

It wasn't the kind of answer that pleased Joyce and Tony Mayhue, publishers of the *Herald*, whom Bernie contacted as soon as the story came over the wire. In a voice that managed to sound at once lilting and strident, Joyce said, "Working a story or not, he represents the *Herald*."

Bernie refrained from reminding her that he had advised against giving Paul an unrestricted contract, predicting that it would encourage an attitude that was already too cavalier. Nobody denied that Stafford was a top investigative reporter—intelligent and resourceful and persevering—but he was *also* egotistical and independent to the point of insult, qualities Bernie felt would be aggravated by an independent contract. But the Mayhues had overruled him and this was the result. All that Bernie could do was call Paul's house and leave messages asking for him to get in touch as soon as possible. He had few illusions that the messages would have effect.

The person most immediately affected by the incident at the InterContinental was Ray Tregerdemain. After he and Paul had parted outside the casino, Ray joined some friends that included Nanci Van Zandt, a Dutch woman of thirty-six with whom he occasionally enjoyed nights of such erotic creativity that for days afterward he was filled with amazement at his good fortune. Because of her, he didn't arrive home until late the next morning. Paul's message was waiting on his machine:

"Ray, Paul Stafford. I went to the Vanilla Rose last night and talked to your friend Wenzler. He gave me a line on my brother. Got a meeting on the eastern side this morning so hold the *anmeld* investigation until further notice. Check with you when I get back."

The message left Ray with mixed feelings. On one hand the story of the two brothers piqued his curiosity and he was eager to learn the outcome; on the other hand he'd spent most of the fifty marks and was afraid Paul might want the money back. So he waited to see what happened, and the next day heard over the radio that Paul Stafford had stolen a car and run into a policeman, breaking the man's hip.

Ray called a friend in the police office and learned that the police had gone to the hotel to investigate a case of false travel documents, that the case was being coordinated through police headquarters at Schoneberg and that the U.S. government was somehow involved. That last was only rumor. Ray called both Schoneberg and the American consulate and got the same "no comment" from each of them.

"Something is fishy in Denmark," Ray sang softly to himself. He sat in his basement apartment, slow thoughts gaining momentum as he considered the possibilities. If Paul Stafford had false passports, why? Either he was involved in some sort of illegal activity—drugs, gun-running, currency exchanges—or he planned to use them to get his brother out of East Germany. That seemed the most logical explanation: the false passports were for his brother and something had gone wrong. Maybe he'd been discovered at the border with the passports, escaped and gone back to the hotel, where the police were waiting. That made sense. And then he'd made things worse by stealing a limo and running down a policeman.

Ray shook his head. That made less sense. Paul Stafford might not care about legal niceties where his hunt for his brother was concerned, but he wasn't stupid. False passports would be an easier rap than car theft and hit-and-run. Particularly if he built up the humanitarian angle of getting his poor, oppressed brother out of East Berlin.

He went to the refrigerator for a bottle of pale local beer known as *Berliner Weisse*. The refrigerator was as cramped as the apartment; the rubber seal around the door had long since deteriorated and the interior walls dripped continually with condensation. Everything about his life had become cramped, depressing. He needed a breakthrough story to reverse his lousy luck. *He needed to find Paul Stafford's brother*.

An inspired idea. He'd promised Paul that he wouldn't do a *Kriegserleidnis* but that was before this most recent shit hit the fan. Besides, the new angle was more hard news than human interest. If he could track down Paul's brother, identify him, maybe even set up an interview, he'd have what he needed to do a story that would command international attention. "Journalist a Fugitive Trying to Save Twin Brother"—he could imagine the headlines.

He took a yellow pad and pulled a chair up to the kitchen table—chipped Formica top, metal legs discolored by rust. He wanted a new kitchen table, a new apartment—a new everything.

He made a list of the newspapers and magazines most likely to be interested in his story, then assigned numbers indicating order of submission according to rates and how likely they were to want the story. Too bad Paul hadn't killed the cop. It would have made a stronger story.

But he was getting ahead of himself. All he had right now was Paul's story of a twin brother—no proof—and his own guesses. Diddly-zilch. He picked up the phone and called Otto Wenzler.

"Residence of Herr Wenzler," a male voice answered. Ray asked to speak to the man and was told that Herr Wenzler was busy. Ray then mentioned Paul Stafford and Wenzler got unbusy, came to the phone.

Ray smiled and began his pitch. "Ray Tregerdemain, Mr. Wenzler. I'm a freelance journalist doing a story on Paul Stafford, the American who was involved in a hit-and-run accident outside the InterConnie? You know what I'm talking about, right?"

"I don't read newspapers except for the arts page."

"Yeah, right, me too. Point is, I happen to know that Mr. Stafford talked with you the day before the hit-and-run. I also happen to know that you told him where to find his twin brother. What I'd like from you is the same information: where do I find the brother?"

"I don't know what you're talking about, Mr. Treasure-dome."

"Tregerdemain. And you can't insult me off this story, Mr. Wenzler. Bulldog Ray they call me."

"I repeat, I don't know what you're talking about."

"That's your statement for publication? I'll quote my tape recording from Stafford that says he's seen you and your response is, quote, I don't know what you're talking about, unquote. Have I got that right?"

"Yes."

Ray could feel his quarry, and his big chance, slipping

away. He needed something Wenzler would respond to. A man involved in so many shady dealings must have—

Suddenly he remembered what his informant had told him about the false passports. Was it possible that Paul hadn't brought them from the States but got them in Berlin? From Wenzler? Ray decided to gamble. "Mr. Stafford said something else. He said you were the one who provided the false passports. Have you got any statement to make on that?"

Silence, and Ray felt a rush of excitement. Was it possible? Had he actually guessed right, that Wenzler *had* provided the false documents? If so, he had Wenzler by the balls. "Listen," he hurried to follow up, "this story is either going to end with Paul's brother or with you and the fake passports. Personally I'd rather find his brother, but if you won't link me, then you end up at the end of the line; you see how it goes? You help me and I help you."

"How many people," Wenzler said slowly, "know about Stafford's allegation?"

"Nobody. And nobody will if you pass me on to his brother."

"Just for the record, Mr. Tregerdemain, the allegation is absolutely false."

Just for your record, Ray wanted to say, I'm not recording the conversation. Although now he wished he was. "Nobody's going to hear about it, Mr. Wenzler, I guarantee you that. You can ask anybody. I've been in Berlin a long time, it's my beat, and I always protect my sources."

"I intend to check. If I'm satisfied I'll see what I can do to help about the man you're looking for. I'm always cooperative with the press if possible. Where will you be this afternoon?"

"I've got an interview this morning," Ray lied, "but I should be back here by three."

"Give me your number, I'll call you."

Ray did, and Wenzler said he'd call between three and three-thirty.

Ray smacked his hands together after they hung up. His lucky guess about the false documents had paid off. Wenzler's reaction told him the smart guess was a fact.

"Mr. Bullseye," Ray said aloud, more pleased with himself than he'd been since he managed a five-minute interview with President Kennedy in 1963. Not even the overcast skies that made the apartment particularly gloomy could dampen his spirits. He sat down with the yellow pad and again began to make headlines for his story. In his euphoria it did not occur to him that his stroke of genius had altered his relationship to Otto Wenzler—from minor irritant to serious threat.

CHAPTER

16

PAUL DREAMED HE WAS FLOATING IN AIR, staring down at himself from the sky. He was alone, lying on a bed dressed only in a hospital gown. There was a room around him with pink walls and no windows and the only furniture was a wicker table beside the bed. He tried to open his eyes but his eyes wouldn't open; then he realized his eyes *were* open and he was lying flat on his back and somehow watching himself from the ceiling at the same time. A feeling akin to vertigo washed over him until he realized that the ceiling was covered in mirrors and he was staring at his own reflection.

He struggled to sit up but something resisted his movement. Thinking that he was tied down, he looked for the ropes that held him. Time slowed and stretched and he became aware that he'd been staring at his arms for a long time, and even as the realization occurred it happened again and he had been staring at his arms for a long time, looking for ropes that weren't there.

Paul struggled into a sitting position. He was weak and dizzy and even the slightest movement took tremendous effort. He thrust his feet over the edge of the bed and stood up. The room tilted and nausea engulfed him. He took one step forward before his knees gave way and he collapsed. For a long time he lay with his face against the floor, staring at the legs of the bed. When he felt stronger he attempted to stand again but the same thing happened. Finally he decided he had been drugged.

At least this realization put his helplessness into perspective. On hands and knees Paul crawled around the room looking for a way of escape. There were two doors. One led to a small bathroom and the other, metal, was shut and locked. Because there were no windows in either room and because the linoleum floor and brick walls were cool to his touch, Paul guessed he was in a basement. But where? Karl's house? Would anyone hear him if he called out? He tried yelling, and the sound he heard scared him. It was slurred and unintelligible, the sound of a mental defective.

There was a rasping sound, the sound of a key in a lock. Paul got to his feet, stumbled, sat down heavily on the bed. The door opened and Madam Tran came into the room followed by Helmut, the man who had taken him to Otto Wenzler's study. Madam Tran wore her elegant Vietnamese costume, the Bao Dai, just as she had when Paul met her at the Vanilla Rose. When she saw that he was sitting up, she gave a satisfied nod.

"You awake now. Good."

She brought the tray to the wicker table beside the bed. Paul tried to talk but his tongue felt like clay and the words came so slowly and garbled that even he couldn't understand them.

"No, don't try to talk," Madam Tran told him. "You can't say nothing anyway. First go to the bathroom, then you eat."

She turned to Helmut, who stood in the doorway wearing pleated slacks and a light sweater with the sleeves rolled up. He looked unhappy. The hallway behind him was silent and empty.

"Go ahead," she said. "Take him before he eats."

Helmut came forward and reached for Paul's arm. As he did Paul tried to get up and push past him, but by the time his muscles responded Helmut had him on his feet and was half-carrying, half-dragging him across the room. Paul made an awkward attempt to jam his elbow into Helmut's side. There was no force to the blow but it did manage to make Helmut angry.

"*Scheisskopf.*" He turned Paul around and shoved him back on the bed.

"He doesn't want my help," he said to Madam Tran. "You take care of him." And Helmut left the room.

Paul rolled to his side, saw Madam Tran shaking her head sadly.

"See what happens," she said. "You don't cooperate, you get treated bad."

"*Get away*," he yelled, but the words echoed only in his mind. From his lips came only slurred nonsense.

Madam Tran stood and picked up the tray.

"You a baby now," she said. "You better learn that quick."

She shut the door and locked it, leaving Paul alone with his helplessness and his rage.

Karl arrived in Washington, D.C., with a new passport, a new driver's license and a new name. As Ron Tednick he rented a car and spent two days with a real estate agent inspecting vacation rentals within a ten-minute drive of Andrews Air Force Base. The one that suited him was a farmhouse on Toons Creek Road. On the crest of a hill overlooking the Patuxent River, it sat well back from the road on two acres of land and was, as the agent Rita Gaylord assured him, "within walking distance of the river."

Ms. Gaylord was an attractive woman in her mid-thirties. The first day he met her, she was wearing a pants suit that showed off her trim figure. The next day she wore a light, clinging summer dress. She was a well-manicured woman with perky features and luxurious, streaked hair swept back in a wave. And she was happy to be of service to Ron Tednick, a divorced father whose children were coming to visit him for a month.

"How old are your children?" asked Rita.

"Eleven and nine," Karl said, choosing ages too old to draw on walls and too young to throw wild parties. His wife, he said, lived in California and he worked for the National Security Agency in Washington. His parents were coming from Philadelphia to be with him and the children and he wanted a large place for them to spend the month.

Karl enjoyed spinning out details of a fabricated life. Pretending to be someone else offered him a strange freedom. For once he could be a part of normal society, an average man, secure, faceless.

Rita Gaylord didn't think of Ron Tednick as an average man. His athletic body and good looks attracted her, and she attached no stigma to his divorce. She was divorced herself. Rita put a lot of energy into finding just the right place for Mr. Tednick. She also offered to show him a beach south of Annapolis.

"It's an out-of-the-way place," she said. "Great sand, a great place to take the kids."

Karl declined the offer. The last thing he wanted was someone getting close. That was why he'd chosen the Toons Creek house: it was private, close to Andrews Air Force Base and had an adjoining building that had once been a stable. The stable had been renovated and the bottom floor was now a garage and work area while the top floor contained storage space filled with articles the owners of the house didn't want to trust to tenants.

They signed the rental agreement at Rita's office and Karl gave her a cashier's check for two thousand dollars. Turning it between a thumb and forefinger, Rita said, "Maybe you should have a house-warming party before your children arrive."

"No thanks," Karl said. "I like privacy." Now that the house was his, he could afford to be blunt. He already regretted telling her that he was divorced. A wife with terminal cancer or Alzheimer's disease would have been a safer story.

Once settled, Karl began putting together the elements needed to accomplish the Redeye mission. He divided his mission into three preliminary operations: finding a launch site, stealing the Redeye, and implicating a third party.

The first operation was more difficult than he had anticipated. Andrews Air Force Base was bordered on the north and south by housing developments and shopping centers and on the south and east by industrial parks, farms and a trailer court. Unfortunately, the approach path of the General Secretary's aircraft was over the most populated areas, and this made the risk of being seen unacceptably high. He couldn't just step out of the car and stand on a street corner with a Redeye missile over his shoulder.

At first he considered using the roof of a house or a store. This would give him a clear shot at the *Ilyushin*, but could he gain access to a roof of a building without alerting its occupant or owner? He investigated renting a house but none was available in the area beneath the approach path. The more he thought about it, the more flaws Karl found in the roof idea. If he did find a place how could he be sure that the police didn't routinely check all recently rented property below the approach path? And how could he get his scapegoat, the person who was to be blamed for the General Secretary's assassination, to rent the house? What about helicopters? On a roof, he would stand out as clearly to them as they would to him. And if he could overcome all those problems, how would he know which place to rent when he couldn't know what runway the General Secretary's plane would use until the day it arrived?

Ultimately it was the consideration that the runway would depend on which way the wind was blowing that inspired Karl's solution. What he needed was mobility, mobility and camouflage—an innocent-looking vehicle that would hide him even while he pulled the trigger; something with an opening through which he could fire the Redeye. Fortunately, the American mania for traveling without leaving home provided just such a vehicle: a Winnebago.

Karl was pleased with himself. Instead of worrying about one or two fixed launch sites, the motor home opened up a number of possibilities. He could park on a neighborhood street or go to a shopping mall or a school or a church or even pull to the side of a freeway and fake a flat tire or engine trouble. And with a skylight he could fire the missile from inside, eliminating the possibility of accidental or chance witnesses.

The only real difficulty he had was finding a motor home with a skylight-escape hatch. It was a luxury option that didn't come with most rental vehicles, and he didn't have the money to buy a Winnebago outright. Uncle Alex and his group did not have unlimited resources. They were patriots, not those favored by the Kremlin and its largess. He located what he needed at Sunshine RV in Fairfax, Virginia. A chubby salesman came with him on a test drive and gave Karl a rhapsodic account of his own family's vacation in a motor home. It was a lumbering, clumsy vehicle but it was everything Karl needed.

The second operation, stealing the Redeye, first required a physical inspection of the Bayonne terminal. For this Karl needed the services of his brother. He rehearsed his story, then phoned the Military Ocean Terminal, asked for the public affairs officer, was handed to a Major Irene Fellows.

"Major Fellows...my name is Paul Stafford. I'm a

reporter for the Washington *Herald* and I'm working on a story about the Military Sealift Command. I would like to make an appointment for an interview."

"I'll see what I can do, Mr. Stafford. Give me the specs again. This is a story for the Washington *Herald*?"

Karl expanded on his theme. He felt an odd delight in pretending to be Paul Stafford, the prize-winning journalist. It turned out that Major Fellows had read a story of Paul's—something about the rebellion in Afghanistan. Karl made a mental note and later, when he was in the library, he looked up all of Paul's articles and read them. They were well done, Karl decided, but ultimately came to nothing. The world responded to actions, not words.

His brother's life continued to hold a strange fascination for him. He drove past the Arlington house and was surprised by its size. It was a two-story brick home with a turret at one corner. On one side of the house was a screened-in porch and on the other an attached garage. The front yard, big as the house itself, was dominated by a huge maple tree.

It was Karl's first evidence of just how successful his brother was. Later when he was in D.C. he stopped by Farragut Square and stood in a Crown bookstore across from the *Herald* Building. He imagined Paul going to work there each day and tried to guess which of the nearby restaurants his brother frequented.

These excursions to the site of his brother's haunts were brief. Most of the time he spent in the library researching American fringe groups and radical movements. What he was looking for was a violently nationalistic organization in desperate need of money.

He found it in the Rank, a white-supremacist group based in Houston, Texas. Its leader, Grant Harkness, had been convicted along with two others of killing a radio talk show host by sending a bomb through the mail. The three men were currently appealing their convictions. One of the articles described a fund-raising auction at which maps of the world were sold with new borders drawn along racial lines. These were the sort of people Karl was looking for, zealots and believers in bizarre causes. There must be others like Grant Harkness. Within the Rank he felt he would be able to find a man gullible and hungry enough to rent the Winnebago.

* * *

Ray Tregerdemain met Otto Wenzler at the Berlin Zoo. It was five o'clock. The skies were overcast and a chilly mist dampened the pavement and caused Ray's nose to run. He dabbed it with a handkerchief as he made his way to Zellerbach Hall, where a reception for the Friends of the Berlin Zoo was in its final stages. Wenzler was at the reception and Ray was to meet him outside the Hall at a quarter past five.

As he hurried along, Ray felt the familiar tingle of excitement at the prospect of an important story. According to Wenzler, Paul's brother was a GDR communist party member with aberrant sexual tastes. In exchange for anonymity, Wenzler was to give him the name of the brother and four other East German heavies who had visited the Vanilla Rose. This was more than Ray had hoped for. This might open the door to an exposé about East German officials who visited West Berlin bordellos. The world press would eat it up. Especially tabloids.

Ray could feel the story unfolding, building. More than one story, really, and that made him feel more secure. Paul was probably back in the States, maybe doing a piece on his brother. Well, now Ray would have his own slant, could put his own spin on it. If Paul came out with the story of his brother or even the InterContinental Hotel incident, Ray could develop the sex-and-politics angle into something all his own. *Special to the Tribune by Ray Tregerdemain.* He'd have a byline on the wire by the end of the month.

Because of the rain, most visitors were leaving. Only the animals seemed oblivious to the weather. Ray turned up the collar of his overcoat, adjusted the angle of his corduroy touring cap and jammed his hands into his pockets. When he got to Zellerbach Hall he waited in the lobby for Wenzler to appear. Inside the hall a string quartet playing classical music served as a background to the noisy chatter of well-to-do attendees who had donated money for the new aquarium. Ray caught a glimpse of them whenever the door opened. They didn't look like the kind of people who visited zoos; they didn't look like the kind of people who visited anywhere without an engraved invitation.

Wenzler came into the lobby engaged in animated conversation with an older couple. He was wearing a dark, well-tailored suit, a silk shirt and tie, but his long flowing hair and thin body reminded Ray of an aging rock star. When he spotted Ray, Wenzler made a casual gesture behind his friends' backs, acknowledging Ray's presence and cautioning him to stay away.

Ray slipped outside and waited. A few moments later, Wenzler came out alone. Now he was wearing an overcoat and carried a briefcase in one hand and umbrella in the other.

"You are Mr. Tregerdemain?"

"That's me."

"Follow me at a distance, please."

Ray started to ask where they were going but Wenzler was already heading down a wide cobblestone walkway toward the sea-lion enclosure. The overcast had grown so thick that wrought-iron streetlamps were on, their gold light gleaming dully from rain-slick stones.

Ray followed about twenty feet behind. The few people who were on the path were heading in the opposite direction, toward the main gate. The bark of sea lions grew loud as they approached. Wenzler went into a low concrete building—public restrooms—and Ray followed.

The restroom was deserted. There was a gutter at the base of a urine-stained wall that led to a cigarette-clogged drain. A row of empty stalls faced six sinks beneath a flickering neon light. After checking to make sure no one was in the stalls, Wenzler set his briefcase on a sink and took out a metal detector that looked to Ray like the sort of thing security guards used in airline terminals.

"You don't mind, I hope," Wenzler said.

"You think I've got a gun?"

"Or a transmitter or a tape recorder. Please."

He had Ray turn slightly while he ran the metal loop up and down his legs, along the small of his back, under his arms and along his chest. The machine beeped twice, once for his massive key ring with its Swiss army knife, the second time for a small microcassette tape recorder in his vest pocket. Wenzler wanted to inspect each item. When Ray showed him the tape recorder, Otto asked him to take the tape out.

"What for? It's not on."

"This way we shall be sure."

Ray hesitated. He didn't like the smell of the restroom

or the way Wenzler kept after him. Still, he had to take some chances if he was going to get a story that would bring back his reputation.

He took the cassette out of the recorder, trying for bravado to boost his confidence. "It's not like we're trading Gary Powers for Colonel Abel, you know."

"It's closer than you think," Wenzler said. "Do you know the name Erich Loerke?"

"Sure, the deputy chairman of the Volkskammer. You're saying *he's* been to the Vanilla Rose?"

"Just so."

Ray let out a low whistle. The Volkskammer was East Germany's legislative body and Erich Loerke was one of its leaders. Loerke was one of the new generation of politicians rapidly achieving positions of prominence.

Wenzler said, "Now you see the reason for my caution. A man becomes more desperate and dangerous the more he has to lose, and Deputy Chairman Loerke has a great deal to lose should this information become public."

"If there's proof," Ray reminded him, but his blood was already racing.

Wenzler nodded toward his briefcase. "In here."

"Let me see?"

"Do I have your assurance that my name will never be mentioned?"

"I told you that before. If you checked me out you know I can be trusted."

"Oh, I checked you out," Wenzler said. "But I like to watch a man's eyes when he talks to me. The telephone is the world's great deceiver—you could tell me you're an animal lover while pulling the wings off a sparrow."

You are one evil fruitcake, Ray thought . . . "Well, now that you know I'm not a spy, let's get out of here. I don't like the smell of this place." In more ways than one, he added to himself.

Without waiting, he went to the door, but not until he was outside beneath the awning and surrounded by the smell of damp leaves and wet concrete, did he relax. Wenzler joined him as a young couple passed, laughing, arm-in-arm, paying no attention to the light rain.

"Ahhh," Wenzler breathed deeply. "Much better out here."

"What about Paul Stafford's brother?" Ray said. "You were going to give me his name."

"Rolf Schmidt, a banker. He has been to the Vanilla Rose on numerous occasions. His sexual preferences run to bondage and S and M and he makes no distinction between fantasy and reality. The result has been some less than savory episodes in which the girls have been damaged."

"Yeah, I know. I met one of them Saturday night. Kristy . . ."

Wenzler raised a negligent shoulder. "So many girls, so many names, who can keep track?"

Ray's attention had already returned to Erich Loerke, a much more important story than Rolf Schmidt.

"What about the others?" he asked. "You said there were six other party members who got their rocks off on this side of the Wall."

Ray deliberately inflated the number but Wenzler caught it.

"Four others."

"Are any of them as prominent as Loerke?"

"I'm sure they will be after you sensationalize their exploits."

A balloon vendor wheeling a tank of helium passed them. Rain dripped from his felt hat and the balloons that struggled after him were huddled and bent like old men. Wenzler moved out from beneath the awning and began walking.

"Wait a minute," Ray called, following him. "What about the proof?"

"All in good time. First I want to see if my coat is dead."

"Your what?"

"Are you aware," said Wenzler, "that you can buy dead animals from the zoo? Perhaps there is another story for you. I am interested in a sick polar bear. I will pay to have it made into a fur coat. Two thousand marks—expensive, perhaps, but how many people in the world can wear the white fur of a polar bear?"

They had reached the polar-bear enclosure where a lone man in a yellow rain slicker was taking pictures of the bears. A three-foot-high wall surrounded the area; on the other side, twenty feet below, a wide moat surrounded a rocky island where the bears went about their business, oblivious to both visitors and rain. Wenzler went to the wall overgrown with ivy and began counting the bears.

"If there are thirteen bears, one is mine," he said. "How many do you count?"

Ray was uninterested in the bears but turned and counted, wondering which one would appear in the society pages next winter wrapped around Otto Wenzler.

The bears were like huge snowmen on the brown rocks. One of them sat on its haunches, scratching like a dog, another broke into a lopsided but oddly graceful run as it loped briefly after its mate. Still another was in the water, head high, snorting noisily as it swam. Ray counted only nine but it was impossible to see what was on the far side of the rocks.

Wenzler turned to him. "How many?"

"I count nine."

"Excuse me, sir." A voice behind him.

Ray turned to find the man who had been taking pictures standing next to him. Holding out his camera, the man said, "Could I trouble you to take my photograph?"

Ray was annoyed but what could he do? Say no, I don't want to take your stupid picture? He glanced around but there was no one else to do it so he reluctantly held out his hand for the camera. As he did, from behind something stabbed his neck and a jolt of electricity caused his mouth to snap open, his muscles to convulse.

Ray collapsed. His body felt numb, burning as though stuck by a thousand pins. A buzzing was in his ears and a gagging taste of metal was in his mouth. Through the haze of pain, he saw Otto Wenzler standing above him. In his hand he held a black plastic device with two sharp metal probes extending from it. Electrical connectors, Ray dimly realized.

It was like looking at the world from the bottom of a well. He saw Wenzler slip the device into his coat and kneel beside him. Ray wanted to tell Wenzler that he was not a brave man, that he was a coward, that he could be scared into silence. He had nothing to prove, he could get by without the story about forged passports or Erich Loerke and the Vanilla Rose. None of it mattered. I don't care, I'll stop... He tried to speak but his ears were clogged, he couldn't hear his own words. He wasn't even talking, he realized, the noise in his ears was only the sound of his teeth grinding.

He watched as Wenzler searched his pockets, handed over his tape recorder to the man in the yellow slicker, then removed all the little scraps of paper, receipts and notes from his wallet, leaving only the credit cards, money, I.D. cards and photographs. Ray wanted to tell Wenzler that the credit cards had expired, maybe if Otto knew how close to poverty he was he'd let him live. A foolish thought for a desperate man.

They lifted him up, the two of them, and he realized what they were going to do. He kicked out hard, barbed wire ran through his muscles, his legs wouldn't respond. They balanced him on top of the ivy-covered wall and looked around to make sure no one was in sight or within earshot.

Please . . . but the plea echoed only inside his own brain.

Tears came. Suddenly, finally, everything in his world was precious: his gloomy apartment seemed familiar and secure; his last assignment, a dumb piece on military wives in Berlin, seemed wonderful, the resulting hack story lighthearted and amusing; his nights with Nanci Van Zandt were like magic, her eager body a gift beyond measure . . .

The cement scraped his neck, he fell, and water engulfed him. He rose to the surface coughing, trying to swim. Water flooded his mouth, he tried to spit it out. He had no more control over his breathing than he did over his arms and legs. The coughing was automatic but he couldn't hold his breath, couldn't spit. Water lapped his mouth and flooded his nose.

He made one last effort to swim, and for a moment it seemed that his arms and legs responded weakly. Maybe the shock was wearing off. From the corner of an eye he caught a flash of white and heard a distant splash. A spreading wave reached him, momentarily covering his face as it passed. Water flooded his mouth. He lashed out, rose to the surface coughing and gasping, eyes wide.

His efforts began to take some effect, moving him away from the wall toward the rocky island where a polar bear stood with lowered head, staring at him. Something off to one side, in the water, was snorting. Ray doubled his efforts, willing his arms forward, his legs to kick. If only he

could breathe. Again a wave choked him and he sank
beneath the surface. His chest heaved and bubbles tickled
his nose as the air left his lungs.

No.

His head was pounding from lack of oxygen, but he
could feel his arms and legs responding now. He struggled
to the surface. His head broke free and he took a gulp of
air. As he did, something struck his leg, a downward force
that submerged him in mid-breath. Water gushed thick
and cold down his throat into his lungs.

His arms and legs responded instinctively. He bobbed
again to the surface, chest convulsed, no longer able to
cough, no air left to expel the water. And then the
strength was gone and his arms and legs grew still. The
world dimmed and the rain-spattered surface rose in liquid craters in front of his eyes. His last thought was that
he had stumbled onto something more important than
twin brothers finding each other or a car theft and hit-and-
run or high-ranking communist officials coming to the
West for sex—and he would never ever know what it
was . . .

Oh, mama, please . . .

Ray lost consciousness before the bear's second tentative
swipe disemboweled him.

CHAPTER

17

KARL WAITED AT THE SECURITY DESK AT THE main gate of the Military Ocean Terminal in Bayonne, New Jersey. Outside the window a uniformed MP waved vehicles through: a snappy salute for officers, a quick flick of the wrist for enlisted men, a gesture toward the security office for anyone without I.D.

A white golf cart turned the corner and sped toward him. The driver was an army officer, a woman in her early thirties. Karl was expecting her, Major Irene Fellows, the public affairs officer, his escort for the day. After slamming her cart to a stop just inches in front of the window, Major Fellows got out and came inside.

"You're Paul Stafford?" she asked.

"That's right."

"Your editor wants you to call," she told him as she signed a visitor's log next to his name.

"My editor?"

"A guy named Bernie Stern. He seems to think you're AWOL." She pronounced it *eh-wall*. Karl tensed... he didn't recognize the term. "You talked to... Bernie?"

"Had to validate your credentials. We're not open to the public except on Armed Forces Day."

Karl, of course, would have preferred that this editor Bernie Stern not know about "Paul" being back, but he knew what his response would be. For some time he had been considering calling the *Herald* and making some excuse for Paul's absence; now he had to do it. He hardly wanted Paul's superior becoming concerned or trying to track him down.

The cart whined as they sped down a road bisected by railroad tracks. Major Fellows had a long, bony face but what she lacked in physical beauty she made up for with an outgoing, cheerful, even chipper, manner. She drove aggressively, weaving around workmen and sounding a high-pitched horn whenever anyone got in her way.

Karl asked how long she had been working at the terminal and barely listened to the answer. His attention was on the surroundings, on the rows of gray warehouses and tall cranes that loomed like metal spiders and moved along metal tracks to the tune of warning bells.

Uncle Alex's map of the terminal was out-of-date. Karl began making mental corrections: location and type of buildings, their age and construction, paths of electrical and telephone lines, types of locks and security systems. He also noted the attitude of the employees and general feel of the place—who blended into the background and who didn't and how security-conscious people seemed. The atmosphere was more businesslike than vigilant. Americans were, as advertised, an unsuspecting people. He was glad he wasn't on the other side, wandering around the Soviet Union trying to wangle a tour of a shipping terminal in Murmansk.

Major Fellows filled him in on the history of the terminal, how it had been used in World War II, what its importance was today, as well as a rundown on the Military Sealift Command, which, she felt, got too little credit for the job it did.

They came to a ship that was loading huge crates on pallets, and Karl expressed his surprise that everything wasn't in closed containers.

"We're a full-service facility," Major Fellows said. "We still do a lot of pallets as well as drive-on, drive-off shipments—automobiles and household goods for officers going overseas, the works. But you're right, containers are the easiest and fastest way to go. They're airtight and waterproof and we can stack them outside if we have to. Don't even need a warehouse."

"Are they safe sitting outside?"

"Each container is locked and sealed. And if it's security cargo, it goes to Warehouse E."

Karl kept the conversation going, never focusing directly on security questions but picking up bits of information. He learned that Warehouse E was locked and alarmed and checked every hour by a security patrol. He would have liked to go inside and look the place over but there was no way to do it without asking. The most he could get was a quick look at the outside of the building as they passed by.

Major Fellows took him to inspect a row of containers stacked on the pier. They were like oversize shoe boxes measuring eight feet square by twenty feet long with full-width doors opening at one end. Karl paid special attention to the way the doors were secured.

"Is this brass?" he asked, hefting a padlock.

"Has to be. The containers are secured on an open deck. If those things were steel they'd be rusted shut by the time some of these cargos reached port."

After noting the manufacturer's name—Eagle Safe & Lock Company—Karl turned his attention to the container itself.

"How can you tell what's in this?"

"I can't. Not without a manifest to check the CDN."

"The what?"

"Cargo designation number. Right there."

She pointed to the letter-number code stenciled on the side of the containers. It was similar to the code Uncle Alex had given him for the Redeye shipment, but Uncle Alex hadn't mentioned that the same numbers were stamped on the security seal, a metal band looped through the hasp along with the padlock. The ends of the security band were crimped together where they passed through a metal ball, which made it impossible to open the door without breaking the seal.

The last stop on their tour was the Cargo Control office located on the top floor of a rust-streaked gray building that commanded a view of the entire terminal. There were half-a-dozen people in Cargo Control. Computer screens glowed green and a teletype machine occasionally clattered into life, but no one seemed particularly busy. One wall showed a map of the terminal; on another was a white Plexiglas scheduling board with names of ships, dates and warehouse codes written in grease pencil. Karl noted with satisfaction that the Redeye transport ship *Coralis* was still due to arrive on the twenty-fifth.

While Major Fellows traded jokes with a lieutenant, Karl moved to the window and got a good look at the roof of Warehouse E. He was pleased to see that there were three metal ventilators that looked large enough to climb through. All he had to do was figure a way to remove them and deactivate the alarm system.

"What are you looking at?" Major Fellows said from behind him.

"Great view of New York," Karl said easily, turning around.

"The best on the base," she agreed. "In Manhattan people pay twenty-five hundred a month for this kind of view. These guys get it for free."

The chatter continued, but Karl's mind was already on ways of breaching the security of the warehouse, breaking into the container and getting a Redeye.

Major Fellows dropped him off at the Main Gate, and Karl drove the shoreline adjacent to the terminal, periodically stopping when he found a clear view of the harbor to make notes on a map. He crossed the Bayonne Bridge into Staten Island, where the land curved until it brought him to a point directly across from the seaward end of the terminal. In Bayonne the shoreline was given over to industry, but here it was more residential.

Finished with his reconnaissance, Karl went to a restaurant and ordered lunch. While waiting for the food, he went to the pay phone near the restroom and called the *Herald*. Since arriving in America he had attuned his ear and adjusted his accent to standard American English. In preparation for talking to Bernie Stern, Karl also brought to mind his brother's speech patterns, which were so similar to his own, and tried to imagine what kind of a relationship Paul might have with this man, his boss. It would not be a normal boss-employee relationship. Paul was some sort of prize-winner and worked independently. He decided on a tone of guarded equality and, as the English idiom went, would play it by ear after that.

The main switchboard at the *Herald* patched him through to the editor's secretary.

"This is Paul Stafford. I'd like to talk to Mr. Stern."

"*Hi*, Paul," the secretary said, startling Karl with her unexpected informality. "You're the man of the hour here. Hold on."

While he waited at the phone he became aware of his unconscious habit that his brother had noticed in the beer garden at Treptow Park. He had taken his spare change and stacked the coins in a graduated cone, quarters on the bottom, then nickels, pennies and dimes, and now he was running his fingers up and down the neat stack. Annoyed, he swept the coins off the narrow ledge and into his pocket. Nervousness was weakness.

Bernie Stern came on the line, using neither preamble nor greeting.

"Stafford, what the hell is going on with you? Where are you?"

"I'm in Bayonne, something important came up—"

"Right. Like going to Berlin and stealing cars and running over German cops. Listen, you want to leave the country, let your people know you'll be missing weeklies and maybe you could even let me know, considering I'm your editor. It doesn't look too good when the only way we can find out what our reporters are doing is by reading it in the *Post*. The Mayhues are all over me about what's going on and what can I tell them? Nothing. As in 'I don't know nothing'—which I don't."

Karl hadn't realized that the incident at the Inter-Continental had been so well reported. "I'm sorry—"

"Wait, let me guess: You're pissed off at the delay in the Rockland-Birdwell piece so you're going to do a prima donna tap dance on company time and I'm supposed to keep time with castanets? You trying to prove a point here or just proving that you're the world's *numero uno* pain-in-the-ass hotshot..."

Karl could feel the panic rise. He had been wrong to call Bernie Stern. It was more than a voice he was impersonating, it was a whole relationship with all its subtleties and nuances and personal history. He didn't even know what Bernie was talking about—Rockland-Birdwell? Mayhues? Weeklies? He was lost and at any moment the editor was going to realize it.

"Listen," he said quickly, "I can't explain now but I had to go underground for a story—"

"Underground?"

Karl winced. Not the right term, not the right term. He pushed ahead. "I'm working on a story about illegal arms sales by ex-CIA officers. It could be very big."

"Very big up my ass. What are you talking about? Where'd this come from? There is no story about arms sales and the CIA. Iran-contra is history, for Christ sake."

He was in trouble, no doubt about it. The more he talked, the worse it got. The only way now was to end this conversation before the editor caught on. But Bernie's next words were like a reprieve.

"Or is it?"

His tone was different, quieter, even uncertain. And Karl began to understand better his brother's relationship with the editor. It was based on verbal jousting and mock battle—and the editor's grudging respect. Bernie's outrage and disbelief were, it seemed, the common currency between them, not evidence of Karl's failure. The pause— Karl's silence—had seemed to change the character of the interaction, tipped the scales, as they said, in his favor.

Karl picked it up. "Bernie, this makes Iran-contra a footnote. That's why I had to disappear. My life's not worth a—" he remembered another colloquialism from his training—"plugged nickel if these guys find out I'm onto them."

"Who, for Christ sake? Can you give me a name?"

"Not yet. It wouldn't be safe."

"A CIA–arms sales link? For real, cross your heart and hope to work for Rupert Murdoch?"

The jargon was still confusing, but Karl ignored it.

"It's real but I've got to disappear for maybe another month. If it's longer than that, I'll let you know."

"Wait just a damn minute. Give me a contact, give me a number."

The editor's eagerness for the story was apparent, as was his belief that the man he was talking to was Paul. Karl's earlier despair turned to exultation. He could do it. He *could* impersonate Paul even with someone who knew him personally.

"No contacts, no numbers," Karl said. "I've got to do this one alone."

"What about the cop in Berlin? What am I supposed to tell the Mayhues?"

"Tell them the CIA planted the story to discredit me. Nothing really happened in Berlin."

"Is that kosher or bullshit?"

"Uh . . . listen, Bernie, I've got to go. Someone is coming." Kosher? Another omission in his linguistic training.

"Keep in touch, damn it."

"When I can."

"He's in *my* charge. You don't hurt him bad until you have permission from Herr Wenzler."

Helmut climbed off Paul's back. "The next time he causes trouble let *me* give him an injection. He'll be good then. Very good."

Paul rolled away, weak, trembling. He wanted to strike out, smash Helmut's face.

The two of them moved to the door, paying no attention to Paul.

"I don't need you no more," Madam Tran told Helmut. "If he tries trouble I can just increase my dosage."

Paul's anger fueled his attempt to get off the bed. He stumbled to his feet and stood half-crouched, clutching the mattress for support. The two of them turned to look at him.

Helmut grinned. "Oh, he wants to fight."

Paul tried to tell him where to stick it, but his tongue was thick and his words were slurred.

Helmut came toward him. "What's that? You want to say something?"

The face danced in front of him, misshapen, taunting. Paul hit out with his fist, but his muscles were spastic and the effort only unbalanced him and sent him sprawling to the floor. Helmut nudged him with his foot, taunting him to get up, easily avoiding Paul's clumsy attempts to grab his leg...

Later, after they had gone and his anger faded, Paul realized he was only risking having the dosage increased, which would turn him into a zombie unable even to crawl across the room. He wondered briefly what they were using on him? Phenobarbital? Some kind of barbiturate... Whatever it was, the drugs held him captive as much as the locked room.

He decided his best, his only option, was to cooperate. He ate his food, ignored Helmut's taunts and handling, even turned dutifully to one side when Madam Tran gave him the injection. He would bide his time until he could collect his energy and find some way to escape. Meanwhile, the days and nights flowed one into the other, forming a white haze in which he drifted, drifted, drifted...

CHAPTER

18

IT WAS HOT AND HUMID IN HOUSTON, TEXAS, not what Karl had expected. His picture of the American West came from movies and television, a land of flat mesas and painted deserts and tubular cacti standing tall against a wide sky. Well, at least a lot of the men wore cowboy boots and Stetsons.

He bought a street map, rented an air-conditioned Thunderbird whose steering and handling disappointed him, and drove to the Federal Court House on Rusk Street. Houston, with its downtown cluster of slab-sided silver-windowed buildings, felt more alien to him than Washington, where the tops of monuments and church spires still dominated a peaceful horizon.

Karl took an elevator to the fifth floor, where a young black woman wearing handcrafted Indian jewelry helped him locate the case number of *United States versus Harkness* and then delivered a transcript of the trial in two volumes. Karl joined two law students at a long table hunched over their research. Locating the names he wanted was easy enough: in back of the transcript was an index of witnesses and exhibits matched to page numbers. Karl turned to the testimony of each witness and wrote down the names of those associated with the Rank.

Two hours later he had a list of seven possibilities and proceeded to look up the names in the Houston phone book. One name was missing, another he discarded after seeing how many people were named "Johnson." He ended up with five addresses, which he located and marked on his map. After lunch he drove to each address. Those who lived in well-tended suburbs with second cars or children's toys in evidence he dismissed, while those who were in depressed areas or whose homes looked in need of repair he carefully noted.

One man, George Lish, lived on the outskirts of Houston in an area of old farms and new housing developments. His home and business were on the same property, half an acre of land bordered by tangled timber and humming power lines. The sign on the chain link fence said "Lone Star Dog-O-Rama: Boarding and Obedience Training." Beneath the letters a crudely rendered German shepherd growled at the world. The same sign was on the door of a pickup truck that sat in the driveway of the house. Clearly business was not booming for George Lish.

Karl checked into a Holiday Inn and further narrowed the selection by calling each person and asking for the wife. George Lish's response pleased him most of all. "There ain't no Mrs. Lish," he grunted, and hung up.

Karl placed a 1 beside the man's name. He remembered from reading some of the testimony that George Lish was one of the founders of the Rank but that he now served only on an advisory council. Not a bright man, not a prosperous man and not a married man—a near-perfect fall guy.

Next morning Karl drove to the Dog-O-Rama. The reception area was as tawdry as the exterior. The furniture consisted of a plastic couch with one leg propped up by a brick and an orange coffee table covered with faded Breeder's World magazines. The pale green walls were plastered with advertisements for pet supplies. The room was empty when Karl walked in so he followed the sound of voices to the open back door.

Two men, one white, one Mexican, stood in front of one of the runs arguing in a mix of Spanish and English. Karl assumed the older man was Lish. The German Shepherd at Lish's feet bristled and bared its teeth when Karl appeared in the doorway. The two men turned.

"King," Lish yelled. "At ease."

The dog stopped barking.

"King, sit."

The dog sat down and Lish waved to Karl. "Come on over. He won't hurt you none."

Karl moved forward, keeping an eye on King just in case the dog didn't understand English.

"He's got perfect training," Lish said. "Don't you worry. He won't eat nothing I don't tell him to eat."

George Lish was a short, thickset man, about thirty. He had the body of a weight lifter and a boyish face that reminded Karl of the preacher he had seen on television the night before. Lish wore soiled, khaki shorts and a black, tight-fitting tee-shirt.

"Didn't see you come in," he said. "What can I do you for?"

"I'm Karl Muller, Mr. Lish. Is there someplace we can talk privately?"

"What about?"

"The Harkness case, for one thing."

Lish's eyes narrowed.

"You with the government?"

"No. I represent an organization whose goals are similar to your own."

"What organization?"

Karl indicated the young Mexican who was now investigating a hole in the fence surrounding one of the runs. "It's a confidential matter. Can we go into your office?"

"Berto," Lish called, "when you get that finished cut Kay-Ray's nails and check that abscess on his ear. I'll be inside."

Lish led him through the reception area to his private office, a room only slightly less depressing than the outer room. There were a couple of chairs, a desk, and a sagging bookcase beneath which clumps of dust and dog hair had grown to the size of tennis balls. A series of photographs on the wall depicted annual meetings of the Rank in which Lish stood arm-in-arm with his buddies, each of them wearing military fatigues and holding a rifle. A brown-stained Mr. Coffee sat on a small table.

"Let's get one thing straight, Mr. Muller, whoever you are, if it's about the Harkness case I don't talk unless I'm subpoenaed."

Karl understood the trap had to be baited with trust—or at least credibility—before he offered any money. Still standing, Karl spread his arms. The dog, which had followed them inside, growled.

"Why don't you search me," Karl said. "I'm not from the government. I'm not carrying a weapon and I'm not wired. Go ahead."

Lish stared at him, and gradually the suspicious look gave way to a smile. "Hell, I know you ain't carrying, otherwise you wouldn't offer."

He pushed a copy of Soldier of Fortune from a chair and motioned Karl to sit down before taking a seat behind the desk. The dog lay down at his feet. Karl put his briefcase on the floor and began his pitch.

"Mr. Lish, I'm sure you know that the Rank is not the first organization or the only one that advocates racial purity."

"Yeah, I know. We're like different chapters of the same book." He smiled, pleased with his clever phrase, which he had read in one of Rank's handouts.

"The attempt to purify America," Karl continued, "goes all the way back to the Civil War, when freed American slaves were resettled in Liberia."

"Where? New Iberia?"

"No, Liberia. In Africa."

"Oh, yeah."

"And more recently Germany attempted a purification plan."

Lish's features hardened. "What are you? Some kind of damn reporter?"

"Not at all, I am merely—"

"Well, we're not Nazis so you can forget that. We're white separatists—*Americans*, hundred percent. We don't say any one race is better than the other, just that God meant them to be separate. And we're *not* Nazis because we're not going to kill any races, including Jews. It says right there in the Bible that the Jews shall inherit the land of Canaan and that's Israel. The Germans lost the war because they went against the Bible."

"You're right," Karl said. "And they realize that now."

"Who realizes it?"

"The men who were once Nazis and escaped to South America. You've probably heard of them—the *Organisation der ehemaligen SS-Angehörigen?*"

Lish looked baffled.

"Commonly known as the Odessa."

"Oh, the Odessa. Yeah, I heard of them."

"And they've heard of you."

"Of me?"

"Your organization—you were, I believe, one of the founding members of the Rank."

"And proud of it. That's no crime."

Lish's quick changes from belligerence to suspicion to defensiveness and back made Karl wonder if he'd chosen someone a little too unstable for the role he had in mind. But along with the instability there was gullibility, and if the story he told fitted Lish's preconceptions he would, he figured, accept it.

Lish picked up a hand exerciser from the cluttered desk and as they spoke he squeezed it, first in one hand, then the other.

"Anyway," he said, "we're not part of *any* foreign bunch. People keep paintin' us as un-American, but all we're after is to keep the racial heritage of this country."

"I understand. Germany took the wrong path, it's up to America now."

"Maybe so, maybe not," Lish said suspiciously. "What'd you come here for, anyway?"

Karl now began building the foundation of lies intended to seduce Lish into his trap. He began by telling Lish that the Odessa felt a comradeship with all "organizations which share your ideals," and that it was aware of the trouble that the Rank's leader Harkness was having. Members of the Odessa sympathized with his plight and admired the strong action he had taken to silence the enemies of racial purity.

"*That's* for sure," Lish agreed. "You should have heard the stuff that radio guy came out with—all kinds of lies. Grant started getting hate mail. People were calling him at night, scaring his kids, all because of this guy on the radio. And whenever Grant would call up to set him straight the guy would say some insult and cut him off in the middle of his answer. I've got tapes—you want to hear firsthand some of the crap he was putting out?"

"Perhaps later."

"Well, anyway, that's not fair, not the American way to use media to attack somebody who can't defend theirself, you know what I mean?"

Of course he did, said Karl. And so did his comrades in the Odessa. Which brought Karl to why he had come. His people wanted to contribute to the defense fund for Grant

Harkness and wondered if Lish would handle the money for them.

Lish suddenly became alert. "What money?"

"Five thousand dollars..."

Karl placed the briefcase on the desk, opened it and turned it so Lish could see the money. The man's Adam's apple bobbed as he looked up at Karl.

"That's for Grant?"

"For his defense fund. Would you be willing to be our conduit for the money and insure that it reaches Mr. Harkness?"

"Well, sure if—" he paused in mid-sentence, frowned. "Yeah, well, we're Americans, not Nazis. My daddy fought the Nazis in the war. If this is going to tie us up with old Nazis, I don't know..."

"Just the opposite. We are as eager as you to keep the source of the money anonymous. Say that you raised it from secret sources, whatever you wish. Not necessary to mention the Odessa, although I assure you we *are* on your side."

Lish chewed his lip and looked back at the briefcase, and Karl quickly picked up a stack of twenty-dollar bills, slid the rubber band off one of them and held it up to him.

"I don't see any German writing on this, do you?"

A brief smile appeared. "Well, like my daddy used to say, green is green..."

"Then you're willing to handle the transaction?"

"I guess, so long as we're quiet about it. But how come you want *me* to do it? Why not just give it to Grant?"

"Can I speak confidentially?"

Lish glanced around, leaned forward. "Sure, what?"

"Without casting any doubts on Mr. Harkness, we have no way of knowing just what kind of pressure the government might bring to bear on that man. We feel it's best, at this point, if he knows nothing of the source of the money. What he doesn't know..."

Lish nodded sagely. "Sure, sure, I can understand that."

I'll bet you can, Karl thought, noting that the man could scarcely keep his eyes off the money. It was time to close. If he had prepared correctly, Lish would accept the next mix of truth and fiction not only because it conformed to his preexisting beliefs but because he stood to gain from it.

"The Harkness matter isn't the only reason I came . . . Are you familiar with the name 'Dr. Mengele'?"

"The Nazi doctor? Sure."

"Good . . . Dr. Mengele, as you may know, escaped to Paraguay after the war. He brought with him a large amount of gold and jewels. Some of this he invested, some of it still survives. When the doctor died his fortune was entrusted to his common-law wife Maria, with the instruction that she distribute it to promote the cause of racial purity. At first she didn't want to do this. Maria is half-Indian, a beautiful woman who grew up in the streets, a beggar, so money has a far greater importance for her than it might for you or me."

Lish nodded, Karl pushed on with his concoction. "For years Maria could only bring herself to give away a thousand dollars here and there, but the bulk of the estate remained intact. In fact, the estate continued to increase in value until today it is worth in excess of one point three million dollars . . ."

Lish whistled appreciatively and the dog lifted its head.

"To get quickly to the point," Karl hurried on, "Maria was recently diagnosed to have leukemia. Her doctor says she has only a few years to live, and now she wants to honor Dr. Mengele's wishes. She is a superstitious woman, an Indian, after all, and she seems to believe the reason she contracted the disease is that she failed to follow the doctor's wishes."

Lish's mind was spinning with zeros—one point three million of them.

"My job," Karl concluded, "is to find someone from the Rank who would be willing to meet Maria and discuss the dispersal of one hundred thousand dollars in the United States. To promote the cause of racial purity."

"A hundred thousand dollars . . ."

"There is only one stipulation: under no circumstances is the money to be traceable to Paraguay, to Maria Mengele or to the Odessa."

"You just want to keep it secret, that's all?"

"We *must* keep it secret. Most of Dr. Mengele's wealth was from Jewish sources—that is to say, Jewish property—all of which was assigned to the Jewish Relief Agency after the war. Some of the property is still in the form of jewels, coin collections, so on. Israel has a claim against all Jewish property not returned or compensated for. If any of the money or the property can be traced to Maria, the Israeli government may attempt to claim it, to steal it . . ."

"Oh, so it's Jewish money."

Karl held up the twenty-dollar bill again. "I don't see any Hebrew on it, do you?"

Lish smiled. "Still green from where I sit."

"All right then, all you have to do, Mr. Lish, is meet Maria and get her blessing."

" 'Get her blessing'? What do you mean?"

"She always meets each recipient in person. Indian, you know. They have to look you in the eye before they trust you.

Lish looked worried. Would this Indian woman like what she saw? Karl noted his expression, assured him there shouldn't be a problem, that from what he knew of Maria they'd get along fine. He said that Maria had just arrived in the United States. She had come to consult with the medical experts at famous hospitals. "She's in Miami now," Karl said, "but she'll be going north very soon for treatment."

Lish frowned. "She's not mixed up in drug traffic, is she? We don't hold with drugs. They poison the mind, like interbreeding poisons the blood."

Lish's unpredictable, near-random thoughts startled and worried Karl. He hoped that the man wasn't too bizarre to be credible as the General Secretary's assassin.

"Maria is a wealthy woman," he reminded Lish. "She doesn't have to traffic in drugs."

"Well, I know Miami. It's gone Cuban now and they're all tied into drugs."

"No, no," Karl said, inventing some as he went along now. "The only reason Maria is in Miami is because passenger ships don't go to Washington, and she's afraid of flying, doesn't trust airplanes. She only travels by ship and by train."

And by Winnebago, he added silently. But he said nothing to Lish about the motor home. Instead he explained that Lish was to come to Washington the next Thursday to meet Maria. This would be after she finished her tests at Johns Hopkins University—he had researched famous American hospitals that specialized in cancer treatment—but before she left for the Mayo Clinic. It would also be four days before the General Secretary's arrival on Monday, which would give Karl time for his final preparations.

Karl was pleased with himself. He felt like a chess master, moving a piece here and a piece there in a deceptively innocent fashion designed to lead his opponent into an inescapable trap. The lure of this particular gambit was one hundred thousand dollars, available in cash as soon as Maria approved Lish.

Lish's eyes gleamed at the prospect, but he forced a frown. "Who's going to pay for the trip?"

"We will, of course. You'll stay at the Marriott-Arlington with us."

"You'll be there?"

"I'll pick you up at the airport."

Lish still seemed preoccupied.

"Is that a problem?"

"Just that I'll have to pay Berto to feed the dogs while I'm gone . . ."

You greedy bastard, Karl thought. He took out his wallet. "How much will it cost?"

"I got to give him a hundred a day, otherwise he'll scab for pipe-fitting down at Lenmore."

Karl separated two one-hundred-dollar bills and made certain Lish got a good look at the rest.

Lish reached for the money but Karl hesitated. "You are certain you can leave here?"

"I'm your man, Karl."

You're my dead man, Karl thought.

He handed over the money and returned Lish's smile, as false as his own.

In Berlin, Paul found it almost impossible to concentrate on any single thought long enough to follow it to a conclusion. He was continuously weak and dizzy, felt as if the drugs were dissolving his muscles and turning his bones to rubber. To conserve his strength he began sleeping for longer and longer periods of time. He was dozing almost constantly by the time he realized that it was the drugs that took his energy, not lack of sleep. And he was growing weaker, not stronger.

Galvanized into action by the thought, Paul slid off the bed and attempted to exercise on the floor. A single push-up was an effort and caused blood to pound in his head. He rested and did another. He managed to do three before Madam Tran brought in the food tray and laughed at his efforts.

"You think you're going someplace? Huh? Not unless you're a worm, maybe. You want to crawl under that door? Come on, now, it's time to eat."

She helped him up onto the bed. In the process his hand struck the table, spilling a glass of orange juice. Madam Tran jumped back.

"Damn no good," she said, inspecting her silk Bao Dai and the drops of juice near the skirt. She went into the bathroom, cursing softly in a mixture of Vietnamese, French and German. It took Paul a moment before he fully realized that she hadn't closed the door. If he could get out of the room, out of the building . . .

He got himself up, bracing himself against the dizziness that made the room spin. The door was twenty feet away but might have been a mile. His legs were weak, his stomach queasy. He dropped to his hands and knees and the nausea passed. He could hear the water running in the bathroom. He focused his attention on the open doorway and crawled. It seemed to take an eternity to cross the room—and when he reached the door, it closed in his face.

He turned, looking over his shoulder like an animal. Madam Tran was staring down at him, hands on her hips, the wet spot on her Bao Dai gleaming darkly.

"You spilled your food, little worm," she said. "Maybe you rather eat off the floor."

She took the tray from the table and carefully emptied the contents onto the floor. As she left, Paul grabbed weakly at her ankle but she kicked his hand aside and slipped out the door, taking the tray and utensils with her. Using the doorknob, Paul pulled himself to his feet and pounded in frustration. All that did was make him dizzy. He slid to the floor, the hospital gown bunching around his chest.

Paul clawed at the door. "Let me out," he yelled, but the strangled sounds that came from his mouth were as pitiful as his efforts. His motor skills were disintegrating, his body failing. He had to find a way out—and quickly.

Exhausted by his struggle at the door, Paul took a plastic glass from the wicker table beside the bed and crawled into the bathroom. He was not an animal. Water would be his breakfast this morning. He wouldn't eat from the floor . . .

Later, he lay in bed and stared at the spilled food reflected in the ceiling mirrors. A fly crawled over the white dome of a broken soft-boiled egg, and the toast was discolored by a puddle of orange juice. The garbage that had been his meal mocked his weakness. He tried to think, to concentrate, but the morning's exertions had worn him out. But then, as he began to doze, an idea came and he sat up, thoughts racing, and stared at the mess on the floor. The food had given him an idea about how to escape.

He lay back down, smiling, and the smile persisted even after he fell asleep.

When he awoke the food was gone, and so was the memory of his escape plan. He had forgotten.

CHAPTER

19

KARL INSPECTED EACH TOOL AND PIECE OF equipment before placing it in a nylon backpack. He was at a hotel in Hoboken, New Jersey, and the equipment was spread before him on the bed. Metal tape, gaffer's tape, surgeon's gloves, dentist's mirror, padlock, caulking compound—the list was a long one, too long for his liking. He preferred simplicity, but for this operation there was no choice. He had to get onto the terminal, break into Warehouse E, steal a Redeye missile and escape, all without leaving a trace. And he had to do it tonight— tomorrow the *Coralis* arrived.

Karl took a taxi to a marina on Staten Island, where he had left an inflatable boat and motor. He had bought the outfit through a newspaper ad. The boat was patched and the motor had been repainted an ugly blue, but its looks were deceiving. He had inspected everything carefully and made two practice runs, the first up Newark Bay to Bayonne Park and the second into Upper Bay, around the Statue of Liberty and back, a route that took him past the Military Terminal.

The boat would get him across the bay but he could not risk leaving it exposed on shore or anchored in the water. To make his escape he had purchased an underwater propulsion vehicle, a Dacor Nereid that lay in the bottom of the inflatable boat covered with plastic. It was shaped like a torpedo with handles extending from the rear. When he bought the Nereid, it had been bright yellow; Karl had since painted it black. The vehicle was battery-operated, silent and would run for some three hours at one-and-one- half knots. Towing the Redeye would cut the speed and endurance, but Karl had made his plans so as to have both the outgoing tide and river's current behind him.

It was a mild weekend night. Nobody paid any attention as he left the marina. The tide was rising and the air was thick with the smell of brine, seaweed and mud. On the larger boats, interior lights glowed and traced rippled patterns across the black water. A motor cruiser moved down one of the slips, the sound of animated chatter drifting from its deck.

Karl twisted the throttle and the roar of the outboard dominated the night. As he moved beyond the confines of Van Kull Kill into Upper Bay, the sea began to heave. Now the Military Ocean Terminal came into view, its bright perimeter lights glancing off obsidian waves and throwing deep shadows into warehouses and streets beyond. A ship was being loaded, and Karl angled away from the activity toward a portion of the pier close to Warehouse E. Before entering the glare of the lights he stopped the motor, removed his outer clothing and shoes, sealed them in a waterproof bag he tucked inside the backpack. Beneath the clothes he wore a torso wetsuit.

He adjusted the straps on the backpack, thrust his feet into swim fins and slipped overboard. The shock of cold, oil-slick water quickly dissipated as the water warmed the inside of the suit. With a knife he sliced open each of the inflatable sections and let the boat sink beneath the waves. The Nereid, which weighed over thirty pounds on land, settled into the water with a slightly negative buoyancy. Karl engaged the vehicle and let his body trail like the tail of a kite. The water swirled and bubbled around his shoulders as the Nereid pulled him toward the pier.

There were no permanent guards along the seaward boundary of the terminal. When his feet touched bottom Karl took off his weight belt and put it in a fishnet bag he then fixed to the Nereid. He tied a fishing line to the belt and let it sink along with the vehicle to the bottom. After noting his position, he made his way to shore, letting the fishing line unwind behind him. He hid the fishing line beneath a rock, removed his swim fins and scrambled over slippery pilings and broken concrete slabs until he gained dry ground. Keeping to the shadows, he crossed the deserted terminal to Warehouse E, where he knew that a security patrol made its rounds once an hour, although he did not know exactly when.

The warehouses were bordered by deserted streets

bathed in pools of light. Warehouse E had loading doors twenty feet high at one end, and next to them was a normal-size metal door inset with squares of frosted glass. Karl stood silent in the shadows, listening and watching. When he was certain that no one was around he went to the door, risking the porch light to inspect the frosted glass. Just as Major Fellows had said, there was a faint outline of metal security tape on the inside.

He moved back into the shadows and made his way to the rear of the building, where he took from the backpack a spider hook attached to a Dacron line. Using the rope as a sling, he lofted the hook onto the roof. It tumbled into the gutter and he winced at the sound. When he tugged on the rope the hook bounced free and fell to the ground. A cat darted silently out from the shadows and disappeared. Karl paused to listen, then threw the hook again. He did this four times before it caught.

Once the the hook was lodged firmly he tied the backpack to the free end, then scaled the rope. The metal gutter gave slightly when he grabbed it, and Karl prayed that whoever the contractor had been he hadn't skimped on materials. For a moment he dangled thirty feet in the air, the gutter sagging under his weight, then managed to swing a heel over the edge, rolled up and over and was on the roof.

He paused a moment to catch his breath before hauling up the backpack. Along the apex of the roof were three metal ventilators capped by hoods. Karl made his way to the one in the middle and took out of the backpack a small oxyacetylene torch and a black asbestos cuff. The oxyacetylene outfit he had bought at a hardware store; the asbestos cuff he designed himself so that the flame wouldn't show while he was working.

He positioned the cuff and lit the torch. After adjusting the flame he began to cut around the neck of the ventilator about six inches above the base. The suit was wet against his skin, and the light wind made him shiver. He was glad for the tendrils of warm air that came drifting from the torch. From his vantage point Karl could see the spread of the terminal, the harbor, and on the far shore, the city of New York, its millions of lights casting a pale glow on the underside of low-hanging clouds.

It took just over ten minutes to cut around the ventilator. Karl placed it on its side and peered into the warehouse. The opening was blocked by iron bars. Using a flashlight and the dentist's mirror, he took a look at the underside of the bars. Shiny metal tape ran their length, each end attached to terminals in the ceiling.

With his own metal tape Karl ran an alternate path between the terminals, bypassing two of the bars, then cut the bars with the acetylene torch and placed each segment on the roof. The opening now large enough for him to fit through, he lowered the backpack to the floor, fixed the other end of the line to the roof and climbed down.

The interior of the warehouse was almost completely dark, the only light coming from the frosted windows in the metal doors. The cargo containers were stacked two and three high, each shipment in a separate area. Using a flashlight to check the Cargo Designation Numbers, Karl found QL 4416 H5. He breathed a large sigh, the Redeye shipment had arrived on schedule. Moving quickly, he cut the padlock with the torch, broke the metal security band and opened the doors.

The narrow beam of the flashlight revealed rows of dark green metal boxes separated by wood frames. Karl removed a wood brace, pulled out one of the boxes and lowered it to the floor. It was five feet long, eighteen inches wide and a foot high. The corners were rounded and there were metal handles at each end. It weighed about fifty pounds but almost half of this was from a battery charger and the box itself.

Karl flipped open the latches and lifted the lid. The smell of fresh paint and electrical wiring reminded him of a new stereo. He was looking at a metal tube about four feet long with a handgrip and eyepiece located one third of the way from the firing end. This was the launch tube; the missile itself was inside it. Karl took out the launcher and inspected it: handgrip, flip-up eyepiece, cable terminals, battery compartment. Removing the end caps, he peered into the barrel with a flashlight. The heat-seeking hemisphere of the Redeye gleamed back at him like a reptilian eye—

The sound of a car. He flicked off the flashlight and waited. Headlights washed across the frosted window and stopped. The security patrol. Karl checked his watch: twelve-forty. Instinctively he moved back against the container, knowing that it would do no good . . . if anyone came in now the operation was blown.

A man's silhouette loomed large against the frosted glass, then shrank as the man approached the door. The sound of the idling engine echoed faintly off the warehouse walls. One man called to another and laughed. The doorknob rattled once, then the shadow moved away. Moments later the engine roared and the window reflected a reddish glow as they drove off.

Karl let his breath out slowly. Now that they were gone, the adrenaline came in a quick rush; his heart raced and a prickly sensation spread across his hands.

He replaced the weapon and checked the four batteries and their charger. He would only need one battery, but the others would serve as backups. When he was finished checking the Redeye, he repacked it and set it aside. The next step was to lock and reseal the cargo container so that no one could tell that it had been opened.

From his backpack Karl pulled out an Eagle padlock, one that matched the army's model, and snapped it into place. Finding a duplicate lock had been a matter of calling hardware stores until he found what he wanted. The security seal had required a more complex although ultimately no more difficult solution. He had a new seal with the correct cargo designation code already embossed: QL 4416 H5. The blank security bands were readily available and so were the individual dies that he used to stamp the correct code. Now he threaded the band through the hasp, slid one end through the slotted metal ball and clamped them together with a crimping tool. Not until the cargo arrived in Costa Rica and the assignee tried to open the lock would anyone discover the switch.

Once the container was sealed, he brought out the caulking compound and sealed the metal box containing the Redeye. He smeared the sticky substance around the seam, applied a strip of gauze and repeated the process. The caulk had a distinctive smell that made him uneasy; he imagined it permeating the building and alerting the security guards. After finishing the job he went to the front door and bypassed the alarm system in the same way that he had earlier, using his own metal tape to trace an alternate path between terminals.

He opened the door and peered outside. The area was

deserted. Moving quickly he took the Redeye around to the side of the building to a metal trash dumpster. Although the air was cool he was sweating inside the wetsuit. Rusty hinges squeaked as he lifted the lid. He had forgotten oil. It seemed there was always something, in this case nothing critical, but it annoyed him just the same.

He stowed the Redeye in the dumpster and closed the lid quickly and firmly to minimize the noise. Then, back inside the warehouse, he retraced each step, removing the metal bypass tape as he went. He scaled the rope to the roof and replaced the security bars, using gaffer's tape to secure the broken segments back in their original position. The tape was dark gray and similar in color to that of the bars. He doubted that anyone glancing up into the shadowy recesses of the ceiling would notice the difference.

Once the bars were in place he ran metal tape along the underside to reconnect the original circuit. Finally, he put the top back on the stump of the ventilator, again using the gaffer's tape. Eventually the sun and rain would dry out the tape and strong wind would topple it, but by then his mission should be accomplished.

He climbed down the rope and tugged a disconnect cord to free the spider hook. He shoved the gear into his backpack, returned to the dumpster and retrieved the Redeye. This, of course, was when he was most vulnerable. The Redeye package with its case and batteries weighed almost sixty pounds. Bending forward so that some of the weight was taken by the backpack, he made his way to the water. At one point he was crossing the street when a car appeared and turned onto the street and it was only a matter of good luck that it turned away rather than toward him. Karl cursed softly and wished again that he'd figured out a better way of transporting the missile. Something less noticeable, something with wheels.

By the time he reached the water, he was breathing heavily. Rocks slippery with seaweed lay exposed by the ebbing tide. Twice he slipped and sat down heavily, trying to cushion the Redeye case with his body. The second time the case slipped free and banged against the rocks. To Karl the sound was as loud as a rifle shot but there was no reaction from the terminal; the only sound to disturb the quiet night was the distant rumble of the crane moving along the pier and the faint jangle of its warning bell.

The cold water was a shock to his overheated body but Karl welcomed it. The water was safety. He followed the fishing line back to the Nereid, put on his weight belt and attached a rope from it to the handle of the Redeye case. With the case floating low in the water behind him, he let the Nereid take them across the narrow channel to Staten Island.

He had parked the car in a residential area along Richmond Terrace near his landing spot, a small park bordering the shoreline. The outgoing current was stronger than he'd anticipated and he had to make a heading change to the west to correct for it. Even so he missed his landfall by a quarter of a mile and ended up beneath a restaurant that sat on pilings overlooking the water. It was two-thirty in the morning.

He hid the Redeye, stripped off the wetsuit and dried himself as best he could with the thin white towel that he'd taken from the hotel and stowed inside the waterproof bag along with his clothes. The clothing soaked up what moisture the towel missed, leaving his shirt clammy against his back as he walked the deserted streets. By the time he reached the car he was shivering. He turned on the heater, returned to the restaurant and retrieved the Redeye.

Exhilarated by his success, Karl drove all night back to Washington. He slept for six hours, ate breakfast at noon and then sat down on the living room floor, the Redeye and its components spread out around him. He had memorized the instruction manual during the holiday at Zinnowitz with Uncle Alex; now he began practicing what he had learned. The launch sequence consisted of a number of operations: gyro spin-up, target ranging, uncaging the gyro, infra-red acquisition and firing. Karl practiced them over and over, and by the end of the day the Redeye felt as familiar in his hands as the steering wheel of the Mercedes.

The next step was to develop a procedure for firing the missile from inside the motor home, a task that proved more difficult than he'd anticipated. After renting the Winnebago he drove at night with the Redeye to Dulles Airport and parked beneath the approach path of the incoming jets. The civilian aircraft appeared in the open skylight framed by a black sky alive with stars, but Karl found that there was no time to track them. By the time he caught the aircraft in the ranging ring, the forward edge of the hatch blocked his view. The only way he would have enough time to track, lock and fire seemed to be to stand on the roof and this he was unwilling to do. Of his four launch sites two were in suburban neighborhoods, one was at a roadside rest stop and the fourth was in a shopping center parking lot. Karl wanted to be able to remain hidden, even during launch, which meant firing through the skylight.

One solution was to modify the opening and make it bigger but this couldn't be done until after he'd duped George Lish into renting the motor home. Once that was done, he could make the modification himself or pay to have it done. If he paid someone, there was no telling how long it would take or if the person would realize that the Winnebago was a rental. The best course was to do it himself, but he hated to do anything that would draw attention to the Winnebago and he had a natural distrust of halfway measures. What if he made the opening so big that it weakened the frame? He imagined a scenario in which the roof gave way when he hit a pothole and the motor home collapsed like a dynamited bridge.

In the end Karl opted for a simpler, more innovative solution that involved a mirror and a lot of practice. The mirror was convex and when he clipped it to the forward edge of the skylight opening it provided a view of the sky behind the Winnebago. It was a distorted view, with tiny planes growing rapidly in size and ballooning outward as they passed overhead, but with enough practice Karl found that he could interpret distances just as easily as he could with the naked eye.

Using the mirror, he practiced the same procedure that he'd mastered at the house. He stood in the Winnebago with the Redeye on his shoulder, one eye at the target ring and the other on the approaching plane. He uncaged the gyro and began leading the aircraft even before it reached the skylight. As it swept into view, the acquisition signal, a thin, reedy tone, indicated that the Redeye was locked on target and that he could fire at will. Once launched, the jet's exhaust gases would act as a hot carpet, leading the heat-seeking head of the Redeye to the aircraft. Once launched, an aircraft without infra-red counter-measures was doomed.

Karl spent three nights locking on one civilian aircraft after the other, each one a trigger pull and three seconds away from destruction. He wondered how many lives passed through his hands? A thousand? Two thousand? Ten thousand? It didn't matter. Only one life was important. Only one life was the target.

His experience with the Winnebago convinced him that while ideal as a launch platform, the motor home was too slow and clumsy to serve as a getaway vehicle. He bought a copy of the local paper, the *Prince George's Journal*, and went looking for used motorcycles. In a neighborhood of permanent house trailers he met a sullen young man who had a Kawasaki KE-100 for sale.

"I wouldn't sell it," the boy mumbled, "only I'm going into the army."

He had pale skin, stringy hair and pouting lips, and Karl had trouble believing that the American army would want him.

The Kawasaki was black with red-and-orange flames dashing across its gas tank, a dual-purpose machine made for off-road work as well as the street. With a one hundred cc engine it wasn't particularly fast or powerful but it wasn't heavy and would be easy to get in and out of the Winnebago. Besides, the motorcycle only had to take him from Andrews Air Force Base to National Airport, just across the Potomac from downtown Washington.

"It's in cherry condition," the kid mumbled.

A ride around the neighborhood convinced Karl, and they quickly settled on a bargain-basement price.

When Karl returned the Winnebago to Sunshine RV, he took the motorcycle and used it to return to the Toons Creek house. It clearly wasn't made for freeway driving, so he stayed on the secondary roads, just as he would when he made his run from Andrews to National Airport.

He also bought a space-age helmet with a full face visor and spent hours riding the country roads that wandered through the wooded hills of Maryland. Twice he rode from Andrews to Washington National Airport to familiarize himself with his escape route.

It was on the second trip that he saw his brother's wife. It was a Wednesday afternoon, and for no reason other than his continued fascination with his brother's life, Karl had detoured past Paul's house in Arlington, Virginia. Dressed in a leather jacket and full-face helmet, he wasn't worried about any of the neighbors mistaking him for Paul.

It was when he turned onto the block that he saw a woman exiting the house. Could it be her? He made a quick U-turn, drove around the corner and returned to a position where he could watch without being seen. The woman had black hair held in place by a red silk scarf worn as a headband. She wore a gray blouse with black slacks and moved briskly to an Alfa Romeo parked at the curb. When the Alfa came toward him, Karl remained where he was and with the visor down, pretended to study a map and glanced up only at the last minute to get a good look at the woman. It was Joanna, all right. He recognized her from the photograph that Paul had given him.

She seemed concentrated on something and he felt sure that she hadn't noticed him. Excited, he allowed himself to follow her across the Key Bridge to an art gallery in Georgetown, the Kawasaki making it easy to slip through traffic and keep hidden by intervening cars. When they arrived at the Gallerie L'Enfant he remembered that Paul had said his wife worked at an art gallery. Paul's wife. Joanna . . .

There was a smile on his face as he rode back to the Toons Creek house and began to speculate on his brother's life. Somehow, from Paul's uneasiness when he mentioned her, he had gotten the impression that his brother and Joanna had separated; if so, she must have returned in Paul's absence. Was she worried about Paul? Did she know that he had gone to Germany? If she called the editor, Bernie Stern, he would tell her the same story that Karl had given him about going underground to investigate the CIA and arms deals. The more he thought about it, the more Karl thought of learning firsthand about his brother's life. If he could sneak into the house while Joanna was at work . . .

But he wouldn't have to sneak; he had Paul's keys. That realization carried its own special excitement and anticipation. He could just walk up to the door and—no, too dangerous. The Redeye mission was far too important to risk for a whim. Paul's life was Paul's life and his life was his and nothing he could discover could change their separate destinies. Karl thrust from his mind the notion of going into his brother's house, but it didn't disappear . . . it took root in his subconscious, and began to grow even as he prepared to meet George Lish.

The idea of his escape returned to Paul with a rush in one of the rare moments of lucidity that preceded his daily injection. It came back to him . . . that day he spilled orange juice on Madam Tran and her first reaction had been concern about her clothes. And that was the key. Praying that she would react the same way if it happened again, Paul made his preparations.

First he filled his plastic glass with water. Since the vertigo made it impossible for him to stand, he crawled to the bathroom and back, putting the glass on the floor each time he moved ahead. When he got to the bed he put the glass against the wall underneath the wicker table. Then he lay down and practiced every movement, over and over. What he had to do was simple but his limbs lacked coordination and his muscles were weak . . . he worried that he wouldn't be able to perform the maneuver quickly enough and without faltering.

But there was no choice: he *had* to do it; somehow he had to make his body obey. It had been so long since he'd been healthy that he couldn't even recall the sensation. Had there actually been a time when he could stand without getting dizzy, walk without falling, and even run? When, if his mind said, *Do it*, his body had swiftly responded with no more concentration on the mechanics than he used in breathing?

He had to regain these capabilities to escape, but everything depended on Madam Tran and whether her reaction would mirror the previous one. When she arrived Paul saw with satisfaction that her Bao Dai was a rich gold decorated with brocade. Good. The more expensive and fancy the dress, the more likely she would react to protect it. Clothes were clearly an obsession with her.

She approached the bed as she always did, businesslike, lips pursed, one eye on Paul. As usual the syringe was on the tray beside the food, beside the glass of milk that came with dinner. Paul struggled to a sitting position and, pretending to be very hungry, reached for the tray just as

Madam Tran put it down, hit the glass of milk and knocked it to the floor, splattering Madam Tran's Bao Dai.

"Damn you!"

She slapped him hard as she could. Paul fell back on the bed, ear ringing from the blow. His face felt numb and one eye was watering so that he had to keep blinking to make it focus. He could see himself in the mirror over the bed, first fuzzy, then in focus, then fuzzy again...

The sound of water running in the bathroom brought him to his senses. How long had he been lying there? How long did he have? Never mind, he had to act. Now...

He rolled to his side. The tray was still on the table, and on it was the syringe. Now came the part he had practiced. He reached out, hand shaking. The syringe seemed such a long way off... He levered himself up on one elbow, and the elbow gave way. He fell against the mattress, got control again, tried again... The syringe. His fingertips brushed the smooth glass, which moved away. He leaned further, felt the muscle in his supporting arm begin to tremble—and then, finally, he had it.

He brought the syringe close to his chest. Through the doorway Madam Tran was partly visible, her back to him, still busily, angrily cleaning the Bao Dai at the sink. Paul turned his attention to the syringe. With clumsy hands he thrust the needle into the mattress and depressed the plunger. There was resistance, it didn't seem to be moving. He pushed harder, his thumb slipped off. Cursing softly, he wiped his sweaty hand on the sheet and tried again. *Easy*, he told himself, don't try too hard, don't break the needle... He kept a steady pressure, and slowly, slowly the syringe emptied. When all the fluid had been expelled Paul rolled to his stomach, head and arms extending beyond the mattress so that he could reach the water glass on the floor. He put the needle into the glass and pulled the plunger. Slowly, ever so slowly, the syringe began to fill.

Too damn long, a voice inside screamed at him. It's taking too *long*, she's on her way out, hurry, for God's sake... He fought the panic and continued the steady pressure. The plunger moved with terrible slowness. His hands trembled; his fingers almost slipped. His head, hanging over the side of the bed, throbbed painfully. He wanted to yank the plunger back but forced himself not to . . .

And then at last it was done.

And the water in the bathroom had stopped.

He shoved an elbow under his chest and levered himself up. In the bathroom Madame Tran smoothed her wet Bao Dai and began to turn. He had to get the syringe back onto the tray. In his hurry his hand struck the underside of the table and the syringe flipped out of his fingers and skittered across the floor.

"You damn trouble . . ." Madam Tran was saying as she came into the room.

The syringe lay by itself, midway between the spilled milk and the bathroom. In a moment she would see it. In a moment she would know. Unless—

Paul lunged and struck the tray, tumbling the chicken and dumplings, the beets, everything onto the floor.

"No more," Madam Tran shouted. She came forward, avoiding the mess on the floor, and shoved him back on the bed.

"Hungry," Paul mumbled.

"You get nothing, you get nothing tonight, maggot-eaten trouble man . . ."

She started toward the door, then saw the syringe and remembered the injection.

"Hungry," Paul said.

"Shut up. Turn around."

She pushed him to his side and Paul felt the familiar sting in his buttocks. A smile tugged at his lips as Madam Tran marched out, slamming and locking the door behind her. Somebody would come to clean up the mess, but Paul didn't stay awake to find out who. Exhausted, he fell asleep, and in sleeping began to become a threat to his brother.

CHAPTER

20

GEORGE LISH ARRIVED AT WASHINGTON NAtional Airport shortly after noon on Thursday, just four days before the General Secretary was due to arrive. As the plane approached low over the silvery brown Potomac he began to pick out familiar landmarks: the Washington Monument, Arlington Memorial Bridge, the Capitol. He strained to see the Vietnam War Memorial, the monument to his own generation's sacrifice in the cause of freedom. George had championed the cause of a Vietnam memorial, only to be disappointed by the author of the winning design—an oriental girl, American by nationality but clearly foreign by race . . . clearly not from the same brave stock that produced the men who fell at Bunker Hill and Iwo Jima.

George shared with other members of the Rank a special world geography in which each continent was allocated to a certain race: blacks in Africa, orientals in China, Mexicans in South America, Jews in Israel, and Aryans in Europe and North America. This was the natural order of things and obviously the way God intended it.

Unlike some members of the Rank, George considered himself a moderate fellow. He didn't want to kill all the blacks and Jews—people were people, after all. No, he favored the "Israeli model," which meant that each race would be put back in its proper homeland. Like he always told people, he *supported* the blacks in South Africa. He was willing for all whites to leave Africa in exchange for all blacks leaving America. "A White America for White Americans." That was the Rank's slogan.

George was proud to say he had invented the slogan ten years ago when he and six others had founded the Rank. He had been the organization's first vice-president, married at the time to a woman named Bobbi who bore him three children and turned failing Dog-O-Rama into a profitable business before leaving George for a pet food salesman. Since then the Dog-O-Rama had gone into a decline, stimulated by the downturn in the Houston economy, which everybody knew was on account of the Arabs and their cheap oil.

George's fortunes within the Rank suffered a similar decline. As the memberships grew he was overshadowed by men like Grant Harkness, men with dynamic personalities, more jazzy, extreme ideas and lots better slogans. In subsequent elections George suffered humiliating defeats, although he was careful to hide his disappointment behind an outward show of good-natured camaraderie. He was demoted to serving in committees and organizing the combat games that took place once a month. He was not part of the inner circle and wasn't a member of the Action Squad that sent the bomb to the radio station. So it was with a secret and understandable thrill that he heard the news of Grant Harkness' arrest.

George smiled as he recalled presenting the Odessa's money—the half of it that he'd parted with—to Grant Harkness. He'd kept two thousand five hundred in reserve, figuring that he could double the satisfaction of seeing Grant's stunned expression if he gave the money in two separate chunks. Asked where it came from, George had smiled and said, "I have secret sources that I'm not at liberty to divulge."

He was vaguely aware that he was fooling himself, that what he was doing with the money was waiting to see if he was approved as a beneficiary for Dr. Mengele's money. If this woman Maria didn't approve him, maybe he would hold back some of the twenty-five hundred in payment for the time and effort he was spending. In fact he had already spent eight hundred dollars to pay off some pressing debts—he thought of it as a loan he would pay back as soon as the summer business picked up...

George's self-confidence began to ebb as the plane taxied toward the terminal. This Karl Muller, so confident and self-assured, represented a larger, secret world of foreign affairs that George only dreamed about. Why should such a man trust him? Why should Maria Mengele?

By the time he stepped into the terminal he was so uneasy that he was almost surprised to find Karl waiting.

The Odessa man, as he knew him, greeted him warmly, and George's doubts began to evaporate.

"How was the flight?" Karl asked.

"The usual bullshit," George said, "Took longer to taxi to the runway than it did to get here... Did Mrs. Mengele arrive?"

Karl gave him a cautionary look. "We'll talk in the car."

"Got it," George said, biting off the words in a clipped, no-nonsense fashion that he hoped would make up for the obvious blunder in mentioning Maria Mengele's name in public.

In the parking lot Karl led him to a gleaming burgundy-and-silver Lincoln Continental. George felt a tweak of jealousy... it didn't seem fair that a Nazi organization had all this money while the Rank had to struggle to pay the printing costs of its newsletter, *Battle Lines*. If he could get his hands on a little of it... his thoughts were full of dreams of what he might accomplish with some real money while Karl paid the parking fee and headed north along the George Washington Parkway. He came out of his reverie when he noticed Karl's preoccupation with the rearview mirror.

"Problem?"

"Someone in a yellow Jaguar. Came out behind us, turned the same way. Let's see if they..." Karl let the words trail off, then relaxed. "No, it's okay, they're going to the city." As he spoke they turned west on Highway 244.

"Aren't we going to the city?"

"We've got a little problem, George."

And George thought, My luck is never any good. They've found someone else to give the money to. "What's wrong?" he asked.

"Take a look." Karl handed him a Xerox copy of a telegram from Buenos Aires addressed to Karl Muller c/o the Marriott Hotel: ISRAELI M AWARE YOUR MISSION. SUGGEST PRECAUTIONS, ADVISE GL. There was no signature.

"*Israeli M?* Who's that—the Mossad?" George knew his spy fiction.

Karl give him an admiring look. "Exactly."

George glowed. "But who's GL?"

"You."

George cringed. It had never occurred to him that he was important enough to be included in a telegram, especially one like this.

Karl was saying something now about a wallet being stolen, and George forced himself to concentrate.

". . . hotel detectives couldn't find a thing," Karl said. "But then, with the Mossad after you, you don't expect them to. The point is, I was supposed to rent a motor home. You know, one of those Winnebagos with a bedroom, kitchen, everything on wheels, as they say?" He glanced at George. "You know what I'm talking about, right?"

"I think I missed the first part, sorry . . . you said your wallet was stolen?"

"From my hotel room. While I was in the swimming pool. It might have been the maid or a professional burglar *or* the Mossad. Who knows? But whichever it was, I must rent this motor home to take Maria to the Mayo Clinic. Now that we know the Mossad is onto us, she does not want to travel by train, and an ordinary automobile would not be adequate, considering her condition . . . I told her I would see if you could do it."

"Do what?"

"Rent the motor home for her."

"*Me* rent a motor home?"

"You would not have to pay for it, of course. I will give you the money: seven hundred and fifty dollars."

"But . . . can't *you* rent it?"

"Not anymore. My driver's license was stolen with my wallet."

"Maybe you could just fly out—"

"Maria is afraid of flying. I told you that."

"Oh, yeah," George said, although the truth was that he had forgotten almost everything about Maria except her one hundred thousand dollars.

"Maria tires easily, she has a special diet, she is often in pain. A motor home makes sense. It may also be a blessing in disguise. If you do her a favor, she is certain to trust you . . ."

George was alarmed by the unexpected request and the responsibility that went with it. "Well," he hedged, "what if you don't get it back in time? Or have an accident?"

"The seven hundred and fifty dollars includes insurance. As for getting back in time, you can take the money out of the bequest if we're late."

George remained silent. He was trying to absorb and sort out this new development. If he signed for the motor home he'd be legally responsible for it. If he refused, Maria Mengele might choose someone else to handle the money. George had already awarded himself a substantial commission and did not want to lose it.

Then he had a darker thought. He gave Karl Muller a surreptitious glance. The man was a stranger. Could this be some kind of scam to steal a motor home and blame it on him? How much did something like a Winnebago cost? Thirty, forty thousand? He'd be bankrupt if he had to pay out that kind of money... Of course, if she gave him the money, the hundred thousand would pay for a couple of Winnebagos.

"Is she... going to give me the money today?"

"If she trusts you, you will have it in a matter of hours."

"And she's got the money with her?"

"Fifty thousand dollars is in cash, the rest is in the form of jewels and precious metals. But, of course, if you don't want to do her a favor—"

"No," George said quickly, "I was just thinking about the Mossad. Whether there would be any danger involved."

"To them, perhaps. Right?"

"What?"

"I have the impression that you are a man who can take care of himself. And of those who would cause trouble for you."

Karl gave him a soldier-of-fortune grin that George returned, faintly. Much as he liked to think of himself as a commanding presence, deep inside George suspected that he was more often the victim of events than their master. He was beginning to have that feeling now, of things moving too fast, of events gone out of his control...

But with the thought of the money to anchor his resolve, George dismissed his fears. He would rent the Winnebago and prove his worth. But if Maria Mengele didn't give him the money, he'd drive the damn thing right back to the lot and tell her to forget it. Right, it was that simple. He'd do it.

* * *

When they reached Sunshine RV, Karl said he had to call Maria and went to a phone booth at the corner. He couldn't, of course, go inside without the salesman recognizing him; further, it was absolutely necessary for his plan that George rent the Winnebago by himself, that George be the renter of record.

Karl was pleased; things were going well. The Maria Mengele story was the most complex, and unlikely, of all the lies he'd constructed for the Redeye mission, and therefore the most vulnerable. But George Lish was running true to form. The lure of one hundred thousand dollars combined with careful ego building had overruled the man's innate caution and cowardice. Karl was proud of the telegram, which he had sent to himself at the hotel and then cut and pasted together in such a manner that the Argentine address, originally part of the message, appeared to be the address of the sender. Photocopying it had made the deception invisible, and Lish had not asked to see the original. Karl smiled as he remembered how proud the man had been about guessing that *M* meant *Mossad*—as if anyone would use such a transparent code...

Karl could see George through the window of Sunshine RV, filling out forms, talking to the clerk. He felt a bit like a cat toying with a mouse, letting it run a few feet and then batting it back to the center of the room to play with it once again. But now the time for play was over. He reached beneath the seat, drew out an ice pick with a shiny green handle and slipped it into the pocket of his sport coat.

The Winnebago was twenty-seven-feet long, beige with a red-and-blue stripe. Karl led the way, driving slowly so that Lish, following in the motor home, could keep up. He had told him that because of the Israeli interest in Maria's movements they had moved from the Marriott to a safe house near the Patuxent River. Karl kept an eye on the Winnebago but George seemed to have no trouble with it; whenever Karl glanced his way, he gave a firm thumbs-up sign.

When they reached the Toons Creek house Karl unlatched the gate and drove on ahead, parked, and as the Winnebago came lumbering up the tree-lined drive opened the stable doors and waved it inside. George gave another thumbs-up. As he passed, Karl opened the side door and stepped inside. It smelled new inside the Winnebago, a mix of fabric, plastic and paint.

Karl came forward until he stood between the two front seats.

George turned off the ignition. "This is a great spot."

"Wait a moment," Karl said. "Before you get out, show me how this machine operates."

He slipped his hand into his pocket and grasped the ice pick as George began to point to the dashboard controls.

"Hell, this thing's a pussy rig, just like driving a car. You got a few more switches is all. This is the master electric, you check it to see..."

As George leaned forward to touch the electrical switch Karl could see the slight notch at the base of his skull, just above the vertebrae. He brought the ice pick into position, aiming like a matador. As he was about to strike, a horn sounded from the driveway and George turned so abruptly that the ice pick grazed his neck. He also saw the weapon.

"What's—?"

And then he saw Karl's expression, and he knew. And in that moment of comprehension, Karl struck, thrusting forward and upward, aiming at George's throat. But the Rank's combat exercises were not altogether without effect. Instinctively George parried the blow, and the pick glanced off his jaw and gouged open his cheek. He grunted in pain.

A car door slammed and a woman's voice called. "Hello?"

It was Rita Gaylord. Karl knew he had to finish this and do it quickly. Too late now to wish he had latched the gate behind the Winnebago. At any moment Rita might find them.

George had both hands around Karl's wrist, holding the ice pick at arm's length. The man, it seemed, was incredibly strong, his compact, weight-lifter's body working to his advantage in the cramped space. But he also fought badly, defensively, his eyes wide with fear, his clenched teeth visible between the torn folds of bloody flesh.

Extending two fingers of his free hand, Karl gouged George's eyes. The man let go of his wrist, trying to protect himself. Karl stepped close and plunged the ice pick into his chest. George lunged upward, hands clawing at the air, and then his eyes glazed and he collapsed onto the steering wheel. Karl reached for the body and lowered it to the floor.

"Anybody home?"

Karl stood. She was visible through the rear window, Rita coming this way. He took off his coat, which had blood on the sleeve, and stuck it under Lish's head. When he stood up she was at the back window, her hands cupped around her eyes. Seeing him, she tapped the window and waved. Karl waved back but kept his position, blocking her view of George's body on the floor between the seats. When she disappeared around the side of the Winnebago he crossed to the door and stepped out before she could enter.

"Well, hello there," she said. "Is this yours?"

"My parents own it," Karl said, closing the door behind him. "They drove down here from Philadelphia."

Rita wore tan slacks and a chartreuse cashmere sweater; in other circumstances Karl would gladly have seduced her. Now he just wanted to get rid of her.

"I've never been in one of these things before," she said.

Karl forced himself to remain calm. This was dangerous, this woman was dangerous.

"It's not mine to show," Karl said. "But let me ask them and see if it's okay to take you for a ride."

To make the point clear, he stepped past and headed to the door. Rita followed.

"You pick the day," she said. "I'll buy the gas."

Get out of here, he wanted to shout, but forced himself to speak casually. "What brings you out this way?"

"I got a box of peaches from one of those Fruit-of-the-Month clubs so I made peach pie. I thought you and your children might enjoy it. Where is everybody, anyway?"

Goddamn you, Karl thought. He was still on edge, keyed up, which made concentration difficult. Trying to remember everything he had told her before, he began fitting a new story together.

"My parents went sailing with some friends and the children are still in California. There's a legal problem of some kind about out-of-state visitation rights. I don't know if they will get here or not."

"So you're all alone right now?"

Karl looked at her. She stared back, the corners of her

wide mouth upturned. She was not going to quit. She was a problem and was going to remain a problem.

He had to kill. Not Rita—that would risk a murder investigation—but himself, Ron Tednick, and the attractive image he had built up. He had to offend Rita, humiliate her so that she would leave him alone, never want to see or hear of him again. She wanted a lover? He would give her one.

"I'm not alone," he finally answered. "You're here."

"Well, then. Can I offer you some peach pie?"

"At least."

"Ahh, yes," she said in a singsong voice.

Rita returned to her car, a blue Peugeot. As she leaned across the front seat Karl could see the outline of her panties, visible beneath the slacks. She had nicely rounded buttocks. He regretted the circumstances weren't different.

They went into the kitchen, where Karl handed her a knife and she began to cut the pie. They were not talking now, but Rita wore a secret smile, even hummed to herself as she worked. Karl moved behind her and slid his hands over hers. She settled gently backward, her body warm and firm against him. With his arms around her, he lifted her hand and moved the knife away from the pie.

"Drop the knife," he whispered.

She tried to look up at him.

"Don't turn around. Just put down the knife."

"Umm, you're full of surprises."

She let the knife fall to the table. Karl guided her hand back to the pie and slowly pushed downward. Rita hesitated as she touched the crust, then relaxed. Pie filling oozed around their fingers. He lifted her hand and brought it to her face.

"Wait," she giggled, turning her head to one side.

He smeared the pie across her lips and let the messy filling fall on the cashmere sweater. She paid no attention to the sweater. Instead of resisting, she joined him, rolling her head and licking his fingers. She turned around, put her hands around his neck and kissed him, smearing the sticky filling across his lips as well.

Rita's unexpected arrival had ruined a clean kill and unnerved Karl. He felt a rush of anger—with her, with himself, with the situation. He shoved a hand up under her sweater, grabbed the front of her bra and tore it. She pulled away but her eyes remained bright.

"Wait . . ."

With one continuous movement she freed herself from the sweater and slid out of the broken bra. Her plump breasts, outlined in white, had upturned nipples. She wiggled her shoulders and sent the soft flesh dancing, watching him with a crooked smile. She was, she believed, good in bed, and she wanted him to know it.

Karl dug his fingers into her breasts and pulled her abruptly toward him. This time she winced. "Easy honey, *easy* . . ."

Putting his hands on her shoulders, he pushed her down.

"Suck me."

"Give a girl a chance . . ."

Karl pressured her to her knees and then unzipped his pants.

"I'm not hard," he said.

And he wasn't. This was not a sexual encounter, it was a defensive maneuver. He was trying to alienate her; trying to be rough without bruising her, to be offensive without assaulting her. But she was too forgiving. She took him in her mouth and began a gentle movement.

Karl's head went back, the warmth began spreading through him. And with it a familiar heady feeling.

No, this was no good, he could not let this happen. Any kind of sexual relationship with Rita would only confuse and jeopardize matters. He had to alienate her but without dangerous consequences. How? He did not want to hit her. That could lead to a police complaint. Besides, so far as he was capable of the sentiment, he liked Rita Gaylord. Another time . . . there had to be—

As soon as he thought of it he was sure it would work, if he could manage it . . .

He relaxed his mind and recalled the day he had been shot by the Russian guard, the day he had met Alexander Ikhnovsky, Uncle Alex, who had sent him here. He remembered the pain of frostbitten toes and the fear of being caught, and he used the memories to stop his body from responding to Rita's erotic manipulation.

"Wait." He took a step back, and still half-hard gave her

what he had heard them call in the bordello a "golden shower." Rita scrambled to her feet.

"Hey, come on," Karl said.

But Rita yanked the cloth from the table and dried her shoulder with quick angry movements. Her breasts still bore the imprint of his fingers.

"I thought you wanted a little action."

Without answering she retrieved her sweater and stood there, breathing heavily, glaring at him. "You did that *on purpose.*" She stepped forward and raised a trembling hand, but did nothing more. Then the anger died and her eyes filled with hurt. "Why?" she said in a tiny, miserable voice, and then she was gone.

Watching from the window, Karl saw her put on the sweater before getting into the Peugeot. Gravel erupted from beneath the rear tires, and the car shot forward and disappeared down the hill. Karl was confident that she would not be back. And that she would not tell anybody what had just happened to her. He had achieved his purpose. And, strangely, felt no pleasure in it.

CHAPTER

21

PAUL WOKE UP WITH A CRY. THE IMAGE OF A man with a torn face and death-glazed eyes slowly faded and he saw himself in the ceiling mirror, lying in bed, his arms outstretched to catch a falling body.

George Lish.

He sat up, confused. It took him a moment before he remembered where he was and what had happened. Then two thoughts struck at the same time. His mind was clear, he was himself again. And his brother had killed a man named George Lish. He could still feel the weight of the body on his arms, still hear the gasp of surprise when the ice pick pierced the heart. The memory was vivid, just as it had been after the other dreams.

George Lish? The name meant nothing to him, but he guessed from past experience that Lish was either a CIA agent who had become a threat, or a KGB asset who had outlived his usefulness. Whichever, whatever, his brother had killed again.

When Paul sat up his body responded normally for the first time in . . . how long had it been? He didn't even know what day it was. But at least he felt whole again. The mental fog was gone, he could think clearly. A faint dizziness told him that the effects of the drug hadn't entirely worn off. He was still weak but at least he could think, and there was still time to recuperate, some twelve hours until the next injection.

The door rattled and he quickly lay back down on the bed as Madam Tran entered with the breakfast tray. When she saw him she frowned. "You going to be good this morning? Otherwise no food, okay? You wait until I feed you."

"Yes," Paul said slowly. He had no idea what he sounded

like under the drug so he decided it was best to speak as little as possible.

After she fed him, Helmut came in and he had to put up with the indignity of being helped to the bathroom. For the first time he saw in Helmut's face how much the man hated this duty. Why had Otto made him do it? Why not some flunkie? The only answer was Karl. This was the way he wanted it. Helmut and Madam Tran and Otto were the only people who knew that Karl had a twin brother. They were the only people Karl trusted with the information.

But the answer raised more questions than it answered. Why the secrecy? Why had Karl kidnapped him? Where was Karl now? And *who* was George Lish?

Helmut returned him to the bed and left the room. As soon as he was alone Paul got up and checked the door. It was locked. Moving upright after crawling on his hands and knees for so long was, literally, a heady experience. That he could stand firmly and move about on two legs seemed miraculous, but moving around the room quickly told him how weak he still was. After only a few minutes of activity he found himself trembling with fatigue, the strength in his muscles exhausted. He would need to wait until his body had recovered more fully before attempting an escape. Trying to control his impatience, Paul spent the day resting and drinking large amounts of water to speed the drugs out of his system. The hours seemed endless but he celebrated each time he walked to the bathroom and back without falling.

When lunch came he suppressed the urge to rush for the door. Not yet. He did take the opportunity to note the lock on the outside of the door: a metal bar, simple, effective—and without a key.

Madam Tran left. He knew the next time she came back it would be with dinner, and the injection. He looked around now for any sort of weapon but couldn't find one. The bedstead was brass but too well secured for him to separate a rod from the frame. The wicker nightstand offered little; besides, its destruction might alert whoever came through the door. Surprise would have to be his weapon; he would make his break when the next person came through the door. Paul hoped it would be Madam Tran.

But four hours later, when the door opened, it was Helmut who came in. Paul pretended to be asleep.

"All right, come on." Helmut shook him roughly. "You want to piss or not?"

Paul allowed Helmut to help him up. The man, he noted, was dressed in a tuxedo and smelled like a flower garden, which explained why he had come in early. He was planning a night on the town and didn't want to do his chores at midnight.

Paul waited until Helmut had him almost on his feet, then abruptly stood up, catching the man's arm behind his back and twisting it around. Helmut grunted in surprise.

"You go first," Paul said quietly, then shoved up on the arm and pushed forward at the same time, forcing Helmut to lurch ahead. Moving faster and faster, his free arm flailing as he tried to get his feet under him, Helmut saw the wall and let out a cry. Remembering the indignity of the needle, Paul didn't let up. Bent forward at the waist, Helmut slammed headfirst into the wall and collapsed. As Paul stepped back, trembling from the exertion, there was a crash behind him. He turned to see Madame Tran in the doorway, the tray at her feet.

Paul started toward her but the woman was quicker than Helmut. She bolted back into the hallway and tried to slam the door. Paul just managed to thrust his arm into the opening and the door rebounded off his forearm, numbing his hand. Madam Tran shouted for help. Keeping her weight against the door, she grabbed Paul's index finger and bent it back. The pain acted as a catalyst and infused his weakened muscles with new strength. He shoved forward and burst through the door into the hall.

The force of his effort threw Madam Tran against the wall, and she quickly pulled a butterfly knife from the folds of her Bao Dai. With a quick flick of the wrist half of the thin handle pivoted in a circle and rejoined its mate, back-to-back now, exposing a long, shiny blade. She jabbed at his face, but it was more a feint than an attack and her eyes looked beyond Paul to the safety of the corridor beyond. She wanted out.

Paul was able to dodge the thrust, then deliberately stepped aside, offering the woman an apparent escape route. As her eyes shifted to the hallway beyond him, he kicked out at her hand and sent the knife flying. She tried to rush past but he grabbed her and for a moment the two of them grappled. Madam Tran was strong and wiry, and as he struggled to hold her Paul couldn't believe his own weakness. She tried to knee him in the groin and would have succeeded except that the long folds of the Bao Dai left her off balance. Paul swung her around and somehow managed to push her back into the room with enough force so that she fell to the floor. Before she could get up he slammed the door and slid the bolt home.

He paused for a moment to catch his breath. To his left, a short dark hallway led to an ancient, cast-iron door that was slightly ajar. He approached it warily. Behind him he could hear Madam Tran beating on the door and yelling. Fortunately the walls were thick enough to muffle the sound.

The iron door opened to a continuation of the same hallway, now carpeted and more brightly lit. Music and conversation drifted down a flight of stairs at the bottom of which were two doors, one labeled *Damen* and the other *Herren*. He was in the basement of the Vanilla Rose.

As Paul climbed the stairs, the air around his legs suddenly reminded him that he was still wearing a damn hospital gown. If Madam Tran hadn't showed up when she did he at least could have traded clothes with Helmut. Well, it was too late now . . .

His senses had been deprived for so long that entering the main room of the Vanilla Rose was like stepping into another world. The gaudy extravagance of the decor and the girls in their colored lingerie dazzled him. Sounds were too vibrant and loud, smells rich and pungent. People turned to stare as he crossed the room and some of the men hooted and laughed. "Tell her to give you back your clothes," one of them shouted happily.

Paul gave him a look that shut him up, for the moment anyway. He would have liked to find Otto Wenzler and happily wring his neck, but his muscles were already trembling and the blood was pounding in his head. Obviously his body was still recovering from the effects of the drug and what he'd been through these past few minutes.

* * *

Outside, it was just dusk, and the smell of fresh air was like a glorious discovery. Dressed as he was, like an escapee from a hospital, people gave him wide berth and he had to ask five times before someone finally gave him directions to the police station. As he walked there he planned what he would do . . . First, swear out a complaint against Otto Wenzler, then back to the hotel for a bath and a shave and a night's sleep. Would the police lend him money for a taxi? Maybe Ray Tregerdemain could help. In the morning he'd call Bernie and tell him why he'd disappeared. He'd also call Hugh Roark and tell him about Karl. All bets were off now. Karl had betrayed him.

Or had he? Karl could have killed him but he'd put him on ice instead. Paul also remembered what Karl had said about the CIA . . . that they would kill him if they found out or even seriously suspected he was responsible for their agents' deaths. Would they execute Karl if he turned him in? And if they did, could he live with the knowledge that he had caused his brother's death? Could he look his mother in the eye afterward? And wouldn't she find out? After all these years of guilt over abandoning Karl . . . Perhaps he could set up a meeting with Roark, feel him out about a deal—Karl's life in exchange for revealing his identity . . .

He was at the police station now, a stone building that looked like an armory. The lobby had high ceilings with corridors leading off in either direction and worn benches along one wall. The sound of a police radio echoed from a distant room. Behind a broad counter sat a policewoman in a sexless uniform of indeterminate green. She straightened up as Paul entered and hunched her shoulders forward when she saw what he was, and wasn't, wearing.

"It's all right," Paul told her, "I'm not crazy. Someone kidnapped me and I just got away. His name is Otto Wenzler and I want him arrested—"

"And who are you?"

"My name's Paul Stafford. I'm an American citizen. Wenzler's guilty of assault, battery, kidnapping—"

The mention of his name clearly interested her.

"You are Paul Stafford?

"That's right, you probably have a missing-persons report—"

Standing now, she brought a whistle to her lips and blew a loud, shrill sound. Paul assumed she was calling a squad to go after Otto Wenzler, but when the police came streaming out of the back room she pointed at him.

"Paul Stafford. He's the one—*Offizier* Dietrich."

Before Paul could explain, before he could even think, they had him up against the wall with his hands behind his back. He caught snatches of conversation . . .

"Who is he?"

"Stafford, remember?"

"He walked right in?"

"Look what he's wearing."

"Where'd he come from?"

"The one who ran down Dietrich."

"*He's* the one?"

It wasn't until they handcuffed him that Paul finally realized what was happening. And it wasn't until the next day that he actually believed it.

With George Lish's death the final stone in the foundation of the Redeye plot had been laid. Before Karl could dispose of the body, however, he had to apply Lish's fingerprints to pieces of incriminating evidence. In his earlier assassinations Karl never had had to deal with the bodies of his victims. Now it was necessary and he found the task distasteful.

He wrapped Lish's body in a plastic sheet and took it to the bathroom, where he placed it in the bathtub with the head next to the drain. After turning on the shower he cut the carotid arteries with a straight razor. When the blood had drained he carried Lish's corpse back to the stable and placed it on a worktable.

He steeled himself for what came next. In order to implicate the man he needed fingerprints. Karl locked the forearms in a vise and used a hacksaw to cut off each hand at the wrist. He forced himself to work as a butcher worked, treating the body as an inanimate object.

When it was done he put on his surgeon's gloves and, cupping the severed hands in his own, applied Lish's fingerprints to areas of the Winnebago that Lish hadn't touched: windows, cupboard, toilet, both sides of the skylight, the convex mirror, even the spare tire.

He did the same thing to the Redeye, pressing the lifeless fingers to all parts of the launching tube, to the batteries, the case, and the connectors. He paid particular attention to the circular battery receptacle, inside of which he placed the print of an index finger. He planned to do a poor job of wiping the missile clean, as if Lish had tried to conceal his identity, but this print would survive no matter how many others he obliterated.

Karl waited until nightfall, then buried the corpse in an out-of-the-way, heavily wooded part of the property. He knew that bodies were often discovered in what newspapers termed "a shallow grave," but these were usually last-minute expediencies resorted to by killers in a state of emotional turmoil. The graves were little more than depressions covered by dirt and pine needles. But a body four feet deep would never be found. And if the forest floor was left intact, the grave itself would not attract attention.

Karl prepared carefully. Before digging he took a shovel and lifted the topsoil in squares that he set to one side. Then he put down a plastic sheet and stacked the dirt on it as he dug the grave. Occasionally an axe was necessary to cut through a root but most of the time he worked with a pick and shovel. The work made him hot and the mosquitos made him irritable. By the time he finished it was after midnight.

He placed the body in the grave and filled it in, layered the surface slightly to compensate for the inevitable settling, then replaced the squares of topsoil and watered them. Finally he carried away the excess dirt and sprinkled it lightly over other areas of the property When he got back to the house it was two in the morning. His arms and back ached and he was hot, tired and dirty.

In the shower Karl stood with head bowed beneath the hot spray of water. His plans were completed. He knew the approach paths to Runways 01 and 19 at Andrews Air Force Base. He had chosen his launch sites, two for each runway, one primary and one alternate. He had the Sony-CIKOP-34F radio with which he could monitor up to three frequencies at once, including the Soviet select air-to-air frequency. And he had George Lish's signature on the Winnebago rental agreement and his fingerprints all over the motor home and the missile. He should have been pleased and optimistic; instead he was uneasy, restless.

Karl analyzed his feelings. It was not the revulsion over the disposal of Lish's body, and it was not the episode with

Rita Gaylord. These were matters of necessity and he accepted them as such. It was something else . . .

It was, he realized, and with some surprise, his role in the sabotaging of the Mutual Defense Treaty. As a German, Karl knew all too well how easily a country could be led to its own destruction while confident of victory. It had, after all, happened to Germany in 1939, and by 1945 Karl and his whole generation had begun to pay the price. He rarely troubled himself with political matters, but now, as so-called Summit Monday approached and the newspapers and magazines filled with details of the Mutual Defense Treaty, it was difficult to ignore the seriousness of what he was about to do. He tried to shut out the pro-treaty talk, but it was there all around him. He had to remind himself that Uncle Alex was still the finest man he'd over known. And above it all, that he *owed* Uncle Alex—owed him his life.

It was Friday morning and the General Secretary would not arrive until Monday. Karl was still restless. Wandering through the house, the notion of visiting Paul's house came back, and unlike his brief second thoughts about his mission, it would not go away. Even as he tried to talk himself out of it—it was a risk, after all—the idea took firm hold and he began making plans. He would make sure that Joanna wasn't home, enter secretly and stay for only an hour. If anything looked too dangerous, or felt out of place, he'd forget the whole thing.

As a precaution he called the Gallerie L'Enfant to make sure that Joanna was working. A woman answered. Adopting a nasal, tenor voice, Karl asked for Joanna Stafford.

"She's not in today," the woman told him. "Can I help you?"

"Actually, a friend in Chicago suggested that I ask her advice on some paintings. Do you know when she'll be back?"

"Friday and Saturday are her days off, but she'll be in on Sunday. Shall I give her a message?"

"My name's Dan Julian, but she doesn't know me. I'll stop in Sunday. Thank you."

Karl hung up before the woman could ask the name of his friend in Chicago. As he fingered Paul's house key, he briefly considered going over now. He could watch the house and wait for Joanna to leave on an errand. No, too dangerous. Even if she left the house there was no way of knowing how long she would be gone.

Curbing his impatience, Karl took the Kawasaki, drove to Chesapeake Bay and spent the day at the beach. Sunday morning would be soon enough to see how his brother lived his private life.

CHAPTER

22

NEWS OF PAUL'S ARREST SPREAD LIKE A GATH-
ering wave. The precinct captain in Neukoln called the
chief of police in Schoneberg who contacted the American
mission in Templehof who communicated the news to the
CIA's West Berlin section who relayed it to headquarters
in Langley, Virginia. Hugh Roark heard about it as he
returned from lunch. What surprised him most was the
report that Paul had walked into the police station and
given himself up. Indeed, Paul's escape from the hotel had
forced him to concede that his ability to analyze people
and predict their behavior had failed him. The false passports, the escape and the stolen limousine all served to
confirm Maurice's early evaluations, a fact the younger
man hadn't let him forget...

"You like the guy and you want to believe him. I've got
no feelings one way or the other so I see right through
him."

"I had the impression you didn't like him."

"I don't like him thinking he can make a fool out of me.
Otherwise I'm neutral."

Neutral or not, Maurice's prediction had been that Paul
would show up in Moscow, and Hugh needled him about
that on the flight to Berlin. "Probably a ploy, huh?"

Maurice, seated next to him working on a crossword
puzzle in the Pan Am Clipper magazine, looked up.

"What's that?"

"Giving himself up like that. Trying to get our trust, you
think?"

"He's not innocent, I know that much."

"Tricky, though. Walking into a police station wearing a
nightshirt. Very damn tricky."

Maurice gave him a black look and went back to his

puzzle. It was the Memorial Day weekend and he had canceled his holiday plans to go with Hugh after the news of Paul's arrest.

Hugh turned to the window. The Atlantic Ocean was obscured by clouds, but Hugh remembered the first time he'd flown this route in an Army C-47. It had been wartime then, the big one, World War II. But after V-Day came Korea and then Vietnam and all the while the cold war and the arms race and revolutions all over the place. And now, something new, the Mutual Defense Treaty with its technology to end all technologies.

Well, maybe so. He remembered a science fiction story in which a benevolent radiation belt enveloped the earth and neutralized all electrical current. That was all it affected, just electricity. The result was no radio or television, no automobiles, planes, space shuttles, computers, *and* no guided missiles. Just the steam engine, the gaslight and the horse and buggy. The nineteenth century preserved forever.

Wasn't that more or less what the Mutual Defense Treaty promised? A more enlightened, less restrictive version of the same scenario? American and Russain technologies in orbit, ready and waiting to pounce on any missiles launched in attack? But neither Star Wars nor the Nevsky technology would change human nature. It was the human factor that most interested Hugh Roark, not new technologies. And right now, that interest was concentrated on solving the riddle of Paul Stafford.

Larry Kincaid met them at the Tegel Airport. Kincaid, with the Berlin section, had a receding hairline, spoke in a soft voice and wore a Pierre Cardin suit and aviator's sunglasses. Hugh and Maurice had met him on their earlier visit and he looked happier then than he looked today.

"We can't keep the lid on this thing much longer," Kincaid told them as they left the terminal. "The police want to bring charges and the press is already nosing around. By tomorrow morning, the word's going to be out."

"Where is Stafford now?"

"In a holding cell at police headquarters in Schoneberg."

"Schoneberg?"

"It's the best we could do."

"Can't we get him in a safe house?"

"It's a civilian offense; the Germans want custody. If you knew the trouble we've caused already . . . the police don't like being told what to do by the Lord Mayor's office, the Lord Mayor hates being usurped by USCAB and USCAB is on our ass for making them play the heavy."

Hugh nodded. He was aware of the delicate relationship that existed between the local Berlin authorities and the United States Commandant, Berlin, known as USCAB. USCAB in person was a two-star general who was officially the ultimate legal authority in West Berlin. Over the years various protocols and accords specified the authority and jurisdiction of the police but in the end every German organization was subservient to USCAB.

An *Offizier* at Schoneberg led the three CIA men to an interrogation room with a table and four chairs and a bottled-water dispenser. A circular fluorescent light in the ceiling buzzed softly. The room had the bright, antiseptic feel of an operating room.

Maurice looked the room over. "Are we wired?"

Kincaid said, "A wall mike patched to a truck in the parking lot. Is Stafford the one who took out some of our guys?"

Hugh gave him a sharp look.

"Where'd you hear that?"

"You give and you get, you know how it goes."

Maurice and Hugh said nothing. Kincaid frowned. "Come on, Roark. I'm giving you backup. How do I bill the time?"

"You want the number?"

"I've got the number, I want the words. Is he the one?"

"He's a direct link," Hugh said. "How and why we still don't know."

Maurice tightened his lips and Hugh knew what he was thinking . . . Kincaid had no need to know. But Hugh remembered from his own experience the resentment of local-station personnel toward the covert action or special investigations boys who came in from Washington and ran cowboy operations without coordinating them locally. And Kincaid was right—they needed his help on this one. Give a little, get a little.

Paul was brought in, dressed in a gray prison uniform. He looked pale, drawn. When he saw them he seemed surprised.

"You guys?"

"Hello, Stafford."

"I asked for the American Ambassador."

"You got us," Maurice said.

"You going to get me out of here?"

Hugh said, "I want you to meet Larry Kincaid. He's with our Berlin section."

"I don't care if he's with the Berlin Circus as long as he can get me out of here."

"Take it easy."

"You take it easy. I've been kidnapped and drugged and arrested as soon as I escaped. I want out of here *now*."

"We don't have that kind of authority—"

"Bullshit."

Kincaid said, "He's right. You're being held by the West Berlin police, which means we have no jurisdiction over you."

"Don't give me that. This is an occupied city and the final authority is an American army general. You going to pick up the phone or not?"

He knows the political landscape, Hugh thought. If nothing else, Stafford's time in Washington had been good training in bullshit detection.

"Let's talk first," Hugh began.

"Let's get out of here first."

Hugh shook his head. "Can't do it, Paul. You know that."

Hugh's tone brought home to Paul the futility of insisting on his freedom until these men were convinced of his innocence... During the past twenty-four hours in jail he had pieced together the story of what happened at the InterContinental... that Karl had returned impersonating him, had been discovered with the false documents and had hurt a police officer in making his escape.

Hugh motioned to a chair. "Why don't you sit down and tell us everything that happened."

"How's this? George Lish is dead."

Paul expected some sort of reaction to the name but he was disappointed.

"Who?"

"George Lish. He's dead and I know who did it."

The men looked puzzled.

"Who's George Lish?" Hugh asked.

"Probably one of your boys. Don't you know?"

They stared at him, waiting.

"Or working for you. One of your assets."

Hugh turned to Maurice. "Know the name?"

"No."

He turned to Kincaid, who spread his hands and shook his head.

"Well, he's dead," Paul insisted.

"How do you know?"

"Two days ago I had another dream. Like the ones before, only this time his name was George Lish, a baby-faced guy, and I killed him with an ice pick. But it's no dream. I was receiving thoughts, direct impressions from the killer." Faced with the reality, there was no room for maneuvering, bargaining about Karl and keeping his identity secret for his mother's sake. For his *survival* he had to convince them of Karl's existence. "His name is Karl Alexander. My twin brother . . ."

"Twin brother?"

"That's what it's been all along," Paul said, pressing forward despite the expression of disbelief on the faces of the CIA men.

"That's why the dreams were so real. I've got a twin brother, and somehow I identify with him when he kills. Intense emotional excitement will—"

The cynical smile on Maurice's face made the anger and frustration of the past weeks boil over, and he moved toward the CIA man with clenched fists.

"I don't *need* this," Paul shouted. "You get out of here—"

"Keep your damn hands—" Maurice began.

Paul tried to grab him, Maurice pushed him off and for a moment they grappled before Hugh moved in and separated them.

"That's enough—"

"Get him out of here."

". . . no position to threaten anybody."

"I said *enough*."

Maurice moved back, smoothing his coat. Paul pointed to him and said, "He waits in the parking lot."

"Mr. Singer is part of the investigation—"

"Mr. Singer's got shit for brains."

Maurice colored. "Only shit for brains would believe some story about a twin brother."

"Talk to my mother, she'll tell you."

"We already did," Hugh said.

The anger left him. "You did?"

"Neither she nor your wife said anything about a twin brother."

"Joanna? You talked to her?"

"We talk to everybody," Maurice told him.

Hugh shot him a cautionary look and added, "We were trying to find you."

"Is Jo home? I want to call her—"

"Let's stay with this, first."

"I want to call my wife."

"So you can tell her what to say?"

"Will you get this asshole *out* of here?"

Hugh sighed and turned to his partner. "Maybe it's best you wait outside."

"You *believe* this crap about twins?"

"I don't know what to believe until I have a chance to hear his story. Neither do you."

"Excuse me," Kincaid said, "I don't want to appear stupid or anything, but what is it we're talking about here, dreams or murders?"

"I'll fill you in later," Hugh said. "Right now I want to hear more about Mr. Stafford's twin brother."

"Karl," Paul said. "His name is Karl Alexander, born Karl Weiss. You can find *anmeld* records up to February of forty-six that will list both of us."

"What records?"

Paul told them about the police registration procedures, but when he mentioned that *anmeld* records were in Pankow, Maurice gave a snort of disbelief. Hugh glanced at him and Maurice said, "Pankow's in the East."

"I know that," Hugh said testily, "I was here after the war." And then before Maurice could respond he turned to Kincaid. "Can we get a check on those records?"

Kincaid slid a hand inside his coat and produced a leather-bound note pad.

"There are ways," he said, and began making notes as Hugh returned his attention to Paul.

"All right, let's go back to the starting gate. What happened after you left Washington?"

Paul took a deep breath and began the story. He told them what he'd found out from his mother and why she had never admitted having Karl. When he got to the part about Ray Tregerdemain and the prostitute hitting him in front of the casino, he sensed a change in his listeners. Kincaid looked up from his note pad and Hugh exchanged a knowing look with Maurice.

"What's wrong?" Paul said.

"You say Ray Tregerdemain was with you?"

"That's right. He heard the girl's story. He can vouch for me."

"No, he can't," said Maurice. "He was killed about ten days ago."

"Killed?" Paul repeated dumbly.

"Reported as an apparent accident," Kincaid said. "At the zoo. He fell into the polar bear cage and either drowned or was mauled to death, the coroner couldn't determine which happened first."

Paul was stunned. Ray killed, in a zoo. The one man who could back up his story.

Hugh was asking a question. He forced himself to concentrate.

"When was the last time you saw Tregerdemain?"

"Saturday night," Paul said slowly. "The first day I got here. He went into the casino and I went to the Vanilla Rose. I was going to call him the next day—I *did* call him, but he wasn't home. I left a message and that's the last . . ."

He let the words trail off. The implications of Ray's death were all too obvious: Karl had found out about Ray and killed him. But how? How could Karl know? Had he told him? He thought back, trying to remember if he'd said anything about Ray to his new-found brother. They had talked about so many things, he couldn't recall mentioning Ray but he might have. And if he had, then *he* was responsible for Ray's death. The thought brought a sick feeling to his stomach.

"When did he die?" Paul asked. "What day?"

Kincaid answered immediately. "Monday night."

"About twelve hours after you escaped from the hotel," Maurice added pointedly.

Hugh held up a hand. "Easy."

"Pretty convenient accident—"

"I was not involved," Paul snapped. "I was drugged. For God's sake, I was a prisoner until the other day."

"Why don't you tell us what happened?" Hugh said quietly.

Paul got a drink of water from the dispenser and went on with his story, describing his visit to the Vanilla Rose and his meeting with Otto Wenzler. When he told them about the false passports, Hugh went to his briefcase, brought out the passports and opened them to the photos.

"You're saying this isn't you?"

"That's Karl."

Maurice and Kincaid crowded close, comparing the photos to Paul.

"The hair is different . . ."

"Just combed different."

"The lighting's kind of flat."

They kept glancing up at him and back to the photo. Paul felt the way he had when Annie Helms hypnotized him, like a freak of nature, a laboratory specimen.

"Can we finish this," he said. "I want out of here."

"All right," Hugh said, "you came back to the hotel and there was a message waiting. The message told you to go to a certain place the next day—"

"The Spree Bowl at noon."

"And your brother was waiting for you?"

"No, he phoned about ten minutes after I got there. He gave me instructions . . ."

As Paul told them about the meeting with Karl, Kincaid noted down the details: type of car, Karl's name, the Eichwalde Combat School, Treptow Park. As for Hugh, he was particularly interested in the name of the man who raised Karl.

"He wouldn't tell me," Paul said. "But I assume his name was Alexander."

"Alexander," Hugh repeated. "Was he Russian?"

"He didn't say, but I got the impression he was well connected, whoever he was."

"Where did Karl go to school?"

"He didn't say."

"You didn't ask?"

"No, I didn't ask. There were a thousand other things to talk about, we couldn't cover everything in one afternoon."

"But he's an instructor at the Eichwalde Combat School?"

"Yes."

"And he's married and has three children?"

"Yes. Wife's name is Magda. Children are Bridget, Katrina and Wilhelm." His journalist's conditioning to remember names helped.

Hugh turned to Kincaid. "Would you have a dossier?"

"Eichwalde?" He shrugged. "If we don't, military intelligence might."

"See what you can dig up."

Kincaid made a wry face. "It's Saturday."

"I know, but I'd like to confirm or deny the brother before the news breaks."

Kincaid folded his notebook. "All I can do is make the request."

"It's a white priority," Hugh said.

"Coded?"

Hugh nodded and Kincaid smiled ruefully. "A little more than a request, then. Be right back."

After Kincaid left Paul said he wanted to make some phone calls.

Hugh shook his head. "Let's finish here first—"

"Look, Roark. I just dropped off the face of the earth for two weeks and I want to let some people know what happened."

"They think you've gone underground to work on a story."

"Who does?"

"Your wife, your editor, your mother . . ."

"You told them I was working on a story?"

"You did. At least we thought it was you until . . ."

Maurice said, "It still might be him."

"What?" Paul demanded.

Hugh told him what Bernie Stern had told them: that Paul had called to say that he'd gone underground on an important story. The editor wouldn't give them any details. Maybe he should have, but Paul hadn't expected this, that Karl would impersonate him, appropriate his name and use his identity for his own purposes. Whatever the hell they were . . .

He began asking questions: What had Karl said to Bernie? How long ago? Had his brother called anyone else? Had he called Joanna? Or his mother?

"Not when we last spoke to them," Hugh said.

"When was that?"

"We did a routine call-back, what was it . . ."

"Three days ago, I think," Maurice said.

"Where's a phone? I want to find out."

"We don't have a secure phone," Hugh said.

"I don't care if it's secure or not as long as I can hear them and they can hear me."

"Well, I'm afraid we do care. Can you limit what you say to these people?"

"Meaning what?"

"Meaning no mention of Mr. Singer or myself or of the Agency or of the murders."

"I just want to find out if anyone else has heard from Karl."

"And I'll have to monitor the conversation."

"How about a urine test?"

They called the *Offizier,* who pretended not to understand Hugh's basic German. Paul interrupted and demanded a phone in brisk *Berlinerisch*. The *Offizier* stiffened and marched off to make the arrangements. A few minutes later he led them to what looked like an accounting office. There were neatly stacked ledgers behind glass-fronted shelves and two computer screens on two spotlessly clean desks.

The *Offizier* took his position just inside the door. Paul asked Maurice to wait outside.

Maurice glanced at Hugh, who said, "Why don't you check and make sure that George Lish isn't one of ours?"

"The *alleged* George Lish," Maurice grumbled as he left the room. After he was gone Paul motioned for the *Offizier* to shut the door, but nothing happened until Hugh nodded approval, at which point the man did as asked. Paul made the call collect. Hugh picked up a phone on the adjoining desk and listened.

Saturday was Joanna's day off but only the answering machine was at home. Paul's message was brief: "Jo, it's me. I'm in Berlin and I've got a lot to tell you. There's no number here so I'll call you later." He paused, then, "I miss you."

He waited in silence for seven seconds in the faint hope that she was listening and would pick up the phone. Then he heard the tape click off.

Maybe Joanna had switched schedules and was working. He called the gallery and got Denise, who told him what he already knew, that this was Joanna's day off.

"I don't expect her until tomorrow," Denise said in her deliberate aristocratic lilt.

Paul's next call was to his mother. She was happy and relieved to hear from him but worried about the reports of the hit-and-run incident in Berlin. She told him that "certain men" had been calling and asking questions about him.

"Are you in trouble? If you need any money..."

Evidently Karl hadn't called her. Paul considered warning her but decided against it. If Karl meant to get in touch with her, he would have done it by now. He hung up and dialed again while the *Offizier* complained to Hugh, who pretended not to understand German.

This one was to Bernie Stern, who was his usual sarcastic self when he came on the line.

"Damned good of you to contact us. Especially since the CIA knows about your arms-deal story and if you checked in more often you'd know they're hot to trot to find you."

"They already found me. I've got one of them right here."

Hugh gave him a warning look.

"Right where? Where are you?"

"I'm in Berlin. In jail. Now listen, Bernie, whoever phoned you last time wasn't me. Okay? We haven't talked since the day you sidetracked the Rockland-Birdwell story. That day in your office, remember? The man on the phone was my brother."

"You don't have a brother."

"Yes, I do. A twin brother. His name is Karl Alexander and he kidnapped me over here and he's been impersonating me in the States—"

"Oh, sure... what the hell are you trying to pull? No, let me guess. There's no story. You've been in bed for two weeks or sucking the sun in Acapulco. There's no CIA connection, no arms sales, no sources, no leads. Am I not perilously close to the truth?"

"Bernie, shut up and listen."

"Better be good, *real* good."

"How about a KGB assassin—"

Hugh waved at him but Paul plunged on without a pause.

"—how about a kidnapping and six—count them—six unsolved murders? How about someone trying to frame me? How does all that sound?"

"Like you're on drugs."

"No drugs, Bernie. This is mainline reality."

Bernie's voice took on a different tone as he considered the possibilities. "A KGB assassin you can actually identify?"

Hugh was looking at him. "Call him a three-letter assassin, Bernie. The phone's not secure."

"So who is this guy?"

Paul gave him an abbreviated, laundered version of what had happened and in return received the details of Karl's phone call. His brother's story about secret arms deals was obviously meant as an excuse for Paul's absence, but the reason for Karl's presence at the Military Ocean Terminal in Bayonne was a mystery. By the time they finished, the *Offizier* was making impatient noises and glancing at his watch.

Bernie had one last question. "Hey, if I believe you, how do I know this is you and not Karl?"

"Who else would tell you to go fuck yourself?"

"At least that makes sense . . . when are you coming back?"

"As soon as the triple-letter gentlemen spring me. I'll call you if and when I get in."

The *Offizier* escorted them back to the interrogation room, where they found Maurice and Kincaid bent over the table paging through an open file. When they looked up there was excitement in Kincaid's eyes but Maurice seemed in shock.

Hugh said, "What's the word?"

"Bonanza," Kincaid said. "We just got a file." And with a near-flourish he brought out an eight-by-ten black-and-white graduation photograph. College students stood on bleachers in front of a wall festooned with ribbons and a bas-relief portrait of Lenin. The students were separated by sex, men in lumpy suits on the outside and women in the center wearing floral-patterned dresses that looked as if they'd been cut from Depression-era window curtains.

Paul didn't need the typewritten identification tag to recognize Karl. His brother stood third from the left in the back row, his head lowered slightly, looking warily at the camera.

"There are three other photos," Kincaid said. "None very good. Stasis men don't like to have their pictures taken."

"Stasis?"

"Yes, it seems your brother was a member of East Germany's KGB counterpart. Nominally they're independent but they dance to whatever tune Moscow plays."

"And that's the magic KGB connection," Hugh said. "Which also proves that your dreams are . . ."

"Are real," Maurice finished in a stunned monotone.

The two of them looked at Paul with a mixture of fear and fascination usually reserved for circus freaks.

"I told you *that* a month ago," Paul said.

"You can really do that?" Maurice said. "I mean, read people's minds?"

"I had dreams," Paul said irritably. "It's not mind reading. Come on, you talked to Dr. Helms."

"I have dreams too, but not like that. Not where I can see what's going on in other people's heads."

"You don't have a twin brother."

Now Kincaid was confused. "Excuse me, but did I miss something here?"

The explanations began again, and Paul had to remind himself that these men were only now coming to terms with a phenomenon that he had been forced to acknowledge weeks ago. Hugh recovered more quickly than Maurice, who remained shaken and suspicious, not so much of Paul but of a world that had suddenly changed the rules and made possible something formerly impossible. Kincaid treated it first as a joke, then became apprehensive.

It took half an hour before Paul could return the conversation to the subject of his freedom. He wanted to get out of prison immediately but the CIA men told him that they didn't have the authority to release him. "We'll get you out," Hugh reassured him. "Just be a little patient—"

"You be patient. After you've been drugged and kidnapped and thrown in jail and haven't done a damn thing."

"The Berlin police still think you ran down one of their officers."

"So show them the picture. Prove that it was Karl. Get me the hell out of here."

"We'll get you out. Even if we have to call Washington and have them pull the right strings. Don't worry."

But Paul did worry. And with good reason. While the CIA men were busy pulling strings, he spent another rotten night in jail.

CHAPTER

23

THAT NIGHT, PAUL DREAMED OF RAY TREGER-
demain. They were standing on opposite sides of a swimming pool and Paul was reaching out, trying to hand Ray
fifty marks. They were separated by twenty or thirty feet
but still they leaned toward one another, hands outstretched,
until Paul slipped and fell into the pool.

In a dizzying shift of perspective he became an observer, standing behind Ray, and the man in the water was
Karl. Karl yelled for help, and Ray, thinking it was Paul
who was in trouble, jumped in to save him.

No, Paul yelled, but no sound came from his lips. He
could only watch as Ray swam to Karl, who had gone limp
and floated facedown, shoulders half-submerged. When
Ray got to him, he slipped his arm beneath Karl's shoulders and began swimming back toward shore. Paul watched
as they came toward him, Ray struggling through the
water, breathing in quick gasps with Karl's head, face
upturned and unconscious, resting on his shoulder.

As he approached, a terrible transformation took place.
Karl's eyes opened and a smile spread across his face. The
smile didn't stop but kept going, distending the features,
pulling back the cheeks and elongating the mouth and
nose until it became the snout of a huge polar bear with
glittering black eyes and blood-red lips.

Watch out, Paul screamed silently.

In the water Ray became aware of the transformation.
He turned, saw the bear and with a cry of terror released
his hold and pushed free. Trying to escape, he swam
frantically toward Paul. The bear rolled slowly, nosed
under the water and became a shifting pattern of refracted
white, moving beneath the surface, beneath the swimming
man. Paul extended his hand to help and Ray reached up,

but before their hands touched, huge white paws grasped Ray from below and pulled him under.

Paul's hand, still extended, now held fifty marks, the money he'd first offered Ray. Suddenly he knew that the only way to save Ray was to throw the money into the pool. The two forms were visible beneath the waves, rolling one on top of the other, white hair and pale flesh alternating beneath the roiling surface.

Paul threw the money into the water, shouting, *Take it, take it*. Instantly the bear disappeared; in the still water he watched Ray swimming upward, swimming toward him, hands clawing the water, bubbles escaping from his mouth, eyes wide, only now it was no longer Ray, it was—

In a flash of white Ray disappeared and the polar bear rose from the water with Jason's lifeless body clenched in its mouth . . .

Paul woke up and fell off the cot as he flung his arms up. He was drenched in sweat. The image of his son's body seemed to fade slowly, and it took a few minutes before he realized where he was. A guard appeared, blinking under the amber lights outside the cell.

"Was ist?"

Paul picked himself up and waved the man away. Alone, he sat shivering on the bunk, wrapped in a pale green blanket. The image of Jason, blue-skinned in death, was the one he remembered from the mortuary where he'd insisted on seeing his son's body, not embalmed or powdered but immediately, right away, the only way he could believe it. Paul had pushed that moment from his mind. He hadn't thought of it again until tonight, until the dream, where it was all mixed up with Ray Tregerdemain's terrible death.

You let him drown . . . The words came with a shock of recognition, they were the same ones he'd used with Joanna. *You let him drown,* he'd told Jo on the night that she'd come to talk about having another child. And now he had let Ray Tregerdemain drown—

But not in the same way, he silently protested. He couldn't have known that Karl would kill Ray. And yet he hadn't told Ray that they were dealing with a killer. He hadn't mentioned the dreams, hadn't protected Ray by letting him know the true situation. He'd made a mistake in judgment and Ray had paid the price. Just like Joanna. Jo . . . Not until now did he realize the full measure of her desolation. Not only from Jason's death, but from his turning away, his implicit condemnation. How many times had she come to him for comfort and in how many subtle ways had he let her know that no comfort was possible from him? When she blamed herself, he was silent. When she was silent, his correct but distant attitude accused her. All these months he had been punishing her for making their lives needlessly painful, something neither of them needed or deserved. If he had gone that weekend to Charlottesville . . . if he had told Ray Tregerdemain about Karl . . .

Suddenly he felt he *had* to talk to Joanna. He stood up, crossed to the door of the cell and called for the guard. When the man appeared Paul demanded a phone call. The guard, a young fellow with tiny eyes and bushy eyebrows, shook his head. "I have no authority for that; you go back to sleep." He hitched up his pants and returned to his office.

But Paul couldn't sleep. He spent the rest of the night pacing, his thoughts alternating among Joanna and Jason and Ray Tregerdemain. He hoped the CIA people would be there early and make good on their promise to spring him, but breakfast came and they still hadn't arrived. It wasn't until almost nine that he was led to a processing room where Hugh, Maurice and Kincaid waited.

"It's about time you got here," Paul said.

"It's the weekend," Hugh reminded him. "We had to call Washington and get people out of bed—"

"Yeah, life's tough in the big city. Let's go."

Kincaid said, "We have to wait for the man from the consulate."

"Who?"

"His name is Walsh, he's the only one who can officially receive you into custody."

"And he's got your temporary passport," Hugh added. "So we can get you back to the States."

"I want to make a phone call."

Hugh looked up with a frown, and seeing his expression Paul added, "Same rules as yesterday."

"Can't it wait?"

"It can; I can't. I've been up since four this morning. Let's go. Let's get something done."

Hugh sighed and turned to the others. "Let us know when Walsh arrives."

They returned to the same office they'd gone to the day before. Paul took one desk and Hugh another. It was after midnight in Washington, early on a Sunday morning. Joanna sounded sleepy when she picked up the phone.

"Hello?"

"Jo? It's Paul."

"Paul?"

"Sorry to call so late. Did you get my message the other day?"

"Umm. Are you still in Berlin?"

"I'm leaving as soon as I can. Listen, there's something I want to know. Forget how strange it sounds but when was the last time we spoke?"

"You know when."

"Please . . . have I called you since you left me the note?"

"It doesn't matter, Paul, I've got my own apartment. I'm moving out . . . We need some time apart. I do, anyway. I can't take the way we've been living so . . . I found a place near DuPont Circle."

"With someone?"

"No, Paul. Alone."

"I see . . . well, whatever you feel comfortable with," he said lamely. "We'll work it out . . ."

"I'm not making any hard and fast decisions," she said. "But I have to stop feeling rotten about myself, and I can't do that the way we've been. I'm not blaming you and I'm not blaming myself—I *can't* blame myself—but you do. I know you do, Paul, and maybe you've got a right to but I can't handle it. Can you understand that?"

"Sure . . ."

"I'm sorry, I didn't mean to tell you like this, but I spent a week alone, wishing I was dead and thinking about everything and . . ."

He could tell from her voice that she was close to tears.

"It's all right, Jo."

Her breath caught and then, in a flat voice, she said, "I wish it was."

He wanted to be with her, to hold her, to feel her

arms around him, to tell her what he felt and finally understood, or at least was beginning to understand. He wanted to tell her that he was sorry; but with Hugh pretending not to listen and the German policeman at the door all he said was, "Whatever's right, that's what we'll do. We can talk when I get back, okay? You're going to be there?"

"When are you coming back?"

"Tonight or tomorrow, it depends."

"You don't have to come back on my account," she said stiffly. Then, aware of the hint of hostility in the response, she added more gently, "Sorry."

"Jo, listen, there's something you should know. This is going to be a lot to take at once, but I've got no choice . . . A couple of weeks ago I found out I've got a twin brother. His name is Karl Alexander and he lives here in Berlin. That's why I came over here."

"But you never—"

"I know. I mean, I didn't know. Mom thought he died right after the war so she kept it secret. But you know those nightmares I have?"

"Where you think you kill someone?"

"Right. Well, it seems that those weren't nightmares after all. Just before you left a couple of people from the"—Hugh glanced up—"a certain organization convinced me that those nightmares really happened. I didn't believe it, Jo, but it's true. The obituaries of those same people— their names, anyway—are in newspapers. You can look them up, see for yourself."

"*What* are you saying?"

"Karl works for a foreign government, he's an assassin and he's in the United States. At least he was ten days ago. He even called Bernie and impersonated me—"

"That wasn't you?"

"I've been in Berlin since the day after you left."

So much had happened, Paul realized. The last time they had talked was the night that she'd told him about Luis de Cuevo—the same day that the CIA men had come to him, the day he'd discovered that the death-dreams were real. And he'd never told her. He'd withdrawn from her, as if she were unworthy of knowing what was happening in his life. Talking to her now, it was as if they were strangers again—or getting acquainted again. There was so much about each other that they no longer knew.

At first, like the rest, she was incredulous. Then, as the details of the situation became real, so did the implications of what he was saying. "That's why you asked when we last talked? You thought he might call *me*?"

"I don't know what he might do. All I know is that he's very dangerous and he's impersonating me."

"You're scaring me now, Paul. This isn't funny."

"I know. Listen, do you think you could find someplace to stay for a few days? Maybe ask Denise or go to your parents."

"Does he really look exactly like you?"

"I've got somebody here who could tell you."

Hugh looked up in surprise as Paul offered him the phone, then waved him away.

"Somebody who's helping me find Karl. Until we do..."

"Well, I do have this new apartment."

"Good." He thought of suggesting she get the Smith & Wesson revolver that he kept in a file cabinet but decided against it. After all, Karl's appearance in New York had been almost two weeks ago and whatever his business was it had nothing to do with Joanna. If anything, he would want to avoid her and anyone else who might recognize him as an imposter.

"I'm probably overreacting," Paul said, trying to reassure both of them, "but better safe than..."

Kincaid stepped into the room and announced that the consular representative had arrived. Paul took down the address of the new apartment and told Jo he'd leave word at the gallery when he was coming back.

Just before they hung up he managed to say what she hadn't heard from him in a very long time. "I love you, Jo."

There was a moment's hesitation. Then, "You're a funny man," she said seriously.

After she hung up Joanna sat cross-legged on the bed. What Paul had said about Karl Alexander worried her as much as his sudden warmth confused her. Two weeks ago his reaction to her affair with Luis de Cuevo—his total, and depressing, lack of anger or jealousy, his cold, unemotional lovemaking had, she thought, told her how little she meant to him. Her brief betrayal had seemed to prove what she most feared, that there was nothing left to betray. And yet, a few moments ago he had told her that he loved her with such conviction that it was impossible to doubt he meant it.

The familiar creak of a tree branch rubbing against the roof startled her. She slipped on a robe and went downstairs and checked each of the doors to make sure they were locked. The empty house felt threatening now... She imagined this new-found brother Karl outside somewhere in the yard, watching. She shut the blinds, pulled the curtains and turned on the radio. Her emotions in a turmoil, she made coffee and sat at the kitchen table seriously wondering for the first time since she'd returned from Maine if she was doing the right thing...

Joanna had died in Maine—that's how she'd thought of it. She had gone to her family's summer cabin for escape, oblivion, release from a dead heart, a dead marriage. The cabin sat at the tip of a narrow peninsula thrust into Penobscot Bay, a single-story rambling structure with a high peaked roof and screened-in porch on tall bluffs overlooking a rocky shoreline and tumultuous ocean. A local handyman usually opened the cabin but Joanna had not contacted him. When she arrived the windows were shuttered, the screens on the porch boarded up and the electricity off. She opened the cottage herself, hoping that the physical labor would somehow relieve the pain. She released the shutters and latched them open and removed the protective sheets of plywood from the porch screens, getting splinters in her palms. She figured out how to turn on the water and electricity, then cleaned the house, sweeping up the dead bugs, washing the refrigerator, airing the bedding.

These routines soothed her some and she managed to sleep pretty well the first night. When she woke up, though, the memory of what had happened with Paul was too much for her. She pulled out the old trunks and began going through them, looking at memorabilia from her childhood, searching for the little girl who'd gotten lost somewhere along the way. But one trunk wasn't hers—it was Jason's. It held his summer toys—the Tick-Tock book, He-Man, Loomis the stuffed dog with its stitched ear. She'd forgotten about them. In Washington they had given

Jason's things to Goodwill and turned his bedroom back into a guest room. Seeing his toys at the cabin brought back too-painful memories: she remembered every toy and how it had come to Jason, the exact occasion. She even remembered the design on the wrapping paper she'd used on some of the Christmas gifts.

The tears came and offered a sort of relief, but one that left her exhausted. She drove to Camden, where nobody knew her, and bought a few cans of Campbell's Hearty Dinners and a case of scotch. Drinking steadily, she courted alcoholic oblivion for days. At some deeper level she realized that she was asking from herself what she felt she'd failed to get from Paul—*attention*. Did she care? Did she care about herself, about anything at all?

The photographs on the mantel above the fireplace showed each of the four generations as children, each one seated on an oddly shaped rock they called Breadloaf: her grandmother, her father, Joanna, and Jason. Each child had been between two and four when the photo was taken. They were a family tradition, and they pierced her heart. Jason's smile, trusting and confident, accused her. Paul's eyes accused her. Her own heart accused her.

She forced the scotch down until she got sick, lay down on the floor and slept for twelve hours.

When she woke up it was an overcast day, raw and windy and cold and she decided to end it, end herself. The decision filled her with a strange exhilaration. She dumped the contents of her father's trunk onto the floor and found his .22 revolver. The gun was unloaded but with it there were two boxes of bullets, one full and one with just a few shells. Selecting the cleanest bullets from the unopened box, she loaded three of the six chambers, every other one. Modified Russian roulette. She would let the fates decide if she was fit to live or not. She no longer could.

The mechanics of what she was about to do gave her momentary pause. If she died in the cabin, who would find her? And after how long? The idea of leaving a mess for someone was distasteful, so she put on a yellow slicker and went outside, where she stood on the bluff overlooking the sea. Forty feet below, the waves crashed against jagged rocks surrounded by angry foam. The tide was just past full, which was good. If she fell, her body would be washed out to sea.

Cold rain and fear made her teeth chatter. She brought the gun from beneath the folds of her slicker. Did bullets fire if they were wet? She didn't know, but she resolved to do this quickly. Holding the gun firmly, she rotated the cylinder, two, three, four times. There was a fifty-fifty chance of a loaded cartridge. Or an empty cylinder.

As she raised the gun and put the barrel in her mouth . . . she began to cry. It was silly, hysterical crying. She felt stupid standing there with the cold metal barrel between her lips so she switched positions and put the barrel to her temple but the tears continued, warm against her rain-soaked cheeks. She could see herself standing there, leaning over the cliff, so melodramatic, so absurd. And she at least knew she didn't want to die.

She moved the gun away from her head, pointed the barrel down at the angry waves and then, about to pull the trigger, she changed her mind. Her hand went around the barrel of the gun, and she threw it as far out as she could into the sea.

"Not my fault," she called after it. "It's not my fault, goddamn it."

Shaking from more than cold, she returned to the cabin and gathered Jason's toys and summer clothing. Each armful she took to the bluff and threw the articles into the sea, one by one. She worked in feverish haste but her mind was clear and she knew what she was doing. After Jason's things came the scotch. She grabbed all the bottles, empty as well as full ones, and threw them into the sea as well.

Back in the cabin, she was shivering so violently that she had difficulty lighting a fire, fingers so numb she could hardly hold the match. Finally the newspaper caught and after a few moments the warmth began to spread across the room. She stripped out of her wet clothes, toweled dry and pulled the blankets off the bed. Wrapping them around her, she sat on the floor close to the fire, staring into the flames. Gradually the trembling stopped.

That night she slept on the floor, curled up with cushions like an animal in its lair. When she woke up eighteen hours later she was no longer the same person, no longer the little girl on Breadloaf rock with fairytale dreams, no longer the young woman in the Ethiopia scrapbook who stood facing the camera with a self-confident smile while somber-eyed Africans looked on. And no longer the bride whose marriage was to be a real-life adventure played out against an exotic, fast-track world of journalism. When she woke up Joanna was a woman who hadn't been able to save her child, who was estranged from her husband, and whose feeling of special dispensation hadn't made her immune from life's natural disasters, after all.

She returned to Washington, considerably saddened but more secure in this new knowledge of herself. She could, she felt, go on from here even if she had to go on alone. She was unsure of how Paul would react to her decision to find an apartment but certain that it was the right thing to do. His two-week absence only reinforced how he felt—or didn't feel—about her...

Now, as Joanna sat at the kitchen table cradling her cup of coffee, she seriously wondered if she'd been hasty. On the phone Paul had seemed so genuinely warm and caring, so different from the way she remembered. *I love you*, he had said. For the first time since...she couldn't remember. Before the accident, probably. Ironic if after everything she'd done to try and please him that her decision to leave had done what no amount of being stoic and guilty could do—

A noise outside the kitchen window startled her and she jumped, spilling hot coffee on her fingers. She put down the cup and shook her hand to cool it. The sound was the branch of a tree rubbing on the outside wall, a familiar sound now made ominous by Paul's warning. She wished she knew more about this brother of his. Was he some kind of madman? A nut? The vision of someone sneaking around outside sent her upstairs to Paul's study to get the gun from a locked filing cabinet.

Crazy, she thought as she climbed into bed and put the gun in the drawer of the night table. There was a hollow clink as the metal touched the glass. Joanna reached beneath a silk scarf and found a pint of Chivas Regal, half full, or half empty...She recalled putting the bottle there during some distant past life, but the memory was dim, more like remembering something she'd been told by someone else.

She slept restlessly, woke up at dawn and then, comforted by the new daylight, slept soundly for three more hours.

When she got up she called the owner of the new apartment and made arrangements to move in that day. Then she called Denise at the gallery and begged off work.

At ten o'clock, she left to get some packing boxes. She paid no attention to the silver-and-burgundy Lincoln Continental parked at the end of the block or to the man inside who averted his face as she passed and then watched her in the rearview mirror until she disappeared around the corner.

CHAPTER

24

AFTER WATCHING JOANNA LEAVE THE HOUSE, Karl drove to a pay phone and called to make sure no one else was there. When he heard the answering machine he hung up. What he was about to do was dangerous, he knew. His background, his training, his instincts all warned against this, but he was powerfully drawn to his brother's existence, as though it were part of his own . . . He had this compulsion to see how Paul lived, how *he* might have lived had their positions been reversed and he had been the one to get sick and Paul been left with Tante Inge. A tiny microbe had changed the course of their lives; he wanted to compare the result. He needed to know. He *deserved* to know.

He did not park on the same street as the house. He left the Lincoln a block away, behind Paul's house. There would be less likelihood of someone connecting him with the car, and if he had to leave quickly he could slip out the back door and cross a neighbor's yard. He had decided against a disguise. A stranger entering the house might cause suspicion, but what could be more natural than Paul Stafford entering his own house? At most he might have to exchange a cursory greeting and he felt confident he could do this. He'd fooled the CIA men.

It was warm and damp as he made his way toward Paul's house. A gang of children played at one end of the street and a man with his back to him was weeding his lawn just two houses away. Karl casually opened the low wrought-iron gate and walked up to the house. He got to the front door without being noticed. The first key didn't work—a back-door key or maybe the key to Paul's office—but the second one slid easily into the lock. Once inside he paused to listen, to smell the air, to let the feel of the place sink in.

The house seemed smaller than it looked from the outside, but by East German standards it was still palatial. There were rooms to either side and a flight of stairs directly in front. As he walked the ground floor it struck him that the house was not so much decorated as arranged. Chairs, tables, lamps, artwork—each piece seemed chosen for itself rather than to fit with a design, yet the effect seemed harmonious.

In the kitchen he reviewed his escape route. There were three doors: one to the cellar, one to the back yard and a third to the garage. Inside the garage he found an Audi. Paul's car, he knew. He had the key on the same ring as the others. The Audi was white, the same as his Mercedes, but it was not a Mercedes, which gave Karl a small satisfaction... He had begun to envy his brother's life and it pleased him that his own car was superior.

Upstairs there was a large bathroom and four other rooms: a master bedroom, guest room, office and an artist's studio that looked as if it were in the process of becoming a storage room. He went first to the bedroom. The bed was loosely made, an empty cup with coffee residue sat on a night table. Beside it was a pint of scotch, Chivas Regal, half full. He licked his finger, rubbed it in the bottom of the cup and tasted it. There was no hint of liquor. Did the woman drink in bed? To help her sleep? To drown her sorrows?

A classified section from a newspaper lay on the floor beside a yellow pad, both sandwiched between the bed and the night table. The newspaper had apartment listings, some of which were circled in red; on the yellow pad were brief descriptions and phone numbers. Karl smiled. The impression he'd gotten from Paul was correct; his wife, Joanna, was leaving. She drank herself to sleep. His brother's life was not so ideal as it seemed.

He replaced the newspaper and pad, opened the drawer to the night table and found a gun. Loaded, and on her side of the bed, the side with the scotch bottle on the night table. Which meant what? That Joanna was afraid of prowlers while Paul was away? Or could it be Paul she was afraid of?

Karl was intrigued. Paul's description of Joanna had not

hinted at this. Scotch and coffee in bed, a search for a new place to live and a loaded gun close at hand. Karl tried to recall what Paul had told him . . . Joanna had been involved in famine relief when they met—a humanitarian cause— but now she worked in an art gallery in a world of egoism and cultural snobbery. More contradiction. Which meant . . . a woman who didn't know herself? And looking to find out? The sort of self-questioning that was all over the magazines these days . . .

There was a photograph on the dresser that showed Paul and Joanna on a sightseeing boat on the Seine. They stood at the rail with Notre Dame in the background. Karl picked up the photograph and stared at Joanna. She was smaller than Magda, with jet-black hair and blue eyes the color of the distant sky. Her smile seemed eager, looking ahead. To what dreams? He couldn't, of course, know. But he did know such people could often be duped by offering them their own dreams.

Satisfied that he had discovered an important clue to Joanna's personality, Karl continued his inspection, going through the dresser drawers, noting that Joanna was more casual with her clothing than Paul and that her lingerie was more delicate and stylish than Magda's. From the closet he took a brown tweed man's jacket and tried it on. The fit was perfect. He found a black silk dress and held it up, imagining Joanna inside it, imagining the two of them together, just as in the photograph. If he wanted to he could slip into his brother's life as easily as he put on his jacket—

The doorbell rang and the illusion shattered.

Quietly Karl replaced the dress and closed the closet door. He crossed the hallway to the office, which overlooked the front yard. Positioning himself to one side of the window, he peered out. Whoever was at the door was beneath him, obscured from view, but there was a power lawnmower on the front walk that hadn't been there when he arrived. Now a boy stepped into view, about twelve years old, wearing threadbare jeans with holes in the knees and an oversize baseball jersey. As Karl watched, the boy bent over the lawnmower, adjusted the throttle, pulled the starting cord and the engine roared into life, destroying the quiet of a Sunday morning.

Karl frowned. With the boy out there he couldn't leave

unnoticed through the front door. Still, he had been fortunate . . . it could have been a cleaning lady or someone with keys to the house. Besides, it wouldn't take the boy long to mow the lawn, ten or fifteen minutes. He should be gone by the time he was ready to leave.

Karl turned his attention to the study, the room to give him the clearest picture of his brother's life. On the walls were plaques and certificates, framed news stories and photographs of Paul on assignment all over the world, from the jungles of the Philippines to the Antarctic, where he stood in a fur-lined parka with another man, both of them surrounded by penguins.

A desk of oiled teak held a Zenith personal computer, a Rolodex and a stack of bills that must have come while Paul was gone. Someone, probably Joanna, had written Paul's name and beneath it a list of names and telephone numbers of people who had called and left messages on the machine. It was difficult for Karl to believe that anyone knew that many people or that his brother was comfortable being *known* by that many people. When Karl was a child his greatest desire was to be invisible. He could remember hearing Tante Inge—Frau Heusner, he corrected himself—returning home at night. He would shut his eyes, hoping that this would make him invisible, hoping that if he couldn't see her, she couldn't see him.

Going through the desk drawers Karl found a box of blank checks and was struck by an odd idea. But the more he thought about it the more it appealed to him. He took out the wallet he had taken from Paul and studied his brother's signature on his driver's license. The handwriting was remarkably similar to his own. He practiced Paul's signature on a blank piece of paper, and when he had it right he opened the bills on the desk and began making out checks: electricity, gas, Visa, American Express, Woodward & Lothrop—he smiled as he thought of Paul's confusion when he discovered the bills had been paid. Paul might guess who was responsible but could never prove it. And who would care? What law had been broken? What harm had been done . . . ?

Karl was so involved in what he was doing that he didn't notice that the variable whine of the lawnmower had sunk to a steady idle, and when the front door opened it took him completely by surprise.

The sound of voices reached him, a woman and a boy. "Just stack them there, that's all right."

"What about that branch? I can cut it down easy."

"I think we better leave it for the professionals, Danny."

"I can do it easy. My dad's got a chain saw, a Black and Decker."

"Then you ask your dad and see what he says."

"Okay."

During the interchange Karl moved swiftly and quietly. No time now to wonder why Joanna had returned early or if she had gone to work at all. He had to leave this house without being discovered. If he could make it to one of the rooms at the rear of the house he could slip out a window, drop to the ground and leave through the back yard.

He returned the checkbook and the bills to the drawer, moved into the hallway just as the front door shut. Too late. Footsteps on the stairs accompanied by the hollow bump-bump of a cardboard box. If he crossed the landing, Joanna would see him. He slipped back into the office and stood behind the door, from where he had a view of the hall into the bedroom.

Joanna appeared then, carrying one cardboard box and dragging another. She took them both into the bedroom and stood for a moment catching her breath. She wore khaki shorts and a red sweater with sleeves rolled to the elbows. As Karl watched she began packing her clothes, from time to time disappearing into the closet.

He considered the options. The stairway began between the two back rooms and was surrounded by a railing. To escape he would have to make his way around the railing and go halfway down the stairs before he was out of sight of someone in the bedroom. Joanna's forays into the closet wouldn't give him sufficient time, he would have to wait until she went downstairs. And then another possibility as the sound of the lawnmower chugged to a stop. The boy had apparently finished the front yard. Karl waited for the doorbell to ring. When nothing happened he made his way to the window. At one point wood creaked beneath his feet and he froze. The sound of Joanna packing continued without interruption. He reached the window and looked out. The boy had disappeared—he would try to get out the front way.

The window was one of the old, double-sash variety

with a movable lower pane. As he unlatched it the sound of metal grating on metal made him wince, but the sounds from the bedroom at least reassured him that Joanna was still busy packing. Placing the heel of his palm against the frame, Karl pushed. Nothing happened. Why couldn't brother Paul live in a modern home with aluminum frame windows? Wasn't this America, all shiny bright and new? And then he heard Joanna coming across the landing toward him. He had just enough time to step back against the wall—and then she was in the room. And he had no place to hide.

Without glancing his way, Joanna crossed directly to the desk, opened a drawer and took out a roll of tape. Her back was to him, but if she gave the room so much as a cursory glance she couldn't help but see him. He fought the urge to crouch, to shrink, to flatten himself against the bookcase behind him. He remained still, barely breathing, willing himself to be invisible just as he once had as a child.

Joanna took the tape and left without glancing his way.

As soon as she was gone a tremor ran through his body and the adrenaline made him dizzy. When he heard Joanna in the bedroom, he quietly returned to his position behind the door and looked out.

He saw her kneeling on the floor, taping the box. Outside the house, in the back yard now, the lawnmower buzzed into life. Good. The noise would cover any sound he might make trying to get the damn window open. He took a step toward the window, then realized that the lawnmower would also cover the sound of Joanna's return if she decided to put the tape back in the drawer. No, he thought, stepping back, better to wait and see what she did next.

He watched through the narrow opening. After taping the box Joanna pushed it into the hallway. He expected her to start packing the next box but instead she went to a linen closet and tried to get something from the top shelf. When she couldn't reach she stepped precariously up on the bottom shelf and managed to grab a small nylon bag, but in pulling it down, a number of boxes tumbled out, raining down on her head.

"Shit," she said, jumping back.

She rubbed her eye, evidently trying to clear it of

something. Shaking her head and blinking, she went into
the bathroom. All right, this was his chance. When he
heard the water running, he moved swiftly onto the landing. All he needed was a moment to get downstairs, then
exit by the front door.

As he passed the partially open door of the bathroom he
could see Joanna bending over the sink.

Don't look up, he thought. Otherwise...

The floor creaked, but the sound of the running water
masked his footsteps. And then he was beyond the doorway, out of sight. It took him an extra moment to step
around the box she had left at the top of the stairs—as he
did the phone rang.

He took two quick steps downstairs and then the water
stopped and he froze. He wanted to make a run for the
door but remembered how badly the stairs creaked. Any
abrupt movement would get her attention. The bathroom
was closer to the office, so she could answer the phone
there. If he kept still she wouldn't see him, unless she
came back to the bedroom.

Which is what she did.

She was toweling one side of her face and was about to
enter the bedroom when she lowered the towel and saw
him. He had turned around to face upward so that from
her perspective it would look as if he had just arrived and
was coming upstairs. When she caught sight of him, she
jumped, then seemed to relax.

"Paul! My God, you—"

She doesn't know, he realized. *She doesn't know*...

"I didn't mean to scare you," he said as calmly as he
could. *Play it out*, nothing else to do except—

"With all the racket I didn't hear—"

And then her expression changed and her eyes widened
and he thought, she knows. And not only that he wasn't
Paul. Her expression shifted again as confusion seemed
replaced by fear. She knew who he was; *she knew he was
Karl*.

The phone was still ringing as they faced each other on
the stairway, neither wanting to admit what he knew to the
other. Awkwardly, the game of deception went on.

"I can't stay," Karl said, knowing as he did that this
probably wasn't going to work. "I just came to get some
notes ..."

Joanna fought to get control of herself. She gestured weakly toward the office. "Go ahead."

"Aren't you going to get the phone?"

"You can get it."

She backed up to give him room, pressing her shoulders against the wall. Karl came upstairs slowly, and as he did there was a click and the recorded message began: "This is Paul and Joanna Stafford. We're not available right now but if you leave your name and number we'll get right back to you."

Karl was barely aware of the tape. His eyes were on Joanna's, and although he kept his expression pleasant, he was thinking: How could she know? How could she know who he was? Unless Paul had lied to him and had told her before he left. Or had she talked to his mother and his mother had told about him? Or—or just possibly Paul had escaped and she'd spoken to him.

And that would account for the fear in her eyes.

He stopped at the top of the stairs. As the message concluded, a beep announced the caller...

"This is Shiela Burney for Joanna Stafford. You can pick up the key from our office anytime after noon today, which is Sunday. Thank you."

At the sound of the voice Joanna said numbly, "It's for me."

She moved to enter the bedroom but he put up his arm, blocking the way.

"Why are you afraid?"

"Paul..." the word was strained.

"No." He smiled. "You know, don't you?"

"The phone..."

She tried to duck under his arm but he thrust his leg forward, blocking the bedroom door. She stepped back, staring at him.

"Let the machine get it."

"Okay." She smiled but Karl caught the quick hard glint of decision in her eyes and a moment later she was running across the landing to the office. He went after her and got to her just as she put her hand on the phone. He slammed his hand over hers before she could lift the receiver.

"How did you find out?" he said quietly.

The answering machine clicked off.

"Find out what?" Her voice was a whisper.

But Karl was looking at the answering machine... He hadn't played back the tape. Now he reached over and flicked the playback switch, and as he did Joanna ran out the door, slamming it behind her. Karl, assuming she was headed downstairs, followed quickly, ready to leap the railing and intercept her on the stairway. Instead she rushed into the bedroom and slammed the door, and he knew immediately what she was after.

Following her into the room, he saw Joanna was digging in the night table for the gun. In two quick strides he reached her as she turned, gun in hand. Cocked, too, he noted with some surprise. As he grabbed the revolver he made certain that his thumb was between the hammer and the cylinder, and the hammer snapped painfully against his thumbnail. She really would have shot him, he realized.

Joanna was strong, fear pumping her adrenaline as they careened around the room. The night table overturned and the coffee cup and scotch and a lamp went crashing to the floor. She let go of the gun and broke away and ran to the window, where he caught her from behind. She slammed an elbow at his chest as he lifted her, and as he swung her around her foot struck the window and the glass shattered, letting in the angry whine of the lawnmower.

He pushed her to the bed, held the gun to her head. "Stop now. Don't make me kill you."

She froze. Outside, the sound of the lawnmower chugged to a halt.

"Mrs. Stafford?" the boy called. "What happened?"

Joanna's eyes shifted from the gun to the window, and Karl understood what she was thinking. "If you say something you will both die."

She hesitated.

"Look at me," Karl demanded. "I will kill you first and him second. He will not get out of that yard."

Her resistance collapsed. She bit her lip and nodded.

The boy called again, "Mrs. Stafford? Are you okay?"

Karl stepped away from the bed but kept the gun trained on her. He motioned to the window. "Tell him it was an accident. Tell him you're fine. Get rid of him. Go ahead, do it."

Keeping her eyes on him, she stood up. Broken glass crunched underfoot as she made her way to the window.

Karl stepped close to the wall so that he could watch her face without being seen. Joanna gave him a glance, then, applying a smile, peered out.

Danny was looking up at her, squinting against the sun and bright sky.

"What happened?"

She took a deep breath. "I stumbled when I was moving the boxes, Danny. It's okay. Are you done yet?"

"Did you cut yourself?"

"No I . . . I hit the window with a box. The yard looks real good, Danny."

"Yeah, I'm almost through. You want me to put the glass in the trash can?"

"That will be fine."

As Karl motioned her back to the bed, the damage already done, the full extent to which the Redeye mission had been compromised, began to sink in. It was not so much what Joanna knew about him that worried him but how she knew . . .

As for Joanna, now that she was over the initial shock, she began to collect and even reassert herself.

"What do you want here?"

"Allow me to ask the questions. Who told you about me?"

She looked at the gun. "What are you going to do?"

"I am going to try and save your life, just as I saved your husband's life. But I won't be able to if you refuse to cooperate. Once more, how do you know about me?"

"You didn't save his life, you made him a prisoner, you—"

Karl's hardened expression stopped her. He felt a burst of anger toward Otto. Not only had he paid five thousand dollars, he had provided the Haloparimine, a powerful Stasis-developed sedative sufficient to keep Paul disoriented and weak as a kitten for months. How was it possible that his brother could escape? Goddamn you, Otto . . .

"When did you talk to him?" he said to her.

Joanna glanced at the gun, then back up at his face, studying him. "You're Paul's brother. Would you really kill me?"

"If I have to."

She stared a moment longer, then folded her arms and just sat there, as though daring him to do his worst. She decided cooperating would buy her nothing, only increase *his* options. Of course she had not had Paul's dreams.

Karl knew he could get the information out of her. He could grab her by the neck and stick the gun in her mouth, terrorize her into talking. But as a professional he knew that terror carried its own risks, that it could release hidden forces and produce unexpected results. Joanna might well become hysterical, alert the boy in the yard, or she might become so crazy he would be forced to shoot her. It would be less risky at the safe house on the Toons Creek property. Whether she talked or not, he could not leave her here.

He moved to the dresser, opened the drawer and pulled out a pair of socks and a handful of pantyhose. Joanna began to object, and then a new look came over her face as she realized that he knew exactly which drawer they were in. At his approach, she drew back. He motioned with the gun.

"Face down on the bed."

"Wait. If you leave now—"

Karl smiled. "If I leave you will be a good lady and not say a word? Please..." He realized it was dangerous to take her, but far more dangerous to leave her. The easiest way was to kill her, but until he knew how much of a threat his brother had become, Joanna would better serve as a hostage.

In the back yard the lawnmower came noisily to life. The boy must have finished picking up the glass. No longer needing to worry about noise, Karl slipped the gun into his pocket, took hold of Joanna by the shoulders and pushed her face down onto the bed, muffling her scream. Sitting astride her back, he wadded a sock into a ball and stuffed it into her mouth, then used a pair of pantyhose to gag her. He tied her hands and feet and bound her in a fetal position by looping a pair of pantyhose around her neck and running it between her knees to her ankles. When he was finished he wrapped her in a blanket and carried her downstairs to the garage. He put her on the floor, opened the trunk of the Audi and after spreading the blanket inside lifted her into the trunk. He closed it and returned to the kitchen—

A knock at the back door...the boy, Danny, stood there, peering in. Karl stepped back but it was too late.

Danny had already seen him. Nothing to do now but play out the charade. He stepped back into the kitchen and went to the door where Danny waited.

"Hi, Mr. Stafford. I didn't know you were home."

"I came in last night. I was asleep."

"I'm all done, I even cleaned up the glass—"

"Good." Karl forced himself to survey the yard. "It looks very good."

The boy stood there, and Karl finally realized he was waiting to be paid. How much? Perhaps he could phrase it ambiguously and Danny would tell him.

Karl said, "Have you change for a ten?"

"Not with me but at home I do. I can—"

"That's all right. Just apply the balance to next time."

He handed over a ten-dollar bill and closed the door. As he turned away, Danny's voice reached him.

"Wait, Mr. Stafford."

What *now*?

Danny stood holding the bill, staring up at him with a worried expression.

"This is only a ten, Mr. Stafford . . ."

"*Only* a ten?"

"I did both lawns."

Damn, how much did these spoiled American kids get for mowing a lawn? He added another ten and Danny finally seemed satisfied.

"I told Mrs. Stafford that I could cut that branch up there. Only five bucks. You want me to do it?"

"No, thanks," he said, and shut the door before Danny could come up with some new bright idea.

Carefully he retraced his steps, wiping away his fingerprints as he went. In the bedroom he righted the table and replaced the lamp and other items that had fallen to the floor. When he got to the study he discovered that the answering machine was still on playback. He returned the tape to the beginning and listened, but the only message was the woman who had just called. If he wanted any more information about Paul, he would have to get it from Joanna.

He returned to the garage and opened the trunk. Joanna had obviously been struggling to free herself; her face was red with effort, she was breathing heavily and her neck was raw from the twisted pantyhose.

"We are leaving now," he told her. "Please do not struggle. You will only wear yourself out and there is not much air coming in. It is a forty-minute drive, then I can let you out."

He closed the trunk and got into the car. The driver's seat, rearview and sideview mirrors were all positioned perfectly. Paul's car. He found a radio-controlled device in the glove compartment that opened the garage door. As he turned onto the street he saw Danny, half a block away and coming toward him.

As soon as Danny saw the car, he waved and called out something. Karl's nerves, already stretched thin, could stand no more. Rather than stop and find out what he wanted, Karl simply smiled, waved and kept driving. As he passed he caught a glimpse of a five-dollar bill in Danny's hand. So it was fifteen dollars to do both lawns. The boy was honest, wanting to give him back his five-dollar overpayment. Honest, and a potential danger.

When the Audi didn't stop, Danny continued on to the Stafford house and rang the bell. He intended to give the money to Mrs. Stafford but she didn't answer. He knew she was home because her car was still at the curb and he hadn't seen her with Mr. Stafford. Maybe she was on the phone and couldn't come to the door. Or maybe she was taking a bath. Or maybe—a sudden, secret thought—maybe she was having her period. She might feel sick or something.

Embarrassed, Danny walked quickly back to the sidewalk, whistling loudly to show that it really wasn't all that important, the errand that had brought him to the door. He'd come back tomorrow to return the money. By then Mrs. Stafford should be feeling better.

CHAPTER

25

ON THE FLIGHT BACK TO WASHINGTON THE three men sat side-by-side, Hugh in the middle, Paul next to the window and Maurice on the aisle. They were in the No Smoking section at Paul's insistence, which meant that periodically Maurice had to leave his seat and go to the rear of the aircraft to smoke a cigarette. He wasn't pleased. It seemed to him as if they had been released in Paul's custody instead of the other way around. While at the airport he had taken Hugh aside and suggested that he was treating Stafford too much like part of the team and not enough like an asset, and a dubious one at that.

Hugh tended to shrug off Maurice's concerns. He was now pretty well convinced that Paul was as much a victim as any of the people murdered, and he had made a decision to treat him as part of the team, sensing that it was the most effective way to get Paul's confidence and thereby his cooperation.

"But you're not controlling him," Maurice complained. "He's controlling us—"

"He's sharp, he's got ideas."

"But he's not one of us."

Neither am I, Hugh wanted to say. He hadn't felt like one of "us" since the Tehran fiasco. Maybe that was why he liked Paul Stafford. A natural outsider, Stafford felt no need to be an insider. He'd been impatient that morning with the consular official, a bald man with a double chin named Walsh, who made it obvious what an imposition it was giving up his Sunday morning to come down there and get an American out of jail...

"It's real tough for him without that second cup of

coffee," Paul whispered loudly enough for Walsh to hear.

With the deputy police chief of Berlin in attendance, Walsh mumbled a short statement about who was cooperating with whom in the matter of Paul Stafford, transfer of custody, jurisdiction of designated agencies, guarantee of appearance within seven days of notification . . . Once formalities were over, Walsh signed his name half a dozen times and disappeared. A police officer with sad eyes and a receding chin then gave Paul a silver plastic bag decorated with a rampant bear, the symbol of Berlin. Inside was the hospital gown he had been wearing on his arrival.

"You can use the restroom," the officer told him. "To change clothes."

"Shove it," Paul told him.

He started toward the door but the officer called loudly after him. "Excuse me, sir, but if you are not returning the uniform issued on your arrival then you must pay for it."

Paul looked down. "Pay for this? You're kidding?"

"Eighty-five marks, sir. Regulations."

"Here," Hugh said, and handed Paul a hundred marks.

Kincaid had gone to get the car, and while they waited for him outside the police station Paul stood with his eyes closed, face tilted toward the sun. A fresh, gusty wind swirled paper debris along the street and pushed patchy shadows of clouds up the face of nearby buildings. Watching him, Hugh could almost imagine the heightened sensation of sun and wind on skin that had been shut from light and fresh air.

"What did you guys find out about Lish?" Paul asked without opening his eyes.

"He's not one of ours," Maurice said. "Not unless he's too recent to be on computer."

"What about the army?"

"Their records show two Lishes, one overseas, the other stationed at Camp Pendleton in California. Neither one's a George and there's nobody at the Military Ocean Terminal by that name. The closest match is a civilian employee named *Litz*—L-I-T-Z. Maybe it looked the same in your dream."

Paul opened his eyes and turned away from the sun.

"It doesn't *look* any way; it's just something I know."

"We're running a check on Mr. Litz," Hugh said. "Just to make sure."

"Why don't you run a check on cargos while you're at it?" Paul said. "I'd like to know what kind of material goes through there."

"You think he was after cargo?"

"He was after something."

It was a good idea, Hugh decided. He turned to Maurice. "Have you called for transport from Dulles?"

"I'll call from the airport. *If* we get there in time."

"When you do, talk to Audrey, have him get a cargo list from the army. Whatever was there the day of Karl's visit."

"And what's come through since then," Paul added.

"Right," Hugh agreed. "The whole works..."

And that was the way the day had gone, with Paul acting as another member of the team, Hugh backing him up and Maurice trying unsuccessfully to maintain the boundaries between them. Now, as they headed over the North Atlantic at thirty-six-thousand feet, Maurice went to the rear of the aircraft for a smoke and Hugh dropped his tray table and pulled out a notebook and a pencil.

"Let's review what we know," he said to Paul. "Karl Alexander, an agent for the Stasis. Officially a combat instructor, primary assignment is assassination. You find him and blow his cover and what does he do? He doesn't kill you, even though you gave him every chance in the world. Instead he makes you a prisoner. Now we know he's not squeamish about killing so either you're a very small threat—which I doubt—or he didn't want to kill his own brother. What's your guess?"

"I guess he felt a connection... with me, my life..."

"You want to be more specific?"

"That depends," Paul said. "Let's assume I cooperate and help you find him. What happens then?"

"Well, if you're right about this man Lish and he was killed in America, we could put Karl Alexander on trial for murder."

"Or you could put a bullet through his head."

"Ah," Hugh said. "*You* feel a connection too. You think we're going to kill your brother—"

Paul looked straight ahead. "Are you?"

Before he answered, Hugh glanced back to make sure that Maurice was still in the rear of the plane, then in a more confidential tone said, "I won't tell you that we would never consider killing Karl Alexander, but that's not my job. My job is to identify him and locate him. After that I've got an option to try and grab him. I don't have the authority to execute him." He didn't add that killing was something he had little stomach for. As distinct, for example, from Maurice . . . "But I want to catch him and I want you to help me do it."

"And if you can't catch him?"

"Then Maurice takes over," Hugh said quietly.

Paul had expected something like this. He glanced toward the rear of the aircraft, where Maurice stood with his back against an emergency exit, the cigarette next to his face, eyes trained on a flight attendant preparing a food-service cart. Paul too easily could imagine Maurice being capable of guiltless murder. All in the line of duty. Now he understood why these two CIA men had been paired. By himself Maurice was too cold and off-putting to win trust or elicit information from anyone. But he'd have no problem getting a gun to a man's head and pulling the trigger.

Hugh said that he'd picked the No Smoking section because he knew Maurice couldn't last without a cigarette and they'd have a chance to talk privately. "I want to bring Karl, your brother, in alive. So does Dr. Helms. If you're willing to help us—"

"You talked to her? To Annie?"

"Last night. She's pretty excited. Wanted to get you under hypnosis as soon as we landed but I told her to leave you alone until tomorrow. Anyway, if you'll cooperate I'm hoping the three of us can bypass the fourth of us and save your brother's life . . ."

Paul looked at him. "Why you? I know that Annie's got her sights set on being another Madame Curie, but why should you be so interested in bringing him in alive?"

Hugh hesitated, then: "Okay, I'll go all the way with you. This is my last field assignment. I'd like to see it through to the end. Besides, I'll admit this whole mental telepathy thing intrigues the hell out of me and I want to see you do those tricks—you know, guess how many bananas your brother's holding behind his back."

Paul made a wry face.

"I'm serious, though," Hugh said. "Your brother's a

slippery fish, but one hell of a catch. I'd like to take him alive. What do you say?"

Paul's instincts about people had usually been good, and his antennae were telling him to trust Hugh Roark. But even if he were wrong, did he really have any good alternatives? All his non-cooperation would get him would be one more very hostile CIA agent... So he proceeded to tell Roark what he knew of Karl's background, his upbringing under Tante Inge and his resentment that Paul had escaped to America.

"He was very curious about my life," Paul said. "He kept staring at me and asking questions. At one point I had this weird feeling that he was looking at me to see who he was supposed to be. It may sound crazy but I think he thinks I stole his life. He kept talking about what would have happened if our positions had been reversed. I think because I was the one who had to go to the hospital he blames me for what happened."

"That's like blaming the stove for burning the stew."

Maurice's return interrupted them, and Paul turned his attention to the New York *Times*. In a box on the bottom of page one was a story about the heart attack the President's father had suffered on Friday. The President was returning this evening from visiting him. It was the first that Paul had heard of it, and reading the account made him realize how out of touch he had become in just a few weeks.

The words began to blur and he found himself getting sleepy. The tension of the past few days caught up with him and the rush of air past the fuselage dulled his senses. Ignoring the two CIA men now, he tucked a pillow against the window and dozed...

He dreamed about Joanna. She was locked in a room and he had the key, but no matter how hard he tried, the door wouldn't open. He became frantic, convinced she was in serious danger. In the odd logic of dreams he knew that he had the right key. Still, the door wouldn't open. Finally he realized he was pulling on a door that opened inward. Pushing forward now, the entire door fell away, hinges and all, but instead of Joanna there was only empty space. Instead of a room, there was sky and clouds and he was staring up at a huge jet airplane plummeting toward him, out of control, one wing tilted toward the ground, its fuselage on fire—

He woke with a start. In the dim light it took him a moment to realize where he was. The cabin was bathed in eerie shadow. The in-flight movie was in progress and most of the windows had been curtained. Roark turned toward him, sliding the earphones to his neck as he did.

"You all right?"

Paul nodded absently, reached up and pushed the call button.

"You had another dream?"

"Not the same kind, not a death-dream."

He explained briefly, while Maurice dozed, and as he did the dream lost some of its frightening impact. It was a more normal dream, the kind where current situations and worries get jumbled around in a surreal blend of fact and fancy. He'd been thinking about Joanna and he was in an airplane . . . the two elements had combined in a normal dream, one of his own dreams, not a reflection of something happening with Karl.

Hugh agreed. "A lot of things can cause dreams. Stress, worry, tension. My wife dreams whenever I'm away and it's no wonder. Half the time I can't tell her where I am, what I'm doing or when I'll be back."

The flight attendant appeared, and Paul asked if the aircraft had an in-flight phone. It did, but they were beyond the range of its use. Paul glanced at his watch. Almost lunchtime in Washington.

Beside him, Hugh had opened his wallet and removed a business card that he held out so Paul could see it. "Ever been to this place?"

The card showed a photograph of an imposing stone structure overlooking a lake. Tennis courts and part of a golf course were visible, and the impression was one of a medieval castle surrounded by a country club. The caption at the bottom read: "Marquand Manor House." It was like calling the Taj Mahal a cozy cottage, Paul thought.

"It's on Lake Champlain," Hugh told him. "A gorgeous view, especially rooms that end in '14'—214, 314, 414 and on up. My wife and I go there every year and spend three days together. The manager, Dave Pellston, is a friend of ours. That's his name on the back."

Hugh flicked the card over so that Paul could read the

name. Paul nodded politely and settled back in his seat. The dream had left its residual feeling of dread that he couldn't entirely shake. Gradually his attention shifted back to what Hugh was saying...

"No one's ever done a study of Company divorce rates," Hugh went on. "But I suspect it's way above average, at least for case officers. That's why Helen and I started doing yearly honeymoons. A chance to renew the marriage and all that. We even had a rule up there, we'd only tell the truth to each other."

The headphones were still draped over his neck and Paul could hear the movie soundtrack, thin and reedy, like midgets talking.

"We have our routines. Breakfast in bed, room service, eggs Benedict with champagne to start the day. Nice tradition. You might want to try it, maybe. You and your wife..."

Paul gave him a sharp look, remembering how Hugh had been a party to his conversation with Joanna.

"Just a suggestion," Hugh said quietly.

For the first time Paul was becoming aware of Hugh as a human being rather than a CIA agent. He noticed the tiny broken blood vessels clustered at each nostril, saw the shift in skin texture that marked Hugh's vanished hairline, and recognized the deep cynicism reflected in his pale brown eyes.

Paul took the business card and slipped it into his pocket.

"How the hell," he said, "did a man like you get involved with the CIA?"

"It was the best job in the world at one time."

"Yeah, during World War II."

"And after."

"And then?"

Hugh looked at him to check if he were really interested, then proceeded to tell him. They were three hours from Washington. The time passed quickly.

Trussed up as she was in the trunk, Joanna tried to control her fear and make sense out of what was happening. The gag bit the corners of her mouth and she was stiff from lying with her knees drawn up to her chest and her cheek pressed against the lumpy blanket. The warm air was thick and stale. Her immobility, the darkness and claustrophobia were worse than having a gun pointed at her. Afraid that she might suffocate if she struggled, she lay still, and tried hard to think...

Why had he done this? She searched her memory for everything that Paul had told her about his brother. He had said that Karl was a killer for a foreign government. But didn't that mean he killed only on assignment? He had no reason to hurt her. But she remembered the look in his eyes when he had threatened to kill Danny and the way he had handled her as soon as the loud noise of the lawnmower drowned out any other sounds.

She saw again the way that he'd gone unhesitatingly to her underwear drawer. He knew which one it was. The implications were obvious—he'd been in the bedroom before. Was it today or had he been there earlier? He had Paul's keys so he could have come anytime, even while she was there, maybe while she was sleeping. The image of Karl entering at night and standing in the room while she slept made her sick. She thought back over the past few weeks, trying to remember if any of her panties or bras were missing. Nothing special came to mind.

She knew when they got to the freeway because the car picked up speed and they were no longer stopping for traffic lights. Immediately she had tried to keep track of how long they traveled in each direction and which way they turned, but it soon became confusing. Now, as they left the city, Joanna became aware of a lump in the floor of the trunk pressing against her hip. She tried to shift her weight but every time she moved, her bonds pulled tighter.

Suddenly, without warning, the Audi braked and lurched to the left. Joanna was thrown forward against the metal cross-braces of the rear of the back seat. The squeal of an approaching vehicle's brakes built and an air horn sounded directly behind them, so close that the trunk resonated with the sound. Joanna braced herself for the rear-end collision that she knew was coming. Instead, the car swerved back to the right and accelerated again, leaving behind the sound of the angry truck horn.

Her heart pounded, her forehead hurt where it had struck the forward wall. Two weeks ago she had wanted to end her life but found the will to carry on. Now, it seemed, she was going to die in a stupid traffic accident, crushed in the trunk of her own car. Either that or Karl would kill her and dump her body on the side of the road or in some empty field.

Her head still pressed against the rear seats; she shifted position, and as she did something pinched the little finger of her left hand. A moment later her fingers identified the object as a bottle cap, left over from some picnic or a vacation that she and Paul had taken together during some distant, safer time. She clutched it like the hand of an old friend.

They turned off the main road, and the farther they went, the more certain she became that he was going to kill her. The muffled wail of a passing train hinted that they were near an Amtrak route but Joanna was too upset to speculate on their location. If only she had a knife or a piece of glass or a—

The bottle cap. She could feel the sharp edges between her fingers. It might be enough to cut through the pantyhose if she could just manage to get it in the right position. She twisted it in her fingers and began pushing at the bonds. She had only limited movement of the fingers of her right hand and couldn't tell if the cap was doing any good.

Then the car slowed and stopped and Karl got out. Joanna struggled to slip the bottle cap into her back pocket before he opened the trunk. The cap was like a charm now. As long as she had it with her she would be safe. She was still trying to reach her pocket when Karl returned to the car, drove forward and stopped again.

She heard him get out once more just as she managed to slip the cap into her pocket. Outside the car she heard a dull metal clang. A moment later, they were driving again, this time slowly. Moments later, the car stopped for the last time and Karl turned off the engine. She would know now if he meant to kill her.

The sound of the key sliding into the lock was magnified by the confined space. She tensed. The trunk opened and she squinted against the light. Karl stood above her, a knife in one hand. She drew a sharp breath and stiffened as he leaned toward her.

"Don't be afraid," he said, "I intend to untie you."

His voice sounded friendly. The knife slid behind her neck and she flinched. There was a sharp tug and the gag came free. Thrusting her tongue forward, Joanna pushed the stocking, wet with saliva, from her mouth. Her lips were raw and her jaw was stiff; she worked her mouth a moment. One by one Karl cut the remaining bonds and then helped her out of the trunk.

"I'm sorry you had to travel that way," he said. "But there was no time to explain and I could not take a chance on your making an upset."

He sounded so pleasant, so much like Paul talking...

They stood before a large, isolated farmhouse that sat on the crest of a shallow hill surrounded by forest. To one side was a stable and beyond it a corral overgrown with weeds. No other homes were visible and no sound of human habitation interrupted the cicada's intemperate buzz or the mockingbird's occasional call. She took a deep breath. The warm air was cool against her damp skin. It was country air, familiar from her childhood, and it struck her with a sweetness and richness that made her dizzy. She allowed a sense of new hope. Maybe Karl meant no harm after all—

And then she saw the gun. Karl had drawn it from his jacket pocket and stepped back.

"Wait..." Joanna gasped.

He smiled, an engaging smile, just like Paul's.

"Don't worry." The barrel of the gun swept upward until it pointed at the sky. Karl pulled the trigger, and a sharp *crack* echoed into the hills.

Still speaking pleasantly he said, "Now you know that we are alone and I know that the gun works. No one will help you if you try to run away."

He slipped the gun back into the jacket and motioned toward the house with a nod of his head, another familiar Paul gesture.

"Please," he said. "You should be my guest rather than my prisoner."

Inside, he led her to the kitchen, a cheery room decorated in a country style with yellow-trim bay windows and blue-checked curtains. The blue-checked pattern was duplicated in the tablecloth. There was a deep double sink, a laminated wood counter and a cast-iron stove with a row of copper-bottomed pans hanging suspended above it.

"Would you like something to drink? I have root beer, ginger ale."

"Water is fine."

"Perhaps wine?"

"Just water."

He got two glasses from the cupboard and filled them at the sink, turning his back to her. She stole a glance at the back door, wondering if it was locked, trying to estimate if she could possibly outrun him in a dash to the wooded area at the bottom of the hill.

"Please don't try to run," Karl said without turning.

She stared at him in amazement. He brought the water to the table, smiling at her confusion.

"Your reflection is very clear in the kettle," he said, indicating the shiny chrome kettle beside the sink.

Again it was like seeing a part of Paul's personality, imperfectly, as if refracted through flawed glass. Paul, too, was incredibly alert and aware of the world around him, but whereas Paul showed his interest openly, Karl kept his awareness hidden, like the gun concealed in his jacket pocket.

Karl was watching her with interest. "I really did not mean for you to see me this morning. If I had known you were not going to work I would never have come."

"Why did you come?"

"To the house?"

Joanna nodded. The question had brought an imperceptible change in Karl's expression, a slight hardening of the pleasant smile that she recognized as one of Paul's defenses against a question he was uncomfortable answering.

"I suppose," he said slowly, "that it was a matter of curiosity. I was curious to know how my life would have turned out if Paul had been the stronger one of us and I the weaker."

"The stronger? What do you mean?"

"Didn't he tell you?"

Joanna shook her head. "There wasn't time."

"Then you haven't seen him."

"No, I—"

He was watching her intently, waiting for an answer. When she stopped in mid-sentence he smiled.

"You talked to him on the telephone," Karl concluded. "Which means he is still in Berlin."

His evident self-satisfaction made her angry. "He's in jail," she said, "because of *you*."

"In jail?"

"For running down a policeman."

"Of course," he said. "They would blame him..."

"For something *you* did."

"Poetic justice, I believe you might call it. Paul lied to me. He told me that he had come to Berlin alone. He said that the Central Intelligence Agency did not know of my existence, but when I went to the hotel, there were CIA agents, who tried to capture me."

"You've got an answer for everything, just like him."

Karl's eyebrows went up in surprise. Then he smiled, genuinely this time. "You think we are similar? Beyond the physical appearances? Let me ask you: Would you have known it was me on the stairs if you had not talked to Paul first?"

"Of course."

"How? How would you have known?"

He leaned forward, watching her eagerly.

"Paul isn't ugly," she said.

"Ugly? What do you mean?"

"He would never have done something like you did to me, on the bed and putting me in the trunk."

Karl shrugged that off. "But on the stairs, or sitting down like this, across the table from one another, would you have known?"

She regarded him closely. Who *was* this man and what was he after?

"Maybe not for the first few minutes," she said slowly. "But after a while..."

"Then what?"

"Paul can be gentle," she said.

He stared at her with an expression that seemed to Joanna a mixture of astonishment and bitterness.

"The world is not a gentle place," he said stiffly. "If you knew that you wouldn't be here, Paul wouldn't be where he is. Gentleness? You find it only when protected by strength and courage. You are lucky, people like you who live under the protection of others, but when that protection is taken away, then you learn."

He stopped abruptly, stood up. "I had no breakfast," he announced. "There is ham and cheese and hard-boiled eggs. Would you like some?"

"No thank you," Joanna said.

She was still thinking about his outburst. One thing was certain: he was eager for her reaction to him and how she thought he compared to Paul.

Joanna said, "Why did you bring me here?"

"So you wouldn't tell the authorities. My presence in Washington is a secret."

"Why?"

"If I told you, your life would be in danger."

"From you?"

"Perhaps."

He began slicing the cheese. She decided to challenge him.

"Paul said you were an assassin for a foreign government. Is that true?"

He paused, turned and his gray eyes regarded her silently.

"Occasionally—rarely—killing is one of my duties."

"Like now—?"

"No," he said with an amused smile, "that's why I brought you here."

But she recognized the smile from Paul's face. It covered a lie. And now she was convinced that unless she got away from this place she would die here.

Surprisingly, the knowledge had a cold, calming effect. She was no longer as frightened as she'd been lying in the trunk of the car. He had revealed something of himself— not enough yet, nothing she knew how to use, but he was no longer as unknown an entity as before. And she felt she had one advantage: she could read his expression better than he could read hers. Living with Paul had schooled her in the subtle art of discerning the truth behind the protective half-truths and reflex deceits that grew like ivy over the invisible walls of their marriage. I know you better than you know me, she thought as she watched Karl, now cutting cheese at the counter. She also knew which of her own responses were effective in dealing with Paul and which were not. She wondered if Karl had any of the same vulnerabilities. If he did . . .

She got up and came toward him. "Here, let me help with that."

He turned, knife in hand, and stared at her. Slowly a smile worked its way across his features. He held the knife toward her. "Would you like to cut the ham?"

Joanna hesitated, then realizing that he expected her to take it, she shook her head.

"I'll tell you what," she said casually. "Why don't I make some coffee? Have you got some?"

"In there." He pointed to a cupboard.

Joanna felt his eyes on her as she crossed the room. All right, she thought. Now it begins. Cat and mouse. Mouse and cat. Her survival would depend on which was which.

CHAPTER

26

THE CIA HAD SENT A CAR TO MEET THEM AT
Dulles International. The driver handed Hugh a briefcase
with an inset combination lock.

"Audrey says this is up to the minute," he said. "You
don't have to come in until tomorrow."

"That's damn nice of him," Maurice said. "He must
have been promoted since we were gone."

Hugh offered Paul a ride, then waited until they were
inside the car before opening the briefcase, which contained computerized cargo manifests from the Bayonne
terminal. The three, including Paul now, studied the information, passing the sheets back and forth. Most of the
cargo that had been shipped during the previous ten days
was household goods for officers going overseas. There was
also a consignment of web belts and leggings and a variety
of food stores going to the navy: gallon cans of spaghetti,
five-pound cartons of cereal, tins of powdered eggs...

"Look at this stuff," Maurice said in disgust. "Powdered
milk, powdered eggs, ice cream powder..."

"What about this?" Paul said, pointing to two cargos
listed as "Contents Classified."

"What about it?"

"Can we find out what they are?"

"We?" said Maurice.

"You find out, somebody find out."

Hugh nodded. "We'll put in a request on Monday."

"Why not today?"

"It's not priority and this is Sunday," Hugh reminded
him. "Any extra manpower is likely working security for
the Mutual Defense summit."

Mention of the summit reminded Paul of how long he
had been away. The drugs had confused his sense of time,

made him feel now like Rip Van Winkle. The summit, still weeks away when he left for Berlin, would begin tomorrow. He hadn't even known that the President's father was in the hospital until he picked up the newspaper on the plane.

As they approached Highway 124 Paul was about to tell the driver to turn right when Maurice leaned forward and gave him directions to Paul's house.

Paul smiled grimly. "I see you know all the best ways to get to my house."

"We know where you live," Maurice said.

"And no doubt how much I've got in the bank."

"Officially, no."

Paul had to restrain himself from making some reference to Maurice's less than savory activities. After what Hugh had told him it was hard to be civil to the man but he didn't want to betray Hugh's confiding in him.

When they arrived at the house the garage door was open and Joanna's red Alfa was sitting at the curb. Paul's first thought was that the Alfa's starter was acting up again. Then he remembered that Jo was moving and probably needed the bigger car to transport her things.

Before Paul got out of the car, Hugh gave him his home phone number. "In case anything comes up," he said.

Considering what Hugh had confided about himself, Paul suspected the man was talking as much about coming to terms with Joanna as he was about finding Karl.

The lawn had been newly mowed, he noticed, as he walked up to the house. It was Sunday; Danny McVey had been here. The familiar neighborhood routines were still being observed. There were times when a neighbor's preoccupation with a manicured lawn or waxed BMW irritated him, but today he found it comforting. It was good to be home.

He reached behind the porch light for the spare key. It wasn't there. He checked the ground beneath the light. Had Jo forgotten to leave it? The anxiety he'd felt on the plane began to trickle back. Then he realized: that's why Jo had left the garage door open, so that she could go in through the kitchen. Maybe she hadn't been able to find the key.

He entered the house from the garage, half expecting to

find a note on the kitchen table. Nothing. He called Joanna's name. No answer, but he hadn't expected one. The house was empty.

In the front hall the empty boxes brought home for the first time the reality of Joanna's leaving. He continued upstairs. There was a box in the hall, this one full, and another in the bedroom, empty but with one side crushed, as if someone had stepped on it. Then he saw the broken window and walked slowly toward it. From the shards of glass left in the frame he guessed that the window had been broken from the inside. What the hell . . . ?

Moving close to look into the yard below, glass crunched beneath his foot. He knelt down and found two chunks of glass next to the wall, but when he looked outside there was no debris in the yard. He turned from the window. The bedspread was mussed, and so was the Chinese rug. Lingerie dangled over the side of an open dresser drawer.

Moving quickly now, he checked the other rooms. The red light was flashing on the answering machine. There were two messages, one from a real estate agent who wanted to coordinate schedules so that Jo could pick up the key to the new apartment, the other from Denise asking Jo to call. Paul called the real estate woman first and confirmed what he already feared: Joanna had never kept her appointment. Then he called the gallery, where an irate Denise complained that Joanna had asked for the morning off and then hadn't shown up at all.

"I just hope it's an emergency," she said, "because I had to cancel my plans this afternoon."

"Yeah," Paul said, "maybe she's been in a car wreck or something."

"I didn't mean *that* kind of emergency," Denise said archly.

He hung up and called Danny's house. His mother, Cassie McVey, answered. Paul asked to speak with Danny.

"Did he screw up the lawn?" Cassie wanted to know.

"The lawn's fine, Cass. I just want to ask Danny a couple of questions."

"No problem, but listen, I told him to bring you your change. I don't want him spending money he hasn't earned— not until he has a credit card, anyway, you know what I mean?"

"What change?"

"For the lawn. You gave him twenty, right? Well, he's not a Savings and Loan—that's what I told him. I said, if you're not paying interest you're not borrowing money."

"*I* gave him twenty? Is that what he said?"

"Well didn't you?"

"Cassie, just put him on, will you? There's some confusion over here. I'll straighten it out."

"If he's lying again—"

"Will you just get him?"

The pause on the other end of the line told him she was hurt by his abrupt tone.

"Please," he added in a conciliatory tone.

She answered with careful precision. "If you'll be patient for one moment."

Paul could hear her in the other room talking over the sound of a televised football game. A normal Sunday afternoon in the suburbs, only nothing was normal anymore. Not since he found out about Karl . . .

Danny came on the line. "I got your five dollars, Mr. Stafford. I was going to bring it over on the next commercial—"

"Danny, listen carefully. I've got a couple of questions for you. They may make no sense to you, it may seem like I should know the answers but I want you to answer anyway, okay?"

"Sure."

"You mowed the lawn this morning, didn't you?"

"Sure."

"How long ago?"

"How long?"

"What time did you mow the lawn?"

"I didn't have my watch on. I guess about ten-thirty."

"Who was here?"

"Come on, Mr. Stafford. You know."

"I was here, wasn't I?"

"Sure. You paid me and everything."

Paul's grip on the phone tightened. "Okay, now listen. Pretend like I've got amnesia, I can't remember a thing. Was Mrs. Stafford here?"

"Sure."

"The window in the bedroom is broken. Did you see what happened?"

"Well, it was like all of a sudden the glass came down right in front of me. If I'd been a little closer it might have sliced my ear off. And Mrs. Stafford said she hit it with something. Not her hand, a box I think."

"She told you that?"

"Sure. I asked if she was cut and she said no."

"Listen, Danny, and this is important. Was anyone else here when the window broke?"

"Besides you and Mrs. Stafford, I didn't see anybody . . . What's going on, Mr. Stafford?"

Paul hung up, then dialed the police. A switchboard operator passed him off to Detective Perlmutter, a man who asked questions with a thick southern accent.

"How old is your wife, sir?"

"She's twenty-nine."

"Any mental or physical impairments?"

"No."

"Why do you believe she's missing?"

"I told you, there's a broken window in the bedroom. There's also signs of a struggle. The bed is all mussed up, the side of a box is smashed and the rug's all bunched up."

"Any sign of physical injury?"

"Like what?"

"Bloodstains, hair or tissue, anything of that nature."

"No, *nothing of that nature*." Watch it, he told himself. You need him . . .

"All right, sir. We'll send an officer over to take your report."

As soon as he was off the phone he had second thoughts. Could he be sure Joanna was with Karl? What if she'd gone to find someone to replace the pane of glass? Or taken a box of clothes to her new apartment? Could she have gone with Karl of her own volition? No, he couldn't believe she would do that. Not after what he'd told her about Karl . . . There was no use pretending. Karl had kidnapped Joanna. But it made no sense unless . . . unless Karl had found out about his escape. He could have talked to Otto or read the story in the newspaper and decided to go after Joanna, take her hostage.

Again, why?

And more important, what did he intend to do with her?

He dialed Hugh Roark's home number and talked to his wife. Roark hadn't gotten home yet.

"Just tell him that Karl surfaced. Ask him to call me at home."

Needing to do *something*, Paul went over the house again, looking for any clues, hoping he wouldn't find any of Detective Perlmutter's kind of evidence. Vague unease had hardened into a ball in his stomach. The more he thought about it, the more he was sure Jo was in serious danger. If only he knew why Karl had come here, why in hell he'd gone to Bayonne and what he was doing in Washington.

He needed answers. Well, this was his town, his territory, and he was supposed to know how to get answers. Let the CIA work bureaucrat's hours, he would track down this George Lish and find out what was in the Bayonne shipments and he would do it now, today, not waiting until Monday.

He got out the *Herald* phone directory and looked up the home numbers of researchers. Kathy Craven was his first choice but she wasn't home. Next he tried Pam Markowitz, who was home and willing to work on Sunday for double-time.

"Good," Paul said. "Are the computers up?"

"They were when I left."

"Here's what I want you to do. Access National Phone Service Directory and find me every damned George Lish in America. Then call and find out which one's dead."

"Which one's what?"

"Dead. I got a tip that a man named George Lish was killed three days ago. I want you to find out the who what where when why. I want a quick and dirty bio."

"Are you serious?"

"Someone's life may depend on it. Can you get down to the office right away? I'll meet you there as soon as I can. If you find anything first call me at home."

When he hung up, Paul felt a little better...at least he was moving, and it made him feel more in control.

The next call was more difficult. Vic Daniloff was a friend from army days. They had flown together in Vietnam, and Vic had then gone career army and transferred to intelligence. Now he was a lieutenant colonel stationed at the Pentagon. Paul had used Vic for confirmation of primary-source information but had never sourced him directly. It was an article of faith between them that he would never trade on their friendship by asking Vic for primary information. Now there was no other way.

"Hello, captain," Vic greeted him cheerily. "What's all this I heard about you in a hit-and-run in Berlin?"

"Wasn't me."

"That's good to know. I tried calling but nobody was home—"

"Vic, listen, something real serious has come up and I need your help. If there was any other way I wouldn't come to you but Joanna's in the middle of it. I think she's in trouble."

"What happened?"

"Someone's holding her as a hostage—I'm sure of it but I can't prove it, not until I get more information. That's where you come in."

"Keep going."

"Two cargos were sent from the Military Ocean Terminal in Bayonne, their contents classified. I've got the lading numbers, shipment dates, all that. What I don't have is what's in them. That's what I need from you."

Vic said slowly, "You want me to access classified information."

"I wouldn't ask if there was any other way."

Vic was silent for a moment, and when he spoke there was an edge in his voice. "I knew you'd do it someday. Come to me for some story that—"

"It's not a story, Vic. It's *Joanna*. Her life's in danger, for Christ sake."

"How in danger?"

"You want the short version or the long version?"

It was an old routine: the short version was *trust me,* the long version was *please trust me.*

"Blind faith, huh?"

"It was enough at LZ Bird," Paul said, reminding Vic of the first time they'd flown together. Vic had just arrived and he'd been assigned area-familiarization as Paul's copilot. They'd gone into Landing Zone Bird at night and Paul had taught Vic how to hold position by tucking in close enough to see the instrument lights on the ship ahead. It was dirty pool, Paul knew, reminding him of Vietnam. Vic knew it too.

REDEYE **291**

"Don't give me that," he said.

"I saved your ass a couple of times."

"I saved yours, too."

"We were a good team, Vic."

"It's not a team, now, Paul. It's not just the two of us in a cockpit. I've got a career, I've got a wife. I've got Linda and the kids and a house with a mortgage. We're not yahoo flyboys now. Passing classified information isn't like faking a terrain familiarization on a beer run to Khe Sahn. Don't come at me with something like this."

"No choice, Vic."

There was a long silence and Paul let it sit there, big and empty enough to fill with memories of LZ Bird.

"Paul . . ." The voice was tight and controlled. "You make a career of bucking the system. I made a career supporting it. I can't live outside the system."

"I'm not asking you to."

"If it gets out—"

"I've never blown a source, Vic."

He sighed. "All *right*, I can't promise anything but I'll see what I can do."

"That's all I'm asking."

"You be at the office tomorrow?"

"Not tomorrow. Today."

"I have to go to the office for this. I don't have a secure line here . . ."

"I'm sorry."

"We almost went to Cape May this weekend," Vic said. "Never mind . . . what are the goddamn cargo numbers?"

Paul gave them to him and Vic repeated them back, then said, "Are you at the *Herald*?"

"No, but I'll be there soon. Leave a message with the operator if I'm gone."

In the background Paul could hear the television: the football game.

"And Vic?" he added, "It needs to be ASAP."

"I *got* the message."

A few minutes after Paul hung up, the police arrived. There were two of them, one a stocky black man with drooping melancholy eyes, the other a white man with a jaw that thrust forward like the prow of a ship. The black man was in charge. Before he spoke, he glanced at a thick note pad he carried in one hand, checking Paul's name.

"Mr. Stafford? You phoned a missing-person report?"

"My wife. She was here this morning with a man who's been impersonating me. I can prove that. Now she's gone and there's evidence of a struggle."

The two officers exchanged a look and Paul knew it was going to be difficult.

The first officer said, "Where was the forced entry?"

"What forced entry?"

Again he consulted his notebook. "Broken window. Signs of forced entry."

"Upstairs," Paul said. "But I didn't say it was a forced entry."

"Are these your boxes, sir?"

"My wife's."

"Is she going somewhere?"

"She just got an apartment in D.C."

The officers said nothing but Paul could sense their growing skepticism. By the time he'd shown them the window and explained about Joanna, their notebooks were back in their pockets. The window looked like an accident, nothing was stolen, Joanna had keys to the Audi, Paul had admitted that they hadn't been getting along...

"That's not the point, damn it. The point is that someone was here in this house with her this morning and she would have never left with him of her own free will. I *know* that. I spoke with her last night and warned her about him."

"About who?"

"A man named Karl Alexander. My twin brother."

It sounded foolish so he added, "He's a murderer," which sounded even more foolish.

"A murderer," the black officer repeated somberly. "Well, sir, that sounds like a job for homicide."

His partner with the bony face clenched his teeth to keep from smiling.

It was useless, Paul realized. The more he said, the more far-fetched it sounded. Given time he could get witnesses. Given time, he could prove that Danny saw a man who was impersonating him at the same moment that he was on Flight 491 inbound from Germany. Given time he could prove he had a twin brother and maybe even prove that Karl was a suspected killer. But by then it would be next week and God knew where Karl would be or what might have happened to Joanna...

The officers began an explanation about freedom of movement for adult Virginia citizens with no history of senility or mental illness. Paul cut them short and ushered them out of the house. Out on the sidewalk some of the neighbors had gathered, curious about the police car. Paul assured them that nothing was wrong and chatted long enough to satisfy himself that none of them had seen Karl earlier or had seen the Audi leave. He went back inside and stood staring at the empty boxes in the hallway, all addressed to the local Safeway store. Danny had said that Jo had arrived with them just this morning. And then what? Karl surprised her? Forced his way inside?

No, of course not. He had my keys.

Anger surged through him. What the hell was Karl doing? He'd taken his wallet, his car, the keys to his house, and now the son of a bitch had taken his wife. He'd impersonated him in Bayonne and even carried off a conversation with Bernie. His brother was taking over his life, stealing his identity like some sort of leech, sucking his existence away bit by bit.

The more he thought about it, the angrier he got. Yes, in the beginning he'd tried to understand Karl, even tried to sympathize with him, with the horror of his childhood, the arbitrary, rotten bad luck he'd had. But no more. This was far more ominous than simply kidnapping him and keeping him prisoner. In some perverse way Karl was beginning to take over and live Paul's life. Including his wife.

He felt he had only a limited amount of time to find Karl and stop him. It was as if Karl was stealing elements of his life until some critical mass would be exceeded and Karl would actually *become* him.

"No you *don't*..."

Two could play this game. He had always been more sensitive to what Karl was doing than the other way around. Well, now he would use that sensitivity to stop him. He returned to the office and called Annie Helms. The business card she had given him had disappeared with his wallet, but her number, in Jo's handwriting, was on the list of phone messages. He sat down heavily, pulled out the bottom drawer and rested his foot on it as he listened to the phone ring.

Be home, be home...

A moment later a low voice answered. "Annie Helms."

"Hello, it's Paul Stafford. I need to—"

He stopped in mid-sentence, his attention caught by the sight of a check inside the drawer. Not just one check but a lot of them, *his* checks, made out and already signed.

"Paul," Annie said eagerly. "I'm glad you called. I talked to Hugh, he told me what happened. The link is your brother, right? A twin brother named Karl Alexander?"

Paul barely heard her. He leaned down, picked up the stack of checks and bills and put them on the desk. The first one was made out to American Express in the amount of his two tickets, from Washington to Miami and Miami through Frankfurt to Berlin. The handwriting looked like his, the signature looked like his, but he had never seen the bill, never made out the check. The check bore today's date.

Annie was calling his name. "Paul? Are you okay?"

Paul stood up slowly, teeth clenched, feeling dizzy.

"God*damn* you," he gritted. "Goddamn you."

"What? What is it?"

"It's him. He even made out my checks. He's paying my bills—"

"Who? Karl?"

"Yes. He took my checkbook—I've got them right here—American Express, the gas, the electricity—he signed *my* name. He's trying to—"

An edge of renewed excitement was evident in Annie's voice. "Karl signed *your* name to *your* checks?"

"Goddamn it, I want him. I want into his mind. How soon can you get here?"

"To your house?"

"Wait, you're in Silver Spring. Let's meet at the *Herald*. You're going to hypnotize me. How long will it take you to get downtown?"

There was an imperceptible pause, then she said, "Give me twenty minutes."

"I'm on my way."

"Wait," she said quickly. "What happened?"

"He's got Joanna. He's...he's trying to steal my life. Trying, hell. He's doing it. I'll see you down there."

"Bring the checks."

He hung up, and when he unlocked the file cabinet to get his gun, it didn't surprise him that the gun was gone. The son of a bitch had his wife, his wallet, his car, his clothes and now his gun.

CHAPTER

27

IT WAS A CAT-AND-MOUSE GAME, AND BOTH
of them knew it. Each wanted something from the other,
but neither was altogether sure what the other knew.

Karl was certain that Joanna was trying to lull him into a
false sense of security, but each time he thought he could
predict her response she surprised him. He had even
given her opportunities to escape—apparent opportunities, anyway—turning his back, placing the knife within
her reach, leaving the room one time—but she made no
move. Mostly she acted almost friendly, engaging, which
he suspected was a ruse, although it intrigued him. As did
her answers to his questions about Paul. The more he
learned, the more he continued to feel drawn into his
brother's life . . .

As for Joanna, she made a decision to try to act as
natural as possible. The effort was exhausting, and the
eerie physical similarity to Paul was more disconcerting
than she'd expected. As he leaned toward her across the
table, he seemed to go in and out of focus, the edges
blurring between him and Paul so that sometimes she all
but lost the sense of Karl as a stranger. There was always
that physical presence, the uncanny likeness to Paul. It
was almost easier to believe that some alien intelligence
had invaded and taken over Paul's body . . .

Karl's hunger to know all about Paul not surprisingly
spilled over into a persistent curiosity about Joanna and he
began questioning her about her life. He seemed particularly pleased to hear she was an only child.

"Did you feel special with the attention of two parents,
or were you lonely without brothers and sisters?"

The question stumped her because she had only her
own experience, there was nothing to compare it to. He

was also intrigued by her knowing how to fly, wanted to
know why she decided to become a pilot. That one was
easier.

"My father had a plane," she told him. "When I was
little I would sit on his lap and he let me handle the
controls. Later I took lessons and got my pilot's license."

"Then you come from a wealthy family."

"Not wealthy. There was land they sold when I was six.
Most of their money came from that."

"Do you think it helped draw you together, you and
Paul, this interest in flying?"

"I don't think so." She felt herself getting edgy, nervous
as he moved into personal areas.

"He said he wanted to fly with you to Ethiopia and you
refused."

Joanna tried to conceal her surprise. One of her problems trying to carry off this exchange with Karl was that
she had no idea what Paul had told him. More than once
he had referred to things she assumed he had learned
from Paul.

"Taking Paul would have meant less space for food," she
said. Besides, the *Herald* was paying his way over.

"Still, I think Paul was attracted by a woman who could
share his interest in flying."

"Did he say that?"

"He did not, but I know that I would be attracted by
someone who shared my interests."

"What are your interests?"

He smiled. "That is what I am finding out."

He turned the conversation back to Paul and his life. He
wanted to know how Paul got along with his parents, why
he had decided to be a journalist, how long he had known
Joanna before they decided to get married, where they
had gone on their honeymoon, why she was moving away
now. Like Paul, she thought, he seemed almost obsessive
about details. Joanna forced herself to satisfy him, alternately
piquing his interest and satisfying his curiosity as she
played for time and looked for a real opportunity to
escape. It was as if Karl was on the trail of something and
she was leading him, but she had no idea where she was
going or what, ultimately, he wanted or intended.

When they moved to the living room Karl offered her
the couch but she sat in an overstuffed chair. Without the

table between them, her bare legs made her self-conscious. She wished she wasn't wearing shorts. To mask her unease, she tried again to turn the conversation around.

"What about you? Are you married?"

"Of course. I have a wife and three children but with none of them have I ever had a conversation such as the one that you and I are having now."

Joanna hadn't thought of it as a conversation so much as an interview, and an extended one at that.

Karl pulled a rocking chair close and settled into it. "Tell me, what was the first thing you noticed about Paul? That first time you saw each other, where was it? The parking lot of the store with the odd name?"

"A Safeway store."

"Safeway, yes. When you saw him there, what first attracted you to him?"

She felt like Scheherazade, spinning stories to save her own life. She had better make them as interesting as she could.

"The contrast between his smile and his eyes. I liked his eyes, disliked his smile."

"Go on. Give me an example."

"Well, he was watching me argue with the store manager and his eyes seemed warm and curious but he had a smile with the downturned lip that seemed cynical. Eyes and smile tended to fight each other. I couldn't figure out which one was the real Paul... What about you? What was the first thing you noticed about your wife?"

"I liked her looks," he said flatly. "But with Paul, at what point did you decide that you were in love with him? How did you know?"

God, this was the same dogged pursuit of a subject that was so characteristic of Paul when he was interviewing someone. Ask ten questions, answer one, ask ten more...

"I think I fell in love the first time we talked," she said. "He asked what I was doing and when I told him he listened with such close attention that I felt like what I was telling him was the most important information in the world. He listened to me like he really cared what I thought. Not many men do that..."

"I care what you think."

"Why?" She tried to sound casual, not at all sure she wanted to hear his answer.

"Because if *I* had been the weaker one and Paul the stronger, then his life with you would have been mine."

She stared at him. So that was the reason for all his questions? To find out what some alternative life might have been like?

Karl misunderstood her expression. "He didn't tell you that part, did he? How my life was sacrificed for his? I am sure he avoided that part."

"What?"

His words were still echoing in her mind: *"His life with you would have been mine."*

"Did he tell you how he came by his charmed life?"

"What charmed life?"

"The famous journalist with awards and plaques all over the walls. Did he tell you why it happened to him and not to me?"

"He earned the awards," Joanna said, trying to hold back her irritation. "I wouldn't call it a charmed life."

"That depends on your point of view. Paul was not the strong one. He was sick. He would have died, but my mother took him to an American hospital and left me with an old woman who used me in ways which would disgust you. Paul's good life is built on my suffering. The strong carry the weak. I saved him twice: once when we were children and again only two weeks ago. I could have killed him two weeks ago but I saved him. Now I pay the price. Just as I did before."

She was stunned. With this outburst she realized how she'd misunderstood what he was after. She had tried to humanize, to make herself and the life she shared with Paul attractive. She'd given a picture of their relationship to win his sympathy. The strategy had backfired. To Karl, every cherished moment was more damning evidence of the life that Paul had stolen. In trying to build a case for Paul and herself, she'd built a case against them.

"Why do you look at me like that?" Karl demanded.

"What?"

"You look at me as if I am some sort of monster."

Think. Pretend to see things from his perspective. *Do* something... "I'm sorry, of course I know you're not a monster—"

"How do you know that?"

Now he was toying with her, and she was the mouse in

the cat-and-mouse game. His tone was light, he smiled, but behind the words she sensed that the answer was important to him. She struggled to appease him.

"I don't believe anyone is inherently evil—"

"What do you believe?"

"I . . . believe in people—their basic goodness."

Wrong answer. Karl's lips formed a condescending smile. "You don't really believe that."

"Yes, yes, I do. Really."

"What about me? Do you believe in my basic goodness?"

"Yes, I do, but I think you try to defeat it—"

His smile hardened. Quickly she saw her mistake. Sympathize, don't criticize.

"I don't say I'm right . . ."

"No, no, do not back down. That is what Paul finds attractive in you, your strength, that you stand by your principles. I find it attractive, also. So go ahead. Analyze me. Tell me why you think I defeat my . . . basic goodness." No smile this time.

"I don't . . . know you well enough."

"Sure, you do. I'm Paul, only stronger."

Oh my God, she thought. He really believes that.

What to do? She couldn't continue this but she didn't dare stop. She had to have some relief from his terribly intense scrutiny. She needed to let her face reflect her true feelings, if only just for a moment.

"All right," she said, "I'll try . . . but first you've got to let me go to the bathroom."

For a moment she thought he might object, then he relaxed, leaned back in the rocker and waved toward the hallway. "Use the one on this floor, beneath the stairway."

She got to her feet, hoping he didn't notice how unsteady she was. But she felt his eyes on her as she crossed the room, and when she turned into the hallway she caught a glimpse of him looking at her legs. After years of living with Paul, Joanna recognized and understood that look . . .

As soon as the door was shut, the fear she'd hidden until now sickened her. The coffee burned her stomach. She gripped the wash basin until her fingers ached. Nausea came over her, and she had just enough presence of mind to turn on the water so that Karl wouldn't hear as she gave in to it.

She flushed the toilet, rinsed her mouth and forced herself to breathe deeply. No more, she had to get away. There was a narrow window in the bathroom. She pushed the curtains aside and inspected it. It was a new aluminum window, small, but if she opened both panes, large enough. One hundred feet away were the woods.

Her fingers had moved to the latch before she noticed Karl standing at the living room window, staring into the distance. The configuration of the house gave him a good view of the exterior bathroom wall. She pulled back, hoping he hadn't seen her, fighting down the panic that came from knowing she was trapped. Karl wasn't stupid. He knew about the window. He wasn't going to let her go anywhere.

She fought to stay calm. Instinct ordered her to act, to get away, to run into the woods until she could run no more. Or to the Audi. She remembered the spare key that Paul kept tucked under the radiator just in case he ever lost his keys in the field or on assignment. The key was in a metal container the size of a matchbox with two thin magnets on one side. Jo recalled that they had once used the spare key when Paul inadvertently locked his keys inside the car. That was two years ago. Now she imagined the key tucked away inside its magnetic container, waiting for her to retrieve it... If only she could break free long enough to find it... But to do that, somehow she would have to put Karl out of commission...

But how? She had never even hit anyone in her life. How much force did it take to knock a man unconscious? And would she be able to do it if she had the opportunity? Karl had said he meant to let her go. But his words said one thing, his tone, expression, body language said something else. He never meant for her to leave here alive...

She had been in the bathroom long enough. Don't arouse his suspicions now, not after working so hard to offset them, refusing opportunities to run away, acting warm and friendly. And he had responded, whether he knew it or not. There was no mistaking the desire in the look he'd given her as she left him.

His life with you would have been mine.

No wonder Karl was attracted to her... all day long he'd been living *Paul's* life. What if she offered him a chance to live Paul's life for real? What if she . . . if she went to bed with him?

The thought made her cringe. She could never do it.

But would she have to? What if she made him think she was willing, then surprise him . . . Maybe a few preliminaries. Could she do that? She would have to. And she would have to choose the right place, somewhere with something hard that she could use as a weapon.

If she failed it would be worse than ever. If she hurt him but didn't get away . . . But she couldn't wait any longer. She had to try.

She checked herself in the mirror, took a deep breath, opened the door and stepped into the hallway. Because he was still at the window, Karl wasn't immediately visible.

"Karl?" She used his name for the first time. "Can I take you up on that glass of wine?"

As he came toward her, he looked surprised, and pleased.

Good, Joanna thought. Be surprised.

"I'll join you," he said.

She followed him to the kitchen, dipping one shoulder in a way that she knew Paul always found attractive. Now all she needed was a weapon.

CHAPTER

28

ON HIS WAY TO THE *HERALD* PAUL WAS FORCED to detour around Seventeenth Street, which was barricaded and guarded by district police in preparation for the Soviet leader's arrival the next morning. The Russian embassy, a five-story brownstone, sat in the middle of the block, its wrought-iron gate temporarily removed to accommodate the armored Soviet limousine that would meet the General Secretary at Andrews Air Force Base. On the roof a security man stood watching the street below.

Normally Paul enjoyed the sense of excitement that permeated Washington during the visits of a foreign leader, but today, intent on his private business, the detour annoyed him. When a confused motorist stopped in the middle of the intersection to ask directions of a policeman, he honked his horn angrily. The policeman gave him a sour look. When he arrived at the *Herald*, Annie Helms hadn't showed up yet. Paul told the receptionist that he would be in research and went to see if Pam had discovered anything. He found her seated at the computer terminal, the remains of a Big Mac lying in its plastic container between her keyboard and the telephone. She sat with one leg tucked under her and, as if to proclaim that this was her day off, wore bluejeans and a checked cotton shirt with rolled-up sleeves. Her eyes brightened when she saw Paul.

"It's a good thing you didn't ask for *Jones*," she said. "I'd be here until Christmas."

"What about Lish?"

She showed him a list of names.

"Eighty-seven Lishes in the United States, almost a third of them up in the Seattle area. They must have come on the same boat—salmon fishermen or airplane designers."

"How many *Georges*?"

"Five Georges, two accounted for by phone—Savannah and Detroit." She lowered her voice suggestively. "Savannah George sounds very nice. I think I'll call him back and see if he ever comes up to Washington."

"What about dead George?"

"Three possibilities: Seattle George, whose roommate says he *thinks* George is on a hunting trip but they work different shifts and he hasn't seen him for a while. That's one. Then there's Nashville George, where nobody answers. Finally we've got Houston George, who left on a business trip and never came back. He runs a boarding kennel and his dogs were starving."

"Sounds good."

"Not for the animals. Dogs and cats mostly and one poor parrot. The SPCA people were there when I called. When Houston George didn't come back there was nobody to feed the animals so somebody called the SPCA."

"Where'd he go? What kind of business trip?"

"They didn't know. They were just there to figure out what to do with God's little dears—that's what this lady called them, '*God's little dears*.'"

"What about the police? Have any bodies been found?"

"Who knows? I haven't had time to call."

Paul reached for the phone. "What's Houston's area code?"

"Seven one three."

Pam stood up and stretched while Paul made the call. The police had no reports of George Lish, dead or missing. As soon as he hung up, the phone rang. It was the receptionist with news that Annie Helms had arrived. Before he left he gave Pam new instructions.

"Check with the police in Nashville and Seattle. If none of those Lishes are missing or dead, get me background on Houston George. I want to know marital state, employer, if he's connected with government agencies or defense contractors, if they're in debt—you know the routine."

"Oh, sure," Pam said. "I'll just give them your name, they'll tell me everything I want to know."

"Pretend you're a prospective employer, pretend you're TRW, pretend you're Publisher's Clearinghouse and you want to give Lish a million dollars, whatever you want. Use your imagination."

On his way upstairs Paul met Dicky Lazarus, the photographer who had been in his office the day the CIA men first showed up. Dicky, wearing two Nikons, did a double-take when he saw Paul.

"Hey," he said. "What are you doing here?"

"I work in the building, remember?"

"This morning somebody said you were in jail in Berlin."

"Must have been my twin brother," Paul said. "Where are you going?"

Dicky wrinkled his nose in disgust. "The President is landing at Andrews. The usual grip-and-grin stuff. Hey, what about the cop? You really run him over?"

They reached the entrance to the building where Annie Helms was waiting.

"Tell you tomorrow," Paul said.

Annie greeted him with a firm handshake and a thousand questions. Ever since Hugh Roark called her from Berlin and told her about Karl Alexander, she'd been berating herself for not coming on her own to the truth. Twins. It seemed so obvious. In college she had done a research project on the twin studies carried out at the University of Minnesota. She remembered the remarkable incidence of shared personality traits and the symbiotic emotional responses that characterized twin groups, and she was irritated that she hadn't immediately investigated the possibility with Paul.

As he escorted her upstairs now, Paul told her what he had found at the house and filled her in on the details of his miserable time in Berlin. The experience had left him the worse for wear, Annie decided. He was pale and drawn, his hair messy, clothes wrinkled and he needed a shave. Tension and worry were evident in the set of his mouth and the narrowed eyes, and his voice was flat with controlled anger when he told her about Joanna's kidnapping.

"He's still impersonating me," Paul finished grimly, "and he's got Joanna."

"But you don't know that for sure."

"I know it. I can't prove it but I *know* it, just like I know a man named George Lish is dead but I can't prove that, either."

"What reason would he have to kidnap her?"

The buzz and staccato chatter of printers swelled as they entered the city room. Annie was surprised at the number of people who were working on a Sunday. A young man called to Paul as they passed. He nodded acknowledgment but continued talking to Annie.

"I don't know, that's why I want you to hypnotize me. I need some kind of clue—where he is, what he's up to, something. We know he's in the area so it should be easier this time."

"Not necessarily," she said. "Mental energy hasn't been scientifically quantified, but the available evidence indicates that physical proximity isn't as critical as the intensity of the emoting experience and the harmony of the receptor."

"Emoting?"

"Forget the jargon. Emotional, will do."

"Whatever, all I know is that I want a look into his mind. I want Joanna."

They reached Paul's office, which was smaller than Annie expected, just enough room for two chairs, a desk and file cabinet. On one wall was a large bulletin board with announcements pinned to it. There was a wire-mesh basket on the desk with pink message slips. Beside it a photograph taken on a merry-go-round showing Paul and a young woman standing beside a child who sat astride a carved unicorn.

"No couch," Paul said, "but the floor's okay."

Annie glanced down. It wasn't ideal but the environment was familiar to Paul and that might help him to relax.

Paul said, "Loosen my belt and all that crap?"

"Whatever makes you comfortable."

Paul kicked off his shoes and lay down.

"I don't guarantee this will work," Annie cautioned him.

"Why not? It worked before."

"Not exactly. We were doing something different. We were searching your memory, and the incidents we discovered all fit the same pattern—your brother was in a state of high emotional excitement and you were asleep."

"Let's just do it, okay?"

Annie looked around the room. "We need something you can concentrate on."

"I'll concentrate on Karl."

But she meant something concrete to focus his attention. There was a Luxor lamp attached to the desk. She swiveled it and extended the arm so that the head was

positioned above Paul. Then she seated herself on the floor
beside him.

"All right, Paul. I want you to relax. Let your mind clear
of thoughts, of worries and fears. Concentrate your attention on the light bulb, listen only to my voice, and relax,
relax . . ."

She led him through the relaxation procedure, calling
attention to each part of his body, working her way from
the extremities inward, through his torso to his face.

"Your eyes are becoming heavy now," she said in a low
lilting monotone. "You are growing sleepy, your eyes are
so heavy you can't keep them open . . ."

Paul closed his eyes, but it wasn't working. He wasn't
becoming drowsy. His mind was racing just as it did when
he was working against a deadline. It was like a search-
light, picking facts out of the darkness. He couldn't dim
the light or diffuse the focus and facts kept reappearing as
clues in different combinations.

"Your arms are growing heavy, the weight is spreading
from your shoulders down to your fingertips, a weight like
lead, so heavy now that you cannot move your arms. Your
right arm is thick and heavy and you cannot move it no
matter how hard you try. You can't lift your arm because it
is so heavy. Your arm, your whole body is like lead. No
matter how hard you try you can't raise your arm. You can
try it now, Paul. Try to raise your arm and feel how heavy
it is, feel how immobile your arm has become . . ."

Paul lifted his arm and opened his eyes. "It's not
working."

"You're fighting the suggestion."

"I'm *trying*."

Annie shook her head. "I can see it in your body. When
your hand relaxes there's a frown on your face; when your
face relaxes your shoulders are tense; when your shoulders
relax your hands are tense. You're not letting it happen.
You're thinking too much."

Paul sat up. "I can't help it. I keep trying to put the
pieces together. George Lish, the Bayonne terminal, Joanna—
they're all connected somehow."

"Stop thinking. Empty your mind."

"I'm trying."

"No you're not, you're not concentrating."

"All right, do it again."

Paul lay down and closed his eyes. This time Annie thought she did manage to induce a light trance. She told Paul to imagine he was watching a signal coming from Karl, a beam of light emanating from Karl's eyes, like a slide projector beaming an image onto a screen inside his mind.

"The image that you see is what Karl sees. You're looking through his eyes now, you're looking through Karl's eyes and you see what he sees. On your own mental screen you can see what Karl sees. Tell me what it is, Paul. Tell me what you see on your mental screen."

Annie could see the movement of his eyes beneath the closed eyelids.

"Let your mind remain blank, a blank screen, and let the image from your brother's eyes play on that screen. Whatever Karl is looking at, right now, that's what you're seeing. Light and shadow, form and color, it's all becoming clear. Karl's world is becoming clear before you. You see what he sees, the two of you are one, the two of you see the same things now. Tell me what's on the screen, Paul. What image do you see?"

He frowned.

"Don't force the image," she said. "Just relax now. Relax and let it appear naturally . . ."

Paul could feel himself fighting her suggestion. There were times when Annie's voice soothed him into something resembling a trance, but all the time he was aware of his mind resisting. He didn't want to relax, he didn't want to give up control. He wanted inside his brother's mind and yet he didn't.

It was no good. He opened his eyes. Annie's face, just a few feet away, was backlit by the curtained windows facing the city room.

"It's not working," he said, and stood up.

Annie was still sitting on the floor, watching him. "We could use drugs—"

"No, no drugs."

"You want to find her, don't you?"

"Not dead."

The words slipped out and surprised them both. A look of new comprehension came to Annie's eyes. She got to her feet. "That's it. That's why you won't go into a trance.

You're afraid you'll experience her death. That's why you can't relax."

As soon as she said it Paul knew she was right.

"That's it, isn't it?" Annie persisted.

Paul nodded. "It's like I've got control over her life. I feel like if I go to sleep or into a trance he'll kill her. As if my conscious will is some sort of a shield. It's crazy but that's how it feels."

"Maybe not so crazy."

Paul gave her a sharp look. Annie's eyes were alive with excitement. "Maybe you *are* keeping her alive," she said. "Maybe your desire for your wife's safety—the importance she has for you as a human being—maybe those feelings are apparent to Karl. Not consciously, but manifested as a feeling."

"Then I *shouldn't* go into a trance."

"It's all speculation," she said in a voice of wonder. "But what if it's true? What if you are keeping her alive?"

Paul was frustrated. To save Joanna he had to find Karl, to find Karl he had to establish a mental link with his brother, but to do that required hypnosis that could endanger Joanna. It was a full circle with no solution.

He picked up the phone and dialed 4478. There was only one way left, the hard way, the plodding step-by-step way, the accumulation of facts until a pattern began to form.

"Research. It's me."

"Pam, what have you got?"

"Not much on Nashville and Seattle Lishes but Houston Lish sounds like a real nut case."

"What do you mean?"

"Come on down, I'll show you."

"Over the phone, Pam. What have you got?"

"Okay, okay. Mr. Houston Lish turns out to be a member of the Rank—you know, the looney tunes who killed that radio guy in Texas?"

"They sent a bomb through the mail, right?"

"And anonymous death threats to the judge who sentenced them. If you're doing a story on these bozos you better start opening your mail with tongs."

"What about Lish?"

"He was one of the founders of the Rank back in the seventies. He wasn't charged in the bombing but at the trial he was forcibly removed from the courtroom twice for demonstrating."

Paul made notes. After hanging up he told Annie what Pam had come up with.

"He left Thursday morning," Paul concluded. "And I dreamed his death Thursday night. With the time difference, that would be Thursday afternoon in Houston."

"You think Karl killed him in Houston?"

"I don't know. Pam's trying to find out where Lish was going. But if he *was* killed in Houston, we've got Karl in three locations: two weeks ago in Bayonne, three days ago in Texas, and this morning at my house. New York, Houston and Washington. There's got to be a connection."

"Never mind the connection," Annie said. "Let's just concentrate on where he is now. We've got to find him and investigate the mental link that exists between you. That's what's important."

Paul's face clouded and Annie added quickly, "And to find your wife, Paul. I know that comes first."

Paul doubted that it did, at least not to Annie. Before he could respond, the phone rang. It was Vic. The first thing he wanted to know was if Joanna was still missing.

"The situation hasn't changed," Paul answered.

"Then I've got your information," Vic said. "But I don't like what I see."

"What?"

"DE 3186 SF is shipment, ten each, Communications/ Data Link Jammer type AN slash MLQ dash T six."

"A data-link jammer? What's that?"

"Security system for radio transmissions. And your second shipment—"

"Wait a minute," Paul grabbed a pen and sheet of paper. "Give me the numbers again. Alpha Mike—"

"Alpha *November* slash Mike Lima Quebec dash Tango six."

"Okay. What's next?"

"QL 4416 HS is two hundred and fifty-six each Redeye tactical weapons, type XM41E2."

As soon as he heard the word *Redeye* the image of a doorway open to the clouds blossomed in his mind.

"Redeye," he repeated.

"X-ray Mike four one Echo two, you get that?"

Paul scribbled quickly. "Yeah, okay."

"Just remember, my ass is hanging in the wind on this one. Don't expose me to Charlie, huh?"

"I won't. Thanks, Vic."

As he put down the phone Annie was watching him closely. "What?"

"A Redeye missile," Paul said slowly. "And a dream I had. On the plane. It came back to me just now."

"What dream?"

Paul explained about the dream and how he remembered it when Vic mentioned the Redeye missile: the room with Joanna locked inside and the door that opened onto the sky with a jet—

He paused, his thoughts churning.

Annie said, "That sounds like a normal dream, not a link with Karl."

Paul wasn't listening. With the news of the Redeye shipment the facts had begun to shift, forming a dim pattern that was gradually emerging like a ship from the fog.

"Wait a minute, wait a minute," he said. He began pacing nervously. "Forget about Lish for a moment and focus on the Redeye. Maybe that's why he was at Bayonne, not for a victim but for a weapon. What if he went to Bayonne to steal a Redeye?"

"And just what is a Redeye?"

"A heat-seeking missile used to shoot down jets. But if that's why he's here, to shoot down a jet . . ."

Thoughts tumbled one after the other, each one modifying the one before, shifting the context, changing the import of his perceptions. *Had* Karl come to America to steal a Redeye and shoot down an aircraft? If so, why? Why not use a bomb? Why not sabotage an aircraft in a way that would look accidental? There was no reason to use a Redeye unless—

Unless the aircraft were impossible to approach in any other way. No . . . unless the *victim* were impossible to approach in any way. A man so well guarded—

Paul stopped. There was only one answer.

"Christ! The President . . ."

"What?"

He turned to Annie. "His target isn't Lish, it's the President of the United States. That's why he needs a Redeye!"

Annie just stared at him. Paul grabbed her by the elbows.

"The *dream*," he said, voice cracking. "The jet falling. It wasn't my dream, it was Karl's. He's planning on shooting down Air Force One."

Paul released her and turned for the phone, taking Hugh Roark's number from his shirt pocket.

"Wait a minute," Annie said. "That's a big leap—"

"It fits, it all fits . . ."

"But was a missile stolen?"

"Yes."

"Is that what the man told you?"

"No."

"Then how do you—"

Paul was already dialing. Annie stepped over and put her hand on the receiver.

"Paul, will you wait? Wait just a minute."

"I'm calling Hugh. The President's in danger—"

"You don't know that."

"I *do* know it. I can't prove it but I know it. I'm sure Karl somehow got a Redeye and he's going to use it to shoot down the President's plane. Anybody else he'd kill another way, one-on-one, like all the others. But the President—how do you kill one of the best-guarded men in the world? You don't. You kill the plane he's on."

Paul turned back to the phone but Annie grabbed his elbow.

"Paul, *why*? You said Karl works for the Russians. Why would the Russians assassinate the President when their leader is coming tomorrow to sign the treaty?"

Paul stared at her. He felt like he'd just walked into a brick wall. He was certain he was right but he saw with equal certainty that what Annie said was true. Why would the Soviets want to shoot down the President now?

"I don't know . . . maybe to stop the treaty, to make a tougher one with a new President . . ."

"You see?" Annie said gently. "You're reaching, jumping to conclusions. I know you had a dream about a jet falling, but that's not unusual. You were on a plane. Considering everything you've been through, it would have been strange if you *hadn't* had dreams. And when you think about this missile, how could one man steal something that big? He'd need help."

"No, no," Paul shook his head. Annie's reading list obviously didn't include *Jane's Weapons Systems*. "It's a shoulder-launched missile. It's portable. You can pick it up with one hand."

"Still, it wasn't reported stolen, was it?"

"I don't know."

The look in her eyes was one of professional understanding, and concern. Paul pulled away.

Annie said quietly, "Why don't you sit down, Paul? Take it easy—"

"Don't patronize me, Annie."

"I'm not."

"You damn well are."

"All right, but before you make any decisions, at least think things through."

Paul looked at his watch. "The President lands in less than an hour. I think there's a good chance that Karl's out there with a Redeye missile waiting to shoot him down. And I know he's got Joanna. What would you suggest? Are you willing to take the responsibility for the President's death? Or for Joanna's?"

Annie's self-assurance began to waver. "What about George Lish?"

Paul had forgotten about Lish. For a moment the scenario he'd built threatened to collapse. Then he remembered something about one of the CIA victims.

"Jim Wilson," he said. "Remember how he was found? In the trunk of his car with his throat slit and a note that was supposed to be from some anti-American Turkish group. Only the note was fake, remember? To throw suspicion on someone else."

"What are you saying? That George Lish—"

"Could be a scapegoat," Paul finished. "Maybe he never was the intended victim."

For the first time the awful implications of what Paul was saying became clear. This time Annie didn't protest when he dialed Hugh Roark. The CIA man had gotten Paul's earlier message and had been calling the house for half an hour.

"I'm not at the house," Paul said. "I'm at the *Herald*. Annie's with me."

"What's she doing there?"

Paul quickly told him what had happened since they'd

parted. He made it as brief as possible but even so it was hard for Hugh to keep up. He kept saying, "Whoaa, whoaa," and asking Paul to repeat or explain something. When Paul told him he thought Karl meant to shoot down the President, he stopped Hugh cold.

"Are you serious? You really think he's got a Redeye?"

"Hugh, I do. I can't prove it and Annie thinks I'm crazy—"

"I didn't say that," Annie called out.

"But your source," Hugh said. "Can't he tell you if one was stolen?"

"Not now. The President lands in forty-five minutes. You want to take the chance?"

"No. You stay there, I'll get right back to you."

"I won't be here. I'll be where *he'll* be. Where the President's plane is scheduled to land. Andrews Air Force Base."

"No, you can't do any good out there—"

"If I find him I find Jo."

"The Secret Service will want to talk to you. You better stay put."

"No way."

"Paul—"

"I'm going after Jo, you take care of the rest."

"Wait. Let me talk to Annie."

Paul held out the phone. "He wants to talk to you."

While she talked with Hugh, Paul went outside to another phone. He dialed the National Weather Service and listened to a tape-recorded forecast and review of current conditions. Only one statistic interested him: the wind direction. He had covered his share of presidential arrivals over the years and was familiar with the runways at Andrews. When he heard that the wind was from the south he knew that Runway 19 would be in use. If Karl positioned himself on the approach path he would be north of the airport.

He put down the phone, called to Annie and started toward the elevator. By his calculation they had less than an hour to find Joanna, and save the President's life.

CHAPTER

29

BEFORE HE KILLED HER KARL WANTED HIS brother's wife. He wanted to possess her in every way, including spiritually. That Joanna had to die was a decision he had made on the way to the Toons Creek house. His failure to kill Paul had already endangered his own life and now threatened the security of the mission. He would not make the same mistake again.

And yet as the afternoon wore on his feelings underwent a subtle change. In the beginning he had been interested in talking to Joanna for the insight she could provide to Paul. By the time they moved from the kitchen to the living room his interest and attention had shifted increasingly to Joanna. They were involved in a battle of wits, he and Joanna. Or were they? Her responses seemed endlessly variable; one moment she was earnest and sincere, a moment later, whimsical and ironic, a moment after that, apprehensive and fearful. Every comment that indicated she misunderstood everything that was going on was balanced by one of such unerring accuracy that he almost imagined that Joanna could read his mind. Her moods were mercurial; attempting to capture her thoughts was like trying to grab a fish from a running river.

It was in the living room that her physical presence took on a sexual dimension—the way she sat, her trim legs tucked beneath her, head thrust forward, the well-defined lips half-parted, sometimes flat, sometimes curling inward, changing form and redefining themselves with every shift of emotion. He was aware of the way the sweater hung on her shoulders and the swell of her thigh where it disappeared into dark recesses beyond the thick cuff of the shorts. His gaze slid over her long hands and restless fingers that kept adjusting the sleeves of the sweater. There was a wedding ring, a gold band inset with tiny diamonds, the same as Paul had. Suddenly he wished he'd taken Paul's ring along with his passport.

Standing at the living room window while she was in the bathroom, he began to fantasize sex with her. He imagined her standing close to him, her desire matching his, her eyes glistening. He would place his hands on her hips, then slowly follow the contours of her body upward, his hands sliding beneath the sweater, feeling the curve of her waist, the faint ripple of ribs disappearing beneath the soft swell of her breasts. She would return his embrace, leaning into him, stretching her arms around his neck, her face turned to his, their mouths joined, teeth sliding against one another, the soft warmth of her cheek against his face.

Lost in the fantasy he paid no attention to the tiny alarm bells sounding deep inside and it wasn't until she came out and called in an obviously seductive voice, "Karl, can I take you up on that glass of wine," that the spell was broken and he knew...

She was going to try to seduce him.

And he also realized with a shock how far he had been drawn into the fantasy that he and Paul were somehow the same person, that Joanna was his wife as much as Paul's, that her attraction to Paul would somehow translate into a corresponding attraction to him. It was an illusion of his own making, he realized, but she had recognized and encouraged it. She had offered the most seductive fantasy of all: that for the first time in his life he had met someone who *understood* him. And he had fallen for it.

Until she overplayed her hand.

"You want wine?" he called, quickly recovering.

Joanna came into view, one shoulder lowered suggestively. "Please."

No, Karl thought, you're going too far. The voice, the shoulder, too much.

"I'll join you," he said.

He stepped quickly past her so that she wouldn't see the satisfaction in his eyes. Or the admiration? What was it Paul had said? That Joanna was the most emotionally astute woman he'd ever known. Now Karl knew what he meant. Joanna had ferreted out weakness where he thought none existed. She had discovered his long-buried need to be understood, perhaps even accepted?

Now that he clearly saw what she was doing, he was amazed that she had brought him this far. A moment ago he had been fantasizing making love to her. Now, he again envisioned the two of them together, but this time she was the aggressor, kissing him, undressing him, running her lips across his body, encouraging him... with her long, delicate fingers, exciting him and then what? Would she try to grab the gun? Smash a knee into testicles? How far would she go?

He went to the cupboard, got out two wineglasses and placed them on the table. Joanna stood at the table, watching.

"It's funny being here with you like this," she said. "I keep thinking you're Paul."

In spite of himself, Karl again felt he was taking over part of his brother's life, but this time he also recognized and understood the reaction. Careful to maintain a light tone, he said, "Except that Paul is nicer and more gentle?"

"Maybe, but of course I haven't been with you in the best of circumstances..."

This time there was no body movement to go with the words, her tone was less obviously suggestive. Had she realized she was coming on too strong, Karl wondered? Had she read him that well and made an adjustment in her performance?

"Maybe we can compensate for that," he said.

Karl opened the refrigerator and took out a chilled bottle of white wine. He had already decided what he would do with her. First, encourage her to drink. If she was playing a role as he believed she was, she would need the courage the alcohol would provide. He remembered the bottle of scotch on the table beside the bed and guessed that she often turned to liquor in times of stress. He hoped so, because it would give more credence to her death. It would look like she broke her neck when she missed a turn and the car tumbled into the Patuxent River. And if she had a significant amount of alcohol in her system, so much the better. In the meantime it would be amusing to watch as she tried to seduce him and discover just how far she would go. He would not be easy to get into a state of sexual abandon—Joanna would have to work very, very hard.

"I hope you like white wine," he said as he placed the bottle on the table beside the two glasses.

When Joanna saw the label she smiled. "I don't believe this."

"What?"

"Did Paul tell you he liked Orvietto Classico?"

"Does he?"

"It's one of his favorites, didn't he tell you?"

Karl shook his head, watching her closely. She seemed to be sincere now.

"Well," she said lightly, "maybe you two have the same tastes in life."

"It seems we do."

He turned to get a corkscrew. Joanna might start the seduction but he was going to finish it. He wanted to see her face when he was deep inside her. He wanted to—

He had just gotten the corkscrew from the drawer when something—a movement reflected in the distant kettle or a rustle of quick-moving fabric or a slight grunt of physical effort—something alerted him. He turned, crouching, just in time to see the raised arm descending, the wine bottle a green blur . . .

As he raised his arm to block the blow he caught a glimpse of her face, the expression now so different from a moment ago. Her teeth were clenched, eyes bright with fear and hate. He was looking at the real Joanna at last—Joanna, the enemy.

His arm partially blocked her at the wrist but the momentum sent the bottle crashing against his temple. A sheet of white sparks jumped before his eyes. As he grabbed for her, his knees buckled, and he collapsed to the floor.

Something moved, something tugged at his coat. He blinked, saw her crouching over him, her arm extended as she tried to get at the gun in his pocket. When she saw his eyes open she moved quickly away, but he managed to grab at her and caught her ankle. She tore free and ran out of the room, leaving him gripping her shoe.

He stumbled to his feet and started after her. In the hall a wave of dizziness made him career off the wall and knock a Winslow Homer reproduction to the floor. He paid no attention. By the time he reached the front door he had the gun out.

She was twenty feet away, running past the stable, heading for the woods.

"Stop, right there," Karl ordered.

She changed direction, veering to the stable. He fired a quick shot as she reached the door. She was thirty feet away. He went into a marksman's crouch but there were still ferris-wheel spots dancing in his eyes. As she threw open the door he squeezed off another shot and saw the wood fly above and to the left.

Then she was gone.

All right, he thought as he stood up. Now she was trapped. The only door to the stable was at his end. He walked deliberately forward. His head throbbed but when he touched his temple he felt no bleeding. He breathed deeply and his eyes cleared. She had managed a lucky blow. She would never have a chance at another.

As soon as he and Annie arrived at Andrews Air Force Base Paul realized what an impossible task he'd set for himself. Less then fifteen miles from Washington, the base was situated in an area where housing developments, shopping centers and industrial parks alternated with small farms, rolling fields and thick forests, any one of which offered too many opportunities for concealment. At least he had had the foresight to bring along a map of Prince Georges County, and though this helped narrow the area of the search there were still too many places beneath the approach path to Runway 19 where Karl could be.

They had made the drive in record time, weaving in and out of traffic, with Paul alternately thinking out loud as he tried to re-create his brother's reasoning and cursing at cars that got in his way. Most of the time Annie sat gripping her seat. She disliked sports cars, and the Alfa Romeo's seatbelts didn't even have shoulder straps.

Paul pulled into the parking lot of a 7-11 store and grabbed the map from Annie's lap. Across the street a tall fence marked the boundary to the air force base. The main gate was visible with uniformed, white-gloved military police waving vehicles through.

"You think it's crazy, don't you?" he said as he pored over the map.

"I don't know," she said. "If you think that he's out here . . ."

Paul frowned in concentration, lifted his head and stared outside.

"No," Paul said slowly, "it's more than him. Jo's in danger, and this son of a bitch has got a Redeye missile. I'm sure of that..." Except the words that had come with increasing conviction now lost some of it. "I don't know if he's *here*. I'm not... responding to it, to this..."

"You mean the base?"

"Everything. I've got this feeling, this urgency the President's in terrible danger—" He stopped, frowned. "Or Jo. It could be her, not him. Except what the hell would Karl be doing with a Redeye unless it's the President's who?" He put his hands to his temples and pressed inward, shook his head and slammed a fist against the steering wheel.

"Hold it, Paul. Just try to let your mind relax," Annie said quietly.

"I can't, can't relax. *Something's* going to happen, and it's got to do with Joanna and the Redeye and Air Force One..."

The Winnebago gave Joanna a moment of hope. It blocked her view of the rear of the stable and it wasn't until she ran around it that she realized there was no back door.

It had been a foolish choice, ducking into the stable, but the gun-shots had unnerved her. Their sharp reports echoed in her ears and her hand tingled from the way the door jumped when the bullet struck it. The stable had seemed her only chance. Now, the folly of that decision became too apparent. In addition to the Winnebago there was a work-table surrounded by shelves and cupboards and three propane tanks standing against one wall, and that was all. There was no place to hide except the Winnebago, and what was that but another box inside a box?

Needing to do something, she opened the door to the Winnebago. And had an idea. Instantly she dropped to the ground and wriggled beneath the motor home. The earth was uneven and smelled of damp dirt; she could feel the undercarriage pressing against her back. With her face turned to one side she could see the base of the stable walls between the underside of the Winnebago and the floor. The narrow band of light that streamed in from the open doorway dimmed when Karl entered.

She froze.

Karl was only visible from the knees down. At any moment she expected he would stop, his knees would bend, and his head would come into view as he looked beneath the Winnebago and found her. But he walked down the right side of the Winnebago, toward the door that she'd left open.

He thinks I'm inside it, she thought.

As he passed her, she began to work her way toward the rear of the motor home, where it was closest to the outside door. Her hair caught in something and she almost cried out. She reached around and tried to free it. No use. Karl mounted the step to the Winnebago and his shoes disappeared from view. She had to move—*now*. She shoved forward, heard and felt the clump of hair rip from her scalp, and crouching low, ducked out the door and around the front of the house to where the Audi was parked.

When she turned around she half-expected to see Karl coming at her. Not yet. The sun was low, long shadows bathed the yard. Tranquility at odds with the reality.

Moving quickly, she located the magnetic keyholder beneath the front bumper. Her fingers fumbled to open it, and when she did the key flipped to the ground. She dropped the holder, recovered the key and got into the car. By habit she slammed the door and instantly regretted it. Karl was sure to have finished looking in the Winnebago and was probably outside by now.

The seat was too far back but she couldn't take time to adjust it. Perched on the edge, she jammed the key into the ignition and started the car. If he hadn't heard her before, he had now. She let out the clutch and the car lurched forward, and died. She hadn't released the parking brake.

She wrenched it free and started the car again. This time when she let out the clutch the Audi shot forward and she found herself holding onto the steering wheel to keep from being thrown back too far to reach the pedals. A glance in the rearview mirror still showed no sign of Karl as she rounded the curve and the farmhouse was lost in the trees.

She let out a deep breath, pushed the button and rolled

up the windows. The skylight was open too, but before she could close it a wrought-iron fence came into view. For a moment she was tempted to smash through it, but crashing the fence might puncture a tire or smash the radiator or shove a fender into the wheel. A glance behind showed her that the road was empty. She pulled to a quick stop, left the motor running, got out and pushed open the gate. Back in the car, she realized how naked she felt outside it.

The road behind was still empty so she took a moment to lock the door and adjust the seat. When she reached to close the skylight a flash of movement caught her eye, not from the empty road but from the woods off to the right.

He was coming toward her, open coat flapping, palms chopping the air.

She threw the car into gear and headed out of the gate, tires spitting dirt, rear end fishtailing as she turned onto the road. The Audi straightened and Karl slammed shoulder-first into the right side of the car. He clutched the door handle, half-running, half-dragged alongside as he tried to get in. But the doors were locked and she had rolled up the windows.

But there was the open skylight.

As the car surged forward he lost his footing and grabbed the sunroof just in time. His legs banged against the car but he held on. When Joanna looked over, Karl's face was pressed against the window, his features flattened and distorted as he struggled to maintain his hold.

She wrenched the wheel back and forth trying to shake him loose. But he had both hands on the sunroof now, and as she swerved toward him he used the motion of the car to help him climb aboard. A moment ago it seemed impossible he could hold on. Now he lay across the roof, his legs visible in the rear window, his fingers curled around the inner lip of the sunroof.

She accelerated and at the same time reached over and activated the switch to close the sunroof. A pickup truck appeared, coming straight at her, horn blaring. Gripping the wheel hard with both hands she swerved back to her side of the road. She slowed down then, thinking that maybe, somehow the people in the truck would help, but it went right past, peppering the side of the Audi with grit. All she got was a glimpse of the driver's face scowling at her.

He thinks we're fooling around, she thought.

Karl's arm plunged through the five-inch gap in the sunroof and grabbed at her face. She ducked away but the hand kept clawing at her. Fingers raked her cheek, then gripped her forehead and went toward her eyes.

She slammed on the brakes, the car skidded wildly. There was a thump, Karl plunged into view, disappeared over the hood. The car was skidding sideways in a slow spin. She fought to regain control and had almost succeeded when the Audi slammed rear-end into a telephone pole.

The impact was solid but not wrenching, like falling over backward in a chair. The engine died and in the new silence the wail of an approaching train sounded. To the left, in the direction that she'd been heading, the road climbed to meet the railroad tracks, and beyond the tracks was a busy highway. Behind her, through a drifting cloud of dust, she saw Karl get to his feet and start toward her.

She started the car and tried to drive ahead. The Audi rocked forward, and stopped, rear tires spinning. The engine roared but the rear wheels only dug in deeper. She began rocking the car, putting it into reverse, then forward, reverse and forward, rocking it back and forth. With each cycle the trunk rose higher. Karl was close now, she could even see the expression in his eyes. Not wild, not crazed. Weirdly calm, professional. Now the car had bounded back onto the road. Joanna swung the wheel to the left and fishtailed away.

Karl was less than five feet from the rear bumper when the Audi began to pull away. She watched in the rearview mirror as he made one last effort to catch up, then slowed and collapsed to the roadside—no, not collapsed. He had gone into a crouch with one elbow braced on his knee, the gun held out with both hands. She hunched down and yanked the steering wheel back and forth to throw off his aim. Any moment she expected to hear the shot, and she wondered if he hit her in the head would she die before she heard the bullet?

He did not fire. Instead he stood up, pocketed the gun, and began coming after her. It was so crazy it scared her more than the gun. He couldn't hope to catch her, then why—?

And then she heard the diesel's wail and saw the train

approaching the crossing. A long train that would cut her off from the safety of the highway. It was over. Unless—

She shifted to fourth and put her foot to the floor. If she stopped, he would kill her. If she died at least it would be trying to get away, not passively trapped like some animal. She leaned forward, pushing the steering wheel, urging the car onward, afraid to shift her gaze from the opening between the two railroad crossing signs, afraid to see the train bearing down on her.

The scream of the diesel's horn was constant now and joined by another sound, the shriek of metal as the train's wheels locked in a final attempt to stop. The road lifted as it met the railroad bed, and she felt her stomach drop as the Audi vaulted into the air. She was aware of a black thundering mass and a single sweeping headlight off to her left and a world of noise. The tracks flashed beneath, and a moment later the car was buffeted by a shock of rushing air. The train's horn shifted in tone as the Audi slammed down on the other side of the tracks, and the train swept past and behind it, a blur of quick-changing colors in the rearview mirror.

Before she could recover from the shock Joanna saw the Stop sign fifty feet ahead, and beyond it the busy highway. She was going over seventy miles an hour.

She slammed on the brakes, knowing as she did that it was useless. All she could do was try not to hit anyone, and with that thought she deliberately steered off the road and into an embankment. The right fender struck, the Audi vaulted into the air and turned slowly on its side. When it hit the pavement, it flipped over again and again and again.

CHAPTER

30

LE SORBET RESTAURANT WAS HALF A BLOCK from the Secret Service field office on G Street. It was here that Agent Eliot Ingerman, assistant director of the Secret Service Protective Division, received news of the Redeye threat to Air Force One. For six weeks he had been working twelve-hour days coordinating security arrangements between the various intelligence agencies in preparation for the Russian General Secretary's visit. He had gotten only five hours' sleep the night before and had been stuck in his office all day. At five-thirty he slipped away and walked to Le Sorbet, where he ordered a seafood croissant and a cup of coffee. The beeper went off before the food arrived. Now, as he stood at the pay phone and listened to the incredible possibility that a Redeye missile had been stolen and would be deployed against Air Force One, he couldn't help feeling that the threat would never have materialized if he had stayed in his office and sent a secretary out for food.

"What's the quality of the intelligence?" he asked grumpily.

"Single source but no confirmation. The officer running him rates him solid but admits it's more gut-level than long-term experience."

"Who's the officer?"

"Hugh Roark. He's one of the old guard, working a special assignment through Security. He seems solid."

The man on the other end of the line was Tommy Lecrazny, CIA liaison officer. Also on the line was Ingerman's assistant, Barbara Ziegler, who had received the incoming call and patched the CIA man through.

The smell of food made Ingerman's stomach growl. He glanced toward his table where a waitress held up his seafood croissant. Ingerman smiled and nodded to her and continued questioning Lecrazny.

"Who's the primary?"

"Paul Stafford, reporter over at the *Herald*."

Ingerman's senses sharpened. Paul Stafford wasn't the most well-loved reporter in Washington—especially by some of the defense contractors and their politician pals— but no one doubted his credibility. Or the accuracy of his sources.

"The tip came through Stafford's source?"

"Not exactly. It's Stafford's brother."

"The tip came through his brother?"

"No, the brother's the assassin."

"*Stafford's* brother?"

"That's how I get it."

"And Stafford called him in?"

"Yep."

"Well, fuck a duck," Ingerman said softly.

All his Secret Service training emphasized avoiding emergencies; advance planning was the order of every day. The President and his family never went anywhere that had not been prepared beforehand. Emergencies were anticipated so that they were no longer emergencies but contingencies. There was a contingency plan for everything, including the substitution of Dulles Airport for Andrews Air Force Base. The question now was whether to activate the Dulles option. It was a matter of individual judgment and the chance of making an error was magnified by both lack of information and the necessity for a quick decision.

Ingerman glanced at his watch. The President was scheduled to land in twenty-eight minutes.

"Okay, I'm on my way back. Leave a number with Barbara and stay close to the phone."

"I told you this one was out of left field."

"Barbara?"

"I'm here."

"Okay, listen. Call the Bayonne terminal and confirm the integrity of the Redeye shipment. Then double-check the PTA for stolen or missing Redeyes or any other kind of ground-to-air missiles."

He was referring to the Potential Threat Analysis, a report prepared by the Office of Protective Intelligence,

which listed all individuals, organizations or activities that
might become a threat. Stolen Redeye missiles definitely
fell into the PTA's jurisdiction.

"Next thing," Ingerman went on, "locate Paul Stafford
and have him stand by. Then alert Kenny—he's doing the
arrival at Andrews—give him a sitrep and tell him we'll
get back. And get a current ETA for the landing. After that
find me Colonel Coswell or Bud Hollingsworth—somebody
who knows the capabilities of a Redeye and how much
threat it poses to Air Force One. Hollingsworth's number
is on a zip card. I'm at Le Sorbet and I'm leaving now."

After hanging up Ingerman detoured past his table,
grabbed the croissant and left a five-dollar bill. Outside,
he walked briskly down the street, wolfing his food as he
went.

Joanna's decision to outrun the train took Karl by surprise. When her car did not slow down but shot across the
tracks he expected it would be crushed like an aluminum
can. Instead, it disappeared from view, leaving him staring
in disbelief, unable to believe that Joanna had gotten away.
Yet there he was, standing in the middle of the road, dirty
and bruised, trying to catch his breath, while she was no
doubt on her way to the police. How she had started the
car he still couldn't figure out . . . the keys to the Audi
were in his pocket.

As the shriek of the train's brakes and wail of its horn
subsided his anger and self-recrimination boiled up. Part
of his arsenal was to recognize and exploit the weaknesses
of his victims, and he was an expert at it. Yet in this case
he had been betrayed by *his* weaknesses . . . especially the
illusion of living his brother's life that had taken such hold
of his imagination. Joanna had recognized it and used it.
She had played to it, built and encouraged it for her own
purposes. He had known that her seduction was false; why
then hadn't he also realized that she would make her move
before it even began?

Because he had so badly wanted the seduction to happen.

He threw the gun to the ground. Everything was in
jeopardy now. She would go to the police and she would
tell them about the Toons Creek property and the
Winnebago. The police would come looking for him; they
might even discover Lish's body. When he thought of the

trouble he'd gone to kidnapping his brother, stealing the Redeye, placing Lish's fingerprints everywhere. And what of Ikhnovsky? The old man had said that his life was in Karl's hands. Had he traded his mentor's life for his brother's?

Karl was still sorting through his angry thoughts when the train passed and he saw several cars stopped on the highway beyond the crossing. For a moment he thought that Joanna had flagged down motorists to come and get him. Then someone lit a purple flare and went running to put it on the road, and Karl suddenly realized: Joanna had not escaped, after all. She had missed the train but hit something else, apparently another car on the highway.

Rage evaporated, relief flooded in. He began jogging toward the accident. He ran easily now. With this reprieve his thoughts regained their equilibrium and he was able to begin planning his next move. Joanna would, he hoped, be dead, and if so his only problem would be getting back to the safe house.

He slowed to a walk as he reached the crest of the railroad tracks. One lane was blocked and someone had taken on the task of directing traffic. His eyes read the story in the long shallow furrows that angled off the road and up an embankment, where they disappeared. The splintered stump of a Stop sign stood at a forty-five-degree angle; beyond it the highway was covered with broken glass and bruised with patches of white paint and silver metal.

She had obviously lost control, gone up the embankment and cartwheeled into the street where she had struck another car, a Ford Escort, he noted. The left front panel of the Ford was staved in, its metal ripped, the engine cocked to one side, its steaming radiator dangling like a broken tooth. Two men were leading a hysterical woman from the Ford. Nearby another man was lying on the ground, alive but clutching his arm.

A larger crowd had gathered around the Audi, which had come to rest in an upright position but was in much worse shape than the Ford. Its wheels were bent almost parallel to the road, all the glass was broken and the openings, which had been windows, were barely recognizable. The roof, buckled and twisted, hugged the car like a metal blanket, and all the corners and sides were mashed inward, as if a giant had used the car for a piece of clay. It seemed unlikely that anyone could have lived through the crash.

As he approached, two men and a young woman eased Joanna's body through the gaping windshield. A fourth man wearing shorts stood to one side giving nervous advice . . . "That's got it. Here she comes, here she comes." . . . Someone called out, "Is she alive?" No one answered but the comments continued as more people gathered around. "Okay, gently now." . . . "Shouldn't we get her away from the car?" . . . "You don't want to move her; if she's got broken ribs you could puncture a lung." . . . "But the car, I smell gas." . . . "No cigarettes."

The man in shorts turned and began yelling importantly, "Nobody smoke, there's gasoline here. No smoking."

Karl moved forward. Joanna was lying on the side of the road, her face cut, blood streaming from her head. She was deathly white and Karl couldn't tell if she was breathing. One arm lay twisted at an impossible angle, the jagged tip of glistening white bone poking out of her sweater. A woman came running with a blanket. Karl took one end and helped cover her with it.

"Is she alive?" he asked.

"Just barely," the man on the ground beside her said. "Has anybody got a bandage? Something to stop the bleeding?"

A young man pulled off a tee-shirt with a picture of Bruce Springsteen on it. Karl placed his index and middle fingers on Joanna's neck and felt for a pulse. It was there, but faint. The man who had gotten the tee-shirt began using it to stanch the flow of blood. He looked up at Karl and shook his head.

"I don't think she's going to make it."

Karl nodded and moved back, letting others fill the role of Good Samaritan. Joanna was a threat. She had made herself a threat. She had to die. This was good. This way it looked like a simple accident without his having to arrange it.

He left the scene and began walking back to the house. When he heard a distant siren he thought what a shame that they had come so quickly. He hoped the man with the tee-shirt was right. That Joanna was almost dead. It would be best if she died on the way to the hospital.

* * *

Air Force One was over Wheeling, West Virginia, when the call came through. The President was in the First Family's lounge, sitting near his wife, who ignored what he was saying. She had good reason: the President was speaking in Russian. He sat with his feet up, eyes closed, wearing tiny earphones and a boom mike, listening to a tape of Russian phrases he intended to use during the meeting with the Russian leader. His father's heart attack, mild as it was, had left him with a heightened sense of mortality that gave added significance to the Mutual Defense Treaty. If he could leave this a more peaceful and secure world than the one he'd been born into he would count his life, and his tenure in office, well spent.

Someone knocked at the door. The President, who liked to travel in casual attire, assumed that it was his valet with a fresh shirt, his coat and tie. Instead he found Lee Knudson, his chief of staff, waiting for him.

"Eliot Ingerman's got something for you."

Lee did not say that it was important but he didn't need to. The layout aboard Air Force One was such that the President's compartment and First Family's quarters were in the forward section of the plane, followed by compartments for the White House staff, Secret Service detail and press pool. By tradition, occupants of one section were free to visit those behind them but did not move forward without an invitation. Unless it was something very important.

The two men went to the President's compartment, a hybrid modern office and communications center. From a single telephone the President could link through the National Command Authority to every communications system, civil and military, closed, ciphered, encrypted or open, in the Western world. In this case the man on the other end of the line was Eliot Ingerman. The President didn't know Ingerman well but what he did know encouraged him to trust his judgment, which was why he was surprised that the Secret Service man thought it necessary to brief him on a situation that seemed farfetched at best.

After explaining the situation Ingerman said, "Colonel Coswell tells me the aircraft has a defense screen that would knock out a Redeye but I've got a detail on the way to Dulles just in case we want to make a preemptive defense."

"What are you saying, Eliot?"

"I'm saying, sir, that if you'd like to order the Dulles option, we can move on it right away."

No, the President thought, that is exactly what I would not like to do. There were four members of the White House press pool aboard the aircraft, not to mention the reporters and photographers at Andrews; any deviation to Dulles would be all over the papers and networks within hours. He could imagine the lead story: "THREAT TO AIR FORCE ONE FORCES LANDING AT DULLES." He could imagine the effect this would have on the Russians, particularly the KGB contingent in charge of the General Secretary's safety.

"You wouldn't ask my opinion if you could confirm a definite threat, would you?"

"No, Mr. President."

"Are you prepared to execute the Dulles plan based on what you know now?"

"Without independent confirmation of reporter Paul Stafford's story, and based on what I'm told about our air defense capabilities, my judgment says no."

"You've been doing this longer than I have," the President said. "We'll go with your judgment.

"Yes, sir." Ingerman didn't sound happy.

The President smiled. "You were hoping I'd make it easy for you?"

"Damn right, sir."

"All right, Eliot. Thanks for the briefing. You'll let me know where all this started."

The President hung up and exchanged a speculative look with Lee Knudson.

The chief of staff said, "Son of a bitch probably taped the conversation to cover his ass in case we go down in flames."

The President shrugged. "It goes on all the time. We just don't hear about it."

"You mean venality, subservience, evasion of responsibility?"

The President smiled again. Lee's exaggerated sarcasm offended some people but the President enjoyed it.

"The threats. They get handled. We never know—"

"We'll know this time if they don't get handled."

The President's smile faded. He turned to look out the window. Some thirty thousand feet below, the country crept silently westward as they began the descent into Washington.

Two Air Force helicopters began circling lazily over the approach area as Paul and Annie checked the spot that seemed best situated for an attack: an industrial park located in a wooded area just beyond the base. There were a couple of older wood homes that once might have been farmhouses but most of the buildings were of concrete construction, one, two or three stories high: a printing company, an auto body shop, a design studio, a self-storage facility and half-a-dozen anonymous warehouses.

Paul was sure that Karl wouldn't be wandering, carrying the Redeye like a fishing pole, but he described the missile to Annie so she knew the size and shape of what they were looking for. They drove slowly up and down dead-end roads and saw dozens of places that Karl might be, but no sign of him or of Joanna. At one point they stopped at the self-storage facility and asked about anyone who looked like Paul, realizing as they did how peculiar the question must sound. A young man with a Jamaican accent said he couldn't help them but let them go up to the roof.

Paul shook his head as he surveyed the surrounding area. "He could be on that roof or that roof or still inside a building waiting for the plane to come in sight. Or he could be out there in the woods."

"We'll know in a minute," Annie said.

Paul followed her gaze and saw a Boeing 707, low in the sky, turning toward them. He checked his watch. It wasn't yet six o'clock.

"Not him," he said. "That's the backup plane. Air Force One will be about ten minutes behind."

Annie gave him a look of renewed appreciation. Paul decided not to tell her that he had worked the White House beat for six months.

They went back to the car and decided to check the roads that passed beneath the approach path: Interstate 95, Highway 337, the Marlboro Pike and Suitland Parkway. It was a rolling terrain, and the roads were usually bordered by woods. They passed a car parked at the side

of the road with its hood open and stopped to inspect it.
Paul peered in the window and walked around the car.
Annie followed. Every time a truck passed, the air buffeted
them and the suction tugged at Annie's skirt.

Paul ran a speculative eye over the back of the car. "The
trunk would probably be big enough to carry the missile,"
he said. "And who knows if anything's really wrong with
the engine?"

"But where would he go?"

Paul turned and looked at the trees some ten feet away.
He began walking toward them. Annie caught up to him
and suggested they spread out. The woods weren't particularly thick but they would cover more area by separating.
And they didn't have much time.

She seemed caught up in the search as much as he was,
and for the first time Paul considered what might happen
if she came on Karl, toting a Redeye missile and with the
38-caliber Smith & Wesson.

"I know you don't want to hear this," he said. "But did it
ever occur to you that he might kill you if you try to stop
him?"

"I won't try to stop him. I just want to find him."

Before he could figure out what she meant by that he
saw over her shoulder, in the distance, the President's
plane, Air Force One. It was only a silhouette as it turned
slowly onto final approach but Paul recognized it. His face
hardened then, and Annie turned to look over her shoulder.

"That's him?"

Paul didn't answer. He was already charging through the
woods, shouting Karl's name. Anything to disrupt him,
flush him from his hiding place. Annie took a divergent
path and followed some thirty feet off to his right. She
added her voice to his, which Paul thought was just as
well. The more people Karl thought were after him, the
more likely he was to bolt.

The earth sloped upward, then began a gentle descent.
There was a flash of color just ahead, through a clump of
trees, and a moment later Paul found himself in the open,
standing on the shoulder of another road, not the freeway
this time but the Allentown Road, which bordered the
base.

The flash of color was a sweeping red light from a
Highway Patrol car parked in the center of the road. Two

officers stood beside the car, chatting. On the road, in the distance, Paul could see another police car blocking the road. This car was turning away traffic.

One of the patrolmen spotted him and his smile died. "The road's closed, sir."

The man's partner turned around just as Annie came out of the woods.

"Karl?" she called out, then stopped short. She saw the police and she saw Paul and she looked confused. The police looked suspicious.

"Can we help you folks?"

Before Paul could answer Annie recovered and gave a quick innocent explanation.

"Someone had trouble on the freeway," she said brightly.

"There's a car with nobody around. We thought maybe they'd come this way."

The older patrolman had heavy jowls, but he was evidently a man of the old school; he tipped his hat and said, "If they did they're not here now, ma'am. This road's closed until the President lands."

"Then maybe somebody gave them a ride," Annie said. "Thank you anyway."

She took Paul's arm and led him back the way they'd come. The whine of the approaching jet made them both look up. Trees pointed like tall fingers at the hazy blue sky beyond. The noise swelled, and Air Force One slid overhead. Now they could see the blue-and-white markings and the presidential seal. Annie took a quick breath and involuntarily tightened her grip on Paul's arm.

The sight of the plane triggered something in Paul, a dislocation of memory, the sense that something was wrong. It had to do with the shape of the aircraft, with the engines, lunging forward from their pylons beneath the sweptback wings. It was wrong...

The plane disappeared from view.

"That's not the one..." Paul said.

Annie turned to him, realized she was holding his arm and released it. Paul was still staring into the trees.

"That's not the plane."

"It's another backup?"

He turned to her. "No, it's not the one I saw. You know, in my dream. Or whatever you call it. I remember *clearly*, one wing was broken and it was heading straight for me.

But there were no engines. No engines on the wing. They were in back, attached to the fuselage. Rear-mounted engines, just below the tail."

"You mean like a 727?"

Paul shook his head. "*Four* engines, two on each side, mounted in—"

It hit him like a physical blow. He knew the aircraft type now: paired engines, two on each side, mounted in tandem. And the sweptback tail topped by a horizontal stabilizer, just like a 727 except it wasn't a 727, it was a Russian jet, an Ilyushin 62. It was Aero-flot...

"My God."

Annie stepped back. "*What?*"

Paul's face was a mask of wonder, and disbelief.

"It's not the President. It's the Russian. Karl's going after—"

"*Who?*"

"*That's* why he's here. *He's going to kill the Russian General Secretary.*"

Annie could only stare at him. She heard what he was saying but it made no sense. For the first time she questioned her own judgment and wondered if Paul was indeed crazy. She felt like Alice running after the White Rabbit. Every time she turned around a pumpkin had become an orange, or a mushroom a birthday cake.

"He's going to kill the Russian," Paul announced. "I'm *sure* of it."

He started back to the car. Annie ran to catch up.

"But you said—I thought Karl was working for the Russians."

"He is."

"Then why—?"

Paul opened the door to the car and turned to her. "I don't know. But I saw four engines mounted in twin pairs and that spells Aero-flot and that means the leader of the Soviet Union. Let's call your boss."

"Wait." Annie put a hand on his arm. "Paul, stop and think a minute. If he's working for the Russians he's not going to shoot down their leader. And if he's not working for the Russians..."

Her reasoning ran into a dead-end. Paul looked at her closely. "What are you saying? That he's working for you guys? For the CIA?"

"No, no," she said quickly, and then, with less assurance, "at least I don't think so."

For a moment they both considered the possibility that Karl was somehow working for the CIA. Paul felt his mind stretch to the breaking point as he tried to juggle the facts into a new interpretation. If Karl was actually working for the CIA, then who were the original victims? KGB agents? And why would Hugh and Maurice need Paul's help in tracking him down? Or were they supposed to be KGB agents too?

No. He'd confirmed Hugh and Maurice's credentials. They were CIA. That was a fact. And he had dreamed the murders; that was another fact. And he had good reason to trust Hugh Roark; that was a fact too.

"No," he said firmly, "it doesn't work any other way. I don't know why he's after his own boss, but I know he is . . . Come on."

He slid into the car and Annie followed him.

"Don't tell anyone but Hugh," Annie warned. "If the Russians hear about it, even if it's not true, they may try to kill him."

He looked at her. "Just as long as they don't kill Joanna."

"He's your own brother," she said.

Paul didn't answer. Annie watched him for a moment, then turned to the window. When she spoke again her tone was almost reflective. Peculiar, he thought, at a time like this.

"You don't realize how rare it is, this link you have with Karl. Maybe in its special form it's unique. The two of you are very valuable people."

Paul shook his head.

"It's true, damn it. I know it sounds extreme, but your lives are one of a kind, worth more than—"

"Than my wife's, than the President's?"

She didn't answer him, but as he looked at her he realized that was exactly what she thought.

CHAPTER

31

BECAUSE OF HIS PREMATURELY GRAY HAIR, AS well as a certain knack for navigating the treacherous political waters of governmental bureaucracy, his colleagues had given Eliot Ingerman the nickname "Gray Fox." Ingerman played to this image by projecting an urbane, authoritative exterior that was sometimes at odds with the turmoil he felt during those rare times he had to put his judgment on the line. This was one of those times.

He had returned to his office on G Street and with Barbara's help had talked to a dozen people in as many minutes. He hadn't been able to get in touch with Paul Stafford, for which he blamed the CIA. After all, Stafford was their source. But he had talked to Hugh Roark and everything that the CIA man told him served to confirm his assessment that the Redeye threat was empty. Stafford's brother, a twin it turned out, was a man Stafford had never met or even known about until a few weeks ago. The brother, Karl Alexander, was supposed to be working for the KGB through an East German organization called the Stasis.

"He's a trained killer," Hugh Roark had told him. "And very effective."

Maybe so and maybe not, Ingerman thought. The CIA wasn't infallible. It put too much emphasis on collecting intelligence and not enough on analyzing it. Stafford was a case in point: what kind of Byzantine plot would have a Russian hitman going after the President now, on the eve of the Mutual Defense Treaty? Hugh Roark had no answer for that one.

No, the whole thing seemed more likely to have sprung full-blown from this Paul Stafford's imagination. The report from the Bayonne Military Terminal was negative: there were no reports of any security breaches or missing cargo. And Colonel Coswell assured him that Air Force One was infra-red protected.

"We've got a Hot Brick system," Coswell explained. "That puts out a variable-frequency waveform that'll confuse the hell out of a heat-seeking missile like the Redeye. Which, of course, is not to say that I'd like to have one fired in my direction."

Or the President's direction, Ingerman thought. Despite the reassurances, the Gray Fox had taken two precautions: he had warned the President about the threat and he had arranged to videotape the landing. If anything *did* happen he wanted a filmed record for both clues and evidence.

Now, as he watched the video monitor, he felt a familiar burning sensation in his stomach. It was going to be a rough week for his ulcer. The scene on the monitor showed the arrival area at Andrews, where a small group of people waited to meet the President. The camera operator, one of their own men, was on the roof of the terminal. He didn't have a tripod and the picture was jerky.

"Tell him to hold still," Ingerman called to Barbara, his assistant. "Give us a steady picture."

Barbara sat at an adjoining desk with a telephone to her ear. She was a plain, middle-aged woman who was as efficient as she looked.

The camera operator's voice reached them through the monitor. "Okay, here he comes."

The image abruptly shifted and settled on the far end of the runway, where Air Force One was visible descending from a hazy sky. Ingerman waved Barbara over and they both held their breath as the plane slowly, imperceptibly approached the runway. As it was about to touch down a phone rang, making them both jump. Barbara returned to her desk to take the incoming call.

The plane touched down and Ingerman's stomach growled in relief. The damn CIA boys had spooked him.

The camera operator said, "Is that it?"

"Stay on it," Ingerman instructed. Just in case. Always, just in case.

He opened his desk drawer, took out a pill for his stomach and walked into the hallway for a drink of water.

When he came back to the office the air force was rolling out the steps to Air Force One.

Ingerman said, "The cooler in the drinking fountain is on the blink again, better call someone."

Barbara looked up from the phone, her face ashen.

"What?" he demanded.

"That was Bayonne," she said slowly. "A security team just inspected the warehouse. They found a ventilator, up on the roof, where somebody broke in. It looks like it happened during the last month."

Ingerman felt icy fingers on his backbone. He turned to the television monitor, where the President stood at the top of the ramp, waving to friends and reporters.

You lucky son of a bitch, he thought. And then he thought it again, this time for the President.

Karl alternately walked and jogged back to the Toons Creek house. He was in good spirits. He had meant to devise a traffic accident to kill Joanna and now it had happened with the added benefit of eyewitnesses. His only concern, of course, was that she might not have died. He had no idea whether she recognized the Redeye packing case in the back of the Winnebago but he didn't intend to take any chances. As soon as he got home he took out the phone book and began calling hospitals. Joanna had been taken to Glenway Memorial Hospital in Upper Marlboro. A nurse in the emergency room told him that she was in surgery.

"How badly hurt is she?"

"I don't know, Mr. Stafford. You'll have to talk to the doctor when he comes out of the operating room."

"Was she conscious when she was admitted?"

"No, sir. She was brought in comatose and in shock."

"But she's expected to survive, is that right?"

"You'll have to talk to the doctor about that, Mr. Stafford."

"All right, I'll come right down."

After hanging up Karl considered the situation. If Joanna survived she would come out of surgery under sedation. Judging from what he'd seen of her injuries they would probably put her in intensive care, where she would be hooked up to a lot of machines and monitors. She would be getting an intravenous solution and would probably be on a respirator. The nurses would be watching, so he had to be careful. He could do nothing physical.

The obvious choice was a drug. A whiff of hydrogen cyanide would induce a heart attack, but there was no way to administer it if she was on a respirator. Besides, he had no hydrogen cyanide, only Haloparimine, the same sedative he'd given Otto to use on his brother.

Karl smiled as the idea took hold. He went to the bathroom and found his toilet kit, a compartmentalized soft leather bag he had purchased in Turkey. He took out a small round bottle with a syringe top. The label indicated that this was medicine for use with an ear infection. In fact, it was highly concentrated Haloparimine. One syringe would induce a sleep so heavy that a man's bedroom could be searched with a crowbar and he wouldn't wake up. Two syringes could induce a coma; the entire contents would kill a person.

All he needed to do was dump the Haloparimine into the IV solution. The first symptoms of the drug, shallowness of breathing, would be masked by the respirator. By the time Joanna's blood pressure began dropping, he would be gone and the drug would have progressed too far to be reversed.

Feeling more confident than he had since Joanna had surprised him that morning, Karl changed clothes and began packing the Winnebago. He wore gloves so as not to leave any of his own fingerprints next to George Lish's. The house itself didn't matter—there was no way he could get rid of all of "Ron Tednick's" fingerprints even if he wanted to. But it wouldn't be necessary. Joanna was the only one who could link him to the Toons Creek house and she was not going to survive.

It was a small and select group of men who gathered in the Briefing Room of the Secret Service field office on G street. Eliot Ingerman had called the meeting after talking to Stafford on the phone and deciding that the man was sane. Unfortunately, Stafford sounded more credible than he looked. When he showed up for the meeting Ingerman was dismayed to find him hollow-eyed and pale and obviously on edge. It didn't help that most of his assertions couldn't be checked, based as they were on dreams and premonitions and hypnosis and what seemed psychological mumbo-jumbo.

The woman, Annie Helms, made a more substantial impression, although her theory about brain waves and genetic compatibility was equally out of left field as far as he was concerned. Ingerman had talked to them both on the phone and decided that if he had to make a decision based on such elusive evidence, he wasn't going to do it alone. It was at that point that he called a meeting of the Summit Security Unit.

The six men who sat around the oval table represented various intelligence and security agencies: the Secret Service, FBI, CIA, Defense Intelligence Agency and the State Department's INR—the Bureau of Intelligence and Research. In addition, Ingerman had asked Colonel Buzz Coswell, an expert in airborne defense systems, to attend. Hugh Roark and Annie Helms were there with Paul Stafford. Conspicuously absent were the KGB security-specialists who had flown in from Moscow weeks ago. Ingerman thought it best to wait until the American contingent had a chance to evaluate Stafford's story before opening themselves up to Russian alarm or criticism. Or ridicule.

Ingerman took off his jacket, unbuttoned his cuffs and rolled them neatly twice to emphasize the importance of the meeting. As soon as the last man arrived, he stood up.

"Gentlemen, thank you for coming on such short notice. Obviously I wouldn't have called this meeting unless the circumstances were extraordinary and they are that. Many of you will recognize the man on my right by name, if not on sight: this is Paul Stafford, from the Washington *Herald*. Next to him are two members of the Central Intelligence Agency, Hugh Roark and Dr. Anne Helms, both of whom are closely associated with the events that have led up to this meeting. In a nutshell, Mr. Stafford has information that leads him to believe that a man—in fact, his own brother—has stolen a Redeye missile and intends to use it to shoot down the Soviet General Secretary tomorrow morning."

There had been some complaints about calling a meeting during the dinner hour but this little bombshell effectively stilled them.

D. L. McNally from the State Department finally made himself heard above the others.

"Wait a minute, Eliot. Where are Vronsky and Dekanozov? Why aren't they here?"

"I think you'll understand the reason when you've heard Mr. Stafford's story."

"Just so you understand, the protocol guarantees the KGB security section a voice in any decisions concerning the General Secretary's safety."

Ingerman was annoyed. He knew as well as McNally what the protocol provisions were.

"That's all well and good," he said, "but according to Mr. Stafford it's the *Russians* who are behind the plot."

There was a moment of stunned silence that Ingerman allowed to linger in the air a bit longer than necessary before he turned to Paul. "All right, Mr. Stafford, the floor is yours."

Paul stood up and looked around the table. "Three weeks ago," he began, "I wouldn't have believed a word of what I'm about to tell you." And then, briefly as he could, he told them about the death-dreams, about Roark and Singer coming to him and about the discovery of his brother. He told them how he had tracked down Karl and how his brother kidnapped and then impersonated him, first at the hotel, then at the Bayonne terminal and finally at his own home. He described the dream of George Lish's death and the most recent dream of a doorway opening to the sky where an Ilyushin 62 was falling in flames.

The reaction of his listeners was mixed. Some of the men masked their reactions with impassive faces while others were openly incredulous. One man sipped his coffee and toyed with the cup while another slumped back in his chair with folded arms and lowered head. At one point Doug Weems, the FBI man, interrupted with a question that Ingerman delayed with the suggestion that they wait until Paul was finished.

"I know that George Lish is dead," Paul said. "I know that Karl Alexander has a Redeye missile, I know that he kidnapped my wife Joanna and I know that he's going to try to shoot down the General Secretary's plane tomorrow morning."

"Is that it?" Doug Weems asked. "That's the extent of your evidence?"

"That's it. I can't prove it but—"

"Then I'd like to know what the hell we're doing here!"

"Wait a minute," Tommy Lecrazny began.

"No, I mean it," Weems said. "We've got a file full of crackpot death-threats six feet deep. That doesn't mean we—"

His words were drowned in a flurry of delayed reactions as several began talking at once. Paul exchanged a glance with Annie Helms, who rolled her eyes as if to say, What did you expect?

Ingerman let the uproar continue for a few moments and then moved to regain order. "All right, all right, let's take things one step at a time. Doug, your point is that there's not sufficient evidence to merit taking any action, is that what you're saying?"

His initial outburst over, the FBI man became more cautious. "Take action how? By investigating, sure. But let's not run off half-cocked. We've got a list of everybody who's made death threats on the Russian and none of them involve anything like a Redeye missile. That takes a conspiracy and conspiracies don't happen overnight and they don't happen without involving a lot of people and a lot of people don't make conspiracies without leaving a trail. I can tell you right now there's nothing in Bureau files and we know there's nothing on the PTA. So, sure, investigate, but why all this? Why an emergency meeting? The only hard evidence is that a warehouse up in Bayonne was broken into."

"Warehouse E," the DIA man reminded him. "That's a security warehouse and that's where the Redeyes were shipped from."

"Shipped intact, isn't that right?"

Ingerman nodded. "Padlocked and sealed before arrival at Bayonne, both intact when they arrived, both intact when the container was loaded."

McNally pulled out a pipe and began a dredging operation in a pouch of tobacco. "Have we checked with the shipment consignee in Costa Rica?"

"The shipment hasn't arrived yet. The *Coralis* is still at sea. We're trying to get authorization to break the container and do a cargo check."

Weems said, "Back to square one. The only hard evidence is a busted ventilator in a security warehouse."

"And six dead CIA assets," Hugh said.

"That's an altogether different case—"

"Not if the same man is responsible."

"Excuse me," McNally said. "But the more important issue here is motivation. According to what I've heard, this Karl Alexander works for the KGB, isn't that right?"

"No," Hugh said. "He works for the East German Stasis."

"I know, but he takes orders from the KGB, correct?"

Hugh nodded. "Assassinations would have to be approved by Moscow."

"So fundamentally we're saying the same thing: he works for the KGB and my question is, what I'd like to know, how does that square with shooting down the Russian leader?" McNally sat back with a satisfied expression.

"I've got a reason," Paul said. "Karl told me the finest man he'd ever known was a Russian. When I pressed him, he wouldn't tell me who it was, but according to his file, Karl was the protégé of a Russian KGB man named Alexander Ikhnovsky."

"What file was this?"

Hugh said, "Our station in Berlin."

McNally raised an eyebrow. "And you passed it around?"

"I passed it to Mr. Stafford."

"Who has a clearance, I assume?"

"Let's get back to the point," Ingerman told him. "What about Ikhnovsky?"

"He worked his way up to Deputy Director of the KGB," Hugh went on. "One of the old guard who was pushed aside when this new guy and his reformists took power. It's possible a group of reactionaries, hardliners, wants to get rid of him."

"And blame it," Paul added, "on George Lish and the Rank."

". . . There's always a wolf waiting to grab the baby," McNally said. "That's nothing new in Russian politics . . ."

Weems looked around the table. "I think we've lost track of the real point, which is that everything we're talking about is based on this man's dreams."

He nodded toward Paul, who again had the feeling he

was an animal in a zoo. Before he could respond Annie spoke for the first time.

"They're not dreams, not in the conventional sense of the word. They're intense impressions that Paul—Mr. Stafford—picks up sporadically and without volition from experiences his brother is having."

"That's reassuring," Weems said. "For a moment there I thought we might have to make a decision based on dreams. Now we can make it on mind reading."

"Or on missing your dinner," Paul added.

Weems shot him a surprised look and Ingerman quickly intervened.

"I think Dr. Helms should give us her view of the psychological aspects of the situation. Mr. Stafford, perhaps you wouldn't mind waiting in my office? I'll have Barbara take care of you. Gentlemen, if you'll excuse us for a moment."

Paul followed the Secret Service man into the next room. It was after normal working hours but there were still a number of people on duty. The low sound of radio communications and zip of laser printers reminded Paul of the *Herald*. There was the same feel of round-the-clock activity.

"I trust you don't mind being out here," Ingerman said. "but you understand the type of controversy that your story generates."

"Yeah, I'm a human mini-series."

Actually now that he'd told his story there wasn't much that Paul could do except try to find Joanna before tomorrow morning. Somehow the two lives were intertwined, he thought . . . such as, if the Russian leader survived, Joanna wouldn't. And vice versa.

Ingerman's assistant, Barbara, took him in hand. She was a matronly woman with soft features and the beginning of a double chin, but she spoke with quick precision and her eyes reflected an intelligence to match. She showed Paul to the couch in Ingerman's office and offered to get him a soft drink or coffee.

"Coffee, please," Paul said. "And I'd like to use the phone."

"You go right ahead. Punch the green button, that'll get you an outside line."

He called home, half-hoping that Joanna had called,

half-fearful that if Karl was holding her hostage, there might be a message threatening her life. Instead the answering machine played back a message from the police:

"Mr. Strafford, this is Officer Cruikshank of the Maryland Highway Patrol . . . There has been a traffic accident involving Mrs. Joanna Stafford. She's been taken to Glenway Memorial Hospital. That's in Upper Marlboro and if you need to get in touch with us, here's a number—"

Paul slammed the phone down and dialed the information operator for the number of the hospital. A traffic accident? Where? How? And what about Karl? Was he in it? Above all, was Joanna all right?

When he got through to the admissions desk Paul explained who he was and the operator put him on hold while she paged the doctor. Paul found himself clenching and unclenching his hand. If Karl had hurt Joanna . . .

Barbara returned with his coffee and put it on the desk. She saw from his face that he was upset and gave him a questioning look. Paul turned away, ignoring her, and she went back to her desk.

"Mr. Stafford, this is Dr. Halby."

"I want to know about my wife. How is she? Is she all right?"

"Your wife should be fine," Halby told him. "A CAT scan showed no skull fracture or cranial bleeding. She did suffer a ruptured spleen that required immediate surgery, but the operation went well and she's recovering now in ICU."

Paul slumped down. "But she'll be all right, you say?"

"Barring any further complications, she'll recover fully."

"What happened, doctor? Do you know?"

"Your wife was in an automobile accident, a fairly serious one by the extent of her injuries."

"Was she alone?"

"As far as I know. You'd have to talk to the police."

"Were there any other injuries?"

"Aside from the concussion and the spleen she has an exterior fracture of the left arm and two fractured ribs, lacerations of the scalp and lip and some minor cuts and bruises. The internal bleeding was the biggest danger but I believe we've stopped that now."

"So she'll be okay?"

"As I say, barring any further complications. We'll know more when she regains consciousness."

"Was she conscious when she came in?"

"I don't believe she was."

"Then she didn't say anything? About the accident?"

"You have to understand, your wife was in a state of shock when she arrived."

"I want to see her."

"You can do that, but only for a few minutes. She's in intensive care."

"You just take care of her. I'll be right there."

"One more thing, Mr. Stafford. Are you the same Paul Stafford who writes for the *Herald?*"

"Yes."

"Well, that article on malpractice suits was right on the money. I wish I could make it required reading for all my patients."

"Talk to you when I get there," Paul said.

Before he left he wrote a brief note explaining to Annie where he'd gone and left it with Barbara. As long as Joanna was safe, the experts could concentrate on the Russian.

CHAPTER

32

AIR FORCE TECHNICAL SERGEANT MARINA Adieva should have been nervous but she felt nothing. She was not a woman who harbored doubts. Outside the window of the Electronic Maintenance Facility she could see Aero-flot 86540, code named *Plamenny*, flame. This was the aircraft which would take the General Secretary from Moscow to Washington, D.C. Marina's crew had just completed an on-board inspection of the electronic systems. Now they sat crowded around an ancient black-and-white television watching a soccer game.

Marina surveyed the brightly lit room with its steel gray work benches and complicated test equipment. There was a tool kit someone had left on the bench nearest the door. Bobokov. He was the most careless and slipshod member of her team. Marina casually drifted over to the table and, when no one was looking, picked a thin screwdriver from its slot and slipped it into her pocket. Then she called out sharply.

"Bobokov, is this your tool kit?"

Bobokov turned with a confused smile.

"I say, is this yours?"

"I was in a hurry—"

"And where is your number four?"

"What?"

Marina picked up the kit and carried it to him. The other technicians either turned to watch or hunched closer to the television.

"Your number-four screwdriver," Marina said. "Where is it?"

Bobokov took the kit and frowned. He lifted some of the other screwdrivers from their slots.

"I'm sure it was here..."

"You didn't leave it in the Wildfire system did you?"

Bobokov paled. It was a cardinal rule that when performing maintenance on a delicate piece of electronic equipment all parts taken out for testing were to be replaced and nothing foreign left behind. An air crew's life depended on such attention to detail, as did the careers of electronic technicians such as Bobokov.

"No, no," he protested, "I know I had it when I left the aircraft. It must be here in the shop."

"I hope so, because I intend to check the aircraft."

Marina left the shop and crossed the tarmac to Aero-flot *Plamenny*. A yellow fuel truck crouched low under one wing as ground crewmen finished making their preparations. The guard, an air force corporal in knee-high boots, paid no attention to Marina as she boarded the aircraft. She was wearing her identification badge and he had seen her before.

Inside the plane Marina made her way to the cockpit. Behind the pilot and co-pilot seats there were two work stations, one for the flight engineer, the other for the ADO, the air defense officer. The ADO's desk faced a bewildering array of switches, lights, digital readouts, display panels, gridded screens and radar scopes. They were all as familiar to Marina as the pattern on her bedspread.

She turned her attention to the Wildfire IRCM system, a defense against infra-red, or heat-seeking, missiles. The system was actually two separate components: DeTect and DeCoy. DeTect consisted of infra-red sensors able to pinpoint any high-temperature heat source moving toward the aircraft at over sixty knots. It would alert the ADO to a potential threat and tell him range, bearing and speed. It was a passive system used for identification and tracking but unable to defend the aircraft.

DeCoy was the active system. It used a heated ceramic element whose radiant energy was mechanically modulated to confuse an incoming missile about the aircraft's whereabouts. Attempting to follow the apparent wild gyrations of its target, the missile would make ever-larger corrections until it exceeded its maneuverability limits and went out of control. DeCoy was Aero-flot *Plamenny's* protection, and it was this component that Marina meant to disengage.

But cleverly. The control panel, the arming switch, indicator lights, frequency selectors, test indicators—all these things must look and respond normally. The ADO would mistakenly think that they were protected, while DeTect would accurately register what was happening... Oh yes, they would see it coming, all the way in. And realize too late that they were naked.

Marina sat down and went to work. She had designed and built a circuit board that would disengage DeCoy's ceramic element without alerting the ADO. All she had to do was remove the cover plate, snip five wires and reroute them through the new board. She had practiced the procedure at the test bench; it would take three minutes and twenty seconds.

Unlike Karl's Uncle Alex and his coterie, it was not politics that motivated Marina. It was strictly personal. Marina was in love with Colonel Feliks Grigorenko. She had been in love with him ever since she graduated from the air force's advanced electronic school and began her duties as one of the maintenance team for Aero-flot *Plamenny*. At the time of their meeting, another Soviet leader was in power and Grigorenko, then a captain, was his pilot. Marina was twenty-two and had never been in love; Grigorenko, in his late forties, was unhappily married and had been in love many times.

Marina was not a beautiful woman, although a hint of Mongol blood gave her features an unusual look that stopped short of being exotic. She was uneasy with people and had few interests, but those she had she pursued with an intensity and singlemindedness that sometimes intimidated her peers. She seemed more interested in microchips and circuit boards than in socializing, which made it all the more surprising when she fell so much in love with Grigorenko, a casually vain and slightly overweight man to whom flying came as naturally as seduction.

The affair blossomed quickly and might have run its natural course, ending in disillusionment for Marina, had not the then General Secretary died. When the new one replaced him, he also replaced the pilot of Aero-flot *Plamenny*. Grigorenko was sent to an air base on the Kamchatka Peninsula, where he distinguished himself as the interceptor pilot who incorrectly identified Korean Air Lines Flight 007 as a U.S. Navy RC-135 reconnaissance aircraft.

Grigorenko's error was never officially acknowledged. In fact, to prove that no mistake had been made, he was promoted to colonel. But he was taken off flight duty and within the Soviet air force his name became synonymous with the English expression "blind as a bat." When he eventually returned to Moscow, it didn't take long for him to gravitate toward Alexander Ikhnovsky and the others plotting to overthrow the current regime.

In the meantime Marina remained steadfast. Without planning or explanation or understanding, she had taken Grigorenko into her heart as she had not done with any man before him nor would do with anyone after him. It was a commitment that could not have been more absolute had it been memorialized with wedding vows and a public ceremony. After his departure she threw herself into her work and devoted herself to the letters she wrote him each day but could not send. She had no close friends; the depth of her pain and the extent of her bitterness on his behalf remained hidden.

It took Marina three months to work up the courage to make contact with Grigorenko after he returned to Moscow. Under the domed ceiling of the Marxistskaya subway station, the former lovers met for the first time in years, and under the peeling ceiling of Marina's apartment they became lovers again. The next morning, with Marina lying exhausted on top of him, Grigorenko asked if she would risk her life for him. Without hesitation she answered yes . . .

A faint vibration shook the aircraft as someone mounted the outside steps. For the first time she felt a twinge of alarm, but she stayed calm and began screwing the cover plate back in place. As long as it wasn't the ADO, no one would know what she was doing. As she finished she heard someone step into the compartment behind her.

"Something wrong?"

Marina finished tightening the last screw and turned around. A burly KGB man in civilian clothes was staring at her. He frowned when he saw her coveralls and her badge.

"We were given an all-clear on electronics. Why are you here?"

Marina stared back impassively and held up the screwdriver.

"One of my men left this aboard. I didn't want it rolling around loose."

The KGB man grunted and turned his attention to the cockpit. "Has the captain been here?"

"I haven't seen him."

When she left, Marina paused at the top of the stairs and ran her hand over the fuselage of Aero-flot *Plamenny*. After so many years, the aircraft was like an old friend. For that brief and only moment, she felt sad.

Annie's presentation didn't last long. No sooner had she begun a discussion of mental affinity in twins than Barbara Ziegler slipped into the room and whispered in Ingerman's ear. When her audience turned its attention to the newcomer, Annie paused.

Ingerman stood up. "Excuse me, Dr. Helms, I'll be right back. Please continue."

Annie waited until he was out of the room and then picked up where she had left off.

"Tests at the University of Minnesota have shown a high correlation of image-affinity grouping in active-passive mental states," she said. "It's similar to the way that iron filings align themselves along the magnetic lines of force when they come into proximity with a magnet. In the case of twins, the passive mental state picks up images from the active mental state."

It was not the most receptive audience she had ever faced. These were practical men whose job it was to defend against concrete realities like bullets and bombs. Annie found herself speaking more and more rapidly in an effort to convince them. Just as she felt she had gotten their attention, Ingerman returned. All eyes turned toward him and Annie paused again.

"Sorry," Ingerman said, "I keep interrupting you. We just got word that Paul Stafford's wife is in the hospital. I spoke to the police who tell me that she was involved in a car accident this evening. She ran a Stop sign at high speed and lost control of the car. Right now she's in serious condition at Glenway Memorial Hospital."

"Where's that?" someone asked.

"Upper Marlboro. It's out near Andrews."

"Near Andrews? What was she doing out there?"

"The police had no idea."

"Where's Paul?" Annie asked.

"He's on his way to the hospital."

McNally took the pipe from between his teeth. "Was Mrs. Stafford alone or was she with this Karl Alexander?"

"She was alone."

Weems nodded. "So much for Stafford's kidnapping theory."

"We don't know that for sure."

"We don't know *anything* for sure. Why call a meeting without much information, that's what I'd like to know."

"Because," Ingerman replied with more patience than he felt, "I wanted everyone to be apprised of the situation and I wanted everyone to meet Paul Stafford since his credibility is a key consideration here—"

"Which at the moment," Weems put in, "is not so high."

Frank Delgado, an overweight man from the Defense Intelligence Agency, was squirming. "Could we abbreviate this, please? If we're here to consider a threat, then let's consider a threat. I don't know about the rest of you but I don't have time for speculating on science fiction—no offense Dr. Helms—but let's keep to what we know."

"He's right," Tommy Lecrazny said. "Let's assume the worst case: there's a Redeye missile out there with somebody who intends to use it. It doesn't matter whose brother he is or how he got a missile or whether he killed or kidnapped anyone. All that matters is, how real a threat is a Redeye missile and what do we do about it?"

"What do you mean, how real a threat? If he can shoot down the General Secretary's plane . . ."

"Can he? My understanding is that the Redeye is pretty much outmoded. I mean, we've got counter-measures for something as primitive as a Redeye missile, don't we, colonel?"

Colonel Coswell, hands folded on the table in front of him, nodded. "That's affirmative."

"So, I assume the Russians have some kind of counter-measures, too."

"I'm sure they do," Coswell replied. "Something comparable to our Hot Brick system. The DIA would have more on Soviet air defense systems."

"We do," Delgado agreed. "But we don't know just what kind of a package they've got on this aircraft."

"There's a good way to find out," Ingerman said. "Let's ask them."

Karl parked the Winnebago in the hospital parking lot. Clouds had crept over the night sky, and from deep within their recesses distant lighting glowed. There was a close, muggy feeling in the air that presaged a change in the weather. Before he went into the hospital Karl walked around the building, familiarizing himself with the layout and the grounds in case a quick escape became necessary. In addition to the main entrance there was a side door, an emergency room entrance and a loading dock on a lower level.

The hospital was a new one with glass doors that opened automatically at Karl's approach. Cool air enveloped him as he entered the reception area. To the left was a lounge made up of slab couches grouped around a planter with abstract graphics decorating the walls. The reception desk was directly ahead, manned by a nurse wearing a green nametag. Karl told her he was Paul Stafford and that his wife had been brought to the hospital after a car accident.

The nurse, a thin black woman whose nametag said "Raylene," typed a few quick entries into her computer and looked up.

"Your wife is recovering from surgery, Mr. Stafford. She's in intensive care. Just sign in and I'll give you a pass and you can go on up."

She handed him a pen and Karl signed Paul's name in the ledger. It didn't even feel odd any more, signing his brother's name.

Raylene also handed him a pink card encased in plastic with the word "VISITOR" on both sides.

"That's on the third floor, Mr. Stafford. You just take one of the elevators down the hall on the right."

"Thank you."

Karl walked down the hallway but rather than stopping at the elevator he continued until he found two double-doors leading to a stairway. He went downstairs and made sure the doors were unlocked. Through the thick windows he could see a long, brightly lit hallway with lab technicians and maintenance people going about their business. The loading dock was at this level. If he needed to, he could escape through the basement.

When he got to the third floor he had to stop at a desk outside the intensive care unit. After showing his pass and explaining who he was, he went through a set of double-doors and entered a hushed environment in which the rhythmic beeps and tones of monitoring instruments seemed loud. The physical layout of the ICU was like the spokes of a wheel, with glass-walled rooms extending outward from the nurses station at the hub. From the ceiling, banks of display screens stared down, each telling its own story of some particular portion of the anatomy.

There were three nurses in the room, one behind a circular desk, the other two standing outside it. They were talking quietly when Karl entered; at his approach a hawk-faced woman with a brittle smile came toward him. Her nametag identified her as "Margaret."

"Mr. Stafford?"

Karl nodded, momentarily taken aback that they knew his name. Seeing his confusion, Margaret said by way of explanation, "They told us you were on your way. Your wife is right over here."

There was only one other patient in the ICU, an old man whose emaciated body raised barely a ripple in the sheets covering him. Joanna was in the adjoining room. She lay pale and still, connected by tubes to equipment on wheeled carts that surrounded the bed. One small tube went into her nose, another made its way between her loosely parted lips and the third, to which Karl paid particular attention, disappeared beneath a white bandage on her arm.

"I know it looks frightening," the nurse was saying. "But she's actually doing very well."

Karl turned and stared down at her.

"Then she won't die?"

"I should say not," Margaret said, apparently offended by the suggestion. "Barring any complications, your wife should recover quite nicely."

After cautioning him that he could stay only a few minutes, she returned to the nursing station. Karl approached the bed. Joanna's head was bandaged and one side of her mouth was swollen and bruised. Her upper lip was drawn slightly where stitches had been taken.

As he stared down at her, Karl noticed the silken strands of black hair that crept from beneath the bandages. Her eyes, shielded behind delicate, translucent eyelids, were still. About to place his fingers against her cheek he caught himself. If he touched her, he might change his mind.

That was the danger in pretending to be Paul; it was making him susceptible to some of Paul's emotions, which had been so alien to him. What was it Joanna had said? Paul was gentle? Well, Paul could afford to be gentle. Everything in life had been handed to him, wrapped and tied like a Christmas gift. He, Karl, could afford no such luxury.

He withdrew his hand and glanced up at the nurses. They were visible through the open door and side window, talking softly, not paying much attention to him but still aware of what was going on. They were sure to notice if he brought out a knife and tried to cut the IV bag. Then he noticed the pale green curtain hanging against the wall that could be drawn around the bed to provide some privacy.

He went back to the nursing station. "Excuse me, Margaret. I would like to pray for my wife. Would it be all right to draw the curtains, just for a few moments?"

She hesitated.

"Please?" Karl added in a low voice.

"All right then, but just a few moments, Mr. Stafford."

Margaret went to the room and drew the curtains around the bed.

"You mustn't touch her."

"I understand. And thank you."

After one last glance at her patient, Margaret left him alone.

The curtain did not completely mask the bed, but it obscured the area in which the clear plastic IV bag dangled from a metal pole. Karl moved close to it, careful not to trip over anything. While the respirator cycled softly in the background, he took out a Swiss army knife, opened the small blade and quickly made an incision along the seam at the top of the IV bag. He then exchanged the knife for the bottle of Haloparimine.

For a moment he hesitated. For a few hours her opinion had mattered to him. But, he reminded himself, it had all been false on her part. Just play-acting to escape. Do it. He squeezed the bag to open the incision and poured the Haloparimine into the bag, creating a faint pattern where the two liquids met. He then gently shook the bag and the disturbance cleared.

Karl stared at Joanna one last time. It would be a painless death. At least he could give her that.

Arkadi Vronsky disliked Washington, D.C. He disliked America and all Western nations in general, not on political grounds but because they made his job so incredibly difficult. Vronsky was the director of security for the General Secretary, a job that was difficult enough in the Soviet Union and almost impossible in America, a society that seemed always to be on the brink of anarchy. Whenever he and his team suggested even the most modest security precaution they were told they couldn't do it without infringing on somebody's constitutional rights. The Americans could not even go to the grocery store without insisting on a constitutional right to overspend and indulge themselves. That was why, when Eliot Ingerman told him about the Redeye plot, Vronsky assumed it to be the work of an American. He was shocked to learn that the suspect, Karl Alexander, was alleged to be a member of East Germany's Stasis.

"That's a very serious allegation," Vronsky said. "The GDR is our ally. To accuse it of planning an attack on the General Secretary's life is as irresponsible as it is absurd."

"I didn't say the GDR planned the attack," Ingerman told him.

"Who, then?"

"We think it's possible that someone in your own government is behind the plot."

Vronsky stared at Ingerman and wondered what kind of a game this man was playing? He found something suspect in Ingerman's expensive and impeccably tailored suits and his well-groomed mane of gray hair. The man was too conscious of himself and the impression he made; Vronsky would have liked a glimpse below the surface of Ingerman's gleaming facade, particularly at this moment. Was he serious in suggesting a Soviet-directed plot against the General Secretary?

"Mr. Ingerman," Vronsky said, "if ever there is a Soviet plot to destroy a Soviet leader, I guarantee that you will be the last to know."

"Could be. But our information is that Karl Alexander is

the protégé of an ex-deputy director of the KGB, a man named Alexander Ikhnovsky."

Vronsky was familiar with the name; he'd even met Ikhnovsky years ago. But the man was retired now and too far removed from the political arena to effect any changes in the government. There were other men, old-line, reactionary members of the Politburo and some army leaders who were much more vociferous in their condemnation of the current leader's policies and who constituted real threats. The KGB was aware of these men.

"What do you suggest we do, Mr. Ingerman? Arrest Alexander Ikhnovsky? And on what charge? Can you give me any proof of this conspiracy?"

"It's not up to me to prove conspiracies. I'm only interested in getting your General Secretary in and out of Washington in one piece. We've got a missile shipment we're going to check, and when we do we'll know if there's a Redeye missing or not. In the meantime maybe you can find out if Karl Alexander is in Berlin."

"You mean you don't know if he's in Washington?"

"We have a single-source report. I'm looking for supporting evidence, one way or the other. Also, I'd like to know how well protected your aircraft are from something like the Redeye?"

"As well as your own aircraft are protected, I'm sure."

"You might want to find out."

After the American left, the first thing that Vronsky did was to contact Air Marshal Lyalin, who actually laughed at the mention of a Redeye missile.

"The Redeye is from the horse-and-buggy era," Lyalin boomed through the phone. "It has no IFF, no narrowband frequency selection, not much range and is a followonly weapon. It's been replaced three times over. I thought the Americans had given them all away."

"That's what they're doing, only now they have one less to give away than before."

"They lost one, did they?"

Lyalin seemed to think this a fine joke. There was something about the air marshal's relentless good humor that grated on Vronsky's nerves. At least Lyalin was able to reassure him that Aero-flot *Plamenny* was protected from a Redeye missile by something called the Wildfire system.

"A blind man chasing a greased pig," Lyalin said. "That's

the Redeye chasing Aero-flot *Plamenny*. The missile will more quickly end up in someone's living room than in the General Secretary's lap."

"Still, you might want to pass along the information to Moscow," Vronsky suggested drily.

"I shall, I certainly shall. But Wildfire will be operating whether the Americans have lost a Redeye or not. That is standard procedure."

The air force had its standard procedures and Vronsky had his. He went to the radio room and encoded a priority request for a copy of Karl Alexander's Stasis file and confirmation of current whereabouts. He could already tell that this would be a long night.

CHAPTER

33

PAUL FELT THE FIRST DROP OF RAIN AS HE crossed the hospital parking lot. From beyond the horizon came the rumble of distant thunder. As he approached the building, an illuminated sign bordered in green caught his eye: "Glenway Memorial Hospital." A feeling of recognition tugged at the edge of his consciousness. Had he been here before? As the sliding glass doors opened automatically at his approach the feeling intensified, along with a vague foreboding.

Paul went straight to the reception desk and announced himself. "I'm here to see my wife. Joanna Stafford. She's in ICU."

The nurse, Raylene, ran an eye over him, and a slow smile spread across her features.

"How'd you do that?" she asked.

"Do what?"

"Change clothes so fast? How'd you do that?"

It took Paul a moment before the full impact of her words struck him.

"*Joanna*. Where is she?"

"Wait a minute now, you got to sign in again."

"It's not *me*, I didn't—"

He saw the ledger on the desk and grabbed it. His own signature stared back at him. Karl had been here. He shoved the ledger aside and turned on the nurse. "Where's intensive care?"

"Calm down, Mr. Stafford. You just—"

Paul reached across the counter and grabbed her by the shoulders.

"Where *is* she, damn it? What floor?"

Raylene tried to pull away, eyes wide. From across the room a uniformed guard approached.

"Just a minute, sir."

Paul turned and headed down the hallway. The guard, a man about sixty, tried to stop him but Paul shoved him aside and ran down the hall. The guard yelled and a couple of attendants turned to look. Paul jumped for an elevator and slipped inside just as the doors closed. A nurse's aide stood behind a patient in a wheelchair.

"ICU," Paul said. "Which floor?"

The aide, scared by his manner and look, seemed tongue-tied.

Paul looked around. Above the doors was a building directory: "Intensive Care" was on the third floor. He jabbed the button and a moment later the elevator bumped to a stop. A maintenance man was mopping a narrow strip of linoleum between two portable signs that read "Caution: Wet Floor." At the end of the hallway there was a desk, and behind it were double-doors leading to the ICU.

A male nurse looked up at his approach but Paul walked right past him. The man called after him, "Excuse me, sir . . ."

Three nurses at a circular desk looked up in mild surprise at his approach.

"Joanna Stafford? Where is she?"

The oldest nurse frowned. "Now, Mr. Stafford, I told you—"

The male nurse had followed him in. "Excuse me, sir. You can't just barge in here."

Paul turned to the windowed rooms as the oldest nurse, Margaret, came toward him. And it was then he spotted Joanna lying with her eyes closed, head swathed in bandages, tubes running into her nose and mouth, another into her arm. Paul rushed to her bedside. She looked so pale and . . . lifeless that he was sure Karl had already killed her. Then her chest moved and he realized she was still breathing, she was alive. Or was it the respirator breathing for her? What could he tell with her hooked up to all these damn machines?

Margaret came in after him and took his arm. "Mr. Stafford, you have to leave here, now. I told you that before."

Paul wrenched free and picked up Joanna's hand. He felt for a pulse.

"Mr. Stafford, please . . ."

Paul turned on her. "He's trying to kill her. The man who was here a few minutes ago, it wasn't me. He's trying to kill her..."

Margaret stared at him. Joanna's heartbeat came to his fingertips, faint. But instead of relief he felt a growing dread. Something was wrong. Karl had come here for a reason...

"All right, Mr. Stafford," Margaret said gently. "Why don't you come out here and sit down—"

"Check her. Find out what's wrong."

His fingers were still on Joanna's wrist, feeling her heartbeat, but feeling, too, something lurking just beyond the boundaries of his consciousness. An image began to form of a narrow opening—

"She'll be all right if you just come outside..."

Margaret placed a hand on his arm and gently but firmly tried to pull him away.

"*Don't.*" Paul yanked his arm free. The male nurse stepped forward, his palms upraised.

"Take it easy, Mr. Stafford. You don't want to hurt your wife, do you?"

The image faded, leaving only a residue of unease. What the hell had Karl done? What?

"Something's wrong with her," Paul insisted. "I don't know what, but the man who was here before, he did something. Check her vital signs, her blood, everything."

Margaret and the male nurse exchanged a glance. Another nurse was watching from the doorway. Obviously none believed him.

"Was I wearing these clothes?" Paul demanded. "I wasn't, right?"

For the first time a faint look of uncertainty crossed Margaret's face.

"You see what I'm saying? I know it sounds crazy but I think he might have poisoned her or injected her with something or—"

He noticed the IV bag and now an image exploded in his brain: the narrow opening, an incision in plastic, something... poison... draining into the bag, into Jo's veins—

The male nurse was motioning to two uniformed guards who had just arrived.

Margaret said soothingly, "She's really all right, Mr. Stafford. The machines tell us that."

"No she's *not*." He moved to the IV monitor and yanked the tube free. An alarm bell went off as the tube snaked across the floor and glucose gushed from the bag. He pulled out the tubes and wires attached to the other machines. The room came alive with beeping and alarm bells and blinking lights.

The guards grabbed him and hustled him out of the room as nurses converged on Joanna.

"Do a blood test," Paul yelled. "See if there's poison."

"Just come along now," one of the guards said.

They had him by the arms, one on both sides with an aide behind him.

"My wife . . . tell them to check the IV—"

"Sir, you're upset, but you're also disrupting this hospital."

As they wrestled Paul to the other side of the room, Dr. Halby arrived. He was younger than Paul imagined, a short, wiry man with bushy black eyebrows and lips too well-formed for his features. He went immediately into Joanna's room.

"Someone's trying to kill her," Paul called to him. "Check her blood and change the IV."

At least there was a flurry of activity in Joanna's room. At least they were paying attention to her condition now.

"I'm *okay*," Paul told the guards, pulling his arms free. After a few minutes, Dr. Halby came out.

"Is she all right?" Paul demanded. "Did you check her?"

"You're Paul Stafford?"

"Did you do a blood test?"

"Wait a minute. Let me try to understand something. You're the Paul Stafford I talked to on the phone? The one who wrote those articles on medical malpractice?"

"Yes, what about my wife? Is she all right?"

"No thanks to you, I'm afraid."

"Did you check her blood and change the IV?"

"The IV was contaminated so we changed it. There's no need to check her blood. Now suppose you tell me—"

"Doctor, I believe someone's trying to kill my wife," Paul interrupted. "A man impersonating me was just here. You can ask the nurses. He was wearing different clothes. He's my twin brother and he has a history of using drugs to incapacitate and kill people."

He could tell Halby didn't believe him.

"I *know* how it sounds," Paul said quickly. "But I can prove what I say. Call the CIA and ask for a man named Hugh Roark. He'll confirm what I'm telling you."

The wrong thing to say. Halby's skepticism turned to incredulity at the mention of the CIA. Paul felt his frustration mount.

"Will you just for God's sake check her blood? If she was poisoned, how could you find out? Where would it show? Just *check*."

Halby rubbed the bridge of his nose. "Mr. Stafford, will you take a moment and consider what you're saying. Just think what you're—"

"I know goddamn good and well what I'm saying."

"You're distraught, which is only natural under the circumstances—"

"And what if she dies? Is that only natural under the circumstances?"

"If you'll allow me to, I'll prescribe something—"

Margaret came out of the ICU holding the empty IV bag.

"Excuse me, doctor, you might want to look at this." She showed Halby the bag. "Either the seam broke or else, maybe . . ."

She let the words trail off. Halby inspected the bag while Margaret eyed Paul.

"That's it," Paul said. "You left him alone with her, didn't you? The first man who was here?"

Margaret gave him a look and said nothing until Halby glanced up. "Was someone alone with her?"

"*He* was. He asked to close the curtains to pray," she said, still staring at Paul. "I didn't see any harm in it."

"Not your fault," Halby snapped, but his face was flushed with anger. "I want an immediate blood test and prepare an emergency transfusion. I want the contents of this bag analyzed."

Margaret returned to Joanna's room and Halby turned to Paul. "If you're right, either I owe you an apology or you owe the police an explanation."

"Just save Joanna, okay?"

Halby was already in motion. The guards took Paul to the security office to fill out a report. He was still there when Annie Helms arrived.

* * *

The problem with the KGB's centralized bureaucracy was that all messages were routed through Moscow. In Vronsky's case, his priority request for confirmation of Karl Alexander's whereabouts brought a quick response from the Berlin Karlshorst section: Karl Alexander was on temporary duty with the KGB training facility at Yaroslavl. Because the night signals clerk in Moscow received the response as he was going off duty, his replacement enciphered the message and transmitted it to Washington. In the process he misunderstood the origination code so that when Vronsky received it, he thought the information came from Yaroslavl rather than Berlin. By midnight, he was on the phone to Eliot Ingerman with the good news: Karl Alexander was six thousand miles away.

It was the second piece of good news for Ingerman. The American and Soviet air defense specialists had already conferred and the consensus was that a Redeye missile wasn't sophisticated enough to pose a threat to the Soviet air defense screen.

"They won't go into details," Coswell told him, "But from what they say and what we already know, it's probably something like our Hot Brick system."

Ingerman didn't pretend to understand Hot Brick systems but he was willing to accept Coswell's assurances. His job was to protect the Russian leader once he was on the ground; it was up to the air force to get him there. Still, he wished they had been able to discover whether or not a Redeye was missing. But the *Coralis*, with the containers lashed to her deck, was battling a tropical storm in the Caribbean. It would be at least forty-eight hours before a physical inventory could be made.

And then there was Paul Stafford, whose credibility had just reached zero. If Karl Alexander was in Yaroslavl, then it must have been Stafford who visited his wife both times in the hospital. He recalled what Hugh Roark had told him about Stafford's marital problems and his wife leaving him. Had Stafford tried to drug his own wife? And then lost his nerve and gone back and saved her? Or had he planned it that way from the beginning? To save his wife and effect a reconciliation as the heroic husband?

A chilling possibility occurred to him: what if Stafford was one of those multiple personalities? The Dr. Jekyll and

Mr. Hyde type, in which neither personality was aware of the other's existence? He had read articles about such people and even studied case histories during a course on criminal psychology. It made more sense than dreams and mental telepathy.

Besides, what reason did anyone else have for killing Joanna Stafford?

When the test results showed a lethal amount of sedative in Joanna's IV solution, Annie's testimony and her CIA credentials helped convince both Dr. Halby and the police of Paul's story. After the reports were filed, Paul insisted on returning to the third floor. He could not stay in the ICU, but Dr. Halby arranged for him to wait in the lounge at one end of the hallway. It didn't matter to Paul as long as he could monitor who had access to Joanna. He had apparently arrived just before much of the sedative had a chance to enter Joanna's system. Now that she was safe he wasn't going to trust fortuitous timing again. He was going to stay there until Joanna regained consciousness, which Halby anticipated might not be until morning. Annie opted to stay with him.

"You should go home," he told her.

"I'll stick around."

"Why?"

"Well, to be truthful, I want to find your brother."

"You think he's coming *back* here?"

"No. But if you fall asleep tonight I'd like to be here in case you have any dreams."

"I'm not going to sleep," Paul said. "Not until I know that Joanna is all right."

They were sitting on the couch. Paul leaned forward, put his elbows on his knees and rested his chin on his palms. Annie sat with him in silence. Later, she said, "They don't think he can shoot down the General Secretary with a Redeye."

"Who doesn't think so?"

"They were talking about it after you left. There's some kind of a defensive screen. The Redeye can't get through it."

Paul nodded absently, his mind on Joanna. Annie became silent, aware that he was not in the mood to talk. Twice she went to the cafeteria and brought back coffee.

Around two in the morning she began to doze off, each time sliding sideways against Paul. He moved to a chair and let her curl up on the couch. Later one of the nurses covered her with a blanket.

Paul's eyes remained transfixed on the entrance to intensive care, and there were times when his mind went blank and he was looking at nothing. Dr. Halby stopped twice to check on Joanna and to reassure him. Just before dawn the fatigue caught up with him and Paul found himself falling asleep, only to wake up with a start when his hand dropped from the arm of the chair or when his head fell forward. He had not had a good night's sleep in three days.

Annie woke up at six-thirty. Unable to persuade Paul to come to the cafeteria for breakfast, she went alone and brought back coffee, a pint of blueberry yogurt and a Danish. At eight-fifteen Joanna regained consciousness, but Paul had to wait until Dr. Halby checked her and the nurses removed her from the respirator before he could go in. When Joanna saw him her first reaction was fear. Her eyes widened and she let out a hoarse cry.

Dr. Halby put a hand on Paul's arm. "Wait."

"Jo," Paul said. "It's me. Paul . . ."

"Paul?"

"Yes, *yes.*"

He came toward her but she drew away.

"Hand," she said, pointing.

Paul held out his right hand but she ignored it and reached weakly for his left. Only after she turned his fingers and saw the wedding band did she begin to relax and her eyes filled with tears. Paul knelt by the bed and pressed her hand.

"You're all right, you're all right, darling . . ."

"He was here," she whispered to him, still hoarse.

"I know."

"Tied me up, I had to get away."

"Joanna, Joanna . . ."

"Tore my hair."

She raised her hand to her head and when her fingers met the bandages she seemed surprised. "That bad?"

"You were in a car wreck, Jo."

"A car wreck? No, I remember my hair . . ."

"Your hair's okay."

"I tore it. One of those motor homes. I crawled underneath it to get away..."

She remembered escaping from Karl but she remembered nothing about the accident. When Paul told her about it she frowned. "I hurt the car?" It struck such a note of incongruity that he had to smile. Jo looked confused for a moment, then smiled too when she realized. The stitches at her lip made her wince.

"Ow."

"Don't smile."

"Don't make me laugh."

She pointed to a pitcher of water. Paul poured her a glassful and watched her sip it, favoring the injured lip. When she was done he put the glass back on the nightstand. He took hold of her hand. "Do you know how much I love you?"

"Tell me."

He leaned close and told her, realizing it was long overdue.

The General Secretary asked to be awakened when Aero-flot *Plamenny* passed over the North American continent. The steward brought dark Turkish coffee, and the Russian leader tucked a lump of sugar behind his lower lip and sat sipping as he stared out the window. Dawn's hard-edged light reflected the plane's white underbelly but had not reached the land below, emerging gray and shapeless from the night.

His wife entered the stateroom then and sat down across from her husband.

"You got some sleep?"

"Enough. What about you?"

"Enough," but the enigmatic smile told him a different story.

She was worried about the trip, he knew that. She had an unerring instinct when it came to sensing the mood of her country. When he graduated from Moscow State University it was she who told him to let their peers go to the high posts in Moscow. He should return to Stavropol and local politics. It had been the most astute move of his career.

She had been correct, too, about the speed with which he carried out his reforms. When he assumed the Soviet leadership she had urged caution. But he had pushed ahead, perhaps too quickly. The high expectations had led to disillusionment and, in the last few months, to feelings of unrest. Which was what worried her.

"The mood is wrong," she had said last week. "Remember the atmosphere just before Brezhnev replaced Khrushchev?"

"I am not Khrushchev," he reminded her. "And this is not 1963."

"You could get sick, postpone the summit."

It was wishful thinking. There was no way to postpone the summit. The Mutual Defense Treaty was the key to furthering the shift from a military economy to a peace-time market economy. The Mutual Defense Treaty, he had said in a speech to the Politburo, was mankind's last great attempt to save itself "from the endless cycle of wars whose battles echoed down the corridors of time." The Mutual Defense Treaty was his legacy to the nation that had given him birth and nourished him and raised him to the highest office in the land.

There was a quotation that he had heard his grandparents use, a biblical reference that stuck in his mind. The words came back to him now: "When I was a child, I spoke as a child and I understood as a child and I thought as a child: but when I became a man, I put away childish things." That was how he felt about the Mutual Defense Treaty. It was time now to put away childish things.

The first rays of the sun touched the land below, setting white fire to mists that ran like veins among the rolling forests. An escort of United States Air Force jets had replaced their own MiG fighters during the night. They were in U.S. hands now.

She reached across the table and took his hand.

"It will be good," she said, wishing she really believed it.

He nodded. It would have to be good. There was no other way.

Karl awoke refreshed after a good night's sleep. It was clear and cool, a good omen. He went to a truck stop called Dixie's Diner, ordered a breakfast of sausage and eggs, and enjoyed his last moments as an anonymous American. The commuter flights left hourly from Washington National to New York, where he would catch a four o'clock flight to Brussels. After that, a connection through Rome to Berlin. By tomorrow at this time he would be home.

The thought brought him no particular joy. His career in the Stasis was over. By now Paul was sure to have talked to the American embassy officials and probably the CIA. Karl had no illusions about his brother. Having been betrayed, Paul would make good his threat to tell the CIA who was responsible for the deaths of their agents. The CIA would send someone, maybe a team, two or three men. His death would appear accidental but to anyone inside the intelligence community the message would be clear: judgment and execution.

Karl could see his future as if looking through a crystal ball. He would take Magda and the children and move to Russia, where Uncle Alex would insure that he was given an adviser's role at some KGB or army training school. In the aftermath of the General Secretary's death, he would be an unsung hero of the new faction, but only as long as Uncle Alex was alive would he be safe. After that he would be a liability to the plotters—the one man who could disprove their legitimacy.

No, Karl thought, from now on, he would be a man on the run. He would have to plan an alternative life while Uncle Alex was still able to protect him. He would need to put away money in a Swiss bank account, he would need false identity papers, and when the time came, a credible death. Otto could help him; he could make amends for letting Paul escape.

Karl paid the bill and left the change stacked neatly in a cone on the table. When he returned home he would have no American money to serve as a tell-tale clue indicating where he had been. He left the restaurant, drove to a shopping center and positioned the Winnebago at the eastern edge of the lot facing the direction from which Aero-flot *Plamenny* would make its approach. The winds were light and from the south, which meant that Runway 19 was in use. The Ilyushin would make its approach from the north and land on a heading of 190 degrees, almost due south.

Karl unloaded the Kawasaki motorcycle, started it and let the engine run a few moments. His escape route would take him out the back of the shopping center and through